Twentieth Century American Wars

TWENTIETH

CENTURY

AMERICAN WARS

Wilbur H. Morrison

HIPPOCRENE BOOKS
New York

For information, address:
HIPPOCRENE BOOKS, INC.
171 Madison Avenue
New York, NY 10016

Library of Congress Cataloging-in-Publication Data

Morrison, Wilbur H., 1915–
    Twentieth century American Wars
                Wilbur H. Morrison.
     p. cm.
    Includes bibliographical references (p.) and index.
    ISBN 0-7818-0120-6 :
    1. United States—History, Military—20th century. 2. United
States—History—20th century. I. Title.
E745.M56 1993
973.9—dc20   93-5305
                                              CIP

Dedicated to the memory of my late mother and father,
Lucy and Martin Morrison.

Contents

Introduction

I WAS BORN IN 1915, DURING THE SECOND YEAR OF WORLD WAR I. Therefore my whole life and members of my generation has been dominated by wars big and small. I served in World War II for four years, flying 38 combat missions as a bombardier-navigator with the Army Air Forces. Most of them were flown with the Twentieth Air Force against Japan for which I received 14 awards and decorations.

I remained in the Ready Reserve after 1945, making myself available for service in any of the wars that followed but I was never called up. Until I retired, I took advantage of the many fine schools offered by the Air Force and completed all their courses except the one for the War College.

I have written extensively about all of the Twentieth Century's wars but this book deals primarily with the causes and effects.

My background is extensive. As a regional radio news commentator between 1935 and 1954—except for the war years—I reported on all of the great events of the times, interviewing hundreds of men and women who were the nation's newsmakers. For the next 15 years, I had responsible management positions in public relations with Douglas Aircraft Company and Lockheed where I associated with many of the world's leaders in the airlines, the military services, and the financial and business worlds. During these years I received an invaluable education in all the sciences. Although this is not a memoir, much of the text of this book is derived from information gleaned from my personal experiences.

There is a chain of events throughout the Twentieth Century that leads from one war to another that can easily be recognized. Although war is a stupid and tragic way to resolve differences between nations, not everyone believes that. Thus we have men like Hitler, Mussolini and Tojo. In more recent times, men like Saddam Hussein of Iraq believe that war is the only way to achieve world power.

Among the Twentieth Century's many wars, two world wars have caused a huge number of deaths and enormous devastation to much of the world's land mass. Although the United States has escaped physical destruction of its mainland in all of these wars it has paid a high price with more than 500,000 dead and approximately 934,000 wounded young men and women.

The apparent end of the Cold War in 1991 has been greeted with hope by a world weary of war, although some parts of the world remain in turmoil. But the eclipse of communism in the Soviet Union offers mankind its first hopeful sign that peaceful overtures may eventually replace war as a means of settling international disputes. Such a change is urgently needed because for the first time in the world's history mankind has developed the means to totally destroy itself. While much of the world remains in a volatile state, wars remain a frightening possibility.

I believe a better understanding of our past conflicts will offer lessons for handling future emergencies. If so, the six years that I have devoted to the research and writing of this book will have been well spent.

—Wilbur H. Morrison, Lt. Col. Air Force, Ret
Fallbrook, California

CHAPTER 1

The Confident Years

"SPEAK SOFTLY AND CARRY A BIG STICK" BECAME THEODORE ROOSE-
velt's trademark in the early years of the Twentieth Century. For most
Americans its meaning had such a strong influence through the years
that it dominated their political thinking throughout the century.

Despite the ravages of the Civil War, the United States had experienced
an unprecedented growth in the final years of the Nineteenth Century,
and vast fortunes were made by enterprising capitalists who helped to
create a freewheeling industrial society.

With optimism running high following the end of the Spanish-American War in the fall of 1898—the war that Secretary of State John Hay
called "a splendid little war"—the new Andrew Carnegie Steel company
was incorporated in New Jersey with a capitalization of $160 million in
defiance of the Sherman Anti-Trust Act. Although this was the largest
incorporation to date, there were many more in the early years of the
Twentieth Century.

The Treaty of Paris ending the Spanish-American War was signed on
December 10, 1898, by the United States and Spain. The following
year a treaty made Cuba an independent republic under United States
protection. The Platt Amendment to this treaty gave the United States
authority to intervene to suppress a revolt. Under the treaty's terms, the
United States acquired Puerto Rico, the Philippines and Guam. Spain
agreed to abandon all claims to Cuba and agreed to assume $400 million
in Cuban debts. The United States Senate, after a bitter battle between
imperialists and anti-imperialists, ratified the treaty.

The outcome of the presidential election in 1900 had been a foregone
conclusion for months. President William McKinley and Theodore
Roosevelt easily defeated the Democratic ticket.

1

President McKinly and his wife attended the Pan American Exposition in Buffalo, New York, on September 5, 1901. Fifty thousand people gathered there, but few heard what he had to say. It was a familiar theme, reiterating his belief that isolation was no longer possible or desirable, and that God and man had linked the nations together. "The period of exclusiveness is past," he said.

The following day McKinley attended a public reception at the Temple of Music. When the doors opened at 4 p.m. McKinley stepped out surrounded by Secret Service men and local police. One of those who walked forward in a double line to greet him was Leon Czolgosz. No one noticed that he had a revolver concealed by a handkerchief in his right hand. When he reached McKinley, the President held out his hand to greet him. Czolgosz brushed the President's hand aside and fired twice through the handkerchief. McKinley stared at the man with contempt, and there was a stunned silence for a moment until the guards jumped on Czolgosz.

Despite his wounds, McKinley called, "Don't let them hurt him!"

Vice President Roosevelt was in the Adirondack Mountains and word of the President's shooting had to be sent over mountain roads, which was time consuming. Once Roosevelt was informed he was brought to Buffalo by special train on September 14. He arrived shortly after McKinley's death. Roosevelt took the oath of office at 3 p.m. in the library of the house where McKinley's body still lay.

This act of terrorism by an anarchist acting on his own was not considered a threat to the security of the United States. Most Americans faced the future with confidence, believing that if their own economic expectations were not realized that their children would inherit a better world.

Although the South had been devastated by the Civil War, the rest of the nation experienced an economic boom at the turn of the century. However, the United States was dominated by privileged Americans, and poverty's ugly reality was visible everywhere.

Still there was an air of abiding hope that new inventions and industrialization would rid America of poverty and open up new opportunities for people of talent, ambition and imagination.

For most Americans, the United States was the finest nation on earth. This feeling of optimism lasted until 1914 when it was shattered by World War I. Actually, this period of unbounded optimism was never recaptured in like manner during the Twentieth Century.

An event occurred on December 17, 1903, that would forever change the science of war. Reclining on the lower wing, Orville Wright made man's first powered flight in a heavier-than-air machine by flying 120 feet in 12 seconds. There were only five witnesses so it took the nation's news media some time to appreciate the significance of this historic flight. It was an outstanding feat, and one of the greatest achievements of all time. The fact that it was accomplished by men of little formal education, and limited funds, makes it all the more remarkable.

Wilbur later flew 852 feet in 59 seconds, and the air age was born.

This was an age abounding in talent as one spectacular invention followed another as America truly came of age.

After Panama declared its independence from Columbia, backed by a United States' threat to intervene militarily, President Roosevelt set up a seven-man commission on February 29, 1904, to complete the canal across the Panamanian Isthmus. America's new international role throughout the world, and especially in the Atlantic and Pacific ocean areas, was expected to take on a renewed importance once the canal was completed. After that warships could transit through the canal from one ocean to another in a fraction of the time it had formerly taken.

Secretary of State Hay and Philippe Buneau-Varilla, Panama's minister to Washington, formalized their negotiations for a canal across Panama, giving the United States government the rights to a 10-mile-wide strip of land for $10 million and an annual charge of $250,000 to be paid after nine years.

In his annual message to Congress on December 6, 1904, President Roosevelt established a new principle for America's conduct of foreign affairs in North and South America. He said that since the United States, under the Monroe Doctrine, had forbidden foreign interference in the Western Hemisphere, that it had the responsibility to insist on proper redress for wrongs inflicted upon a foreign state by any country within the American sphere of influence.

Roosevelt, using the "Corollary" to the Monroe Doctrine that he had promulgated the year before, announced in early 1905 that the United States Government would take over the Dominican Republic's debt payments, customs and finances until its debt with Great Britain was resolved, and it was free from the threat of bankruptcy. This was a dangerous precedent, and the United States Senate withheld approval of the protocol. But the President ignored the Senate and reached an agreement with the Dominican Republic. Roosevelt's interference in the affairs of another nation was unfortunate, to say the least, because his intercession was based upon the premise that if only 50 percent of all receipts were stolen by corrupt Dominican officials, the government would survive, but if 90 percent were taken off the top, it could not. Roosevelt's decision created friction between Latin and South American countries and the

United States that was never fully resolved even after the State Department repudiated the protocol in 1930. By then, the damage to the credibility of the United States and its integrity was almost irreparably harmed.

A final agreement to end the Russo-Japanese War was reached on September 5, 1905, in Portsmouth, New Hampshire. Japan was given protection rights over Korea, and received the South Manchurian Railway and the southern part of the Liaotung Peninsula. Roosevelt's personal diplomacy was so skillful that he prevented Japan from acquiring all of disputed Sakhalin Island—giving them only half of the strategic island— while Japan agreed to make financial restitution to Russia.

Roosevelt richly deserved the Nobel Peace Prize that he received for his efforts. Most importantly, America's international reputation for justice and fair play was considerably enhanced.

The American people were warm in their praise of their President for intervening so successfully in the dispute, and obtaining a settlement acceptable to both sides. It is possible that the end of the conflict in 1905 saved a quarter of a million soldiers' and sailors' lives who otherwise would have perished if the war had continued.

Wilhelm II of Germany and Nicholas II of Russia now reached agreement to provide mutual help in Europe, which also strengthened Russia's position in the world after its devastating defeats in the Far East.

The Great White Fleet, composed of 16 battleships of the United States Navy with their gilt bows, (most of the fleet) set out on December 16, 1907, on a world cruise to show the flag, and to demonstrate America's naval might. In part, President Roosevelt wanted to demonstrate to Japan that the United States's concessions in recent international relations were not the result of weakness or fear of Japanese power. There was some concern, at first, that Admiral Togo's Japanese fleet might attack the American fleet, but these fears proved groundless. Commanded by Admiral Robley D. "Fighting Bob" Evans, who had earned the nickname in several engagements, and who had long fought for a steel-ship Navy, was named commander-in-chief of the United States fleet. During the long voyage, however, he was forced to retire due to illness.

The fleet was met with enthusiasm everywhere, including stops in South America, Australia and Japan where the Japanese got the message that the United States was an up-and-coming world power.

Navy officials learned to their dismay that the fleet was heavily dependent upon foreign supplies. As a result, they decided that the Navy needed a more balanced distribution of ships—and not just battleships— but including destroyer escorts and supply ships. It was an error in judgment that the Navy continued to make throughout the century. On the whole the trip was a huge success and the fleet did not return until February 22, 1909, just 13 days before President Roosevelt had to leave office.

To no one's surprise, Republican William Howard Taft defeated Democrat William Jennings Bryan in the presidential election on November 3, 1908, with an electoral vote of 323 to 162.

Taft's popular majority was only half what Roosevelt had gained four years earlier because there was unrest among the people of the West. A number of Democrats were elected as governors.

The United States Naval Air Service was created officially on March 4, 1911, when Congress approved $25,000 for the new Naval flying corps. The following year Congress increased the amount to $65,000 because of their concern about the country's lack of airpower. A minuscule sum compared to the $16 million allotted by European governments to their military aviation, but unfortunately the Navy Department refused to even spend this amount.

Territorial disputes had long been simmering in the Balkans and war broke out in 1912. Turkey was defeated by an alliance of Bulgaria, Serbia, Greece and Montenegro. In a peace treaty signed in London the following year most of European Turkey was partitioned among the victors. War broke out again in 1913 as Bulgaria attacked Serbia and Greece and was defeated when Romania intervened and the Turks captured Adrianople.

The explosive situation merely awaited the proper spark to ignite the whole continent. It was not long in coming.

President Taft's efforts to stabilize Latin and South American economies was called "Dollar Diplomacy" by opposition parties, but the President preferred to call his efforts "substituting dollars for bullets," by using private American capital. The net effect was not what he envisioned because it kept corrupt governments in power, and was resented by these nations as an American intrusion in their internal affairs.

When Taft considered it necessary to protect American interests in Cuba under terms of the Platt Amendment, he sent in United States Marines on June 5, 1912. Such a step was against his own policy that he had spelled out in his "dollar diplomacy." American intervention was wrong and terribly misguided. It started a chain of events in the coming years in which the United States supported corrupt governments with dishonest admininistrations, leading inevitably to the creation of long-lasting animosity in most of these nations toward the United States.

Theodore Roosevelt re-entered politics in 1912 for another run at the presidency but he was defeated at the Republican convention.

He organized the Progressive Party and polled more votes than Taft, but succeeded only in splitting the Republican vote, and assuring the candidacy of Democrat Woodrow Wilson.

Roosevelt had helped to usher in a new age of social justice—often in an arrogant and high-handed manner—but the American people turned to a new man on the political scene who, they believed, would better guarantee the kind of future they all sought.

Wilson's victory was a landslide. He won 435 electoral votes to Roosevelt's 88 and Taft's 8.

Woodrow Wilson set the theme for his Presidency in his inaugural address. "We have been proud of our industrial achievement, but we have not hitherto stopped thoughtfully enough to count the human cost. . . . The great government we loved has too often been made use of for private and selfish purposes, and those who used it have forgotten the people."

The American people reacted with enthusiasm to the words of this intense and scholarly man whose idealism, piety, and obvious intelligence were so refreshing.

Taft left office largely discredited by the American people, although his accomplishments were formidable. From the start of his Presidency Taft had instructed his attorney general to prosecute violators of the Sherman Anti-trust Act, and he accomplished what Roosevelt was unable to achieve in almost two terms of office. Taft's reforms saved the government millions of dollars as he made changes in the operation of the government that resulted in greater efficiency. One of these changes brought 8,000 assistant postmasters under Civil Service, and he had fought to legalize a general income tax by proposing a constitutional amendment. After it was ratified by the states, the amendment became law in February 1913, as the 16th Amendment. Taft's greatest failure as President was his endorsement of the principle of high tariffs. President Wilson, who succeeded him, did not agree.

By the time the Panama Canal was opened for service in 1914 the United States Army Corps of Engineers under Colonel George W. Goethals had spent more than $366 million. Prior to its completion Goethals was confirmed by Congress as the first governor of the Permanent Civil Government of the Panama Canal Zone.

President Wilson pressed an electric button in the White House on October 10, 1913, to set off an explosion of the Gamoa Dike to link the waters of the Atlantic and the Pacific. But the first steamer did not use the 40.27-mile canal until August 3, 1914.

It was a magnificent undertaking because much of the canal had to be blasted out of solid rock. Construction had been started on the Atlantic side and the canal was dug 11½ miles due south to the 104-square mile Gatun Lake where the canal turns southeast before heading for the Pacific coast. The canal lifts ships 85 feet above sea level through a series of three locks on the Pacific and Atlantic sides.

The Wright brothers won an important decision on January 13, 1914, against Glenn Curtis. It involved airplane balancing patents that had been in contention for several years and interrupted the free-flow of ideas in the industry.

President Wilson publicly refused in 1914 to recognize General Victoriano Huerta as the rightful President of Mexico, saying he had not been elected by the people, and implying that he was a dictator, which was true.

For some time, European leaders had urged Wilson to recognize Huerta because he had been a strong ruler and seemed to be the only official capable of keeping the peace in Mexico. The country was in a state of siege, threatening the heavy foreign investments in Mexico's natural resources, by Pancho Villa and Venutiano Carranza.

Much to the surprise of most Americans President Wilson asked Congress for authority to use armed force to make Huerta comply with American demands, and it was readily granted.

United States Navy ships were dispatched to Veracruz, Mexico, and Marines took control of the city. In the fighting, four Americans were killed and 20 wounded.

This action complicated an already tense situation because Germany used this port on the Gulf of Mexico to send arms to Huerta. But wiser heads prevailed and representatives from Argentina, Brazil and Chile mediated the dispute and war with Mexico was averted.

The occupation of Veracruz had one positive aspect. It stopped German supplies to Huerta.

Archduke Francis Ferdinand, Austria's Crown Prince, was murdered on June 28, 1914, by Gabriel Principe and Pan-Slav fanatics in Sarajevo. The Austro-Hungarian government sent an ultimatum to Serbia on July 23, and declared war five days later. The situation quickly worsened as Russia mobilized its armed forces. Ferdinand's assassination was just the trigger that ignited the conflict. The real causes were age-old imperial, territorial and economic rivalries.

The London Stock Exchange, the world's most influential at this time, closed on July 31, due to the war. The United States Stock Exchange followed suit. After several weeks all important exchanges had closed their doors.

Any hope that all-out war could be avoided ended on August 1 when Germany declared war on Russia, and the German Kaiser ordered his army to march on Belgium with the idea of later invading France. Two days later Germany declared war on France.

As German troops moved into Belgium on August 4, Great Britain honored its treaties and declared war on Germany.

The United States formally announced its neutrality on August 5, and President Wilson offered the nation's services to mediate the spreading conflict, but European nations were too intent on war to even seriously consider a peaceful solution.

Austria-Hungary declared war on Russia on August 6 as the United States proposed that all belligerents stand by the 1902 Declaration of London that the open seas were neutral areas, and that neutral shipping would be protected.

Thousands of Americans were stranded in Europe without funds and, as the war progressed, they found it impossible to return home. The American government authorized the shipment of $5 million in gold to help pay their expenses, and their return fares.

Secretary of State William Jennings Bryan wrote to J. P. Morgan on August 15 to announce that loans to belligerents were against the United States policy of neutrality. Two months later, officials of the government changed their minds, saying that shipments of gold or extensions of credits, would not be prohibited.

President Wilson, adamant about maintaining complete neutrality, advised Americans on August 19 to be "impartial in thought as well as in action . . . neutral in fact as well as in name."

It was easier said than done as pro-and-con sentiment in the United States quickly polarized, mainly along ethnic lines. Some supported the Allies, while others favored the Germans. But most Americans, including former President Roosevelt, wanted to remain neutral.

Belgium succumbed quickly as her army proved no match against Germany's armed forces that drove like a juggernaut through the country and then swung toward France. Many Americans changed their attitudes about non-involvement in the war after stories of German atrocities in Belgium were published. Most were not true, but some had a basis in fact.

During the early days of the conflict airmen flew back and forth across the battlelines making notes of enemy troop movements and taking photographs. For a time there was a gentleman's agreement that neither side would fire upon the other.

Such a situation could not last. The inevitable happened when a pilot took a gun along and shot at an enemy plane. By August, pilots were routinely shooting at one another with rifles and pistols, but doing little harm to one another.

No one recalls who dropped the first bomb, but there are numerous accounts of French reconnaissance pilots strafing soldiers in the German trenches or while they marched along roads.

After Belgium was overrun, former President Roosevelt, writing in *Outlook Magazine,* said "the United States has not the smallest responsibility for Belgium," and he strongly advised the nation to remain neutral.

Japan declared war on Germany August 23 but the Germans seemed invincible everywhere as they defeated the Russians three days later at Tannenberg on the Eastern Front. This defeat seriously undermined the Allied cause.

As the Germans appeared ready to overwhelm France in early September, the United States Treasury Department established the Bureau of War Risk Insurance to provide up to $5 million insurance for merchant ships and their crews.

September 5, President Wilson ordered that wireless stations be provided by the United States Navy for direct transatlantic communications. In a controversial agreement, Wilson told German diplomats they could use those facilities even for encoded messages. The President was naive in assuming that Germany would use these facilities without abusing the privilege. Later, Wilson was informed by the British just how naive he had been.

The seemingly invincible German army ground to a halt that same day just 25 miles from Paris when France's army stopped it at the Marne River. The German general staff had counted on a quick victory before the Allied forces could array their full might against Germany. The French Army denied them a quick victory by its stubborn resistance and the bravery of its men. In one of the most strategic battles of the war— quite possibly of all wars—the Germans were forced to retreat to the Aisne and quickly build defensive positions. Thus began a stalemate on the Western Front that lasted three years while the Kaiser called for an increase in submarine warfare to cut off supplies to Great Britain from its overseas empire and the United States.

The Germans continued to be more successful on the Eastern Front winning another important victory against the Russians at the Masurian

Lakes. With this overwhelming defeat, the Russians were effectively out of the war as a viable military force for the Allies.

Americans continued to have mixed emotions about the war, and their loyalties were divided along ethnic lines: most German-Americans sided with the pacifists in advocating neutrality although their interests were mainly with the Germans. But, many of them reasoned keeping America out of the war was the best way to help achieve a German victory.

Some of those who favored the Allies took a more martial stance. They joined either the British Army or the French Foreign Legion. Some served as ambulance drivers, while others worked zealously in war relief efforts. In 1916 American fliers formed the Lafayette Escadrille in the French Air Force, and their exploits became legendary.

The Hearst newspapers and the Chicago Tribune advocated neutrality, and used their considerable influence to keep the United States out of the conflict.

President Charles W. Eliot of Harvard proposed an offensive and defensive alliance with the Allied powers early in the war, but nothing came of his proposal. If he had accepted President Wilson's offer to become ambassador to Great Britain, he might have been more successful in promoting the idea, but he turned it down.

With the ground war in Europe stalemated, the first bombing raid was flown when Britain's Royal Naval Air Service sent Lieutenant C. H. Collett to bomb German airship sheds at Düsseldorf. A month later three British Avro-504 biplanes bombed the Zeppelin airship works at Friedrichshaffen. The Germans retaliated, their aviators hurling small bombs upon the cities of Dover and London.

These bombings, although limited in scope, heralded the start of the air war, despite government agreement by most major European powers to refrain from aerial bombardment of any kind.

After the First Battle of the Marne in September 1914, the German drive was stopped 25 miles from Paris. Now the war was largely confined to the trenches with little or no change in the front lines. Germany increased its submarine warfare against Allied shipping, prompting Great Britain to declare the North Sea a military area. The British Admiralty announced that neutral ships bound for neutral ports would travel at their own risk and be subjected to search and seizure.

The United States continued to trade with all belligerents, including Germany, and some American industries were reaping unexpected profits although farmers were suffering because many of their normal overseas markets were now restricted.

For Great Britain, control of the seas was mandatory and its government officials early in the war had established an Order in Council to enlarge the list of goods going to Germany that it considered contraband and subject to confiscation. When such goods were removed from ships, the British paid for them. Among items listed as contraband was cotton that was used to make munitions.

Secretary of State William Jennings Bryan protested the Order in Council September 26, but some United States businesses were making so much money out of the war that Bryan was pressured into formally withdrawing the protest, which he did October 22.

The situation resolved itself because the British fleet succeeded in bottling up the German fleet in its harbors so it could not protect ships bound for Germany from being seized by elements of the British Navy. The flow of overseas goods to Germany was effectively stopped.

Germany turned to the only weapon it had to counter Britain's control of the seas—its submarine fleet. In 1914, hoping to keep America neutral, Germany had attacked only warships.

On January 28, 1915, Congress approved legislation authorizing the establishment of the United States Coast Guard. Later, it was charged with the prevention of contraband trade, and was given responsibility for assisting persons and ships in distress at sea.

For the first time, the danger of shipping American goods to Europe was forcefully revealed with the sinking of the merchant ship "William P. Frye." It was taking a cargo of wheat to Great Britain but it was torpedoed by a German submarine in the South Atlantic.

President Wilson sent his good friend Colonel Edward M. House to Europe January 30 on the "Lusitania" in an attempt to get the warring powers to settle their differences without further war. He was disturbed to learn that neither side was interested in peace talks, each believing they could win the war. House was shocked to learn that German leaders insisted upon acquiring Poland and Belgium in any settlement, and really hoped to dominate all of Europe.

With Great Britain's Royal Navy blockading Germany's ports, the Germans retaliated February 4 by proclaiming the seas around the British Isles a war zone where all neutral shipping could be attacked.

Six days later, with American shipping under constant attack, President Wilson warned Germany that the United States would hold it "to a strict accountability" for "property endangered or lives lost." He was forced to take this step despite pressure from pacifists who accused him of taking sides.

German U-boat commanders were faced by a classic Catch-22 situation. If they abided by the normal rules of war and warned ships prior to launching torpedoes so their crews and passengers could take to lifeboats, they would expose themselves to Allied warships. U-boats were particularly vulnerable to guns on the surface. To assure their own safety, they were almost forced to attack silently and without warning.

The war at sea intensified March 11 as Britain declared a blockade of all German ports, and announced they would stop all German ships before they reached the North Sea or the English Channel.

President Wilson protested Britain's blockade March 30 because it would interfere with American shipping and ships of all noninvolved nations even though they were heading for neutral ports.

The British refused to change their policy, declaring that cargoes of most of these ships would end up in Germany.

German officials protested to the United States April 4 that it must insist that Britain lift its blockade and permit Germany to trade with the United States. At the start of the war, the Germans had not been concerned about a blockade because they expected the war would be short as its armies overran the continent. That situation failed to materialize due to France's stubborn resistance once German troops were on French soil.

Seven months after the start of the war in Europe, and despite recommendations by a board headed by Captain Washington I. Chambers, the Navy still had only 12 planes for training. This brilliant engineer had been assistant to the Secretary of the Navy's Aide for Material in 1909. When the Navy Department decided to follow air developments more closely the following year, he was the logical man for the job. He was intimate with most of the air-minded civilians and officers of that day. Glenn Curtiss, hearing of his appointment, offered to train an officer in a Curtiss plane at no cost to the Navy. Chambers quickly accepted and Lieutenant Theodore G. Ellyson was taught to fly by Curtiss pilot Eugene Ely in San Diego, California.

Captain Mark Bristol, who was operating a bombing course for aviators at Pensacola, Florida, pleaded with the Navy for two planes for each of the fleet's 16 battleships. He was named Director of Naval Aeronautics November 23, 1914, and used his new position to seek support for building up his air service.

After thorough study, the Navy's General Board agreed that the situation was deplorable, claiming that aircraft were the eyes both of armies and navies, and finding there was no limit to their offensive capabilities. While the board urged the Navy Department to make $5 million available to aviation, they pointed out only a third of previous allocations had been spent.

No action was immediately forthcoming but several officers were sent to Europe to study the military situation.

In Europe, following British and French bombing raids, the German

Navy decided to use its huge Zeppelin airships in organized attacks against Allied cities. Ten bombs were dropped on Antwerp September 28, but the first large scale bombing wasn't flown until Christmas Eve, 1914, when bombs plunged from the sky on Dover, England.

Germany had 30 airships available. Some of them had been constructed originally for the commercial transport lines of Delag, the German civilian carrier prior to the war. The five-ton load-carrying capability of the Zeppelins gave the Germans a decided advantage and they moved swiftly to capitalize on it.

In subsequent flights they became a menace beause the British had no fighter plane to reach the high-flying Zeppelins. But dropping bombs from such altitudes prohibited accurate bombing. When they came in at lower altitudes, the inflammable gas bags encountered fighters and anti-aircraft guns that made each mission hazardous.

There was only one solution—night attacks. The Germans launched their first night raid April 14, 1915, on Tyneside, England.

During the summer of 1915 Germany increased its airship attacks, hoping to bring England to her knees by destroying morale at home. Although raids were made regularly on several English cities including London, the raids were more of a nuisance than anything else.

The British developed new fighter planes, and the attacks dropped off as Zeppelins routinely were shot down, but this was not the end of the attacks because the Germans were developing new Zeppelins that would be less vulnerable.

The Naval Appropriations Act of 1915 at last recognized the dire need for expansion of the U.S. Naval Air Service. A million dollars was approved but, equally important, the act authorized a committee later to be known as the National Advisory Committee for Aeronautics. Two of its 12 members were Navy men and it soon began its historic record of contributions to aeronautical research.

Early aviators like Bristol, Chambers and others had long fought for adequate compensation for men who risked their lives flying. This new act recognized these risks and authorized a 50 percent allowance for qualified pilots along with survivors' benefits. It was a welcome reward for the Navy's 48 eligible officers and its 96 enlisted men plus the 12 officers and 24 enlisted men of the Marine Corps.

During the second year of the war in Europe, all powers began an intensive buildup of their large bombing planes. Italian engineers at first held a commanding lead after Giovanni Caproni, pioneer designer and builder of airplanes, converted his latest passenger plane to a bomber. A giant triplane with a 130-foot wingspan, it could carry up to one-and-a-half tons of bombs, some of them mounted internally.

Russian-built Sikorsky four-engine bombers carried their first loads over German lines during February 1915. Seventy-three of them attempted to fly from Russia for delivery to Allied airfields, but only three completed the trip. Engine trouble plagued the "Illya Mourometz" bombers and crash landings were common in hay fields and cow pastures.

The Sikorsky bombers that did get into combat were never shot down. Their five machine guns, capable of firing at every conceivable angle, made them impregnable to German pursuit planes. They even had a tail gunner, a concept not used in United States bombers until World War II.

The Sikorsky bombers would have posed an extreme threat to Germany if production had not been halted because of the Russian Revolution in 1917. The Italian "Caproni" bombers maintained a production lead until 1917 when German "Gothas" and British "Handley-Pages" went into service.

In a routine action, President Wilson created Naval Petroleum Reserve No. 3 in Wyoming on April 30, 1915. It was known as Teapot Dome and it covered 9,481 acres. It would become world-renowned years later in a political scandal that would rock another presidency.

CHAPTER 2

"Lafayette, We Are Here."

A U-BOAT SANK THE AMERICAN TANKER "GULFLIGHT" WITHOUT WARN-ing May 1. Germany hastened to offer reparations, and promised that its U-boats would not attack another American ship without warning unless it tried to escape. When pressed by President Wilson to stop undersea warfare, German officials refused because their submarines were the only German ships that could penetrate the British blockade.

The British passenger ship "Lusitania" was sunk without warning six days later. Eleven-hundred-and-ninety-eight of its 1,924 passengers lost their lives, including 128 Americans. The Germans charged that the ship was carrying munitions, although the British denied it. Years later, it was revealed that the "Lusitania" was carrying munitions. Americans should not have been on board a belligerent ship, although they had not been advised that the "Lusitania" had some military cargo on board. However, the German Ambassador, Count von Bernstorff, had printed a warning in New York's newspapers May 1 advising Americans that it would be unwise to travel into a war zone on ships carrying cargoes to the Allies.

Count von Bernstorff offered his condolences to the families of those Americans who perished in the sinking, but there was a widespread anti-German reaction.

President Wilson still hoped to avoid war. Three days later he stated the United States' position in a speech in Philadelphia by saying, "There is such a thing as a nation being so right that it does not need to convince others that it is right."

Secretary of State Bryan demanded in a note to Germany May 13 that it disavow the attack on the "Lusitania." He warned that America would omit no word or deed that might be necessary to uphold the rights of its citizens anywhere in the world.

Despite his strong words, Bryan confided to the Austrian ambassador, whose country was allied with Germany, that his note to Germany "means no harm, but had to be written in order to pacify excited public opinion. The Berlin government therefore need not feel itself injured, but need only make suitable concessions if it desires to put an end to the dispute."

The Austrian ambassador immediately contacted Arthur Zimmermann, Germany's undersecretary of state for foreign affairs, and passed along the information. This occurred before the American ambassador in Berlin reached him to give him Bryan's antagonistic note. When the American met with Zimmermann, he was advised of what Bryan had told the Austrian ambassador, thus totally destroying the effects of Bryan's tough memorandum. As a result, the Germans never disavowed the attack on the "Lusitania" or made reparations.

Former President Roosevelt at first had approved of Wilson's neutrality, but now he called the sinking of the "Lusitania" murder " murder on the high seas." He told newsmen that he was "sick at heart" over Wilson's actions and his pacific Secretary of State William Jennings Bryan.

Wilson and some members of his cabinet prepared a new note of protest for Bryan's signature June 8, but Bryan refused to sign it and handed in his resignation, saying that as a pacifist he could not sign such a strong note. Wilson sent it the following day, demanding that Germany cease its procrastination over the sinking of the unarmed "Lusitania" and demanded reparations. He said Germany must "prevent the recurrence of anything so obviously subversive of the principles of war." In the note, Wilson said he refused to recognize the previously non-existent "war zone" that Germany had established around the British Isles. "The lives of non-combatants cannot lawfully or rightfully be put in jeopardy by the capture or destruction of an unresisting merchantman."

Bryan had disliked this part of the statement in particular, saying, "A ship carrying contraband should not rely upon passengers to protect her from attack—it would be like putting women and children in front of the army." Sixty-three infants were drowned when the "Lusitania" sank.

German officials refused to give the pledges sought by Wilson but they did agree to permit Americans to travel in well-marked neutral ships.

America's plastics industry boomed as a result of the war, and cellulose acetate was particularly in demand to coat the fabric of airplanes to tighten them. With the expansion of the automobile industry, crude oil was needed in quantity not only to make gasoline, but to provide a large number of chemicals for the plastics industry.

Although aviation was still in its infancy in the United States, due to government apathy, rapid strides had been made in Europe even before the war. On the eve of World War I, France's Louis Bleriot had already built over 800 airplanes of 40 different types.

In America, Commander Jerome C. Hunsaker was starting to build M.I.T.'s first wind tunnel and had initiated a course in aerodynamics and aeronautical engineering. He brought in Donald W. Douglas, an M.I.T. graduate, to assist him. It was soon evident to both of them that they had meager information to support their efforts. The new tunnel's balance was unattainable in the United States and had to be procured from Great Britain's National Physical Laboratory.

America's limited basic knowledge of aircraft design had been gained primarily from wind tunnel work in England, France and Germany. Hunsaker's and Douglas's first tests, therefore, only confirmed the results of previous foreign experiments.

The Wrights had built a small tunnel in the early 1900s, and there was another at the Washington Navy Yard, but the M.I.T. tunnel at Cambridge was more advanced in style and operation.

Douglas had gone to college with Thomas Alva Edison's son, where they shared a room. When the famed scientist offered him a job, Douglas declined because he wanted to make a career as an aeronautical engineer.

Glenn L. Martin, who had moved his plant to Santa Ana, California, in 1907 where he made gliders, moved again to what later became Los Angeles International Airport. There he constructed an aircraft plant prior to the start of World War I where he was building Army training planes by 1915.

That year Hunsaker received a letter from Martin asking him to recommend an aeronautical engineer. He asked Douglas if he wanted the job, and Douglas eagerly assured him that he did.

Martin had heard of Douglas so he promptly hired him. His new chief engineer immediately changed the company's way of designing and building airplanes. He made stress analyses to replace the physical tests that had been used to determine a structure's inherent strength, and factory workers were given detailed drawings for each part. In the past, each airplane had been practically hand-made. They called him the "boy engineer" behind his back.

When the first airplane that Douglas designed for Martin exceeded its performance specifications, Martin's engineers were convinced that their new chief engineer knew what he was doing. The aircraft was designed to fly 70 miles an hour, and it attained a speed of 72.

Douglas had often said that designing an airplane was 99 percent mathematics, and his fellow engineers grudgingly conceded that maybe he was right.

Pusher-type planes now were giving way to tractor designs, although many pushers continued to be built. Virtually all planes were small, and with relatively low-powered engines. A big order for a firm was six or eight airplanes a year, and they were priced between $10,000 and $15,000 each.

On the war fronts, a newly organized Russian army of 800,000 men had headed for Prussia January 31 to start a new offensive. Six months earlier they had lost their first battle with Germany even though they outnumbered the Germans two to one.

On the Western Front, A French offensive in Champagne began February 12 and captured 20,000 unwounded German prisoners on the first day. Meanwhile, British troops attacked on a five-mile front on both sides of the La Bassee canal to the north and managed to get within 12 miles of Lille. These were the first heavy attacks on the Germans in this area since the Allies were defeated on the Marne the previous year.

Turkish forts on the Gallipoli Peninsula were attacked February 19 by French and British battleships as a preliminary bombardment prior to an attempt to take Constantinople. These forts guarded entry to the Sea of Marmara and their elimination was vital if the campaign was to have a chance of success. Winston Churchill, First Lord of the Admiralty, had conceived the plan to force the Germans to ease pressure on the Russia forces defending the Caucasus front.

British troops went ashore April 30 at six points on the Gallipoli Peninsula while French troops drove Turkish troops back from strategic positions on Cape Kum Kale on the Asian side of the Dardanelles Strait. Aggressive Turkish troops eventually forced the British and French to end their campaign the following January. The campaign ended in disaster for them when all troops were withdrawn January 8, 1916.

Armenians, a Christian minority in mostly-Muslim Turkey, were considered traitors. This was just an excuse to order their deportation, but even worse was to befall the Armenians. They had been scapegoats for centuries, and 300,000 were massacred in 1890. Talaat Pacha, Turkish Minister of the Interior, announced June 17, 1915, that "those who are innocent today may be guilty tomorrow." Since the first of the year hundreds of Armenians in the Turkish army were charged with spying, disarmed and executed. The German Ambassador told his government the truth in a telegram, saying, "The Ottoman Court wants to profit from the war by putting an end to its interior enemies, the Christians, without any diplomatic interference."

The Russian offensive on the Eastern Front turned defensive as German troops smashed through Russian lines to capture Warsaw, and fell back across the Vistula River. The loss of the strategic city of Warsaw weakened the whole Russian front as four German and Austrian armies prepared to renew the attack. A huge number of Russian prisoners were taken by the Germans and Austrians, indicating a drastic fall in Russian morale.

To relieve the pressure on the Russian front, an Allied offensive moved forward as British and French troops occupied 20 miles of German trenches, penetrating the German lines in some places to a depth of two-and-a-half miles. France's army swept forward in Champagne in an attempt to weaken the German positions around Verdun. But the Germans had 1.8 million men defending this sector and the fighting was fierce. The front remained much the same as the year before.

The attempt to help the Russians failed because their poorly equipped troops were no match for the Germans. Reports indicated that 30 percent of Russia's troops were without weapons. As Russian troops started to retreat, Czar Nicholas II personally took command of his armies but he was unable to stop the Germans from seizing parts of the Ukraine, Lithuania and Byelorussia. Even worse, by September 6 the Russians had lost six million men.

The French General Staff still hoped to reclaim the territory lost to Bismarck's Germany in 1870 by attacks against the Germans in Alsace-Lorraine. Despite their failure in 1914, repeated attempts were made again this year with mixed results.

During fighting in the Argonne the Germans used gas shells prior to an infantry attack, helping them to make limited advances. Use of poison gas was a new element in a war that was already known for its viciousness.

With the Western Front in a state of uncertainty, Field Marshal Sir Douglas Haig was appointed Commander-in-Chief of the British forces in France and Belgium. Two weeks earlier General Joseph Joffre was named to the same post as head of the French army.

The Allied changes came none too soon because the Germans were massing seven army corps of 280,000 men for an offensive against the forts guarding Verdun. These forts guarded the principal invasion routes into France. If they were lost, the Allied position throughout France could become untenable.

Winston Churchill, who had been denounced for the failure of the Gallipoli campaign, resigned from the British cabinet November 12. He said he would join his regiment to fight in France. Dissension within the coalition government had been strong for some time. Prime Minister Asquith, who headed it, had asked Churchill to participate in a small War Council, but Churchill had refused. He said that the council's role had changed and he "could not accept a position without an effective share in its guidance and control."

The League to Enforce Peace, a prototype of the later League of Nations, was organized June 17 at Independence Hall in Philadelphia with William Howard Taft as president. Its promoters drew an analogy between the success of the United States and the need for a somewhat similar organization of the world's nations to preserve peace. It was a visionary approach to a universal problem, but most nations weren't prepared to give up some of their sovereignty for the good of all people.

The war was brought closer to home to Americans July 2 when a German instructor at Cornell University exploded a bomb in the United States Senate's reception room, and escaped. The following day, Erich Muenter shot J. P. Morgan for representing the British government in war contract negotiations. This time he was captured, but he committed suicide three days later.

Dr. Heinrich F. Albert, responsible for German propaganda in the United States, created a diplomatic incident July 15 when he left his briefcase on a New York City subway. A Secret Service agent recovered it and learned from its contents that Germany had established an extensive spy network in the United States. Involved were members of the German consulates, the Washington Embassy and the steamship lines. Even more shocking was the revelation that many German-Americans were involved in espionage. Secretary of the Treasury William G. McAdoo leaked the contents to the New York *World*, and their revelation shocked the American people.

The so-called "grandfather clause" that was added to the constitutions of Oklahoma and Maryland, was declared unconstitutional July 21 by the United States Supreme Court. The clause stated that anyone whose grandfather did not vote in an election could not vote. It was aimed principally at blacks, but it also had an impact against immigrants.

President Wilson sent his third note to Germany on this date about the sinking of the "Lusitania." He warned that future infringement of American rights would be considered "deliberately unfriendly."

Four days later relations between the two countries worsened when a U-boat sank the American ship "Leelanaw" with a load of flax off the coast of Scotland.

Wireless communication was established July 27 between the United States and Japan, thus bringing the two nations closer together as "instant" communication with many nations of the world became an increasing reality.

United States Marines were ordered into Haiti July 28 to quell a revolution. What began as a short-term intervention to initiate administrative changes ended as a 19-year occupation that produced no worthwhile changes in Haiti's chaotic government operations.

Conditions in Mexico were so unstable by August that a Latin-American Conference was called on the 5th as revolutionary forces roamed the countryside causing havoc everywhere. Officials of Argentina, Brazil, Bolivia, Chile, Guatemala and Uruguay joined the United States to discuss the matter. Conditions among Mexico's poor had reached an appalling state and corruption was widespread. American "Dollar Diplomacy" was blamed for much of the problem, and suspicion about American motives almost precluded a just settlement.

The Díaz regime had tried to modernize Mexico when it took power in 1876 by permitting development by foreign interests. By 1910, American interests owned 100 million acres, including much of the country's mining, timber and agricultural lands, totaling 22 percent of Mexico's territory. William Randolph Hearst owned almost eight million of these acres. Foreign ownership helped to impoverish Mexico's peasants, and 90 percent became landless. To maintain control, Díaz used dictatorial powers to hold down the legitimate rights of Mexico's workers. In 1910, workers joined with peasants and many members of the middle class in a rebellion that overthrew Diaz. This revolution was an agrarian, small-town revolt led by Pancho Villa and Emiliano Zapata who sought to restore village rights to the nation's resources. At first, it was a conservative revolt because it favored decentralized self-rule.

Taft had imposed an embargo on arms to Mexico while he was President, but Wilson ignored the ruling until it became apparent that Huerta was not only incompetent but a tyrant who could never impose law and order on Mexico. Despite huge amounts of arms sent to Huerta between March and September in 1913 for use against forces under Carranza, Villa and Zapata, Huerta failed to establish law and order and Wilson was forced to stop America's support for him. Without it, he was quickly overthrown and Carranza became head of the government.

President Wilson then ordered the occupation of Mexico's port city of Veracruz and stocked a large arsenal with American weapons.

Wilson was under great pressure from American interests represented by William Randolph Hearst, William F. Buckley, Sr., of the Texas Oil Company and Senator Albert B. Fall to guarantee American interests in Mexico. Fall even asked for outright seizure and annexation of Mexico.

A military training camp was set up in Plattsburgh, New York, August 10 to train civilians. It had been initiated by Grenville Clark, Theodore Roosevelt, Jr., and several others despite Wilson's adamant refusal to endorse the idea of "preparedness." "The Plattsburgh Idea" caught on and it was duplicated at many other military installations by

General Leonard Wood. The first 1200 trainees went to Plattsburgh where they paid their own travel expenses. Meanwhile, William Jennings Bryan and Robert La Follette spoke out strongly against the practice, but in a year's time 16,000 men were taking part in this unofficial military training.

In Europe, Bulgaria became a participant October 14 when Britain and France declared war on her.

War fever in the United States against Germany rose when it was announced that the Italian ship "Ancona" was sunk November 7 without warning by an Austrian submarine. Twenty-seven Americans died in the sinking.

Tempers were further inflamed on November 30 when an explosion ripped the DuPont ammunition plant in Wilmington, Delaware, because sabotage was suspected.

Henry Ford believed that he, alone, could end the war in Europe. A strong pacifist, he conceived the idea of a "peace ship" that he fitted out at his own expense, that would carry distinguished Americans to Europe to convince the war's leaders that they should seek peace. His goal was "to get the boys out of the trenches by Christmas." By the ship's departure time, no one of importance had joined him on his peace crusade, and the whole idea was ridiculed in the press and by responsible persons.

President Wilson, although sympathetic to the Allied cause, still was determined to keep America out of the war. Privately, he had doubts his goal was achievable because Germany kept making aggressive acts against American ships and citizens. To be prepared for any eventuality, the President asked Congress on December 7 for a standing army of 142,000 men, with a reserve of 400,000 more.

With some industries expanding due to the war, unions demanded an eight-hour day and other concessions from steel firms. The Iron and Steel Workers Union in East Youngstown, Ohio, was first to get its demands approved December 27 because skilled workers were in short supply.

President Wilson had long demanded of Germany that it cease its attacks upon neutral shipping, and particularly American ships, but throughout most of 1915 his demands were ignored. But on January 7, 1916, German officials notified the State Department that it would adhere to strict international rules of maritime warfare.

While war raged in Europe, involving millions of men on both sides, a much smaller—but equally deadly—war continued in Mexico. January 10 General Francisco "Pancho" Villa forced 18 American mining engineers off a train and murdered them. He committed this atrocity deliberately to embroil the United States in Mexico's civil war.

Representative McLemore introduced legislation in Congress February

2 to seek Wilson's approval for banning overseas travel by Americans in ships of warring nations. It was his hope that this would eliminate the deaths of Americans thereby reducing America's chances of being brought into the conflict. The President objected because he considered such legislation as an attempt to tie his hands on foreign affairs and the proposal was tabled.

In Europe the war heated up in February and, at the Battle of Verdun, the Germans and the French each lost about 350,000 men for no worthwhile advantage.

Pancho Villa led an attack into New Mexico on March 9 and killed 17 more Americans, this time on United States soil. President Wilson ordered Brigadier-General John J. "Black Jack" Pershing to take 6,000 men and pursue Villa into Mexico and to capture him. Although Pershing made a valiant attempt to find the revolutionary general, he failed to apprehend him.

Meanwhile, economic conditions in Mexico worsened during 1916 as workers defied their government and staged the largest general strike in Mexican history. They sought to establish a worker's self-government, but the idea was anathema to Washington that feared loss of the huge foreign holdings in Mexico.

The matter of preparedness took a big step forward on March 15 when the House of Representatives passed the Army Reorganization Bill, and the Senate agreed to bring the Army up to full strength.

The National Defense Act was passed on June 3 and authorized a standing army of 175,000 men. The National Guard, which could be called up in the event of a national emergency, was established at a strength of 450,000 men.

American emotions were further heightened against the Germans as a U-boat sank a French ship on March 24 with the loss of three Americans. The ship was unarmed, and steaming through the English Channel.

Secretary of State Robert Lansing warned Germany that the United States would break off diplomatic relations unless these attacks were discontinued.

From then on American diplomatic notes became increasingly severe as American officials began to think the unthinkable that perhaps the United States should take an active part in the war. Slowly but surely the American people were changing their attitude and were about ready to follow their President in whatever step he decided to take. They all fervently hoped to prevent American involvement in the war, and none more so than the President.

1916 was a presidential year, and the war complicated the political situation in the United States.

The Republican Party held its convention June 10, 1916. A little-known Charles Evans Hughes—at least on the national level—was nominated to head their ticket with Charles Fairbanks of Alaska as their nominee for vice-president.

Privately, President Wilson held out little hope that the United States could avoid the war in Europe. He was not re-assured by German claims that neutral merchant ships would no longer be attacked without warning. With America re-arming to prepare for any eventuality, he personally led a preparedness parade June 14 in Washington.

In May, one of the great sea battles of all times had been fought between the British and German navies at Jutland. The British lost the most ships but they emerged victorious because the German surface fleet never again ventured out of its ports.

In the United States, Navy airmen had fought for years to obtain funds for aircraft carriers. They asked for $13 million in early 1916 to build up the Navy's air arm, with $6 million to be set aside for two carriers. The Naval Appropriations Bill of August 29 approved three-and-a-half million dollars for aviation, but the appeal for carriers was stricken. The bill also provided for a true naval flying corps and a reserve corps. Despite the fact that the bill called for a separate corps, it was never created, although it did provide openings for 150 officers and 350 enlisted men from the Navy and the Marines.

By the end of the year, 60 planes were on order and Curtiss had the greatest share with its order for 30 seaplanes.

Army aviators served as part of the Signal Corps, and they were dominated by ground officers, so their situation was even worse.

It was a foregone conclusion when the Democrats met in St. Louis June 16 that they would renominate Wilson to head their ticket. Most Americans appreciated his efforts to remain out of the war so their backing for a second term was done with enthusiasm. Thomas R. Marshall was also renominated for vice-president.

Another preparedness parade the following month in San Francisco ended disastrously when a bomb explosion on July 22 killed nine people and wounded about 40 others. Thomas J. Mooney, a labor leader who had joined the Socialist Party, and Warren K. Billings were convicted of responsibility for the bombing. Mooney was condemned to death and Billings to life imprisonment, although California's governor in 1918 reduced Mooney's sentence to life imprisonment. Both men denied complicity in the crime and a number of investigations were held through the years. Mooney was pardoned and released in 1939 and Billings was also released. The latter was officially pardoned in 1961.

President Carranza ordered his troops to attack American soldiers in

Mexico and 18 were killed or wounded on June 21 at Carrizal. Despite American protests, the Mexican government announced that the killings would continue unless Americans withdrew from Mexico. President Wilson refused the Mexican demand until order was restored along the border. The following month both nations agreed to submit their dispute to arbitration to avoid all-out war.

Starting in June, and continuing through the summer months into September, General Aleksey Alekseyavich led a successful offensive against the Austrians on the Eastern Front, but at the cost of a million men. The losses served to further demoralize the Russians so it was a Pyrrhic victory.

On the Western Front, during the Battle of the Somme from July through November, the British lost over 400,000 men, the French 200,000 and the Germans 450,000 with neither side gaining a strategic advantage.

Wilson was re-elected in November, but it was a close race. Hughes, the "bearded iceberg," had given him a run for his money. Wilson's search for peace, and his dual focus on preparedness, matched the mood of a restless people not sure of what the future held in store for them. The Democrats also won control of Congress, and Jeannette Rankin of Montana became the first woman to be elected to the House of Representatives despite the lack of woman's suffrage in most states.

In December, the German Kaiser offered to enter into peace negotiations rather than "to continue the war to the bitter end."

Thus encouraged, President Wilson sought from both sides the terms they would consider to end the war. But the German government refused to be specific, and Allied nations offered such stiff terms that the Germans refused to even consider them. Furthermore, the Allied powers distrusted America's motives, and refused to cooperate.

With the war in Europe fostering increased concern for the defense of the Panama Canal, President Wilson authorized the purchase January 17, 1917, of the Virgin Islands. They were strategically located for bases to guard the canal, and they were available from Denmark for only $25 million.

President Wilson appeared before Congress January 22 and outlined a plan for a league of peace. He envisioned an organization that would unite peace-loving nations. He said he was appealing once again to the warring nations to put aside their differences and to end the war without an aftermath of bitterness. He called his concept "Peace without victory." It was a grand gesture, but ignored by both sides although they desperately needed peace. But each side still expected to be victorious on Europe's battlefields although the war was stalemated in endless trench warfare on the Western Front.

Any hope of peace, or compromise, evaporated January 31 when Germany declared that it would resume unrestricted submarine warfare. Officials warned that neutral ships, armed or unarmed, who sailed into a German war zone, would be attacked without warning.

Wilson broke off diplomatic relations with Germany February 3, saying that further unrestricted submarine warfare was sufficient cause to intervene in the conflict. He told the nation, "This government has no alternative consistent with the dignity and honor of the United States." He still insisted that this action did not mean that war was inevitable.

But that same day the American steamship "Housatonic" was sunk without warning by a German submarine.

Despite Wilson's opposition to a bill that called for a literacy test for immigrants, and excluded Asiatic laborers except those from Japan, the Congress over-rode his veto and passed the Immigration Act February 5.

With America's involvement in the war at sea gaining momentum, Wilson recalled American troops stationed along the Mexican border. Earlier, Pershing had been called back from Mexico after his unsuccessful pursuit of Pancho Villa.

Unstable conditions continued in Mexico even after the war and in 1920 Venustiano Carranza was forced to fight opposition forces under Álvaro Obregón. His army was defeated and Carranza was assassinated. Zapata was murdered in 1919, and Villa met the same fate in 1923.

President Wilson had earlier given Germany permission to use the nation's wireless transmission system, but the Germans used it to send coded diplomatic notes to Mexico against the United States. The American government was unaware of this violation of their agreement with Germany until British Secret Service agents intercepted a telegram from Foreign Minister Arthur Zimmermann to the German ambassador in Mexico. Zimmermann had long believed that America's involvement in the war was a foregone conclusion—which it was not—so his telegram had instructed the ambassador to urge Mexico in the event of war between Germany and the United States to take military action against its neighbor to the north. In return, he promised that Germany would restore the American states of New Mexico, Texas and Arizona to Mexico. The telegram was incredibly stupid, but Wilson had been naive in permitting the Germans to use the nation's transmission system.

British officials had waited for an opportune time before revealing the contents of the note, and when the United States broke off diplomatic relations with Germany February 3, they decided the time was propitious in the hope that it would provide the final lever to get the United States fully involved.

Wilson was appalled by this flagrant violation of the courtesy he had extended German officials and, at first, he refused to believe it. He thought it was a British propaganda move. If it were true, he realized, he would look ridiculous in the eyes of the people of the world. An investigation revealed that the telegram had been sent, although President Carranza had turned down such a suggestion.

When the Zimmermann telegram was released to the press February 24, the public was aroused to a fever pitch against Germany.

Two days later Wilson asked Congress for permission to arm merchant ships in order to safeguard American lives and rights at sea. Senator La Follette of Wisconsin, long-known as a pacifist, led a filibuster against such a bill in the Senate.

Wilson responded angrily, saying, "A little group of willful men have rendered the great government of the United States helpless and contemptible."

Before the bill could be passed the Senate had to adopt the cloture rule—permitting a majority to terminate debate—before the bill could be seriously considered.

Meanwhile, the attorney general ruled that the President already had authority to arm merchant ships and March 9 Wilson issued the directive without congressional approval.

The citizens of Puerto Rico had been in a quandary about their true status since their islands had been taken over by the United States. The Jones Act, passed March 2, finally made Puerto Rico a part of United States territory, and its people at last became citizens.

Wilson began his second term March 5 as tensions rose between those who believed the United States should become involved in the war in Europe and those who were adamantly opposed.

Seven days later emotions were fanned by Germany's sinking of the American merchant ship "Algonquin" without warning.

Three more American ships were sunk March 18: the "City of Memphis," "Vigilante" and "Illinois" in the same fashion. And the sinkings continued as the American "Healdton" was sunk off the Dutch coast three days later.

In the middle of this increase in submarine warfare came news that revolution had broken out in Russia, and the Czar was forced to abdicate, and he and his family were executed in 1918. Aleksandr Kerensky of the Socialist Revolutionary Party and his associates formed a new Russian government that the United States recognized March 22. In July, Kerensky became its prime minister.

Inevitably, with submarine warfare at its peak, it no longer was a question of whether the United States should join the Allied powers against the Central Powers, but when.

President Wilson reached his irrevocable decision and called a special session of Congress for April 2, 1917. That night, his limousine drove down Pennsylvania Avenue with an escort of cavalry. Thousands of Americans stood on the curbs in the rain, many carrying American flags, and solemnly watched their president drive toward the Capitol where he arrived at 8:30 p.m. He asked Congress to declare war on Germany saying, in part, "The world must be made safe for democracy."

Two days later the Senate gave its approval and, on Good Friday, April 6, the House of Representatives joined the upper house in voting overwhelmingly for war.

Congress passed the Selective Service Act May 18, authorizing the registration and draft of all men between the ages of 21 and 30 for military service.

General John J. Pershing was named to head the American forces in Europe. He had been a cavalryman in the Southwest during the last days of the Indian resistance, and then taught military science at the University of Nebraska and at West Point where he had graduated years earlier as president of his class.

During the Spanish-American War Pershing had served in Cuba, where he won a reputation for bravery, and then in the Philippines against the Moro uprising.

Pershing had been named official observer during the Russo-Japanese War in 1905 and his thoughtful dispatches brought him to the attention of President Roosevelt who promoted him to brigadier general.

During his involvement with the border problems with Mexico, Pershing's wife and three of his four children died in a fire. The tragedy forever changed him and he became aloof and taciturn, but his brilliance as a commander soon became legendary, and he developed the tactics to fight a modern war that are still followed.

When the United States declared war on Germany, a wave of optimism swept Allied Europe. Losses in human life and material had been staggering, and there seemed no hope of winning the war solely with ground troops. The free world was enthralled, therefore, by rumors that the United States would send 100,000 bombing planes to Europe within six months.

Among top Allied military commanders, there were some who said "Large numbers of heavy bombing aircraft can bring about a quick German surrender." Admiral Fiske said, "Aerial bombardment and aerial torpedoes are the key to defeating the Germans."

Italian authorities claimed large warplanes could do at long range what ground and naval guns could only do at short range. The Italians, world leaders in the production of large bombers, urged the United States to purchase Italian bombers as soon as possible and win the war. By this time, the Italian Air Force was flying Caproni bombers over Austria directly across the Adriatic Sea.

With the declaration of war April 6, the Navy had only 201 aviation personnel, of whom 38 were aviators and 163 had enlisted aviation ratings. There were six flying boats, 45 seaplanes for training, three land planes and two kite balloons.

So much for rumors about 100,000 bombing planes. Government insensibility had put the United States far behind other nations despite the fact it had flown the first heavier-than-air machine.

In May, at the urgent request of the French government, seven officers and 122 men in training at Pensacola were organized into the First Aeronautic Detachment, United States Navy. With Lieutenant Kenneth Whiting in command, this first flying unit arrived in France on June 5. Only four officers were qualified pilots and they had no planes.

Donald Douglas had left the Martin company in November 1916 to accept a position as chief civilian aeronautical engineer for the Army Signal Corps.

In Washington he was told that he must pass a Civil Service examination before he could assume the responsibilities of the office. Signal Corps officials sought in vain for someone who could make out such a test. It was finally agreed no one in government knew as much about aeronautical engineering as Douglas so they decided to forego the examination.

Douglas then was sent on a tour of all eastern aircraft plants to collect information on what everybody was doing, thus broadening his knowledge, to his immense satisfaction.

During this period, the government brought over quite a few well-known British and French aircraft; types then in service on the Western Front. Rather quickly, Douglas was able to gather extensive information about what was going on in the world of aviation.

When some of these foreign planes were gathered in a building belonging to the Smithsonian Institution, he was instrumental in seeing that all American aircraft officials had a chance to benefit from the latest knowledge and techniques of aircraft design and construction.

Douglas worked diligently to improve the status of the Aviation Section. It was not in high favor among Army brass, despite the efforts of the Army's first aeronautical engineer, Grover Loening, who was one of the most brilliant engineers of his time. Douglas strove to improve the

Aviation Section's image although he was frustrated more than once by failure of Army generals to understand the importance of airpower.

United States industries, therefore, were not prepared for the mass-production of airplanes, and when Congress passed an appropriation of $649 million to build them, Douglas and others wondered how 20,000 combat planes and 9,000 trainers could ever be built.

Standardization was the word most often used to get the job done. In other words, airplanes should be built like automobiles.

One product of this period was the Liberty engine that later became famous. At L.W.F Engineering Company, College Point, Long Island, a company airplane was redesigned as a test bed for the Liberty and made its first flight August 21, 1917. Although the first engine had eight cylinders, it was decided production models should have 12 to provide more power. Each engine weighed 844 pounds but produced 420 horse-power, and they were of good design. Production lagged behind because it took so long to "debug" the engine before it could be produced.

Douglas's main job during the year he spent in Washington was to work on redesigning British airplanes. During his government service, he argued forcefully for the design of stronger airplanes but, each time he had a new airplane to propose, orders came down from above to scrap it. Douglas was often bitter, but he stubbornly kept up with new designs although all of them were rejected.

Throughout this period he was made particularly unhappy by the fact that automobile executives were brought in to run the aircraft production program. Good men at mass production techniques, he readily conceded, but he also was aware these men knew little or nothing about the production of airplanes.

The first soldiers of the American Expeditionary Force landed in France June 24. They were sent to Allied units at a time when the war was going badly for the Allied cause, but it would be fall before an appreciable number of American men could even start to make a difference.

On July 4, Colonel Charles E. Stanton went to the tomb of Lafayette, the French officer who had resigned from the French army and gone to the United States in 1776 to serve in the American army during the Revolutionary War. He was commissioned a Major-General in the Continental Army and became one of General Washington's intimates. Stanton spoke quietly, but with immense feeling, when he said, "Lafayette, we are here."

CHAPTER 3

A World Safe for Democracy

WITH THE NATION AT WAR, TRAINING CAMPS PROLIFERATED AROUND the United States. Rantoul, Illinois, opened the first field on July 4 to train aviators. The long delay in developing military aviation had to be overcome quickly because the Army had only 55 planes and 4,500 aviation personnel. Congress quickly passed an appropriations bill calling for the expenditure of $640 million for military aviation programs.

The first American soldiers went into combat in Europe on October 27, and the first Americans to die in action were killed on November 3.

On the Italian front from October to December, the Italian army retreated following the battle of Caporetto after losing 600,000 of its troops to the Germans as prisoners and deserters.

On the Western Front there were battles at Arras, Champagne, and Ypres (for the third time), with little change in the front lines. British tanks made their first large-scale attack in November, but made little impact on the entrenched Germans.

The American Rainbow Division, representing every state in the nation, arrived in France November 30 with Colonel Douglas MacArthur as chief of staff.

War plans called for 180,000 American soldiers to be in France by the end of 1917; an insignificant number compared to the need, but still an incredible achievement by a nation that only the year before had seriously started its war preparedness drives.

In Russia, the Bolsheviks under Vladimir Ilyich Ulyanov Lenin and Leon Trotsky staged a coup d'etat against Kerensky because of his moderate policies and indecision as prime minister, and he was forced to flee.

The revolutionaries then appealed to Germany for an armistice, and it was granted December 15.

The United States declared war against Austria-Hungary December 7, and now all adversaries were clearly defined.

An unlikely hero, who would gain extraordinary recognition in 1918, had been a racing car driver before he attended pilot's school because he sincerely wanted to be a combat pursuit pilot. Edward V. "Eddie" Rickenbacker got his wish and, while flying French-made planes and later as commander of the famous "Hat-in-the-Ring" 94th Pursuit Squadron, was credited with 26 aerial victories against the Germans. For his incredible valor, Rickenbacker received his nation's highest award—the Medal of Honor. By war's end, he had shot down more German planes than any other American pilot.

Woodrow Wilson had been re-elected in 1916 as a peace president, and he had tried to mediate between the warring nations. Now he was a war president and he tried to use his influence to assure a lasting peace. In his "Fourteen Points" that he released on January 8, 1918, he announced definite terms to obtain an armistice. They involved specific rules for determining the German border, the matter of Polish, Turkish and Belgian sovereignty, war reparations and other helpful suggestions. Each of these recommendations was viewed by the parties involved in the conflict as how best they would advance their own selfish ends. But Wilson's final recommendations upset officials of Europe's governments to an extent that surprised him and most Americans who had long been aware of the value of unity among disparate groups such as existed in the United States. He called for "a general association of nations . . . under specific covenants for the purpose of affording mutual guarantees of political independence and territorial integrity to great and small states alike."

For centuries the politics of Europe had been governed by historical hatreds so Wilson's call for a league of nations was met with hostility by most Europeans. They considered that such an association would threaten their existence as independent nations.

France's Prime Minister, Georges Clemenceau, was typical of Europe's leaders who responded. "President Wilson and his Fourteen Points bore me. Even God Almighty has only ten!"

Ever since the draft was authorized by Congress there were those who challenged the government's right to draft men for service in the nation's armed forces. Selective Service Law violations reached the point where the Supreme Court agreed to review the law's constitutionality. In a decision announced January 7, the Justices announced that the Constitution does authorize conscription during wartime because it gives Congress the power "to declare war . . . to raise and support armies."

For years there had been proposals to dam the Tennessee River to provide electricity. The war effort, demanding huge amounts of energy, hastened the project. Wilson gave approval to the Muscle Shoals Dam February 24.

On March 3 Russia made it official as her communist regime signed a peace treaty with Germany, thus relieving the Germans from fighting a two-front war.

With the end of the war in the East, and the Italian forces effectively routed, the German High Command felt free to throw the full weight of its military might against the Allies on the Western Front before the Americans could introduce their armies in strength. In what proved to be its final offensive, Germany assaulted the Allied lines March 21 with 207 divisions against the Allies' 173. The assault began against the British between Arras and La Fere and forced them to withdraw 40 miles to the rear.

In Russia, civil war broke out between the communists and the anti-communists. Troops from the United States, France and Great Britain were dispatched in March to support the anti-communists, but they were withdrawn in 1919 without taking much of a part in the civil war. Japanese troops took advantage of the situation by occupying Vladivostok which they held until 1922.

On the Western Front, the British were forced to withdraw April 9 from Ypres to Armentieres.

The following month the French armies found it impossible to repulse the Germans as heavy fighting continued between Noyon and Rheims.

Throughout the war, the main problem with the Allies had been one of leadership. With the situation at the fronts growing more desperate each day, the Allies named General Ferdinand Foch as supreme commander of Allied forces, including the Americans.

After reviewing the situation, General Pershing made a special plea to President Wilson to get more American troops into France, even if they were untrained. This was done and 313,000 American troops arrived in July.

In its first independent action, the 1st Division on May 28 was thrown into the Battle of Cantigny. American troops quickly gained a reputation for bravery, but they were fresh and idealistic, not worn down by years of trench warfare like French and British soldiers.

The tide for the Allies turned June 25 when the Marine Brigade of the United States's 2nd Division captured Bouresche and Belleau Wood. The fighting lasted two weeks in a square-mile area. The Marines suffered terrible losses of 9,500 dead and wounded, almost 55 percent of their brigade. They not only stopped the Germans, but went on the offensive.

In conjunction with the French, American troops distinguished themselves at Château-Thierry and helped to stop the German advance there.

During the Second Battle of the Marne, German troops again took the offensive and on July 15, they attacked on both sides of Rheims. They almost reached their objectives but American units stopped them after two days of vicious fighting.

Marshal Foch ordered a counterattack at Soissons July 18, and the Germans had to fall back all along their front lines. Heavy losses in the Argonne and at Ypres panicked the German leadership.

Much later it was revealed that the German chancellor had said at the time, "On the 18th even the most optimistic among us knew that all was lost. The history of the world was played out in three days."

General Pershing, who had long argued to keep Americans in their own units, and not have them integrated into foreign organizations while fighting the Central Powers, had encountered stiff resistance. But President Wilson had supported him and, on August 10, Pershing was given permission to establish an independent American army. He was placed in command and Colonel George C. Marshall was named his operations officer.

The summer of 1918 was a desperate time for the Allies and, with aircraft production almost at a standstill in the States, the Army was forced to buy French airplanes. Unfortunately, these airplanes had been discarded by the French two years before, and new French aircraft could not be spared for sale to the United States. Fortunately, the United States Army was also able to procure the English Sopwith Camel; one of the finest fighters in World War I.

Congressional committees raged about the aircraft production pace, and charged there was favoritism in the award of some contracts. They were particularly incensed because it was obvious that profits on some airplanes and engines were too high.

It was an embarrassing period for the aircraft industry, one in which they were not wholly at fault because they had been asked to do an impossible job in too short a time. Even the Military Affairs Sub-Committee admitted they didn't imply their criticism should be directed at all companies because much had been accomplished. One of the problems was within the government itself and the sub-committee recognized it, recommending that a single man be placed in charge of a department of aviation. The chairman said, "Aviation should be organized similar to our Departments of the Army and Navy." Officials of these services fought stubbornly and unrealistically against such an independent air force, and were successful in keeping such an organization out of the military system until after World War II.

Despite the debacle in aircraft procurement, there were some excellent planes. The Thomas-Morse MB-2 was comparable to the French Spad. The Chance Vought VE7 trainer was also outstanding, as was Grover Loening's M-8 monoplane. In addition, Aeromarine and Burgess made some good airplanes for the Navy.

After Glenn Martin opened a new plant in Cleveland in the spring of 1918, he asked Douglas to join him again, and he readily accepted.

Douglas's first assignment was to help design a large twin-engine bomber. When the design was offered to the Aviation Production Board Douglas and Martin were told there were no plans to order another bomber. After the board was later reorganized, Martin was authorized to build the new bomber with Liberty engines.

The Douglas-designed Martin bomber flew in August 1918, and it proved to be superior to anything produced in Europe or the United States, but the war ended before it could be used in combat. The Army decided to keep it in production because it surpassed the performance of every competitor. It proved the utility and practicability of large aircraft for all uses, both civil and military. Actually it was so versatile that it could be used as a night bomber, a day bomber, or a long-distance reconnaissance airplane.

In Europe almost a million men died in the last three months before July 31, 1918. The German High Command had launched their last big offensive in March, but Allied resistance blunted the drive everywhere. Between the Marne and the Vesle the Allies had pushed the Germans back two miles in what was called a "brilliant operation" against some of Germany's elite Prussian and Bavarian Guards.

General Pétain's army had faced General Hindenburg's crack troops July 28 at the Marne and soundly defeated them. When Pétain saw an opening for a counterattack, he sought Marshal Foch's approval to exploit it. The Allied Commander-in-Chief did so and Hindenburg's army was forced to retreat so precipitately that the Germans barely escaped disaster. Throughout Germany there was deep despair and melancholy as the German people, exhausted by four years of war, awaited the inevitable end.

With the war winding down, the record number of women in the nation's factories wondered what peace would mean for them. Some of the suffragists had objected to their work, particularly pacifists like Carrie Chapman Catt and Jane Addams. Several employers said it was women's patriotic duty to leave their jobs as soon as the men returned from the war. No one seemed to care what happened to these hardworking women who also served at lower wages than their male counterparts.

The United States had created a sorry spectacle in the eyes of the world by its much-vaunted claims of mass production of airplanes. The truth was that by July 1, 1918, only 67 of 601 American-made DH-4 aircraft had reached the battlefronts, but not a single one had been in combat. Congress had approved the production of 8,500 DH-4s, but work had to be stopped until defects in design and workmanship were resolved.

On August 7 a squadron of 18 American-made DH-4s did make it over the German lines for the first time.

Although Navy and Army flying units performed well in Europe, (Army aviators mostly flew foreign aircraft) the grandiose claims that airpower would end the war were not realized. The principal problem was lack of aircraft and trained personnel. World War I was won primarily on land and sea. The total contribution of all aircraft participating in this "war to end all wars" was negligible.

Navy flying-boat squadrons made a worthwhile contribution to the war effort, achieving extraordinary performance records during the final 10 months. Only three Allied ships were lost to enemy submarines or naval gunfire in their patrol area off the coast of France. In contrast, one year earlier, an average of a ship a day was sunk.

The Allied powers, flushed with the warm glow of victory, for the most part discounted the potential of aerial bombardment. (It really hadn't lived up to its supporters' predictions.) The Germans thought otherwise and the Allies were to learn 21 years later how well the Germans had learned a vital lesson.

The government's Naval Aircraft Factory at Philadelphia made significant contributions to the war effort by helping the Naval Flying Corps to grow from 54 airplanes at the start of the war to more than 2,000 by the time of the armistice.

Although $1½ billion had been spent on aviation, only 200 American-built aircraft ever reached the front. There's no doubt, however, that if the war had lasted another year, America's aircraft industry would have proven itself, because a rate of 21,000 aircraft a year had been reached in 1918.

In one of the least known operations of World War I, 10,000 Americans joined Japanese forces to occupy Vladivostok on Russia's Pacific coast. Some Americans were later dispatched to Siberia. Reluctantly, these forces became involved in Russia's internal affairs at a time of civil war between the White Russians, who represented the past, and the communists who had set up a government. The American government advised its military forces to side with the White Russians in a campaign around Archangel and Murmansk that lasted until May 1919. It was a futile gesture that solved nothing.

The Allied offensive continued on the Western Front and September 14 the St. Mihiel salient was taken by independent American forces under General Pershing. Although 15,000 Germans were captured, the Americans suffered 8,000 casualties.

The Allied command now drew up plans for a knock-out blow against Germany from Ypres to Verdun. In the attack on a sector between the Argonne Forest and the Meuse River September 26, some 896,000 American troops joined with 135,000 French soldiers in the largest battle fought up to this time. The Germans were forced to retreat but the cost was high—120,000 casualties. To the north, along the Hindenburg Line—Germany's last line of defense—British troops breached it and it was evident that Germany's collapse was imminent.

Inside Germany, a parliamentary government headed by Prince Max of Baden was formed October 3 as resistance at the fronts collapsed, and German sailors mutinied, and there was open rebellion against authority in Munich. Six days later, Kaiser Wilhelm II abdicated. The new government promptly initiated peace overtures with President Wilson based on his "Fourteen Points."

At home, in this election year for members of the House of Representatives and a third of the Senate, plus local contests, one of the major issues was women's suffrage. Carrie Chapman Catt, and the outspoken Alice Paul, zeroed in on Wilson's failure to support their cause, and now his compromising policies backfired.

In an ill-timed partisan move October 25, Wilson called on the nation to elect a Democratic Congress to back his peace negotiations.

The Republicans, sensing a vibrant issue that would gain them converts, supported women's suffrage. The party pledged that, in the new Congress, they would submit an amendment to the states for ratification. It was a wise move and one that, they hoped, would help them in 1920 during the presidential election. The ploy worked, and the Republicans gained a majority of 43 seats in the new Congress.

While Allied negotiations proceeded with German officials to end the war, Austria sued Italy for an armistice and on November 4 surrendered. After a month of discussions, the German government signed an armistice treaty with the Allies at 5 a.m. November 11 in a dining car in the forest of Compiègne. Six hours later, hostilities ceased and unmitigated joy swept the ranks of the men in the front lines, and people everywhere.

Although America's involvement had been relatively brief, the cost was high. One hundred and sixteen thousand, five hundred and sixty four Americans had died, (63,114 were non-battle deaths) while another

204,002 were wounded. The United States had spent more than $41.75 billion.

World War I had caused the deaths of 8.5 million people, with another 21 million wounded, and 7.5 million were either prisoners or missing in action. On a dollar basis, the war had cost more than $232 billion.

At the start of the war in 1914, the United States owed Europe $4 billion, but its agricultural and industrial exports had tripled during the war, and now it was the world's principal creditor with European nations owing it $10 billion. In addition, the United States was now practically self-sufficient.

The world's trading practices had seen a drastic change. In the Pacific, Japan had displaced European traders in China and India. Its huge sales of munitions to Russia during the war had brought it enormous financial rewards.

In addition to the tragedy of war, disease took an equally deadly toll as an influenza epidemic began in 1918. Before it had run its course in 1920 nearly 20 million people died, including 500,000 Americans.

President Wilson embarked for Europe December 4 to attend the peace conference with a large group of historians, geographers, political scientists and economists. With the American Commission to Negotiate Peace there were Secretary of State Robert Lansing, General Tasker H. Bliss, who had served as a member of the supreme war council in France and Colonel Edward M. House. The latter was Wilson's friend and confidante who had served as the President's personal representative to European nations during the war. House had been appointed to act for the United States in negotiating the armistice with the Central Powers in 1918, and he had secured Allied acceptance of Wilson's "Fourteen Points" which he had helped to draft.

Wilson made a major and unforgivable error in not including anyone in his group from the now largely Republican Congress.

In France, Wilson was greeted everywhere with great enthusiasm when he spoke for the hopes of mankind to live in peace without another war. He became known as "Wilson the Just."

The Peace Conference began in Paris at the Palace of Versailles January 18, 1921. Germany had agreed to negotiate a treaty based upon Wilson's "Fourteen Points," but at the start of the conference there was no representative from the Central Powers. Although the Armistice had been signed the previous November, it had to be renewed each month for six months. During that time, the blockade—including vital food for the German people—remained in force. Inevitably, this caused conditions in Germany to deteriorate with a growing bitterness among the German people towards their victors.

Wilson, surrounded by dozens of top people, chose to involve himself in all of the conference's small details, thereby causing him to lose a certain dignity that he had so ably won during the war years.

A landmark Supreme Court decision March 10 ruled that the Espionage Act did not violate the First Amendment. Oliver Wendell Holmes, known for his vigorous, lucid opinions, often in dissent, agreed with the majority that in war there exists the "clear and present danger" that is referred to in the Constitution. He added that, in any event, free speech was always under restraint."

The Peace Conference ended with the signing of the Versailles Treaty, and it cost Germany Alsace-Lorraine her overseas colonies and $15 billion in reparations. The Germans also had to admit their guilt in starting the war.

Inside Germany, since the November 11, 1918, armistice, the nation was ripe for revolution and the communists tried to take power in several cities.

Although General Pershing had expressed a wish to continue the war right to Berlin before the Armistice, he had been overruled by Marshal Foch. Once it was signed, however, the Allies entered Germany and its economic system was placed under Allied control.

Wilson's "Fourteen Points" were not adhered to in the final treaty and some of the clauses, such as those forbidding German rearmament, and an indemnity of an indeterminate amount, were impossible to administer. The fact that the Germans had agreed to an armistice based upon the "Fourteen Points," but were forced to sign for terms unsatisfactory to Germany's future economic and political well-being, was used by Adolf Hitler later as the basis for his charge that Germany had been betrayed, and not defeated.

President Wilson had fought for the establishment of a league of nations, and the concept was accepted by all signatories although the United States Senate had to approve it.

The League of Nations Covenant, signed by the nations involved in the Treaty of Versailles, called for an assembly of nations to "promote international co-operation and to achieve international peace and security."

At this stage, such outstanding Republican leaders as Senator Henry Cabot Lodge and former President Roosevelt backed the League of Nations Covenant. In fact, financial, industrial and most intellectual leaders agreed that it was a surprisingly good idea.

With such initial backing, all Wilson needed was to rally their support to his cause and show some flexibility. Incredibly, he took an adamant stand against even minor changes that might have made the Covenant more supportable by members of the opposition party. The inevitable happened. Support for the Covenant began to erode.

Although few Americans knew it, Wilson was a sick man and, despite the advice of his doctors, he insisted upon taking his case to the American people during a grueling whistle-stop tour starting September 3, 1919. He had done this before, and quite successfully, but physically he wasn't up to such a rigorous schedule and his stubbornness had disastrous consequences for himself, and the nation.

CHAPTER 4

"This Statesman's Ancient Cup of Hemlock"

DURING A NATION-WIDE TRAIN TOUR, WILSON GAVE FOUR OR FIVE speeches a day. He had been well received in California where he faced isolationist Senator Hiram Johnson and his arguments head on, and finally began to gain sizable numbers of converts to his cause. Then he turned back toward Washington. Although his stamina was declining, he was buoyed up by crowds in the Far West who were receptive to his message. At the fair grounds in Pueblo, Colorado, Wilson's words rang true and made a strong impact September 25. "Again and again my fellow citizens, mothers who have lost their sons in France have come to me and shaken my hand and said, 'God bless you, Mr. President.' I advised the Congress of the United States to create the situation that led to the deaths of their sons. Why, my fellow citizens, should they pray God to bless me? Because they believe that their boys died for something that vastly transcends any of the immediate and palpable objects of the war." This was his 40th speech, and the best of his entire trip, but his exhaustion was all too evident. Those close to Wilson on the train were not surprised when Wilson's physical condition deteriorated to the danger point and he could not continue his whistle-stop tour. The train was ordered to return to Washington without any additional stops. In the White House, a few days later, Wilson suffered a crippling stroke.

For five weeks the President's life hung in the balance before he slowly began to recover. But in those weeks the United States was practically without a President, although the Congress and the American people were not advised of his serious condition.

Fortunately for the nation, there was no serious international crisis, although Wilson's inability to press for passage of the peace treaty, and approval for joining the League of Nations, did much to determine the fate of both.

The United States Senate reached a decision about ratification of the Versaille Treaty and the League Covenant on November 19, 1919. Republican Senator Henry Cabot Lodge's campaign had doomed it from the beginning and, to the surprise of few people, both the treaty and the league covenant were voted down 55 to 39. This was 15 votes short of the two-thirds majority needed to ratify the treaty. Many Wilson supporters voted against it because Lodge's proposal had so watered down its provisions that they were totally unacceptable to Wilson and officials of the Democratic Party.

And so a great opportunity to preserve the peace was lost after the almost unbearable sacrifice of so many millions of people during the war. Other nations did approve the League of Nations and it was established, but without the United States it became fundamentally incapable of performing its primary role as an arbiter of international disputes before they reached the crisis stage.

Kansan William Allen White—the Sage of Emporia—had developed his *Gazette* into one of the most notable small newspapers in the country through his distinguished editorials and policies. He now put the Senate's action against President Wilson into enduring perspective. "With calumny rampant around him, he tasted the ingratitude of his republic; this statesman's ancient cup of hemlock. No wonder that on the high and empty altar where the flame of his fame was quenched, and the cold charred ashes were strewn, he lay helpless while the high priests of the temple cut out his heart."

President Wilson's efforts did not go unrecognized outside of the United States becuase he was honored for his peace efforts with the award of the Nobel Peace Prize.

Many Americans were convinced that since the communist takeover of the Russian government that radicals, anarchists and communists were out to destroy law and order, not only in the United States but in established democracies throughout the world.

In South Braintree, Massachusetts, a shoe company's paymaster and a guard were murdered April 15 during a holdup. Two admitted anarchists, Nicola Sacco and Bartolomeo Vanzetti, were arrested on charges of robbery and murder three weeks later.

Varied viewpoints complicated the case, and there was obvious bias on both sides. But, in the final analysis, jurors decided that the circumstantial evidence was too strong to be ignored and they voted unanimously for murder convictions in the first degree for both men. In Massachusetts, this meant the death penalty.

Mass demonstrations were held in Europe following their conviction as the defense moved for a new trial, but the judge denied it. International labor unions donated money, as did other organizations and individuals, as the appeal process continued for the next six years while Sacco and Vanzetti remained in prison.

The Massachusetts Supreme Judicial Court considered the case January 27, 1927, and upheld the judge's decision. On April 9 they were sentenced to death.

While Sacco and Vanzetti prepared to die August 23, Vanzetti issued a final statement. "If it had not been for these things, I might live out my life talking at street corners to scorning men. I might have died, unmarked, unknown, a failure. Now we are not a failure. Never in our full life can we hope to do such works for tolerance, for justice, for men's understanding of men as now we do by accident; the taking of our lives, lives of a good shoemaker and a poor fish peddler. All that last moment belong to us. That agony is our triumph."

There seems little doubt that Sacco was guilty, but Vanzetti's guilt is not so easily established because they remained steadfast in their loyalty to one another until the end.

The tragedy of the Sacco-Vanzetti case is that both men were badly used by those whom they most trusted—the anarchists and the communists. Their deaths did not result from any failure of America's judicial system that tries to protect the innocent. The appeal process was thorough and prolonged, and there is every indication that justice prevailed.

Republicans generally approved of presidential candidate Warren G. Harding's belief in protective tariffs, his opposition to the League of Nations, and high taxes on war profits. Some of Harding's plea for a return to normalcy was already taking effect even though Wilson was still President.

Congress passed two measures to restore peacetime conditions. The Army Reorganization Act was approved on June 4, 1919, to establish a peacetime army of approximately 300,000 men, while the following day it passed the Merchant Marine Act to continue the wartime shipping board and permit it to sell the government fleet to private owners or to operate the ships they could not sell.

Although the aircraft production program during the war had proved a disaster—through little fault of the manufacturers who were asked to do an impossible job with little or no preparation—the Federal Government had done a remarkable job of building up the nation to war preparedness in record time. Most boards that ran the war effort had been operated efficiently. Actually, the war had brought a loosely-federated nation of states more closely together as a nation with their common goal of achieving victory. Congress went a step further with its regulatory bureaus June 10 by enacting the Water Power Act, and by creating the Federal Power Commission to oversee power plants.

Women got the right to vote in 1920 after the 19th Amendment to the Constitution was ratified by the necessary number of states. President Wilson, who had long opposed woman's suffrage, had recently recognized the importance of ratification. He knew that without its support, the Democratic Party faced certain defeat in November. Therefore, when Tennessee delivered the needed 36th and last state certificate to ratify the amendment to Secretary of State Bainbridge Colby on August 26 at four in the morning, Wilson told him to announce immediately that women had won the right to vote. His decision to back the amendment came too late because most women never forgave him for his earlier lack of support when they needed it. The National League of Women Voters was organized shortly thereafter to educate women about how best to use their hard-won right.

Harding won a landslide victory on November 2 with 404 electoral votes to James M. Cox's 127.

The bitter struggle between battleship admirals and the new aviation-minded junior officers broke into the open following the war. It reached such intensity that the controversy threatened the very foundations of the Navy's traditional military mission. The problem was primarily how to administer Naval Aviation within the Navy Department.

Commander J. C. Hunsaker, dedicated officer of both the surface fleet and Naval Aviation, was blunt in his demands for action. He had been aware of army Brigadier General William S. "Billy" Mitchell's plans for establishing a separate air force. Mitchell had commanded Army aviation in Europe.

The Navy's part in the coming struggle over the relative effectiveness of bombers versus battleships, that was to last seven years and rock the nation, began innocently enough. Lieutenant Commander H. T. Bartlett suggested a series of aerial bombing experiments using older warships destined for the scrap heap. He recommended that the U.S.S. "Indiana," a veteran of the Spanish-American War, and captured German warships be used as target ships.

The first tests were underwater concussion tests against the "Indiana's" hull to simulate near-misses by aerial bombs. They caused the ship to sink slowly so she was towed to shallow water and run aground. Large 1,800 pound bombs were set off on deck and inflicted heavy damage to turrets and superstructure. These tests were only preliminary, but the consensus of opinion among air enthusiasts was that a warship could be put out of action or sunk. The next step was to use bombers.

Brigadier General "Billy" Mitchell unleashed an attack upon government bureaucracy when he returned to state-side duty.

There were many in government who tried to shut him up. They quickly learned the caliber of the man with whom they were dealing. "Was it not true," he said, "that America failed to deliver a single combat aircraft worthy of the name to her own Army and Navy fliers risking their lives in Europe?" Mitchell was mad, and he had every right to be. No one could deny that he spoke basic truths, although he sometimes embellished them for effect. A juicy national scandal, promoted avidly by the nation's press, began in earnest.

Admiral W. S. Sims, President of the Naval War College, and naval inventor Admiral Fiske, shared most of Mitchell's views except his proposal for a unified air service. Sims, in particular, had fought for modernization of the Navy since the turn of the century. When his advice was sought as to whether battleships should be discarded, he said, "I would prefer right now to put money into airplane carriers and the development of airplanes. The airplane carrier will become a more powerful capital ship than the battleship. It is my belief the future will show that the fleet with 20 carriers, instead of 16 battleships and four carriers, will inevitably knock the other fleet out."

To quell the bitter controversy, the War Department ordered tests to start in the spring of 1921, first against a submarine that Navy planes quickly sank, then against a German destroyer that Army pilots sank. The German light cruiser "Frankfurt" was sunk in two hours July 18 by both Navy and Army planes.

At last the big moment arrived on July 20, 1921, and tests were scheduled against the German battleship "Ostfriesland." It was the most modern warship of its time. Would it finally resolve the arguments over whether bombing planes could sink a battleship? The world would soon know, but it was years before the argument was settled to everyone's satisfaction.

The bombers remained in the sky for 57 minutes before the order for attack was given at 3:42.

After repeated attacks, the "Ostfriesland" listed astern, but she had suffered no fatal injuries. It appeared to many that Mitchell was wrong. One Navy expert said the ship could not be sunk by bombing. Among high government officials, it was obvious that little impression had been made. General Pershing and Secretary of War John W. Weeks didn't even remain for the following tests.

The next day might provide the proof of Mitchell's contentions because his 20th Squadron at Langley planned to use one and two thousand-pound bombs.

Mitchell noted with satisfaction that his bombardiers were getting the range as bombs four and five dropped on the port side near the mainmast and 25 feet off the port side.

The ship shuddered with the force of these bombs as the massive battleship reared upward by water displacement pressures far in excess of the weight of the battleship. Mitchell was in a state of exultation as water poured entirely over the ship as she rocked back and forth.

The "Ostfriesland" seemed in bad shape the next day after several direct hits and near misses as she settled down and rode the waves gently.

The sixth bomb landed near the starboard side and lifted her stern high in the air. When she fell back, there was an obvious list to port.

"She's sinking!" came the agonized cry from the control ship. Most Navy officers refused to concede. They had seen warships stay afloat in wartime even after cruel wounds had been inflicted.

The "Ostfriesland" rolled again to port, her bow rising higher in the air. Thousands of spectators crowded the decks of the Atlantic Fleet staring incredulously as the indomitable dreadnought prepared for her final plunge. The ship filled rapidly with water and her bow was high enough for all to see the large hole in her hull as she slowly sank.

Army General Charles T. Menoher turned to Secretary of the Navy Edwin Denby, "I guess the Navy will get its airplane carriers now."

Rear Admiral William A. Moffett, new chief of Naval Aviation, was the only participant to speak out publicly. "We must put planes on battleships and get aircraft carriers quickly."

"Day of battleship ended!" cried the nation's press as General Mitchell continued his fight for a single air force.

Admiral Moffett, in his new position as head of Navy aviation, testified before an investigating committee that at least three-fourths of his service's planes were either obsolete or unfit for effective use. "The safety of ships in the next war will depend," he said, "to a great measure on aviation."

Mitchell released a 6,000-word statement September 25, 1925. He was determined to crucify government aviation officials, the War and Navy departments who, he charged, were responsible for "incompetency, criminal negligence and almost treasonable administration of national defense!"

He expected to be courtmartialed and he was not surprised when the War Department issued orders for him to stand trial for his "unmilitary behavior and gross insubordination."

Mitchell was found guilty of violating the 96th Article of War. He was sentenced to five years suspension of rank and loss of command and pay.

He promptly resigned from the Army to continue his fight directly to the American people through books, articles and speeches.

Although more and bigger carriers had long been sought by chief of naval aviation Rear Admiral William A. Moffett, the Navy's first carrier, a flush deck, electrically-driven ship, was commissioned March 20, 1922, as the U.S.S. "Langley." Originally a collier, its deck measured 535 feet by 64 feet, roughly the size of the "baby" flattops of World War II.

An orderly buildup of the Navy's aviation service in direct ratio to its fleet expansion was initiated in 1926. This was a five-year program establishing a goal of 1,000 airplanes for Naval Aviation.

Ever since the war ended in 1918 the economy had deteriorated. One of the problems of joblessness was the practice of manufacturers of working its employees 12-14 hours a day, often expecting them to work weekends. Instead of cutting back on hours to make more jobs available, industrial concerns cut wages instead. In the steel industry, workers were called upon to work 24 hours straight during a "stretch-out." Children and women faced the same problems as men, particularly after the Supreme Court in 1918 ruled that the law to protect children was unconstitutional. The New York Central was one of the worst offenders. It cut wages of approximately 43,000 employees July 1 by almost 23 percent. At the same time, the Railroad Labor Board authorized a 12 percent cut. Clothing workers, already burdened by sweat-shop conditions, were forced to accept a 15 percent cut. Before the end of 1921, United States Steel cut wages three times. The economic impact was predictable as 20,000 businesses failed during the year, increasing unemployment on a massive scale. By August, there were 5.74 million unemployed. Henry Ford felt that the crisis was past, and for him personally this was true. The Ford company had closed its plants earlier because dealers were unable to sell cars, but the company's assets rose to $345 million.

Although Congress had refused earlier to approve the Versailles Treaty, with the League of Nations covenant, President Harding finally signed a joint resolution of Congress on July 2 that declared an end to the war with Germany, although negotiations about reparations were not resolved and became a continuing irritation. The peace treaty was officially signed in August, and the end of the war with Austria and Hungary was also proclaimed.

With a complete lack of common sense, the Reparations Commission assessed Germany's liability for World War I at $33.25 billion. How this prostrate nation could be expected to pay such a sum was not seriously considered.

Although Senator William Borah had worked overtime to prevent the Versailles Treaty from being approved, along with the League of Nations covenant, he called for a Washington Disarmament Conference to discuss arms limitations with Britain, France, Italy, Japan and four other nations, but no invitation was sent to Russia. The conference met on November 12, 1921, and agreed that ships over 10,000 tons displacement should be based on a ratio of five for the United States and Great Britain, three for Japan and with France and Italy each given a ratio of 1.67. France refused to limit smaller ships or land armaments. All powers agreed not to build large ships for 10 years, placed restrictions on the use of submarines and outlawed the use of poison gas. The conference also defined the rights to Pacific island territories, and called for a joint consultation in the event of aggression in the Pacific. They all agreed to respect the open-door policy for China, but a short time later Japan ignored it and invaded Manchuria. The other powers protested this infringement, but they could not agree to take positive steps to enforce the agreement. United States officials signed this agreement with the reservation that "there is no commitment to armed force."

CHAPTER 5

"Black Tuesday"

THE ALLIED WAR DEBT HUNG OVER THE WESTERN WORLD LIKE THE proverbial sword suspended by a single thread over the head of the Greek courtier Damocles as he attended a banquet in the 4th Century B.C. He had been invited by Dionysius the Elder, a tyrant who resented Damocles's comment about his good fortune in rising from humble origins to his position of power through conquests. Great Britain owed the United States over $4 billion, France $3 billion and Italy more than $1.6 billion. These were the big indebtednesses, but several smaller countries owed the United States lesser amounts. Meanwhile, other countries owed Great Britain approximately $10 billion.

Great Britain had twice offered to remit her debts and reparations if the United States would not hold it to repayment, but while Woodrow Wilson was President he insisted upon full repayment.

After the war, it became increasingly apparent that no nation could pay the full amount it owed, and some adjustments seemed advisable.

America's refusal to appreciate the effect of this monetary problem on European nations created an anti-American feeling that, in turn, engendered isolationism in the United States. Most Europeans felt America had profited from the war, and that its manufacturers had received lucrative contracts for war supplies and postwar relief. They had hoped that Harding, after he became President, might be more reasonable, but he also refused to cancel the debts.

Germany was in such dire straits that it was unable to pay even the interest on the amount agreed upon for her reparations. That nation's economy was still in chaos, and the German mark had dropped to an exchange rate of four million to one American dollar.

Harding further removed the United States from Europe's affairs on January 10, 1923, by calling home the last American troops stationed in Germany.

Shortly thereafter, French and Belgian troops occupied Germany's Ruhr Valley, claiming it as part payment on that nation's reparations.

President Harding left Washington on June 20 for a tour of the West and Alaska. He was deeply upset by the scandals in his administration that were being unveiled in Congress, and he needed to get away.

Upon his return from Alaska August 2, Harding stopped in San Francisco to recover from an attack of ptomaine poisoning, but when he developed pneumonia he became a very sick man.

That night in Los Angeles Harding's secretary started to read a speech the President had planned to give before he became ill. It was a typical Harding speech, full of his confident assurance that despite the depression the nation's economy was on the right track. "I am a confirmed optimist. . . . We do rise to heights at times when we look for the good rather than the evil of others."

One of his aides rushed up to the secretary and handed him a note. He quickly read it, and was shocked by its contents. He turned back to his audience. "Ladies and gentlemen, you must excuse that. . . . President Harding. . . . the President is dead." There was a shocked silence, with the hundreds of men and women in the audience not at first comprehending the magnitude of the revelation.

Later it was announced that the President had died of apoplexy, but this condition was later known more correctly as one caused by an embolism.

Vice President Calvin Coolidge was in Vermont on a fishing trip when he got the word that Harding had died of a stroke on August 2. The following day, in a small white cottage of a justice of the peace, Coolidge was sworn in as President with only eight people in attendance.

Harding was not personally dishonest, but he had surrounded himself with too many cronies who were, as would soon be revealed in detail. He was a product of the times who, to his credit, admitted that he was a man of limited talents. The American people had wholeheartedly elected a man who looked and acted like their vision of a President, never seeing the lack of substance beneath his surface veneer of charm and polish. But the corruption issue has distorted his administration's accomplishments. He balanced the budget, and reduced taxes to their lowest level in the nation's history. The Naval Disarmament Conference, set up during his administration, resulted in four treaties. He fought for full citizenship for blacks, although his efforts weren't successful.

Donald Douglas left the Martin company in early 1920 to move to

California to establish his own company. One of his motivating factors was his conviction that the airplane had a bright future as a civilian transport. He had a vision that airplanes could bring people all over the world closer together and, through greater understanding, eliminate disastrous wars. Such an idea was extremely radical in the early 1920s.

In Germany, it now took more than six million German marks to match the value of one pre-war mark. An egg cost the equivalent of 30 million marks when compared to values in 1913. By October money had deteriorated so rapidly that few banks would exchange German marks for any amount of hard currency. Workers and older people in Germany suffered terribly from this inflation.

Adolf Hitler and his fledgling Nazi Party tried to take advantage of this situation, but the "Beer Hall Putsch," Hitler's first attempt to overthrow the Munich government in 1923, failed. In 1924, Hitler was sentenced to five years in prison, less six months that he had already served, but he was released after a total of eight months.

At Landsberg Prison where he was confined, Hitler started a diary, "When a world comes to an end, then entire parts of the earth can be convulsed, but not the belief in a lost cause." This led to a book that he called *Mein Kampf,* or "My Struggle." This volume covered his childhood years, his years in Vienna, the war years, the revolution in Russia and the start of the Nazi movement in Munich. In it, he referred to himself as a poor boy—which he was not—and he discussed Jews, Marxism and racism. He denounced the futility of parliamentary government and the monarchy; detailing his views on why Germany lost the war. In a rambling account, he discussed syphilis and the decline of the theater. When the book was later published, it was condemned for its turgid prose and its pompous oratorical style, but it found a receptive audience. It became the bible for the Nazi movement, saying, "The trial of common narrow-mindedness and personal spite is over—and today starts. . . ."

After Benito Mussolini's successful march on Rome the previous year, resulting in the formation of a Fascist government in Italy, followed by Hitler's attempt to assume power in Germany, Europe's future seemed bleaker than ever to most Americans who now wished to divorce themselves as much as possible from the region's age-old economic and political problems.

Calvin Coolidge was overwhelmingly elected President on November 4, 1924, with a 15.7 million popular vote to Davis's approximately 8.4 million.

With "Cautious Cal" as President, for whom a display of emotion was almost unknown, the American people settled back "to keep cool with Coolidge" and enjoy "The Roaring Twenties."

Although Germany had agreed to pay reparations of 132 billion gold marks, prompted by French and Belgian threats to take over the Ruhr with its huge coal and iron industries, by 1923 the German mark was worthless.

President Coolidge's stand on war debts remained the same as his predecessors until the fall of 1924. He had repeatedly said, "They hired the money, didn't they? Let them pay it. I don't propose to make merchandise out of American principles. But while the favor of America is not for sale, I am willing to make concessions for a chance to do a little profitable economic and moral rescuing."

As the financial depression worsened in Europe, Coolidge reversed his position November 24, 1924, by approving a lower repayment figure of $11.5 billion at just above 2 percent interest, with repayment stretched to 62 years.

The economy was booming, except for the farm belt, and with it a bull market was developing, prompting humorist Will Rogers to say, "Two-thirds of the people promote while one-third provide."

This economic resurgence was due, in part, to American industrial expansion and the development of new and novel technological inventions.

Although the United States Navy's General Board had recommended five 23,000-ton aircraft carriers in the mid-20s, plus five 13,800-ton smaller carriers, only the U.S.S. Ranger was authorized in 1925.

The United States and France reached an agreement on April 29, 1925, to resolve the French debt. Eventually 60 percent of the debt was cancelled, and France agreed to pay $4 billion over 62 years at 1.6 percent interest.

One of the truly great heroes of the 1920s was Richard E. Byrd who explored unknown polar regions. With private backing, Rear Admiral Byrd and Floyd Bennett made the first successful flight over the North Pole on May 9, 1926, and Byrd was awarded a Medal of Honor. This was just the start of an illustrious exploration career.

Nicaragua was going through another of its perennial periods of revolt this spring, and President Coolidge sent United States Marines to restore order, starting a military presence in this Central American country that lasted until 1933.

The cornerstone for modern commercial aviation in the United States was laid May 20, 1926, when Congress passed the Air Commerce Act. It created a Bureau of Aeronautics in the Department of Commerce authorized to license all American planes and pilots, set up and enforce air traffic rules and regulations, investigate accidents and test all new engines and aircraft for safety.

Long considered a "crank" scientist, Robert H. Goddard for years tried to elicit interest in the development of rockets. In 1919, he experimented with solid-fuel rockets. His paper on the subject, "A Method of Reaching Extreme Altitudes," was ridiculed by the media. The *New York Times* called his conclusions laughable, or at best "a naive fantasy." Although most Americans did not take him seriously, scientists in other nations— particularly Germany—followed his continuing experiments with strong interest.

Goddard launched the world's first liquid-fueled rocket in 1926 at his Aunt Effie's Massachusetts farm. The flight lasted only two-and-a-half seconds and, like the Wright's first powered flight, it attracted little attention although it was an event of equal importance to science and the future of the world.

Despite frustration, and often ridicule, Goddard continued his experiments until he died in 1945, developing 200 patents in the field including gyroscopic steering and power-driven fuel pumps. Recognition came long after his death when it became evident that he had anticipated many of the developments that later came into being, such as rockets propelled by hydrogen and oxygen, rockets designed in stages, unmanned spacecraft and the feasibility of building a base on the moon.

No event of the 1920s surpassed the drama of Charles A. Lindbergh's solo flight from New York to Paris as millions of people anxiously awaited word of his safe arrival in the French capital.

The 3,600-mile flight was feasible only if every pound of excess weight was removed from the plane and was replaced by all the fuel it could hold. Lindbergh took off from New York's Roosevelt Field May 20, 1927, his "Spirit of St. Louis" so over-loaded that he barely cleared the telephone lines at the field's far end. An unlikely hero, the 25-year-old Lindbergh was shy and reticent, but a superb pilot.

He later described his 33½-hour flight by saying he knew he could make it if his engine kept running and, much to his satisfaction, it performed perfectly throughout the long flight while he fought off fatigue and tried to keep awake and alert. It was almost a losing battle as he droned across the Atlantic at an average speed of 100 miles per hour, concentrating on his navigation.

As he approached Le Bourget Field he stared at the mob of people assembled to greet him, still not comprehending the enormous excitement his flight had generated among the people of the French capital. Later, he learned that at least 100,000 people jammed the roads to Le Bourget to watch him land.

Through the determined efforts of Admiral Moffett, head of the United States Navy's Bureau of Aeronautics, two aircraft carriers, the

U.S.S. "Saratoga" and the U.S.S. "Lexington," were commissioned December 14, 1927, and January 5, 1928. They had been converted from two heavy cruiser hulls that had been scrapped under terms of the Washington Disarmament Conference treaties in 1922. Weighing 33,000 tons each, their flight decks were 800 feet long and 100 feet wide, with control islands far to starboard.

By the end of 1928 the Navy had 829 aircraft of all types, close to the number set for the end of their five-year plan. Two hundred eighty-five of these airplanes were operated from carriers.

Dive-bombing tactics had been developed to a fine art and were demonstrated by Navy fliers at the National Air Races at Mines Field, later Los Angeles International Airport. Throngs of spectators gasped as each plane hurtled earthward toward a whitewashed target circle in front of the reviewing stand. Moments later, the bombers pulled out in front of the roaring crowd while their bombs slammed into the circle.

When the demonstrations were repeated the following year at the National Air Races in Cleveland, one interested observer made notes for future use. Major Ernst Udet of the German Air Force was so impressed with this new bombing technique that he took the idea back home to Germany.

Aerial bombardment now entered three definite stages and set the pattern for the future. Horizontal and dive bombing were accomplished from high altitudes, while torpedo bombing became a "just-above-the-water" operation.

Dive bombing was a natural for the Navy because aircraft could fly out of anti-aircraft range and the dive itself, almost straight down at high speeds, offering the best elements of a surprise attack. This technique proved successful even against warships as they twisted and turned at high speeds on the ocean's surface.

More powerful bombers were desirable so in 1928 the Bureau of Aeronautics issued formal specifications for a new series of aircraft capable of carrying bombs up to 1,000 pounds.

Republican Herbert Hoover was inaugurated as President on March 4 along with Charles Curtis as vice-president. Hoover received international recognition when he headed relief work during and after World War I. Through his brilliant management, he directed efforts that fed and clothed millions of people whose lives had been devastated by the war. At his inauguration he assured the world that the United States had "no desire for territorial expansion, for economic or other domination of other people."

At the international conference in Paris in early 1929 considering a new and reduced schedule of payments of German reparations, financial experts agreed on terms proposed by Owen D. Young that would ease Germany's plight but not solve it. The Young Plan wasn't signed until January 1930, by Germany and its former World War I enemies.

1929 started off with an aviation "first" and several more new records were set before the year's end. Army Air Corps Major Carl Spaatz and Captain Ira Eaker set a new endurance record between January 1 and 7 in an Army Fokker by remaining aloft 150 hours and 40 minutes over Los Angeles, aided by serial refueling. James H. Doolittle proved the feasibility of flying solely by instruments on September 24 when he took off and landed from New York's Mitchell Field without seeing the ground.

The president of New York's National City Bank spoke confidently of the nation's economy on October 22, 1929, "I know of nothing fundamentally wrong with the stock market or with the underlying business and credit structure." But there were several tell-tale signs that he should have noted. There were heavy withdrawals of capital from the United States to England in September after the British interest rate was raised to 6.5 percent. Stock prices had obviously peaked this same month, and there had been a steady decline in the value of stocks ever since. American growth during the 1920s had been at the expense of its international trading partners, many of whom were forced to turn to their own form of protectionism that adversely affected the sale of American farm products. With the United States a net international lender, with a gain in gross national product of 40 percent in this decade, the world's economy remained stagnant resulting in weak prices and outright deflation of the commodity markets. As a result, foreign money was invested in United States securities, and stock prices rose 497 percent from 1921 to 1929. When the British pound became overvalued, Great Britain returned to the pre-war gold standard. This action forced the United States Federal Reserve to artificially hold down interest rates to prevent a flight of capital to the United States. It encouraged stock investment, rather than bond buying, and made it attractive to borrow money for the speculative buying of stocks. Thus stocks reached exorbitant heights not justified by economic factors. The problem was further exacerbated by insider trading.

The first signs of panic occurred on Wall Street October 24 when stock prices collapsed on the New York Stock Exchange and some 13 million shares were traded and the day became known as "Black Thursday."

Richard Whitney, representing four large banking houses, put in a bid for steel, and the market rallied. Five days later on "Black Tuesday," the bottom fell out of the market, and 16 million shares were sold at declining prices. Although it wasn't recognized immediately, this proved to be the most catastrophic day in the market's history.

Wave after wave of panic selling brought prices tumbling down as billions of dollars were lost. Traders watched with horror as their holdings were wiped out, and the floor of the exchange became a bedlam of shocked and incredulous people. For a time it was hoped the resistance barriers would stop the wild tumble, but stock leaders abruptly crashed through them.

The following week *Variety*, the entertainment industry's publication known for its provocative headlines, put it succinctly: "Wall Street Lays An Egg."

CHAPTER 6

Collapse of the American Economy

THE UNITED STATES NAVY WAS STILL CONSIDERED THE NATION'S FIRST line of defense but planes from the carrier "Langley" in 1929 proved the vulnerability of the Panama Canal to air attack. Within the Navy, there was a growing awareness of the primary importance of Naval Aviation, promoted in large part by Admiral Moffett's untiring efforts as head of the Bureau of Aeronautics.

This was also the year that Moffett fostered increasing technical improvements within the bureau. It marked the use of wheel brakes and tail wheels for carrier aircraft, which greatly increased pilot safety.

Norden Mark II gyroscopic bombsights were tested at the Naval Ordnance Proving Ground. Both Norden and Sperry sights evolved from earlier devices dating back to World War I. They proved so reliable that two bombs out of three landed within 25 feet of the aiming point on the first try. Carl Norden's bombsight, in particular, became the first effective high-altitude sight used by the Navy, and later models were adopted by the Army Air Corps.

When the beloved Knute Rockne, Notre Dame's celebrated football coach, was killed in the crash of a commercial airliner on March 31, 1931, there was a tremendous hue and cry in the world's press about the inadequacy of American-built aircraft. There was almost universal condemnation of airlines and plane manufacturers that all aircraft were obsolete and unsafe. The public outrage was so great that the crash of the Fokker trimotor, which suffered a major structural failure because of its mostly wood construction, dealt an almost mortal blow to the infant airline industry. Although the framework of the Fokker's fuselage was made of tubular aluminum, the rest of the plane was constructed of wood. Cassein glue (a phospho-protein precipitated from milk), was used to bond the wing's wood spars and outer "skin," but after water penetrated the wing's interior over a long period of time the glue produced fungus growths that eventually weakened the structure and brought about a total collapse. Aircraft manufacturers were forced to build all-metal airplanes for the airlines and the military services.

German industrialists turned inward to seek surcease from their economic problems in 1931 by financing the growing Nazi Party that under Adolf Hitler now had 800,000 members. Once ridiculed for his plans for Germany's future, Hitler represented the future power structure in Germany.

Japan's aggressive moves in the Far East escalated on September 18, 1931, when her armed forces marched into Manchuria in northeast China. This action was in direct violation of the Kellogg-Briand Pact that Japan signed in 1928, but in reality turned out to be the first of many Japanese violations in the next decade.

Japan was on the march after years of patiently waiting for the opportune moment. Viscount Tani had said in 1891 that "Japan must with patience wait for the time of confusion in Europe to gain its objectives."

The Japanese premier in 1915, Count Shigenobu Okuma, had inspired Japan's militarists for years with his ringing cry, "Japan will meet Europe on the plains of Asia in the Twentieth Century and wrest from her the mastery of the world."

Secretary of State Henry L. Stimson sent notes to Japan and China on January 7, 1932, that the United States would not recognize any territory taken by armed force in violation of the Kellogg-Briand Pact that both nations had signed in 1928. Japan's occupation of Manchuria in 1931 prompted the note. Japanese officials not only ignored it but expelled Chinese forces from Shanghai on March 3. Eight days later the League of Nations adopted Stimson's non-recognition policy. Japan then withdrew from China but not from Manchuria. In October, the Lytton Commission appointed by the League to investigate Japanese activities in Manchuria denounced them and designated Japan as the aggressor.

Mrs. Nettie W. Caraway was appointed a Senator from Arkansas on January 12 to fill the unexpired term of her late husband. When she ran in the fall elections in her own right she became the first woman ever to be elected to the Senate.

For the first time the United States Government became a major source of business capital after President Hoover signed a bill on January 22 creating the Reconstruction Finance Corporation. Both houses of Congress had earlier passed the bill and the agency started operations on February 2 with $500 million in funds, with authorization to borrow up to $2 billion in tax-exempt bonds. This was another belated effort to stimulate the economy by authorizing the RFC to lend money to banks, insurance companies, building and loan societies, agricultural credit corporations, farm mortgage associations and railroads. By signing the bill, President Hoover acknowledged that government aid was needed to stimulate the American economy, and get it moving on an upward spiral. The RFC moved quickly and, by year's end, it had loaned $1½ billion to financial institutions.

New York's governor, Franklin D. Roosevelt, gave a speech on April 7, 1932, that set the theme for his upcoming fight to be nominated by his party as its presidential candidate. He called attention to "the forgotten man at the bottom of the economic pyramid." This reference struck a responsive chord in millions of Americans who felt alienated from the Republican administration, but who were disturbed by politicians like "Al" Smith who were becoming more conservative.

Pioneer aviatrix Amelia Earhart thrilled all Americans, particularly women, when she flew across the Atlantic by herself on May 20 from Newfoundland to Ireland; a distance of 2026 miles that she covered in 12½ hours. This was "Lady Lindy's" second flight across the Atlantic. Four years earlier she had flown it as a passenger with two men. There were many women who had learned to fly, but few achieved her worldwide fame. Buoyant and nonchalant, Earhart said she flew for "the fun of it," but she was always conscious as a feminist of her importance as a "role model." She married publisher G. P. Putnam in 1931, but she made it clear that she intended to pursue her flying career, becoming one of the century's most beloved personalities.

Roosevelt was privately appalled by the way Hoover had ordered the "Bonus Army" removed from Washington. When asked later by Rexford Tugwell, one of his "brain trusters," what should have been done, he replied that Hoover should have sent out coffee and sandwiches to the 200 veterans who marched up to the White House gate and invited a delegation to sit down with him. "Instead," he said, "he let 'Doug' MacArthur do his stuff."

After Huey Long called to protest Roosevelt's supposed turn to the right following the 1932 convention, Roosevelt told Tugwell, "That is one of the two most dangerous men in America."

"Who's the other?" Tugwell said.

"Douglas MacArthur."

President Hoover's action in dealing with the "Bonus Army" subjected him to much criticism. Typical was Malcolm Cowley's article in the *New*

Republic. He said one thousand homeless veterans, or 50,000, can't make a revolution. If such ever comes, he said, "it will come from a different source—from the government itself. The Army in time of peace at the national capital has been used against unarmed citizens—and this, with all it trends for the future, is a revolution in itself."

By July 1932, farm purchasing power was half what it was in 1929, and monthly wages were down to 60 percent of that pre-depression year. With the market's collapse in the fall of 1929, dividends paid to stockholders had been reduced to 57 percent, with business losses $6 billion, while industry was operating at half its volume of that year. Unemployment was rising.

On election day, November 8, 1932, CBS's New York station televised the election returns starting at 8 p.m., using pictures of the candidates and issuing bulletins as the counting of ballots went on. Most Americans still got the news from their favorite radio station.

Roosevelt was elected by a popular vote of 22.8 million to Hoover's 15.7 million with an electoral vote of 472 to 59. He won in all states except Delaware, Pennsylvania, Connecticut, New Hampshire, Vermont and Maine. The Democratic victory was widespread as they won control of Congress by electing almost two thirds of the Senate and almost three-fourths of the House.

In Germany, the Nazis were a growing power, gaining 232 seats in the Reichstag, but not enough to warrant their assumption of the Chancellor's office. President Paul von Hindenburg had long resisted any attempt by Adolf Hitler to gain power in Germany, but now the nation was threatened by economic chaos and a growing communist conspiracy. There were also rumors of a military coup the morning of January 30, 1933, and panic spread through the capital of Berlin. Hindenburg regarded Hitler as the best alternative to the breakdown of law and order threatening Germany's survival as a nation. In the president's office, Hitler was sworn in as Chancellor in what could only be construed as a shot-gun wedding. Hindenburg was so upset that he didn't even directly offer the job to Hitler, nor did he greet members of the new cabinet, or give his views about what should be done. To everyone's surprise, Hitler spoke briefly. He swore to uphold the Weimar Constitution, and he promised to get a majority in the parliament so the nation would no longer have to operate under emergency decrees. He also said that he would solve the economic crisis and unite Germany.

Throughout America there was hope for a better future with the new administration, and despair at the state of the nation's economy. Bread-lines and soup kitchens had been common since 1931, and the only constant was the ever-increasing number of unemployed. In the plains states, the harshness of farm conditions was magnified by a lingering drought that had started in 1930.

Japan had often threatened to walk out of the League of Nations and it took such action February 24. After voting to reject the Lytton Commission's report, accusing Japan of aggression in Manchuria, the Japanese delegation walked out of the Assembly meeting in Geneva.

The United States Navy's first true aircraft carrier built from the keel up was launched at Newport News, Virginia, February 25. It was christened "The Ranger" by Mrs. Hoover to honor America's earliest naval hero, John Paul Jones, whose ship was so named.

An arsonist set fire to the German Reichstag in Berlin the night of February 27. When Hitler was informed, he said, "It's the Communists!" It burned throughout the night and was totally destroyed. Now Hitler cast caution aside and sought to grab total power, still under the guise of destroying the Communists. At a cabinet meeting, Hitler said the crisis was such as to warrant "a ruthless settling of accounts" with the Communists which "must not be dependent on legal considerations." He proposed an emergency decree that, in effect, suspended the civil liberties granted by the Weimar Constitution such as free speech, free press, secrecy of mail and telephone communications, freedom of assembly and the inviolability of the home. The decree also authorized the Reich Minister of the Interior to seize control temporarily of any state government unable to maintain order. Not all members of the cabinet were Nazis, but none opposed him, although the former chancellor, Franz von Papen, pointed out that the threats to intervene in state business would be deeply resented.

That evening Papen and Hitler reported to President von Hindenburg that such action was necessary to put down the Communist rebellion and the President signed it. The Weimar Republic, which had such a tortured existence, was dead.

The Nazis' assertion that the Reichstag fire was caused by Communists was widely believed in Germany, but not in the rest of the world. Diplomatic and foreign press associations were convinced that the Nazis had ordered the Reichstag burned as a pretext for crushing the Communists.

America's favorite comedian, Will Rogers, understood the American people very well, and he put it in words that will always ring true in describing the situation as it existed in 1933. "America will hold the distinction of being the only nation in the history of the world to go to the poor house in an automobile."

Chief Justice Hughes administered the oath of office to Franklin D. Roosevelt March 4 on the steps of the Capital before a crowd of hopeful people, while millions anxiously waited by their radios at home. Roosevelt's rich, cultured voice had never been more vibrant: "President Hoover, Mr. Chief Justice, my friends. This is a day of national consecretion . . . and I am certain that on this day my fellow Americans expect that upon my induction into the Presidency I will address them with a candor and a decision which the present situation of our people impels. This is pre-eminently the time to speak the truth, the whole truth, frankly and boldly. Nor need we shrink from honestly facing conditions in our country today. This great nation will endure, as it has endured, will revive and will prosper . . . Our greatest primary task is to put people to work.

"So, first of all, let me assert my firm belief that the only thing we have to fear is fear itself—nameless, unreasoning, unjustified terror which paralyzes needed efforts to convert retreat into advance."

For a beleaguered America, a ray of hope rose up throughout the land, instilling in its people an air of confidence in the future that had all but disappeared.

CHAPTER 7

Roosevelt's "Hundred Days"

WITH THE UNITED STATES FACING ECONOMIC COLLAPSE IN EARLY 1933, President Franklin D. Roosevelt declared a four-day "bank-holiday" effective Monday, March 6. It was later extended to seven days to permit the Treasury Department to make new regulations. His order closing the nation's lending institutions was taken under authority of a 1917 wartime measure and was necessary to stop the panic "run" on banks by depositors demanding gold in exchange for their deposits. The closing-out of accounts had forced almost half of the nation's banks to close or suspend payments, further worsening the already acute financial crisis that had reached the desperation stage. The situation was particularly acute in small cities and in rural areas. The President also ordered an embargo on the export of gold, silver and currency and called for a special session of Congress to convene March 9 to consider further emergency measures.

The Congress, now that Democrats controlled the House and Senate (three-quarters of the House and almost two-thirds of the Senate), proved pliant in Roosevelt's strong hands, at least for the first 100 days. When it met in emergency session March 9, it further legalized Roosevelt's action of closing the banks by approving the Emergency Banking Relief Act, giving the President broad powers over all banking transactions and foreign exchanges. Under its terms, banks were allowed to re-open when they proved they were solvent. Within three days of Roosevelt's order over 1,000 banks reopened for business, and by the end of March three-quarters of the nation's banks were operating. Once confidence was restored failures and runs on banks ceased. The Stock Market rallied, and hoarded gold began to return to the Treasury. Most Americans breathed a collective sigh of relief, believing the worst of the crisis was over.

At a time when the world's most powerful nation was bogged down in economic difficulties, unable to take an active role in the settlement of international crises, forces inimical to the free world were marshalling their resources to contest for mastery of the world. For those who kept up with what was happening in Europe and Asia, the outlook was frightening. But most Americans were more concerned with just finding the means to exist.

One of Roosevelt's priorities was to "put people to work" and, at his instigation, Congress nine days later approved the Reforestation Relief Act establishing the Civilian Conservation Corps. Three hundred thousand young men (ages 18-25) by August were being paid $30 a month to perform badly needed reforestation projects, helping to prevent soil erosion and improve flood control, and to build roads and develop the national park system. Army officers at first operated the work camps despite criticism that the CCC resembled Hitler's youth program. This wasn't true because the men were volunteers and there was a minimum of regimentation, no propaganda and no military drills or weapons training. Wages matched the pay of Army privates but their upkeep, including medical care, was paid by the program. Recruits were obligated to send as much as $25 a month home to needy dependents. Leaders received more monthly pay, but the amount still was at the subsistence level. They served a minimum of six months, and a maximum of two years. One little-known aspect of the program later paid dividends. The men received vocational training and remedial classes in elementary and secondary education. Thus positive steps were taken to prepare them to enter the private job market once their terms expired in the Civilian Conservation Corps.

The program was quickly established and by the time it phased out at the start of World War II more than 2.5 million men, including thousands of American Indians, had planted 200 million trees that reforested 17 million acres, helped to check serious soil erosion in many parts of the country and brought the nation's parks up to a state of excellence they had never known. This was one of Roosevelt's finest programs because it helped to solve a pressing problem, and paid long-range dividends that are incalculable.

In his message to the House March 10, Roosevelt had warned that the deficit "will probably exceed one billion dollars unless immediate action is taken." At the time this was a shocking figure, although dwarfed years later by deficits in the hundreds of billions of dollars.

The deficit was considered so serious that a special "Economy Committee" was created to take steps to reduce the government's budget. A bill was passed that, among other things, sharply cut the defense budget from $752 million in 1932 to $531 million in fiscal 1934, with the army bearing the brunt of the cuts.

Secretary of War George H. Dern and Army Chief of Staff Douglas MacArthur sought a meeting with the President to protest the Army's cuts.

Dern tried to argue with the President, but Roosevelt was adamant and he refused to consider an increase in the Army's budget. MacArthur broke in, claiming that the "country's safety is at stake," saying that the United States was now militarily in 17th place. Roosevelt still refused to change his position and MacArthur was furious. The words came out of him without control: "When we lose the next war, and an American boy, lying in the mud with an enemy bayonet through his belly and an enemy foot on his dying throat, spits out his last curse, I want the name not to be MacArthur but Roosevelt."

Roosevelt exploded in a mighty roar. "You must not talk that way to the President!"

MacArthur promptly apologized, believing that his outburst had ended his career, and wishing he could take back those hasty words. He offered his resignation, fully expecting it would be accepted.

As the general walked to the door at the end of the meeting, Roosevelt spoke. He seldom lost his temper and now his voice again was perfectly under control. "Don't be foolish, Douglas. You and the budget must get together on this."

With 15 million unemployed—a quarter of the nation's work force—President Roosevelt issued a proclamation April 19 that the United States would no longer adhere to the gold standard. The Emergency Bank Relief Act passed March 9 had already authorized withdrawal by the Treasury of all gold and gold certificates, and prohibited the hoarding of gold. Now that the dollar was no longer redeemable in gold in the United States, holders were advised to turn it in at Federal Reserve banks for $20.67 an ounce. The embargo on exports of gold was maintained except that earmarked for foreign countries.

Germany announced on October 14, 1933, that it would withdraw from the Disarmament Conference in Geneva and that in two years it would resign from the League of Nations. National Socialism under Adolf Hitler was on the march, boding ill for the rest of the world.

An expansion of the United States Navy was proposed March 27, 1933, by the Vinson Naval Parity Act that authorized the construction of ships and planes approved by the naval treaties of 1922 and 1930 that were renounced that year by Japan. Under terms of the Act, 100 ships and a thousand airplanes were to be built over the next five years. But Congress failed to appropriate sufficient funds, so construction didn't get under way until 1938.

While the news from Europe worsened each year, Japan denounced the Washington Naval Treaty of 1922 and the London Naval Treaty of 1930. Further, her government announced that it would withdraw completely from these treaties' terms effective December 1936.

These war-like moves by Germany and Japan boded ill for the free world, with the United States caught in the middle.

Airpower had stirred the imagination of the world's leaders since World War I, both for its commercial possibilities and for its potential for waging war in a new and decisive manner.

But the United States had been the slowest of all nations to appreciate the possibilities of airpower. In 1933 appropriations for military funding had dropped to 50 percent of the needs projected by military leaders for the 1926-1932 period. Secretary of War George H. Dern, in his annual message to Congress in 1934, recommended purchase of 600 airplanes for the Army Air Corps to give it a total of 2,320 aircraft. By the end of the year, the Air Corps had fewer than 1,500 operational aircraft, 300 short of the 1,800 Congress had authorized 10 years earlier. In 1936, the "Corps" had only two bombers in production, Martin B-10s and Douglas B-18s, both small two-engine airplanes whose short range limited them to coastal defense.

With the death of Germany's President Paul von Hindenburg August 2, 1934, Chancellor Adolf Hitler repudiated the Treaty of Versailles and began full-scale rearmament. An Austrian war veteran and a fanatical nationalist, Adolf Hitler had fanned German discontent for years by claiming that the Weimar Republic following World War I had been imposed upon Germany whose legitimate aspirations to world leadership had been thwarted by a world conspiracy. Until Hitler's rise to power as chancellor January 30, 1933, Germany had been crippled by currency inflation, and the tremendous burden of war reparations that resulted in acute economic distress for most Germans.

In 1935 Hitler withdrew Germany from the League of Nations and incorporated the Saar following a plebiscite. Germany's former adversaries agreed to its return as a concession to Hitler's demands for restoration of Germany's pre-war boundaries. He backed up his growing militancy with compulsory military service for young Germans, and authorized the passage of the so-called Nuremberg Laws depriving Jews of their citizenship.

In recognition of the growing military threat in Europe Roosevelt signed the Neutrality Act August 31 that denied shipment of any arms and munitions—but not raw materials—to belligerents once the President had declared that a state of war existed. American citizens were also prohibited from traveling on ships of a belligerent nation. If they did so, it was made clear that they traveled at their own risk. A basic goal of the Neutrality Act was to separate United States financial interests from foreign wars. It specifically was aimed at Italy's designs on Ethiopia.

The Neutrality Act was invoked October 5, 1935, two days after Italian forces invaded Ethiopia, by President Roosevelt who said that "a state of war unhappily exists" between the two nations.

Six days later the League of Nations in Geneva voted to declare Italy the aggressor, but without the backing of the United States the League was helpless to take effective action.

Meanwhile, Japan's occupation of China was resisted by Mao Tse-tung and his Red Army and the Nationalist Chinese under Chiang Kai-shek, but their main battles were among themselves. To escape entrapment by the Nationalists, Mao Tse-tung led his Red Army to the north in a "Long March" noted for the incredible hardships suffered by his Communist troops.

The much-maligned Works Progress Administration was now of great assistance in the maintenance of an effective fleet air arm in the United States Navy. Roosevelt had directed in 1934 that WPA funds be used to engineer and construct two new carriers. As a result, the U.S.S. "Yorktown," laid down May 21, and the U.S.S. "Enterprise," July 15, were completed in time to be available for World War II. That same year the Navy was authorized to add 650 planes to its previous authorization for a thousand planes. This action permitted the Navy to bring its air strength up to the amount approved by the London Treaty of 1930 but, most important of all, it specified no exact limit.

Although some individuals in the Navy's Bureau of Aeronautics clung stubbornly to the obsolete biplane configuration, it had to be replaced, despite its advantageous slow landing-speed characteristics aboard carriers because they inhibited increased performance. The bureau circulated specifications for a new dive bomber in 1934. They stated specifically that the airplane should be for dive bombing and scouting only, that it must possess substantial range, high payload, and include a bomb displacement or swing-down gear to toss bombs away from the airplane and free of its propeller. Dive brakes to reduce speed in steep dives were considered absolutely necessary. Vought entered the competition but its dive-brake system—a reversible propeller—was not satisfactory. The Martin entry was an improved version of its earlier T5M, later re-designated BM-1. It proved to be the first dive bomber capable of pullouts with a 1,000-pound bomb attached.

The Douglas-Northrop XBT-1 was flown for the first time during July 1935. It showed promise even at first and its designers' hopes were realized far beyond their fondest dreams when it led later to the famous SBD Dauntless.

Naval Aviation really came of age when the first ship designed from the keel up as an aircraft carrier was commissioned in 1934 and assigned to the Pacific Fleet. The U.S.S. "Ranger" had longer decks than previous carriers to accommodate larger and more powerful aircraft and was urgently needed because the aging "Langley" was reduced to limited duty.

When the airship "Macon," sister ship of the "Akron," was lost off Point Sur, California, in February 1935, it marked the end of production for the huge dirigibles. Now the airship "Los Angeles" was the only rigid airship in the Navy and its days were numbered.

In 1934, Charles Egtvedt, Boeing's president, had accepted his engineers' suggestion for designing a four-engine commercial transport to be called the Model 300. Shortly afterwards, when the Army asked Boeing to enter the competition for a multi-engined bomber, Egtvedt proposed a four-engine bomber that would be the military derivative of its Model 300.

Boeing unveiled her entry as Model 299, a four-engine bomber that later became known as the B-17 Flying Fortress.

During flight evaluation tests, the 299 crashed so the decision was delayed until almost the end of the year. The decision was made to give the big contract to Douglas for 103 B-18As, an improved version of the original two-engine bomber. Boeing remained a future contender with a contract to build 13 YB-17s.

Tension in the Far East increased markedly in December 1935 when Japan, which had earlier denounced the Washington Naval Treaty it had signed in 1922 to reduce the size of navies and maintain the "Open Door" policy in China, formally withdrew from the London Naval Conference. Thus the conference was made ineffective although in March 1936, Britain, France and the United States agreed to limitations of their navies, but they were so insignificant that they were meaningless.

Congress passed its second Neutrality Act February 29, 1936, extending its provisions until May 1, 1937, and adding a prohibition against granting any American loans or credits to belligerents. This same date Congress passed the Soil Conservation and Domestic Allotment Act to replace the Agriculture Adjustment Act declared unconstitutional by the Supreme Court. Under this new act, farmers would be paid for withdrawing land planted with soil-depleting crops such as cotton, tobacco, corn and wheat, and for their assistance in controlling erosion by planting soil-conserving crops.

Panama's authority over the Canal Zone was enhanced March 2 when the United States signed a treaty with that country's leaders. But Congress balked at some of the terms, and the Senate refused to ratify it until 1939.

Addis Ababa, capital of Ethiopia, fell to the Italian Army May 9, an action condemned by most people of the world. Emperor Hailie Selassie fled the advancing troops and sought sanctuary abroad. He spoke eloquently to the League of Nations, seeking its support against Italy. Although condemnation of Mussolini's action was strong, his appeal for justice was ignored.

CHAPTER 8

"A Rendezvous with Destiny"

WHEN ROOSEVELT ACCEPTED HIS PARTY'S 1936 NOMINATION FOR A SEC-
ond term there were 100,000 people at Philadelphia's Franklin Field.
He spelled out his campaign's theme by attacking moneyed interests who,
he said, were trying to cripple reform. "They created a new despotism and
wrapped it in the robes of legal sanction. . . . The royalists of the economic order have conceded that political freedom was the business of the
government, but they have maintained that economic slavery was nobody's business. . . . These economic royalists complain that we seek to
overthrow the institutions of America. What they really complain of is
that we seek to take away their power."

He brought the convention to its feet when he said. "To some generations much is given, of other generations, much is expected. This generation of Americans has a rendezvous with destiny."

A revolution against Spain's leftist-oriented Popular Front government
began on July 17 when Spanish Army units revolted in Morocco. It was
started because of Army dissatisfaction with the government's failure to
stop the rising tide of violence by disaffected citizens. After conservative
groups headed the opposition, General Francisco Franco was placed in
charge and took action against the Loyalist forces of the government. The
United States Government announced on August 7 that it would not
interfere in what soon became an all-out civil war.

Despite polls predicting an Alfred E. Landon victory, Roosevelt won
by a landslide with 27.7 million popular votes to 16.6 for Landon.

Elections in Germany gave Adolf Hitler 99 percent of the vote. His
ambitious plans for Germany began to unfold with the occupation of the

71

Rhineland, and the signing of a pact with Mussolini. Hitler also inaugurated a four-year plan to boost Germany's economy.

King George V of England died January 19, 1936, and was succeeded by his son Edward VIII. The King later abdicated because the British government refused to let him marry a divorced woman, Wallis Warfield Simpson.

With the Neutrality Acts of 1935 and 1936 about to expire, Roosevelt signed the third neutrality act May 1, 1937, to keep them in force. The prohibition on the export of arms to belligerents remained intact and such nations were forbidden to sell their securities in the United States. American ships were also prohibited from carrying arms to war zones, and belligerent nations were required to pay in cash for certain non-military goods purchased in the United States and to carry them in their own ships. The act thereafter was referred to as "the cash-and-carry- law."

Earlier, Roosevelt had signed the Reciprocal Trade Agreements Act that extended the Trade Agreements Act of 1934 to June of 1940. It also authorized the President to negotiate foreign trade agreements.

In July the Japanese had invaded China on a trumped-up charge and seized major cities. Although the prime minister, Prince Konoye, tried to control the aggressive policies of the Japanese Army, he was unable to do so. At first the invasion united Chiang Kai-shek's Nationalists and Mao Tse-tung's communists as the capital was moved to Chungking and they tried to contain the Japanese invasion. When the Japanese took over Nanking 200,000 Chinese civilians were killed. Twenty thousand women were raped and then murdered in what became known as "The Rape of Nanking." On September 14 Roosevelt issued an executive order that barred United States ships from carrying arms to both China and Japan.

Impotency of the League of Nations was never more fully evident than when it voted December 11, 1937, against Italy's occupation of Ethiopia, but refused to grant sanctions. Mussolini simply withdrew his country from the League, and ignored their protestations.

A more immediate threat to the peace involving the United States occurred in China December 12 when the American gunboat "Panay" was bombed by Japanese planes and sunk in the Yangtze River. Even some of the isolationists were aroused by this action but Japan's prompt apology two days later, and her agreement to pay indemnity with a promise not to repeat such an incident, cooled emotions for the time being.

The political situation in Europe reached the explosive stage March 18, 1938, when Austrian Chancellor Kurt von Schuschnigg was forced from office and Hitler sent German troops into Austria to "preserve order." Hitler announced defiantly that Austria was now united with

Germany in an Anschluss and denounced Allied claims that Austria had been conquered.

Nearer home, Mexico rocked the American business community by nationalizing oil properties owned by foreign companies without agreement to pay for them. A financial settlement wasn't reached until 1941.

Roosevelt's growing internationalism, first expressed in a Chicago speech October 5, 1937, outraged conservative Republicans. Former President Herbert Hoover responded for them March 31 in a speech to the Council on Foreign Relations. In it he advised the United States not to make any alliances with European countries who were starting to form alliances against Hitler's Germany, Mussolini's Italy and General Franco's Spain. He warned that such action would only lead to America's involvement in another war.

Earlier treaties limiting the size of the world's navies had failed because some countries—notably Japan—had refused to obey them. Now a broad expansion of the U.S. Navy was authorized by Congress May 17 in what became known as the "two-ocean Navy" bill that provided funds for a broad expansion over a 10-year period.

The economic recession that had hit the United States a year earlier was still causing distress to millions of Americans. Roosevelt approved the Emergency Relief Appropriations Act June 21, 1938, that extended previous efforts to deal with the recession. In April, Roosevelt had addressed the Congress and the American people and requested such action. Economic conditions in the South were particularly bad. A report on conditions there said the region's rapidly growing population was faced with the problem of finding work that would give most southerners a decent living on the farm or in the factory. Thousands of people, the report stated, had to shift each year from their farms to mills or mines and back again to their farms. As a result, low wages and poverty had become self-perpetuating.

Europe's newest trouble spot turned out to be the Sudetenland, an area of Czechoslovakia largely inhabited by German-speaking people. Urged on by Adolf Hitler, many of them demanded autonomy.

As the political crisis deepened in Europe, Hitler appeared September 12 in Nuremberg at what was called the "First Party Rally of Greater Germany." He arrived at the huge outdoor stadium just before 7 p.m. to the hysterical "Sieg Heils" of the Germans assembled for the party congress. He walked toward the rostrum with his right arm raised in salute.

Foreign observers at first were lulled by his mild tone as he spoke about the party's struggle. His manner changed as he started to denounce the Czechs. "I am in no way willing that here in the heart of Germany a second Palestine should be permitted to arise. The poor Arabs are defenseless and deserted. The Germans in Czechoslovakia are neither defenseless nor are they deserted, and people should take notice of that fact." The crowd roared its approval. Hitler insisted that he was only interested in justice. "We should be sorry if this were to disturb or damage our relations with other European states, but the blame does not lie with us!"

Czech, British, French and Italian politicians believed that his relatively mild words indicated Hitler would seek a political solution. How wrong they were soon became apparent.

Hitler had mobilized Germany to an unprecedented extent by 1938. The Hitler Youth numbered 7.7 million. At first, four million German youth had refused to join youth organizations but reluctantly did so after Hitler threatened to conscript all youth. He warned their parents that their children would be taken from them and put into state orphanages.

Germany was now a police state under control of the Nazi Party and Heinrich Himmler, chief of the Secret Police and the S.S. He was a small man, with thick glasses through which peered small but animated eyes. Joseph Goebbels, a swarthy man with a crippled foot, had a quick mind and a neurotic personality. He controlled everything the Germans read, saw or heard. A genius at propagandizing the Nazi party, Goebbels used his vast powers ruthlessly.

President Roosevelt sent a personal message September 21 to the governments of Great Britain, France, Germany, Italy and Czechoslovakia asking them to negotiate a peaceful settlement of their differences.

Prime Minister Neville Chamberlain of Great Britain had long adopted a policy of appeasement of Hitler, and now as the Sudetenland crisis erupted with the possibility of war, he spoke to the British people. "How horrible, fantastic, incredible that we should be digging trenches and putting on gas masks here because of a quarrel in a faraway country between peoples of whom we know nothing."

Americans awakened each morning to the rantings of Adolf Hitler whose hysterical outbursts were almost caricatured by shortwave transmission. One such appeal was typical. "For 20 years," Hitler said, "German people in Czechoslovakia had to be traitors to their own cause because they were defenseless against Herr Beneš' persecutions. Either Beneš will accept my offer and give the Germans in the Sudetenland freedom or we'll take it!"

Ignoring President Beneš' protestations, Chamberlain swapped Czech freedom for what he called "peace in our time." He and French Prime Minister Edouard Daladier attended a conference in Munich September 30 and signed an agreement that permitted Germany to take over the Sudetenland.

Upon his return to England Chamberlain spoke to the British people. "Tomorrow, Parliament is going to meet and I shall be making a full statement of the events that have led up to the present anxious and critical situation. And first of all I must say something to those who have written to my wife or myself these last weeks to tell us of their gratitude for my efforts and to assure us of their prayers for my success. After my visits to Germany, I realize vividly how Herr Hitler feels that he must champion other Germans. He told me privately, and last night he repeated publicly that after the Sudeten question is settled that is the end of his territorial claims on Europe."

Hitler entered the Sudeten with German troops on October 3 and most Europeans outside the Third Reich breathed a sigh of relief. In the United States, a Gallup poll showed that only a minority of Americans disapproved of the Munich Pact. It would soon become apparent that appeasement of Hitler only worsened the international situation.

A foretaste of events to come was given German Jews the night of November 9 when Nazi stormtroopers attacked them, and their institutions, throughout Germany. The Nazis called it "Kristallnacht" or "crystal night" because it was commonly referred to as the "night of the broken glass." It was not just a night of shattered windows but an unprovoked, vicious attack by Nazi thugs who destroyed or damaged 1,118 synagogues throughout Germany and Austria, and made personal attacks against many of Germany's 550,000 Jews. Jewish homes were destroyed, and possibly 1,000 Jews were killed although the German government admitted to only 36 deaths.

The following day about 30,000 Jews were sent to concentration camps. It was the start of a program by the Nazis who eventually put to death approximately six million Jews in Europe along with nine to 10 million non-Jews including Gypsies, Slavs (Poles, Ukrainians and Belo Russians) and even some Allied prisoners of war who had tried to escape. The rest of the world did not then realize the true extent of the catastrophe.

In the middle of November American relations with Germany reached such a low point that the ambassador to Germany was recalled for "report and consultation." Four days later Hitler recalled the German ambassador.

Anthony Eden, who had recently resigned as Britain's foreign minister to protest Chamberlain's actions at Munich, gave a radio address in New York City on December 6 in which he warned Americans that all democracies were threatened by Adolf Hitler and Benito Mussolini. His words were largely ignored because most Americans remained strongly opposed to involvement in Europe's escalating crisis.

CHAPTER 9

Strict Neutrality

DESPITE HITLER'S WAR-LIKE ACTS IN EUROPE, AND JAPAN'S GROWING involvement in the occupation of China, most Americans began 1939 with a strong conviction that their country should remain neutral regardless of what happened in the rest of the world.

President Roosevelt, privy to secret intelligence unknown to most Americans, was not so naive. In his annual State of the Union address to Congress January 4, 1939, he shifted emphasis from a discussion of the economy to international affairs, calling upon all democracies to be prepared.

The following day he submitted his $9 billion budget to Congress, including $1.319 billion for defense.

Five days later the President requested an additional $552 million for defense, including funds for an air defense program.

The German Army invaded Czechoslovakia March 14, an action that came as no surprise to most world leaders after the Allied "sell-out" at Munich the previous fall over the Sudentenland. The country was annexed seven days later. The Baltic port of Memel, a part of Lithuania, and adjacent to East Prussia, was annexed at the same time. Two days later, Hitler demanded permission from Poland for passage through the Polish Corridor to Danzig.

These actions prompted Roosevelt to again seek additional defense appropriations.

Tension in Europe increased dramatically when Great Britain and France promised to help Poland if it was threatened.

Not to be out-done by Hitler, Benito Mussolini invaded Albania April

7, and six days later Great Britain and France offered to help Greece and Romania in case of aggression.

These actions by Germany and Italy aroused strong anti-German and anti-Italian feelings in the United States but official policy remained one of strict neutrality; a viewpoint shared by most Americans.

Meanwhile, the Civil War in Spain came to an end in victory for General Franco's Fascist forces and the country joined the Anti-Comintern Pact and resigned from the League of Nations.

In an attempt to keep Spain from becoming a full-fledged partner with Germany and Italy, the Franco government was recognized by Great Britain and France, and the United States followed suit April 1.

Roosevelt interjected himself again into international affairs when he wrote Hitler and Mussolini April 14 and suggested that they offer a 10-year guarantee of peace for Europe and the Middle East in exchange for American cooperation to talk about world trade and armaments. Specifically he asked them not to attack 31 European and Near Eastern nations. Hitler responded that Germany was only righting the wrongs of Versailles. To further demonstrate their unity Germany and Italy formed a military alliance on May 22. Hitler showed his contempt for the President's intervention by revoking Germany's non-aggression pact with Poland and the Anglo-German Naval Agreement.

A number of prominent physicists prevailed upon Dr. Albert Einstein, who had moved to America from Germany in 1933, to write President Roosevelt on August 2 advising him that atomic fission could be used to make highly destructive bombs, and that two German physicists had shown that the bombardment of uranium with neutrons actually fissioned, or split apart, the uranium nucleus, releasing energy and actually creating more neutrons to form a chain reaction.

After Einstein's letter was delivered to the White House it did not go directly to the President because it was decided that someone Roosevelt knew and respected should make the proposal. Dr. Alexander Sachs, vice president of Lehman Corporation, was selected to make the presentation. Sachs was a biologist and an economist, and an excellent choice.

He was ushered into the oval office on October 11, 1939, and was warmly greeted by the President. "Alex, what are you up to?"

Sachs had decided not to use Einstein's letter, but instead he summarized it. First, he emphasized the power aspects of nuclear energy, then related the medical benefits to be derived from the use of radioactive materials, and lastly he spoke of "bombs of hitherto unenvisaged potency and scope." He advised the President to make arrangements with Belgium for uranium supplies, and to accelerate experiments which he believed industry or private foundations could pay for. Finally, he suggested that the President designate an individual and a committee to serve as a liaison between the scientists and the administration.

In conclusion, he read the last lines of Francis Aston's lecture which he had given in 1936, but that wasn't published until two years later. Called "Forty Years of Atomic Theory," the Nobel prize-winning English physicist said, "Personally I think there is no doubt that sub-atomic energy is available all around us, and that one day man will release and control its almost infinite power. We cannot prevent him from doing so, and can only hope that he will not use it exclusively for blowing up his next door neighbor."

Roosevelt nodded his understanding. "Alex, what you are after is to see that the Nazis don't blow us up."

"Precisely."

The President called in his aide Colonel Edwin M. "Pa" Watson. "This requires action," he told him.

Watson initially set up a committee composed of the director of the Bureau of Standards—the nation's physics laboratory—and a representative from the Army and Navy.

But the establishment of an organization to perform atomic research on a highly secret basis with the full financial backing of the government wasn't established until 1941 when the Manhattan Project was charged with responsibility to develop atomic bombs.

The possibility of war increased dramatically on August 23, 1939, when Germany and the Union of Soviet Socialist Republics signed a nonaggression pact in Moscow. People everywhere were shocked when the announcement was made the following day. American communists, in particular, found it almost impossible to justify while nations all over the world were dismayed by the news. The two nations agreed that neither would attack the other nor remain neutral in case of an attack by another nation.

Attention now focused on Poland because Nazi propaganda had risen to hysterical heights during the same time about the perfidy of the Polish government in refusing to cooperate with the Third Reich.

President Roosevelt sent personal appeals to Poland, Germany and Italy urging arbitration of their differences, and conciliation or negotiations to resolve German-Polish differences to avoid war. The Polish government had few options, caught between its two powerful neighbors. Poland accepted conciliation, but Hitler ignored appeals for a peaceful solution.

The German Army invaded Poland September 1, 1939, at 4:45 a.m. and Hitler charged the intervention had been precipitated by an attack by Polish personnel which was not true.

Officials of Great Britain and France immediately demanded that Germany withdraw its armed forces from Poland, but Hitler ignored their demands, instructing his armed forces to continue their drives. The Polish armed forces, totally unequipped to resist a modern army led by tanks and protected overhead by massed waves of aircraft, quickly disintegrated as the Germans swept triumphantly through Poland.

Great Britain and France declared war on Germany September 3, but Belgium declared it would remain neutral.

President Roosevelt spoke to the nation by radio on that date saying he was aware that the nation was not neutral in thought, but that Americans must remain neutral in policy. Two days later he declared the United States would officially remain neutral in the conflict.

The following day the war was brought home to Americans when the British passenger ship "Athenia" was torpedoed by a German submarine off the Hebrides Islands and 28 American passengers were killed. Secretary of State Hull immediately advised Americans to travel to Europe only when it was absolutely necessary.

The President declared a limited national emergency September 8 to give himself, he said, "certain powers to act more quickly in the developing world crisis."

Germany demanded surrender of Poland's armed forces after its troops captured Warsaw September 17, and Polish resistance collapsed. Germany and the Soviet Union now signed a new treaty to divide Poland into German and Russian sectors while Russian troops invaded Poland September 17. All resistance ceased a week later when the last of Poland's army surrendered.

Secretary of State Hull announced October 2 that the United States did not recognize the partition of Poland by Germany and the Soviet Union. He said the American government would maintain diplomatic relations with the Polish government in exile in Paris.

At the Inter-American Conference in Panama City October 2 and 3, conferees issued a "Declaration of Panama" that established safety zones in the seas of the Western Hemisphere, proclaiming they were off-limits to naval forces of the belligerent nations. It was one thing to issue a proclamation, but something else to expect that these nations would honor it. They immediately proceeded to ignore the warning.

The American Federation of Labor, mirroring the strong feeling of neutrality throughout the nation, adopted a resolution October 11 that called for the United States not to become involved in the war in Europe but then interjected American sympathies by calling for a boycott of goods from Germany, Russia and Japan.

Little action took place in Europe after Poland capitulated, but the war began to spread to the Atlantic. Roosevelt issued a proclamation October 18 saying that American offshore waters, and all American ports, were closed to submarines of all belligerents. It was promptly ignored by both sides.

The United States took its first important step toward involvement in the war when President Roosevelt signed the Neutrality Act of 1939. It repealed the general embargo on arms called for in previous neutrality acts, and now permitted the sale of arms to belligerents on a cash-and-carry basis although not in American ships. In effect, this so-called "neutral" plan favored Britain, France and their allies because they had access to lines of credit denied the Germans and Italians.

Now the war accomplished something all of Roosevelt's New Deal programs had failed to achieve—it ended the long depression as factories started to expand to produce arms and war equipment for Great Britain, France and their allies. In the West, and California in particular, aircraft factories were producing at an accelerating rate and there was now a shortage of workers.

Most people throughout the world were outraged when it became known on November 30 that the Soviet Union had invaded Finland and bombed its capital Helsinki. American hearts went out to the Finnish people as they doggedly resisted the Red Army and its air force during the winter months when Russian armor bogged down in deep snow drifts, bringing the invasion to a virtual halt. The United States Government extended both private and governmental aid to Finland but the end was inevitable. The brave Finnish people were defeated on the battlefield in March but not in spirit. Under peace treaty terms control of about 10 percent of the small country was assumed by Russia but Finland remained free.

Appropriations for expanding America's defenses dominated the $8.4 billion budget President Roosevelt submitted to Congress on January 3, 1940, amounting to more than 21 percent of the total or $1.8 billion.

America's relations with Japan deteriorated even further at the start of the new year, culminating in the expiration of the 1911 trade treaty that had offered Japan special terms. Secretary of State Hull informed Japanese officials that the treaty would not be renewed but that trade between the two countries would continue.

Admiral William D. Leahy, chief of naval operations, had formed the Atlantic Squadron in 1939 to protect the United States' inherent rights to the sea lanes. Rear Admiral A. W. Johnson, the same man who had been in charge of the 1921 bombing tests, was given seven cruisers and seven destroyers to cover his vast responsibilities, but his command had only 80 airplanes.

A few weeks later, following the Munich conference where "peace in our time" was predicted, a doubtful United States quietly strengthened the squadron. But by 1940 there were still no carriers to adequately secure a strong defense line in the Atlantic.

The ships of Great Britain and her allies suffered terribly during the first two months of 1940 as German U-boats waged the "Battle of the Atlantic." Ship losses steadily mounted until they reached almost disastrous proportions with the loss of 440,000 tons of Allied shipping.

On land, the war remained on a "sitzkrieg" basis. Roosevelt dispatched Undersecretary of State Sumner Welles to Europe on February 17 to survey conditions between the warring nations and he reported the findings on March 28 to the President.

Americans had not as yet seriously suffered as the war escalated around the world, although some imported products became scarce. Silk stockings were an early casualty, but DuPont's development of nylon resolved that situation.

Although Germany had a non-aggression treaty with the Soviet Union, that nation's failure to quickly defeat Finland caused Hitler to reassess the U.S.S.R.'s military capabilities. Both he, and Allied leaders, decided that in a war with Germany, Russia would be overrun quickly.

Italy's dictator, Benito Mussolini, met with Hitler at the Brenner Pass on March 18, and they agreed to a secret pact to defeat the Allies.

The Germans invaded Norway and Denmark on April 9 and Denmark soon surrendered. Norway fought back with British and French forces but two months later Norway's King and his prime minister ordered his country's forces to cease fighting.

President Roosevelt appealed to Mussolini April 29 in another attempt to persuade him to use his influence to find a peaceful solution to Europe's problems. His request was rejected.

Hitler's true intentions were revealed May 10 when Germany's armed forces invaded Luxembourg, the Netherlands and Belgium. To keep the assets of these nations out of German hands, the President froze them in the United States.

Prime Minister Neville Chamberlain, whose appeasement of Adolf Hitler had helped to create the present situation, spoke to members of the Parliament on this date after they had roundly condemned him and removed him from office. "It was clear that at this critical moment in the war that what was needed was the formation of a government which would include members of the Labor and Liberal opposition. His Majesty has now entrusted to my friend and colleague Mr. Winston Churchill the task of forming a new administration on a national basis."

Members of Parliament cheered as Churchill rose to speak. "I speak to you for the first time as prime minister in a solemn hour for the life of our country, of our empire, of our allies, and above all of the cause of freedom."

During the previous years Churchill had become the conscience of England, but his warnings had been ignored.

"I have nothing to offer," Churchill said, "but blood, toil, tears and sweat."

The German army crossed the French frontier two days later using its typical blitzkrieg tactics of airpower, tanks and heavily-armed infantry, and quickly swept British and French forces into pockets of resistance. Belgium's King Leopold ordered his army to surrender May 28, thus stranding about 400,000 Allied soldiers who were forced to withdraw to France's channel port of Dunkirk.

With the Nazis sweeping toward Paris, Premier Paul Reynaud made a radio appeal to the United States. He had replaced Daladier in March. He said that France would fight on. "Our generals are commanding battalions," he said. "Send us waves of planes and we shall hurl back the invader. France will never die."

It was an emotional speech, but one that didn't relate to reality. There were no waves of planes available in America, even if the American government had been inclined to become involved in the war that, at this stage, it definitely was not. Roosevelt asked Congress for appropriations in late May to train 50,000 pilots, and to build 50,000 warplanes per year, but no airplanes were immediately available to avert the present emergency.

Italy declared war on the Allies June 10, and Mussolini's troops invaded France.

In a speech at the University of Virginia, with his voice quivering with outrage, President Roosevelt condemned Mussolini's action: "On this 10th day of June, 1940, the hand that held the dagger has struck it into the back of its neighbor."

The President admitted that United States policy was emerging from "neutrality" to "non-belligerency." In other words, the United States would now openly support the Allies without actually becoming involved in the war. Americans accepted his words with resignation, most believing that the United States eventually would become involved in the war. Isolationists remained strong in their convictions but even they had to admit that times had changed.

In Europe, French troops withdrew from Paris, and the Germans entered the undefended city June 14. Marshal Henri Pétain succeeded Reynaud as head of France's government at Vichy. The two nations signed an armistice June 22 at Compiègne, site of the World War I surrender.

During the fall of France, Winston Churchill sent the first of many telegrams to President Roosevelt May 15, signing himself as that "former naval person," and thereby establishing a strong bond between them. Churchill urged the President to supply Britain with military hardware, saying he hoped that eventually America would participate in the war.

The President went to Congress the next day and asked that its members appropriate more money for defense, particularly to increase the production of aircraft.

When General George C. Marshall became chief of staff of the United States Army the day Germany invaded Poland in 1939 he told the President that he had inherited the army of a third-rate power, with fewer men than Portugal's army (approximately 125,000 men.) In training exercises trucks were labeled "tanks" and artillery pieces were represented by stove pipes mounted on wheeled vehicles. There were only 28 real tanks in the Army, and they had long been obsolete. The Army Air Corps had only 1200 regular and reserve officers on duty, with a total complement of 11,000 men. Its aircraft were largely outmoded because funds to develop new fighters and bombers had been restricted for years.

The Navy was in better shape, and its air arm had over 5,600 aircraft and more than 6,000 pilots.

As the evacuation of Allied troops began at Dunkirk on the coast of France President Roosevelt established the Office for Emergency Management, believing that war involving the United States was inevitable.

In one of the most incredible feats of all time all available naval and civilian ships were dispatched from Britain to assist in embarking the troops who were under constant bombing and shelling. Of the 400,000 who had been been in Belgium, 338,226 were evacuated. Eighty naval and merchant ships were lost to enemy fire, and 80 Royal Air Force pilots died protecting the beachhead.

When the German Army overran Dunkirk June 4, thus ending the evacuation, Churchill paid tribute to all those who had taken part in a radio address heard throughout the world. "We shall fight on the beaches, we shall fight on the landing grounds, we shall fight in the fields and in the streets. . . . we shall never surrender."

The shock of France's quick defeat prompted Congress to agree that millions of dollars worth of surplus or outdated arms, munitions and aircraft could be sold to Great Britain through the War Department.

Although France's government had surrendered to the Germans, General Charles de Gaulle, who had escaped to England, pledged June 18 that he would carry on the fight against the Germans for a completely free France.

In a further escalation of the war, the Soviet army occupied the states of Lithuania, Latvia and Estonia on the Baltic Sea, forcing them in August to become part of the Soviet Union.

Two more defense appropriation bills were approved by Congress in June with the Naval Supply Act authorizing $1.5 billion for naval defense, and the Military Supply Act providing $1.8 billion for military defense projects. The national debt limit was now raised to $49 billion.

With the possibility of America's involvement in the war, Roosevelt strengthened his administration with the appointment of two prominent Republicans—Henry L. Stimson as Secretary of War, and Frank Knox as Secretary of the Navy. Stimson had been Taft's Secretary of War, and the department had been reorganized and reinvigorated by his actions. In the '30s he spoke out strongly for preparedness after Hitler came to power, although his words were largely ignored. Roosevelt now shrewdly formed a "coalition government" to demonstrate to the rest of the world that the United States was united, and to enhance his own prospects for a third term in this election year.

With the growing concern about German and Russian infiltration in the United States, Congress passed the Alien Registration Act June 28 to require all aliens in the country to register periodically, and made it illegal for individual organizations to advocate the overthrow of the United States Government by force.

Although the situation in Europe was stark for Great Britain, the losses of ships and vitally-needed cargoes in the Atlantic reached its peak from July through October. Germany had 28 operational U-boats at sea and they were sinking ships almost without opposition.

Roosevelt again went to Congress July 10 for additional funds for defense, seeking $4.8 billion on the day that Nazi warplanes attacked England in what was to become "The Battle of Britain."

Later, as the German Air Force sent masses of planes over England to bomb its cities, and were met by the outnumbered fighters of Britain's Royal Air Force, Winston Churchill spoke eloquently of this massive challenge to the British people. He said that "The Battle of Britain" was about to begin, and that Hitler would have to take the British Isles or lose the war. "Let us therefore brace ourselves to our duty, and so bear ourselves that if the British Empire and its Commonwealth last for a thousand years men will still say this was their finest hour."

The American Democratic National Convention met in Chicago from July 15 to 19 to nominate Roosevelt for an unprecedented third term, and to name Secretary of Agriculture Henry A. Wallace as the vice-presidential candidate.

Congress was in no mood to deny the President anything to increase the security of the United States, and it approved another $4 billion for a two-ocean Navy of 200 ships. This bill authorized the Navy to start the greatest expansion in the country's history by approving funds to build $1,325 billion of new combat ships.

Delegates to the Pan-American Union met in Havana July 30 to discuss ways of preserving the independence of nations in the western hemisphere. In a "Declaration of Havana" representatives of these countries announced that they were prepared to resist the transfer of any European colonies in the hemisphere to German control.

With "The Battle of Britain" at its height, and the war at sea in a state of chaos, the United States agreed to give 50 over-age destroyers to Britain in exchange for 99-year leases for naval and air bases on various British possessions in the western hemisphere. Earlier, Roosevelt hadn't dared to take such a partisan stand in the war, but now the American people were becoming more and more concerned about the possibility of a Hitler victory in Europe. So, the time was ripe to initiate the first step of what later would evolve into a lend-lease agreement.

Secretary of State Hull, keeping a wary eye on the Japanese, warned Japan's leaders in September that the United States would oppose aggression in French Indochina. Japan ignored the warning. Three weeks later she signed an agreement with France's Vichy government for sea-and-air bases there.

The effects of the war in Europe were felt in a more personal way when Congress approved the Selective Service Training and Service Act that Roosevelt signed September 16. Under its terms 16.4 million men between the ages of 21-35 were required to start registering for military training a month later for what was called a year of military service for the first group of 900,000 men.

Ten days later the President announced an embargo, effective October 16, on the export of scrap steel and iron outside the western hemisphere—except to Great Britain. Such action was taken to deprive Japan of much-needed supplies, and her government promptly protested, but took even more decisive action by signing a military and economic pact with Germany and Italy pledging mutual assistance.

By October 12, the Royal Air Force's Fighter Command had won "The Battle of Britain," and Hitler's plan to follow the aerial assault with an invasion of the British Isles had to be indefinitely postponed, and eventually cancelled. The German Air Force had sustained very heavy losses despite their superiority in numbers of war planes. Britain's use of radar for early warning of raids, their direction and anticipated time over England, had helped to defeat the Germans in addition to the incredible bravery of RAF fighter pilots. Without control of English airspace, such an invasion was impossible. Many of England's cities and war plants had been devastated, and the loss of pilots and aircraft was particularly acute. German bombing raids continued throughout the war, but never at the intensity of "The Battle of Britain."

Germany now moved in another direction, occupying Romania while Italy invaded Greece. Great Britain promptly landed forces on several Greek islands, including Crete.

In December a nationwide poll revealed that 39 percent of Americans believed it had been a mistake to become involved in World War I, and most of them were opposed to involvement in the new war. The poll indicated, however, a reduction in isolationist beliefs because a similar poll in 1937 had shown that 64 percent thought American participation in the earlier war was a mistake.

Meanwhile, Great Britain's armed forces attacked the Italians in North Africa on December 9 and destroyed Marshal Rodolfo Graziani's army, taking about 130,000 prisoners.

President Roosevelt established the Office of Production Management on December 20 and placed William S. Knudsen in charge to coordinate and expedite defense production. The Germans used this pretext to charge that the United States was guilty of "moral aggression" by providing aid to Great Britain. For once the Germans were not guilty of propaganda but stating a fact that most Americans agreed was all too true.

There were few doubters on December 29 when President Roosevelt gave one of his popular "Fireside Chats." His voice rang with conviction as he said, "We must be the great arsenal of democracy. For us this is an emergency, serious as war itself."

In his annual message to Congress on January 6, 1941, President Roosevelt sought additional aid for the Allies and spelled out what he called the "four essential freedoms" that Americans and all similarly-inclined people were dedicated to preserve. He listed them as: Freedom of speech and expression, freedom of worship, freedom from want and freedom from fear. His rallying cry to free peoples everywhere struck a responsive chord, and none more so than in the hearts and minds of most Americans. The President's call for support of a lend-lease program for the Allies—important to Great Britain whose credit was close to exhaustion—received less than the usual vituperation from members of Congress. Even his $17.48 billion budget with $10.8 billion for defense, was greeted with only minor outrage.

During February and March American and British leaders held secret talks in Washington to lay plans for joint strategic action in the event that the United States became involved in the war. Such meetings, if they had become known, would have been denounced by most Americans whose isolationism remained strong. But officials of both countries believed such plans were necessary. It was agreed at these meetings that even if the United States became involved in a two-ocean war that both countries would focus their major offensive efforts against Germany first, and maintain only a holding action against Japan.

CHAPTER 10

A Day That Will Live in Infamy

AFTER WAR ERUPTED IN EUROPE IN 1939 THE UNITED STATES ARMY AIR Corps was permitted to hold design competitions for offensive bombers. The Air Corps ordered 460 new bombers from four companies, including Boeing B-17s, Convair B-24s, North American B-25s and Martin B-26s. Such was the urgency that all but the B-17 were ordered without first testing them.

In the early part of 1940 the Air Corps asked five companies to bid on a new long-range bomber that could attack Japan if that should become necessary. To keep the isolationists quiet, the bomber was presented as a defensive weapon to provide long-range reconnaissance, and to make strikes against the fleet of a potential invader. Boeing and Convair each won a contract to design and produce two prototypes. The Boeing design was called the XB-29 and Convair's airplane was the XB-32. The Lockheed, Douglas and Martin entries failed to meet specifications. Each company selected the Wright R-3350 engine because it was the only engine under development with sufficient power, and it had already been used in the XB-19.

The Convair XB-32 flew first on July 2, 1942, and the Boeing XB-29 on September 21. Developmental problems were horrendous, particularly with the Convair bomber, but most problems were centered around the Wright engines in both planes which tended to overheat and to catch fire.

In effect, by early 1941 the Army Air Corps was largely a paper air force.

The President's request for a lend-lease program to aid any nation whose survival was considered necessary to the defense of the United States was approved March 11 by Congress which at first authorized $7 billion, but once the United States became involved in the war the program expanded to $50 billion in aid money with one-half going to Great Britain, and a quarter going to Russia.

Passage of the Lend-lease Act came at a critical time because Axis forces began a counter-offensive March 24 against British troops in North Africa, forcing them to withdraw to Egypt. For a time, even Egypt's survival was at stake. German forces invaded Yugoslavia and Greece April 6 and British troops were forced to withdraw April 23 to Crete. But by using airborne troops the Germans captured Crete by June 1.

Greenland was considered so necessary to the defense of the United States that Secretary of State Cordell Hull, and other western hemisphere officials, signed an agreement with Washington's Danish minister Henrik de Kauffman April 9 that the United States would undertake its defense although Danish sovereignty would be maintained throughout the war. Kauffman agreed to permit the construction and maintenance of military installations by armed forces of the United States.

Two days later President Roosevelt told Prime Minister Churchill that the United States would extend its patrolled security zone to longitude 26 west, or a line about half-way between England and the American east coast. Known as "The Sea Frontier" of the United States, such action was deemed necessary because of the enormous damage "wolf-packs" of German U-Boats were inflicting upon allied and neutral shipping in the Atlantic. Losses were particularly heavy in the North Atlantic. The Germans ignored the line and May 21 sank the American merchant ship "Robin Moor."

With the economy in danger of over-heating as American industries strove to build up quickly to supply unprecedented orders for the Allies in Europe, the Office of Price Administration and Civilian Supply—later just OPA—was established April 11 to recommend price controls to prevent inflation. Steel prices were frozen and rubber rationing was insti-tuted. By September it was apparent that price controls had to be more stringent.

From the middle of May President Roosevelt took a series of partisan steps in the war. After denouncing French collaborationists May 15 for their support of German occupying forces in their homeland, he placed all French ships in American ports into "protective custody," including the luxury liner "Normandie." Twelve days later, after Greece and Yugo-slavia were occupied by the Germans, he issued a proclamation declaring that a state of unlimited national emergency existed in the United States. He had thought earlier of such a step, but he didn't feel the time was ripe, but the sinking of the "Robin Moor" a week earlier had given him an excuse to take such a bold step.

That month the President wrote the War Department recommending the buildup of heavy bombers with a production quota of 500 a month. The new B-29 Superfortress, designed to reach all areas of Germany from England, was still only in preliminary design. Now Roosevelt called for production of 26,000 combat planes and 37,000 trainers by 1944. That was shocking enough to officials of the infant aircraft industry which, in the past, was lucky to count production contracts in terms of a few hundred airplanes a year, but the Air Corps also recommended production of 17,000 warplanes for the Royal Air Force! (By the end of the war, the United States had built 297,000 warplanes, vastly exceeding Roosevelt's goal.)

Perhaps the most provocative airplanes of all were contracted for in the spring of 1934—the Douglas B-19 and the Boeing XB-15. Basically they were designed as flying laboratories for the development and testing of airplane ideas for the future. For their time, they were the largest, most powerful airplanes ever built, and they cost $3 million. They were designed to fly 7,750 miles, more than three times the distance World War I destroyers could travel without refueling. Fully loaded they weighed in excess of 160,000 pounds, and they could carry a bomb load of 19 tons.

These airplanes, which first flew in 1937, were underpowered because available engines were inadequate to power such huge aircraft, but they paved the way for the big bombers of World War II, and the great ocean-spanning commercial transports of the post-war era.

Under the broad mandate granted him by Congress to take whatever steps he considered prudent for the security of the United States, the President froze German and Italian assets in the United States June 14, and two days later ordered all German consulates closed by July 10. Germany and Italy retaliated by closing American consulates, and Italian consulates in the United States were closed July 20.

These actions were all just short of war, and were roundly denounced by some Americans and supported by others. For two years Charles A. Lindbergh had spoken out strongly against the war, particularly at America First rallies. At one meeting in Madison Square Garden he had said, "These wars in Europe are not wars in which our civilization is defending itself from some Asiatic intruder, there is no Ghengis Khan or Xerxes marching against our western nation. This is simply one more of those age-old struggles within our own family of nations. If we enter fighting for democracy abroad, we may end by losing it at home."

In outright violation of the 1939 non-aggression pact signed by Germany and the Soviet Union, Hitler ordered an attack against Russia June 22, 1941. German forces moved methodically into the communist nation as Russian forces gave way before the huge Nazi juggernaut as it advanced along an 1,800-mile front from Finland to the Black Sea. Later, Romanian, Italian and Finnish troops took part in the invasion.

Two days later President Roosevelt pledged American assistance to the Soviet Union and on July 13 Great Britain and the Soviet Union signed a pact in Moscow that neither would make a separate peace with Germany.

American factories were now working toward peak capacity as peacetime plants converted to the production of war material in record time. Plants that made a full range of civilian products quickly began the production of airplanes, tanks, ammunition and uniforms. Synthetic rubber replaced non-available natural rubber, and synthetics such as nylon and rayon easily supplanted silk that had come mostly from Japan. The West Coast boomed as never before as over 1.2 million workers thronged its cities to work in its new factories.

By war's end, American factories had produced 297,000 airplanes, 86,000 tanks, 12,000 ships and an enormous volume of special vehicles for the armed services, along with a constant flow of ammunition and munitions.

This rapid growth soon resulted in problems, most of which were promptly controlled as much as possible. The Fair Employment Practices Committee was established June 25 to promote black equality in defense plants and in government employment. It was the first positive step taken to address the problem, and it was the forerunner of later laws that tried to establish economic opportunities and effective equality for blacks.

Charles A. Lindbergh carried his anti-war crusade to New York. "I know I will be criticized by the interventionists in America when I say we should not enter a war unless we have a reasonable chance of winning. That, they will claim, is too materialistic a viewpoint. They will advance again the same arguments that were used to persuade France to declare war against Germany in 1939. I do not believe that our American ideals and our way of life will gain through an unsuccessful war. And I know that the United States is not prepared to wage war in Europe successfully at this time . . . it is not only our right but it is our obligation as American citizens to look at this war objectively, and to weigh our chances for success if we should enter it. I have attempted to do this, especially from the viewpoint of aviation. I am forced to the conclusion that we cannot win this war for England regardless of how much assistance we extend."

By executive order June 28 President Roosevelt established the Office of Scientific Research and Development to coordinate scientific-technological work for the war effort. Chairman Vannevar Bush became responsible for research on radar, sonar and the first stage of development of the atomic bomb. Roosevelt secretly proposed to Great Britain October 11 that they join forces to develop the atomic bomb.

United States Marines occupied Iceland July 7 by an agreement between its government and American officials to prevent its use by the Axis powers for military bases.

Japan completed her occupation of French Indochina July 26. Great Britain and the United States retaliated by halting all trade with Japan and froze that nation's assets. This action was later used by Japan to justify its decision to go to war.

On the following day Roosevelt nationalized the Philippine army and called it into service with the United States Army because the Philippines were still a dependency. Lieutenant General Douglas MacArthur, who had earned a reputation for bravery in World War I, and had served in the Philippines from 1922 until 1930 when he was appointed Army chief of staff in Washington, was placed in command over the joint forces. With the increasing war threat in the Far East, MacArthur was given a fourth star and named commander of United States forces in the Far East.

The United States then warned Japan's ambassador in Washington that any further aggression in the Far East would lead to a move by the United States to protect American rights.

There was little pretense now about American involvement in the war although it was considered prudent by officials of the Roosevelt administration to hold secret meetings between August 9 and 12 on American and British warships off the coast of Newfoundland. After a series of historic meetings between President Roosevelt and Prime Minister Winston Churchill eight goals for the world were set forth in an Atlantic Charter, including the renunciation of aggression, the right of people to chose their own government, the support of access to raw materials, guarantees of freedom from want and fear, freedom of the seas and disarmament of all aggressors. The "charter" was announced in a joint statement August 14 and by September 24 fifteen anti-Axis nations— including the Soviet Union—had endorsed the Atlantic Charter. It later became the blueprint for the post-war United Nations. Basically, Great Britain and the United States pledged themselves to the common goal of the destruction of Nazi Germany.

In a move that fooled no one in Washington, the Japanese ambassador to the United States presented a note to President Roosevelt August 28 stating that Japan's Premier Konoye wished "to pursue courses of peace and harmony" with the United States.

Upon his return to the capital, President Roosevelt was sobered by news that the House of Representatives had passed the six-month extension of the draft by only a single vote. Isolationists had fought its extension in a final desperate move to keep the United States out of the war. The Senate had passed the bill 45 to 30, but the House voted 203 to 202 for extension.

Isolationist Senator Burton K. Wheeler had sent a million postcards on his congressional frank urging citizens to write the President that they were against entry into the European war. This was a flagrant abuse of the privilege, but he wasn't challenged.

The extension was unpopular because young men had been promised the year before they would only have to serve one year. Parents of many drafted men wrote the President, and signs began to appear throughout the nation listing the letters OHIO (Over-the-hill-in-October.) By urging draftees to desert, the campaign was in open defiance of the law.

Prior to the House vote, Speaker Sam Rayburn appealed to members, calling upon them to support the extension. "Do this for me," he said, "I won't forget it." He appealed to their patriotism when he realized he was four votes short of passage. "You cannot allow the Army to be disbanded," he said, in an emotional appeal. Such was his prestige among House members, and despite the visitor's gallery jammed with flag-carrying mothers and young men in uniform, four representatives switched votes, but it was a squeaker. It indicated the depth of the anti-war feeling in the nation.

The President ordered United States ships and planes September 11 to shoot on sight any Axis ships within the zone he had declared April 11 would be defended. He considerd such a step vital to the nation's security because American naval and merchant ships had come under increasing attack by Axis ships.

Five days later, the United States Navy announced it would be responsible for protecting all ships as far east as Iceland.

Enormous sums had been approved by Congress for building up America's defenses, and for lend-lease aid to its allies, so the Revenue Act of 1941 was passed September 20 to raise taxes to support some of this huge expenditure.

Despite repeated warnings to Germany about unrestricted U-Boat attacks, the American destroyer "Kearney" was torpedoed October 17 off Iceland although it didn't sink. Eleven Americans were killed.

Ten days later, the President broadcast to the nation on Navy Day saying, "America has been attacked, the shooting has started." Despite his words, he had no illusions about the feeling of most Americans who desperately wanted to remain out of the war. Therefore, he didn't dare to call for a declaration of war against the Axis powers.

Even the loss of 100 Americans on October 30 when the United States destroyer "Reuben James" was sunk by a German U-boat while on convoy duty off Iceland did not appreciably raise the pro-war sentiments.

Moscow was placed under a state of siege on October 20 as German armies approached the capital, although bad weather had slowed their advance. The German armies expected to easily capture Moscow, although the government had been moved to Kuibyshev. Kiev and Odessa had already been captured, but German losses were much higher than anticipated and the Russians proved to be a tougher foe once their homeland was invaded than Adolf Hitler had expected.

American Ambassador to Japan, Joseph Grew, warned Washington November 3 that the Japanese might be planning a sudden attack against United States positions. Four days later Secretary of State Cordell Hull repeated Grew's warning to President Roosevelt and his cabinet.

With tension running high the first two weeks of November, negotiations began November 17 between Japan's ambassador in the United States, Kichisaburo Nomura, and a special envoy, Saburo Kurusu, to resolve their differences. Three days later the Japanese envoys proposed that the United States remove restrictions on trade with Japan and refrain from interfering with Japan's activities in China and the Pacific.

President Roosevelt took still another partisan step on behalf of the Allies November 17 by amending the 1939 Neutrality Act to permit American merchant ships to be armed and to call at Allied ports.

The Japanese proposal to give Japan a free hand to do as it pleased in the Pacific was rejected November 26. Secretary of State Hull demanded instead that the Japanese withdraw their forces from China and Indochina and, if they did so, he promised that the United States would remove its trade restrictions.

Japanese officials rejected this American proposal December 1, but did not immediately inform the United States. The decision to go to war had been made long before the proposal was originally made to American officials.

Two days later, Japanese consulates in the United States began to burn their secret documents.

German forces penetrated within 20 miles of Moscow by December 5, but Russian counterattacks forced them to fall back from their forward positions. Kalinin, northwest of the capital, was recaptured as the Nazi armies faced rejuvenated Russian forces and the typical fierce Russian winter came to their aid. General Fedor von Bock sent word to Adolf Hitler in Berlin that "it would be inconceivable that anyone could reasonably hope to have this operation succeed after our serious losses and our lack of officers."

Adolf Hitler, the former corporal, had made one mistake after another since the start of the invasion of Russia. His field generals had urged him to make a lightning attack on Moscow, which probably would have succeeded. Instead, he couldn't make up his mind at first, and when he did reach a decision he ordered part of his armies to seize Leningrad, while others moved into the Crimea. Russian troops fought savagely to hold Leningrad, giving their forces time to marshal defenses in front of the capital. There Russian troops under General Georgi Zukhov were dug in and, with new T-34 tanks, Katyusha mortars, and a revitalized air force they went on the offensive against Germany's hungry, exhausted and dispirited troops. They did not stand a chance against the aroused Russian people whose civilians served as partisans behind the lines while others dug tank traps.

Hitler raved against his generals, refusing to believe the reports coming back to him. What was happening to his armies before Moscow was unbelievable to him, making a mockery of the statement he had released two months earlier that Russia "had been struck down and will never rise again."

American officials were fully aware that Japan would strike somewhere in the Pacific (they had earlier broken her diplomatic code, but not her military code), but they did not know the specific point of attack. Therefore President Roosevelt appealed directly to Emperor Hirohito on December 6, asking him to exercise his influence to avoid war.

The announcement that the Japanese had attacked the United States came at mid-afternoon in America as radio networks read a bulletin. CBS announced, "We interrupt this program to bring you a special news bulletin. The Japanese have attacked Pearl Harbor, Hawaii, by air, President Roosevelt has just announced. The attack was made on all naval and military activities on the principal island of Oahu."

The specific details of the attack were shocking. It had begun at 7:55 Honolulu time that morning and it was now mid-afternoon in the East. Eventually Americans learned that 19 ships, including six battleships, had been sunk or disabled, about 150 planes destroyed, 2,403 soldiers, sailors and civilians were killed while another 1,178 were wounded. Meanwhile, Japanese planes and ships attacked United States bases in the Philippines, Guam and Midway, as well as British bases in Hong Kong and the Malay Peninsula.

Japanese envoys in Washington had been instructed to deliver the note rejecting the November 26 American proposal by 1 p.m. Washington time—shortly before the attack on Pearl Harbor was expected to begin. They didn't arrive in Secretary of State Hull's office until 2:05 p.m. after he had been informed of the unprovoked attack. That evening the obvious was made official as Japan declared war on the United States.

No single act could have so united the American people as this one against Pearl Harbor. President Roosevelt spoke for almost all Americans December 8 when he went before a joint session of the Congress. "Yesterday, December 7, 1941, a date that will live in infamy, the United States of America was suddenly and deliberately attacked by naval and air forces of the empire of Japan. . . . The attack yesterday on the Hawaiian Islands has caused severe damage to American naval and military forces. Very many American lives have been lost. In addition, American ships have been reported torpedoed on the high seas between San Francisco and Honolulu. . . . hostilities exist. There is no blinking at the fact that our people, our territory and our interests are in grave danger. . . . with confidence in our armed forces, with the unbounded determination of our people, we will gain the inevitable triumph, so help us God.

"I ask of the Congress to declare, since the unprovoked and dastardly attack by Japan on Sunday, December 7, that a state of war has existed between the United States and the Empire of Japan."

There was only one dissenting vote as Congress declared war on Japan. The Senate voted 82 to 0 for approval, while the House of Representatives voted 388 to 1 for war. Pacifist Jeannette Rankin, the first woman to be elected a representative, and who also voted against war in 1917, was the lone dissenter.

Japanese forces invaded the Philippines December 10, landing first at Luzon, but moved quickly inland. Even with the advanced warning MacArthur's forces were caught unprepared for war with heavy losses of planes and ships.

The next day Germany and Italy declared war on the United States and Congress passed a resolution that a state of war existed between them.

The year's third supplementary budget was passed December 15 with approval of another $10 billion.

Admiral Husband E. Kimmel, in command at Pearl Harbor during the Japanese attack, was replaced December 17 by Admiral Chester Nimitz in command of the Pacific Fleet. The 56-year-old Nimitz was a vigorous man whose face had a pink complexion and whose blond hair was starting to turn white.

After the disastrous losses suffered December 7 by the Pacific Fleet, the President decided the Navy had become too hidebound, conservative and protective. Admiral Ernest J. King, who had been passed over for the top command post prior to the war because he had a drinking problem, despite the brilliance he had displayed in a number of commands, was now placed in charge of the United States Fleet and December 20 he was also named Chief of Naval Operations. Roosevelt had said he needed men with new ideas, and he got them with King in Washington and Nimitz as the ideal buffer between the caustic King and admirals in the Fleet. When King was informed he had been placed in charge of the Fleet, he said, "When war breaks out, they look for the sons of bitches."

The success of the Japanese attack on Pearl Harbor should have been foreseen because it had been simulated in 1938, but pleas to devise countermeasures had been ignored by Admiral Kimmel. A war warning had been sent from Washington November 27 telling Kimmel to expect an aggressive move by Japan within the next few days. Hawaii was not specifically mentioned but the Philippines, Thailand, the Kra Isthmus, and Borneo were named as possible targets of Japanese attacks. The warning had ordered Kimmel to prepare to "execute deployment preparatory to carrying out the existing war plan."

Neither Kimmel nor Lieutenant General Walter Short, commander of all army forces in Hawaii, believed the threat would be directed against them. The warning hadn't been transmitted to their air units, and Short ordered all Army aircraft parked wing-to-wing tip for protection against sabotage, which made them particularly vulnerable to air attacks.

Flying boats had gone out on patrol, but largely to train their flight crews. Incredibly, no system had been set up to seek out unfriendly ships or submarines.

Short and Kimmel were brought home to face an inquiry. Associate Justice Owen Roberts was appointed chairman of a special commission December 18 to investigate Short's and Kimmel's conduct. Both were charged January 26 with dereliction of duty, but no further action was taken against them because they had already been dismissed from active duty.

President Roosevelt established an office of censorship by executive order December 19 to control all matters that might provide valuable information to the nation's enemies.

The Pearl Harbor attack united Americans behind the President, and there were few dissenters when he signed the Draft Act December 20 that required all males between the ages of 18 and 65 to register, while those between 20 and 44 were liable for active duty.

Charles A. Lindbergh, who had earlier that year resigned his Air Force commission, now sought to regain it, but Secretary of War Stimson blocked his request for a return to active duty. Now thoroughly discredited in the minds of most of the American people, Lindbergh's isolationist views had been used and distorted by America's enemies and he had destroyed any chance of regaining his "hero" status. Henry Ford gave him a job at one of his aircraft factories, and he later worked for Lockheed where he helped to develop liquid-cooled engines and a cruise-control system.

In 1944, at the age of 42, Lindbergh managed to get to the New Guinea battlefront as a civilian technical representative ostensibly to compare the range, firepower and other characteristics of Lockheed's P-38 "Lightning" fighter versus single-engine fighter aircraft. He had been told by nervous Air Force generals—some of whom were old friends—to avoid combat.

Lindbergh believed there was only one way to find out the information he sought and that was to fly actual missions. In the process, he flew 50 missions as a civilian totaling 178 combat hours, normal for a fighter pilot in uniform, and once shot down a Japanese fighter that came at him head-on.

President Eisenhower, at the instigation of Air Force Friends, commissioned Lindbergh a brigadier general in 1954. This action was later approved by the United States Senate.

Prime Minister Winston Churchill joined the President in Washington for conferences December 22 to discuss joint war efforts. While they conferred, Wake Island, an American territory in the Pacific, fell to the Japanese, while the British colony of Hong Kong succumbed to superior Japanese forces. Army Air Forces Chief of Staff General Henry H. Arnold pressed for an aerial bombardment of the European continent, promising to get the first group to England in March and 800 bombers by the end of the year. Both Arnold and Roosevelt were anxious that Americans become quickly involved in operations, believing that airpower was the only way to make an early impact. Admiral King presented the Navy's viewpoint that the Pacific should receive major attention but a "Europe-first" strategy was reaffirmed by Roosevelt and Churchill. Both knew that any land-invasion of German-held Europe in 1942 or 1943 would have to be primarily British. Plans called for no American ground troops in England by July 1, 1942, and only 70,000 by October 1.

Twenty-six nations, including the United States, Great Britain, China and the Soviet Union agreed January 1, 1942, to a Declaration of United Nations and pledged to wage a maximum effort war against the Axis Powers, and agreed not to sign a separate armistice or peace treaty.

CHAPTER 11

Turning of the Tide

THE WAR NEWS WAS RELENTLESSLY BAD. MANILA FELL TO THE JAPANESE January 2, 1942, and American and Philippine troops withdrew to the Bataan Peninsula and MacArthur set up his headquarters on Corregidor, a fortified island at the entrance to Manila Bay.

In his State of the Union address a month after the Pearl Harbor attack, President Roosevelt called for production of a vast number of war weapons costing over $52 billion out of a total budget to run the nation in wartime of $58.9 billion.

Now the government began to regiment almost all aspects of American life as new wartime agencies were established during the year to further war efforts through the institution of controls on wages, rents and rationing of food. Most of these steps were necessary, and there was a minimum of government bureaucracy as Americans united in their resolve to win the war. One serious mistake was made in March when the government moved more than 110,000 Japanese from the West Coast to relocation camps in Colorado, Utah, Arkansas and other inland areas. Sixty-eight percent of them were American-born citizens of the United States, although of Japanese ancestry. This action was taken as part of Roosevelt's proclamation January 14 that all aliens in the United States must register with the government. Fears and suspicions were rampant against the Japanese. They had caused some of the problem through their long-ingrained habit of living by themselves without assimilation into the American mainstream, and a few of their race, at least in Hawaii, had served as spies for Japan.

Foreign ministers of the 21 American nations, including the United States, met at Rio de Janeiro, Brazil, from January 15 to 28, to consider relations with the Axis powers. All but two nations agreed to break relations immediately. Chile waited until 1943, and Argentina until March 27, 1945, until their officials were certain who would win the war.

The Office of Civil Defense was established January 28 to coordinate the various tasks that might be performed by civilians such as plane-spotting, and handling fires in the event of raids on American cities.

It had long been evident that a single staff was needed to coordinate military activities by the United States, Great Britain and their allies. The Combined Chiefs of Staff was established February 6 and performed well throughout the war, keeping inter-service rivalry and bickering to a minimum.

Daylight Saving Time was approved February 9 on a year-around basis for the duration of the war in an attempt to conserve needed energy sources.

On this date, the French liner "Normandie" caught fire and capsized at its dock in New York while undergoing conversion to a troop ship. It had been seized after France fell to the Nazis and sabotage was suspected at first, but never proven. It is more likely that a careless workman started the fire.

The war was brought home to Americans to a limited degree February 23 when a Japanese submarine shelled an oil refinery near Santa Barbara, California. The attack caused little damage but created consternation as the first attack by the Japanese against the continental United States.

Far more deadly was the major naval battle fought by Allied forces in the Java Sea from February 27 to March 1. The allied fleet of 18 warships was reduced to two during the battle against a superior Japanese fleet, and these ships were sunk shortly thereafter.

Even worse news came March 11 when it was revealed that General MacArthur had been ordered to leave the Philippines because his forces were in imminent peril of being over-run. He was taken to Australia by boat and plane to assume command of the Allied Forces in the Southwest Pacific. Vowing "I shall return" he left General Jonathan Wainwright in charge.

Admiral King and General George C. Marshall, chief of staff of the Army, had met with Roosevelt February 22. It was at this meeting that MacArthur had been ordered to escape. They had painted a bleak picture of the war in the Pacific, and stressed the importance of maintaining a lifeline with Australia and New Zealand.

King met with the Joint Chiefs March 2 and read them a memorandum. "The general scheme or concept of operations is not only to protect the lines of communications with Australia but, in so doing, to set up 'strong points' from which a 'step-by-step' general advance can be made through the New Hebrides, Solomons, and the Bismarck Archipelago."

He outlined the strategy that was later followed in the Pacific, and recommended that Marines seize and occupy strong points in the southwest Pacific and advance in a northwesterly direction toward Japan. After each strong point was seized, he said, Army troops should garrison it, thereby freeing Marines for further conquests in an island-hopping campaign.

Such a plan obviously was in conflict with the Allied strategy of emphasizing the war in Europe and defeating Germany before major campaigns were initiated in the Pacific. But King insisted that the United States should go on the offensive, saying bluntly that the Allies were getting licked in the Pacific.

Marshall disagreed, saying Germany was a far greater threat to Allied powers than Japan and that a policy of containment in the Pacific should be followed. Once Germany was defeated, Marshall said, the United States could go all out to defeat Japan. But the meeting ended without a decision to increase operations in the Pacific. Through King's persistence, the war was fought on two fronts but the Pacific theater always ended up with limited resources.

MacArthur's escape to Australia was greeted with a public demand that he be appointed supreme commander in the Pacific. Marshall supported such a course but King was adamantly opposed. He insisted that the United States Navy had been preparing to fight a Pacific war for 20 years, and he absolutely refused to subordinate the Navy to an Army commander. He stated flatly that MacArthur didn't understand sea power, and that he would never agree to turn the Pacific Fleet over to him.

Actually, no military or political man wanted MacArthur as supreme commander, and the President was opposed to it. He had never trusted MacArthur, and he also knew that the general had political ambitions and might be selected by the Republicans to run against him in 1944. MacArthur refused to take a subordinate's role under a Navy admiral so the decision was finally made that Nimitz and MacArthur would share command responsibilities. Marshall supported this decision—quite possibly with some relief—and MacArthur was selected to take command of the defense of Australia and its approaches through New Guinea and the Netherlands East Indies, and to the east, for defense of the territory between the Solomon Islands and the New Hebrides. Nimitz was given responsibility for all other operations, although the Philippines later were transferred to MacArthur's command. The compromise violated the time-honored "unity of command" and, like all such decisions, caused constant bickering in the years ahead.

While 75,000 Philippine and American troops surrendered April 9 on Bataan, after holding out for three months against superior Japanese forces, their commander General Jonathan Wainright moved with a smaller contingent to Corregidor for a last-ditch stand in the island fortress. Those taken prisoner were forced by the Japanese to march 100 miles to a prison camp, many of them severely wounded, and all suffering from insufficient food. Thousands died on what became known as the Bataan "Death March."

The war news was unrelievedly bad until April 18 when it was revealed that 16 American bombers led by Lieutenant Colonel James Doolittle had bombed Tokyo and five other Japanese cities. Although it was not revealed at the time, they had taken off from the carrier "Hornet" in a spectacular move to bring the war home to the Japanese people. Unfortunately the carrier was spotted 650 miles from Japan and Doolittle's planes had to launch earlier than they intended, thus making it difficult to land safely at Nationalist bases in East China. Most fliers had to bail out, many in territory occupied by Japanese troops, while one crew landed in Soviet Manchuria. One man died in bailing out while two drowned. Eight were captured. All were tortured, three were executed by a firing squad and a fourth died in captivity. With the assistance of the people in East China the other fliers were rescued. The Chinese paid a heavy price later as the Japanese Army went on the offensive and without any mercy destroyed cities and villages in Chekiang and Kiangsu Provinces for assisting the fliers to escape. It is possible that a quarter of a million Chinese civilians were killed in retaliation. At least 10 million Chinese died as a direct result of Japan's invasion and occupation of a large part of China between 1931 and 1945.

The raid on Japan did little damage. It killed 50 civilians and wrecked 90 buildings but Admiral Yamamoto was forced to apologize to the Emperor because the Japanese homeland had been bombed. More importantly, the Doolittle raid influenced the Japanese decision to attack Midway.

With Allied ships suffering heavy losses from German submarines along the eastern seaboard, a "dim-out" or "black-out" was ordered nightly along the Atlantic Coast. The bright lights often had highlighted ships as they hugged the shore while moving toward their ports.

Admiral Isoroko Yamamoto, commander-in-chief of Japan's Combined Fleet, had used large aircraft carriers as the prime offensive weapon for a new type of war at sea. His activities had cost the American and British navies dearly and Allied leaders were beginning to believe that nothing could stop the Japanese from completing their conquest of the South Pacific and then occupying Australia. But before Japanese troops could occupy Port Moresby and the remainder of New Guinea, the Australian-American lifeline had to be cut. This meant sweeping the Coral Sea free of Allied warships. Although this lovely area was an unlikely setting for a major battle, the Coral Sea's strategic value was well known to commanders on both sides. The nearby Bismarck Sea, with its forbidding islands of lava and volcanic ash, was dominated by Japan with its key base at Rabaul in New Guinea.

Yamamoto had been making long-range plans since the first of the year to control the South Pacific. He received approval from Tokyo to establish a naval air base for control of the Coral Sea's northern section. First, he ordered the occupation of Tulagi in the southern Solomon Islands, and then began plans to land an invasion force at Port Moresby on the southeastern coast of New Guinea. With Port Moresby in Japanese hands the northern part of Australia could be attacked by air.

The Japanese admiral had long envisioned a great battle between the Imperial Fleet and the United States Navy's Pacific Fleet. To him it was obvious that a decisive battle had to be fought to give Japan any hope of winning the war. He had decided, therefore, to attack the island of Midway—with a simultaneous diversionary move against the Aleutians—to force the American navy into a decisive confrontation.

In addition, he decided to overrun the Fiji Islands and Samoa, thereby cutting the lifeline between Australia and the United States.

In the "Battle of the Coral Sea" May 4 through 8, the United States Navy inflicted heavy losses on the Japanese fleet and prevented the Japanese landing at Port Moresby. The American carrier "Lexington" was lost, and the "Yorktown" seriously damaged, but the Japanese lost one carrier, two others were seriously crippled, and several smaller ships sunk or damaged. They had also lost more than 5,000 men.

It was a truly great victory and Admirals King and Nimitz were now convinced that the aircraft carrier was the prime offensive weapon in sea war. This strategic battle was the first naval battle ever fought entirely by air without surface ships engaging one another.

Of greatest significance, it soon became clear that the Japanese had finally overstretched their military resources and found it impossible to occupy Port Moresby and the southeastern coast of New Guinea, from which they could have severed the Australian-American lifeline. The battle gave a needed boost to Allied morale, but the crippling of two Japanese carriers proved a severe blow to Japan's plans for future operations. Japan's southward drive had been halted. Later it was evident that she had reached the limit of her aggression against the Allies in the Pacific.

While this battle was being won General Jonathan Wainright was captured by the Japanese and broadcast to his remaining troops on Corregidor May 7 that they surrender. Wainright and his troops had waged a brave fight against impossible odds, but the news was shocking to most Americans.

An act passed by Congress to establish the Women's Auxiliary Army Corps (later redesignated Women's Army Corp, or WAC) was signed by the President May 15. The other services followed suit and volunteers were accepted by the Navy, Coast Guard, Marines and Air Force.

The Japanese diplomatic code had been broken prior to the war, and in the spring their military code was also broken, so some of Japan's Navy moves could be plotted in late May as Japanese ships headed for Midway, a small island in the Central Pacific, while others headed for the Aleutian Islands in Alaska as a diversionary sweep to draw American ships away from Midway. They were in position June 3 and one of the most historic sea battles was about to be fought.

Yamamoto had ordered the attack to force America's Pacific Fleet to a decisive battle, one which he was confident his Imperial First Fleet would decisively win, forcing the United States to sue for peace.

By June 3 the Allied military position had improved in many theaters. Russia had successfully defended Moscow and Stalingrad, and British general Sir Claude John Eyre Auchinleck had won the first battle of El Alamein in the Egyptian desert.

Although the United States Navy lost the carrier "Yorktown," all four Japanese carriers were sunk June 4 during the Battle of Midway with the loss of a significant portion of Japan's best pilots.

Rear Admiral Raymond A. Spruance, who had been in over-all charge of the American ships, had won a great victory due to his experience and intelligent decisions.

Admiral Nimitz's decision to face most of Japan's navy at Midway with only three American carriers had turned the tide of the Pacific war. It had been a decisive defeat for the Japanese, and their attempt to pierce the outer defenses of the United States had met with disaster. In addition to the loss of their four carriers, they had lost a cruiser. The battleship "Kirishima" and the destroyer "Tanikaze" were badly damaged. Two thousand Japanese sailors died, along with 100 irreplaceable pilots, and 322 carrier planes. American losses included the carrier "Yorktown," 109 carrier planes, 38 shore-based airplanes and 307 men.

Carriers had proven themselves despite overwhelming opposition, and airpower reached maturity in the minds of those who had doubted its effectiveness. It was a great victory, resulting in large part from the work of the SBD dive-bombers, 19 of whose well-placed bombs had destroyed the four Japanese carriers.

During the Battle of the Coral Sea when the carriers "Zuikaku" and

"Shokaku" were damaged, the Japanese had lost one third of their air-power. Unquestionably, these losses contributed to their defeat at Midway.

The Japanese had also lost half their carrier strength during May and June, and they were forced to remove the battleships "Ise" and "Hyuga" from operations and convert them to carriers.

The Japanese had been outguessed at Midway. The breaking of their code played a part in the victory, but Admiral Nimitz had not dared to put full reliance on decoded messages for fear of being misled. Like most intelligence data, reports of Japanese ship movements were voluminous and of mixed quality.

Yamamoto's fleet withdrew from Midway but with the occupation of Attu and Kiska in the Aleutians the Japanese still had a battle line stretching from Alaskan waters to the Solomons in the South Pacific.

At Pearl Harbor, Nimitz studied the Navy's next move. Japan's losses at the Coral Sea and Midway battles seemed to preclude another all-out assault against Australia for the time being. After consultation with Admiral King in Washington, he decided to commit his forces to the South Pacific where the Japanese posed a more immediate threat. Japan's bases in the northern Solomons and New Britain posed a stumbling block to the Allied command—one that would become serious if the Japanese continued to press forward.

Nimitz addressed his staff on the problem. "The chain of islands to the east of New Guinea is the logical route to return to the Philippines."

He wired precise instructions to his new commander in the South Pacific, Vice-Admiral Robert L. Ghormley. "Hold the island position. Continue to support operations in the southwest and central Pacific. Amphibious operations should be planned against positions now held by the Japanese. D-Day is tentatively scheduled for August 1."

General MacArthur proposed a different plan. He recommended to General Marshall that Rabaul should be invaded. Marshall approved the plan June 12, believing Admiral King would provide the necessary ships. He should have known better.

The war in Europe reached a new stage of horror when Lidice in Czechoslovakia was brutally destroyed June 10, to avenge the killing of a member of the Gestapo, by German troops who killed all men and removed the women and children to prison camps.

The Oregon coast was shelled by a Japanese submarine June 21, but without the panic of the earlier attack on Santa Barbara. Both attacks did minimal damage and were hardly worth the effort.

American military leaders now began to plan ahead for the eventual invasion of the Axis-held continent of Europe, and one of the first steps was taken June 25 when Lieutenant General Dwight D. Eisenhower was appointed commander of American forces in the European theater although his command was minuscule in size at this stage of the war.

Nine days later American pilots made their first appearance over the continent on July 4 with Eisenhower on hand to send them off. Six American A-20 light bombers, borrowed from the Royal Air Force, bombed German air fields in Holland to kick off the Eighth Air Force's projected daylight bombing of German-occupied Europe. Two planes were shot down, a third was badly damaged, and only two planes bombed their assigned targets.

The administration let up on its stringent wage and price controls by permitting a 15 percent increase for certain steel workers because of an increase in the cost of living. The "Little Steel Formula" was approved by the War Labor Board.

In the Pacific war theater it was becoming clear that Japan was on the defensive in the South Pacific, and Admiral Nimitz was granted permission to land American troops on Guadalcanal and two other smaller islands in the Solomons to start offensive operations. The fight for Guadalcanal, on land and at sea, was bitterly contested August 7 but American troops established a precarious beachhead that was extended during some of the war's most murderous fighting.

The fighting dragged into the fall of 1942, and the Japanese suffered a number of setbacks, particularly after Admiral William Halsey was placed in charge of the American fleet in the Guadalcanal area. In the middle of November (12–15) the Japanese lost 28 warships and transports and their leaders faced a dilemma. Should they accept defeat or continue their drive toward Australia despite the necessity of further costly attempts to drive the Americans out of Guadalcanal?

Admiral Osami Nagano, chief of the naval staff, and General Hajime Sugiyama personally appeared before Emperor Hirohito on December 31, 1942, to make their apologies for the failure of their commands to retake Guadalcanal. They asked permission to abandon the island, and it was granted.

The Japanese secretly withdrew their forces during the first week of February 1943.

Airpower was the decisive factor in taking Guadalcanal from the Japanese, even though Allied squadrons were constantly outnumbered in the air. Allied airmen, particularly those of the United States Navy and Marines, and the Air Forces' 11th and 19th Bombardment Groups, made up for their disparity in numbers by their skill and tenacity against the Japanese in combat. On the ground the superbly led United States Marines, and their Army comrades who joined them during the fiercest battles starting in October, proved their mettle against Japanese ground troops who, until then, had been considered almost invincible. Now, for the first time, the Japanese had been decisively defeated on land because of the teamwork between land, sea and air forces of the Allied nations. The battle for Guadalcanal had taken six months but, like the battle of Midway, it marked another important milestone in the war.

Although Japan had suffered setbacks, she still controlled an area that extended from Burma on the west to the Marshall and Gilbert islands on the east, the western Aleutian Islands on the north, and the Dutch East Indies on the south. This vast Pacific Ocean area included Korea, Manchuria, Thailand, French Indochina and much of mainland China.

Now that tension in the Far East had eased after the Japanese suffered severe losses in the battles of the Coral Sea and Midway, and the onset of the monsoon season had lessened the Japanese threat to India, more attention was focused on the European theater. On the Russian front, the German offensive during the summer months was in full stride as Feldmarschall Erich von Mannstein conquered the Crimea, and his armies were at the inner defenses of Sevastopol. Russian Marshal Semën Timoshenko's winter campaign below Kharkov had failed, and now the German armies were driving toward the Caucasus with its strategic oil fields.

Feldmarschall Erwin Rommel had opened the North African offensive in May, driving the British back and defeating them at Knightsbridge June 13. After Tobruk's large garrison surrendered June 21, the British Eighth Army a week later dug in for a last stand at El Alamein, only 75 miles from Alexandria, Egypt.

Churchill was deeply concerned about the German threat to the Middle East, with possible loss of the area's oil reserves, the cutting of the lend-lease southern route to Russia, and the severance of Britain's land link with India. He was fearful that the Russian front might collapse, and then the Germans could throw their full weight at the British and the Americans.

Although an invasion of the continent by the British would reduce the pressure on the Russians, realistically at this stage of the war it had little chance of success.

Roosevelt was anxious to get Americans involved in large-scale ground operations before the end of 1942. Stalin's appeals could not be ignored, and there was a growing demand by the American people for more forthright action. Forgotten now were the days of isolationism, Americans were unrealistically demanding action less than a year after they were resisting all appeals for a buildup of the nation's miltiary strength.

After much discussion, the British and American military commands agreed that a cross-channel invasion would be considered for 1943, with emergency invasion operations kept under active consideration for 1942. In lieu of such a 1942 invasion, it was agreed that a combined attack should be launched against North and Northwest Africa prior to December 1 and Lieutenant General Dwight D. Eisenhower was appointed to command the operation.

In July, the British reiterated a contention they had first brought up April 1 that an intensified bomber offensive over Germany was, in fact, the second front that the Americans wanted. They pointed out the success of their own one-thousand-plane raids against Cologne and Essen as examples of what could be accomplished from the air to alleviate Russian problems in the east.

The first American heavy bomber raid was set for August 10 against German-occupied France but it had to be delayed, much to General Arnold's exasperation in Washington. August 14 Major General Ira Eaker wrote Arnold that the theory of daylight bombing was about to be tested with men's lives at stake and that he still had faith in the concept. (The British had adopted night operations for their bombing attacks, and had objected strenuously to the American plan as too risky.)

Twelve B-17 Flying Fortresses took off August 17 with Eaker flying in "Yankee Doodle" in the second element. With four squadrons of protecting British fighters, they attacked the Sotteville railroad marshaling yards near Rouen, inflicting some damage but also inadvertently dropping some bombs on the village of Rouen.

Marshal Harris sent Eaker a wire following the raid. "Congratulations from all ranks of Bomber Command on the highly successful completion of the first all-American raid by the big fellows on German-occupied territory in Europe. 'Yankee Doodle' certainly went to town, and can stick another well-deserved feather in his cap."

Eaker's private assessment was more realistic. "The raid went according to plan, and we are well satisfied with the day's work. However, one swallow doesn't make a summer."

Prime Minister Churchill and United States Representative W. Averell Harriman had spent three days during the middle of August in Moscow conferring with Stalin, and planning future joint war efforts. It was obvious that the war in Russia was reaching its decisive stage.

A few days later, the Germans launched a massive assault on Stalingrad, hoping to complete their conquest of Russia before winter set in.

The German U-boat war at sea had grown progressively worse, reaching the catastrophic stage. Between September 10 and 14 a group of 13 U-boats attacked a convoy en route from North America to Britain, sinking 12 freighters and a destroyer escort. Only one U-boat was destroyed.

Losses escalated in October, and reached their peak in November when the Allies lost over 800,000 tons of shipping. (Throughout the war years the Allies lost 24 million gross tons of shipping to the Axis powers, over half of it to German U-boats.)

President Roosevelt let Axis leaders know October 7 that certain types of action would not be excused as conventional acts of war when he announced a plan to set up a United Nations Commission for the Investigation of War Crimes after the war. His action was taken because certain "crimes against humanity" were already being reported in Germany involving death camps.

An increase in taxes was announced by the government October 21 that would add $9 billion to the increasingly heavy burden placed upon taxpayers as a result of the war. This five percent "Victory Tax" was assigned against all individuals with incomes over $624 a year.

China was granted equal status among the world's powers October 9 when Great Britain and the United States declared they would give up extra-territorial rights. Treaties were signed later in January 1943 to formulize the historic agreement.

Democrats maintained their edge in the November 3 elections by keeping their majority rule intact in the House and the Senate, although the Republicans gained nine seats in the Senate and 26 in the House. Thomas E. Dewey was elected Republican governor of New York and was promptly hailed as the man to oppose Roosevelt for the Presidency in 1944.

Ten days later the draft age was lowered to 18 and now all men between the ages of 18 and 38 were eligible. Volunteer enlistments were ended but some industrial and agricultural workers, as well as clergymen were exempt from the draft.

More than 80 American and British navy ships and transports landed 400,000 Allied troops on the shores of Morocco and Algeria on both the Atlantic and Mediterranean sides November 8 against only light opposition. The few casualties were at Oran and Casablanca where the embittered Marshal Henri Phillippe Pétain, who ruled unoccupied France as a virtual dictator, ordered French North African forces to resist. General Henri-Honoré Giraud had been smuggled out of France and now persuaded France's 14 North African divisions to cease fighting. Heavy bloodshed would have resulted on both sides if they had not done so. Admiral Jean Louis Darlan, who had been a Nazi collaborator, was caught in Algiers visiting an ailing son. He promptly switched sides again and was placed in command of political affairs for France. On Christmas Eve, a French royalist assassinated Darlan, ending his brief reign. The politically inept Giraud was no match for General Charles de Gaulle, head of the Free French forces in England, who now broadened his authority to North Africa.

Italian scientist Enrico Fermi, who had first discovered atomic fission in 1934, had just arrived in New York and he realized that under the right conditions uranium fission might create a self-perpetuating chain reaction with an accompanying release of enormous quantities of energy. When he heard the scientific news from Germany he looked out at the city of New York below him from his Manhattan office. Almost unconsciously he cupped his hands, and said to himself, "A little bomb like that, and it would all disappear."

Fermi later went to work at the University of Chicago to assemble a device that he believed would start a chain reaction. The reactor, or pile, took shape under his direction with a huge, layered lattice of grimy, black bricks impregnated with lumps of uranium.

He and his colleagues were set to start their "pile" December 2, 1942. This was the final stage of their experiment in a squash court beneath the stands of an abandoned football field on Chicago's South Side. He stood on a balcony above the ceiling-high pile and ordered a control mechanism—a rod of neutron-absorbing material—withdrawn from the pile by a few inches, then by a few more, and a few more as tension was reflected on their faces. At 3:40 p.m. the pile "went critical." There were no explosions, just the silent motion of a neutron recorder as the neutrons multiplied, splitting more and more uranium atoms. Fermi had created the world's first self-sustaining nuclear chain reaction.

His calculations were soon brought to bear upon the problem of designing and building an atomic bomb.

German hopes for victory in Russia were dashed November 25 when the German army besieging Stalingrad became virtually surrounded by Russian forces. In one of the bitterest ground campaigns ever fought, the Germans had failed to dent Stalingrad's defenses despite three months of constant attacks. Once German divisions started to surrender, the huge German army slowly disintegrated and the last German unit surrendered February 2, 1943. Three hundred thirty thousand Germans were killed or captured.

It had been a tragic year for many American families who had lost loved ones on the worlds' battlefronts, plus the tens of thousands who had been wounded.

CHAPTER 12

Bombing Around the Clock

RATIONING OF FOODS AND MATERIALS ESSENTIAL TO THE WAR EFFORT such as gasoline had begun the previous year, although leather shoes weren't on the list until February 3, 1943, when each civilian was limited to three pairs annually. By now, it was evident that all aspects of American life needed to be tightly controlled to prevent inflation. Americans were taxed as never before, but there were few gripes on the homefront about the necessary sacrifices as inflation was kept in check. In his January 11, 1943, budget the President submitted to Congress, $100 billion was requested to prosecute the war while only $8.9 billion was sought to run other agencies of the government.

Roosevelt joined Prime Minister Churchill and other Allied representatives from January 14 through the 24th for a conference at Casablanca, Morocco. The biggest disagreement arose over the question of strategic bombing of Germany. Churchill had insisted that Americans should forego daylight bombing of the Third Reich and join the Royal Air Force at night and he had about convinced Roosevelt. The Eighth Air Force's Major General Ira Eaker had been brought to Casablanca by Air Forces Chief of Staff General H. H. Arnold to talk to Churchill and seek to change his mind. At their meeting Churchill said he was disturbed because there had been so few American missions, and that as yet the Eighth Air Force hadn't bombed Germany.

Eaker explained that the Eighth's limited operations were due to inexperienced crews, loss of planes and crews to support the North African invasion, bad weather during the fall and early winter months, diversion of his command to attacks against submarine pens and bases, and the lack of escort fighters. He assured the prime minister that these were temporary problems that would be overcome.

In conclusion Eaker said day-bombing raids imposed a severe strain upon the Luftwaffe, despite American losses, because the accumulation of German losses would eventually decimate the German air force.

Churchill listened carefully and then he read comments that Eaker had written out for his perusal. When he came to where Eaker had written, "If the RAF continues at night, and the Americans by day, we shall bomb them around the clock, and they will get no rest." He repeated, "bombing around the clock," and reread Eaker's words wherein he said, "Bear in mind that by your intelligence estimates, a million men are standing on the Westwall to defend against our bomber effort. Those defenders—firefighters—can be greatly reduced if we stop daylight bombing." He paused, and then read those last words again slowly.

Churchill put down the paper and turned to face Eaker. "General, I want you to know that the reason I have taken this position is because I have been heartsick because of your tragic losses. My mother was a United States citizen, so I'm half-American. Marshall Harris tells me you are sometimes losing 10 percent on a mission, while his losses are only two-and-a-half-percent. You've made a strong case here. While you have not convinced me that you are right, you have convinced me that you should have further opportunity to prove your case. When I see your president at lunch today, I shall tell him that I withdraw my suggestion that you discontinue your daylight bombing, and that you will not be joining the Royal Air Force night-bombing effort. I suggest that your Eighth Air Force continue this daylight-bombing experiment for a time."

The meeting with Eaker cleared up several points that had been troubling Churchill. Prior to this meeting, he had thought the Eighth Air Force had 500 bombers and 20,000 men in East Anglia. Actually, the bomber force was less than 100, because so many had been sent to North Africa.

With Churchill temporarily satisfied about the American daylight bombing campaign, a plan to bomb Germany was put into effect under the "Casablanca Directive" to "bring about the progressive destruction and dislocation of the German military, industrial and economic systems, and undermine the morale of the German people to the point where their capacity for armed resistance is fatally weakened."

Airpower advocates were jubilant because this was a war-winning concept, not just a plan for the preliminary bombing of Germany prior to an invasion to which Churchill was opposed. At this meeting, nothing was said about a cross-channel invasion of the Continent. Churchill's support for "around-the-clock" bombing of Germany was evidently given in the hope that a successful strategic air offensive would make an invasion unnecessary.

After Eaker returned to England he authorized his command's first attack against Germany. Colonel Frank Armstrong led the B-24 attack January 27 along a North Sea route to hit the submarine plants at Vegesack, 30 miles up the Weser River. Cloud cover forced the formation to divert their attack to the port of Wilhelmshaven and one bomber was lost to a fighter attack en route home. It was not an auspicious beginning of the Eighth's campaign to attack German targets.

When the Casablanca Conference ended seven days later the Allies agreed to demand the unconditional surrender of the Axis powers without an armistice such as had ended World War I. They further agreed to invade Sicily and Italy, although American military commanders were opposed. They preferred an across-channel invasion of France from England. A possible invasion of southern France from the Mediterranean was left open. And General Dwight D. Eisenhower was given command of the North African theater.

The German Army debacle in Russia became a catastrophe for the Nazis when the last units surrounding Stalingrad were forced to surrender February 2. A dispirited German high command had reached a turning point in Russia, and its only sensible recourse was to order a methodical retreat from the Eastern Front, despite exhortations from Hitler that all was not lost.

The American Air Forces' hopes for their new B-29 Superfortress bomber were given a setback February 18 when the second prototype crashed in Seattle after a fire in the wing's leading edge got out of control. Boeing's top test pilot, Eddie Allen, and 13 other crew members died in the fiery crash. All B-29s were grounded while experts assessed the problem. This was a serious setback because the bombers were scheduled to go to the Pacific to start the bombing of Japan in about a year's time. Steps were taken to solve the engine's cooling-system problems, and some of the aircraft's other deficiencies, although they were never fully resolved by the time the Twentieth Bomber Command went to India in the spring of 1944.

Eventually 4,221 B-29s were built, at a total cost of $3 billion. Five hundred twelve B-29s were lost during combat operations, while another 260 were lost in training accidents in the United States for a loss rate of more than 18 percent of those produced.

General Rommel's Afrika Korps dealt Eisenhower's North African forces a sharp defeat between February 14 and 25 when American troops were pushed back in the Kasserine Pass in Tunisia. Churchill was upset, telling aides that he couldn't understand how the Americans lost 2,000 prisoners while suffering casulaties of only about 100.

British criticism was strong, and it was valid. In the Maknassy area, 240 Sherman tanks were held up by 20 German tanks. The condition didn't last and the Germans were forced to retreat after they were caught in a two-sided attack between Allied forces in the west and General Montgomery's British Eighth Army in the east who linked up in April. The American II Corps, which had fought badly during February, was taken over by Lieutenant General George S. Patton and old "Blood and Guts" whipped them into shape. He had been an innovative tank commander in World War I and been assigned to an armored division at the start of this war. In Africa, he was first named Commanding General of I Armored Corps near Casablanca prior to his promotion. A tough, hard fighting general who believed himself to be the reincarnation of ancient warriors, Patton was feared and admired in equal measure by his troops. Before he was finished, members of I Corps were professionals.

Joseph Stalin wasn't happy with the decisions that were made at Casablanca and he cabled Churchill March 18 that while the Anglo-Americans were twiddling their thumbs in North Africa, Germany had transferred 36 divisions, including six armored divisions, to the eastern front. "Now as before I see the main task in hastening of a second front in France. . . . Uncertainty of your statements concerning contemplated Anglo-American offensive across Channel arouses grave anxiety in me about which I feel I cannot be silent."

In the Pacific theater, American and Australian planes scored a major victory over a Japanese convoy in the Bismarck Sea off New Guinea by sinking eight transports and four destroyers, and shooting down at least 25 Japanese planes. In all, Japan lost 3,500 men, but of greatest significance to the Allied cause The Battle of the Bismarck Sea dealt Japan's forces a major setback in trying to hold New Guinea.

After American troops captured Bizerte, Tunisia, May 7, and British troops captured that country's capital, Tunis, all organized Italian and German resistance collapsed in Tunisia May 10, and their commanders took part in a formal surrender of 250,000 Axis troops. The Axis had tried for two years to control North Africa and its vital Suez Canal, and under General Rommel they almost succeeded. Rommel was not captured, but was flown back to Germany. But the long effort had cost Germany and Italy 500,000 casualties or prisoners.

Prime Minister Churchill and his top military planners came to Washington May 11 for a two-week conference with President Roosevelt and the Joint Chiefs of Staff to plan for operations in 1944. At the Trident Conference the invasion of Europe was planned, and forces allocated to both major theaters. Despite disagreements, both sides agreed on the general strategy to defeat the Axis. Churchill spoke to a joint session of Congress on May 19 and predicted the total defeat of Germany and Japan.

Almost a year earlier the Japanese had landed in the Aleutians but plans to evict them had been postponed because they posed little threat to the mainland. American troops invaded Attu May 11 and three weeks later all Japanese resistance ended.

Jews in the Warsaw ghetto rose up May 16 where they had long been incarcerated by the Germans, but their attempt to liberate themselves was brutally put down and those who survived were sent to concentration camps, and the ghetto was leveled.

Roosevelt established the Office of War Mobilization May 27 to coordinate the nation's total war efforts. He also directed that all war contracts must include clauses to prohibit racial discrimination in war industries. This ruling was directed at the upgrading of blacks who were working in factories in larger numbers than ever.

The "pay-as-you-go-act" passed earlier went into effect June 9 and introduced withholding of federal income taxes on wages and salaries. Workers learned from now on their paychecks would be smaller as taxes were deducted under the Current Tax Payment Act. The act became a permanent part of United States tax policy as a means of financing the government.

Federal efforts to upgrade blacks in war industry jobs were challenged in several cities by whites who protested the employment of blacks. In Detroit riots became vicious June 20 and for the next two days there was widespread rioting and rampage in which 34 persons died before Federal troops could put down the insurrection.

Congress had adopted the War Labor Dispute Act (Smith-Connally Act) requiring unions to give a 30-day notice before calling a strike in a war plant and outlawing any strike in government-operated plants. The President vetoed the bill but Congress July 25 overrode him. The act authorized the President to prevent labor disputes from interferring with war production by taking over struck plants and have them operated by the government. Later, the act was used in mine and railroad disputes.

The German Army launched a massive attack in Russia July 5 at the Kursk salient. A week later, the Germans had to admit they couldn't crack the stout resistance even though Russian losses were heavier in men, planes and tanks than those suffered by the Germans. But Nazi losses on all fronts were so high that there was no longer a reserve of young recruits to fill the ranks. Russia, with its vastly superior numbers of people, didn't have the same problem.

The world's longest oil pipeline was dedicated in the United States

July 19, traveling over 1,300 miles from Texas to Pennsylvania. En route the "Big Inch" crossed 230 rivers and streams.

American, British, Canadian and French troops invaded Sicily July 10 under General Eisenhower as supreme commander of the landing forces. Twenty-five hundred ships and hundreds of warplanes took part and several cities in southern Sicily were captured on the first day.

President Roosevelt and Prime Minister Churchill issued a joint message July 16 calling upon the Italian people to surrender. Millions of leaflets were dropped all over Italy.

Three days later a more persuasive move was taken when 500 American bombers raided selected targets in and around Rome. Rome had been off-limits to bombers because of its historical, religious and artistic significance. The bombing this time sought to attack only military targets, and this was done. Only one church near a railroad yard received minor damage.

Both these steps—the leaflets and the bombing—had their effect and King Victor Emmanuel forced Benito Mussolini to resign July 25, and the Fascist Party was dissolved three days later. Marshal Pietro Badoglio was appointed prime minister. While pretending loyalty to Germany, he secretly sought ways to get Italy out of the war.

Thirty-eight days after the Allies landed in Sicily Messina fell to the Allies and all of Sicily was in their hands. The island now could be used to provide safer ship passage through the Mediterranean and become the stepping stone to invade the Italian mainland. The Allies paid a price of 25,000 casualties although the Italians and Germans lost 167,000 men.

Race riots now began to escalate in the United States. A rumor that a black had been murdered in Harlem set off riots August 1 that only ended after five people were killed, 410 were injured, and $5 million worth of property was damaged.

In the Pacific theater, the Japanese suffered heavy losses at Wewak, New Guinea, from August 17-21 when American Air Force planes destroyed or disabled approximately 300 Japanese planes, and killed 1,500 Japanese pilots and ground crew. This heavy loss at Wewak, a base vital to Japan's strategic plans, was one the Japanese high command did not minimize.

General Patton, commander of II Corps during the Sicilian invasion, almost lost his command when he slapped a shell-shocked American soldier in a hospital, accusing him of cowardice and of shirking his duty. Only Eisenhower's personal intervention, and Patton's apology to Corps members, saved him.

Allied forces crossed the Strait of Messina September 3 and invaded Italy's mainland. To further their cause, Marshal Badoglio signed a secret armistice on this date with the Allies, agreeing to cease Italian military resistance five days later.

When the surrender was announced September 8 Germany accused Italy of betrayal, and immediately began to treat the country as enemy territory.

Hoping to complete the occupation of all of Italy, Allied troops moved up the "boot" September 9 in about 700 ships to land at Salerno, south of Naples. This time resistance was strong by seasoned German troops but they were forced to abandon Salerno September 14. Five days later Sardinia fell to the Allies, and the French on Corsica rose up on that date against the Italians and Germans.

With the war in Europe proceeding methodically, the House of Representatives adopted the Fulbright Concurrent Resolution September 21 that called for American participation in a world organization to further peace. The resolution advocated the formation of international machinery to achieve and keep a just and lasting peace.

Naples, Italy, fell October 1 to the United States's 5th Army under General Mark Clark. Before departing, the Germans damaged many cultural institutions and burned thousands of books for their "betrayal" by the Italians.

Marshal Badoglio turned his country over to the Allied side October 13 when Italy declared war on Germany. However, it remained under control of the Allied Military Government for the rest of the war.

The foreign ministers of Russia, Great Britain and the United States plus China's ambassador to Russia met in Moscow October 19 for a series of meetings to discuss their problems. When they convened on the 30th they signed a declaration in which the four nations agreed on conditions that would be applied to the Axis powers once they were defeated. They all agreed to support an international organization to work for peace.

Unlike the aftermath of World War I when most of the Congress was strongly opposed to American involvement in a world organization, this time there was almost unanimous agreement for a union of nations to preserve the peace. The House of Representatives had adopted the Fulbright Concurrent Resolution September 21 calling for such U.S. participation, and now the Senate passed the Connally Resolution that supported much the same thing. The Senate resolution specified, however, that it should preserve its right to ratify such an agreement.

President Roosevelt and Prime Minister Churchill journeyed to Cairo, Egypt, November 22 to meet with Generalissimo Chiang Kai-shek, leader of China's Nationalists whom they met for the first time. During their five-day meeting they agreed to demand that Japan surrender unconditionally, restore all Chinese territory seized during the century, give

Korea its independence, and give up all the Pacific islands it had seized since 1914.

Roosevelt and Churchill then flew on to Teheran, Iran, to meet with Premier Joseph Stalin of the Union of Soviet Socialist Republics for the first time.

They convened at 4 p. m. November 28 in the main conference room of the empire-styled Russian legation in Teheran an imposing yellow brick edifice guarded by Sikhs from the British Army. They agreed to sit at a round table to avoid protocol arguments, and the room was heavily guarded by Red Army guards and American Army military police. This was Stalin's first trip outside of his country since 1912.

The 61-year-old Roosevelt acted as chairman. "We are sitting around this table for the first time as a family with the one object of winning the war," he began. He added that he hoped they would publish nothing so they could freely speak what was on their minds.

Churchill spoke next, saying, "We represent here a concentration of great world powers. In our hands we have, too, the future of mankind. I pray that we may be worthy of this God-given opportunity."

Stalin addressed them as host, saying that he took pleasure in welcoming those present . . . stressing that "I think history will show that this opportunity has been of tremendous import."

During a review of the war, Roosevelt said that the American effort against Japan was absorbing the majority of his country's capital ships and one million men. He told Stalin that he and Churchill had discussed during their meeting in Cairo a plan to drive the Japanese from Burma, and open supply lines to Chungking. He said that the United States would have a million men in Great Britain by the end of 1943, and 1.25 million by March of 1944 to "proceed inland and liberate France." He said that planning for such a complex operation had encountered many problems, which were slowly being resolved but that "Overlord" (code-name for the invasion of France) was "possible before August 1."

"The 'Channel' is such a disagreeable body of water," the President said. "No matter how unpleasant, however, we still want to get across it."

Churchill interrupted. "We were very glad it was an unpleasant body of water at one time."

Stalin said he welcomed the news about the Pacific theater, saying that Soviet armies in Manchuria were purely defensive. They would need to be increased threefold to undertake an offensive, he said, but he promised to participate by war's end in Europe "then by our common front we shall win."

Stalin said that he was surprised by the success of British and American operations against the Germans and he said that Russia was making elaborate preparations for a summer offensive the following year. He said that German lines were weaker, and had buckled under Russian attacks. But he emphasized that the Axis still had 260 divisions in Russia which he termed a formidable force.

When Churchill and Roosevelt asked him how their nations could help, Stalin replied that their Italian operations were valuable in opening shipping lanes in the Mediterranean, but not of great value to further the war against the Axis. "The Soviet Union has never regarded the Mediterranean as of secondary importance. It is of the first importance, but not from the point of view of invading Germany."

When Churchill pressed for further operations in the Mediterranean, Roosevelt reminded him of the "further project of moving up the Northern Adriatic and then northeast to the Danube."

Churchill said he agreed once the Allies had "destroyed the German armies south of the Apennines in the narrow part of Italy." Then, he said, the Allied armies would be able to advance to points "where they could either strike into southern France or, as the President suggested, attack northeast from the head of the Adriatic."

When Stalin asked about the timing of such an operation, Churchill said an invasion of southern France might be done in conformity "or simultaneously with 'Overlord.'"

When the subject came up about getting Turkey involved in the war, Stalin said he had little interest in getting that nation on their side. He cautioned against the scattering of British and American forces. "Overlord," he said, should be the "basis of operations in 1944 while all others should be considered diversionary." On balance, he said, "Overlord" held out the greatest possibilities "especially if supported by an invasion of southern France," which, he suggested, if Allied strength in Italy were reduced to 10 divisions, would leave Rome to be taken at a later date.

Churchill and his British advisers privately were concerned about Stalin's interest in the invasion of southern France, instead of completing the conquest of Italy and then moving into the Balkans. They believed such a move into France might open the Balkans to Russian occupation. Churchill was adamantly opposed to any diversion of Allied forces outside of the Italian theater because the Russians then would have a free rein. The British were also privately opposed to the suggested date of May 1, 1944, for the channel invasion of France.

On the second day of the talks it was obvious to Churchill and Roosevelt that Stalin and his advisers had stiffened their demands and pressed hard for firm decisions on "Overlord," demanding to know who would command the operation and insisting upon the establishment of a date to demonstrate good faith. The three leaders agreed on May 1, and no

later. Now Stalin refused to discuss anything but Roosevelt and Churchill's commitment to the invasion, and their agreement to abandon further
Mediterranean projects east of Italy. Once Stalin was convinced the British
and the Americans would abide by their agreement he agreed on the
30th for a large-scale offensive to begin in May 1944 to prevent the
Germans from transferring divisions to meet this new threat in the West.

When it came time to discuss post-war plans there was no dispute
that Germany should be divided. Stalin and Roosevelt said they preferred
a seven-way partition, but Churchill sought a more moderate solution.
He claimed that a policy with the single-minded objective of punishing
Germans would harm Europe as a whole, and become itself a source for
further difficulties. He and Roosevelt said they hoped that the Russians
would be satisfied with Polish territorial concessions, and they suggested
that political independence for Poland would be in Russia's best interests
in terms of both Russian security and relations with the West. Stalin
said he saw no contradiction and that Soviet policy was for a strong,
independent and friendly Poland. He reminded them that Poland had
been a corridor for German invasion of Russia twice in 20 years, with
the latest invasion still unresolved. The Russian premier said repeatedly
that he expected a German recovery in less than 20 years, and he called for
radical, long-range political, military and economic controls to prevent a
German revival. The question was, he said, how this could be accomplished.

Churchill suggested that the United States, Russia and Great Britain
"keep a close friendship and supervise Germany in their mutual interest."

The first full year of the war had seen incredible achievements on the
home front and on the world's battlefields. Men and women who a year
earlier knew nothing about making implements of war were now turning
out airplanes, tanks, ships and everything the military needed in record
numbers and generally of an exceptional quality. This year two million
women went to work in war plants, and "Rosie the Riveter" became a
figure to be admired. From catastrophe at Pearl Harbor, American forces
were beginning to win battles that would eventually defeat the Axis
powers.

The home front was far removed from the battlefronts, although Japanese submarines made two ineffective attacks on the West Coast. There
were blackouts along the coasts, with civilian air raid wardens to patrol
neighborhoods to assure that everyone complied. School children regularly crouched under their desks or in corridors and basements in practice
drills in case a real air-raid should strike in the United States.

Few complained about censorship as all mail to and from overseas was
opened, and there were constant reminders that "loose lips sink ships."

Rationing was borne with good humor as price and wage controls maintained a non-inflationary economy despite the huge expenditures to fight the war. Scrap drives helped to relieve the rubber and metal shortage, and many people grew "victory gardens" to supplement their diets. Drives to sell war stamps and bonds were always successful, and $156 billion was collected in this manner. Meanwhile taxes kept the lid on inflation, especially on luxury items such as cosmetics and jewelry.

America's love affair with sports was a casualty of the war years although games were played, but with the best athletes in uniform the games were rarely worth the time and money spent on them.

The Axis powers had believed that Americans were too decadent and lazy to put up a real fight against them. They learned again that the American people, once they are fully aroused, are an unbeatable adversary. The unmatched United States industrial base had been a sleeping giant during the depression, but now it was out-performing anything the world had ever seen.

On January 10, 1944, President Roosevelt submitted a $70 billion budget to Congress, most of which would be spent on the war effort, and the American people accepted it with few complaints.

With the invasion of Europe secretly planned for spring, General Eisenhower arrived in London January 16 as supreme commander of the Allied Expeditionary Force to make the final preparations for "the crusade in Europe."

In the Pacific, American forces invaded the Marshall Islands January 31. These islands were Japanese owned, and not gained as the result of military occupation, but ownership changed hands after three weeks of fighting. Meanwhile, other American warships shelled Japan's northern Kurile Islands to mark the begining of attacks on Japanese home territory. The war was being brought home to the Japanese in a fashion that was most unsettling to their leaders.

In Italy, Allied forces tried to sweep around the right flank of the Gustav Line January 22 and land two divisions 33 miles south of Rome at Anzio and Nettuno to outflank the German forces. But German leaders committed their full forces February 6 in an endeavor to destroy the Anzio beachhead and to stop the American troops advancing inland at Cassino. This prompt action by the Germans almost drove the Allied troops into the sea.

United States Air Forces in the European theater were now strong enough to make a difference in the air war. General Arnold's dissatisfaction with Eaker's performance as head of the Eighth Air Force, and Eisenhower's preference for Lieutenant General Carl Spaatz who had served under him before he became Supreme Allied Commander, brought about Eaker's transfer at the start of the new year to command allied air forces in the Mediterranean. Spaatz set up a series of massive daylight air raids against the centers of the German aircraft industry between the 20th and 27th of February. Losses were heavy, but the Germans lost even more. Postwar analyses showed that during "Big Week" almost 10,000 tons of bombs were dropped on industrial targets that damaged or destroyed 75 percent of the buildings that accounted for 90 percent of all aircraft production.

Total impact of these February attacks on the German air force was catastrophic when actual air battle losses of more than 600 fighters are considered along with the destruction of plants. The German air force was never able to get back to its previous ability because "Big Week" broke its back.

Spaatz's courage in making the vital decision stands with that which Eaker had shown in his battle to preserve daylight precision bombing against opponents like Winston Churchill and the leaders of the Royal Air Force. If Eaker had not persevered when he was beset on all sides by grave misgivings by many American and British leaders, Spaatz would not have been able to institute "Big Week." If Spaatz had faltered, almost certainly there would have been no successful invasion of the continent, and the destruction of primary targets of the Combined Bomber Offensive might not have been achieved. Underlying both decisions was the inspirational courage of the bomber crews both generals commanded.

Spaatz's decision to launch the offensive directly against the German Fighter Command, in the air and on the ground, was made under the most adverse circumstances. He could have lost the war for the Allies if "Big Week" had failed because control of the air over the continent was considered by all Allied leaders as absolutely necessary to achieve victory.

When Spaatz gave the order to start that momentous week, he knew that with the icing conditions above the fields and the difficulties of assembling above the clouds, the mission posed a tremendous tactical risk. He was aware that if the weather at the bases did not improve as predicted, there was no assurance that any of the bombers would be able to get home safely.

He alone made the decision, one of the most crucial decisions any bomber commander ever had to make. If he had been wrong in his judgment, and the weather had worsened and failed to lift at the bases, the whole Eighth Air Force and most of the Ninth could have been lost in one afternoon. Quiet spoken, always decisive, Spaatz not only had courage but common sense. He had an uncanny knack for arriving at the best possible solution to a difficult problem.

Berlin had long been attacked by the Royal Air Force at night but

600 American bombers, with 800 fighters to protect them, bombed the German capital March 6 in daylight. The raid was repeated two days later and American losses averaged 10 percent on both raids, but now the almost daily attacks against German cities were having a devastating effect on morale and starting to affect the German war effort.

CHAPTER 13

"We Who Hate Your Gaudy Guts, Salute You."

ALLIED OPERATIONS AGAINST THE AXIS'S "SOFT UNDERBELLY," A TERM coined earlier by Winston Churchill, had found German defenses in central Italy anything but soft. The town of Cassino had long anchored the Gustav Line across Italy and it was manned by crack German troops. The Allies had been stalemated there since February 6 but now they launched another major offensive with a massive bombing raid and a tank assault.

A monastery built by Saint Benedict in the Sixth Century had a commanding view of the area. From its heights below the monastery German 88s and smaller guns had pounded the advancing infantry. When ground commanders insisted the abbey be attacked by air, General Mark Clark expressed his doubts that the Germans actually occupied the abbey.

Ground officers insisted that it be destroyed, and it was attacked and totally demolished. All post-war evidence indicates that there never had been enemy occupation of the abbey itself.

The bombing had no effect on the ground fighting because Allied troops failed to penetrate German defenses, and the Allied offensive ground to a halt March 26.

With more and more attention being given to the post-war world, Secretary of State Cordell Hull revealed a 17-point program March 21 for a United States foreign policy that stressed international cooperation.

In European areas already overrun by Allied forces, it was becoming evident that millions of people, whose lives had been disrupted by the war, would be in dire need once the conflict ended. In recognition of the problem, Congress authorized $1.35 billion for the United Nations Relief and Rehabilitation Agency.

The long battle for black voting rights inched forward April 3 when the Supreme Court ruled that a person could not be denied the right to vote in Texas's Democratic primary because of his color.

In the Pacific war theater, the Japanese were caught off-guard when Allied troops landed in the Netherlands part of New Guinea, and quickly established control.

On the Italian war front, the Germans were finally driven back from Cassino May 18 after two months of Allied attacks, and the Gustav Line across central Italy was finally cracked, although it still held strongly in other places.

Three days later the forces at Anzio, bogged down since their landing January 22, went on the offensive and broke out of their beachhead and moved slowly but surely toward Rome. Advance units of the United States Army entered Rome May 23, but the main armies held back because it was a Sunday to give the German troops a chance to evacuate the "Eternal City," and spare its destruction. Allied armies swept through Rome June 5 in pursuit of the German forces fleeing northward.

In England, preparations were underway for the invasion of France. There were 39 divisions of Allied troops numbering 2.8 million men plus air, medical, transport and communictions units waiting "tensely as a coiled spring" to move to concentration areas, then marshalling areas and finally to their assault positions. Four thousand invasion ships waited to transport them, supported by 600 warships, and at least 10,000 airplanes. The assault force numbered 176,000 Allied troops who, once they established beachheads, would be followed by several million more held in reserve.

D-Day for "Operation Overlord" was June 6, 1944, and it began shortly after midnight as two United States airborne divisions, the 82nd and the 101st, were landed behind the coastal defenses of the Cherbourg Peninsula to cut off rear-area communications and to block German reinforcements to the beach areas. Eisenhower had told commanders that airborne actions behind the front lines were essential to success of the landings at Utah Beach. While small units assembled on the ground, they were able to accomplish most of their vital missions despite dispersal from assigned areas. In spite of confusion and mistakes, losses were far below expectations.

The Eighth Air Force sent three bomber divisions to hit coastal batteries and shore defenses on Omaha Beach, and those the British were preparing to assault. The big bombers took off as late as 5:29 a.m., dropping their bombs until 10 minutes before the troops landed. Medium bombers started operations at 3:43 a.m., but the beaches east of Omaha were not hit, and V Corps suffered heavy losses as a result.

This combined sea and air bombardment against a series of beaches in Normandy between Cherbourg and Le Havre shook the entrenched Germans as nothing had done before. Weather and beach conditions had been so unfavorable that the German High Command had actually reduced the state of alert, assuming that no one, even Americans, would be so foolish as to launch a hazardous invasion under such circumstances. They were stunned by the attack.

The situation at Omaha Beach was so serious that the IX Bomber Command was assigned rear choke points and bridges to prevent reinforcements, and their attacks were helpful.

Utah Beach landings went more smoothly, and by day's end, most of the beaches had been secured by 155,000 Allied troops occupying 80 square miles of France.

General Eisenhower went on the radio after the troops landed to speak to the people of western Europe. "A landing was made this morning on the coast of France by troops of the Allied Expeditionary Force. This landing is part of the concerted United Nations plan for the liberation of Europe, made in conjunction with our great Russian allies. I call upon all those who love freedom to stand with us now. Together we shall achieve victory." His statement was broadcast in a number of languages to reach as many people as possible.

Prior to the invasion, the Royal Air Force had devoted three-fourths of its strikes against the railway system, and these attacks and those by the American air forces proved crucial because it took the Germans several days before troops and supplies could be brought into the Normandy sector from other parts of France.

German officials said they had 40 reserve divisions available to move up to the front, but it was impossible to move them rapidly because of air attacks, and some could not be moved at all to meet Allied troops.

Americans woke up with news of the invasion June 6, and before they went to bed that night they knew it had been an overwhelming success.

Eisenhower had told the troops prior to the invasion that "if you see fighting aircraft over you, they will be ours."

Only one allied aircraft was shot down on D-Day, and General Arnold, speaking of the failure of the German air force to contest the amphibious landings on Normandy, said, "D-Day should have been a field day for a strong Luftwaffe. Thousands of ships and boats and landing craft crowded the Channel. A dominant German air force could have created incalculable havoc."

The cost in ground troops was still high, and the amphibious landings resulted in 10,700 casualties—about half the number suffered by fliers in their attacks on "Fortress Europe" to prepare the way for the ground troops prior to the invasion.

This was the largest invasion force in history, and its success prompted Premier Joseph Stalin to utter one of his rare praises of western military operations. "The history of war does not know of any undertaking so broad in concept and grandiose in scale and masterful in its execution."

By June 10 the armies at the Omaha and Utah beachheads broke out and linked up. They moved out as one force against the Germans and, with some setbacks, hardly ever wavered in their drive eastward after Cherbourg fell to the Allies June 27.

A new threat faced England June 13 when German V-1 flying bombs, launched from occupied France and Belgium, made their jet-propelled journey across the English Channel. The first day only one pilotless bomb landed in London, but soon they were exploding in the city with regularity.

Since August 1943, the combination of air and sea power in the Pacific had brought vast destruction to the perimeter defenses of the Japanese Empire. Amphibious forces had freed 800,000 square miles of Japanese-held territory. The islands now in Allied hands had three good fleet anchorages and countless airfields that would soon be put to good use. Japanese airpower had lost supremacy, and its fleet had to remain in the extreme western part of the Pacific Ocean.

After their inner defense line was breached by attacks against the Marianas for the first time, Japanese naval leaders viewed the future April 18, 1944, with consternation. Imperial Fleet Commander Mineichi Koga, who had replaced Admiral Yamamoto after he was shot down by American fighter pilots, ordered his fleet to evacuate Truk and to move westward to the Palaus which were closer to the Philippines.

Koga, who lacked the imagination and drive of his predecessor, then flew to Japan for consultations with government leaders. He advised officials that the new defense line had to be held because the Palaus lay across MacArthur's path as he moved north along the coast of New Guinea. He also warned that maintenance of this defense line was vital to prevent Admiral Halsey's ships from moving toward the home islands.

The fact that the Marianas now faced invasion, and that they were within bombing distance of Japan's cities, was not lost on Japanese government leaders.

When Koga returned to the fleet, he ordered that the destruction of American aircraft should be given top priority, and he devised a new plan to destroy America's Pacific Fleet.

After a high-level conference in early March in Washington, Admiral

Nimitz received direct orders to seize more Japanese-held territory. Mac-Arthur had been invited to discuss future operations, but he had declined. Instead, he made the mistake of sending his Chief of Staff, General Richard Sutherland, no match for Admiral King who dominated the conference. With Air Force General Arnold's strong support for occupation of the Marianas this operation was approved by the Joint Chiefs.

For once there was quick agreement about future operations. The Joint Chiefs agreed with King that Rabaul should be isolated and that MacArthur should proceed westward along the northern coast of New Guinea to seize Mindanao by November 15. Nimitz was ordered to bypass Truk, seize the Marianas on June 15, isolate the Caroline Islands, and invade the Palaus on September 15 in support of MacArthur's Mindanao attack. Nimitz was ordered to invade Formosa on February 15, 1945, and if necessary attack Luzon by air that day. The Joint Chiefs further agreed that the next objective should be on the China coast.

The plan to invade Formosa was not realistic, and was later abandoned, as was the plan to invade China. The Japanese were dug in along defensible shores in both places, and the losses to dislodge them would have been prohibitive. King's plan to occupy parts of the China coast was even more unrealistic. The Japanese were rapidly extending their control of China all along the coast.

Admiral Koga never had a chance to put into operation his plan to destroy the American Pacific Fleet. While flying from Saipan to Davao in the Philippines on March 31, his plane was lost in a storm.

Admiral Soemu Toyoda was selected to replace him. Unlike Koga, Toyoda was an aggressive officer. He was also a realist, saying, "The war is approaching areas vital to our national security. Our situation is one of unprecedented gravity. There is only one way of deciding this struggle in our favor."

Toyoda had been opposed to war with the United States, agreeing with Yamamoto that Japan could not win a prolonged war. As head of the Combined Fleet, he told his superiors that the Americans must be stopped in the Marianas.

General Hideki Tojo, Japan's prime minister, ridiculed Toyoda's comments, calling them hysterical. He refused to permit army aircraft in the Marianas to take part in a showdown with the Americans.

Task Force 58, with Admiral Marc Mitscher in charge, left Majuro on June 6 to join the rest of Admiral Raymond Spruance's Fifth Fleet of 644 ships. Spruance told him, "Your job is to clear the air over the islands."

Mitscher's huge armada had 890 combat aircraft aboard seven heavy carriers and eight light carriers. In addition, he had seven new battleships, eight heavy cruisers, and numerous smaller ships.

Vice-Admiral Richard Kelly Turner's amphibious forces, which would invade the islands of Saipan, Guam and Tinian were supported by numerous ships. Several old battleships that had been sunk or damaged at Pearl Harbor on the first day of the war were ready again for action.

Japanese patrol planes located the huge fleet on June 10 headed toward the Carolines. Admiral Toyoda now believed his suspicions were confirmed that the Americans intended to invade the Palaus, and any landings in the Marianas would be made only to divert attention from General MacArthur's moves in New Guinea. Therefore, he instructed his commanders to prepare for an annihilating battle off the western Carolines, southwest of Guam near the Palaus Islands, where they would be supported by Japanese bases at Yap and Woleai.

Spruance's destination, of course, was not the Palaus but the Marianas. Near the Carolines, therefore, his fleet, with two American heavy cruisers and destroyers under command of the Royal Navy's Rear Admiral Crutchley aboard his flagship the H.M.A.S. "Australia," turned toward the Mariana Islands of Saipan, Tinian and Guam.

Mitscher's first fighter sweeps were launched 200 miles from the Marianas at 1 p.m. on June 11.

The Japanese were caught by surprise, and 150 Japanese planes were destroyed on the ground. Toyoda was astonished to learn that Task Force 58 was attacking the Marianas, and his carefully laid plans to trap Spruance's Fifth Fleet had to be hastily revised.

Because they lost so many planes the first day, the Japanese were unable to launch attacks against the American fleet. When American attacks devastated island installations on the 12th and 13th, and Spruance's battleships also moved in on the 13th to shell the beaches, Toyoda ordered his fleet to leave Tawaitawai on a northerly course and head for the Marianas. The Japanese plan to retake the strategic island of Biak off the northwest coast of New Guinea was likewise hastily abandoned and Vice-Admiral Jisaburo Ozawa was ordered to rush with his carriers at full speed to the Marianas.

Japanese land-based navy squadrons were decimated during the pre-invasion American attacks, a loss of 500 planes.

Thousands of miles away on June 15 Air Force B-29s struck Japan for the first time from bases in China in an attack on Kyushu's Yawata steel mills. The author of this book was the bombardier in the first plane to bomb the target. That same day, Saipan was invaded by the United States Army's 27th Infantry Division and the 2nd and 4th Marine Divisions.

In overall charge on Saipan was Vice-Admiral Chuichi Nagumo who had led the raid on Pearl Harbor. He had told his troops the day before the landings that the Marianas were the homeland's first line of defense, but that he did not expect the Americans to land until later that month or in July. The Americans landed the next day, proving that his intelligence information was totally unreliable.

Admiral Mitscher had moved Task Force 58 around to the west so that it could counter any Japanese attack from the Philippines while Japanese ground troops contested every foot of ground on Saipan.

When an American submarine reported Ozawa's carriers and the Combined Fleet on their way to the Marianas Spruance canceled the June 18 landing on Guam for the time being and sent Mitscher out to meet the Japanese threat.

Spruance released his major battle plan June 17. "Our air will first knock out enemy carriers, then attack battleships and cruisers." That night Spruance received new word about the enemy fleet and ordered Mitscher to position his force 160 miles west of Tinian and attack with three of his four carrier groups.

Ozawa launched his fighters and bombers on the 18th while still 400 miles from the Marianas with instructions for them to land on Tinian and Guam for refueling prior to their return. In the resulting battle, Ozawa lost two of his carriers while 346 planes failed to return in what became known as the "Marianas Turkey Shoot." He reported these facts to Admiral Toyoda at Combined Fleet Headquarters at Hiroshima and was ordered to withdraw to the west. He was bitter about the battle's outcome and resolved to refuel his ships and resume the attack on the American fleet the following day.

Mitscher ordered his planes to follow, despite the extreme range, and another Japanese carrier was sunk along with the shooting down of more Japanese planes, bringing the total to 480. The Japanese had now lost most of their best pilots and crew members, and their carrier aviation declined steadily after this action. The loss of planes was bad enough, but they could be replaced far more readily than the experienced airmen.

For days, troops encountered heavy fire while they fought off daylight attacks and, even worse, screaming banzai charges at night. For the foot soldiers, it was as bad as anything they had experienced in the Pacific. United States losses were 3,400 dead, but the Japanese lost 27,000 dead and only 500 surrendered. Tinian was secured August 1 with heavy losses on both sides, but with the Japanese losing by far the greater number. Guam was retaken on August 10 with 1,214 Americans killed versus 17,000 Japanese. Vice-Admiral Nagumo, who had led the Pearl Harbor attack, was one of those who committed suicide rather than surrender to the Americans.

It was not known until after the war that the Japanese on Guam executed at least 684 Chamorros during the occupation years. These proud people, with a civilization at least 4,000 years old, had endured 400 years of military colonialism prior to World War II. But their pride in being Americans—although they were not made citizens until 1950—never wavered and they resisted the Japanese occupation in every way they could. They also helped American troops to secure the island after the invasion began.

General Tojo, Japan's prime minister, was shocked by the loss of the Marianas. He told the Japanese people that they were now threatened by a "national crisis without precedent." The Emperor, when advised by elder statesmen that Tojo and his cabinet had to be removed, readily agreed. Tojo's resignation was accepted on July 18.

With the fall of the Marianas, Hirohito's naval adviser, Admiral Osami Nagana, said "This is frightful. Hell is on us."

Meanwhile, bases like Truk and others in the central and eastern Carolines were neutralized. Like Kavieng and Rabaul, they were left to stagnate in the backwash of the war.

In mid-July, Admiral King flew from Washington to Pearl Harbor for a conference with Nimitz and then flew on to Saipan. King met Spruance and brought up the subject of an invasion of Formosa. Spruance and Turner both objected that such an invasion might interfere with the occupation of the Philippines. Spruance told King that if Formosa had to be taken, Luzon should be invaded first to provide a fleet anchorage at Manila Bay. He explained that there were no suitable harbors in the Marianas.

King asked Spruance, "What do you recommend now that the Marianas have been taken?"

"Okinawa."

King lifted an eyebrow. "Can you take it?"

"I think so if we can find a way to transfer heavy ammunition at sea." He explained that Okinawa, in the Ryukyu Islands just south of Japan, was 1,400 miles from Saipan and there was no suitable anchorage at which such a transfer could be made.

Spruance also brought up the subject of Iwo Jima, claiming that it should be seized before Okinawa. He said that the occupation of Okinawa would complete the blockade of Japan and that in his opinion the war could then be won without an invasion.

President Roosevelt, who had been renominated by his party for a fourth term on July 20, announced that he would meet with Nimitz and MacArthur six days later at Pearl Harbor.

When they met MacArthur pressed for an invasion of the Philippines but Roosevelt protested that the United States could not stand the heavy losses involved in retaking Luzon. "It seems to me we must bypass it."

MacArthur told the President that such a decision would break a promise to the Filipino people.

When Roosevelt returned to Washington he told Admiral King that he now favored an attack on the Philippines. This decision made King unhappy because it meant his plans to occupy Formosa, and part of the China coast, had to be abandoned.

While the Allies were moving toward eventual victory on all fronts President Roosevelt signed the Servicemen's Readjustment Act June 22 or what later became known more familiarly as "The GI Bill of Rights." It provided educational, housing and other benefits for veterans after demobilization. By the end of 1946 following the war two million veterans had become beneficiaries under the law, most of them attending colleges and universities that otherwise would have been denied them.

The Republicans met in late June at Chicago and nominated Governor Thomas E. Dewey of New York for President, and Governor John W. Bricker of Ohio for Vice-President. One of the few things both major parties agreed on in their platform was membership in a post-war international organization.

Forty-four nations sent delegates to a resort hotel at Bretton Woods, New Hampshire, July 1, for a monetary and financial conference. During their three-week stay they hammered out an agreement to govern policies and plans for mutual assistance in the post-war world to assure economic recovery and to restore world trade. An International Monetary Fund was established for currency stabilization, along with an international bank for reconstruction and development. The Soviet Union sent a delegate but refused to join any of the financial institutions. It was one of the most successful conferences ever held because it effectively governed international finances for the next quarter of a century.

General de Gaulle arrived in Washington July 6 for several days of conferences with American officials. His reception was mixed; many American officials including President Roosevelt considered him a prima dona. But he had a chance to present his plans to govern France once the Germans were driven out.

Saint Lô, a crucial road junction linking Normandy and Brittany in France, was captured by American forces July 18, permitting a breakout by armored forces seven days later, resulting in the isolation of German units in Brittany. Patton's Third Army led the breakout giving the Allies a chance to move toward Germany.

Patton's instructions to his Third Army were explicit. "The commander who fails to obtain his objective, and who is not dead or severely wounded, has not done his full duty."

A bomb almost killed Adolf Hitler in his headquarters in East Prussia on July 22. He escaped serious injury but the threat to his life made him more paranoiac than usual. A group of officers and politicians had tried to assassinate him and seize power but he miraculously escaped. That same day several of the alleged plotters were executed, but this was just the start of his revenge that eventually cost the lives of thousands of alleged conspirators.

Port Chicago, the small town of mostly white people in an isolated area of San Francisco Bay, had suffered terribly when an ammunition ship exploded July 17. During the war it had become crowded with blacks who were brought there to load and unload ammunition ships. The situation had long been tense because the white population made it obvious that they resented the presence of the blacks and constantly harassed them. Their white officers repeatedly insulted them, and threatened to shoot those who violated their orders. In addition, there were no recreational facilities. There had been ample warnings of a brewing crisis even before the ammunition ship blew up.

August 9 the situation erupted in violence in the United States Navy's first mass mutiny when 400 blacks refused to load any more ammunition ships. Their white officers and Marine guards threatened to shoot those who refused to sign documents that incriminated them. When faced with imprisonment, most blacks returned to work, but 50 held out and were given general court martials "for conspiracy to commit mutiny." Blacks who sought a change of duty from their hazardous work were denied. All 50 hold-outs were given 15-year sentences when they flatly refused to return to duty. Forty blacks had their sentences reduced to eight to twelve years after appeals to the Navy's Judge Advocate General's office. Later, Secretary of the Navy James Forrestal reduced the sentences of seven men to 29 months and the rest to 17 months. The entire affair was badly handled from the start, and created a situation that should never have been allowed to develop.

Except for choice cuts of beef, meat rationing had ended in May, and August 14 the production of various domestic appliances was allowed to resume although subject to the exigencies of the war.

Now that the breakout from Normandy was going well, the Allies launched a new front on August 15 against the Germans with the invasion of Southern France at beachheads between Cannes and Toulon. Resistance was light and Allied troops headed quickly up the Rhône Valley.

Dumbarton Oaks, an estate in Washington, D.C., was the scene of an international conference that opened August 25 and lasted until October 7. Representatives from the United States, Great Britain, the Soviet Union and China met to discuss the formation of an international organization to promote peaceful and legal methods to resolve international problems without resorting to war. The proposals they eventually agreed to later served as the basis for the United Nations charter. A security council was recommended as such an organization's executive branch, but the Soviet Union's representative refused to agree to the proposed voting plan that specified that a security council member could not vote on an issue involving itself.

With Allied armies closing in on Paris, Adolf Hitler ordered his commanding general to resist, although such an action might have destroyed the city. General von Choltitz ignored the order and vacated the city. The French 2nd Armored Division under Major General Leclerc was first to enter the city August 25 as Parisians crowded the streets singing the Marseillaise while tri-colored flags hung proudly from government buildings after the German troops had departed. Capture of Paris had no strategic significance so Allied leaders let the French liberate it in their own way. General DeGaulle arrived the following day and marched in a ceremonial parade. General Eisenhower and other Allied leaders waited until the 27th to put in an appearance.

Germans in Toulon and Marseille surrendered to the Allies August 28, turning over most of Southern France to the Allies. With 190,000 men now moving north, American units pushed toward Lyon, France's major city on the Rhône River.

Despite the success of the invasion, England was undergoing new and intensified attacks from rocket-propelled missiles. German V-2s, faster and more powerful than the earlier V-1s, were causing considerable damage to English cities, with the death toll rising daily, although they caused less blast damage than the V-1s. At first, the Allies did not believe the Germans had V-2s in significant numbers, so the Royal Air Force didn't embark on massive retaliations. It was thought that Allied advances on the ground would quickly overrun these bases.

When more and more V-2s continued to fly over England, causing thousands of casualties and destroying hundreds of buildings, Eisenhower ordered emergency priority be given to attacks against these sites. Until these installations, too, were overrun, 1100 V-2s were launched against England. They caused extensive damage, but they arrived on the scene too late to alter the war's outcome.

Allied armies were forced to stop their advances by the middle of September because they were too far ahead of their sources of supply. The drive across France and Belgium had brought them to or near the borders of Germany. Most of France and Belgium now was in Allied hands, as was nearly all of Luxembourg and even a small part of Holland in the Maastricht region. The United States First Army had penetrated Germany September 12 for 10 to 15 miles after breaking through the outer defenses of the Siegfried Line in the vicinity of Aachen on the Belgian border.

The Germans had suffered heavily, but Eisenhower knew they were still a formidable threat and would be even more so the farther the Allies pushed into the German homeland. While the tempo of the air war increased during the fall of 1944, the ground war remained in a state of stagnation.

Meanwhile Roosevelt and Churchill met in Quebec at the Octagon Conference September 11 through 16 to draw up final strategies for defeat of Germany and Japan, and to delineate some of the terms of the peace that hopefully would follow.

In Washington Congress and the administration were drawing up plans for a return to a peacetime economy. In March, the War Production Board had authorized a partial conversion of war industries to production of more civilian goods. The process was stepped up in October in anticipation of an early end to the war, and to the specific problems that would be encountered by the nation in the transition period. It was high time because inflation had reached 30 percent, due in part to a thriving black market that was absorbing $1.3 billion of scarce consumer items. Congress passed the Surplus War Property Act October 1, and the War Mobilization and Reconversion Act to provide for the removal of various controls that had been imposed during the war.

Republican candidate Thomas E. Dewey tried to wage a hard-hitting campaign against Roosevelt in 1944, concentrating on the fourth term aspects of the election, but the President ignored him, except on a few occasions. Roosevelt's sarcastic comment that the prim-and-proper Dewey reminded him of a bridegroom on a wedding cake, (the little statues of bride and groom that were usually used on such cakes in those days) brought snickering looks to the faces of most Americans who, as a result, found it impossible to take the pompous Dewey seriously, but the prize comment of all came when Roosevelt spoke to the Teamsters Union.

During a trip to Alaska, Roosevelt's little dog "Fala" was left behind by mistake, and a presidential plane was dispatched to pick him up. At last Dewey thought he had an issue. He charged that the plane had been sent at great cost to taxpayers. Roosevelt was in rare form, despite his declining health, when he responded to Dewey's charges. "These Republican leaders have not been content with attacks upon me, or on my wife, or on my sons. No, not content with that, they now include my little dog 'Fala.' Unlike the members of my family, he resents this."

On the Pacific war front, MacArthur's forces invaded the island of Leyte in the Philippines on October 20, fulfilling his promise that he made to its people in March of 1942 that "I shall return."

Three days later the Japanese sent a major naval force through Leyte Gulf to disrupt the invasion. In a series of engagements the Japanese Navy was dealt a crushing blow with the loss of 24 large ships, including four carriers, three battleships and 10 cruisers.

After this "Battle of Leyte Gulf" the Japanese Navy ceased to exist except as a suicide force whose kamikazes (Japanese pilots who dedicated themselves to crashing their planes on Allied ships) sought in vain to destroy the American and British fleets.

President Roosevelt easily won an unprecedented fourth term November 7 by defeating Thomas E. Dewey by 25.6 million votes to the Republican candidate's total of 22 million. The electoral votes were even more one-sided—432 to 99. Several million servicemen sent absentee ballots back home from the war fronts.

The Sixth War Loan Drive was announced November 19 to borrow approximately $14 billion through the sale of war bombs, and it was over-subscribed.

A new five-star military rank was approved by Congress December 15 and Marshall, Eisenhower, MacArthur and Arnold were named Generals of the Army while King, Nimitz and Halsey were named Fleet Admirals.

The Allies had become lulled to a false sense of security as their troops headed for Germany through Belgium, but they soon learned they still had some hard fighting ahead of them. General von Rundstedt counterattacked December 16 in the Ardennes Forest, forcing the center of the Allied line to fall back, thereby creating a vulnerable bulge in their lines that the Germans sought to exploit. Hitler hoped to sever the communications lines of the United States First and Ninth Armies and the 21st Army Group, and possibly destroy 20 to 30 Allied divisions.

While clouds covered the front, grounding Allied airpower, the Wehrmacht drove a 60-mile wedge through thinly-held American lines in the Ardennes Forest in an operation later dubbed the "Battle of the Bulge."

When the weather cleared December 23, the full weight of the Allied tactical and strategic air forces was thrown into the battle. The Germans were forced to abandon their drive toward the Meuse River by the end of the month, and elected to concentrate their strongest forces against Bastogne, defended by the 101st Airborne Division, to widen the salient along III Corps' front. Brigadier General Anthony McAuliffe's famous reply to a demand from the Germans that he surrender his men surrounded at Bastogne was a contemputous "Nuts!" They were relieved by Patton's Third Army on December 26, and began a counterattack four days later.

The battlefield was in such a fluid state that there was confusion everywhere at first, compounded by Germans in American uniforms infiltrating the Allied rear. The heroic defenses put up by Allied troops at Saint-Vith and Bastogne, both important highway-network hubs, plus massive air raids, doomed the offensive.

The Germans launched their last counteroffensive in the Sixth Army sector on New Year's Day. While GIs, British Tommies and other Allied soldiers fought well, the back of the Ardennes offensive was broken by tactical and strategic airpower that virtually paralyzed all traffic west of the Rhine River and caused a critical supply problem for the German armies.

During the first week of January 1945, the lines seesawed back and forth while bad weather impeded the movement of General George S. Patton's armored corps.

After Patton's breakthrough at Bastogne, and under pressure from four American corps against the German southern and northern flanks, with the British XXX Corps exerting pressure on the center of the line, the Germans were forced to retreat, but they withdrew slowly with three rear-guard actions that set up roadblocks, booby traps, and obstructions in a disconcertingly efficient manner. After delaying the Allied timetable for six weeks, German troops fell back, drained of vitality, with the loss of irreplaceable reserves.

Once the last German resistance collapsed, Allied superiority in tanks, men and combat aircraft brought an end to Hitler's desperate gamble, prompting Churchill to say that the "greatest American battle of the war" was won.

The setback on the Allied western front caused disillusionment in high Allied military circles about an early end to the war, and advances were made with more caution.

General Omar Bradley, who headed the 12th Army Group, the largest force ever commanded by a field commander, and World War II's finest army commander, said later that after the Ardennes offensive both the Russians and the Allies in the west were able to continue a war of movement because Allied air attacks had denied oil to the Germans. He said that the German retreat from the Ardennes was slow and costly to them because supply trucks had to be drained to fill the tanks of fighting vehicles.

Bradley told officials of the United States Strategic Bombing Survey after the war, "The withdrawal of the Sixth SS Panzer Army, begun in daylight on 22 January 1945 was marked mainly by success of the United States fighter-bombers against its tanks and trucks. When the Allies' threat shifted north of the Aachen sector, the enemy was unable to side-step his mobile formations to meet it in the measure he sought—again for lack of gasoline. When the Allied breakthrough followed west of the

Rhine in February, across the Rhine in March, and throughout Germany in April, lack of gasoline in countless local situations was the direct factor behind the destruction or surrender of vast quantities of trucks and tanks and thousands upon thousands of enemy troops."

In early 1945 Germany was all but defeated, but her true situation was not known to the allies. Even General Arnold had doubts about the effectiveness of the air war. He had noted reports that seemed to indicate factories all over Germany had been destroyed, yet the Germans still appeared capable of resistance on the ground and even of mounting an offensive like the recent one in the Ardennes.

By the end of 1944 military goods represented about 65 percent of all United States production compared to only two percent in 1939. Aluminum production, primarily for aircraft, had risen by 500 percent. Synthetic rubber production had risen from a low of 2,000 tons in 1939 to more than 900,000 tons. It was an incredible achievement.

Russia's Red Army was now deployed from Stettin to Trieste. General Zhukov's armies began to close on the Oder River on a broad front within 60 miles of Berlin. General Konev's drive had reached the Neisse River, poised to seize the Silesian coal fields and the city of Dresden. His army's approach caused millions of Germans to flee westward to a hoped-for sanctuary among American and British troops. Many German government officials, meanwhile, tried to flee from Berlin to Austria. But then the Red Army's progress slowed as it outran its supply lines, and they faced the bulk of German armor on the eastern front. Stalin announced that his Russian armies would pause to bring up supplies while liquidating vast pockets of German troops behind the lines.

A disturbing early indication that post-war relations with the Soviet Union might become difficult was given when Stalin told British and American officials that Polish boundaries had been settled in 1939 (when Russia and Germany divided up the country), and that these territories merely restored to Russia what had been taken in 1917. Stalin insisted that Russia was entitled to full military and political cooperation from Poland since her armies were liberating the country from the Nazis.

President Roosevelt decided to take his fourth oath of office January 20, 1945, in the White House instead of on the Capitol steps, and he called off the usual parade saying it would save time and money. What he didn't say publicly was that such arrangements would be easier on him because of his declining physical condition. In the nation's early years, the oath of office had often been taken in different places.

After he took the oath of office, he spoke briefly, "We have learned to be citizens of the world, members of the human community. We have learned the simple truth as Emerson said that 'the only way to have a friend is to be one.'" He was helped by his son back to his chair.

Labor Secretary Frances Perkins had watched him with tears in her eyes. Woodrow Wilson's widow turned to her and said, "I feel terrible. I feel dreadful. Oh, it frightens me. He looks exactly as my husband looked when he went into his decline. Don't say that to another human soul."

Roosevelt had served longer than any President in history, and he had given far more of himself than most of his predecessors despite his limited energies. The man most responsible for winning the war—and there was no doubt about the inevitable victory now—was one of its victims.

With stepped-up bomber attacks on Germany, including a 1000-plane raid on Berlin February 1 by American bombers, 180 Russian divisions moved toward Germany from the East, while Eisenhower's armies inexorably came from the West. Germany's last months were at hand.

Allied leaders met at Yalta in the Russian Crimea February 4 for a week of talks to discuss the final phase of the destruction of the Third Reich. Roosevelt hoped to enlist the Soviet Union's early entry into the war against Japan because the atomic bomb was still in the testing stage, and his Joint Chiefs of Staff were planning an invasion of the Japanese home islands which they had told him would take 18 months with possibly a million American casualties. He hoped to convince Stalin to enter the war in Manchuria where two million crack Japanese troops were stationed, and to permit air bases for American bombers in eastern Siberia. The President did not intend to give top priority to keep the Russians out of Eastern Europe because he was a realist. They already controlled these areas, and it would take another war to dislodge them.

Trust in Stalin had been dwindling ever since Averell Harriman sent his first warning message in the spring of 1944 that Stalin had adopted a policy of "aggressiveness, determination and readiness to take independent action" in regards to Poland. In August, Harriman wrote about Stalin, Foreign Minister Vyacheslav Molotov, and Deputy Foreign Minister Andrei Vishinsky that they were "men bloated with power who expect that they can force acceptance of their decisions without question upon us and all countries."

Roosevelt also had been warned by Stimson that the Russians were aware of some aspects of the atomic bomb project. Stimson told him that he "believed it was essential not to take them into our confidence until we were sure to get a real quid-pro-quo for our frankness." Roosevelt readily agreed.

The conference at the time was considered to have gone well for the Americans and the British because Stalin had wanted a firm commitment on German reparations and he didn't get it. The Russians wanted to exclude France from the control machinery over Germany, and this was denied them. The Russians fought hard to get a statement in the "Declaration of Liberated Areas" to exclude governments-in-exile from the new governments formed in these areas. This statement was denied them. Although the British and Americans had no bargaining room in Poland because it was occupied by the Russians, Stalin agreed to free elections for the determination of the new government.

Russian leaders privately conceded at the time that Yalta had been a defeat for them. The problem after the war was that Stalin failed to honor his commitments, and he violated every aspect of the agreement.

Stalin agreed that Russia would join the war against Japan after Germany was defeated but he imposed stiff terms, mostly against Japan. They involved the southern half of Sakhalin Island, and the return of the Kuriles, but they also involved rights in Manchuria for warm-weather ports and the use of Dairen and Port Arthur with the latter to be used as a Russian naval base. The Manchurian part of the agreement was signed by Roosevelt without the knowledge and concurrence of Chiang Kai-shek.

A War Department memo was marked "very important" when it was issued by Stimson about the Yalta Conference April 3, 1945, to describe the results of the conference. "The State Department feels that Stalin made very big concessions at Yalta in granting the United States and Great Britain tri-partite interests in liberated areas adjacent to Russia, particularly with respect to the Balkans and the new Polish government. They believe that he did so when he had it in his power to merely sit tight and force the Lublin government down our throats."

The Yalta Conference also agreed to call a meeting of the United Nations in San Francisco April 25 to establish an international peace organization. (American public opinion polls showed that 81 percent of the American people favored such an organization, compared to only 26 percent who supported such an organization in 1937.)

On the war fronts, Manila, capital of the Philippines, was taken February 24, and United States Marines completed the capture of the Pacific island of Iwo Jima March 16 after one of the hardest-fought campaigns of the war. March 7 units of the United States Army crossed the Rhine River at Remagen, and all German forces were driven east of the Rhine by March 25. Patton's Third Army now moved deeply into the heart of Germany and headed for Czechoslovakia and Austria, thus splitting the Nazi armies.

Upon his return from Yalta, President Roosevelt went before a joint session of Congress to report on the conference. His fatigue was obvious and members were shocked by his appearance.

"I hope you will pardon me for an unusual posture of sitting down during presentation of what I want to say, but I know that you will realize that it makes it a lot easier for me in not having to carry about 10 pounds of steel around on the bottom of my legs. Also because of the fact that I have just completed a 14,000-mile trip. . . . Speaking in all frankness, the question of whether it is entirely fruitful lies to a great extent in your hands."

William Allen White, publisher of Kansas's *Emporia Gazette,* once gave President Roosevelt his finest accolade. "Biting good Republican nails, we are compelled to say that Franklin Roosevelt is the most unaccountable president the United States has ever seen. He has seen more of this amazing world than Marco Polo. Well, darn your smiling old picture, here it is. We who hate your gaudy guts, salute you."

CHAPTER 14

"Enduring the Unendurable and Suffering the Insufferable"

AFTER THE MARIANAS WERE CAPTURED IN THE SUMMER OF 1944, HUGE airfields were prepared on the three main islands of Saipan, Tinian and Guam, awaiting arrival of the first Twentieth Air Force B-29 Super-fortresses.

The Committee of Operations Analysts in Washington had drawn up a series of target systems on November 11, 1943, but almost a year later the tides of war had changed drastically in the Pacific so General Arnold called for a new look, particularly since the XXI Bomber Command would soon be operating out of the Marianas.

Nimitz's and MacArthur's forces were by-passing islands once thought crucial in a step-by-step approach to the main islands of Japan. By leap-frogging over great distances, huge enemy-held areas were left to stagnate in the backwash of a rapidly changing war.

Nimitz's Central Pacific forces were forging ahead on the seaways to Japan, while remnants of the Japanese fleet scuttled to the doubtful secu-rity of home ports.

Earlier in the war, President Roosevelt supported General MacArthur's views about a return to the Philippines on an island-by-island approach because MacArthur was a possible Republican presidential candidate in 1944. But the King/Arnold position of occupying the Marianas, and using their bases to bomb Japan into submission, won out in the end.

Thereafter, Nimitz was instructed to move toward the home islands on routes that led through the Marianas, the Carolines, and the Palaus island groups. While these stepping stones were acquired, MacArthur was ordered November 15 to advance his forces from New Guinea to the Philippines.

Brigadier General Haywood S. Hansell, Jr., flew the first XXI Bomber Command Superfortress to Saipan October 12, 1944, and the 73rd Wing followed him to prepare for bombing operations against the main islands of Japan.

Hansell sent his B-29s to Japan for the first time November 17. They flew an average of 3,200 miles to and from Japan, despite primitive communications, virtually no accurate weather forecasts, and fighting their way in and out.

The mission achieved little in the way of effective bombing results, but it did prove the feasibility of conducting daylight precision strikes against military targets in the home islands. Only two B-29s were lost and eight others were damaged. But bombing of the primary target, Nakajima's Musashino-Tama plant in the suburbs of northwest Tokyo, was very poor amounting to destruction of only one percent of the building area. Weather was bad over the target as formations tried to get through at altitudes of 27,000 to 35,000 feet. Wind velocities of 150 mph. raised downwind ground speeds to 445 mph., thus making it almost impossible for the 24 bombardiers who could spot the target to synchronize.

Unfortunately for the rest of the year damage to vital aircraft plants and other primary targets fell far short of expectations because of the same problems of high-altitude bombing.

General Arnold grew impatient with Hansell that he wasn't achieving greater success, and he sent word January 6 that he was through, and that he would be replaced by Major General Curtis E. LeMay who had been commanding the XX Bomber Command in India and China.

Those who expected a dramatic turn-around with LeMay in command were disappointed. The next two missions against aircraft plants in Nagoya and Tokyo were no more successful than those under Hansell.

Aircraft losses rose to 5.7 percent of all B-29s dispatched on 22 missions during January. They resulted from the concentration of Japanese fighter forces and the long over-water flights which were costly in planes once they developed mechanical difficulties or tried to return after being badly shot up.

Arnold, with his customary impatience to get on with the job, pressed LeMay to improve operations. Privately LeMay told his staff, "With those jet-stream winds over Japan, you could go on forever trying to get up to a target. General Arnold has crawled out on a dozen limbs a thousand times to get the physical resources and funds to build these airplanes and get them into combat. Now he finds they're not doing well. He's determined to get results out of this weapons system. The turkey is around my neck. I've got to deliver."

LeMay continued to run the type of operations during February that Hansell had started, while he concentrated on training inexperienced crews. He set up the same kind of lead-crew training he had initiated in England and later brought to India for the XX Bomber Command.

Losses remained high in early February as 360 B-29s went out on a series of missions that achieved little. These flights at above 20,000 feet may have offered some protection to crews under fire from anti-aircraft guns, but the strong winds aloft often made the bombers sitting ducks for Japanese fighters which frequently couldn't be beaten off despite electronically-controlled gun turrets.

The amphibious assault against Iwo Jima began February 19 and its later conversion to an island bomber base permitted B-29 crews to use it as a fuel stop on their return if such became necessary.

After another futile mission to the Musashino-Tama plant near Tokyo in late February was frustrated by clouds (more and more a common occurrence while flying at high altitudes) LeMay's operations officer, Colonel John B. Montgomery, soberly talked to his boss. "Our whole campaign will fail unless something is done to get a better delivery of bombs on the target. We can bomb secondaries forever by radar and it would have little significant impact on Japan."

LeMay agreed. He told Montgomery that he was considering lowering the bombing altitude to 5,000 feet and using incendiaries to attack urban areas. He said that Brigadier General Thomas S. Power, who had brought his 314th Wing to Guam, and Colonel Hewitt T. Whelass had come up with a plan for a low-level attack that would use radar to direct planes along the east side of Tokyo Bay, and then on to Tokyo. Each plane, he said, would have its own heading, fly at a predetermined speed and altitude, and bomb at a specific time. LeMay said he liked the idea, and they had given him an overall plan within 24 hours. "What do you think, Monty?"

"It has great advantages of going against highly inflammable urban areas at low altitudes that will assure vast destruction. Bomb loads would increase by a factor of three to four because we don't have to lift the airplane to altitude, thereby saving fuel."

On March 9 LeMay sent out 334 B-29s over Tokyo at an altitude of 5,000 feet that dropped incendiaries all night long. Sixteen hundred and sixty tons of fire bombs were dropped. Although 14 B-29s were lost, 16 square miles of the city, containing numerous industrial targets, were destroyed or gutted by fire.

It had been a big gamble, many people believing that the losses would be staggering, but General LeMay had confidence that this was the way to destroy the Empire and he had the courage and vision to try it. If he had planned wrong, hundreds of men's lives would have been lost and several hundred million dollars' worth of airplanes. His foresight, however, proved him to be a man of great vision. The success of the Tokyo mission set the pattern for all future fire attacks.

After the March 9 Tokyo mission, B-29s repeated such low-altitude attacks against Nagoya, Osaka and Kobe. On March 11 two square miles of Nagoya were burned out. On March 13, 8.1 square miles of Osaka, Japan's second largest city, were gutted. And on March 16 some 306 B-29s left 2.9 square miles of Kobe in ashes.

Of the 11 high-priority targets, such as aircraft factories and aircraft engine plants, none had been completely destroyed. But production had been interrupted from time to time by attacks by the 21st Bomber Command.

The 313th Wing started mining operations in the Inland Sea March 27. The wing carried on the only mining operations of the command throughout the rest of the war, and caused tremendous damage to the Japanese Merchant Marine.

The 58th Wing, to which the author was attached as a lead bombardier at first and later as a group bombardier, was still in India. In May we were ordered to move to the Marianas while the 315th Wing was scheduled to arrive in July from the United States. Eventually one thousand B-29s were scheduled to bomb Japan in five wings, plus the 509th Composite Group with its atomic bombs that was scheduled for Tinian.

With the invasion of Okinawa set for April 1, Nimitz exercised his right to call on the Twentieth Air Force for assistance to bomb airfields and their installations on Kyushu. Kamikaze suicide attacks in the Philippines against Navy ships were still fresh in his memory and he wanted to avoid a repetition as much as possible.

When Marines and Army troops went ashore Easter morning at Hagushi they found little opposition because the Japanese had decided not to contest the beaches and set up first-line defenses farther inland. The Tenth Army held a beachhead 15 miles long and 3 to 10 miles wide by April 4, including two airfields that were quickly put to use by the Americans.

At first kamikaze attacks weren't serious, but April 6 the Japanese sent 335 suiciders over the invasion area, and about an equal number of conventional fighters and bombers. Losses of ships and men mounted to the critical stage. To further complicate matters the giant battleship "Yamato," and its accompanying warships, slipped out of Tokuyama and headed for Okinawa. Task Force 58 ended this foray by sinking the battleship, the light cruiser "Yahagi," and four of the eight destroyers.

Russia renounced its neutrality pact with Japan April 5. And, a week after the invasion of Okinawa, the Koiso cabinet was dismissed and a new cabinet under Admiral Kantaro Suzuki, former navy chief of staff, was formed.

Alternately aiding the invasion of Okinawa and bombing targets in Japan, LeMay was convinced that his Twentieth Air Force could destroy Japan's capacity to continue the war provided its maximum capacity was exerted unstintingly during the next six months which he considered would be the critical period. He wrote General Lauris Norstad in Washington, Arnold's Twentieth Air Force chief of staff, "Though naturally reluctant to drive my force at an exorbitant rate, I believe that the opportunity at hand warrants extraordinary measures on the part of all sharing it." In effect, he sought a three-months aerial blitz of Japan to knock her out of the war and make the proposed invasion of Kyushu, and then Honshu, unnecessary.

At Warm Springs, Georgia, April 12, an artist was finishing a portrait of President Roosevelt who sat 10 feet away in his favorite brown leather chair.

"Another 15 minutes and that will be it for today," he told the artist, as he lit a cigarette and turned back to the script of a speech he planned to give the next day.

Then his hand went to his head. "I have terrific headache," he said. He slumped unconscious in his chair at 1:15 p.m. He was rushed to a bedroom, but he died two hours and twenty minutes later.

The American people were shocked when they were told later that President Roosevelt had suffered a massive cerebral hemorrhage at Warm Springs and died. He was only 63.

Since his death everything in the house has been kept just as it was on the day he died, with the same roll of faded toilet paper in the bathroom, the partially-burned logs in the fireplace and his books lining the shelves, unopened since the day he died. Elizabeth Shoumatoff's painting stands on the same easel just as she left it. The house is filled with ship models and paintings of famous ships because he had a life-long love of the sea.

Immediately after Roosevelt died Harry S. Truman was sworn in as President.

The new President spoke to Congress April 16. "Mr. Speaker, Mr. President, members of the Congress. It is with a heavy heart that I stand before you my friends and colleagues of the Congress of the United States." He assured them that there would be a quick termination of the war, and he promised to continue Roosevelt's foreign and domestic policies. "Within an hour after I took the oath of office I announced that the San Francisco Conference would proceed. In the memory of those who have made the supreme sacrifice, in the memory of our fallen President, we shall not fail."

After Roosevelt's death Secretary of War Stimson told President Truman that an immense project had been underway for several years to develop a new explosive of almost unbelievable destructive power. Truman was puzzled by the disclosure but Stimson didn't enlighten him further. Later, the new President was thoroughly briefed by Secretary of State James Byrnes.

Truman's ascension to the Presidency appalled most Americans because Roosevelt had been so popular, always the born leader, and Truman's quiet ways seemed ineffectual in contrast. What little was known about him turned people off even more, although they didn't know the full story. He had been sponsored by Thomas Pendergast, the Democratic boss of Missouri, and he had held several local offices after serving as a captain of artillery in World War I. In 1934 Pendergast had helped Truman to get elected to the United States Senate where he became a quiet but loyal supporter of Roosevelt's New Deal. Throughout his early career his personal honesty was never questioned although he was sponsored by a notoriously corrupt political machine. But when he was re-elected to the Senate in 1940 Truman displayed the qualities that later made him famous as President. As head of the Senate committee to investigate war production his associates admired his personal honesty, common sense and hard work. But to the general public, he was almost an unknown when he was named to run as Roosevelt's vice president on the 1944 ticket.

Meanwhile in Europe, advance patrols of the armies of the United States and the Soviet Union approached Strehle and Torgau on the Elbe River April 25 as delegates from 50 nations met in San Francisco to draw up a document that they hoped would become the charter of a united nations organization. The following day representatives of the two Allied armies met formally and toasted one another in recognition that Hitler's Third Reich had been cut in two.

In the following days through June 26 a charter for an organization known as the United Nations was approved, and it gave the people of a war-weary world hope that future wars could be avoided. "We the peoples of the United Nations, determined to save succeeding generations from the scourge of war which twice in our lifetimes has brought untold sorrow to mankind, and to re-affirm faith in fundamental human rights in the dignity and worth of the human person, and the equal rights of men and women and of nations large and small and to establish conditions under which justice and the respect for obligations arising from treaties and other sources of international law can be maintained and, to promote social progress and better standards of life and larger freedom—have resolved to combine our efforts to accomplish these aims. Accordingly, our respective governments, through representatives assembled in the city of San Francisco who have exhibited their full powers found to be in good and due form have agreed to the present Charter of the United Nations and do hereby establish an international organization to be known as the United Nations."

It became effective October 24.

Russian ground forces were approaching Berlin April 29 in three main spearheads from the east, south and north, and the devastated city was mostly in ruins from Allied air attacks.

Adolf Hitler and his former mistress Eva Braun, whom he had just married, were hiding in a bunker with Dr. Joseph Goebbels and his family, Martin Bormann and others close to Der Fuehrer. Earlier that evening Hitler received word that Mussolini and his mistress had been assassinated by Italian partisans and strung up by their feet in a Milan gas station. He told his group that he and his wife would commit suicide.

"I will not fall into the hands of the enemy dead or alive!" Hitler said. "After I die, my body shall be burned and so remain undiscovered forever!"

Nearby wrecked cars had to be drained of their gasoline to provide the fuel for their bodies' cremation.

When urged by some of his followers to try and escape the following day, Hitler refused, saying, that the military situation was hopeless. "After my death, I don't want to be put on exhibition in a Russian wax museum."

After midnight Hitler bade farewell to a group of 20 officers and women secretaries by shaking hands with each one before descending the curving staircase to his suite.

The Tiergarten was reported overrun by Soviet troops by late morning of April 30, and one advance patrol had been seen in the street next to Hitler's bunker.

Hans Baur, Hitler's personal pilot begged him to escape to Argentina or some country where his anti-semitism was appreciated.

Hitler shook his head. "One must have the courage to face the consequences—I am ending it all here! I know that by tomorrow millions of people will curse me. Fate wanted it that way."

Eva died first by taking cyanide poison. Then Hitler shot himself with his pistol. Their two bodies were taken outside, soaked with gasoline, and set on fire, while Russian shells exploded around the area.

That evening their remains were wrapped in canvas and placed in a shell hole outside the bunker and covered with earth. Despite concealment, their charred bodies were discovered by the Russians. Martin Bormann, whose escape from Berlin was long rumored, also died and his remains were identified years later.

Goebbels and his family escaped from the bunker but, after his attempt to negotiate with the Russians failed he, his wife and six children committed suicide May 1.

The last of the German armies surrendered to the Allies May 7 at Rheims, France. Eisenhower, who had represented the Allied governments, sent a telegram to the Combined Chiefs of Staff. "The mission of this allied force was fulfilled at 3 a.m. local time, May 7, 1945. Eisenhower."

President Truman proclaimed VE Day the following day. He told the nation, "I only wish that President Franklin D. Roosevelt had lived to witness this day. General Eisenhower informs me that the forces of Germany have surrendered to the United Nations. The flags of freedom fly all over Europe."

After VE Day, Colonel Cecil E. Combs, target specialist for the Twentieth Air Force, advised Chief of Staff Arnold in Washington that fire raids should be intensified to bring the Japanese war to a quicker conclusion.

Arnold agreed, saying we must "capitalize on the present critical situation in Japan." He wired LeMay to concentrate attacks on aircraft plants and urban areas.

An inscription discovered by a *Yank* magazine reporter at Verdun in 1945 spoke for all Americans, "Austin White—Chicago, Illinois, 1918. Austin White—Chicago, Illinois, 1945. This is the last time I want to write my name here."

Plans for the occupation of Germany were drawn up June 5 by the United States, Great Britain, France and the Soviet Union. They agreed to split Berlin into control areas—Berlin was in the Russian zone—while accepting occupation zones for the rest of Germany.

A grim reminder that the war in the Pacific was still on came when the American aircraft carrier "Bunker Hill" was attacked by a Japanese plane off Okinawa, killing 373 sailors.

Okinawa finally fell to Allied troops June 21 after 12,500 Americans died in the assault and 160,000 Japanese perished.

The Philippines were recaptured July 5 by General MacArthur's forces after 10 months of hard fighting and the loss of over 12,000 American lives.

In Europe, Patton was made a four-star general after VE Day but he promptly got himself into trouble again with his superiors. He pressed them to let him attack the Soviet Army in collaboration with German forces, because he was convinced that the Soviet Union was the United States' worst enemy. This preposterous proposal got him relieved from active duty and he died in December in an automobile accident in Germany. The people of the Allied nations would not have tolerated the start of another war after what they had just been through.

On Guam General LeMay had been hard at work for weeks on a new plan to cover the remaining days of spring and the summer months ahead after the heavy attacks against Japanese military targets during April and May. The doctrine remained the same. During clear days the aircraft industry would be attacked. When weather was bad, and radar runs necessary, the command would drop incendiary bombs on urban areas. No longer was it necessary to send a maximum effort to one target, so on each mission LeMay divided his command to hit separate targets. The "Empire Plan" started June 9 and, as it turned out, served as the governing document for all operations until war's end.

General Arnold flew to the Marianas in early June. LeMay and his staff gave him a briefing, explaining their operations, and what plans they had for the future.

LeMay told Arnold in response to his question about when the war would be over that "we'll run out of big strategic cities and targets by October 1. I can't see the war going on much beyond that date."

The Potsdam Conference opened July 17 with Truman, Churchill, Stalin and Chiang Kai-shek. For the most part they reviewed plans already made and approved them. For planning purposes, the conferences agreed on November 15, 1946, as the date when the war was expected to end.

Secretary of War Stimson handed Truman a telegram from General Leslie Groves's Washington office that first day.

Top Secret
Urgent
WAR 32887
For Colonel Kyles Eyes Only. From Harrison for Mr. Stimson.
Operated on this morning. Diagnosis not yet complete but results seem satisfactory and already exceed expectations. Local press release necessary as interest extends great distance. Dr. Groves pleased. He returns tomorrow. I will keep you posted. (Local press release was

deemed necessary because explosion of atomic bomb attracted local attention. Decided to say an ammo dump had accidentally exploded.)

July 19 Stimson received the following:

Top Secret
Priority
WAR 33556
To Secretary of War from Harrison. Doctor has just returned. Most enthusiastic and confident that the little boy is as husky as his big brother. The light in his eyes discernible from here to Highhold and I could have heard his screams from here to my farm."

"Big Brother" was the atom bomb that was exploded at Alamogordo Air Base in New Mexico. "Little Boy" was atom bomb number two, ready to be used against Japan. "From here to Highhold" meant from Washington to Stimson's estate "Highhold" on Long Island, 250 miles away. "From here to my farm" meant from Washington to George Harrison's farm at Upperville, Virginia, forty miles away.

The secret $2 billion program to develop an atomic bomb had paid off. J. Robert Oppenheimber had been in charge of the weapons laboratory at Los Alamos, but some of the world's leading scientists had paved the way. The first bomb was exploded on a tower and proved to be as powerful as the scientists had hoped it would be. Moreover, the bomb proved to be a practical weapon that could be delivered by a B-29.

Truman talked to his chief advisers and asked whether the atomic bomb should be used against Japan. They were unanimous that it should be. Many of the scientists who had helped to deliver the atomic bomb were strongly opposed to its use, insisting instead that it be demonstrated to the Japanese in an isolated spot. But the chances that it would be a dud, and Truman's strong feelings that its use would end the war without an invasion, outweighed scientific protestations.

Stalin told Truman at the Postdam conference about Japan's efforts to use the Soviet Union as mediators, a fact that the President was already aware of after the decoding of cables to and from Tokyo and Moscow.

The Soviet leader also told Churchill that the Russians would attack Japan soon after August 8.

Truman waited until July 24 to tell Stalin casually that the United States had a new weapon of unusual destructiveness. Stalin showed no interest, saying merely he was glad to hear it and hoped the United States would make good use of it against the Japanese. It wasn't learned until years later that Soviet spies had obtained atomic-bomb secrets and Stalin was well aware of what the United States was doing.

Two days later the Potsdam Declaration was released demanding Japan's unconditional surrender. Secretary of War Stimson's July 2 memorandum to the President served as the basis for the release about terms for Japan's surrender, but no reference was made about the Japanese retaining their Emperor. Secretary of State James F. Byrnes had objected to any such reference because he thought it smacked of appeasement. Neither was there any reference to the atomic bomb. The Japanese were just warned that continued resistance would lead to Japan's prompt and utter destruction.

General Arnold requested at the meeting that General Spaatz be given responsibility for delivering the atomic weapons once the President reached his irrevocable decision, and that he be given as much latitude as possible as to choice of target. There was no argument, and Arnold's request for such authority was granted.

The Potsdam Declaration caused near-panic in Premier Suzuki's cabinet. The military insisted that the government denounce the declaration and Suzuki did so publicly the following day.

The Allies took his statement as a complete rejection of their peace terms and were convinced that the military continued to dominate the Japanese government.

The Potsdam sessions established a Council of Foreign Ministers to meet regularly, consisting of representatives from the United States, China, the Soviet Union, France and Great Britain.

In the middle of the conference, Great Britain's Prime Minister Winston Churchill was voted out of office, and he was replaced by Clement Attlee.

When Stimson confided in General Eisenhower about the atomic bomb he was surprised by his reaction. The general said the news depressed him. When his opinion about its use was sought, Eisenhower said he was against it on two counts. First, he said, the Japanese were ready to surrender, and he thought it "unnecessary to hit them with that awful thing." Second, he said he hated to see the United States be "the first to use such a weapon."

Stimson, who had fought for years to continue development of the atomic bomb, was furious. Eisenhower understood his feelings after his long support of the project.

Eisenhower was right about Japan's condition. She was a defeated nation with her mighty navy destroyed by the United States Pacific Fleet, her merchant ships either sunk or confined to harbors after extensive mining around her home islands, and most of her cities were in ruins following massive bombing attacks by B-29s of the Twentieth Air Force. By this date her destruction was almost total as B-29s roamed at will over her main islands.

The continued efforts during the war to get Soviet Russia to declare war on Japan were unnecessary, and may have helped to give the Soviets a stronger foothold in the Far East. However, it must be recognized that Russia would undoubtedly have moved as she did at the end of the war without any prodding from the United States.

President Roosevelt, and later Truman, sought Soviet intervention because they both were appalled by the prospect of possibly a million American casualties if Japan's islands were invaded. Such a thought was uppermost in Truman's mind when he agreed to drop the atomic bombs. Then, too, losses among the Japanese military and civilians would undoubtedly have gone into the millions. When the counsel of his advisers is considered, and everything the President was told at the time by Generals Marshall and MacArthur that an invasion of Japan was a prerequisite to victory, there's no doubt that Truman made the correct decision.

The extent to which American political opinion had changed since World War I, representing a drastic turnabout in the average American's views about involvement in world affairs, was never more evident than on July 28. On that date the United States Senate gave its consent to the United Nations Charter by a vote of 89 to 2.

General LeMay was designated to pick the date for the first atomic mission. The training of the 509th Composite Group's crews had been completed, and LeMay believed that all was in readiness. When weathermen said August 5 it would be clear over the target city of Hiroshima the next day, he told Colonel Paul Tibbets, who would lead the mission, to proceed as planned for a 2:45 a.m. takeoff.

The true nature of the mission was not revealed to the crews. They were merely told that they would drop a new bomb that would shorten the war by at least six months. Chaplain William Downey stood before them at the briefing. "We pray thee that the end of the war may come soon, and that once more we may know peace on earth. May the men who fly this night be kept safe in thy care, and may they be returned safely to us. We shall go forward trusting in thee, knowing that we are in thy care now and forever. In the name of Jesus Christ, amen."

An hour from Hiroshima, Tibbets received a report from a weather plane over the city at 8:15 a.m. that there were only scattered clouds over the city so, if the weather held for another hour, he knew they could hit the primary target at Hiroshima, and not have to go to Kokura or Nagasaki which had been selected as second and third alternates.

Navy Captain W. S. Parsons and his assistant, Lieutenant Morris B.

Jeppson, had assembled the atomic bomb after takeoff. "Little Boy" weighed 9,700 pounds. It was an armored cylinder, dull black in color, with a slightly rounded nose. A triple-fusing system had been designed to arm it at 7,000 feet.

Captain Parsons advised Tibbets that all was in readiness once "Little Boy" was fully assembled and ready for its historic release.

Hiroshima was Japan's eighth largest city, and headquarters for the Second Army. LeMay had earlier been instructed not to bomb it, for reasons he didn't understand until later. The city was an important port and contained vital industries.

Seven B-29s of the 509th Composite Group had been assigned to the mission, one as a spare airplane at Iwo Jima in case Tibbets' plane the "Enola Gay" got into trouble. Three Superforts had taken off first to serve as weather planes, and the others flew with the "Enola Gay" as observation planes. "The Great Artiste" was piloted by Major Charles W. Sweeney, and the other Superfortress was flown by Captain George W. Marquardt. Both were filled with cameras and scientific instruments, plus military and civilian observers.

Other B-29s were ordered to fly at least 50 miles from Hiroshima four hours prior to the scheduled release, and six hours afterwards. LeMay scheduled two F-13 photo-reconnaissance airplanes to obtain post-strike photographs of the city.

The "Enola Gay" reached the initial point at 9:11 a.m. and Tibbets turned the airplane over to bombardier Major Thomas W. Ferebee, navigator Captain Theodore J. Van Kirk, and radar operator Sergeant Joe A. Stiborik. After a smooth, tense run at 31,600 feet, the "Little Boy" bomb was released.

Set to go off at 2,000 feet, it exploded at 8:17:02 Hiroshima time, 43 seconds after it dropped from the airplane. Crew members felt two distinct shock waves seven seconds later as they were pulling away from the city. Then a huge mushroom cloud erupted above the city and rose quickly to 50,000 feet as the crews stared in awe.

"Tibbets to crew. Fellows, you have just dropped the first atomic bomb in history."

Observers on the ground first saw a huge pinkish glare in the sky, followed by a wave of intense heat and wind that withered everything in its path. Seventy-one thousand, three hundred and seventy-nine Japanese died instantly, and 68,023 others were horribly burned or seriously injured and, suffering from the effects of intense radiation, writhed in agony on the scarred ground. Debris whirled into the sky as a massive cloud of smoke, fire and pulverized matter ascended thousands of feet in seconds. Fires quickly burned what was left of the city and only devastated land remained. Here and there on a pavement was the outline of what had once been a human being, now completely disintegrated and only a shadow remaining to prove that the person had ever existed.

Tibbets sent a radio message back to the Marianas. "Mission successful. No hostile fighters, few flak bursts."

As "Enola Gay" headed back to Tinian the co-pilot wrote only two words in his diary, "My God!"

B-29 photo-reconnaissance planes took pictures five hours after the bomb exploded. Although smoke and dust were so heavy over the city that an accurate damage assessment could not immediately be made, it appeared that 4.7 square miles of Hiroshima had been destroyed. Later it was determined that the number of dead was lower than after the March 9 fire raid on Tokyo, but the number of injured was higher.

President Truman was immediately informed of the successful mission and he authorized a statement for release to the press. "The world will note that the first atomic bomb was dropped on Hiroshima, a military base. We won the race of discovery against the Germans. We have used it in order to shorten the agony of war, in order to save the lives of thousands and thousands of young Americans. We shall continue to use it until we completely destroy Japan's power to make war." The President warned the Japanese that if they didn't surrender they could expect a "rain of ruin from the air, the like of which has never been seen on this earth."

Premier Kantaro Suzuki again advised the Emperor that Japan should accept the Potsdam formula for ending the war, but the Army stubbornly resisted such a move.

Some Japanese leaders had been searching for a way to end the war for months. Emperor Hirohito, who had earlier tried to get the military to agree to a cessation of hostilities, called a meeting of his inner cabinet after Russia declared war on Japan August 10. Although he had little authority, he used his vast prestige as Emperor with the people to insist that the war be stopped.

While B-29s continued their bombing of Japan, the Japanese cabinet sent messages to the Allies through Switzerland and Sweden that Japan would accept the Potsdam terms if they didn't threaten the prerogatives of the Emperor.

The United States didn't reply immediately because it was felt that any Japanese qualifications might be construed as a lessening of the terms agreed to at Potsdam. Truman and his cabinet had never insisted that the office of Emperor should be abolished, but the whole matter needed a thorough review.

While Japanese militarists talked about taking over the government,

President Truman authorized release of the second atomic bomb with Kokura, on the northern tip of Kyushu, as the primary target because of its huge Army arsenal, and Nagasaki as secondary target.

Major Charles V. Sweeney's "Bock's Car" ran into foul weather August 9 over Kokura, and despite three separate runs looking for a hole over the target, Captain Kermit K. Beahan had to admit failure.

Sweeney noted that fuel was running low so he turned his B-29 toward Nagasaki on Kyushu's west side. Although the city of Nagasaki had been bombed several times, it was not appreciably damaged and the Mitsubishi plants had hardly been touched. It was not a good target because the city's valleys were deep within hills across up-and-down terrain.

Beahan sought the aiming point frantically because the countryside lay under an eight-tenths cloud cover and he hoped that radar was bringing them in properly. During the last few seconds, he found a hole in the clouds and "Fat Man" left the airplane at 10:58 a.m. Nagasaki time. The bomb missed the aiming point by three miles but 35,000 Japanese died instantly while 60,000 others were injured. An area of 1.45 square miles, or more than 43 percent of the city, was obliterated, including more than two-thirds of the industrial section. Due to the hilly terrain, destruction spread laterally through the valleys, and was less than a normal fire raid with incendiaries.

An imperial conference was held in Japan the next day. Although no agreement was reached, the Emperor made it clear that he wanted the war brought to an end. He said Japan's only course was to accept the Potsdam Declaration.

With B-29s continuing to devastate Japan with conventional bombs, Emperor Hirohito's views prevailed and the Japanese government accepted the Potsdam Declaration August 14. Once considered a god and father of his nation, and nominally an absolute ruler and commander of Japan's 8.2 million imperial troops, in truth Hirohito had little but moral authority; a symbol of the unity of the Japanese people.

The Emperor made a recording for broadcast over Japanese radio August 15. The people of Japan listened to their Emperor for the first time as he said, "It is according to the dictate of time and fate that we have resolved to pave the way for a grand peace for all generations to come by enduring the unendurable and suffering the insufferable."

Japan's formal surrender was accepted on board the battleship "Missouri" September 2 in Tokyo Bay with Douglas MacArthur officiating as the newly-appointed Supreme Commander of Allied Powers in Japan.

Before he signed for the Allied powers, MacArthur said, "Will General Wainwright and General Percival step forward and accompany me while I sign?" The two emaciated officers, only recently released from Japanese prison camps, stood behind MacArthur as he stepped again to the microphone and said, "Let us pray that peace may be now restored to the world, and that God will preserve it always. These proceedings are closed."

Although the dropping of the world's first two atomic bombs was given credit for ending the war, Japan had already been defeated. The sea-air blockade of the Japanese home islands and the direct bombing attacks on industrial and urban targets had brought about this defeat by the end of July. The production of civilian goods was down so low that the nation faced economic collapse, and munitions output had been reduced so severely by the destruction of factories that military operations could no longer be sustained.

The urban incendiary attacks by the Twentieth Air Force had profound repercussions on civilian morale, weakening Japan's will to remain in the war. Sixty-six cities, virtually all those of economic significance, were subjected to bombing raids and suffered destruction ranging from 25 to 90 percent.

After the war, following months of conducting a thorough survey, officials of the Strategic Bombing Survey reached the conclusion that Japan would have surrendered prior to December 31, 1945, and in all probability by November 1 even if the atomic bombs had not been dropped and even if no invasion had been planned or contemplated.

It is frequently overlooked that the two atomic-bomb attacks gave Japan's militarists a convenient excuse to claim that Japan's army was never defeated and that the nation was forced to surrender by a force for which there was no defense. The facts do not support such an allegation. No nation on earth was ever more thoroughly defeated than Japan once the Allies built up their forces following the Pearl Harbor debacle.

Russia's entry into the Far East war August 8 set up new possibilities for later conflict between the war-time allies. The first step in that direction was taken August 17 when Korea was divided at the 38th parallel with United States troops taking over the southern portion, and the Russians occupying the north.

As tragic as the losses were during the war, the proportion of deaths to wounded Americans was less than one to four, or less than half that of World War I. This was due to more efficient and rapid methods of evacuation of wounded, the use of bloodplasma, and the control of diseases and infections with penicillin and sulfa drugs. In the first five months of 1943 only 400 million units of penicillin were produced, but in that year's final months the total rose to 21 billion units. By August of 1945, after six months of production for civilian use, American pharmaceutical houses were making 650 billion units of penicillin per month.

After the war had ended in Europe President Truman had ordered that the United States start to convert to a peacetime economy. Rationing was ended as each individual item became more plentiful. The War Production Board lifted the ban on the manufacture of civilian goods, manpower and raw materials and ended controls August 20 except for materials in short supply. Controls on all materials ended September 30.

The Lend-Lease Program ended August 21 after $50 billion had been allocated to America's allies to aid the war effort. Receipts had totaled only $8 billion. It soon became evident, however, that other aid programs would be needed for the recovery of war-ravaged nations. At war's end about 10 million European civilians were in countries other than their own as refugees, prisoners or slave laborers.

The Western Allies had lost 10.65 million military personnel either killed or missing, while the Axis powers had lost 4.6 million. There were an equal number of civilian deaths due to starvation, bombing of cities, and mass murders in Hitler's concentration camps. These camps destroyed about six million Jews, but also an additional nine to ten million non-Jews, a fact that is rarely mentioned. Of the approximately 16 million Americans who served in the war the United States lost 405,399 dead or missing in action and presumed dead, but total casualties were over a million. (Almost 18 million Americans were inducted but 6.4 million were rejected as physically or mentally unfit.) The Russians suffered most with more than 27 million casualties, including more than six million battle deaths. Although a true figure probably will never be known, it is possible that as many as 57 million people died in the war.

The American people and industry had been taxed heavily during the war but the revenue from all taxes amounted to less than half of wartime expenditures that had cost the United States approximately $350 billion in loans and military supplies. The Government had borrowed the rest, raising the national debt from the 1940 level of $325 per capita to $1,849.

The end of the war also found the government a huge property owner. The Defense Plant Corporation had financed about 85 percent of the new war plants. Now it owned about nine-tenths of all aircraft, shipbuilding, magnesium and synthetic rubber plants, three-quarters of all aluminum plants and about half of the machine-tool manufacturers.

President Truman was appalled by the plight of emaciated survivors released by the Allied armies in Europe before and after VE-Day, as were free peoples everywhere. Of particular concern were the 100,000 Jewish refugees in Western Europe. He appealed to Great Britain August 31 to permit them to enter Palestine which was under British control.

The President submitted an economic recovery plan to Congress September 6 to aid in getting people back to work in civilian jobs, and called for the building of houses for the nation's more affluent and growing population.

As the Allies prepared for war crimes trials in Japan against those who had abused their authority during the war, Japanese communists staged demonstrations against Emperor Hirohito. He had no idea what fate held in store for him, and he waited for General MacArthur to call him to a meeting.

MacArthur ignored the Emperor, forcing his staff to ask for a meeting with the Allied Supreme Commander of the occupation forces. Once this was done MacArthur agreed to meet with Hirohito September 27.

At their meeting, the General treated the Emperor with respect, but he was dressed only in an open-necked khaki uniform while Hirohito wore a cutaway with striped trousers and a top hat.

The Emperor was obviously nervous and MacArthur dismissed everyone but his own interpreter as they sat by an open fire at one end of the long reception hall. The General offered him an American cigarette that he accepted with thanks. MacArthur took note that the Emperor's hands shook as he lighted it for him. MacArthur realized that Hirohito was suffering the agonies of humiliation and he hoped that he would not plead his case against indictment as a war criminal.

Instead, the Emperor said, "I came to you, General MacArthur, to offer myself to the judgment of the powers you represent as the one to bear sole responsibility for every political and military decision made and action taken by my people in the conduct of the war."

MacArthur was moved by the Emperor's assumption of responsibility and his courage in doing so. He told his staff later that he knew that Hirohito was an emperor by inherent birth, "but in that instant, I knew I faced the First Gentleman of Japan in his own right."

CHAPTER 15

An Iron Curtain

THE FIRST GENERAL ASSEMBLY OF THE UNITED NATIONS MET IN LONDON on January 10, 1946, with Secretary of States James F. Byrnes heading the American delegation that also included Mrs. Eleanor Roosevelt. Fifty-one nations took part, and the Security Council met for the first time later that month. Trygve Lie of Norway was elected as secretary-general and New York was accepted as the site for a permanent United Nations headquarters after $8.5 million was donated in December for acquisition of an 18-acre tract in Manhattan alongside the East River by John D. Rockefeller, Jr.

The bombing of Hiroshima and Nagasaki had brought a sober realization to members of the United Nations of the awesome power of atomic energy, and its potential for misuse. The UN agreed to an international Atomic Energy Commission January 24 that would impose restrictions upon atomic energy to peaceful uses in the future.

The world organization was further sobered March 5 when former Prime Minister Winston Churchill spoke at Westminster College, Fulton, Missouri, to warn about the growing domination of the Soviet Union in Eastern Europe. With President Truman in attendance, Churchill said, "A shadow has fallen upon the scenes so lately lighted by the Allied victory. Nobody knows what Soviet Russia and its communist international organization intends to do in the immediate future, or what are the limits, if any, of their expansive and proselytizing tendencies. . . .

"We understand Russia's need to be secure on her western frontiers from all renewal of German aggression. We welcome her rightful place among the leading nations of the world. Above all, we welcome constant, frequent and growing contacts between the Russian people and our own people on both sides of the Atlantic.

"It is my duty, however, to place before you certain facts about the present position in Europe . . . from Stettin in the Baltic to Trieste in the Adriatic an 'Iron Curtain' has descended across the continent. Behind that line are all the capitals of the ancient states of central and eastern Europe: Warsaw, Berlin, Prague, Vienna, Budapest, Belgrade, Bucharest and Sofia. All these famous cities, and the populations around them, lie in the Soviet sphere, and all are subject in one form or another not only of Soviet influence but to a very high and increasing measure of control from Moscow. Athens, alone, with its immortal glories, is free to decide its future at an election under British, American and French observation.

"The Russian-dominated Polish government has been encouraged to make enormous and wrongful inroads upon Germany, and mass expulsions of millions of Germans on a scale grievous and undreamed of are now taking place."

Churchill concluded with a clarion call for resisting the further encroachment of communism in Europe. "If the populations of the English-speaking commonwealths be added to that of the United States with all that such cooperation implies in the air, on the seas, and all over the globe, if all British moral and material forces and convictions are joined with your own in fraternal association, the high road of the future will be clear not only for us but for all; not only for our time, but for a century to come."

To test the effect of atomic bombs against warships, the United States began tests in July 1946, at Bikini in the Marshall Islands. Two atomic bombs were exploded and 11 large Navy ships were sunk and six others damaged. It was now evident that their destructive power could destroy a fleet unless it was widely dispersed at sea.

Wernher von Braun, a pioneer rocket experimenter in Germany during the war, was brought to the United States in 1945 and assigned to develop rockets for the United States Army. The V-2 ballistic missile was developed at the Peenemünde test facility under his direction during the war.

After he was captured he was asked where he got his ideas to develop the V-2. He looked at his interrogator with amazement. "Don't you know about your own rocket pioneer? Dr. Goddard was ahead of us all." He was referring to Robert Goddard who had been ridiculed for his early work on rockets in the United States.

After a 10-month trial at Nuremberg, Germany, 24 major Nazis were charged with crimes against the peace, humanity and the laws of war, and 12 were sentenced to death. Those who were consigned to death included Ribbentrop and Göring but the latter committed suicide on the evening before his execution. The others were hanged October 16. Rudolf Hess and Walther Funk were given life imprisonment while Hjalmar Schacht and Fritz von Papen were acquitted. In the American zone of occupation there were 12 other trials of major war criminals under international courts of justice.

Korea, which had been divided at the 38th parallel by earlier agreement at the end of the war as a temporary measure, appeared to be headed for permanent division with Russian troops in the North and Americans in the South. This situation prompted acting Secretary of State Dean Acheson to announce on October 1 that the United States intended to keep its occupation forces in South Korea until North Korea was evacuated by Soviet troops and a free government was formed by a unified country.

Although the fighting had stopped after VJ-Day the year before, the war was not officially declared over until December 31, 1946. President Truman formally issued a proclamation to that effect on that date.

President Truman had been concerned since the war's end that more countries would fall under the domination of the Soviet Union unless some drastic American action was taken to prevent it. He went before a joint session of Congress March 12, 1947, to express his concern, and to offer a new program to counteract growing communist infiltration of Greece and Turkey. Economically, like most other countries in Europe, they were almost destitute and prime targets for communist takeover. He told the Congress, "I believe it must be the policy of the United States to support free peoples who are resisting attempts to subjugation by armed minorities or by outside pressures." He said he believed that free peoples should work out their own destiny in their own way, but he added, "I believe that our help should be primarily through economic and financial aid which is essential to economic stability. It is necessary only to glance at a map to realize that the survival and integrity of the Greek nation are of grave importance to a much wider situation."

His wise, and far-reaching program immediately became known as the "Truman Doctrine."

Charges that the United States Government was infiltrated with communists, or communist sympathizers, forced Truman to issue an executive order March 21 that required an investigation of all employees and those seeking jobs in the government. These loyalty checks went on until 1951. The vast majority of the three million employees who underwent the investigation were cleared. Three thousand resigned in protest, not necessarily because they were guilty, but because they considered the investigation a violation of their civil rights. Two hundred twelve were considered suspect and were dismissed.

Historian Bernard de Voto in 1949 spoke out in *Harper's Magazine* to protest the loyalty investigation. "I say it has gone too far. We are divided into the hunted and the hunters. There is loose in the United States today the same evil that once split Salem Village between the bewitched and the accused and stole men's reason quite away."

The devastation wrought throughout Europe during the war had created an economic crisis beyond aid to Greece and Turkey. President Truman, fully recognizing the dire need to get democratic nations back on their feet, sought congressional approval for a plan to help them recover from the war.

And thus was born the Marshall Plan, one of the most unselfish acts ever conceived by the people of any nation. With economic disintegration and political chaos threatening Europe, the nations of Western Europe and the United States conceived a cooperative venture to literally rebuild the economy of the continent. It was a program fraught with risks, but the alternative of communist dominance was even worse. It was America's finest hour in foreign affairs, and one that has not been repeated since.

As conceived by the President and Secretary of State George C. Marshall, American aid would be used to carefully stimulate shattered economies to avoid political upheaval and/or starvation of the people of Western Europe. Marshall, chief architect of the plan that bore his name, initially sought $13.3 billion. This was a huge amount for the time, perhaps worth almost five times that amount four decades later.

The plan succeeded because the United States, magnanimous in victory, sought by its efforts to overcome the errors of past wars and resurrect the economies of defeated nations whose cities and factories were largely destroyed, and help some of the victors to restore their ravaged economies. By its act, the United States assumed leadership of the western world.

The debt cycle following World War I literally created the conditions for World War II. By demanding war reparations from the Germans and the nations that fought with her, and payment for goods provided by the United States to Great Britain and France, the post-war world in the 1920s suffered due to the inability of all but Finland to make payments on their war debts. Inevitably overseas markets collapsed and the United States faced its worst depression in history. The Marshall Plan was the complete antithesis to the age-old theory that to the victor belongs the spoils.

Two years after the plan was inaugurated Western European nations were 18 percent ahead of their pre-war economic levels.

A milestone act was passed July 26 designating that a National Military Establishment of all military services be formed under a secretary of defense with cabinet-level status. In the past, military aviation had been part of the Department of the Army. Effective September 18, 1947, the United States Air Force was established under the new law as an independent service. The Navy had bitterly fought such a move, but the Army Air Forces' role in World War II had won them the right to become independent. Navy Secretary James V. Forrestal was sworn in the day before as the nation's first Secretary of Defense. President Truman later signed an executive order that integrated the armed forces so that all young men, regardless of ethnic and economic backgrounds, would be treated the same.

Ever since the war ended problems had escalated in the Far East. Truman had sent General Albert C. Wedemeyer to China on still another exploratory mission to make recommendations to him as to what steps should be taken to defuse the tense situation between the Nationalists and the Communists. When Wedemeyer reported to the President he denounced the Communists' use of force and the corruption of the Nationalists but he recommended a five-year American military aid program for the Nationalists.

In a related issue in that part of the world, the United States referred the problem of Korea to the United Nations. Divided at the 38th parallel, Russia was rapidly building up local communists for an eventual takeover of the southern part of the peninsula. The UN passed a resolution September 17 that called for free elections throughout Korea.

Representatives of 23 nations met at Geneva October 30 to consider tariff reductions. They agreed that reductions should take effect on two-thirds of their international trade items. This positive step was taken because they all remembered the 1929 depression caused in large part by high tariffs. These nations handled three-fourths of the world's trade so their action quickly revived international trade.

When Communist Party leaders in Czechoslovakia seized control of the government February 25, 1948, it was just another indication that the post-war world was becoming increasingly violent, with little hope for change. The new Prime Minister, Klement Gottwald, rejected complaints from the western democracies that condemned the takeover. He said that the United States, France and Great Britain did not have "the slightest legal right to intervene in Czechoslovak affairs or even to criticize. We will never take any lessons in democracy from those with Munich on their conscience, who dealt with Hitler to divide us up." His reference was in regard to Neville Chamberlain's attempt to appease Hitler prior to World War II.

With the communists in control, and threatening a general strike,

President Edvard Beneš was forced to permit Gottwald to form a "govern-ment of the workers." But he resigned when he refused to sign the communist constitution.

Foreign Minister Jan Masaryk, the populist leader of the Czech nation whose father was co-founder and President of the Czechoslovak republic, remained in office and tried to reassure the country that the communists would maintain democratic institutions.

He said, "We older ones have no reason indeed to be proud of the heritage we are leaving behind for the youth of the world. Will we be proud of the victory which again, of course, will be brought into being by the very youth of all united nations? We were willing to die for an ideal and we would die for it again but we prefer living for it, working for it, safeguarding it."

At 6 a.m. March 10 his body was found three floors down from an open bathroom window in the Foreign Ministry. Gottwald said Masaryk was depressed by the foreign criticism of his decision to join the govern-ment and claimed that he had committed suicide. It is far more probable that he was murdered by communist hirelings.

After Romania's King Michael was forced to abdicate by Soviet-backed communists on December 31, 1947, and Czechoslovakia's takeover by a communist regime, all of Eastern Europe was behind the "Iron Curtain."

These acts had one positive effect in the United States. They galvanized members of Congress into action. Republican Senator Arthur Vanden-berg, for many years a leading isolationist, exerted his enormous prestige toward convincing Congress that President Truman's plan to rejuvenate Europe, and to keep more nations on the Allied side, was in America's best interest. For a cost of $46 per capita Vandenberg said that Truman's plan was a good buy to assure a healthy Europe. He fought hard for passage, and eventually convinced most of his colleagues. It was a coura-geous political act because some Republicans never forgave him.

With Vandenberg's help in the Senate, Congress passed a law on April 2 establishing the Economic Assistance Cooperation Administration. It provided $5 billion in aid to Western Europe under the Marshall Plan.

The United States had long had a touchy relationship with its Latin and South American neighbors and on April 30 a step was taken to improve that relationship. Twenty-one nations met in Bogota, Colombia, to form the Organization of American States, with the United States as just one of the group. A regional group for the mutual defense of the two hemispheres, and for general cooperation, it became legally effective in 1951 when two-thirds of the nations ratified the OAS Charter.

The fact that Truman's foreign policy was sound was never better demonstrated than after the Italians went to the polls in April to elect a new government. American aid, along with strong intervention by the Catholic Church, brought a resurgence of support for the Christian Democratic Party and, much to everyone's surprise, it garnered 48.7 percent of the popular vote. With a number of smaller parties, which had similar pro-Western views, control of the Chamber of Deputies was denied the communists who only received 31 percent of the vote.

Although boycotted by the North Koreans, South Korea held elections on May 10 under the jurisdiction of the United Nations Temporary Commission. On August 15 the Republic of South Korea was proclaimed at its new capital, Seoul, with Syngman Rhee as its first President. A People's Republic was established in North Korea on September 9 that claimed jurisdiction over the entire country despite formation of the United States-backed Republic of South Korea.

In the Middle East, the British flag was lowered over Palestine on May 14 and Israel announced its independence. The United States was the first nation to recognize it. Chaim Weizmann was elected President and David Ben-Gurion became the nation's Premier. Egypt attacked the next day and within two weeks the new state was fighting five Arab nations. They refused to accept Israel's existence. Meanwhile the Arab League rejected an appeal from the United Nations for a ceasefire. Thus Israel was reborn as a state after 2,000 years as its citizens were told to "proclaim liberty throughout the land, and to all the inhabitants thereof."

After extensive, and sometimes vitriolic debate in Congress, the Selective Service Act was passed and Truman signed it June 23, 1948. Men 19 to 25 could be inducted for 21 months service while 18-year-olds were permitted to volunteer for one year in any of the regular services. The new law was needed to provide men for the occupation of Germany and Italy, and to fill the needs of an expanded military program.

The necessity for the new law became apparent the next day when the Soviet Union began a blockade of Berlin by denying Allied access to the city—deep in the heart of the Russian occupation sector—by land and water routes. Stalin had decided on this move to force the Western Allies to give up control of the western part of the city. To counteract the blockade, and not force a confrontation on land, the Allies ordered their air forces to fly in food, fuel and other supplies to the beleaguered city in "Operation Vittles." And thus began one of the most incredible airlifts of all time. In the next 16 months aircraft airlifted 1.6 million tons of supplies to Berlin's 2½ million residents. The Soviet Union's hope for an easy victory was thwarted by the airlift and Stalin cancelled the blockade in May 1949, although the airlift continued until that September to bring the total tonnage to 2.3 million. Stalin had tested the will of the western powers, and he found it far more resolute than he had been led to believe.

The Republican Party began its convention June 21 at Philadelphia. Its platform stressed the party's dedication to the maintenance of peace and the principles of the Taft-Hartley Act.

There was deep gloom among delegates to the Democratic Convention when they met July 15 in Philadelphia. But Senator Alben W. Barkley brought the convention to life with a ringing speech by taking a word the Republicans were using against them and flinging it back in their faces. "What is a bureaucrat? A bureaucrat is a Democrat who holds an office that some Republican wants."

But the convention grew vitriolic over the civil rights issue. A plank had been added to the party platform and it was splitting the party. Handy Ellis of Alabama led the Southern Democrats out of the convention crying out, "The South is no longer going to be the whipping boy of the Democratic Party. And you know that without the votes of the South you cannot elect a President of the United States." He called other Democrats to join them, saying, "And we bid you goodbye."

In addition to the civil rights issue, the platform demanded repeal of the Taft-Hartley law that not all delegates supported.

Truman was nominated with Barkley as his running mate and the President spoke to what was left of the convention, and the nation by radio at 3 a.m. "Senator Barkley and I will win this election and make these Republicans like it, don't you forget that."

Nine days later the newly-formed Progressive Party, made up partly of Democrats who opposed Truman's foreign policy, met in the same city to nominate a presidential candidate. Henry A. Wallace was nominated and he promised party members "a century of the common man," vowing to raise a "Gideon's Army" in the cause of peace and domestic equality.

The Southern Democrats who walked out of their convention met July 17 in Alabama to form the States' Rights Party or "Dixiecrats" as they became known. They nominated Strom M. Thurmond of South Carolina for President, and proposed a platform of racial segregation.

President Truman alienated many Southern voters July 26 by courageously issuing an executive order barring segregation in the armed forces, and calling for an end to racial discrimination in government jobs.

On this date he also called Congress into special session to consider legislation to control inflation, enact civil rights laws and to repeal the Taft-Hartley Act. The rebellious Congress, dominated by Republicans, refused to go along on any of his legislation.

The growing disagreements between the Soviet Union and the western democracies now had become so severe that Bernard Baruch, speaking before a Senate committee, told the lawmakers that "we are in the midst of a cold war which is getting warmer."

After Labor Day the presidential campaign's rhetoric heated up, and the odds were 15 to 1 against Harry Truman.

Republican Thomas E. Dewey told enthusiastic crowds, "We're going to have a spring house-cleaning in January. We're going to have the biggest untangling, unsnarling, weeding and pruning operation in our history."

Truman said of Dewey, "He opened his mouth and closed his eyes, and he swallowed the terrible record of that good-for-nothing 80th Congress."

Dewey was wildly cheered when he told huge crowds that turned out to see and hear him, "Your next administration is going to go forward to make more adequate provisions against the hazards of old age and unemployment."

Dewey didn't realize it at the time but his failure to spell out in detail how he would implement these changes began to cost him votes.

Truman never let up on Dewey. "He says in this campaign that he's for a minimum wage. And I think the smaller the minimum the better it will suit him."

Truman traveled 10,000 miles on a "whistle-stop" re-election campaign, made 140 stops, spoke 147 times and shook hands with at least 32,000 people by October 5. Then he took off for his final swing through upstate New York and then on to Kansas City where his tour would end on October 31.

On election day the *Chicago Tribune* had been so certain of Truman's defeat that it had gone to press with a headline announcing a Dewey victory.

When Dewey finally conceded, President Truman met the press corps in Washington. He convulsed them with his imitation of radio commentator H. V. Kaltenborn. "I had my sandwich and glass of buttermilk and went to bed at 6:30. And along about 12 o'clock I happened to awaken for some reason and the radio was turned on and Mr. Kaltenborn was saying, "While the President is a million votes ahead in the popular vote he has yet to hear. . . ." Laughter drowned out the rest as Truman's clipped speech perfectly mimicked the commentator. When it died down, he continued, "We are very sure when the country vote comes in Mr. Truman will be defeated. . . ." He was again interrupted by gales of laughter. Finally, he said, "I went back to bed."

Truman received 24.1 million votes, Dewey 21.97 million, Strom Thurmond 1.1 million and the Progressive Party received about a million votes. The electoral college gave Truman 303, Dewey 109, Thurman 39 and none for Wallace. It was in impressive popular response, and a great personal victory for President Truman and the American form of democracy.

CHAPTER 16

Home by Christmas

IN MAY THE UNITED STATES HAD TESTED THREE NEW ATOMIC WEAPONS at Eniwetok Atoll in the Pacific, thereby reaffirming the tremendous power of the atom bomb in war. At this time the nation's stockpile of atomic bombs was only 48. The United States proposed international controls for atomic energy on November 4, and the United Nations General Assembly approved the recommendation.

A mutual security pact was signed on April 4, 1949, by representatives of the United States, Canada, Great Britain, Denmark, Norway, Iceland, France, the Netherlands, Luxembourg, Belgium, Italy and Portugal. The North Atlantic Treaty Organization (NATO) was ratified by the United States Senate on July 21 by a vote of 82 to 13. Later, Greece and Turkey joined the alliance. While reaffirming their support of the United Nations, these nations agreed that an attack on any one of them would be considered an attack against all of them.

Secretary of State Dean Acheson said of the pact, "It is clear that the North Atlantic pact is not an improvisation. It is a statement of facts and the lessons of history. We have learned our history lessons from two world wars in less than half a century. That experience has taught us that the control of Europe by a single, aggressive, unfriendly power would constitute an intolerable threat to the national security of the United States. We participated in these two great wars to preserve the integrity and independence of the European half of the Atlantic community, in order to preserve the integrity and independence of the American half. It is a simple fact, proved by experience, that an outside attack on one member of this community is an attack on all members."

Four days later the United States occupation zone in Germany was merged with the zones of France and Britain, assuming the establishment of a West German government. The Federal Republic of Germany came into being at Bonn on May 23, 11 days after the Soviet Union lifted its blockade of Berlin. Dr. Konrad Adenauer later was elected Chancellor while Theodor Heuss was elected President.

American troops were withdrawn from Korea on June 29, except for 500 advisers, because a decision had been made at the highest level that Korea was outside the U.S. defense perimeter in the Pacific.

Events in China had long been predictable since the Nationalists turned over Peking to the communists January 22, 1949, and Generalissimo Chiang Kai-shek announced that he was retiring as China's President in hopes that his departure would end hostilities. The Nationalists had been outmaneuvered repeatedly by dedicated communists so their demise was anticipated. The loss of Peking to the communists forced the departure of 8,000 United States Marines. The communists then began a country-wide campaign to rid China of the Nationalist armies, and they were successful by the end of May.

The United States Government issued a "white paper" through the State Department that blamed the Chiang regime for the Nationalists' defeat. The State Department called it corrupt and indicated that its ineptitude lost mainland China to the communists.

The Nationalists moved most of their forces to Formosa (later renamed Taiwan) where they established a government. Meanwhile, Chinese communist leader Mao Tse-tung proclaimed a new People's Republic October 1 with Chou En-lai as its premier.

A Russian spokesman called the occasion a "failure of U.S. calculations upon atomic monopoly." The Soviet Union immediately recognized the new regime saying, "The victory of the Chinese people deals a cruel blow to the aggressive plans of imperialists in the Pacific Region."

Great Britain and France followed suit but the United States refused. It was a bitter blow to American prestige, but the administration had gone through a series of political setbacks.

A United Nations commission had announced September 8 that it was unable to settle differences between North and South Korea and a spokesman said it was feared the country was close to civil war.

President Truman revealed another bit of shocking news September 23 when he announced that the Soviet Union now had developed a nuclear capability, and that they had just tested an atomic device.

Further bad news was revealed October 12 when East Germany became the Democratic Republic of Germany.

It had been rumored for some time that American scientists were working on a hydrogen bomb. President Truman confirmed the fact

January 31, 1950, that an even more powerful weapon than the atomic bomb was under development by the Atomic Energy Commission. It had been known for some time that atomic energy could be released in two ways; the fission of elements with very heavy atoms such as uranium and plutonium that can be split when struck by a neutron or a subatomic particle, or by fusing four light atoms of hydrogen into the next heavier element helium. Fusion requires enormous heat and high pressures but with the development of the atomic bomb such heat and pressure could be obtained by exploding a fission bomb.

The announcement was greeted with mixed emotions by the scientific community, many of whom deplored what they considered was a misuse of science to make war even more horrible. Three years earlier Albert Einstein warned in the *Atlantic Monthly* that atomic bombs had already been made more effective. "Unless another war is prevented," he said, "it is likely to bring destruction on a scale never before held possible and even now hardly conceived—and little civilization would survive it."

Government officials in Washington, and most Americans, had always been tragically uninformed about the legitimate aspirations of the people of Asia. Instead of seeking the truth on its own, the United States relied upon two of its western allies—France and Great Britain—to determine its policies for the region. When the people of Indochina hopefully looked to the United States for help in freeing themselves from colonialism, the American government ignored their pleas. Although communism had always been rejected by most of the deeply-religious people of Asia, two charismatic communist leaders—Mao Tse-tung in China and Ho Chi Minh in Vietnam—began to gain adherents throughout the Far East.

Under pressure from the communists, France had agreed to recognize Vietnam in 1946 as a "free state" within the French union. The Chinese also reached an agreement with France to withdraw its forces from the northern part of Vietnam in exchange for France's agreement to drop its extra-territorial rights in China. Ho Chi Minh also agreed to permit the return of French troops to the north for five years to replace the Chinese.

In later negotiations in France that September the French refused to grant unification of Vietnam and war broke out. Ho Chi Minh appealed to President Truman for help, but he never received an answer.

Some officials of the Truman administration sympathized with the aspirations of the nationalists in Vietnam for independence, and they were reluctant to see the French gain control of the country by force, but they were concerned lest the communists gain control of Vietnam. Instead, State Department officials urged France to seek an end to guerrilla warfare by agreeing to a political solution acceptable to both sides.

It was American policy not to provide war material to Ho Chi Minh's army, or the French, but such arms regularly went to France and undoubtedly found their way to Vietnam.

Ho Chi Minh turned to renegade Japanese officers, and even some former Germans and French Foreign Legionnaires, to train his nondescript army. They already had American, French and Japanese weapons they had acquired after World War II. They became increasingly effective against the 150,000 French troops who controlled only the cities and their lines of communication. Thus a stalemate resulted.

As the "cold war" intensified with a civil war in Greece, a coup d'etat in Czechoslovakia and the Berlin blockade, Truman was more inclined to accept French control over Indochina. The Far East received a low priority in the minds of his administration officials because it was preoccupied with rehabilitation of western Europe to resist possible Russian aggression.

In April 1949, President Vincent Auriol of France had negotiated with Indochina's anti-communist parties and former Emperor Bao Dai was named chief of state of an association of states that included Tonkin, Annam and Cochin China, but France retained control of the armed forces, finances and foreign policy.

Mao Tse-tung's success in China in defeating the Nationalists and driving their armies from the mainland now convinced officials of the Truman administration that Ho Chi Minh's drive to communize Indochina had to be stopped. With passage of the Mutual Defense Assistance Act by Congress to deal with the "cold war" Truman had the authority to dispense funds to nations in the general area of China who were resisting communist expansion.

The President was concerned that the continued guerrilla war in Vietnam would weaken French support for the North Atlantic Treaty Organization which had been formed the previous year in August for the defense of Europe.

After Ho Chi Minh declared January 14, 1950, that the Democratic Republic of Vietnam was the sole legal government of Vietnam, and China and the Soviet Union immediately recognized the new government, the President's worse fears seemed to be coming true.

Secretary of State Acheson told the American people February 1 that China and the Soviet Union's support of the Vietminh should remove any "illusions as to the 'internationalist' nature of Ho Chi Minh's aims, and reveals Ho in his true colors as the mortal enemy of native independence in Indochina."

It was not revealed at the time that Ho Chi Minh controlled two-thirds of Vietnam, and that the State Department had recommended that the United States support the French in Indochina, "or face the extension of communism over the remainder of the continental areas of Southeast Asia and, possibly, farther westward." The secret report recommended that the United States furnish military aid, but not troops, to the anti-communist governments of Indochina.

Acheson recommended to the President February 2 that Vietnam, Laos and Cambodia be recognized as independent states to encourage the national aspirations of the people of those countries under non-communist governments. He also urged support for France as a friendly country and a signatory to the North Atlantic Treaty Organization. He said the United States should demonstrate its displeasure at communist tactics that, he charged, were aimed at the eventual domination of Asia, while working under the guise of indigenous nationalism.

Truman approved Acheson's recommendations at a cabinet meeting the next day that recognition be made of the states of Indochina.

France informed the Truman administration that the status of French forces in Vietnam was serious and military assistance was needed from both the United States and Great Britain.

After the French Parliament ratified agreements that granted a degree of autonomy to the associated states of Indochina the United States extended diplomatic recognition February 7 to these states with their capital at Saigon, and to the kingdoms of Laos and Cambodia. Great Britain promptly followed suit.

This was a tragic decision because it perpetuated the hated colonial role in Indochina. But the partnership between China and Russia in the Far East, and the communization of all of Indochina was considered by the Truman administration to be a threat to the interests of the United States.

The Soviet Union walked out of the UN Security Council January 13, 1950, when it refused to oust the representative of the Chinese Nationalists. The Russians also refused to take part in any other deliberations with its war-time allies. When foreign ministers of the United States, Great Britain and France met May 14 they acted without Russia in announcing the admission of West Germany to a system of international cooperation and mutual defense.

The world's uncertain peace was shattered on the morning of June 25 when seven North Korean divisions of infantry and an armored brigade of Soviet-built tanks crossed the border at 4 a.m. at the 38th parallel separating North and South Korea. The North Korean Peoples' Army advanced rapidly because the Republic of Korea Army was caught by surprise and was unprepared for the assault. The Soviet Union had provided the North Koreans with the most modern arms, while the United States had failed to equip the South Koreans with comparable military equipment when it withdrew from the peninsula the year before. Unfortunately there were few Air Force combat wings in the Far East and the United States Navy had only one cruiser, four destroyers and a few minesweepers in the Sea of Japan. However, there were substantial fleet units, including an aircraft carrier, in the Western Pacific.

The communists made two amphibious landings with 10,000 troops at Kangnung and Samchok on the east coast as they reached the outskirts of Seoul in the west on June 28.

When the border was violated in force the United States was informed immediately. The State Department requested a meeting of the United Nations Security Council which, by a vote of nine to nothing, with one abstention, and the Soviet Union representative absent, demanded withdrawal of North Korean forces. The council went on record June 27 as saying that North Korea's actions constituted a breach of the peace and asked members to render every assistance to the UN in executing this resolution.

In a message to Congress that day, President Truman said, "The attack on Korea makes it plain beyond any doubt that communism has passed beyond the use of subversion to conquer independent nations and will now use armed invasion and war. It has defied the orders of the Security Council of the United Nations—accordingly I have ordered the Seventh Fleet to prevent any attack upon Formosa. I've also directed that United States forces in the Philippines be strengthened and that military assistance to the Philippines government be acclerated. I have similarly directed acceleration of the furnishing of military assistance to the forces of France and the Associated States of Indochina, and the dispatch of a military mission to provide close working relations with these forces. I know that all members of the United Nations will consider carefully the seriousness of this latest aggression in Korea in defiance of the Charter of the United Nations. A return to the rule of force in international affairs would have far-reaching effects. The United States will continue to uphold the rule of law."

Truman's worst fears seemed to be coming true that the invasion of South Korea presaged an all-out communist offensive in the Far East.

The President met with representatives of the State and Defense Departments that evening. The Joint Chiefs of Staff recommended sending American armed forces to Korea and Truman ordered the United States Air Force and Navy to prepare to fight in Korea. The President's decision was communicated to General MacArthur in Japan, and he was instructed to assist in evacuating U.S. dependents and noncombatants. "You are authorized to take action with the Air Force and Navy to prevent the Inchon-Kimpo-Seoul area from falling into unfriendly hands."

The North Koreans beat them to it and Seoul was captured the following day.

MacArthur, Commander-in-Chief, Far East, was given permission the following day to use elements of his command to attack North Korean targets south of the 38th parallel, and the President authorized the use of ground troops, and gave permission for American aircraft to bomb targets north of the 38th parallel.

The United Nations Security Countil adopted a resolution July 7 that stated, "We welcome the vigorous support which member nations have given to the Republic of Korea. All members are requested to render additional assistance."

The council again called for an immediate ceasefire, but it was ignored.

Now that it was apparent that the conflict would not soon be resolved, Truman issued orders July 7 to increase the draft to supply additional men for the UN forces in South Korea.

The next day General MacArthur was chosen as the head of all United States forces in Korea and 11 days later the President urged a partial mobilization and the Army called up 62,000 reservists. Earlier Truman had extended the draft for another year.

MacArthur quickly realized that the South Korean Army had no recourse but to retreat to a defensible perimeter in the south and hold until American divisions could be landed. In the first 82 days, he advised his commanders to maintain a bridgehead around the southern port of Pusan.

While units of the UN command beat off waves of North Korean attacks around their dwindling perimeter at Pusan, the island of Guam was approved by the Congress August 1 as an unincorporated area of the Department of the Interior. Guamanians were now American citizens although they were not represented in Congress, and could not vote in national elections.

Task Force 77, a combined British and American Fleet, arrived off the coast of Korea July 1. In the next few days carrier attack planes bombed airfields at Taeju and North Korea's capital city of Pyongyang. The propellor planes were followed later by F9F2 jet planes that, due to their superior speed, didn't need as much time to fly the distance to the targets. This was the first time American jets were used in wartime and they destroyed five planes on the ground at the North Korean capital.

While the defense perimeter continued to shrink around Pusan carrier pilots during July claimed 38 aircraft destroyed and 27 damaged, but only two of these were in the air.

The North Koreans, with their limited airpower, found it impossible to ward off attacks and provide air assistance to their ground troops.

The Russians and Chinese had planned to give their North Korean friends large numbers of older propeller aircraft for ground support but the appearance of UN jets over North Korea made this inadvisable.

On the ground, 700 men of the United States 24th Division went into action July 7 after they were flown from Japan. They were hopelessly out-gunned, with little combat training after growing soft consigned to garrison duty in Japan. Their first objective was to block the communists from advancing along highways in the south.

Three days later, it was obvious that the outnumbered Americans and ROK troops could only take up defensive positions around Taejon.

MacArthur realized on the 18th that the 24th Division, fed piecemeal into the front action, and suffering severe casualties as a result, couldn't possibly hope to fight off four enemy divisions. Therefore the 25th Division was shuttled from Japan to Pusan by the Military Sea Transportation Service to help out.

It was also obvious that additional reinforcements would have to be thrown into the battle if American and ROK troops were not to be driven into the sea.

Pusan was so clogged with troops and military supplies that another landing site was selected. Phang, 70 miles north of Pusan, was still held by South Korean troops which held the port until the 1st Cavalry Division landed and were introduced into the fighting to reduce the enemy's drive down the Taegu-Pusan highway.

It was touch-and-go for the UN troops but they managed to hold after Air Force and Navy planes provided excellent close support on all fronts.

Meanwhile, the President asked Congress July 20 to pass a $10 billion rearmament program as a partial mobilization of American resources.

While MacArthur completed plans for an amphibious invasion of Inchon in the north in the hope of trapping the North Korean Army in the south, the communists launched their last and greatest offensive to crush the beachhead around Pusan.

MacArthur, who personally conceived the Inchon operation, had to resist opposition by the Joint Chiefs of Staff. He had considered all possibilities. He knew there were risks in such a daring maneuver but he also knew it would turn the tide in their favor. He told his staff that enemy supply lines were over-extended. "If we can seize Inchon by sea assault, those enemy lines will be severed. It will shorten the war, and save thousands of lives. The whole course of the war will be reversed, and we won't have to fight a winter campaign."

Inchon, only 15 miles from South Korea's capital of Seoul, was deep in enemy territory. Harbor tides undoubtedly are the worst in the Far East, and Inchon can be reached only through a narrow, tortuous channel.

MacArthur refused to reconsider his tactical plans and the Joint Chiefs reluctantly gave their consent.

The amphibious operation began September 15 and the Marines captured Wolmi-do, the strategic island that guarded the harbor, and Inchon fell the next day. For MacArthur the bold gamble paid off. The invasion was brilliantly conceived and masterfully executed. He wired his amphibious commander Admiral Arthur D. Struble, "The Navy and Marines have never shown more brightly than today."

In a matter of days the entire half of the peninsula below the 38th parallel was recaptured by UN forces. The North Korean army, badly beaten and almost in complete rout, fled to the north. Their greatest general, Kang Kun, was killed and his death completed the demoralization of the army.

MacArthur's imaginative strategy had transformed defeat into an overwhelming victory. The North Korean Army, which had been at Pusan'a doorstep, now ceased to exist as an effective force. Its commanders struggled to reassemble the shattered remnants for defense of the territory north of the 38th parallel.

The Republic of Korea's I Corps, near the parallel on the east coast, waited impatiently to drive into North Korea while other divisions were eager to liberate the entire peninsula.

With the North Korean Army defeated, their diplomats tried to stop the UN forces at the former dividing line. Most UN delegates felt this was an unrealistic boundary that ceased to exist after the invasion.

President Truman spoke for the United States when he said, "UN forces have a legal basis for crossing the parallel."

Andrei Vishinsky, president of the UN General Assembly, thought otherwise. He said if UN troops crossed the border, they would be the aggressors.

Warren R. Austin, United States Ambassador to the United Nations, called for the establishment of a free and independent nation to be united under a UN commission supervising general elections throughout the peninsula. He said if the Soviets were sincere in their desire for a termination of the conflict, they should agree to an eight-point proposal for unifying the nation.

While politicians fought over the issue, MacArthur made his own plans to move into North Korea. He was certain neither Russia nor Red China would interfere.

In Washington, the Joint Chiefs of Staff gave him authority to cross the parallel and complete the destruction of North Korea's armed forces. They forbade use of air or naval action, however, against Manchuria or any part of Russian territory.

General George C. Marshall, whom Truman had brought out of retirement September 21 to be Secretary of Defense, advised MacArthur eight days later that he should feel unhampered tactically and strategically.

Before MacArthur moved into North Korea he called upon the enemy to surrender.

Indian Ambassador K. M. Pannikar warned the United States October 1 that Chinese Foreign Minister Chou En-lai had told him that his nation would intervene if UN forces crossed the parallel. He said, however, they would take no action if only ROK troops crossed into North Korea.

MacArthur believed that this warning was just another threat by the communists and he advised the Defense Department not to take it seriously. When MacArthur issued his second surrender ultimatum two days later and it was ignored he prepared for the final step of moving his army all the way to the Yalu River. American troops crossed the border October 7.

Meanwhile, the Peoples Republic of China warned that they would not "stand idly by."

On the homefront the Senate Foreign Relations Committee published a report July 20 on its findings following its investigation of Senator Joseph McCarthy's statements about communism in government that he had made in February. They reported his accusations had no basis in fact.

President Truman and General MacArthur met on Wake Island on October 15 to plan the next step in the Korean War, and both men agreed on the strategy to be followed. MacArthur again assured the President that the Chinese communists would not enter the war.

On the war front itself, Lieutenant General W. H. Walker's Eighth Army ran into stiff resistance in its drive toward Pyongyang, but the capital city fell on October 19. As Walker prepared for the final push to the Yalu, UN victory over the North Koreans seemed certain by the end of October. MacArthur jubilantly told his troops they'd be home for Christmas.

When advance units of the Eighth Army neared the Yalu River disquieting reports came in October 26 that Chinese army units had crossed the river. While Major General E. A. Almond studied the reports, elements of his X Corps swept to the Manchurian border on the east coast.

Attempts to strangle enemy supply lines by UN aircraft proved futile, despite constant attacks against the rail system and highway supply points. Fast carriers were successful in destroying six major bridges across the Yalu River linking Manchuria and North Korea. But the loss of the bridges didn't stop the Chinese because they swarmed across the river after it froze over.

The bitter Korean winter made it difficult to supply the United Nations forces. For the enemy, it was a relatively simple matter because the average communist soldier needed only 10 pounds of supplies each day whereas members of the UN command used a daily average of 60 pounds. The Chinese and North Koreans, with untold millions of laborers to draw upon, used manpower to bring their supplies down the peninsula on trails and paths through the mountains. Animals were also used extensively, so even though highways and rail lines were also used, communist supplies could not be totally choked off.

In the east, United States Marines headed for the Chosin Reservoir to link up with the Eighth Army in the west for the final combined drive to the Yalu River. It wasn't until November 7 that they met strong resistance. During the latter part of the month a human wave of Chinese attacked the Marines. The hills seemed alive with Chinese troops, giving the impression to pilots overhead that the hills themselves were moving. There was only one thing for the men of the 1st Marine Division to do. They began to retreat but it was a fighting withdrawal as they headed for Hungnam where Navy transports were assembling to remove them from their untenable position.

For two weeks while they sought to avoid entrapment in bitter cold, waves of bugle-blowing, screaming Chinese tried to surround them. Marines stacked frozen Chinese bodies as "sandbags" to protect their foxholes as they continued their fighting retreat at times against 15-to-1 odds.

CHAPTER 17

A Nation Divided

THE UNEXPECTED APPEARNCE OF CHINESE SOLDIERS OCTOBER 26 brought the conflict in Korea to a sudden and shocking state, possibly heralding another world war. Although Peking radio called them volunteers, it was evident that entire Chinese divisions were involved as the 7th Regiment of the ROK 6th Division was surrounded by enemy forces after they arrived at Chosan on the Yalu River.

Advance units of the American 1st Cavalry Division were also attacked the first week of November by Chinese horsemen.

United Nations troops reached the Yalu River in force November 20. Six days later 200,000 Chinese communists ushered in a massive offensive that forced the UN troops to withdraw, and the retreat came close to being a rout because the various UN armies were so widely dispersed across the peninsula in violation of all the rules of warfare.

In New York the UN General Assembly adopted a resolution asserting its power to act on threats to peace if the UN Security Council, where the Soviet Union had a veto, was deadlocked or its proposed action was vetoed by any power.

Intelligence sourcs now identified four Red Chinese armies, prompting MacArthur to inform the United Nations November 6 that organized Chinese units were attacking its troops.

The latest bad news from the war fronts had an effect on elections November 7, and the Republicans gained five House seats and 31 in the Senate, although the Democrats maintained control of both houses. Among those elected to the Senate was Richard M. Nixon of California.

Six months earlier France had refused to agree to the rearming of West Germany for service in the North Atlantic Treaty Organization but on

December 6, with the worsening war situation in Indochina and Korea, its leaders accepted a plan for German rearmament but within the European defense community under its supreme commander.

A ban on shipment of American goods to China was imposed November 10 by the President, and on December 16 he declared a national emergency. The President also appealed to Dwight D. Eisenhower to assume command of NATO in Europe. The general took an indefinite leave of absence from Columbia University on this date. Three days later the North Atlantic Council named him supreme commander of the armed forces in Western Europe. NATO's foreign ministers had met the day before in Brussels and agreed on rearmament plans, including West Germany and the United States. Eisenhower set up SHAPE (Supreme Headquarters Allied Powers in Europe) in Paris in the spring of 1951.

With the war in Korea still going badly for United Nations forces, MacArthur sought permission to use his command to attack communist China. The ground situation worsened steadily, and the Eighth Army was soon in critical condition. It was judged so bad that General Almond's X Corps was selected for sea-lift out of North Korea with redeployment from Wonsan and Hungnam on the east coast while the Eighth Army embarked at Chinnampo and Inchon on the west coast.

During evacuations the Seventh Fleet provided daylight close air support and air cover of the embarkation areas while its planes disrupted enemy supply lines in the rear. The Hungnam evacuation was accomplished December 24. It was a humiliating defeat for American forces when they were forced to recross the 38th parallel in the western sector. It was bitterly cold and even food was in short supply as American troops had to live off the land which had already been picked clean. Weapons and ammunition froze and often became useless. The troops couldn't light fires at night to keep warm for fear of betraying their positions, and they had to wait for daylight. Winter clothing had not been provided the troops because it was believed they would be on their way home by Christmas. MacArthur had told them so months before. So they still wore summer trousers, stuffing their jackets with newspapers to keep warm. The Chinese had winter clothing, so the weather was no problem for them. By the time the Americans reached Seoul it was virtually deserted because most of the inhabitants had fled south. American jet fighters had once strafed a column of refugees and for a mile retreating vehicles had to push bodies out of the way.

The communists recaptured Seoul January 4, 1951, and continued to pursue troops of the UN command. They called the American troops "Capitalists—running dogs of Wall Streets."

The last UN ground units departed Inchon in the west on January 5 for the Pusan area.

With this dramatic reversal in Korea, new concern was voiced in Washington about Vietnam where the French were losing their war against the Vietminh to control the southern section, particularly in the hamlets. President Truman therefore authorized the signing of an agreement with France December 23 to provide Vietnam, Cambodia and Laos with military assistance, plus financial help to the Saigon government.

Although the wars in the Far East overshadowed the problems of the Middle East, temporarily resolved through the efforts of Ralph Bunche as UN mediator, Americans were reminded of his efforts in Palestine December 10 when he was given the Nobel Peace Prize in Oslo, Norway. The first black to win such a prize, he had come up the hard way by working as a janitor while he gained an education at the University of California and at Harvard.

MacArthur had been repeatedly warned about his remarks claiming that his command was being hampered by President Truman's refusal to allow the bombing of communist supply depots in China. The controversy became a political issue when the Republicans picked it up and supported the general. Truman stood fast, backed by the unanimous decision of the Joint Chiefs of Staff, that such an action would further escalate the war. MacArthur was warned again not to discuss the issue publicly, but he later openly defied the President.

February 1 the United Nations charged that communist China was responsible for aggression against Korea, despite strong objections by the Soviet Union and other members of the communist bloc.

The American people were divided on the issue of the Korean War because it continued to drag on without a resolution, although UN forces had regrouped in the south and now were fighting their way up the peninsula toward Seoul. With control of the battle lines re-established, Inchon and Kimpo air base again fell into United Nations hands, along with the industrial suburbs of Seoul although the capital didn't actually fall until March 14 of the following year.

The communists then launched an offensive in the central sector but it was brought to a standstill in savage fighting. UN forces now moved ahead on all fronts and, by the end of March, they again approached the 38th parallel.

Korea had always been a miserable place to fight a war, but no area was worse then the one along the 38th parallel with its steep hills. Many of them were of solid rock, and on top of each hill the Chinese were dug in. They fought tenaciously, extracting a terrible price on the Americans and other members of the UN command for every yard they gained.

Now a large number of replacements came to Korea, many of them veterans of World War II, who had seen a lot of combat. They were welcomed enthusiastically by those who had fought up and down the peninsula but most of the reservists who had been recalled were not happy about it.

Chinese infantry charges were particularly unnerving. At night enemy tanks would move in while bugles blared and flares lit up the battlefield. Then wave upon wave of Chinese infantry would strike at the UN lines. The Chinese lost enormous numbers of men to American artillery and small arms fire, but they kept coming.

By the end of March, with UN forces at the 38th parallel, MacArthur proposed to the communists that hostilities cease and a truce be negotiated. When his request was ignored, the Eighth Army pushed closer to the communists' main supply and assembly area. This became known as the "Iron Triangle" between Chorwon, Kumhwa and Pyongyang.

Seventh Fleet carriers were given responsibility for isolating the battlefield as well as routine support. Bridges were given top priority along the west coast.

When the Seventh Fleet was alerted to a possible invasion of Formosa it had to leave its interdiction work until the middle of the month. This gave the communists a chance to repair their bridges and to prepare for a big offensive.

The feud between MacArthur and the administration about the general's request to make attacks on mainland China reached the explosive point April 11 when Truman fired MacArthur saying he was acting "with deep regret" but that he had concluded that the general was "unable to give his whole-hearted support to the policies of the United States government and the United Nations." Lieutenant General Matthew B. Ridgway was named Far East commander. He had headed the Eighth Army in Korea.

This precipitate action was taken after House minority leader Joseph W. Martin, Jr., released a statement in which MacArthur had openly challenged the President's foreign policies in advocating a Korean truce, saying "there was no substitute for victory." MacArthur urged the United States to concentrate on Asia instead of Europe and to use Generalissimo Chiang Kai-shek's Formosa troops to open a second front on the mainland. The assumption that Chiang's troops could mount an invasion of the mainland after their failure to defeat the Chinese communists earlier was almost laughable.

The uproar that resulted brought Truman's standing with the American people to a new low. He held fast, however, saying that full and vigorous debate on national politics is "a vital element" in any free government. He warned that military commanders must be governed by policies and directives issued to them in the "manner provided by our laws."

MacArthur was invited to speak April 19 to a joint session of Congress.

"It has been said, in effect, that I am a warmonger," MacArthur told them. "Nothing could be further from the truth. I know war as few other men now living know it, and nothing to me is more revolting. I have long advocated its complete abolition as its very destructiveness on friend and foe has rendered it useless of settling international disputes. . . . But once war is forced upon us there is no other alternative than to apply every available means to bring it to a swift end. War's very object is victory . . . not prolonged indecision. In war, indeed, there can be no substitute for victory. . . .

"I am closing my 52 years of military service. When I joined the Army, even before the turn of the century, it was the fulfillment of all my boyish hopes and dreams. The world has turned over many times since my appointment at West Point and my hopes and dreams have long since vanished. But I still remember the refrain of one of the most popular barracks ballads of that day which proclaimed most proudly. . . . that old soldiers never die; they just fade away. And like the old soldier of that ballad I now close my military career and just fade away; an old soldier who tried to do his duty as God gave him the light to see that duty. Goodbye."

Members of Congress cheered him madly, and most Americans reacted likewise.

The next day he was cheered by millions in New York where he was given a "ticker-tape" parade with signs saying, "Welcome Home. Well Done."

In time the emotionalism of the moment gave way to a more sensible appraisal of the man and his long military career, and he will be largely remembered for trying to impose his will on the civilian authority of the government. President Roosevelt's earlier assessment that MacArthur and Huey Long were the two most dangerous men in America was reaffirmed.

Starting January 5 the United States Senate began debating the issue of America's military commitments in Europe, and the relative authority of the President and Congress in fulfiling the nation's obligations. Although the issue of collective security had been established after World War II, it still had its critics. But the majority of Senators April 4 endorsed the dispatch of American troops for the defense of Europe. The Senate resolution demonstrated a remarkable understanding that world peace depended, in large part, on American military participation in defending it.

Announcement in August 1949 that the Soviet Union had exploded an atomic bomb created fear and indecision in many quarters because United States possession of these deadly weapons was considered the only deterrent to the massed armies of the Soviet Union and the People's Republic of China. Most Americans had assumed that the Russians were too technologically backward to develop atomic bombs. This proved to be untrue, but the Russians had received an enormous assist from a few British and American traitors.

Klaus Fuchs, a former physicist with the Manhattan Project during development of the atomic bomb, had revealed to Great Britain's Scotland Yard that he and co-workers had passed along highly-secret data about the atomic bomb to the Soviet Union. He implicated David Greenglass, his wife, and a chemist named Harry Gold. The FBI picked them up and they were charged with espionage. They agreed to testify, if their own lives were spared. When their request was granted they revealed that Greenglass's sister Ethel and her husband Julius Rosenberg had run the spy ring. Rosenberg was investigated and it was noted that he had been discharged from the Signal Corps in 1945 because it was alleged that he was a communist. He denied the accusation, but he and his wife were arrested and charged with passing top secret information to the Soviet Union, including highly-classified secrets about the atomic bomb. The Rosenbergs denied these accusations, even when they were promised leniency if they admitted their guilt. They were tried and found guilty and sentenced to death. A fellow defendant, Martin Sobell, was sentenced to 30 years in prison. Judge Irving R. Kaufman told them their crime was "worse than murder."

Their trial was greeted with outrage by some Americans who claimed that the FBI had changed evidence to cover up discrepancies in the testimony by Gold and Greenglass.

They were electrocuted June 19, 1953, after President Eisenhower twice denied their pleas for clemency. The first Americans ever to be executed for espionage in peacetime, they died still proclaiming their innocence.

In Korea, General Van Fleet's "Lincoln Line" five miles north of Seoul stopped the Chinese offensive May 1. Deep trenches, bunkers and heavy field fortifications protected by minefields and barbed wire were established much like the front lines in World War I. By the end of May UN forces in the eastern sector were routinely defeating the enemy in their battles, while forces in the west were putting the squeeze on the communists.

Leaders on both sides realized in June that the war in Korea was stalemated. The Chinese had found it impossible to drive UN forces out of Korea and they had been defeated so badly that they were desperate. Morale was so low that 10,000 Chinese troops surrendered. It was also realized by the heads of the UN forces that they had no hope of uniting Korea by force without extending the war beyond the peninsula.

The Soviet delegate to the United Nations, Jacob A. Malik, proposed immediate discussions June 23 for a ceasefire between the parties involved in the conflict.

Armistice discussions started July 8, 1951, at Kaesong with Vice Admiral C. Turner Joy, Navy commander in the Far East as chief of the UN delegation. These discussions were transferred to Panmunjom in October.

There were limited attempts to change certain tactical positions but the front stabilized along a line between Munsan and Kosong. Meanwhile, the sea and air war continued.

While truce negotiations convened at Panmunjom, many UN commanders feared the Chinese would stall the negotiations while they prepared for a big offensive.

Rear Admiral Perry, commander of Task Force 77, described the situation by saying, "Operations resolved themselves into a day-by-day routine where stamina replaced glamor and persistence was pitted against oriental perseverence."

Although airpower failed to disrupt ground action during the preceding months due to failure of military supplies, the fact that Manchuria was politically "off-limits" should be considered as a contributing factor.

While jet aircraft made the headlines, the Douglas AD Skyraider proved to be the war's most outstanding performer. Its versatility was unusual in an attack airplane and it could carry an ordnance load of 5,000 pounds for an average carrier mission and an overload on shorter missions up to 10,000 pounds.

Air supremacy was attained early in Korea and while the ground forces fought magnificently, Navy and Air Force planes destroyed every worthwhile target.

General James Van Fleet, who had taken command of the Eighth Army April 22 just before the Chinese launched their huge offensive, said after the offensive failed, "The Chinese had unlimited manpower to keep highways and rail systems operating. If we had ever put on some pressure and made him fight, we would have given him an insoluble supply problem. Instead, we fought the communists on their own terms, even though we had the advantage of flexibility, mobility and firepower. Interdiction failed because of the primitive nature of the enemy's exposed supply network."

Both sides agreed to send negotiators to Panmunjom and try to find a common ground for agreement to end hostilities. There was sporadic fighting, often bloody, but the ground action was limited to raids and patrols.

Forty-nine nations—not including the Soviet Union—took part in drawing up the Japanese Peace Treaty that recognized Japan's full sovereignty and independence although Japan agreed to give up control of all territories outside of her main islands. The United States was given the right to occupy the Ryukyu and Bonin Islands with the understanding that they might be placed under UN trusteeship with the United States as sole administrator. Japan also agreed to permit the United States to maintain military forces in her country. The Pacific war ended officially April 15, 1952, when Truman signed the treaty.

President Truman signed the Mutual Security Act on October 10 to provide $10 billion worth of aid to foreign countries. Now the Federal Republic of Germany became a full-fledged partner in Allied defense plans as Truman declared the war with Germany officially over two weeks later.

With Presidential elections scheduled for November, General Dwight D. Eisenhower let it be known January 7 that he would accept a draft for the Republican nomination.

Republicans had been urging the general to make known his present political views, in part because they believed he was the only candidate who could defeat the Democrats, and their conviction that only he could resolve the impasse in the Korean War.

Although President Truman could have legally run for another term in office—his first term after assuming the Presidency when Roosevelt died was not a full term—he announced March 30 that he would "not be a candidate for re-election." For the first time since 1932 the nomination was wide open to any Democrat who wished to seek the highest office in the land.

General Eisenhower's request to be relieved from his duties as supreme commander of Allied troops in Europe was accepted by Truman April 28 and the President named General Ridgway to the post. On this date, Truman also formally announced the end of the state of war between the United States and Japan.

The United States, Great Britain and five other European nations agreed May 27 to form a European Defense Community with joint armed forces. In August, Truman signed the protocol to the North Atlantic Treaty that extended its defense guarantees to include the European Defense Community, but France rejected these guarantees.

The use of atomic weapons in support of ground troops gained more credibility May 8 when Secretary of the Army Frank Pace announced that such weapons had been dramatically reduced in size to fit into a new atomic cannon. But even more disturbing to many Americans was the April 6 announcement that the United States was developing a hydrogen bomb.

With Ridgway's appointment as NATO commander, General Mark Clark was appointed May 12 to head United Nations troops in the Far East. Meanwhile, the war in Korea remained a stalemate as the third year was ushered in June 25. Opposing armies were still dug in, Navy ships were blockading the coastline, while UN planes roamed North Korea seeking targets to prevent a massive buildup of Chinese troops while negotiators haggled at the conference table.

In the early days of the war, when victory seemed assured, 13 major electric power plants in North Korea were spared. Commanders knew their destruction would be needless and costly to a unified nation.

While negotiations continued to drag, reconsideration was given to these strategic targets. They were legitimate military targets, providing power for factories in North Korea and Manchuria, so their destruction was ordered in June. In a magnificent display of precision bombing during a two-day period the power complexes were destroyed. North Korea's electric power output was reduced to the point that even the capital of Pyongyang was without power.

With no progress in the armistice talks, Far Eastern Air Force Headquarters in Tokyo authorized an attack on the North Korean capital. Pyongyang had been spared while the truce talks continued but commanders hoped to add a further note of persuasion by striking hard at the capital.

In a joint Navy/Air Force operation a total of 1,400 tons of bombs along with 23,000 gallons of napalm were dropped on the capital by 1,254 aircraft. Pyongyang radio stations called the attacks "brutal," charging they were ordered in retaliation for the failure of the armistice talks. They didn't minimize the damage, claiming 1,500 buildings had been destroyed while another 900 were damaged.

They hadn't seen the last of these bombers because Pyongyang was struck again August 29 during an "All United Nations Air Effort" in which 1,400 planes took part. After the raid much of Pyongyang was a rubble heap.

These strikes, more than half the total air effort during the summer of 1952, were credited with disrupting several major communist buildups.

While this state of affairs existed in the Far East, President Truman met with General Eisenhower on June 1 after the general relinquished his European command. Eisenhower's decision to accept nomination as a

Republican was a bitter disappointment for Truman, who had once offered to support the general as a Democratic Party candidate.

Two weeks later the President attended ceremonies at Groton, Connecticut, as the keel was laid for America's first atomic-powered submarine, the "Nautilus." It was the first of many such affairs that were to drastically change the United States Navy's ability to account for itself in a rapidly-changing world for future wars at sea.

Eisenhower won easily July 12 on the first ballot at the Republican National Convention in Chicago and Richard M. Nixon of California was selected as his running mate. The Republican platform called for a balanced budget, a reduction in the national debt and retention of the Taft-Hartley Act.

When the Democrats convened in Chicago on July 21 interest centered on Adlai E. Stevenson of Illinois now that Truman had taken himself out of the running. He had served in the State Department as an assistant secretary in 1945, helped organize the United Nations, and had been elected governor of Illinois in 1948.

For their platform the Democrats agreed to advocate continuance of Roosevelt's New Deal and Truman's Fair Deal policies, repeal the Taft-Hartley Act and seek federal civil rights legislation.

Stevenson easily won the nomination of his party for president and Senator John Sparkman of Alabama was nominated for vice-president.

In October Eisenhower spoke in Detroit, stating his political beliefs. "The first task of a new administration will be to review and re-examine every course of action open to us with one goal in view—to bring the Korean War to an early and honorable end. That is my pledge to the American people. For this task, a wholly new administration is necessary. The reason for this is simple. The old administration cannot be expected to repair what it failed to prevent.

"Where will the new administration begin? It will begin with the President taking a simple, firm resolution. That resolution will be: to forego the diversions of politics, to concentrate on the job of ending the Korean War. . . . until that job is honorably done. That job requires a personal trip to Korea. I shall make that trip. Only in that way could I learn how best to serve the American people in the cause of peace. I shall go to Korea."

It was a grandstand attempt to win the election, but it was far more politically sensible than Stevenson's vague platitudes. The people listened carefully and made their decision as to which candidate seemed most qualified to assume the Presidency in this solemn hour in the nation's history.

The American people were confused and angry by what was happening to their country. Senator McCarthy's accusations about communists in government had upset them, but Senator Estes Kefauver's crime probe the previous year that a syndicate of racketeers controlled gambling casinos in America was equally disturbing.

CHAPTER 18

"I Shall Go to Korea."

WHEN THE ELECTION RETURNS WERE IN ON NOVEMBER 4 EISENHOWER had won handily with 33.9 million votes out of the 61.3 million cast versus Stevenson's 27.3 million. Smaller parties accounted for the remainder. Eisenhower carried all but nine states and his electoral count was even more impressive—442 to 89.

President-elect Eisenhower kept his promise to the American people and went to Korea in mid-December. During a three-day visit he toured the battlefields, was briefed by field commanders, and met with diplomatic leaders in Seoul including South Korean President Syngman Rhee.

Eisenhower reported that he had found "no panaceas, no trick solutions" to bring about an end to the war, but that he was confident much could be done "and will be done" to improve the UN's position. He warned that a definitive victory could not be achieved without "enlarging the war." He said he was confident, despite differences between the allies, that the war could be ended, saying, "we are all here together to see it through."

Premier Joseph Stalin, dictator of the Union of Soviet Socialist Republics, died March 5, 1953, and the administration had to review its thoughts about containment of communism. It soon became apparent with the elevation of Georgi Malenkov that the hardliners were still in power in Russia.

Eisenhower made a fateful commitment March 26 when he offered to aid France in its war with the communist forces in Indochina. The war had been going badly for the French, and France's premier René Mayer had sought such support.

Truce talks in Korea, which had resumed in early April following the

197

communist acceptance of a UN invitation to exchange seriously sick and wounded prisoners, reached agreement five days later. In "Operation Little Switch" starting April 20, 1953, some 6,670 communist and 684 UN prisoners were exchanged.

Now steps were taken to reopen the main truce talks and, after negotiations recessed, they began again April 26. While truce talks bogged down on the question of disposition of the Chinese and North Koreans who refused repatriation, Task Force 77 and Air Force groups continued their rail cutting, close air support and attacks into North Korea. Just when it appeared that hope for a settlement was futile, the communist representative at Panmunjom asked May 7 for the establishment of a neutral commission to discuss the problem of those 114,500 Chinese and 34,000 North Koreans. They suggested it be called the National Repatriation Commission to be composed of the four that had already been agreed upon as members of a neutral supervisory commission.

UN negotiators made a counter-proposal May 13 that all non-repatriates be released immediately after an armistice.

Syngman Rhee, president of the Republic of Korea, announced his government would never consent to an armistice that left his nation divided. He threatened to continue the war with his own troops. This further complicated the situation but June 4 the communists agreed to interview the Chinese and Koreans who refused repatriation under supervision of a five-power commission. In this way they hoped to induce them to come home.

The demarcation line posed another stumbling block and heavy enemy action was initiated to gain new ground before the armistice was signed.

During this period the United States Navy's carriers and Air Force units engaged in intense air activities to help throw back the communist armies.

At last a truce agreement was reached June 16 at Panmunjom.

President Rhee promptly released 27,000 anti-communist prisoners in his custody. He said if the United States signed the armistice his government would consider it an act of betrayal and appeasement. The communists reacted furiously and immediately began one of the heaviest attacks of the war. It was directed particularly at the ROK II Corps. While they fought courageously, giving ground only when it was absolutely essential, American Air Force and Navy planes went to their assistance.

Two days after Rhee released the prisoners President Eisenhower sent him a message that he had violated United Nations command authority.

The communist offensive subsided July 19, and their hard-won miles were quickly reduced by vigorous counterattacks by UN armies.

Unfortunately President Rhee's release of the prisoners prolonged the war for five weeks and UN troops suffered 46,000 additional casualties and the communists at least 75,000.

The armistice was signed July 27, ending a war that had cost the United States 142,091 casualties and $20 billion. It had been one of the most savage wars in American history and no clear-cut military victory was achieved.

Regardless of whether the United States won a victory or not, it was a remarkable demonstration of collective security by the new United Nations. Expansion of the war had been prevented, and the horror of a nuclear holocaust had been averted.

Premier Georgi Malenkov's disclosure August 8, 1953, that the Soviet Union knew how to produce a hydrogen bomb was met by fear and concern in America, with some doubts that they had truly done so. Those doubts were laid to rest when the United States Atomic Energy Commission confirmed the Soviet Union's announcement on the 12th that such a bomb had indeed been exploded.

Major Charles E. "Chuck" Yeager flew more than 1600 miles an hour December 16, a new airspeed record. He made the flight in the Bell X-1A rocket-powered plane.

Secretary of State John Foster Dulles caused an uproar January 12, 1954, when he announced a basic shift in the foreign policy of the United States. Instead of the Truman policy of containment, he revealed the Eisenhower administration was committed to a policy of "massive retaliation." Criticism from the communist bloc aligned with Russia was predictable, but there were many other critics among members of nations who had long backed American politics, as well as many Americans who decried a policy that relied almost solely on nuclear retaliation. Adlai Stevenson called the new policy "The power of positive brinking."

The situation in Indochina had deteriorated all through the Korean War and now France's military situation was acute. At a meeting in Berlin February 18 the United States, Great Britain, France and the Soviet Union met to discuss what could be done about the situation. They also reviewed again their long-standing disagreement about the reunification of Germany, with the Russians adamantly opposed to such a move.

France's military situation in Indochina had deteriorated markedly since the first of the year, and the French people were fed up with the continued drain on their country's manpower and resources. This attitude, despite the fact that the United States had borne the greater portion of the military expenses, was crucial in demands by the French people to their leaders that the war be ended. French leaders had sought a negotiated settlement, but the Eisenhower administration resisted such a move, believing it would turn Southeast Asia over to the communists.

Although the United States Air Force now had separate status in the Defense Department, there had long been a need for its own academy similar to West Point for the Army and Annapolis for the Navy. The President approved the United States Air Force Academy on April 1 and plans for its construction got under way at Colorado Springs, Colorado. The first class convened in Denver the following year, and the academy moved to its permanent site three years later.

Although the administration had resisted France's efforts to negotiate a settlement with Ho Chi Minh and his communist government in North Vietnam, promising more military aid, members of Congress voiced objections to further military assistance unless Great Britain made a similar commitment. Secretary of State Dulles repeatedly urged American support to prevent the fall of Dien Bien Phu, the base in North Vietnam where the French foolishly sought to make a stand in a desperate attempt to destroy the Vietminh forces.

Eisenhower's reluctance to intercede with American combat forces on behalf of the French in Vietnam was based on military studies within the Department of Defense that stressed that France still followed an arrogant colonial policy that had so alienated the Vietnamese people that victory was impossible. Military strategists were critical of the French commander's failure to interdict Vietminh supply lines to Dien Bien Phu and to use air strikes against concentrations around the beleaguered bastion.

Eisenhower sent a fact-finding team under Major General James M. Gavin to Vietnam. Their conclusions, reported later to the President, were that eight United States divisions, plus 15 engineer battalions, would be necessary in the Hanoi delta, and that Hainan Island (a part of the People's Republic of China) would have to be seized if the situation were to be reversed. Gavin's team reported that support requirements for such a large force would pose enormous problems because Southeast Asia had no good seaports, airfields and land communications.

As a former military man, Eisenhower recognized the problems.

Gavin said later, "We finally decided when we were all through that what we were talking about doing was going to war with Red China under conditions that were appallingly disadvantageous."

Although the President refused to commit American combat forces, he authorized Far East commanders to furnish all-out logistics support to the French even when it meant removing vital equipment from American units. Sizable numbers of aircraft were involved, plus missiles and ammunition.

Actually, the French had more fighter-bombers and light bombers in the Hanoi area than they could keep in commission due to personnel and maintenance problems.

While a 19-nation conference was meeting in Geneva attempting to work out a truce, the Vietminh began their final attack May 7 at Dien Bien Phu. That afternoon, 55 days after the attack began, General de Castries and his staff surrendered. The French had lost 5,000 troops, including colonials. Eleven thousand men surrendered and most were severely debilitated by wounds, malaria and malnutrition. The conference in Geneva had convened in April to formally end the Korean War, and to seek a compromise settlement for Indochina. A spokesman for the Vietminh insisted that the French had to withdraw from all parts of Vietnam. For the present, he said, the country should be partitioned at the 13th parallel and elections should be held six months after an armistice.

An armistice was signed July 21 after seven years of fighting in Indochina. Its terms divided Vietnam at approximately the 17th parallel into northern and southern parts. The northern section was turned over to the Vietminh and French troops withdrew.

After the formal peace treaty was signed only 4,000 of the 11,000 men who surrendered at Dien Bien Phu were still alive for repatriation. For Ho Chi Minh and the Vietminh it was a decisive victory. When France drastically reduced its military operations in Indochina, the United States on June 15 cut off all military aid.

CHAPTER 19

"Have You No Sense of Decency?"

SENATOR JOSEPH MCCARTHY'S SENSATIONAL WITCH-HUNTING CHARGES about communists in government had reached the hysterical stage in the spring. But when he made charges about infiltration of communists into the United States Army, specifically its base at Fort Monmouth, New Jersey, the televised sub-committee hearings took on a new character. Out of a desire not to become involved in McCarthy's tactics of making accusations without proof, far too many responsible Americans—including the President and most members of Congress—had permitted his unwarranted allegations to go unchallenged. The legal rights of the innocent were ignored until Joseph N. Welch, a noted trial lawayer from Boston, was hired by the Army as its counsel.

Welch turned the hearings around June 9 when committee counsel Roy Cohn was in the witness chair trying to parry Welch's barbed thrusts of sarcasm. The discussion centered on getting communist agents out of war plants before the sun set that night. Welch's line of seeming good-natured ridicule had a serious intent that wasn't apparent to Cohn at first, and McCarthy didn't realize that they were being set up. Both sides had agreed that Welch would not bring up the subject of Cohn's non-service in the military and that he had avoided the draft if McCarthy refrained from bringing up the name of Fred Fisher, a young Harvard Law School man who worked at Welch's Hale and Dorr firm in Boston. Fisher had been a member of the National Lawyers Guild, an organization on the attorney general's list as a communist front. Whether the guild was such a front had not been proved but such a charge, proven or not, could destroy a person's chances for earning a living. By now Fisher was a solid Republican, and certainly no communist, and his law firm considered him too valuable to let him go.

McCarthy broke in. He said to Welch, "I have been rather bored with your phony requests to Mr. Cohn here that he personally get every communist out of government before sundown. Therefore, we will give you information about the young man in your own organization. Whether you knew he was a member of that communist organization or not, I don't know. I assume you did not, Mr. Welch, because I get the impression that, while you are quite an actor, you play for a laugh, I don't think you have any conception of the danger of the Communist Party. I think you are unknowingly aiding it when you try to burlesque this hearing in which we are attempting to bring out the facts."

Welch sought to intervene, but McCarthy cut him off. Turning to an aide, he said, "Jim, will you get the news story to the effect that this man belonged to this communist-front organization. Will you get the citations showing that this was the legal arm of the Communist Party, and the length of time that he belonged, and the fact that he was recommended by Mr. Welch? I think that should be in the record."

Welch's tone changed from his usual bantering, scornful approach. Now he was serious and there was accusation in his words. While Americans stared expectantly at their television sets Welch said, "You won't need anything in the record when I have finished telling you this. Until this moment I think I never really gauged your cruelty or your recklessness. . . . Little did I dream you could be so reckless or so cruel as to do an injury to that lad. . . . I fear he shall always bear a scar needlessly inflicted by you. If it were in my power to forgive you for your reckless cruelty, I would do so. I like to think I am a gentleman, but your forgiveness will have to come from someone other than me."

McCarthy suddenly realized that he had trapped himself, and his attempts to recover his dignity were pathetic. "Mr. Welch talks about this being cruel and reckless. . . . He was just baiting; he has been baiting Mr. Cohn here for hours. . . ."

Welch was unforgiving. "Senator, may we not drop this? . . . Let us not assassinate this lad further, Senator. You have done enough." There were tears in Welch's eyes, and in the eyes of most of the millions who watched this travesty of justice on television. "Have you no sense of decency, sir, at long last? Have you no sense of decency?"

Although Welch's approach to the hearings had seemed to be ineffectual at first, with many people in and out of government highly critical of his casual approach, his actions were successful and deliberately planned. When that day's hearing ended, for all intents and purposes

Cohn and McCarthy were finished, although their hearings continued to drag on, but the "four-year binge of hysteria and character assassination" was about to end.

Senator Arthur Watkins, who had headed the Special Senate Committee to investigate Senator McCarthy's Permanent Subcommittee on Investigations, and his committee members voted unanimously September 27 that McCarthy should be censured by the Senate. This action was taken by the whole Senate December 2 after Republican leaders abandoned him and the Republican defeat in the fall elections had caused McCarthy to lose his position as head of the committee.

The committee's report was devastating: "The Senator from Wisconsin, Mr. McCarthy, in. . . . charging three members of the Select Committee with 'deliberate deception and fraud'. . . . in repeatedly describing this special Senate session as a 'lynch bee' in a nation-wide television and radio show. . . . and in characterizing the said committee as the 'unwitting handmaiden,' 'involuntary agent,' and 'attorneys in fact' of the Communist Party, and in charging that the said committee in writing its report 'imitated Communist methods' . . . acted contrary to senatorial ethics and tended to bring the Senate into dishonor and disrepute, to obstruct the constitutional processes of the Senate, and to impair its dignity; and such conduct is hereby condemned."

The vote for censure was 67 to 22. The door finally closed on a chapter in American history where few of the thousands who had taken part in hearings, emerged with any dignity.

Three years later McCarthy died of alcoholism in obscurity, lamented only by a few friends and members of his family. But McCarthyism has become synonomous with violation of civil rights through his investigative excesses.

The United States had long supported French military operations in Indochina, but now that France had decided to pull back its forces below the demilitarized zone agreed to at Geneva, Eisenhower agreed to increase United States assistance to South Vietnam. The agreement had called for reunification elections, but the communists ignored this section of the treaty. The President agreed January 1, 1955, to send aid to Southeast Asia along with civilian advisers. Later, military personnel were dispatched to train South Vietnamese troops. Thus began an escalation of support to Southeast Asian nations that reached heights not foreseen at the time. Cambodia, Laos and South Vietnam received $216 million in aid during 1955 through the United States Foreign Operations Administration.

The Southeast Asia defense treaty, signed the previous September, became effective in February after ratification by Congress. Dulles hoped that the new organization (SEATO) would be an effective shield against internal aggression and that South Vietnam would only need military forces against such aggression. But the treaty was not as strong as he would have liked. He was particularly disturbed by Article IV because it did not pledge automatic response to aggression with force. The article was weasel worded, saying, in part, that each signatory agrees to "act to meet the common danger in accordance with its constitutional processes."

The American Joint Chiefs of Staff disagreed. They believed that military assistance should provide not only internal security, but limited defense against external attack. With money scarce to build up the armed forces of the United States, the Joint Chiefs did not recommend the expenditure of funds for South Vietnam until a stable government was formed.

Dulles understood the view of Defense Department officials, but he believed that well-trained Vietnamese armed forces would strengthen Ngo Dinh's government. At the time the Vietnamese Army was a collection of former French colonial troops with little command experience and little or no support forces. Therefore, the secretary insisted that the Joint Chiefs provide funds to establish five Vietnamese divisions for internal security that could also be used to provide a limited response for external attack, plus the buildup of an adequate air force. He was aware that such forces would take two to three years to train. Most Vietnamese pilots still flew with French squadrons.

The National Security Council backed Dulles and political considerations were allowed to override military objections. An agreement was reached for a Vietnamese army of 94,000, and the United States agreed to train it.

A Military Advisory Group was split into two parts, one for South Vietnam and the other for Cambodia, to adjust to the political realities when the United States and Cambodia signed an agreement May 16, 1955, for direct military aid.

In South Vietnam the Military Assistance Advisory Group was given two objectives—to create a conventional army of divisional units and supporting forces by January 1956, and to establish programs to maintain the efficiency of this force.

The fact that the French military budget for calendar year 1956 made no provision for Indochina was a sure indication to Americans that France's military presence in Vietnam was coming to an end. The French High Command left Saigon by the end of 1955, and officials were given six months to decide on French or Vietnamese citizenship. The last French forces departed April 28, 1956, ending 94 troubled years that had brought frustration and tragedy to both countries.

Now it was America's war.

Hydrogen bomb tests had been conducted in the Pacific, but much of their results remained classified. However, February 15 the Atomic Energy Commission revealed that a hydrogen bomb had the capacity to devastate a 700-square-mile area.

Although the exact number of atomic bombs held by the world's major nuclear powers was highly classified, there were reports that the Soviet Union and the United States between them had more than enough to kill everyone on earth many times over. The Russians were said to have 1,000 atomic bombs, while the United States had 4,000 bombs and missile warheads.

The threat of their use became a strong possibility when President Eisenhower announced March 10 that in the event of war the United States would use nuclear weapons.

The uneasy peace between the Arabs and the Jews in the Middle East was broken February 28 when Israeli and Egyptian troops clashed on the Gaza strip. The following day Israel was condemned as the aggressor. A ceasefire wasn't worked out until September 4.

April 1 the United States Senate ratified the treaties ending the occupation of West Germany and the nation became the Federal Republic of Germany. The former occupation forces now became security troops, and a month later West Germany became a member of NATO.

President Eisenhower signed a peace treaty with Austria on June 25 after prolonged negotiations involving all major powers. The treaty established Austria's borders at the pre-1938 lines and guaranteed the nation's independence.

The President's long-sought summit conference with the Soviet Union was held in Geneva during July with representatives of the Soviet Union, Great Britain and France.

In addressing the meeting, Eisenhower offered to provide within our country facilities for aerial photography to the other country—we to provide you the facilities within our country, ample facilities for aerial reconnaissance, where you can take all the pictures you choose and take them to your own country to study; you to provide exactly the same facilities for us and we to make these examinations—and by this step to convince the world that we are providing as between ourselves against the possibility of great surprise attack, thus lessening danger and releasing tension. Likewise, we will make more easily attainable a comprehensive and effective system of inspection and disarmament, because what I propose, I assure you, would be but a beginning."

His "Open Skies" proposal was scornfully rejected by the Soviet Union.

The United States and its allies also discussed reunification of Germany with officials of the Soviet Union but met with strong resistance. The Russians said they opposed such a step because of Germany's remilitarization, and rejected Allied proposals for ensuring European security. Instead, they insisted on a European mutual defense alliance to include Germany but not the United States. The western nations rejected this attempt to divide them, and the conference ended on July 23 in failure although it was agreed that their foreign ministers would meet again in October to discuss the issues dividing them.

The United States announced on July 29 that it was prepared to become involved in space projects. It was revealed that the first earth-orbiting American satellite would be launched some time in 1957.

Americans were shocked to learn on September 24 that the President had suffered a heart atatck in Colorado. His illness precipitated a minor crisis in government because the Constitution was not clear about presidential incapacity during an illness. The rule about succession was clear in the event of a President's death, but not when he was physically unable to perform the duties of his office when he was ill.

The impact of his heart attack, and rumors about the seriousness of his condition, dropped like a bombshell on the stock exchanges. Stocks suffered their sharpest decline since 1929, with a loss of $14 billion. This was the greatest loss in American history as more than 7.7 million shares were traded on September 26.

With an uncertain peace in the world, America continued to build up its defenses. The "Sea Wolf," second of the United States Navy's nuclear submarines, was launched on July 21 and the carrier U.S.S. "Saratoga" was launched at New York's Naval Shipyard in Brooklyn. One of the huge new carriers designed for jet aircraft, the "Saratoga" had a displacement of 59,600 tons.

In the Middle East, President Nasser's Egypt received military equipment from the Soviet Union. Israel promptly sought to purchase military arms from the United States but President Eisenhower refused their request.

The administration's international relations continued to deteriorate when Iceland on March 28 demanded removal of all NATO forces from the island. The United States maintained that its air base there was an important link in a network of bases around the world. After strong protests, the government of Iceland agreed in November that the Keflavik Air Base could remain.

The United States had never developed a coherent foreign policy for Indochina and by the middle of 1956 there was still no agreement among American political and military officials as to whether subversion or invasion posed the greatest threat.

Concern for Eisenhower's health had been strong ever since his heart attack the previous year. It surged anew on June 9 when he was hospitalized with an attack of ileitis. This inflammation of part of the small intestine was not serious, although it required surgery.

An important pact was signed July 22 by the President when he approved the "Panama Declaration" along with 18 other heads of state. It confirmed principles established by the Organization of American States, and guaranteed use of the Panama Canal.

The United States's action a week earlier in cancelling the Aswan Dam project had infuriated President Nasser. In defiance, he nationalized Egypt's Suez Canel and warned that Israel would not receive protection for its shipping. Nasser said revenues from the canal would be used to finance the Aswan Dam.

When the Democrats met in convention August 16 in Chicago they again nominated Adlai Stevenson for President although former President Truman had backed Averell Harriman. Tennessee's Estes Kefauver was nominated as the party's candidate for vice-president, defeating Senator John F. Kennedy from Massachusetts who had made a strong bid for the office.

The Republicans met on August 22 in San Francisco and there was no contest for nomination of the President and Vice-President. The convention voted overwhelmingly to support the ticket of Eisenhower and Nixon. Representatives of 70 nations met in New York City October 26 to sign the Statute of the International Atomic Energy Agency. When it went into force July 29 in the following year it helped to promote the peaceful uses of atomic energy as each nation agreed not to use atomic energy to further any military purposes.

In the fall war threatened to engulf the world again. Violence had escalated ever since Polish workers rose against the communists in Posnan June 28, although the uprising was quickly crushed. Then, a month later, Egypt had taken control of the Suez Canal, and October 29 Israeli forces attacked the Egyptians in the Sinai Desert while British and French forces invaded Egypt November 2 at Port Said. Eisenhower was incensed by these actions because he opposed the use of force to solve the area's problems. He used the full power of American diplomacy—in blunt terms to the governments involved in the invasion of Egypt. A ceasefire was arranged November 5 in the Sinai Peninsula, and a UN force was dispatched to keep the antagonists apart in Egypt.

Police in Budapest, Hungary, fired upon demonstrators October 23 when they demanded that the government form a democracy and expell the Russians. A week later the government promised free elections and a policy of neutrality and Soviet troops supposedly began to leave Budapest and the rest of Hungary. Instead, Soviet tanks and troops swept through the capital November 4 and brutally crushed all opposition. Three days later the Soviet Army was in control of the nation. Premier Imre Nagy had appealed to the United Nations for help, but there was little it could do without precipitating World War III. The Soviet Union established a communist dictatorship in Hungary and 160,000 people—mostly students and workers—fled across its borders, principally into Austria. It wasn't announced at the time but Nagy and the leaders of the revolt were executed.

Although President Eisenhower's re-election had never been in doubt, his strong stand against the warring nations in the Middle East helped him to easily defeat Adlai Stevenson with a plurality of 9.5 million votes and an electoral count of 457 to 73. It was a great personal victory, but the President's popularity didn't extend to most Republican candidates for Congress. Democrats retained control of the Senate and the House; the first time in 108 years that the winning candidate for President failed to help his party to establish control of at least one house of Congress.

The United States faced another crisis in the final days of 1956 that was quickly appreciated. Fulgencio Batista, an army sergeant who had led a revolt in 1934 that overthrew the regime of Cuba's President Gerardo Machado, had then established a police state. Corruption was rampant on the island as officials accepted payoffs to permit gambling in Cuba. Cubans were forced to pay bribes for public services and Batista and his cohorts enriched themselves with frequent raids on the nation's treasury. It was a brutal regime in which dissenters were routinely murdered.

Fidel Castro Ruz, an attorney in his 30s, landed a band of 12 revolutionaries in Cuba on Christmas Day. The small group evaded Batista's armed forces and set up headquarters in the jungles of the Sierra Maestra mountains. Within two years he had a force of 2,000 guerrillas including his brother Raul and Ernesto Che Guevara. The latter was an Argentine physician, but most of Castro's followers were young and from Cuba's middle class. Businessmen and landowners, who detested Batista, gave Castro's followers the money to equip them with modern weapons. United States Government aid helped Castro's rise to power by cutting off arms shipments to Batista's Army. Initially, Castro's attempts to overthrow the Batista dictatorship were welcomed by United States officials because they believed he would bring democracy to Cuba. They were soon disillusioned when Castro established military tribunals for political opponents, and sent hundreds to prison when they disagreed with his growing communism. The final disillusionment came when Castro disavowed Cuba's 1952 military pact with the United States, and confiscated American investments in banks and industries. He seized large American landholdings which he first turned into collective farms and then into Soviet-style state farms. But this was just the beginning of Castro's plans for Cuba and his attempts to eliminate all American interests.

President Eisenhower faced these challenges to American power and diplomacy with a forthright proposal January 5, 1957, when he addressed a joint session of Congress. What became known as the "Eisenhower Doctrine," was a proposal that the United States aid Middle Eastern nations who were threatened by communism, and provide arms to any country requesting such aid.

Five days later in his State-of-the-Union address, the President called upon Congress to pass his proposal. But he also warned of the dangers of inflation to the nation's economy.

Secretary of State Dulles re-emphasized the administration's concern about the Middle East as a "powder keg" January 14 when he declared that the threat of communism in the region was at its most critical point in years.

Eisenhower's inauguration was a low-keyed affair this year because January 20 fell on a Sunday and he was sworn in during a private ceremony. But there was a public swearing-in the next day at the east portico of the White House and 750,000 people watched the inaugural parade.

In January the Soviet Union proposed that North and South Vietnam be admitted to the United Nations as separate states. This proposal surprised American officials because it was contrary to the line long taken by North Vietnam's Ho Chi Minh that all of Vietnam should be unified. To achieve this end, the communist government had organized 37 armed companies in the Mekong Delta in South Vietnam. Throughout the year they were successful in killing a great many minor South Vietnamese officials.

The "Eisenhower Doctrine," presented to Congress in January, was approved March 9. In seeking to prevent subversion or conquest of Middle Eastern states, the Congress approved funds to supply economic and military assistance to those nations threatened by communist aggression, and even authorized the use of America's armed forces if they were needed.

With the "Cold War" heating up, Secretary of States Dulles reassured America's allies May 2 that Europe would continue to receive American economic and military backing. At a meeting of the North Atlantic Council in Bonn he said that the United States would maintain its military forces in Europe at their current levels.

South Vietnamese President Ngo Dinh Diem was warmly greeted in Washington nine days later. During meetings between Eisenhower and Diem their commitment to one another was reaffirmed and Eisenhower assured South Vietnam's leader that the United States was dedicated to preventing the spread of world communism.

CHAPTER 20

Troop Pull-back in Far East

PRESIDENT EISENHOWER AND HIS SECRETARY OF STATE JOHN FOSTER
Dulles in 1957 seriously considered pulling all American forces out of
Japan and the rest of East Asia. This was not revealed until 1991 when
secret United States Government files were declassified.

The accidental killing of a Japanese woman by an American soldier
on guard duty initiated serious discussions within the administration
about a pull-out because the woman's death while scavenging for spent
rifle shells aroused indignation among the Japanese people. Eisenhower
called Dulles to tell him, "We have to look at the Asiatic countries and
see if they (American troops) should stay there. If they hate us, (we) can't
do it."

The President discussed the matter with congressional leaders, telling
them that the incident "gave reason for a pressing review of the desirabil-
ity of maintaining U.S. forces in the Far East." Dulles also called for a
full review about the stationing of American troops in Asiatic countries.

In the 1950s, American government officials mistakenly viewed Japan
as a defeated power that would remain economically weak and dependent
upon the United States but incongruously believed it should be built up
militarily to take over most of the United States's defense responsibilities
in the Far East.

Dulles expected that Japan's trade deficit with the United States would
be permament. This incredible misjudgment went against all economic
factors because in 1965 Japan had its first trade surplus with the United
States. It was not the last, and later surpluses reached the tens of billions
of dollars.

Two leading scientists reported on June 24 that a smaller hydrogen bomb could be produced that essentially would have no radioactive fallout. Doctors Edward Teller and Albert L. Latter claimed that in a limited nuclear war that radioactive fallout would probably kill many innocent bystanders but since development of a hydrogen bomb through fusion and not fission, that 95 percent of the fallout would be eliminated. With further development, they claimed, fallout could become essentially negligible.

In Laos, Prince Souvanna Phouma dissolved his government. The situation in Indochina became even more volatile when his neutralist regime was replaced on July 22 with one headed by Phoui Sananikone who, with American support, agreed to take an anti-communist stand in the Far East.

For the first time since 1875 Congress passed a law to protect blacks' civil rights by creating a commission to investigate denial of voting rights because of race or religion. The law made interference with such rights in a national election a federal offense, and provided stiff penalties for violators. Although the number of blacks registered to vote had increased in recent years, it was far below the number who were eligible. President Eisenhower signed the Civil Rights Act of 1957 on August 29.

Black militance throughout the nation rose to new heights during the 1950s and 1960s and whites were forced to face the issue of civil rights to which they had long played lip service.

The Soviet Union startled Americans October 4 by launching the world's first artificial satellite to study the upper atmosphere as part of the Geophysical Year. "Sputnik" went into orbit beeping its way around the world, causing consternation in America whose people had long believed their nation was far ahead in advanced technologies. Soon critics were saying that America's educational system was at fault because of a lack of discipline in the schools, and failure to teach scientific fundamentals.

About a month later the Soviet Union launched another satellite, this time carrying a dog "Laika," that started to orbit the earth November 3 every hour and 42 minutes. It was six times heavier than "Sputnik." The Russians said its instruments were being used to measure cosmic rays, temperatures and pressures.

The Russian success in space was due to a decision at the highest levels to provide the funds and resources for space exploration. Their success came as a rude shock to American complacency, but all that was needed was a similar commitment on the part of the nation's leaders. It wasn't long in coming, and one of the fallouts was more emphasis on science and mathematics in the nation's schools and the recruiting and training of its brighter students.

The United States Office of Education published its findings November 10 about a two-year survey of education in the Soviet Union. It showed that emphasis on scientific and technical education in Russia was far ahead of the United States in its schools and colleges. These findings were confirmed the following June by American educators who toured the Soviet Union.

President Eisenhower, who had resisted pleas by American scientists to make large sums available for space research, changed his mind on November 7 and ordered preparations for America's first launch into space. He also created a panel of experts to explore what direction America's space program should take, and what it should try to achieve.

In July of 1958 Congress used the panel's recommendations to establish the National Aeronautics and Space Administration (NASA) to oversee the nation's future space programs.

Meanwhile, troubles escalated in the Middle East and the United States Navy's Sixth Fleet was dispatched May 14 to the Mediterranean. This doubled America's strength in the area. Eisenhower, in an effort to safeguard Lebanese independence and ensure the safety of Americans, the next day sent arms to Lebanon in an airlift.

Lebanon's President Camille Chamoun appealed to President Eisenhower for additional military assistance July 15 after an uprising threatened to topple his government. Arab nationalists were involved and they also tried to overthrow the government of neighboring Iraq.

President Eisenhower agreed to send more than 5,000 Marines to help restore order in Lebanon under the Eisenhower Doctrine. He explained his action in an address to the American people in which he said that the presence of these Marines would encourage the Lebanese government to defend its sovereignty and integrity, and protect the approximately 2,500 Americans there.

He told the nation that his action would be reported immediately to an emergency meeting of the United Nations Security Council. He assured the people that the Marines would be withdrawn as soon as the Security Council took the necessary measures to maintain internal peace and security in the Middle East.

Great Britain, in a simultaneous action, sent British troops to Jordan when rebels threatened to overthrow King Hussein's government.

Great Britain and the United States withdrew their forces in October when the situation stabilized in the Middle East.

While these actions were under way America's growing nuclear-powered undersea fleet was establishing some historic firsts. The "Nautilus" completed the first submerged crossing of the North Pole under the ice August 3 when it cruised from Hawaii to Iceland. Eight days later the

"Skate" made a round trip to the North Pole and back. That fall, the "Sea Wolf" completed a 60-day underwater trip October 6 to prove that atomic-powered submarines didn't have to surface because there were no batteries to be recharged such as in older-type subs.

This year the Eisenhower Administration seemed at times to be beset by crises all over the world. Chinese communists resumed their bombardment of the offshore Quemoy Islands August 23. The American Pacific Fleet was ordered to escort supply ships from Formosa to Quemoy, up to the three-mile territorial limit of China's waters.

America's rapidly expanding role in space received a boost on October 11 when the "Pioneer" moon rocket was launched. Although it failed to reach the moon, it attained an altitude of more than 79,000 miles. This was 30 times as high as any earlier man-made object.

A slight reduction in tension in the Far East occurred on October 25 when Communist China withdrew the last of its troops from North Korea. But the following year North Korea was charged with 218 violations of the armistice by the UN's Military Assistance Commission.

In Indochina, North Vietnam's army continued its buildup, and South Vietnam's Army reached a total of 150,000 by the end of 1958. At that time President Diem released it from internal security duties.

Regular commercial jet service began in the United States on December 10, 1958, as National Airlines inaugurated flights in two Boeing 707s. As a precursor of the future, Pan American World Airways began daily transatlantic service from New York to Paris on October 26 with a Boeing 707. This year, for the first time, airlines carried more transatlantic passengers than surface ships.

Premier Krushchev upset the West on November 10 when he announced that the Soviet Union would turn over East Berlin to East Germany. Alarmed by the prospect that the East Germans would blockade Berlin, the United States Government promised to protect its sector of the city. The Soviet Union carried the war of nerves a step further by proposing on November 27 that West Berlin become a free, independent city, and Krushchev said East Berlin would be turned over to East Germany the following June.

Proof that the United States was closing the gap between it and the Soviet Union in heavy missiles, an Atlas intercontinental ballistic missile was fired on November 28. It soared a distance of more than 6,000 miles and landed in a test zone in the Atlantic Ocean.

The National Aeronautics and Space Administration selected seven pilots for training as astronauts this year. The first manned space capsule was scheduled for launching in 1961.

Recognition that future wars could well become atomic conflicts caused the United States to sign agreements with some of its allies in May to supply information and equipment to them. Canada, the Netherlands, Turkey and West Germany received assistance under the agreement to permit them to train their forces in the use of atomic weapons. Great Britain, Canada and the United States had cooperated similarly since World War II.

Relations between the United States and Egypt had improved to the point in 1959 where Eisenhower approved economic and technical aid. The previous year Egypt had joined Syria to form the United Arab Republic. By the end of the year the International Bank had authorized $56 million for work on the Suez Canal.

The United States and the Soviet Union made a number of advances in space this year. One Russian spacecraft went into orbit around the sun, becoming the first artificial planet, another landed on the moon, while a third passed around the moon to get photographs of its unseen opposite side. There were four American space probes, all smaller, that transmitted photographs and the first television pictures of the earth while providing information on various aspects of the atmosphere.

America's growing expertise in space was evident August 7 when a 142-pound satellite, Explorer IV, was launched from Cape Canaveral. The new National Aeronautics and Space Administration had built the satellite and successfully placed it in orbit, justifying the decision to set up the agency.

Soviet Premier Krushchev came to the United States for a six-day tour of the nation starting September 15. In a speech to the United Nations, he proposed an end to the armaments race. He mentioned the horrors of war and his desire to spend money for peaceful purposes. His speech was pure propaganda, and not even good propaganda.

America's growing atomic undersea submarine fleet received an important new weapon June 9 when the "George Washington" was launched. It was the first submarine to be equipped to fire Polaris missiles.

The year ended with a startling and sobering statistic. It was revealed that automobile accidents through the years had killed 1.25 million Americans. This total exceeded the number of Americans who had been killed in all of America's wars.

Japan's basic industries were so devastated by World War II bombing raids that they took a long time to recover in the highly-competitive post-war world. A little-known program of vast significance, initiated by the United States State Department, brought thousands of Japan's top industrialists to the United States for detailed briefings by successful American manufacturers. Douglas Aircraft Company, where the author worked as public relations manager for the Long Beach Division, was then building the DC-8 Jetliner. The division became a prime focal point for Japanese executives because of Douglas's reputation for quality products. The author was assigned to set up these company sessions— often week-long affairs—involving 10-25 of Japan's most promising executives from department managers to board chairmen. The program was at its peak throughout the United States. At Long Beach top Douglas managers freely gave of their expertise to help Japanese businesses get back on their feet. During a three-year period I must have met every top executive in Japan because our sessions were so popular. (Douglas was a famous name in Japan whose airlines had been good customers for years.) Our managers talked to the Japanese executives through an interpreter who, in turn, translated their comments through an elaborate earphone system. The Japanese took an incredible amount of notes, and all of their questions were answered forthrightly and in depth.

In later years I was amused to hear how the Japanese had taught Americans how to run their factories in new and innovative ways. In fact, we in this country taught them most of what they know about competing in world markets with top-quality products. Unfortunately for the United States, while they were learning their lessons well from the American factories, the nation was forgetting the very lessons that had once made the United States the envy of the industrialized world. While the United States was letting its factories decline in productivity due to failure to modernize them, it sold the Japanese the most modern production equipment the nation possessed to replace what American fliers had destroyed during the war. It was a classic case of selling someone the rope with which to hang himself.

Lieutenant Don Walsh of the United States Navy and Jacques Picard set a new ocean diving record on January 23, 1960, with their bathyscaphe "Trieste." It descended to a depth of 15,500 feet in the Marianas Trench near Guam in the Pacific Ocean.

Vice President Nixon had announced in January that he would be a candidate that year for the Republican Presidential nomination, and Senator John F. Kennedy announced on April 18 that he would seek the Democratic nomination. Kennedy had aroused interest in several states with large Democratic majorities although his Catholicism disturbed many people. There had never been a Catholic President; Alfred E. Smith had blamed his defeat in the 1920s on his religious background. Kennedy said on April 18, in reply to a question about his Roman Catholic faith, that "I don't think that my religion is anyone's business." But he could not pass it off so easily and hope the issue would go away. It soon became a factor in the campaign.

A classic international crisis erupted on May 5 when Premier Krushchev announced that a U-2 American spy plane had been shot down on May 1 inside the Soviet Union. It could not have happened at a worse time because the President and the Soviet Premier were about to have a summit conference in Paris.

At first President Eisenhower denied that the United States was conducting photographic reconnaissance over the Soviet Union but when Krushchev revealed on May 7 that the plane's pilot, Francis Gary Powers, was alive and had confessed that he had been on a spy mission, the United States State Department tried to limit the diplomatic damage by saying it was known that a U-2 was missing but there had been no authorization for such a flight over Russia. The statement said it appeared that in endeavoring to obtain information now concealed behind the Iron Curtain that a flight over Soviet territory was probably undertaken by an unarmed civilian U-2 plane.

It was an inept handling of a delicate situation, but May 9 Secretary of State Herter admitted that such flights had gone on for years to gather information for the West to prevent a surprise attack. He said such flights would continue until the Soviet Union lessened the danger of aggression. Two days later Eisenhower admitted that he had personally authorized the U-2 flights.

When Eisenhower and Krushchev met at Paris May 16, the President announced that U-2 flights had been suspended and would not be renewed. Krushchev would not be appeased and he withdrew his invitation for Eisenhower to visit the Soviet Union. The summit ended the next day amid charges and countercharges between officials of the two nations.

Eisenhower spoke to the American people May 25 to explain what had happened after he had been roundly criticized for his administration's handling of the situation. "Our first information about the failure of this mission did not disclose whether the pilot was still alive, was trying to escape, was avoiding interrogation, or whether both plane and pilot had been destroyed. Protection of our intelligence system and the pilot, and concealment of the plane's mission, seemed imperative. It must be rememberd that over a long period these flights had given us information of the greatest importance to the nation's security. In fact, their success has been nothing short of remarkable.

"For those reasons, what is known in intelligence circles as a 'covering statement' was issued. It was issued on assumptions that were later proved incorrect. Consequently, when later the status of the pilot was definitely established and there was no further possibility of avoiding exposure of the project, the factual details were sent forth."

Francis Gary Powers was put on trial in Moscow August 17 and was found guilty of espionage for the United States. He was sentenced to 10 years' loss of liberty, three years to be spent in prison, and the remainder at labor in a restricted area.

A year later, with a new President in office, Krushchev said he would no longer make an issue of the U-2 affair in hopes of bettering relations with the United States. Powers was exchanged for Soviet spy Rudolf Abel in 1962.

Eisenhower was furious because he had been made to look ridiculous and he and other administration officials vented their wrath on Powers whom, some said, had agreed to commit suicide to avoid capture and supposedly had a poison capsule to kill himself. These innuendos were grossly unfair, and just not true. Powers did exactly as he was briefed by the Central Intelligence Agency.

The super-secret U-2 was designed by Clarence "Kelly" Johnson's Advanced Development Projects, home of Lockheed's "Skunk Works," in Burbank, California. In effect it was a powered glider with a huge, flexible wing that permitted it to fly above 70,000 feet. At that time the Russians had no airplane that could fly that high, or anti-aircraft guns that could shoot it down. Its high-tech cameras reported on the Soviet Union's military installations, and they were highly perfected. The government called the planes weather reconnaissance aircraft, claiming the "U" stood for utility, to guard their true nature as spy planes operated by the Central Intelligence Agency and the United States Air Force.

Officials of the Department of Defense were shocked when Powers' plane was shot down by a ground-to-air missile that exploded close to his U-2, forcing him to bail out.

Lockheed's chief test pilot, Tony LeVier, first flew the U-2 in August, 1955. It proved to be a tricky plane because of its inherent instability, and a number of later planes were lost as a result. But it was designed for a specific job and it performed well for the next 35 years. Engineers had learned prior to the first flight that all of the usual jet fuels would vaporize at the altitudes to be flown by the U-2 so the first flight was made with cigarette lighter fluid. The fuel was designated LF-1. LeVier's first flight almost ended in diaster because the U-2s landing characteristics were so tricky. Then, too, he found that the plane's wings had so little lift in the thin air at high altitudes that he had to keep the plane at near maximum speed or it would stall and the engine flame out.

LeVier said later that such a condition "puts you in a coffin corner," because going too fast causes buffeting that can shake the plane apart. Thus to remain in the air at those extreme altitudes above 70,000 feet, a pilot had to maintain his speed within four or five miles an hour to survive.

A United States-Japanese mutual security treaty, ratified in June, provided for possible wartime uses of American bases in Japan, and equipment of Japanese forces with atomic weapons. These features triggered anti-American riots in Japan. They became so intense that Eisenhower cancelled his Japanese trip. Despite opposition by some Japanese the fall elections in Japan indicated that the majority of the Japanese people approved the treaty.

The United States now had a stockpile of 18,000 nuclear weapons, including more than 3,000 strategic bombs and missile warheads, plus smaller devices in torpedoes and artillery shells. They were deployed throughout the world, but most of them were in Europe.

Relations with Castro's Cuba had been deteriorating ever since his election as Premier, and his communist leanings became more apparent with his closer association with the Soviet Union. The United States protested to the Organization of American States June 29 that Cuba was now trying to export communism into other Caribbean countries. Castro retaliated by seizing an American-owned oil refinery. The American government cut Cuba's sugar quota July 6 and later suspended all sugar imports. Castro announced August 7 that he had authorized "forcible expropriation" of all American-owned companies. The game of one-up-manship continued after the United States acted October 19 to block shipment of all goods to Cuba with the exception of medical supplies and food.

As the Democratic Convention convened in Los Angeles July 13, 1960, it quickly became apparent that Senator John F. Kennedy held the inside edge to the nomination although Senator Lyndon B. Johnson of Texas had the enthusiastic backing of the party's old guard. But Johnson didn't have a chance against the charismatic Kennedy who won the nomination on the first ballot. For sake of party unity, Johnson was nominated for vice-president. The Republicans met in Chicago two weeks later and Richard M. Nixon was nominated as their candidate, with Henry Cabot Lodge of Massachusetts as the vice-presidential nominee.

While politicians were busy determining who should run the nation in the next four years, a new and far more deadly aspect of submarine warfare emerged July 20. On that date the first successful underwater launch of a Polaris missile was completed. The missile was fired while the submarine was submerged and it hit a target 1,100 miles away.

The 15th session of the United Nations General Assembly opened September 20 and before it ended December 21 most of the world's leaders had used it as a forum to espouse their pet causes and hatreds.

In speaking to the United Nations General Assembly September 23, Nikita Krushchev warned about the danger of colonial wars escalating into a new world war. It wasn't realized in Allied circles at the time that there had been a growing debate between officials of the People's Republic of China and the Soviet Union about such a danger. But their divergent views resulted in a compromise that was not revealed until January 6, 1961. Krushchev told the UN Assembly that world wars and local wars that might end in a world thermonuclear war must be avoided. He made another statement that caught American officials by surprise. He said that national liberation wars to permit colonial peoples to attain independence were not only "admissable but inevitable," and that such wars should receive full communist support.

The same month Krushchev was speaking to the Assembly the Lao Dong Party in North Vietnam revealed that it had formed in South Vietnam a "broad national, united front" of workers, peasants and soldiers to overthrow the Diem government.

From then on North Vietnamese infiltrations of the South increased at a rapid rate, and President Diem's government soon was unable to contain the Vietcong and infiltrating communists from the North.

Ngo Dinh Nhu, President Diem's brother, now introduced some reforms that had long been demanded by the United States, but he refused to reduce the government's authoritarian controls, and unrest among South Vietnamese reached new heights. One of Diem's worst faults as President was his failure to delegate authority and he kept his armed forces fragmented in small commands controlled by 33 province chiefs. Actually, 42 armed forces leaders reported directly to President Diem.

A record number of Americans voted on November 8 to give John F. Kennedy a narrow 50.1 percent victory over Richard Nixon in the popular vote. More than 68 million Americans had gone to the polls, and the race was so close that the electoral vote could not at first be ascertained. Some states demanded recounts but in January the total was announced as 303 for Kennedy with 23 states, and 219 for Nixon with 26 states. The final tally showed that Kennedy had won by about 100,000 popular votes.

In one of his last official acts President Eisenhower directed the United States to break off diplomatic relations with Cuba. Cuba had accused the American government of planning an invasion, and demanded that its Cuban embassy be reduced to 11 members.

In his farewell address to the American people January 17, 1961, Eisenhower surprised most people by warning against the growing power of the military-industrial complex, and his warning became one of his best legacies to the American people.

At John F. Kennedy's inauguration January 20, he made an eloquent plea for vigorous action on domestic issues, while creating an international alliance to combat the world's problems.

"Let every nation know, whether it wishes us well or ill, that we shall pay any price, bear any burden, meet any hardship, support any friend, oppose any force to assure the survival and the success of liberty . . .

"And so, my fellow Americans—ask not what your country can do for you—ask what you can do for your country.

"My fellow citizens of the world—ask not what America will do for you but what together we can do for the freedom of man."

Soviet Premier Krushchev's support for wars of national liberation was recognized by President Kennedy as a threat to the United States. He ordered his Secretary of Defense Robert S. McNamara February 1, 1961, to train and equip more United States troops for counter-insurgency operations. The new President's concern was heightened by the increase in fighting in Laos between Phoumi Nosavan's pro-American government forces and those of the pro-communist Pathet Lao. Much of Kennedy's first two months in office were directed to this crisis. He considered use of American military forces, but rejected the idea because the Joint Chiefs expressed their adamant opposition.

In March, President Kennedy announced that the United States would support Laos's sovereignty, but Great Britain and the Soviet Union proposed instead an international conference to be held in May to resolve the crisis rapidly building up in Indochina.

The Congo, independent since June 1960, when Belgium relinquished control, now was in a state of civil war. To prevent other countries from capitalizing on the Congo's distress, Kennedy announced February 15 that the United States would uphold the UN Charter by opposing any intervention by any country in that nation's affairs. The UN Security Council then authorized international police action to terminate the civil war.

Kennedy proposed a new program March 13 to involve the United States in widespread support for joint social and economic developments in the Western Hemisphere. His "Alliance for Progress" was well received by Latin American nations whose representatives met in August to confer about the program at Punta del Este, Uruguay.

The Soviet Union announced another "first" in space April 12 when it revealed that one of its astronauts had been placed in orbit around the earth. Major Yuri Gagarin made only one orbit before he was safely brought back to earth, but it was a milestone achievement.

While the Soviet Union was reaping the worldwide plaudits for its latest achievement in space, the United States was about to make itself ridiculous in the eyes of the world. The Eisenhower administration had authorized an invasion of Cuba by 2,000 Cuban exiles trained by the Central Intelligence Agency. In theory the Cuban populace was supposed to rise up against Castro and overthrow his communist regime. This incredibly naive plan was given the go-ahead by the Kennedy administration after he took office. The landing was made April 17 at the Bay of Pigs, but without the American planes the CIA had proposed to provide air support. At the last minute Kennedy had rejected their use, and Castro's tanks and artillery slaughtered many of the invaders and captured the rest. The invasion lasted less than 48 hours.

America's first spaceman, Navy Commander Alan B. Shepard, Jr., completed a sub-orbital flight May 5. He accomplished the mission in the first of the Mercury capsules.

After Sheperd's flight, President Kennedy announced that his administration would initiate a program to put a man on the moon by the end of the decade. Such an achievement, he said, would help to restore America's prestige as the world's foremost technological power. Costs were estimated at $25 billion. At first NASA scientists were concerned by the impact on its unmanned satellite programs that would achieve more immediate scientific results, but the support of Congress and the American people was so strong that both programs became a reality.

Air Force Captain Virgil Grissom reached an altitude of 116 miles in space July 21 in a Gemini capsule. But these accomplishments were eclipsed August 6 when the Soviet Union sent up a manned space capsule that orbited the earth 17 times. The pilot returned by parachute suffering no ill effects, he said, although he admitted he had been "seasick" during the 25-hour flight.

With the situation in Europe getting worse as Krushchev threatened to sign a separate peace treaty with East Germany, events in the Far East forced the administration to momentarily divert its attention to Indochina. At the Geneva Conference it proposed May 17 a revised international neutrality program for Laos. Efforts had been futile since 1954 to guarantee neutrality in the region, and efforts had been suspended because of the Laotian political crisis and the 1958 communist uprising.

Although most of his military advisers spoke out against sending American troops to Indochina unless the United States committed itself to an all-out military effort, including the possible use of nuclear weapons, in 1961 Kennedy wasn't ready for such a major escalation of the war. He asked McNamara and the Department of Defense May 11 to assess the value and cost of increasing South Vietnam's armed forces to 200,000 men. The same day he committed an Army Special Forces group of 400 to help clear and hold Vietcong areas, mainly along the Cambodian and Laotian borders. Step by step President Kennedy was getting the

United States further involved in the war, but still without clear and definite goals.

President Kennedy met with Nikita Krushchev in Vienna June 4 in an attempt to resolve their differences. The subjects of Berlin, Laos and disarmament were on the agenda but the conference ended in mutual recriminations. Krushchev continued to insist that the Soviet Union would sign a separate peace treaty with Germany.

Kennedy learned a bitter lesson in dealing with the Soviet leaders, and it was not his last, that they could be arbitrary and inflexible as long as it suited their interests.

The President spoke to the American people of his frustrations and concerns on television July 25, seven weeks after his meeting with Krushchev in Vienna. He followed up his speech with a request to Congress July 25 for a $3.5 billion increase in defense funds, and the request was quickly approved six days later. Congress also authorized the President to call 250,000 reservists to active duty for up to a year, and to increase the length of duty for the regular forces. This authorization was later extended in 1962.

In retaliation, the Soviet Union and East Germany began construction of a wall to seal off East Berlin and East Germany from free access to the West as guaranteed by the Four-Power agreement on Germany's status. The United States, Great Britain and France jointly protested the Berlin Wall August 15, but it was completed three days later. Since 1949 2.7 million people had used their privilege of free access to the West to pass from East Germany to West Berlin. Now the exodus practically ceased although a few who tried to breach the wall made it to freedom although many others were brutally murdered.

The Soviet Union renewed atmospheric testing of its nuclear arsenal on September 1 despite an appeal by the United Nations not to do so. The Russians tested nuclear bombs of about 30 to 50 megatons. Kennedy authorized resumption of limited underground tests, to prevent fallout, but said the United States might be forced to resume atmospheric tests in 1962.

President Kennedy's plan for a Peace Corps of American volunteers to serve in undeveloped countries throughout the world was approved by Congress on September 22 with an initial appropriation of $30 million. The idea for the program was to provide education and technical assistance to help promote the social development of these countries.

CHAPTER 21

Cuban Missile Crisis

NEAR THE END OF 1961 THE SITUATION IN SOUTH VIETNAM BECAME critical as the Vietcong surrounded Saigon and other urban centers and blocked highways. The North Vietnamese now fully expected to take over the South.

Secretary of Defense McNamara recommended to the President that no Americans be sent there unless the United States was ready to make an affirmative decision to support military action that might involve 200,000 American troops in a long war.

Kennedy disagreed and on January 4, 1962, he decided to offer South Vietnam more limited support. A Military Assistance Command was approved with a thousand advisers under the Commander-in-Chief, Pacific, with Lieutenant General Paul D. Harkins in command effective February 8. These "advisers," Kennedy said, were not combat troops but they could defend themselves if attacked. McNamara called Harkins an "imaginative officer, fully qualified to fill what I consider to be the most difficult job in the United States Army."

After Harkins assumed command he pressed for a centralized, counterinsurgency strategy to be developed on a national basis, not only to secure Saigon and South Vietnam's other major cities, but to keep the Vietcong off-balance in the countryside by tactics that would seize and hold vital areas.

South Vietnam's President Diem had earlier established his "strategic hamlet" plan but it had failed because of his insistence upon top-level control. Such a plan dated back to the days of the Chinese domination of Vietnam, and was similar to the "combat village" defense system used during the years the Vietnamese resisted the French. This time the program failed because villagers resented being forced to leave their homes for security reasons and relocate in unfamiliar areas.

In rejecting a greater military involvement at the time, Kennedy said some of his military advisers wanted an open-ended commitment to send troops to South Vietnam. He likened such a force to the units he sent to Germany in 1961 when Soviet Russia threatened to close the Allied corridor to Berlin. "They say it is necessary in order to restore confidence and maintain morale. But it will be just like Berlin. The troops will march in, the bands will play, the crowds will cheer; and in four days everyone will have forgotten. Then we will be told we have to send in more troops. It's like taking a drink. The effect wears off, and you have to take another."

Kennedy was convinced the war could be won only so long as it remained Vietnam's war. Otherwise, he said, the Americans would lose just like the French. In retrospect it is regrettable that he didn't follow his instincts. Instead he continued to send combat advisers without seeking a share in South Vietnam's decision-making policy.

Kennedy authorized the removal of American tanks from the Berlin Wall January 15 to ease tension in the divided city. Two days later the Soviet Union removed its tanks. The wall made it more difficult and dangerous for East Germans to escape to the West because of East Germany's "shoot-to-kill" policy, but by October 13,000 had done so, in addition to another 52,000 East Germans who refused to return home after visiting West Germany.

The Organization of American States recognized the growing problem with Cuba February 14 by excluding it from its activities. Cuba remained a member because the OAS charter didn't provide for expulsion of any member for any reason. Ten days earlier the United States had banned all Cuban imports. Kennedy said the loss of $35 million in trade would inhibit Cuba's efforts to subvert hemispheric nations.

Lieutenant Colonel John H. Glenn, Jr., became the first American to orbit the earth February 20 when he circled it three times in a Mercury space capsule. But this was just the beginning of America's manned space endeavors that would soon eclipse the Russians.

When fighting broke out again in Laos May 12 after a year-long ceasefire the United States sent 4,000 troops and air units to neighboring Thailand for possible use against the communists in Laos plus a Navy task force to the region. Kennedy said this action was taken to assure the territorial integrity of Thailand with which the United States had a mutual defense treaty.

Before the Americans could get into action, the communists decided they had more to gain by discussing a peace treaty in Geneva July 23 and agreed to abide by the 1954 accord. American officials who supported such a treaty were naive to believe that it would be upheld by the communists. North Vietnam ignored it and continued to support their forces in Laos and in South Vietnam.

President Kennedy publicly confirmed August 22 that Soviet supplies and technicians were in Cuba ostensibly to aid in that nation's defense. But this announcement was just the start of shocking revelations to come. An Air Force U-2 spy plane, flying a routine reconnaissance mission over Cuba October 14, brought back photographs of fully-equipped missile bases capable of attacking the United States with nuclear warheads.

President Kennedy met secretly with his Joint Chiefs of Staff two days later to discuss this development. The military chiefs recommended an immediate air strike, and there were suggestions that the United States should invade the island. Attorney General Robert Kennedy, the President's brother, spoke against such action, reminding them of the fiasco at the Bay of Pigs. He said an attack against Cuba would destroy America's moral position in the world. The President opted instead for a naval quarantine of Cuba to block further installations of such weapons. He made it clear that the United States would not tolerate the presence of such missiles so close to its shores and that a quarantine would give the Soviet Union a chance to remove the missiles.

Kennedy demanded that Russia remove all its missiles and dismantle its Cuban bases, and he asked that the UN Security Council and the Organization of American States take a stand in support of this action by the United States.

The Soviet Union immediately denounced the United States and Premier Krushchev warned that Russia would not accept the quarantine. While Soviet ships continued toward Cuba with more missiles and support equipment, the threat of a nuclear war hung over the world.

A top Soviet diplomat unofficially approached John Scali, an American newsman, October 26 telling him that the Soviet Union would dismantle their bases if Kennedy would promise not to invade Cuba.

Kennedy received a telegram from Krushchev that evening saying much the same thing, but in another letter the next day the Russian Premier demanded the withdrawal of NATO missiles in Turkey in exchange. Kennedy privately told his key aides that such a quid pro was unacceptable, so he ignored the second letter. Instead, he responded to the first Krushchev offer.

Two days later Krushchev accepted Kennedy's terms and agreed to withdraw the missiles, and return them to the Soviet Union under UN supervision. Although Castro refused to permit on-site inspection of their removal, Kennedy authorized daily aerial inspection of the sites and naval inspection of ships.

Kennedy announced November 20 that all missiles had been embarked for shipment to Russia and that Krushchev had agreed to remove 42 Russian bombers capable of carrying nuclear warheads within 30 days. Kennedy lifted the blockade on this date.

It had been a close call and any misstep might have thrown the world into the horrors of a full-scale nuclear war.

Intelligence estimates at the time predicted that the Soviet Union had 10,000 men in Cuba and that Castro's army had 100,000 men under arms. Actually there were 40,000 Soviet troops in Cuba and 270,000 Cuban soldiers. The Cuban army expected an American invasion, and believed that 800,000 Cubans would be killed, but Castro supposedly was willing to pay the price.

Although it was not definitely known at the time whether nuclear warheads were on the missiles, this was confirmed years later, along with the fact that the missiles were targeted against New York, Washington, and other American cities.

The Soviet Union had shipped 40 missiles to Cuba, a fraction of the 10,000 warheads each side later aimed at one another.

Edward Teller, the "father" of America's thermonuclear weapons, told a large gathering of NATO's military and civilian leaders that "the scientific world" would soon bring forward a class of weapons that the Russians could never counter. Years later these weapons were revealed as "neutron" bombs.

With American military assistance South Vietnam defied its critics by remaining in existence throughout 1962 although its control over large areas was shaky. The National Liberation Front, North Vietnam's political organization in South Vietnam, changed its propaganda. That fall the communists were saying that a neutral state should be created in the South much like Laos. Of special interest was Ho Chi Minh's statement praising Diem's patriotism. Three years earlier Ho Chi Minh had predicted South Vietnam's defeat within a year. By September 1962, he was saying that victory might take 15 to 20 years.

For the rest of the year in Vietnam and into 1963 the North Vietnamese continued to infiltrate personnel and equipment to the South. They supplied the most modern weapons they could get from China and the Soviet Union.

In the Kennedy administration, optimism was running high that a phased withdrawal of American troops was a possibility. By then American military strength had risen to 11,412. McNamara set 1965 as the planning date for ending American military involvement in Vietnam. Privately, Air Force and Navy officials were skeptical.

At home there was disagreement about the war on college campuses. Students for a Democratic Society called for "participatory democracy," and called themselves members of the new left. They started out with 200 members and initially were involved in community work, notably in Newark where one member, Tom Hayden, concerned himself with slum poverty among blacks. Idealistic at first, the group turned more radical as the American participation escalated in Vietnam.

Two professors of psychology at Harvard, Timothy Leary and Richard Alpert, experimented with hallucinogenic drugs to "liberate the young." They tried various drugs but preferred lysergic acid diethylamide (LSD). It caused the mind to divert to a fantasy world, and distorted and terrorized some individuals although Leary claimed that LSD opened the door of the mind. It was Alpert who coined the word psychedelic.

The Kennedy administration had privately sought a means by which Cubans captured during the Bay of Pigs invasion in 1961 could be released to American authorities. A committee commenced negotiations with Castro's regime and 60 ill Cubans were released early in the year. Now Castro agreed to release the rest after the committee raised $62 million to provide medicine, fuel and cash in exchange for the remaining 1,113 prisoners. They were released starting on December 23.

During the Cuban missile crisis the United States and the Soviet Union realized that they needed a quicker way to handle crises between them. At times, with the world on the brink of another world war, communications between the leaders of the two nations often were delayed for six hours. Now both sides agreed to set up a "hot line" or direct teletypewriter contact between Washington and Moscow to avoid the risk of accidental war. They reached agreement April 5 to lease a cable line from commercial companies that would transmit their messages via England, Denmark, Sweden and Finland.

The situation in Indochina had not improved by early 1963. If anything it was even worse in Laos. The Kennedy administration joined with the Soviet Union in urging renewed neutrality of Laos. Despite their agreement, the Laotian government remained split into three military factions—royalist, neutralist and pro-communist. Each group controlled a separate zone of the country.

The South Vietnamese suffered their first serious setback in 1963 near the village of Ap Bac in the IV Corps area where they had earlier won control of the Plain of Reeds from the Vietcong in the Mekong Delta. The battle was lost because there had been no prior air-ground planning, and no fighter escort to cover the operation. An American helicopter company, which had agreed to fly in the Vietnamese, lost heavily and a number of Americans were killed. The Vietcong's ability to fight against American helicopters and armored vehicles gave them confidence and marked a major turning point in the conflict. After Ap Bac they often deliberately invited battle.

Following this battle there was a lull in the fighting on both sides. Americans urged President Diem to launch operations to exploit opportunities to overwhelm the Vietcong, but Diem was not anxious to involve his troops in other than defensive actions.

Unrest among religious minorities began to spread and the Diem government cracked down. This action only served to increase the tension. In attempting to restore law and order, without resolving the root of the problem, tension increased and violence continued at Hué and spread to all of the northern provinces. When a saffron-robed Buddhist monk soaked himself with gasoline June 11, and the aged man committed sacrificial suicide by fire, the Buddhist cause gained international attention. Then six more monks immolated themselves. People everywhere were shocked when Madame Nhu, wife of Diem's brother, said, "I would clap my hands at seeing another monk barbecue show."

Optimism for an early withdrawal of American troops remained high throughout the early part of 1963, and some American units were scheduled to leave by the end of the year. By June the Military Assistance Command had 16,652 military personnel, with one-third from the Air Force. But McNamara froze the strength on the 28th.

South Vietnam's Joint General Staff ordered all ground force units to operate a minimum of 20 days every month starting July 1. This was to be the start of a general offensive to attain "complete annihilation of the enemy," and to "saturate the countryside" in order to "complete Vietnamese control."

But the Vietcong had been biding their time, and in July they struck hamlets south of Ban Me Thuot and ambushed the roads leading to the area. The same type of activity now spread to other areas.

The Buddhists demonstrated again July 16 and monks and nuns milled in front of Ambassador Nolting's residence in Saigon demanding that the United States compel the Diem government to keep its promises. Violence broke out again the following day.

Diem addressed the nation by radio July 19 but his address was uncompromising. Despite criticism from religious minorities, Diem still enjoyed the support of a majority of the South Vietnamese people, although his brother and his wife were disliked by many people.

President Kennedy went to Europe during the latter part of June and one of his first stops was Berlin where 200,000 Berliners turned out to welcome him on the 26th. In expressing his solidarity with the isolated people of this beleaguered city within the Soviet-controlled area of East Germany, they cheered him wildly, particularly when he said, "Ich bin ein Berliner," (I am a Berliner) claiming that all free men, wherever they may live, are citizens of Berlin.

For years there had been one conference after another to discuss a nuclear test ban treaty. The United States, Great Britain and the Soviet Union finally agreed to one August 5 that banned nuclear tests in the oceans, the atmosphere and outer space. It was signed into law September 24 when the United States Senate approved it and it went into effect October 10. Eventually 113 nations signed it although it was rejected by France and Communist China.

Two satellites were launched by the United States October 16 to detect violations of the treaty.

Martin Luther King had dedicated his adult life to the cause of equal rights for black Americans. The son and grandson of a respected Baptist minister in Atlanta, he had gone on to receive a doctorate at Boston University. An adherent to Ghandi's principles of non-violent protests, he had organized and participated in boycotts and sit-ins as part of his campaign to end segregation.

He was frequently jailed and he and his family were constantly harassed. No matter what they did to him, he counseled his followers, "We must love our white brothers no matter what they do to us."

By 1963 King was a formidable leader of a powerful force because he gave the civil rights movement power and credibility.

He led a march on Washington August 28 of civil rights leaders to promote jobs and freedom. Before 200,000 people at the Lincoln Memorial he delivered one of the most moving speeches any human being has ever given.

"When we let freedom ring, when we let it ring from every village and every hamlet, from every state and every city, we will be able to speed up that day when all of God's children, black men and white men, Jews and Gentiles, Protestants and Catholics, will be able to join hands and sing in the words of the old Negro spiritual, "Free at last! Free at last! Thank God Almighty, we are free at last!"

The rally, which could have erupted into violence, remained peaceful through Dr. King's influence.

Henry Cabot Lodge, an old friend of the President's, was appointed to replace Ambassador Nolting in South Vietnam. Kennedy advised him that the United States would no longer tolerate the systematic suppression of the Buddhists, or Nhu's domination of the government. Lodge was authorized to threaten Diem with a shut-off of American aid unless the jailed Buddhists were released. Lodge replied that the chance of Diem's meeting such demands was "virtually nil." By making them, he said, we give Nhu a chance to forestall a coup, and Lodge suggested that we "go straight to the generals with our demands."

After Lodge returned to Saigon, he spoke to several Vietnamese generals who hinted that a coup against Diem was in the making. They sought American reaction, but Lodge put them off. In response to a further query from President Kennedy about the situation, Ambassador Lodge replied that "United States prestige was publicly committed. There is no turning back."

After the National Security Council reaffirmed the United States' basic course that a coup would be supported if it had a good chance of succeeding, President Kennedy sent a private message to Lodge. He pledged "everything possible to help you conclude this operation successfully." He asked to be given continuing reports in case he wished to reverse the decision.

President Kennedy's problem began to increase when Diem appointed Tran Van Don as chief of staff August 20 to head South Vietnam's armed forces, and his brother Nhu invited senior generals to sign a paper calling upon the government to seize and silence Buddhist leaders. At midnight, Diem declared martial law and a state of siege. Under his authority Vietnamese Special Forces and the police stormed Buddhist pagodas in Saigon and Hue before dawn. Monks, nuns and students were rounded up, but Buddhist leaders escaped and took refuge in the American Embassy.

After weighing the recommendations he had received, Kennedy ordered Lodge and General Harkins to support a coup if it had a good chance to succeed, but to avoid any direct American involvement. He further authorized them to suspend American air support to Diem whenever they thought it was prudent.

South Vietnam's President Diem and his brother were picked up in the early morning hours of November 2 by members of the dissident group. They were brutally murdered although they had been given assurance of safe passage out of the country. Madame Nhu was out of the country so she escaped a similar fate.

Ambassador Lodge reported to President Kennedy November 4 that the change in regime would shorten the war against the Vietcong because of improved morale in South Vietnam. Within three weeks his assessment would prove to be tragically wrong.

Although Diem's government had maintained a high degree of stability, it had failed to achieve national unity. However, none of the nine governments that followed enjoyed the popularity necessary to assure the nation's survival. After the demise of Diem's First Republic, South Vietnam had 62 political groups vying for power. Although operating under a single name, many of these parties were split into irreconciliable splinter groups.

After a group of generals took over the government of South Vietnam following President Diem's assassination, Secretary of State Rusk and Secretary of Defense McNamara went to Honolulu for a meeting on November 20th to review the situation in Indochina. They needed to determine how to intensify Vietnamese participation in the war and end America's combat involvement. In addition, Cambodia the day before posed another problem by severing economic and military relations with the United States. Its government said the United States was attempting to undermine its regime by sponsoring subversive activities against Cambodia from bases in South Vietnam. It was now apparent that Cambodia was turning more to communist North Vietnam.

McNamara informed the group at the meeting that "a certain euphoria had set in since the coup, but actually the generals headed a fragile government." Lodge agreed, but he said the Vietnamese need "greater motivation."

The day before Prince Norodom Sihanouk had convened a special national congress in Cambodia and renounced American aid in an attempt to avoid American interference in the Khmer nation's domestic affairs.

Privately Sihanouk was convinced the communists were his real enemies. But his persistent derogatory comments about the United States aggravated American officials. Secretary of State Rusk told Cambodia's ambassador that he must remember that small countries are not the only ones capable of outrage. "Big countries can get mad, too."

President Kennedy spoke to the Fort Worth Chamber of Commerce November 22 during a political trip to Texas. "So this country, which desires only to be free, which desired to live at peace for eighteen years under three different administrations, has borne more than its share of the burden, has stood watch for more than its number of years. I don't think we are fatigued or tired. We would like to live as we once lived. But history will not permit it. The communist balance of power is still strong. The balance of power is still on the side of freedom. We are still the keystone of the arch of freedom, and I think we will continue to do as we have done in our past, our duty. . . ."

Kennedy had gone to Texas because there were reports that his popularity was down, and the Democrats would need the state's support when he ran for re-election the following year.

It was a bright, sunshiny day and as the Kennedy motocade drove through downtown Dallas there were enthusiastic crowds to greet him and his wife as they drove by. But as the President's limousine drove by the Texas School Book Depository, a shot rang out. It came from the Depository's sixth floor. Kennedy's body stiffened and lurched forward. A second bullet struck the President's head and he collapsed on his wife Jacqueline's lap.

His limousine sped off to Parkland Memorial Hospital where at 1 p.m., November 22, the President was pronounced dead.

The nation was stunned by the news, and at first there were fears of a conspiracy, but they proved unfounded. Lee Harvey Oswald, who was accused of the shooting, was shot and killed that weekend as he was being transferred to another jail. A local nightclub owner, Jack Ruby, killed Oswald. Ruby was later sentenced to death for killing Oswald, but the ruling was overturned by a higher court. Ruby died of natural causes before he could be re-tried.

Once it was learned that Oswald, an ex-Marine, had lived in the Soviet Union, had a Russian wife, and been active in the pro-Castro Fair Play for Cuba Committee, there was concern that the assassination had been part of a communist conspiracy. This was denied by Premier Krushchev in Russia, and there is no evidence that the Soviet Union was involved. In fact, Krushchev ordered that his government provide whatever facts it had on Oswald to the committee that the new President, Lyndon Johnson, had sworn in shortly after Kennedy's death, set up to investigate the assassination. Ten months later the commission reported that both Oswald and Ruby had acted alone.

At 2:30 p.m. that afternoon Lyndon B. Johnson was sworn in as President on Air Force One, the plane taking Kennedy's body back to Washington.

Some Americans have speculated since Kennedy's death that if he had lived he would have withdrawn support from the South Vietnamese government. They quickly forget that it was Kennedy who intensified the war by sending more than 16,000 so-called advisers to South Vietnam, including helicopter pilots who flew combat missions. His last public words belie such talk.

Soon after taking office President Johnson renewed Kennedy's pledge to withdraw some American armed forces, but further solicited plans from the Joint Chiefs of Staff for increased clandestine warfare against North Vietnam, and for cross-border incursions into Laos to check infiltration.

The deaths of President Diem and his brother brought South Vietnam to the brink of collapse, averted only by the United States' later decision to commit combat troops to fight the ground war. Diem had been the only South Vietnamese leader with sufficient stature to oppose Ho Chi Minh, and his death was a disaster for the Republic of Vietnam.

Although American officials were appalled by the brutality of Diem's death, President Johnson recognized the newly-formed government in Saigon November 24 to maintain diplomatic relations. He restored about $500,000 in yearly aid funds, but it was soon evident that South Vietnam's faltering economy, adverse military situation and the failure of the strategic hamlet program called for a reappraisal of American actions.

Meanwhile, Vietcong activity in the countryside increased and the situation through South Vietnam rapidly worsened.

So chaotic were conditions in South Vietnam that it would have been sensible on the part of the American government to adopt a policy of winning the war, or to end its participation. Every previous American government had insisted that South Vietnam had to establish a sound government and fight the war on its own, but President Johnson instead escalated the American involvement instead of insisting that South Vietnam's armed forces take over responsibility for defending their country. It was a tragic mistake that put the United States into a classic no-win situation.

By the end of 1963 American combat deaths reached their highest level yet. Four-hundred-and-eighty-nine were killed during the year compared to 109 in 1962.

The political situation in South Vietnam continued to deteriorate in January when the provisional government of General Minh was brought down by Major General Nguyen Khanh. Now the Joint Chiefs in Washington recommended to the President that the United States take over the fighting in South Vietnam. The Minh government had floundered since it took office and it was removed without popular protest. Politicians who had been loyal to former President Diem had high hopes that Khanh, once known as Diem's adopted son, would vindicate him. A three-man military junta was appointed to run the government. It included Major General Duong Van "Big" Minh, Major General Tran Van Don and Major General Le Van Kim. Khanh later was appointed the group's leader as Chairman of the Revolutionary Military Council while Minh remained as nominal chief of state.

President Johnson revealed on February 29, 1964, that Lockheed Aircraft had developed a new jet capable of flying at 2,000 miles per hour. Everything about the SR-71 all-titanium airplane was new. Even a new fuel, oils and greases had to be developed especially for it. Although research planes could fly at brief spurts of such speed, the SR-71 and its figher derivative the YF-12A could fly continuously at such speeds hour after hour. It was an achievement that the Russians could never match, and so there was no need for a fighter version. But the SR-71 served throughout most of the rest of the century as a reconnaissance airplane and, until satellites took over the job, as a spy plane.

Another 2,000-mile-an-hour plane was revealed in May when the B-70 bomber, made by North American, was unveiled. The 275-ton bomber, capable of flying 6,000 miles at 70,000 feet, was called obsolete by many critics.

An American policy of gradual response to communist aggression was established in March in South Vietnam despite opposition by the Pentagon's service chiefs, and a campaign of covert and naval military pressure against North Vietnam was approved by McNamara.

Meanwhile, on March 6 General Khanh fired three corps commanders and five of nine division commanders. Next, he ordered the wholesale removal of 23 province chiefs. Such indiscriminate action disrupted South Vietnam's leadership and shook the confidence of the people in their armed forces. Military desertions soared, and Vietcong prestige reached a new high as North Vietnam increased its support to its followers in the South.

President Johnson's "war on poverty" that he had proposed in his State of the Union address was offered to Congress on March 16. His plan for a special attack on poverty in the 11-state Appalachian region was estimated to cost $962 million. Congress acted on August 11 with passage of the Economic Opportunity Act to set up a Job Corps, a Domestic Peace Corps, and work-training and work-study programs for youths. An appropriation to implement the act for Appalachia was not passed until the following year.

In the Far East, with various factions in Laos engaged in continued fighting, the United States announced on May 19 that it would use every means short of military action to halt the fighting and preserve Laos's independence. When the fighting continued the State Department revealed on May 27 that light military planes had been sent to the pro-American group in Laos to use against the communist forces.

Southern Senators filibustered for 75 days during the spring on civil rights matters. It was not until June 19 that a majority vote ended the filibuster. This was the first time cloture—limiting debate by calling for a vote—had been used in a civil rights case. The Senate passed the Civil Rights Bill of 1964 by a vote of 73-27 to ban racial discrimination in voting, in education, in public places, in employment, and in all federally aided programs. It was a great victory for President Johnson because the bill was far stronger than one sought by President Kennedy. Johnson called its passage "a challenge to all Americans to transform the commands of our laws into the custom of our land." When he signed it on July 2 he said, "Its purpose is not to divide, but to end divisions."

Republicans met in San Francisco on July 13, 1964, to elect a slate for the coming Presidential election. Arizona's Senator Barry Goldwater, an arch-conservative, was nominated and William E. Miller of New York was named as his running mate.

The Democrats met in Atlantic City August 29 and by acclamation nominated President Johnson. He chose Senator Hubert H. Humphrey of Minnesota as his running mate.

Before dawn August 2 the old American destroyer "Maddox" was investigating coastal activity in waters off North Vietnam. Eight miles offshore, it encountered hundreds of North Vietnamese junks. Her skipper, Captain John H. J. Herrick, steered eastward to avoid a clash and he requested of his superiors that his ship's itinerary be changed. His request was denied.

South Vietnam's fast patrol boats had been in North Vietnam's waters since July 31, but 120 miles north of the "Maddox," intercepting junks and fishing vessels used to ferry arms to the Vietcong in South Vietnam.

The "Maddox" was attacked by three high-speed Vietnamese patrol boats in international waters approximately 28 miles from shore. They were first detected on radar and were tracked at a closing speed of 40 knots. When the boats fired on the "Maddox," the destroyer took evasive action and fired warning shots. When these shots were ignored Herrick ordered his ship to return the fire. He also sent an emergency appeal to the carrier "Ticonderoga" for air support and Task Force 77 went into action for the first time. The pilots reported that one boat was sunk and that the other two were damaged.

President Johnson warned the North Vietnamese the next day that "United States ships have traditionally operated freely on the high seas in accordance with the rights guaranteed by international law . . ." He warned the communists of grave consequences if they continued these attacks.

The destroyer "C. Turner Joy" joined the "Maddox" August 3 in the Gulf of Tonkin with orders to fire in self defense, but was advised not to pursue attackers.

The night of August 4 the "Maddox" reported at least five high-powered contacts 36 miles away. "Ticonderoga" pilots again responded but they reported that they could find no evidence of enemy attackers.

Two hours after the start of the supposed second attack Admiral U.S. G. Sharp was given authority by the Joint Chiefs to take immediate punitive air action against North Vietnam at dawn the next day.

But then Sharp received a report from Captain Herrick about his doubts that there actually had been a second attack.

In Washington the Joint Chiefs decided that a second attack had taken place, although reports from the scene were inconclusive.

Four torpedo boat bases and oil storage facilities at Phuc Loi and Vinh were attacked August 5 in retaliation.

A later review of all facts convinced Navy officials that the second attack never occurred, and that destroyers' guns had fired at radar "shadows."

Despite this later appraisal, President Johnson sent a message to Congress August 5 and asked for a joint resolution of support for his Southeast Asia policy. A resolution was prepared by the administration and introduced by the chairman of the Senate Foreign Relations Committee, J. William Fulbright, and the chairman of the Foreign Relations Committee of the House of Representatives, Thomas E. Morgan.

Congress passed this joint resolution almost unanimously, terming the attacks on the American destroyers part of a "deliberate and systematic campaign of aggression that the communist regime in North Vietnam had been waging against its neighbors and the nations joined with them." The resolution assured the President of the Congress's determination to "take all necessary measures to repel any armed attack . . . and to prevent any further aggression" until the President determined that peace and security of the area was reasonably assured.

This resolution gave President Johnson authority he should not have had without a declaration of war by Congress. It is inconceivable that his administration did not know at the time that the so-called second torpedo boat attack never occurred. In effect, the resolution was passed under false pretenses.

Opposition to the war was growing in the United States. In Oakland, California, 200 demonstrators tried to block a trainload of Vietnam-bound troops. "Suckers!" they shouted, brandishing signs that said, "Off to the slaughter!" During the summer months 15,000 protesters had picketed the White House in Washington calling for an end "to United States aggression in Vietnam."

The Reverend Martin Luther King, Jr., was honored on October 14. He was awarded the Nobel Peace Prize for his efforts in "furtherance of brotherhood among men" through his advocacy of black civil rights. He said that "every penny" would be given to the civil rights movement.

Despite the growing problem of America's involvement in Indochina, an overwhelming majority of the American people voted for Lyndon Johnson for President. The plurality of the Johnson/Humphrey ticket was 15½ million as Goldwater and the Republicans suffered an overwhelming defeat. The electoral vote was equally lopsided with 486 for Johnson and 52 for Goldwater. Democrats gained two seats in the Senate and 38 in the House, and won 17 out of 25 governorship contests.

When Johnson spoke to the nation January 4, 1965, it was with the firm conviction that most Americans were solidly behind his policies. He offered his own program to improve the quality of life in America. He called it "The Great Society" and spelled out federal efforts in education, health care and the arts as well as projects to break down regional pockets of poverty—particularly in cities—and a reduction of pollution in the nation's rivers and lakes. He specifically appealed to Congress to eliminate obstacles in the right to vote.

He had long waged an aggressive campaign for social programs while he served in Congress, and now he used his vast persuasive powers as a politician, and the prestige of the Presidency, to gain those ends. Raised in rural Texas as the son of a schoolteacher, he had first been elected to the House in 1938. For five full terms he earned the respect of his colleagues. His constituents admired his shrewd political maneuvering that he used to gain passage of various legislative proposals. Then he had been elected to the Senate where he ultimately became Senate Majority Leader.

His beliefs were simple: that in an integrated and inter-related society anything that hurts one segment ultimately hurts everyone. Poverty and ignorance, he believed, reduce the nation's strength and must be reduced and, hopefully, eliminated.

Some of the programs had been initiated earlier by other Democratic presidents, including John F. Kennedy. But Johnson got them passed through his political skills earned in large part in both houses of Congress.

North Vietnamese officials believed at the start of 1965 that it marked the beginning of the war's final phase, during which South Vietnam's army would be destroyed by direct military action, and the government and its people would lose their will to fight. They correctly judged that the government of South Vietnam had been weakened by a series of coups following President Diem's assassination in 1963. Since then the South Vietnamese Army had suffered a series of defeats that had led to widespread demoralization. Government control of rural areas was continually eroding as the Vietcong expanded their control. With the start of the new year North Vietnam's army units for the first time moved into the Central Highlands in regimental strength. Infiltration from the North increased and soon reached a rate of more than 1,000 a month. They attacked Pleiku and killed eight Americans and wounded 126 others.

American authorities now were convinced that South Vietnam's armed forces no longer could contain the rising military threat to the security of their country without extensive American military and economic assistance. Ambassador Maxwell Taylor and General William C. Westmoreland recommended the commitment of American ground troops and the President agreed.

The explosive situation in South Vietnam erupted again in February as another power struggle began. Dissident military leaders revolted against Khanh and troops seized Saigon. The Armed Forces Council declared February 15 that it alone had responsibility for selecting the prime minister and the chief of state. While veteran politician Phan Khao Suu remained as chief of state, the council appointed a Saigon physician, Dr. Phan Huy Quat who had formerly served as foreign minister in 1964, as prime minister. Then February 25 a group of senior generals led by Major General Nguyen Van Thieu, commander of IV Corps, and Air Vice Marshal Nguyen Cao Ky who commanded the Air Force, deposed Khanh, the veteran of other coup attempts, as commander-in-chief of South Vietnam's armed forces.

With the military and political situation assuming disastrous proportions, Westmoreland recommended to Admiral Sharp that Marine battalions be sent to Da Nang because of the "questionable capability of the Vietnamese to protect the base."

At the end of February, President Johnson agreed to commit two battalions of the Marine Expeditionary Brigade to Da Nang to protect it.

A new phase of the war began. With the landings of 5,000 troops March 31 a third of the Marine ground forces and two-thirds of its helicopter squadrons in the Western Pacific were committed to South Vietnam. Now there were 23,000 "advisers" in South Vietnam. But the Joint Chiefs made it clear March 7 that "the United States Marine Force will not, repeat, will not engage in day-to-day actions against the Vietcong."

With the situation growing more desperate in late February President Johnson, Secretary of State Rusk and McNamara approved a strategic air offensive to be called "Rolling Thunder," but only against targets below the 20th parallel. McNamara also insisted that the size and frequency of the air offensive be decided in Washington, and that he personally must approve each target. This was an ill-advised decision because after attacks were authorized later above the 20th the threat to American planes had multiplied and it became a perilous area for fliers. President Johnson placed even further restrictions by saying that strikes against surface-to-air missile targets could only be made if they were firing at American planes. All other sites were off-limits. McNamara was convinced that the air campaign would make little difference to United States operations in the South, and that the risk of Chinese confrontations against American fliers was too great.

Years later, when President Richard M. Nixon authorized massive bombing of the Hanoi-Haiphong area in December 1972, the Chinese did not intervene. The Americans were out-bluffed, and this decision extended the war and increased the casualties on all sides.

CHAPTER 22

Johnson Increases American Involvement in Indochina

PRESIDENT JOHNSON PROPOSED TO OFFICIALS OF NORTH VIETNAM APRIL 7 that "unconditional discussions" be started to end the war. The communists ignored the offer, believing they were winning.

After meeting with his defense advisers, the President agreed to step up military and economic aid to South Vietnam. His proposal included the use of troops to protect bases and to train the South Vietnamese armed forces.

Violence erupted in the Dominican Republic April 28 between the American-supported government of Donald Rei Cabral and rebel troops under ex-President Juan Bosch. Johnson sent in a contingent of Marines. He charged May 2 that the leftist guerrilla movement had been taken over by communists who wished to exploit the civil war to gain power for themselves. Eventually the United States was forced to dispatch 20,000 troops to control the situation. American troops withdrew after the Organization of American States agreed May 26 to provide a peace-keeping force to enforce the truce.

Meanwhile the ground situation in South Vietnam worsened and it was decided May 9 in Washington to approve an 18,000 to 20,000 increase in American forces, and to permit Marine forces to take part in combat operations. This brought the number in South Vietnam to 42,200 personnel, and an additional 20,000 were authorized in June. With new American combat and advisory forces, Westmoreland initiated a program to train South Vietnam's armed forces, hopefully to make them capable of defending their country with minimal outside assistance.

General Westmoreland ordered search and destroy missions June 15, and by the end of the month activity was stepped up in all three Marine enclaves.

Johnson advised the American people July 26 that the American troop level would be raised to 125,000 and that Westmoreland would receive whatever reinforcements he needed. To achieve these goals he called for a doubling of the draft from 17,000 to 35,000. The President informed the American people that the non-communist nations of Asia were incapable of resisting the "growing ambition of Asian communism." Then, on August 4, the President asked Congress for an additional $1.7 billion to support the war.

Blacks in the Watts ghetto of Los Angeles began a riot August 11 that lasted for six days. It began when a white police officer stopped a black driver for drunkenness. Before it was over the riot killed 34 people, injured 1,000, and caused $175 million in property damage. All those killed in Watts were blacks, and they were killed by police and National Guardsmen who tried to put down the riot. Approximately 4,000 blacks were arrested. Cornell Henderson, a black worker for the Congress of Racial Equality, gave one reason for the outbreak: "There were a lot of young thugs and agitators but there were a lot of others who were just discontented and took advantage of the situation for emotional release." He charged that the Black Muslims had preached hate and disorder.

These riots in the North were in sharp contrast to the mostly peaceful demonstrations by blacks in the South. As a result many whites who had supported President Johnson's anti-poverty programs now turned against him, and he lost their support for further legislation to provide more jobs, better housing and more educational opportunities which was the root of the problem. Investigators found that these riots were not caused by outside agitators but were "an explosion, an all but hopeless violent protest." Unemployment of black males was 30 percent in Watts, and certainly contributed to the unrest.

Chinese Defense Minister Lin Piao revealed that the People's Republic of China would not intervene directly in Vietnam as Mao Tse-tung began the Great Proletarian Cultural Revolution and unleashed "Red Guards" in a devastating purge of Communist Party ranks. This disclosure should have been used to put the "squeeze" on North Vietnam but unfortunately its impact was either misunderstood or not understood at all. Failure to act by the Johnson administration to take advantage of the situation proved to be a tragic mistake.

American bombing raids against strictly military targets in the southern part of North Vietnam had gradually moved farther north covering most of the country, but not Hanoi or Haiphong and the most important strategic targets.

Secretary of Defense McNamara wrote a detailed memorandum to President Johnson November 7 saying he was convinced that the United States would never achieve its desired goals with a force of 160,000 Americans in Vietnam, and the 50,000 who were scheduled to be sent. He insisted that more men would be needed and he called for a halt to the bombing of the North, saying such bombing would not force Ho Chi Minh to sue for peace.

Johnson was skeptical as were Ambassador Lodge, Admiral Sharp and the Joint Chiefs of Staff. Lodge spoke for all of them: "An end to the bombing of the North with no other quid pro quo than the opening of negotiations would load the dice in favor of the Communists, and demoralize the government of Vietnam. It would in effect leave the Communists free to devastate the South with impunity while we tie our hands in the North."

But Soviet Ambassador Anatoly Dobrynin and a Hungarian diplomat told Rusk that a "few weeks" of bombing halt would be enough to bring North Vietnam to the conference table. They offered no guarantees—just hope.

A truce in the fighting in Vietnam was approved by all parties to start December 24. The Vietcong and American officials agreed to the truce at the urging of Pope Paul VI. Five days later President Johnson sent top officials to Rome, Paris, Warsaw, Ottawa, Moscow and Belgrade to confer with heads of state about a permanent peace.

The war in Indochina had brought about unprecedented protests throughout the United States as more than 100,000 people marched in anti-war parades and took part in rallies. The movement was not entirely communist manipulated. The greatest number of protesters acted out of moral and humanistic reasons.

The "Rolling Thunder" air bombing campaign had achieved only limited success because the most important targets still remained off-limits. In 1965 an average of 200 tons of bombs were dropped each week. The tonnage increased to 1,000 the following year when more lucrative targets were authorized. The Navy alone lost 105 planes and 82 pilots and crew members who were needlessly sacrificed on the altar of political expediency. Many of the targets were worthless and pilots took the same risks as they would against high-value targets. All too many air strikes merely splintered thousands of trees in Laos and South Vietnam. Despite the bombings, the Vietcong still controlled the same areas in South Vietnam it had held the previous year.

The last strike of 1965 against North Vietnam—before President Johnson's seven-week bombing pause—was made against the first industrial target authorized by the Joint Chiefs when the Uong Bi thermal power plant was bombed north of Haiphong. Heavy damage was caused and Haiphong's electrical power was reduced for weeks. All further attacks were suspended to help the peace talks that had begun again.

Martin Luther King's non-violent campaign to gain equal rights for his people got caught up in the anti-war protests. Therefore his leadership and non-violent tactics came under increasing criticism from more militant black crusaders and members of the white protest movement. As a result the black movement became splintered after the ghetto riots. This was unfortunate because the Voting Rights Act, for the first time since Reconstruction days following the Civil War, gave blacks full participation in state and federal elections. Thus further reforms were undermined although legal denial of fundamental civil rights could never be practiced again.

The growing cost in lives of the American involvement in Indochina disturbed the American people when casualty figures for 1965 were released the first day of the new year. One thousand, three-hundred-fifty Americans had died, another 5,300 were wounded and almost 150 were either missing or prisoners. The South Vietnamese government also revealed that 11,100 of their young men had died, with twice that many wounded, and 7,400 reported as missing. It was estimated that the Vietcong had suffered 14,600 killed in action while another 5,750 had been captured.

When it became clear January 31, 1966, that Johnson's peace offensive for Vietnam had failed, the President ordered a resumption of American bombing over North Vietnam. He had hoped to open peace talks with the communists but instead he said his efforts had brought "only denunciation and rejection." During the 37 days of the bombing halt, the United States had conferred with the heads of 115 governments, as well as officials of the Vatican, the United Nations, the Organization of American States and the North Atlantic Treaty Organization.

Despite renewal of the bombing, the same restrictions that had hitherto governed the selection of targets, remained in force. The President again called upon the United States to seek a peaceful solution to the conflict.

Conservation and environmental protection received the President's attention February 23 in a special message to Congress. He called for projects to clean America's waterways, federal grants to preserve historical landmarks and funds to finance pollution-control research. The Congress followed up on his proposal and the President signed the Clean Waters

Restoration Act into law November 3. It was a long-overdue attempt to purify America's polluted rivers and lakes.

Johnson signed the "Cold War Bill of Rights" March 3 to give Vietnam veterans the rights enjoyed by those who fought in World War II and Korea. The new bill permitted special education, housing and health and job benefits for veterans who spent at least 180 days in service since January 31, 1955.

The Department of Defense admitted March 9 that more than 21 percent of the American Army's enlisted men killed in combat in Vietnam were blacks, although they made up only 11 percent of America's male population between the ages of 18-29. The department denied that blacks were given more combat assignments than whites. Blacks had enlisted in large numbers, however, and their poverty backgrounds had deprived many of them from taking advantage of educational opportunities. Therefore they often ended up in infantry units where casualties were higher.

France upset NATO officials March 31 by announcing that she was withdrawing all her toops from the organization's integrated command structure by July 1. This was unsettling, but even worse was France's insistence that all foreign bases including American, Canadian and West German, plus two NATO headquarters, must be removed from France by April 1, 1967. President de Gaulle declared, however, that France would remain a member of NATO. This decision proved costly to the United States because hundreds of millions of dollars had been spent on French bases, and now it had to bear the cost of their relocation.

Buddhist opposition to Premier Ky's regime in Vietnam resulted in a government crackdown on May 15 in Da Nang. Ky had announced the week before that he would not resign after elections to set up a civilian government. The next day Buddhist leaders appealed to the United States for support but they were told that it would only use diplomacy to bring the two factions together. During the week-long battle in Da Nang 75 people were killed and 500 wounded. Buddhist opposition was not crushed until June 23 when their last stronghold in Saigon was overrun.

During the spring months as the bombing of North Vietnam continued American planes encountered increasing resistance from surface-to-air missiles, communist fighters and anti-aircraft guns that took their toll. But with these air operations, and more effective ground operations, the southward flow of men and supplies from North Vietnam began to show a drastic reduction. Still, many of North Vietnam's most vital targets remained off-limits.

Although it wasn't revealed until later, the world's fastest and highest flying aircraft went into production at the Lockheed plant in Burbank, California. The SR-71 "Blackbird" was designed as an unarmed reconnaissance aircraft with a speed in excess of 2,000 miles per hour in sustained flight and cameras that could cover an area of 100,000 square miles in one hour. In service, it flew over communist countries, or along their peripheries, at Mach 3-plus speeds at altitudes between 80,000 and 100,000 feet. The first "stealth" aircraft, its arrow-shaped frame makes radar detection difficult and its black epoxy paint—for which it gets its "Blackbird" nickname—absorbs hostile radar emissions and limits heat emissions that could be detected by an enemy radar tracking system. It is also capable of deflecting incoming anti-aircraft missiles.

Secretary of Defense McNamara announced June 11 that military strength in Vietnam would be increased to 285,000. Seven days later President Johnson announced that the bombing of North Vietnam would be intensified "to raise the cost of aggression at its source."

The Supreme Court made an historic decision June 13 affecting the rights of criminal cases. In Miranda vs Arizona, the court ruled 5 to 4 that an accused must be apprised of his or her rights before interrogation. The majority said this was inherent in the Fifth Amendment rights of individuals against self-incrimination. The ruling stated that a suspect must be told that his remarks may be used against him, and that he has the right to a lawyer during interrogation.

People of many countries now began to protest the growing contamination of the atmosphere as new nations continued to explode nuclear devices in the atmosphere. France completed a series of tests October 4, claiming that they were necessary for "world equilibrium." Three weeks later the People's Republic of China joined the "atomic club" by exploding a nuclear bomb.

Congress approved nearly $3 billion for foreign aid October 7, 28 percent of it for military aid. Four days later Congress passed an appropriation for the Department of Defense totaling $50 billion that was $400 million more than the President had sought. The bill authorized the President to call up as many as 789,000 reserve forces without a declaration of national emergency or approval by Congress.

The House Armed Services Committee had authorized an investigation of the nation's draft in late June, reporting later that it was basically sound. It did recommend that young men be drafted at an earlier age— 19 or 20 instead of 22 or 23—and made those who had been deferred to attend college eligible until age 35. Lewis B. Hershey, Selective Service Director, testified before the committee that he opposed the lottery system. Although it had its shortcomings, namely in the matter of deferments, most Congressmen believed it was the fairest possible way to draft eligible young men for service. Mental standards for draftees were reduced November 29 from a score of 16 to 10, and this prompted the Defense

Department to announce that 2.4 million men who had been rejected would now be reexamined.

President Johnson met in Manila on October 25 with the heads of six other nations involved in the war in Vietnam. At the end of the conference they issued a four-point declaration of peace to announce the goals of the nations involved—the Philippines, Thailand, New Zealand, South Korea and South Vietnam. The goals, they said, were to foster political self-determination as well as economic, social and cultural cooperation to break the "bonds of poverty, illiteracy and disease." They also pledged to withdraw their troops six months after North Vietnam ceased its aggression.

The growing unpopularity of the war in Indochina had an impact on the fall elections. The Republicans gained three Senate seats, 47 in the House, won eight governorships and 540 seats in state legislatures. Edward Brooke of Massachusetts became the first black since Reconstruction days to win a seat in the Senate. And, he won by a large margin. The Democrats still maintained control of both houses by a margin of 65 in the House and 30 in the Senate.

It had been a good year for the United States in space. NASA had made 62 successful launches of spacecraft, five of them manned, for a grand total since 1962 of 267. Four weather satellites had been launched, and one was providing photographs of the weather of the entire world every 24 hours. The Soviet Union and the United States both made soft landings on the moon, and both sent satellites into orbit around the moon. Gemini's last capsule flight lasted about 100 hours. During the year the Soviet Union announced no manned flights, leading to speculation that its astronauts had encountered medical problems. Instead, two dogs had gone into space, and their capsule had been recovered after 22 days.

For the first time American casualties exceeded those of South Vietnam's armed forces. In 1966 some 5,008 Americans had been killed and 30,093 wounded. Total casualties since January 1, 1961, were 6,664 dead and 37,738 wounded. The Defense Department said that troop strength in Southeast Asia was 380,000 by January 1, 1967. A week later Americans launched their largest offensive to date as 16,000 American and 14,000 South Vietnamese troops participated in "Operation Cedar Falls" in the Mekong River delta. This was a drive against enemy positions in the "Iron Triangle," 25 miles northwest of Saigon. The offensive lasted until January 19. Six thousand civilians were sent to refugee camps and their homes were burned or flattened by bulldozers. The area became a vast wasteland as thousands of acres of forests were defoliated.

Admiral Sharp made a new attempt in early 1967 to get permission to deny North Vietnam access to supplies from China and Russia. In particular he wanted to curtail the flow of men and supplies from North Vietnam into Laos and South Vietnam. Through channels he said there were six basic target systems in North Vietnam: electric power, war supporting industries, transportation support facilities, military complexes, petroleum storage depots and the air defense system. He reminded the Joint Chiefs that attacks against these target systems—all of which needed approval by higher authority—should be approved as a package and not doled out a few at a time.

The Joint Chiefs agreed but each time McNamara turned them down. Sharp continuously pointed out that more than 85 percent of the war materials that arrived in North Vietnam came by sea through Haiphong. Cargoes were unloaded on a 24-hour-a-day basis from Russia and her satellite countries. He had strongly recommended that North Vietnam's harbors be mined, but this request was rejected.

In 1972 when President Nixon authorized such operations it cost less than $1 million and not one person on either side was killed. It should have been done in 1965 when mining might well have been decisive in ending the war.

The space program had established a remarkable safety record although three astronauts had been killed in unrelated airplane crashes. That record was broken January 27 when three astronauts, Virgil Grissom, Edward White and Roger Chaffee were trapped on top of the Saturn 1-B and died within 13 seconds when their Apollo 1 spacecraft was swept by fire. The craft was being readied for a launch when the disaster occurred during a full-scale simulation of the launching process. The fire spread quickly because of the rich oxygen atmosphere in the capsule, and a tape recording of their voices indicated that the fire was so intense that they didn't have a chance to unscrew the exit hatch. NASA called for an investigation and a board on April 9 denounced "deficiencies in design and engineering, manufacture and quality control of the entire Apollo project" which, it was hoped, would put Americans on the moon. Specifically the fire was blamed on a defective electrical wire.

Death came to Soviet cosmonaut Vladimir Komaroz April 24 when he was killed after his spacecraft's parachute failed to open upon reentry. This was the only manned flight this year because American flights had been suspended following the Apollo disaster.

The growing opposition against the war in Indochina prompted General William C. Westmoreland, commander of American forces there, to criticize anti-war factions as "unpatriotic." Senator J. William Fulbright, who had become more and more vocal in opposition to the war, accused the Johnson administration of prompting Westmoreland to speak out because they wanted to escalate America's involvement in the war.

With the United States involved more and more in Southeast Asia, government officials paid little attention to the Middle East where sporadic fighting had continued between Israel and its neighbors Egypt, Syria and Jordan. With renewed terrorist raids, Israel warned Syria May 11 in the Security Council that it would defend itself. Six days later the United Arab Republic's President Gamal Abdal Nasser demanded that UN peace-keeping forces be removed immediately from the armistice line between Israel and Egypt. He was upset by allegations from Jordan and Saudi Arabia that he was using these forces to protect his country. Secretary General U Thant reluctantly agreed and the UN Emergency Force was discontinued May 19. Three days later Nasser declared that the Strait of Tiran was closed, thus blocking shipping to Elath in Israel, that country's only outlet to the South and East. Efforts to mediate the crisis were blocked by the Soviet Union which charged that Israel was at fault.

Israel's government decided June 5 that further negotiations were fruitless. When Jordan and Syria shelled Israeli positions, Israel attacked the Arab nations on all fronts. The United Nations Security Council passed a ceasefire resolution the following day and the United Arab Republic broke off diplomatic relations with the United States and denounced Great Britain. Nasser charged that Great Britain had taken part in the air war on Israel's side which both nations denied.

The Soviet Union broke diplomatic relations with Israel June 10, the day both sides accepted a ceasefire. But in six days Israel had captured territory four times its size including the Sinai Peninsula, the old city of Jerusalem, all Jordanian territory west of the Jordan River, and the heights in Syria which that nation had used for years to shell Jewish settlements.

In a lightning war, reminiscent of German blitzkrieg tactics in World War II, the Israelis destroyed hundreds of Arab planes and Soviet-built tanks. Thirty-five thousand Arab soldiers were killed while Israel lost only 679 dead and 2,600 wounded.

Congress extended the draft law June 20 to June 30, 1971. Johnson was given authority to cancel deferments of most graduate students, but not undergraduates, unless it was necessary because of a military manpower shortage.

President Johnson met June 23 with Soviet Premier Aleksei Kosygin at Glassboro, New Jersey. This site was a compromise because Kosygin had refused to go to Washington and Johnson had declined to go to New

York. There Johnson was informed by Kosygin that he had received a message from the North Vietnamese an hour earlier saying that, if the bombing of the North ceased, Hanoi's representatives would talk with officials of the United States. This was no time to let up on the pressure against North Vietnam. Air attacks had hurt her economy but, due to restrictions on targets, her ability to wage war in the South had not seriously been impaired. They met again two days later for talks that were described as cordial, but they failed to reach a meeting of the minds on controversial items such as the war in Indochina.

Despite use of the world's most sophisticated weapons in the hands of the 448,800 Americans in Vietnam by July 1, 1967, a highly disciplined and motivated enemy who employed no airpower in the South, little naval support and, during this period, comparatively few mechanized vehicles, still managed to fight on.

The carrier "Forrestal," on duty off Indochina in the Gulf of Tonkin, lost 134 crewmen July 29 when a fire ravaged the huge ship. A punctured aircraft fuel tank ignited the blaze that swept the flight deck. This was the worst naval accident in a war zone since World War II.

Thurgood Marshall was confirmed by the United States Senate August 30 as the first black justice to sit on the Supreme Court. The great-grandson of a slave, Marshall was Solicitor General before his appointment.

American planes began attacks on some targets along the border between North and South Vietnam August 11 that had previously been off-limits, although some high-priority targets still remained in that category. The Soviet Union called the bombing "a new and extremely serious step."

In March, General Westmoreland asked for 200,000 more troops for a total of 671,616. The Joint Chiefs forwarded his request to McNamara and they also recommended mobilization of the reserves. They also proposed extending the war into Laos and Cambodia and possibly North Vietnam.

The President turned down the request. "When we add divisions, can't the enemy add divisions? If so, where does it all end?"

During August some targets were released within the buffer zone sanctuary along the border between Red China and North Vietnam. In that month the Navy lost 16 aircraft; the highest number for a month in the war.

Throughout August and succeeding months strikes were made against bridges, rail lines and warehouses near Haiphong to isolate the port, although its facilities remained off-limits and could not be directly struck.

In early September Admiral Sharp, commander-in-chief, Pacific, called

General Wheeler, chairman of the Joint Chiefs of Staff, to tell him that he did not agree with the limited bombing objectives approved by Secretary of Defense McNamara and the administration. He said, "What we should do is to destroy North Vietnam's economy."

Sharp pressed for a plan that would deny external assistance to North Vietnam, destroy in-depth resources within North Vietnam that contributed to their aggression, and disrupt the movement of men and materials in South Vietnam and Laos. He sought the mining of three deep-water ports: Haiphong, Cam Pha and Hon Gai. His plan called for destruction of war-supporting industries within Hanoi's and Haiphong's prohibited zones, and air strikes against major lines of communication between these two cities.

John Colvin, consul general of the British mission in Hanoi during 1966 and most of 1967, said long after the war that by September 1967, the Americans had won the war, and then renounced victory by ending the bombing. Prior to that time he said Hanoi's streets were lined with war material from China, but by September there was none at all. He said the key to the effectiveness of the bombing in 1967 was its consistency that "for the first time allowed the North Vietnamese no time to repair war-making facilities." He said their will had been eroded to near extinction, and that their capacity to wage a major war had been broken by the continued cutting of railroad lines from China and Haiphong to Hanoi and by putting its ports out of action.

Colvin said that in his opinion that prompt use of airpower against North Vietnam's industrial northeast would have won the war in 1965 and would have spared both sides the agonizingly higher costs of gradualism advocated by McNamara.

Navy carriers had launched an unprecedented barrage of major attacks against North Vietnam's vital northeast industrial sector, hitting railroad yards, petroleum storage yards as well as bridges and trans-shipment points.

Almost five million South Vietnamese voted September 3 to elect Nguyen Van Thieu as president, and Nguyen Cao Ky as vice-president. They had been opposed by 10 non-military candidates, and there were the usual charges of fraud. But 22 Americans who observed the election called it "reasonably honest."

Secretary of Defense McNamara revealed a "thin" antiballistic missile system, composed of the Nike and Spartan missiles, to shield the United States from a possible nuclear attack from Communist China. In a speech in San Francisco he said the system would cost $5 billion over the next five years and was selected in lieu of another system that would have cost eight times as much. He added that the more expensive system undoubtedly would encourage the Soviet Union to increase its own missile production.

On October 21, some 50,000 anti-war protesters gathered in Washington for a march from the Lincoln Memorial to the Pentagon. There they were met by solid lines of troops with fixed bayonets. There were sporadic acts of violence that resulted in the arrest of 650 marchers.

But thousands of New Yorkers drove through their city with their lights on to demonstrate support for American troops fighting in Vietnam.

The Second Republic of Vietnam came into official existence November 1, four years after the end of the first following Diem's assassination, with Thieu as President and Ky as Vice President. Its Constitution, approved a year earlier by delegates to a constitutional assembly, called for a two-house legislature and a powerful president.

By the end of 1967 American troops in Vietnam numbered 486,000 men and women, an increase of 100,000 since the start of the year. Deaths reached a new high for a total of 9,350, almost 3,000 more than the total for the previous six years.

Secretary of Defense McNamara submitted his resignation November 29 to the President. It was the only logical course for someone who found himself so far out of line with administration policy. It was announced that he would become president of the World Bank January 19, 1968.

North Vietnam's minister of foreign affairs declared the last day of 1967 that if the United States unconditionally ceased its bombing, North Vietnam was prepared to talk. This was a smoke screen to hide her true intentions of developing a theme that the United States was ready to make a deal with North Vietnam. Of course, with cessation of the bombing, North Vietnam could speed up infiltration movements into the South during the dry season without heavy losses.

After discussions between President Thieu and Ambassador Bunker, General Westmoreland issued a joint declaration of a 36-hour cease-fire from the evening of January 29 through the morning of the 31st for the Tet holiday.

In early January 1968, South Vietnamese forces captured Nam Dong, a political commissar assigned to one of the Vietcong's principal headquarters. He disclosed that North Vietnam was switching its strategy from a protracted war to a general offensive-general uprising. This was a radical departure, indicating there was now no hope in Hanoi of another victory like the one over the French at Dien Bien Phu, but a growing belief among communist leaders that a protracted war would cause them unacceptable losses and might end in their regime's collapse. It was now believed that a general military offensive, coupled with a popular uprising, could succeed. They believed that the United States presidential election in November could be used to their strategic advantage and that a communist victory before the election would make it impossible for the Johnson administration to authorize more American troops for South Vietnam.

CHAPTER 23

Tet

COMMUNIST FORCES BEGAN A SIEGE OF KHE SANH JANUARY 21, 1968, a strategic stronghold 14 miles south of Vietnam's demilitarized zone. Months of savage fighting resulted until the siege was lifted April 5. Then the base was abandoned to the communists.

A grave international incident took place January 23 when the U.S.S. "Pueblo," a Navy intelligence ship with 83 Americans on board, was seized off the Korean coast but in international waters by North Korean patrol boats. It was taken into port at Wonsan. North Korea claimed that the ship had violated its waters, a fact denied by the United States. But North Korea had arbitrarily set its territorial limits as 10 miles at sea. Three days later the United States government appealed to the United Nations Security Council to obtain the ship's safe return. Negotiations continued for months after the crew was charged with crimes against North Korea, imprisoned and beaten.

The Senate Foreign Relations Committee had voted unanimously November 16, 1967, to require approval of Congress any time a President sought to send American troops abroad except to repel an attack on the United States, or to protect American citizens. The war in Indochina was excluded, but many Congressmen now had second thoughts about their blanket approval of President Johnson's actions following the Gulf of Tonkin incident in 1964. January 30 the committee voted to re-examine the incident, believing the President may have overreacted as a result of inaccurate or insufficient information.

Before the North Vietnamese initiated their attacks throughout South Vietnam January 30 they had expected that Ho Chi Minh's three-point battle cry, "Defend the North, Free the South, and Unite the Country"

259

would have a patriotic and emotional appeal to the South Vietnamese. Although the United States was labeled another imperialist power like France, the communists were quickly disillusioned. Their attacks were not fully coordinated, probably to deceive the South Vietnamese, as 28 out of 48 cities and provincial capitals were targeted.

The initial phase of the offensive abated during the first week of March, and it was apparent to allied leaders that in view of severe losses the enemy needed a respite to reorganize and refit his battered units.

During Senate confirmation hearings in January for Clark M. Clifford, Johnson's recommendation to replace McNamara as Secretary of Defense, Clifford expressed the fervent hope that the bombing of North Vietnam could be stopped if some kind of reciprocal action came from the communist leadership indicating they were ready to bargain for peace in good faith.

Such a statement was incredibly naive and the administration was falling into the same trap that officials of the Truman administration encountered with the communists during the Korean War. It was learned then that in negotiations with communists that you never weakened your pressure when they sought a cessation of activities.

In a speech at San Antonio Johnson said the United States was ready to talk peace at any time, any place, any where. He said he would stop the bombing but he expected no counter action by the North Vietnamese. In effect the President was telling the communists that all they had to do was to be patient and more concessions would be forthcoming.

North Vietnam's failure to win over the populace in the South, and its losses on every battlefield, called for a re-evaluation of the war. Communist leaders focused on the American homefront and tried to impress upon the American people that the United States was losing the war and that it should withdraw. Communist propaganda now won battles for them that their military forces were unable to achieve. President Johnson was convinced that the majority of the American people were not behind him, and he sought to bring North Vietnam to the peace table. He hoped that a cessation of bombing in the North would be an inducement to North Vietnam to halt its attacks on villages and cities throughout South Vietnam.

The Joint Chiefs reluctantly agreed although they told Johnson that North Vietnam would probably continue to fight until enough force was applied to threaten their existence as a power base. Since the start of 1968, bombing had been seriously curtailed because of the northeast monsoon. While a bombing halt was discussed, the weather changed from the northeast to the southwest monsoon so conditions over North Vietnam would be poor for another month and all but a few strikes would be cancelled anyway. The Air Force agreed to stop bombing during the month of April, and all agreed it would be resumed without reservations unless North Vietnam ceased its activities in the South.

Much of the 1968 Tet offensive in the southern provinces was broken by the middle of February through the combined efforts of South Vietnam's and America's armed forces.

The National Security Council abolished most draft deferments February 16, along with suspension of most occupational deferments. This action was denounced by some universities who claimed this action would seriously harm their graduate programs.

American and South Vietnamese troops went on the offensive March 11 in the largest operation yet in the Saigon area. It was not without its toll and March 14 the United States command announced that the number of American casualties in Vietnam now exceeded the total for the Korean War.

Senator Eugene McCarthy surprised the political pundits by running strongly March 12 in the New Hampshire Democratic presidential primary, although President Johnson won it. He had campaigned against the war in Vietnam, and pulled 42 percent of the votes.

Four days later Senator Robert F. Kennedy of New York threw his hat in the ring. He had skillfully directed his brother's campaign for the Presidency and became his closest confidant while serving as attorney general. He had played a crucial role in the Cuban missile crisis, and was active on behalf of his brother in the civil rights protest movement in the South.

Johnson spoke to Congress and the nation March 31, 1968, "I am taking the first step to de-escalate the conflict," he said. "Tonight I have ordered our aircraft and naval vessels to make no attacks on North Vietnam except in the area north of the demilitarized zone where the continuing enemy buildup directly threatens Allied forward positions, and where the movement of their troops and supplies are clearly related to that threat. Our purpose in this action is to bring about a reduction in the level of violence that exists."

What he did not say was that his order would spare 80 percent of all targets in North Vietnam.

Johnson also announced that he would not be a candidate for reelection. "With America's sons in the fields far away, with America's future under challenge right here at home, with our hopes and the world's hopes for peace in the balance every day, I do not believe that I should devote an hour or a day of my time to any personal partisan causes, or to any duties other than the awesome duties of this office—the Presidency of your country. Accordingly, I shall not seek, and I will not accept, the nomination of my party for another term as your President."

His decision recognized a political truth that he probably would not receive the nomination of his party and that, even if he did, he could not be elected in the fall. A Gallup poll released on this date showed only 29 percent of the American people approved of his handling of the war, and that 63 percent disapproved.

The communists had lost every battle in Vietnam during the Tet offensive but they had won a resounding psychological victory in the United States. On April 3 they agreed to discuss an armistice and immediately took advantage of the peace talks to improve their military positions while they increased their political warfare through propaganda. Thus the United States missed a golden opportunity to deal a death blow to an enemy in agony. More troops were not needed now, and it was time to turn most of the fighting over to the South Vietnamese. The missed opportunity proved tragic in loss of lives and prestige for the United States.

North Vietnam's overwhelming defeat in South Vietnam was not recognized by most people in the United States, but it should have been. The combined forces of the Allies were so overwhelming that it exceeded the communists' manpower by almost three to one and it should have made their defeat a foregone conclusion.

Basically the Vietnamese armed forces did most of the fighting, and most units fought well. Not one Army unit broke under intensive pressure, or defected to the North Vietnamese. In the first phase of the attacks the communists lost 32,000 killed and 5,800 captured. By the end of the second phase in May another 5,000 lost their lives. The communists failed to hold any city except Hue and that was for only 25 days. The general uprising that they had confidently counted upon to achieve success did not occur. It was a military defeat for North Vietnam and even the Vietcong headquarters admitted that they had failed to seize a number of primary objectives, and had not been able to destroy any South Vietnamese units. Most galling of all was the fact that the people of South Vietnam had refused to join the uprising. The fighting did disrupt pacification of the countryside, generating 600,000 new refugees.

Prior to Johnson's address to the nation, in which he took himself out of the presidential race, he announced that Westmoreland would be replaced in June as Military Assistance Commander by his deputy, General Creighton W. Abrams. Westmoreland was named chief of staff of the United States Army in Washington.

Prior to his departure from Vietnam Westmoreland requested an additional 200,000 American troops. Although he wanted to exploit the gains made by Allied troops, his request made no sense. It only fueled anti-war resentment at home. If a gradual reduction of that amount had been requested, it would have been far more logical. Since the enemy had been soundly defeated, fewer United States troops were needed—not more.

South Vietnam's leaders had regained the confidence of most of its people and they should have taken immediate steps to free the South of the communists. Now politics again reverted to intrigues and power struggles as if oblivious to every present threat of conquest. Meanwhile American politics had irreversibly changed from commitment to disengagement. President Thieu should have exploited the military victory gained at such cost. If he had done so his country would have been unbeatable. He, and his political leaders, lost South Vietnam in 1968 because his failure to act aggressively led directly to North Vietnam's final victory seven years later.

Dr. Martin Luther King went to Memphis, Tennessee, April 3 to support a sanitation workers' strike for higher pay. Although he had won the Nobel Peace Prize he had been harassed by the FBI and placed under constant surveillance by J. Edgar Hoover. The FBI director had long tried to discredit King by connecting him with alleged communist infiltrators in the civil rights movement, although no evidence was ever found.

In his speech in the Masonic Temple he discounted the threats against him by "some of our sick white brothers." But he reminded his listeners that he had been stabbed in New York and the knife blade almost reached his heart, and that morning his departure from Atlanta had been delayed by a bomb scare aboard the plane.

"Well, I don't know what will happen now. We've got some difficult days ahead. But it really doesn't matter with me now. Because I've been to the mountain top. I won't mind.

"Like anybody, I would like to live a long life. Longevity has its place. But I'm not concerned about that now. I just want to do God's will.

The next day, as he stood outside on the balcony of his motel, James Earl Ray assassinated the black leader. Ray was later convicted and sentenced to life in prison.

Five days later 150,000 mourners attended King's funeral in Atlanta, Georgia, while riots erupted in 63 cities. But the non-violent cause for which he paid the price lives on, and is strengthened by the memory of this fundamentally decent human being.

A civil rights bill, including prohibition against racial discrimination in the sale or rental of about 80 percent of United States housing, was signed into law April 11 by President Johnson. Such a bill had been proposed for years, but its passage in the House was expedited by King's assassination.

In response to President Johnson's call for peace talks between warring parties in Vietnam, delegates gathered May 10 in Paris. Averell Harriman represented the United States and Xuan Thuy was assigned by North Vietnam.

It had been a year of violence in the United States and it seemed June 8 that it would never end. Robert F. Kennedy, who claimed victory over Eugene McCarthy in the California primary, was shot by an assassin in a Los Angeles hotel. A Jordanian Arab, Sirhan B. Sirhan, was immediately seized by Kennedy aides. Despite attempts to save his life Kennedy died the following morning. President Johnson set aside June 9 as a national day of mourning and appointed a commission to investigate the shooting. Sirhan was convicted of murder and he was sent to prison.

Before his assassination in Memphis, Martin Luther King had planned a "Poor People's Campaign." As a memorial to him the climax of the campaign occurred in Washington, D.C., June 19 when more than 50,000 people, half of them white, took part in a "Solidarity Day March."

In July, Secretary of Defense Clark Clifford, formerly a strong supporter of the war, became convinced that the war could not be won militarily. He decided to propose to President Johnson that all bombing of North Vietnam should be stopped—not just those targets north of the 20th parallel—and that the United States should begin withdrawal of its ground forces and turn over responsibility for the war to the South Vietnamese.

It had long been debated in world councils, but July 1 some 36 nations signed a nuclear non-proliferation treaty. The agreement included the United States, the United Kingdom and the Soviet Union. Final approval awaited action by the United States Senate which postponed its decision until after the presidential election.

Direct airline service began July 15 between the United States and the Soviet Union. This was a small but welcome improvement in relations between the two countries. The Soviet airline, Aeroflot, joined Pan American World Airways in establishing the link.

The Republicans held their convention in Miami Beach this year starting August 8. After a skillful primary campaign Richard M. Nixon was nominated and he named Governor Spiro T. Agnew of Maryland as his running mate, and the convention accepted his choice. The platform was the usual platitudes about a need for a change.

But, in his acceptance speech Nixon promised to make ending the war in Indochina his first order of business. "After an era of confrontation the time has come for an era of negotiations with the leaders of Communist China and the Soviet Union." He stressed law and order, supported civil rights and opposed busing.

The true nature of life under communism was displayed for all the world to see August 22 when Soviet tanks brutally crushed the hopes of Czechoslovakians for more freedom. Several hundred thousand troops had crossed the border the day before under command of the Soviet Union's vice minister of defense, General Ivan Pavlovsky. They came from the Soviet Union, Poland, Hungary and Bulgaria. They met no resistance at first, but when they stormed the national radio station in Prague some Czechs fought back and 30 were killed, while 300 others were wounded.

When the Democrats gathered in Chicago August 28 some 10,000 anti-war protesters converged on the city to disrupt the convention. Mayor Richard Daley mobilized an equal number of city police and National Guardsmen. There was violence in the streets that reached the stage of chaos, and it became worse when the party's "hawks" on Vietnam adopted a platform supporting the war. This particular "plank" called for a halt to the bombing of North Vietnam only when "this action would not endanger American troops there." Anti-war demonstrators outside the convention were beaten and hundreds arrested by Chicago police under orders from Mayor Daley to stop the violence at all costs. Reporters covering the convention expressed their shock and dismay at the police tactics.

As is so often the case, the truth lies somewhere betwen these extremes of criticism.

George C. Wallace was nominated for president on September 17 at the convention of his American Independence Party. On October 1 he named retired General Curtis E. LeMay as his running mate. Wallace's campaign emphasized alleged welfare statism of the two major parties and he appealed to some Americans with his views on racism.

Apollo 7 made a successful 11-day, 163-orbit flight starting October 11. Only a few technical difficulties marred the flight, one of several to be taken prior to a moon landing in 1969 or 1970. The three astronauts had no serious health problems during their stay in space, although they all caught bad colds.

Acting on the advice of Secretary of Defense Clifford, President Johnson announced an end to all bombing of North Vietnam effective November 1. As a result North Vietnam agreed to widen the Paris talks to include South Vietnamese government and National Liberation Front (Vietcong) representatives. At first, South Vietnam's government officials refused to participate, causing a brief delay.

American negotiators at the Paris peace talks became deadlocked over the shape of the negotiating table, and how the parties should sit around it. This was of significance to South Vietnam's leaders who considered themselves the legitimate government, and they refused to accord equal status to North Vietnam's National Liberation Front. Meanwhile the war dragged on.

Although he had ordered a halt to all bombing of North Vietnam Johnson did authorize continuance of reconnaissance flights and interdiction of supplies through Laos. North Vietnam quickly took advantage of the bombing halt and increased the flow of traffic along its major coastal routes to the demilitarized zone. After the bombing ceased in the North small harbors became crowded with boats shuttling supplies to the South.

The Joint Chiefs of Staff had opposed the halt, saying they were convinced North Vietnam was accumulating large stocks to make another major offensive. Their pleas fell on deaf ears.

Richard M. Nixon and his running mate Governor Spiro T. Agnew of Maryland defeated the Democratic ticket headed by Vice President Humphrey and Senator Muskie of Maine by 812,000 votes—less than one percent of the total cast during the election.

Between the election and Nixon's inauguration, 300 GIs died each week in Vietnam, but the peace talks in Paris couldn't proceed because of arguments over the shape of the negotiating table.

Apollo, with astronauts Frank Borman, James A. Lovell and William Anders, lifted off from Cape Kennedy December 21 bound for the moon. It went into lunar orbit three days later, circling it 10 times while sending pictures and reports back to earth. On Christmas Day one of the astronauts read a passage from the Book of Genesis. The spacecraft returned to earth two days later.

While Apollo was headed for its rendezvous with the moon, North Korea released the crew of the "Pueblo" which they had captured the previous January. For 10 months, while the crew was tortured, the United States negotiated for their release. The United States finally admitted and apologized for intruding into North Korean waters while it simultaneously repudiated the admission.

Throughout the fall of 1968 the South Vietnamese government, with major American support (United States losses were averaging 200 dead a week), launched an accelerated pacification program. As a result, two years later at least some measure of government control was evident in all but a few remote regions.

Nixon had campaigned on the promise of a new look at the war and he was expected to bring about a change in the tempo of the fighting in

Vietnam. Therefore both sides had marked time in preparation for what was believed would be an about-face in American strategy.

After the election President Johnson had ordered fighter escorts for reconnaissance flights over North Vietnam, but the escorting fighters were authorized to attack only if they came under attack.

In December, and early January 1969, President-elect Nixon initiated exchanges with the North Vietnamese, stressing his willingness to engage in serious negotiations, but he was rebuffed. North Vietnam's leaders had achieved a unilateral bombing halt, so they were not about to be cooperative. Instead, they again demanded that the United States overthrow the government of South Vietnam.

By mid-January the Soviet Union offered a compromise on behalf of North Vietnam to the problem of the shape of the conference table that had deadlocked negotiations since the bombing halt. They suggested a circular table without nameplates, flags or markings. North Vietnam took this action out of fear that President Nixon would again start bombing North Vietnam. Secretary of State Dean Rusk appealed to President Thieu on behalf of President-elect Nixon to accept this compromise before the inauguration. Thieu agreed and formal truce negotiations got under way January 25, 1969.

But the war continued as if there were no peace negotiations.

Now the nation looked hopefully to their new President when he was sworn in January 20. The United States had passed through a heady period as the world's most powerful nation in which it had tried to be its policeman. Such a unilateral assumption was doomed to fail despite the rightness of its causes in Indochina and the rest of the world, because Americans have never been comfortable in such a role. From the days of isolationism following World War I, to the reluctant consensus after World War II that the United States must use its power and resources to create a better world, the inexorable drift toward America's inherent conservatism gradually became a reality. It was reflected in Nixon's election to the Presidency. Remarkably, it did not affect America's belief that it must maintain a broad participation in the world's affairs, and work within a world organization to preserve the peace. Isolationism had finally been renounced.

CHAPTER 24

Dissent on the Home Front

AFTER RICHARD M. NIXON BECAME PRESIDENT IN 1969 HE VIEWED with growing concern the unresolved war in Indochina, and the proliferation of nuclear weapons. He immediately set forces in motion, following his inauguration on January 20, to establish a measure of control over both problem areas. While he ordered his advisers to take a whole new look at America's involvement in the war in Asia, he also sought to place restrictions on the nation's nuclear arsenal that had grown haphazardly to approximately 33,000 weapons compared to the Soviet Union's 22,500. He was aware that the numbers didn't tell the whole story because Russia's available megatonnage appeared to be about 40 percent greater than the American arsenal. (The Russians had concentrated since the beginning of the nuclear competition on larger warheads.)

Since the days of the Eisenhower administration, massive nuclear retaliation had become the keystone of the United States' strategy to prevent another world war. Its details were spelled out in the "Single Integrated Operations Plan" to assure victory against all potential enemies. But since it was approved technological break-throughs had made nuclear weapons smaller, more efficient and cheaper to make. Thus they became more attractive to military planners as weapons. Exotic new weapons were designed not to fulfill a military need, but because they were "cleaner" or more efficient. In most cases, Pentagon officials found uses for them after they were produced. This was a dramatic, and disturbing change in weapons procurement. It upset many people in and out of government. Although President Eisenhower signed the integrated plan he said it "frightens the devil out of me."

By the end of the Korean War, America's nuclear arsenal had reached

1,000 bombs; an increase from the 50 atomic bombs available in 1948. Then the arsenal grew at a rapid rate to 18,000 nuclear weapons by 1960, including 3,000 bombs and missile warheads, while thousands of other devices were built for installation in torpedoes and artillery shells. The probable total reached 32,500 nuclear weapons at a time when the Soviet Union's arsenal was believed to exceed 22,500 weapons.

Actually there were insufficient targets in the Soviet Union (the United States' most likely enemy at the time) to warrant such an arsenal. The armed services sought to justify it by listing 42,000 potential targets, but the vast majority were military bases, air bases, and targets of such insignificance that they didn't merit an atomic attack. Among the targets listed as high priority were 200 urban areas that contained 50 percent of Russia's key industries, plus six railroad yards that loaded 80 percent of the nation's freight. In an all-out war, such targets were justified along with attacks against electric power stations, steel mills and plants that manufactured war materials. But in addition the Pentagon listed 700 cities with populations in excess of 25,000 people as possible targets. By no stretch of the imagination could such cities be justified as legitimate targets for nuclear weapons. This would be terror bombing at its worst. For example, the Strategic Air Command claimed that sixty 300-kiloton bombs would be needed to destroy Moscow. The bomb that destroyed Hiroshima in World War II was a 20-kiloton bomb, or the equivalent of 20,000 tons of TNT. The central sections of both cities are approximately the same number of square miles although the Hiroshima Prefecture is vastly larger because it includes some off-shore islands with 3,268 square miles compared to Moscow's 386 square miles. The World War II atomic bomb destroyed five square miles of central Hiroshima so it is inconceivable that 60 bombs each with a destructive capacity 15 times greater should be needed to wipe out Moscow. But that's the kind of overkill thinking that was used to justify the huge nuclear arsenal.

The original Eisenhower plan was predicated on the United States absorbing a surprise attack (i.e. letting the Soviet Union be first to start a nuclear war), and then responding with 3,500 to 5,000 nuclear weapons from its submarine and bomber fleets. Twice that many weapons could be sent on their way to targets in Russia if the United States received advance warning of an impending attack. This was the basic theory behind President Eisenhower's plan for massive nulcear retaliation that experts claimed would have killed between 360-450 million people in the Sino-Soviet States bloc. At the time it made sense as a deterrent because the United States had an overwhelming superiority in nuclear weapons for a short period after 1959.

Whether this concept of massive nuclear retaliation helped to prevent

World War III is beside the point because the strategy brought America to the brink of such a war several times, and Americans were forced to fight conventional wars twice in the Far East fomented in large part by the Soviet Union.

President Nixon strove now to find a way to end the war in Indochina, and rein in the Pentagon's avid insistence on more and more nuclear weapons. He was responsible for starting the elimination of defensive nuclear weapons, such as anti-aircraft weapons, that the Russians were frantically producing. The total number of nuclear weapons in the American stockpile was eventually reduced by a third. Unfortunately Nixon approved a new category of targets that called for the destruction of economic facilities whose loss would prevent an enemy from recovering from a nuclear war. This posed a problem for Pentagon planners who found there was insufficient data to determine what were the most critical targets. As a result, all economic targets were listed. Typically, the list included such non-war targets as fertilizer plants because they would be needed to restore a defeated nation's agriculture. With such reasoning it seemed natural for the Pentagon to demand four times the number of weapons to destroy its vastly expanded list of targets.

President Nixon tried to hold the line, and he was largely successful in reducing the huge number of requests for new weapons, although the nuclear arsenal was constantly modernized. This decision to update the nuclear weaponry was a tragic mistake because it burdened the United States with hundreds of billions of dollars of unneeded nuclear weapons that offered no real deterrent to war. As the United States improved its nuclear weaponry, the Soviet Union expanded its nuclear stockpile with thousands of new defensive battlefield weapons. The preposterous arms race expanded almost out of control to the detriment of both nations, bringing them both to the brink of bankruptcy.

Few people realize that most nuclear weapons are targeted at one another's atomic sites, and not at each nation's war-making industries. An across-the-board reduction by both sides in total numbers of nuclear weapons at this time would have maintained each nation's ability to defend itself at far less cost.

Life in the fragile earth's atmosphere, already showing the effects of industrial pollution, could never provide the quality of life most of the world's people have come to expect if 50,000 to 60,000 nuclear weapons were exploded during an all-out nuclear attack. They would cause irreparable damage to the earth's environment. Smoke and dust alone would create climate changes for years to come that would make normal life almost impossible for survivors, while radiation would make vast areas uninhabitable for decades.

In the frantic haste to rearm the nation to survive all contingencies in the event of another world war, few military and political leaders have given serious thought that their plan to help their nation survive is instead a blueprint for economic and ecological disaster.

An accident in the waters off Santa Barbara, California, January 28, 1969, caused extensive property damage, water pollution and wildlife destruction when offshore oil-drilling installations began to leak. By February 5 a huge oil slick closed the Santa Barbara harbor. This was the first of several such massive leaks in various sections of the country as environmentalists called for controls to spare the nation further tragedies. They charged that conservation of natural resources would make off-shore drilling for oil unnecessary.

An historic first flight was made March 2 when the French-British Concorde completed its maiden trip, ushering in limited supersonic air travel. Designed to fly across the Atlantic Ocean in three-and-a-half hours at twice the speed of sound, the plane's $1½ billion development costs were three times what had been projected. But its pilot, Andre Turcat, said the swept-wing craft performed beautifully.

President Nixon returned to Washington on this date after an eight-day trip to Europe where he visited the leaders of Great Britain, France, Belgium, Italy and West Germany.

President Nixon proposed March 14 the construction of an anti-ballistic missile system (ABM) to protect United States offensive missile sites against attacks by either the Soviet Union or the People's Republic of China. He said this "Safeguard System" would replace "Sentinel" that the Johnson administration had authorized to protect American cities from an attack by unsophisticated Chinese missiles. Nixon recommended the immediate construction of two ABM sites, but his plan eventually called for 12 such sites. Fears were expressed in Congress that "Safeguard" would escalate the arms race.

The Senate had ratified Nixon's nuclear non-proliferation treaty the day before the President announced the ABM proposal despite strong objections by some senators. Its purpose was to prevent the spread of nuclear weapons among nations that as yet had not acquired them.

The nation went into mourning March 28 for the death of former President Eisenhower. The 34th President, and retired General of the Army, died of heart failure at Walter Reed Hospital in Washington. He was given a state funeral attended by dignitaries from all over the world. He was buried in Abilene, Kansas, his boyhood home.

It was announced April 3 that the death toll in Indochina had exceeded the number who died during the Korean War. As of the end of April the Pentagon said 33,641 Americans had died since 1961.

The war of nerves between the United States and communist nations grew hotter April 15 when North Korean MIGs shot down an American Navy intelligence plane over the Sea of Japan, killing 31 crew members. Officials of the Pyongyang government claimed the plane had violated North Korean airspace, but the United States denied the allegation. President Nixon sent a naval task force into the area and announced that reconnaissance flights would continue but with air and sea protection.

A Congressional hearing was told April 29 of a shocking $2.1 billion cost overrun on the C-5A cargo transport under construction for the Air Force by Lockheed Aircraft Corporation. This proved to be just the tip of the iceberg of similar overruns on other projects.

On May 14, 1969, President Nixon went on national television to report to the American people about the war in Vietnam after he had offered a proposal to the North Vietnamese through Ambassador Dobrynin to begin secret, two-party peace negotiations. They did not respond. Nixon said he had offered a simultaneous withdrawal, followed by an exchange of prisoners of war, and free elections in South Vietnam.

While Congress was studying the ABM proposal, research was underway on multiple, independently-targeted reentry vehicles or MIRVs. In this field it was far ahead of the Soviet Union. MIRV showed promise of adding to America's offensive capability while the Russians had little or nothing to counteract this devastating new weapons system. Each intercontinental ballistic missile (ICBM) with three to 10 separately targeted nuclear warheads was a formidable jump in the state of the art. Both systems were not needed.

After years of debate, a Strategic Arms Limitation Treaty (SALT) was signed in Washington on October 3, 1972, with the Soviet Union. It limited each side to two ABM anti-ballistic missile systems to defend their respective capitals, (the United States never built its system) along with an interim agreement to set limits of a temporary nature on strategic offensive forces. This resolution proved to be a worthless document because it wasn't binding on either party. At the signing, President Nixon called the agreement "a first step in reducing the danger of war." He said the next vitally important step was consideration of the whole range of offensive nuclear weapons and to look ahead "to the possibility of reducing the burden of nuclear arms and eventually the possibility of limitations and restrictions on the use of such arms."

The war in Vietnam caused renewed criticism to erupt throughout the country when United States and South Vietnamese forces launched a 10-day assault May 10, 1969, against "Hamburger Hill" in the A Shau Valley. Although it had little strategic value, it became one of the bloodiest battles of the war. The hill was abandoned on May 28.

After the battle for "Hamburger Hill" Senator Edward Kennedy spoke out against the level of military activity in Vietnam, claiming that it was opposed to our stated intentions and goals in Paris. "But more important," he said, "I feel it is both senseless and irresponsible to continue to send our young men to their deaths to capture hills and positions that have no relation to ending this conflict."

While the war in Indochina was still going badly for the United States, America's space program was moving from one triumph to another. Apollo 10 splashed down in the Pacific May 26 after 18 days in space, including 31 orbits of the moon. This mission was designed to be a complete rehearsal for a manned lunar landing.

President Nixon met with South Vietnam's President Nguyen Van Thieu on the island of Midway on June 8 to discuss the Vietnam war. After the conference ended, Nixon announced that 25,000 American troops would be withdrawn from South Vietnam by August 31. This was the first withdrawal of combat troops since President Johnson sent Americans to fight there in March 1965, except for those who had completed their combat tours. President Nixon also revealed that this was the first step of his administration's plan to turn combat operations over to the South Vietnamese. Later withdrawals were announced on September 16 for an additional 35,000 troops, and 50,000 more on December 15.

In 1968 Dr. Benjamin Spock was convicted of conspiracy to counsel draft evasion. His conviction was overturned on July 11 by the Boston Court of Appeals with one of his co-defendants. Others were granted a retrial of their charges.

A boyish-looking astronaut with an engaging grin became the first human being to set foot on the moon on July 20 1969, at 10:56 p.m. Eastern Daylight Time. Neil Armstrong, a member of Apollo 11, made the historic journey with Colonel Edwin E. "Buzz" Aldrin and Lt. Col. Michael Collins. Their spacecraft was lauched four days earlier from Cape Kennedy and Armstrong and Aldrin made man's first descent to the moon in their "Eagle" lunar landing module. From the moon's rock surface, Armstrong spoke for America when he said it was "one small step for a man, a giant leap for mankind." He and Aldrin deposited a lunar capsule and an American flag on the moon while three-quarters of a billion people listened to a description of the historic event or watched the landing on television. The astronauts set up scientific experiments and collected rock specimens. Armstrong read the words engraved on a plaque that was left on the moon: "Here men from the planet Earth first set foot upon the moon July, 1969, AD. We came in peace for all mankind."

President Nixon returned to Washington August 3 after a 12-day trip around the world. As he made stops in Thailand, India, Pakistan, Indonesia and South Vietnam he outlined a new foreign policy of self-help for the United States. He assured communist countries that he would negotiate with them in an atmosphere of "mutual respect." In Eastern Europe he visited Romania, the first President to set foot in a communist nation since World War II. He told the Romanian people that "nations can have widely different internal orders and live in peace."

On the day Nixon returned home America's growing achievements in space were highlighted once again when NASA's Mariner 7 passed within 2200 miles of Mars, transmitting breath-taking pictures of the planet back to earth.

In Vietnam, American losses reached 100 dead in one week as the conflict became the living room war because it was brought by television each night into the homes of most Americans. They now became more and more disenchanted about this bloody war that was being fought without definite goals. It became the most widely-reported war in history—and the most unpopular. President Ho Chi Minh's death on September 3, 1969, increased the calls for an end to America's involvement. Nixon's earlier announcement that he would continue to remove Americans from the war zone was reaffirmed when he ordered the withdrawal of another 35,000 troops.

In early September anti-war activists called for a moratorium or suspension of combat until American troops were out of Vietnam.

Nixon responded by announcing on September 16 that he was withdrawing another 60,000 American troops by December 15. He said of the call for a moratorium, "As far as this kind of activity is concerned, we expect it. However, under no circumstances will I be affected by it."

Nixon further explained, "Once the enemy recognizes that it is not going to win its objectives by waiting us out, then the enemy will negotiate and we will end this war before the end of 1970."

His critics were not appeased. There were anti-war demonstrations on most college campuses, and even the presidents of 79 colleges signed an appeal to Nixon "for a stepped-up timetable for withdrawal from Vietnam." Tens of thousands of activists against the war marched around the White House on October 15 while thousands of others attended anti-war rallies across the nation. Although millions were involved, fortunately there was little or no violence. For the first time moratorium adherents included many from America's middle class and older Americans.

Although the President's policy of "Vietnamization" of the conflict in Indochina was met with approval, anti-war activists continued to press for total removal of all Americans from the war zone. Observance of the first National Moratorium Day on October 15 brought out large crowds of anti-war demonstrators throughout the country and they were joined by some Senators and Congressmen. Mrs. Martin Luther King, Jr., led a march of 45,000 people from the Washington Monument to the White House.

A month later, on the second Moratorium Day, more than 250,000 people gathered in Washington. This figure eclipsed the number who had turned out for the civil rights rally in August 1963. San Francisco held the largest protest movement in its history against the Vietnam war while similar demonstrations were held in other cities. President Nixon ignored the rallies which fortunately were relatively free of violence.

President Nixon spoke to the nation on November 3, 1969. He described the secret talks that had taken place with officials of North Vietnam, and that he had asked the Soviet Union for help in achieving peace. He also revealed that he had written privately to Ho Chi Minh but that his plea to seek a solution for ending the war had been flatly rejected.

He described his plan to bring peace. Based on his Nixon Doctrine, he said, Vietnamization had reduced infiltration, and therefore American casualties. He said he would not announce a timetable for withdrawals, as the pace of withdrawals would be tied to the level of enemy infiltration and American casualties. He said if these went up, "I shall not hesitate to take strong and effective measures . . . This is not a threat. This is a statement of policy.

"Therefore," the president continued, "I have rejected the easy way in favor of the right way." To America's youth he said that he respected their idealism and shared their concern for peace. "I want peace as much as you do."

Vice President Spiro Agnew delivered a scathing attack against network television news coverage when he spoke November 13 in Des Moines, Iowa. "A small group of men, numbering perhaps no more than a dozen anchormen, commentators, and executive producers settle upon the 20 minutes or so of film and commentary that's to reach the public. . . ."

A week later Agnew lashed out specifically against the *New York Times* and the *Washington Post* in Montgomery, Alabama, but actually against all members of the print media with almost identical charges of manipulating the news.

While Agnew was denouncing the news media, the largest anti-war rally in United States history was taking place November 14-16 in Washington, D.C. A quarter of a million protesters gathered there to demand an end to the American involvement in the war in Indochina. Some carried coffins printed with the names of America's war dead. Inside the Justice Department and the Pentagon hundreds of paratroopers stood by in case of a violent confrontation with the huge crowd. But the protesters remained peaceful, and only one demonstrator was arrested. He was caught drawing a peace sign on the Washington Monument.

Anti-war hysteria rose to a fever pitch the next day when it was revealed for the first time that on March 16, 1968, American troops under Lieutenant William Calley had killed 567 unarmed men, women and children in the South Vietnamese village of My Lai. Calley was charged with ordering the death of everyone in the village which he said were all Vietcong. Calley and Sergeant David Mitchell were ordered to stand court martial to face charges of assault and murder while an Army investigation was ordered.

Preliminary talks between the Soviet Union and United States negotiators began November 17 in Helsinki, Finland, to establish ground rules to continue Strategic Arms Limitation Talks scheduled for the following April in Vienna, Austria. A breakthrough was achieved a week later when the superpowers agreed to limit nuclear weapons under terms of the United Nations-sponsored Nuclear Non-Proliferation Treaty. Both nations pledged not to spread nuclear know-how or material.

The United States Army announced on November 24 that Lieutenant William L. Calley had been charged with premeditated murder in the massacre on March 16, 1968, of Vietnam civilians at My Lai. Sergeant David Mitchell had already been tried and acquitted of killing 30 people in the massacre.

The following day President Nixon renounced the use of bacteriological agents in war, and ordered destruction of such weapons. He revealed that first-strike use of certain chemical agents were now outlawed although tear gas and chemical defoliants, both widely used in Vietnam, would continue to be authorized. In making the announcement the President said he had asked the Senate to consent to the 1925 Geneva Protocol prohibiting biological and chemical weapons. He reserved the right to use lethal chemical weapons in retaliation if they were ever used against American troops.

The President issued an executive order on November 26 establishing a lottery for choosing men to be drafted into the armed forces. The first lottery drawing was held on December 1 with New York Representative Alexander Pirnie withdrawing the capsules. It was hoped that this lottery in New York City would be the answer to mounting criticism of inequities in the Selective Service System. Nineteen-year-old men became eligible according to their birthdates, with each day in the year represented by a capsule. The order in which birthdate capsules were withdrawn during the lottery determined the order in which men would enter service.

And so ended the 1960s, a decade of violence throughout the world, and unprecedented discord at home with the rising specter of world-wide inflation casting a shadow on the next decade. The world's population was growing at the rate of 2 percent a year despite wars in many areas of the world, and poverty in much of the Third World. Despite these handicaps the total number of people on planet earth had reached 3.5 billion, and of this number 204,334, 344 were Americans who faced the 1970s in as troubled a state as they had ever known due to the divisiveness created by the war in Indochina.

CHAPTER 25

A Drastic Change in American Policy

IN HIS STATE OF THE UNION ADDRESS JANUARY 22, 1970, PRESIDENT
Nixon spoke of a "new American experience" of equality of opportunity
and government responsiveness to meet the needs of the American people.
He called upon the nation to "begin to make reparations for the damage
we have done to our air, to our land and to our waters." To further those
ends he asked Congress to enact a family assistance plan to replace the
present welfare system and guarantee a minimum income to every family.
He insisted, however, that the nation's first priority must be to "bring
an end to the war in Vietnam."

The Nixon budget that he presented to Congress on February 2 showed
a $2 billion surplus. He had cut $6 billion from military and space
programs. Johnson's "Great Society" programs weren't cut. Actually
Nixon spent more on welfare and food stamp programs than Johnson had
done. Spending for defense was reduced from 45 percent of the budget
in Johnson's presidency to 37 percent.

Although the Paris peace talks were not proving fruitful President
Nixon continued to withdraw American combat troops from Vietnam.
He promised that by the end of the year the American presence would
be reduced to 340,000 military personnel. This would mean a reduction
of 210,000 from the peak strength in 1968. In his Vietnamization program, Americans were ordered to take a more defensive posture in Vietnam. Such a posture was already reducing the weekly casualty toll from
a 1968 weekly average of 280 to a year-end death toll of 25 a week.

When four students at Kent State were killed by National Guard troops called out to quell a reported riot, student unrest was fanned when Press Secretary Ron Ziegler read a statement, "This should remind us all once again that when dissent turns to violence, it invites tragedy. It is my hope that this tragic and unfortunate incident will strengthen the determination of all the nation's campuses—administrators, faculty and students alike—to stand firmly for the right which exists in this country of peaceful dissent and just as strongly against the resort to violence as a means of such expression." Unfortunately some of the victims were not participating in the anti-war rally but were merely changing classes. The Guard had been called out earlier in response to the burning down of the ROTC building on campus.

Nixon spoke to the nation on April 30 to try to justify an invasion of Cambodia that he had authorized. He said he had ordered the operation to attack "the headquarters for the entire Communist military operation in South Vietnam." He assured Americans that "this is not an invasion of Cambodia." He claimed that he would not occupy the area and that once enemy forces were driven out of their sanctuaries, and their military supplies were destroyed, "we will withdraw."

Nixon said that "no one is more aware than I am of the political consequences . . . It is tempting to take the easy political path: to blame this war on previous administrations and to bring all our men home immediately. But I have rejected all political considerations in making this decision . . .

"Whether I may be a one-term President is insignificant compared to whether by our failure to act in this crisis the United States proves itself to be unworthy to lead the forces of freedom in this critical period in world history. I would rather be a one-term President and do what I believe is right than to be a two-term President at the cost of seeing America become a second-rate power, and to see this nation accept the first defeat in its proud 190-year history."

The Cambodian excursion uncovered insignifcant enemy resistance, and certainly the headquarters was not found although large quantities of supplies were destroyed.

After an investigation into the deaths of four students at Kent State May 4 it was determined National Guardsmen, sadly lacking in leadership and inexperienced in riot control, had over-reacted. They had been called out to put down a student anti-war demonstration, and had fired into a crowd of hecklers who should have been dispersed by less lethal means.

Two more students were killed and 12 others injured May 14 when violent demonstrations erupted at Jackson State College in Mississippi, a predominantly black college, when state police fired into a crowd of bottle— and rock-throwing youths.

During this period of violence on the nation's campuses, President Nixon signed into law a bill giving 18-year-olds the right to vote in federal elections. Young people had long campaigned for such a right, claiming that if they were old enough to be drafted, they were old enough to vote.

A daring, but fruitless raid into North Vietnam on November 23 to rescue American prisoners held 23 miles west of Hanoi failed to achieve its objective. American soldiers overran a camp where prisoners supposedly were being held, but none were found. Air Force and Navy planes provided cover for the operation by conducting seven-hour bombing raids. Although no prisoners were found—they had been moved to another camp—the heavy bombing raid served as a warning to the Communists that, despite troop reductions, the United States still packed a lethal punch.

Meanwhile the second year of peace talks in Paris dragged on, establishing no basis for an honorable end to the war.

Opposition to the war in Indochina remained strong in 1971 despite Nixon's plan to gradually withdraw American combat troops. Expansion of the war to Laos and Cambodia, and heavy bombing raids against North Vietnam, had infuriated those opposed to the war. More than 20,000 South Vietnamese troops had entered Laos on February 13, supported by American planes and artillery, to cripple North Vietnam's supply line down the Ho Chi Minh Trail. President Thieu called the attack "an act of legitimate self-defense," which it was, but anti-war activists denounced the invasion in no uncertain terms although they had never criticized North Vietnam for persistent use of Laos and Cambodia since the war began. An anti-war rally was held on April 24 in Washington. Ten thousand people demonstrated against the war, and demanded a total pull-out, wholly oblivious to the fact that fellow Americans in North Vietnam's prison camps would be at the mercy of their nation's enemies.

Various moves had been quietly taken by the Nixon administration to improve relations with the People's Republic of China, including a secret visit by adviser Henry Kissinger. An indication of China's interest in reducing tensions was its earlier agreement to host the American table tennis team. The Nixon administration took a more important step on June 10 by lifting the 21-year-old embargo on trade with China. Five days later the President surprised the world by announcing that he had accepted "with pleasure" an invitation by Premier Chou En-lai to visit the Communist country. Later that fall, the United States dropped its stand against seating the People's Republic of China in the United Nations.

In late June the Supreme Court ruled on two important issues. On June 28 it voted 8-1 that the Constitution prohibited states from reimbursing private schools for non-religious education, and two days later ruled that the *New York Times* and the *Washington Post* could resume publication of the top secret Pentagon papers about Vietnam. These revelations implicated high officials of the Kennedy administration in the overthrow of President Diem of South Vietnam in 1963, and in general revealed the chaos within the Kennedy administration in their conduct of the war in Indochina.

President Nixon's plan to reduce world tensions received a boost on October 12 when he announced that he would go to Moscow in 1972 to meet Soviet leaders. This was a drastic change in American policy, marking the first time since World War II that an American President had gone to the Soviet Union to meet with its leaders. The historic visit was made possible by a Soviet concession on September 3 that the USSR would guarantee western access to West Berlin, and the pledge was made in writing. Berlin had been a source of friction between the two superpowers since the Berlin blockade in 1948-49. The United States responded with a promise not to try to incorporate the western section of that city.

Later, on November 5, tensions were further reduced by Nixon's order releasing $136 million of feed grains for sale to the Soviet Union.

President Nixon announced another withdrawal of 45,000 men from Vietnam on November 12, reducing the number in the war zone to 139,000. These planned reductions had sharply reduced the casualty rate from 1968's high of 14,592 American deaths to 1,302 this year.

The People's Republic of China became a member of the United Nations on November 15 after the Nationalist Chinese were expelled. Its chief delegate, Chiao Juan-hua, rebuked fellow members for permitting the major powers "to manipulate and monopolize" the organization.

American Ambassador George Bush welcomed the Chinese delegation by saying that member nations were divided on the issue of Taiwan's expulsion but that nearly all countries, including the United States, "agreed that the moment in history has arrived for the People's Republic of China to be in the United Nations."

Chiao criticized Japan and the United States for their efforts to "create two Chinas in the United Nations." He vowed that his country would "liberate Taiwan." He also pledged support to Arab countries that, he said, were opposed to "Israeli Zionism." In his first address Chiao said that his nation opposed "the power politics of big nations bullying small ones or strong nations bullying weak ones." In a bid for leadership of "Third World" countries, he said that these countries desire independence, and seek liberation through revolutionary means.

A strong stand against inflation was taken December 18 when the United States devalued the dollar by 8.57 percent. With dollars now cheaper in comparison to foreign currencies, the Nixon administration hoped to increase American exports and reduce the $5 billion negative balance in its trade with other nations, to an $8 billion surplus. The imbalance had been caused by the value of imports exceeding the value of American goods exported overseas.

President Nixon approved production of a space shuttle on January 5, 1972. NASA had sought permission to develop a reusable spacecraft that could be lifted into space by rockets, but land as an airplane. It was expected to take six years to build and test the $5.5 billion craft.

The war in Indochina continued to occupy much of Nixon's time as he grew more concerned about failure of the peace talks in Paris to reach agreement. Although the North Vietnamese continued to press their attacks on South Vietnam, Nixon announced that he had ordered the withdrawal of another 70,000 American troops by January 13, reducing American strength to 69,000 men and women.

The cost of continuation of the war was reflected in his proposed budget for fiscal 1973. It called for a deficit of $25.5 billion, the largest in peacetime American history.

On January 25 President Nixon announced that his administration would present an eight-point peace proposal to the North Vietnamese and the Vietcong when they resumed their sessions in Paris on February 3. His proposal called for a ceasefire and release of all American prisoners in exchange for a United States withdrawal. After American troops had been withdrawn, the President proposed that South Vietnam should hold new elections in which the United States would remain neutral. He also revealed for the first time that Henry Kissinger and the communists had been meeting secretly since June.

Attorney General John N. Mitchell resigned from the Nixon cabinet on February 15, to take over as chairman of the Committee to Re-elect the President. He was succeeded by Richard Kleindienst of Arizona.

Thousands gathered at Andrews Air Force Base in Washington to wish President Nixon Godspeed on the morning of February 17, 1972, as he prepared to leave for his trip to China. Top officials of the government joined rank-and-file Washingtonians and heard him say before he boarded his plane that the United States and China must "find a way to see that we can have differences without being enemies in war." He spoke without notes. "If we can make progress toward that goal on this trip, the world will be a much safer world." He compared his trip to the flights to the moon by American astronauts. And, using the words on the plaque that they left on the moon to describe the purpose of his trip, Nixon repeated, "We come in peace for all mankind."

Air Force One landed in Peking February 21 at 11:30 a.m. which was 10:30 p.m. Sunday night by Eastern Standard Time. And so he began a week-long visit that he called "a journey for peace." Since 1949 the United States had had no diplomatic relations with the People's Republic of China after the Nationalists were driven from the mainland to set up a separate Chinese government on Taiwan. As he disembarked from his plane Nixon extended his hand to Chou En-lai. He wrote later of his impression of that meeting, saying, "One era ended and another began."

They drove into the city through empty streets. After lunch the President received word that Chairman Mao would receive him. He took Kissinger with him, and they were both surprised to find that Mao was a sick old man, barely able to stand. They met in the chairman's austere study surrounded by books. They talked for an hour but half the time was devoted to translation. No matters of substance were brought up as their conversation dealt with generalities. Kissinger told Mao that he had assigned his writings when he taught at Harvard.

Mao replied, "These writings of mine aren't anything. There is nothing instructive in what I wrote."

Nixon disagreed. "The chairman's writings moved a nation and have changed the world."

"I haven't been able to change it. I've only been able to change a few places in the vicinity of Peking. Our common old friend Generalissimo Chiang Kai-shek doesn't approve of this. He calls us Communist bandits."

Nixon asked, "What does the Chairman call Chiang Kai-shek?"

Chou En-lai broke in. "Generally speaking we call them 'Chiang Kai-shek's clique.'"

Nixon reminded Mao that the Soviets had more troops on the Chinese border than they had in Eastern Europe.

Mao nodded his agreement.

Nixon noticed that Chou En-lai was anxiously glancing at his watch so he said to Mao that he knew he had taken a risk in inviting him to China, "but having read some of your statements I know that you are one who sees when an opportunity comes, and then knows that you must seize the hour and seize the day."

Reiteration of some of his own words by Nixon pleased Mao.

Nixon continued, "I would also like to say in a personal sense . . . you do not know me. Since you do not know me, you shouldn't trust me. You will find I never say something I cannot do. And I always will do more than I can say."

In parting, Nixon said like Mao he came from a poor family but still became head of a great nation.

Mao replied, "Your book, *Six Crises*, is not a bad book."

Nixon looked at Chou and smiled. "He reads too much."

That night Nixon exchanged toasts with Chou En-lai while a Chinese band played "America the Beautiful" and "Home on the Range."

During a week of sightseeing and banquets, Nixon was impressed by the vastness of China and its thousands of years of culture. He and Chou met frequently and each explained their outlook on the problems dividing their nations. The talk was blunt, but friendly, so neither side could doubt the views of the other.

Their differences made a final communique difficult, but the problem was solved by using separate paragraphs to express their views. They did agree on the mutual threat posed by the Soviet Union which was basically the reason for their get-together. Nixon told Chou that he would "turn like a cobra on the Russians, if provoked, or if the Red Army marched either west or south." In the communique they agreed on the following language that neither nation "should seek hegemony in the Asia Pacific region" and that each was opposed to efforts by any other country or group of countries to establish such hegemony. The word "hegemony" was constantly used by the Chinese against the Soviet Union so this veiled language was understandable to all.

Of great importance to the Chinese was the status of Taiwan that was recognized by the United States as the government of China. Nixon had long been a strong booster so he couldn't accept strong language about the Chiang Kai-shek regime. He reminded Chou about his problem, and the Chinese foreign minister understood his position. Therefore he agreed to words that almost skirted the subject. In the communique his words reaffirmed the Communist claim to be the sole legitimate government of China and that Taiwan was a part of China. He demanded the withdrawal of all American military forces from Taiwan, and said he was opposed to any "two Chinas" formula. The United States position was added, acknowledging that all Chinese on either side of the Taiwan Strait maintain there is but one China and that Taiwan is part of China. "The United States Government does not challenge that position," it was stated. "It reaffirms its interest in a peaceful settlement of the Taiwan question by the Chinese themselves. With this prospect in mind, it affirms the ultimate objective of the withdrawal of all U.S. forces and military installations from Taiwan." In the meantime the United States agreed to progressively reduce its military installations on Taiwan as the tension in the area diminished.

Nixon scored well in the final draft because the Chinese agreement brought them into the problem of finding a way to end the Vietnamese war.

Nixon attended a farewell banquet February 27 in Shanghai. In his toast to his Chinese hosts, he said, "We have been here a week. This was the week that changed the world."

Ever the realist in foreign affairs, Nixon had been wise enough to realize that the old policy of ties to the Nationalists on Taiwan had long outlived their usefulness, and that it was time to face the reality of the real world in the Far East and drastically change his thinking, and that of the people of the United States.

In Vietnam, Communist troops launched a massive attack across the Demilitarized Zone March 30, but the South Vietnamese fought back, holding gains by the North Vietnamese to 22 miles after five weeks of fighting. President Nixon ordered bombing attacks renewed against North Vietnam, the first in three years, and May 9 ordered the mining of North Vietnam's major ports.

The conservative leader of southern causes, whose "segregation forever" views were expressed as he tried to bar the registration of the University of Alabama's first black students, Governor George C. Wallace of Alabama, decided to run for President of the United States again this year on an independent ticket. His attempt in 1968 failed when he garnered only 13 percent of the popular vote.

He was shot while campaigning on May 15 in a shopping center in Laurel, Maryland. Although he was paralyzed for life after the shooting, he remained on the ballot. Arthur H. Bremer was convicted of the shooting and sent to prison. In Bremer's home police found a notebook with random thoughts about Nixon. One of them said, "Happiness is having George Wallace arrested for a hit-and-run accident."

President Nixon followed up his triumphant visit to the People's Republic of China with a visit to the Soviet Union starting on May 22. He met with Communist leaders in Moscow and four days later signed a pact that pledged the two nations to freeze nuclear arsenals at current levels. He announced that the two countries would also work out a trade agreement, and that he had agreed to a joint Soviet-American space mission in 1975.

In one of the most bizarre events of the Twentieth Century, whose impact was not at first appreciated, five men raided the Democratic National Headquarters in the Watergate complex in Washington. It was later learned that all of these men were employed by the Committee to

Re-Elect the President, and that they had burglarized the headquarters to seize Democratic political material. Police arrested the men, plus two others later, in connection with the break-in. G. Gordon Liddy and E. Howard Hunt did not take part in the robbery but they were charged with planning it. When it was learned that both Liddy and Hunt had worked as aides in the White House, the break-in became a growing scandal.

President Nixon's campaign to reduce tensions between the United States and the Soviet Union went into high gear on July 8 when he authorized the sale of $750 million of corn, wheat and other grain products to the USSR.

The Democrats met on July 10 in Miami Beach to nominate candidates for the fall's national election. Hubert Humphrey and George McGovern had the most delegates, but in the end it was McGovern who won out. Senator Thomas F. Eagleton was nominated as his running mate. With McGovern's nomination, the American people had a clear-cut choice between two men of entirely different ideologies. McGovern had campaigned against the Vietnam War throughout the year for the "immediate and complete withdrawal" of American troops.

On July 25 Senator Eagleton admitted that he had undergone electric shock therapy for depression. McGovern said he would continue to support his running mate but the American people responded negatively to the news. Eagleton resigned on August 1, and later H. Sargent Shriver replaced him as the vice-presidential candidate. Shriver was the late John and Robert Kennedy's brother-in-law, and he had served well as head of the Peace Corps.

The first strategic arms treaty signed by President Nixon with the Soviet Union during his visit to Moscow was approved on August 3 by the Senate. It set limits on anti-ballistic missile systems for both countries. The second treaty was approved by the Senate on September 14 and it placed a ceiling on offensive weapons. Both treaties were noteworthy, not so much for what they achieved, but because they started a trend in the right direction.

The President announced on August 12 that the last units of America's ground forces had been withdrawn from Vietnam. The United States Navy still maintained its presence off-shore, plus some Air Force units in Thailand and Guam that were still available for whatever punitive action the President might choose to take. This year the military draft was phased out as the services became all volunteers.

President Nixon and Vice President Spiro Agnew were renominated at Miami Beach by almost unanimous votes after the Republican Convention opened on August 21. Anti-war demonstrators tried to disrupt the convention two days later but 1,129 were arrested outside of the hall.

President Nixon approved an amendment to the Social Security Act on October 10 that increased benefits for the nation's elderly by $5.3 billion a year. His signature authorized other important changes, including an increase in the annual amount a beneficiary can earn while Medicare benefits were extended to disabled Americans under the age of 65. Three months earlier Nixon had increased Social Security benefits by 20 percent.

For these and other reasons the American economy was in better shape and, with the Vietnam War winding down, the American people overwhelmingly selected Nixon as President over Senator McGovern. The election was a triumph for Nixon who received 47 million votes, or 60.7 percent of the total to McGovern's 29 million, or 37.5 percent.

The Dow Jones Industrial Average reflected the optimism of the American people as it exceeded 1,000 for the first time. The victory was a vindication of Nixon's handling of the war, his foreign policy and the economy. But it was a success story without a happy ending as the political fabric of the Republican administration began to unravel.

CHAPTER 26

A Matter of Life and Death

ALTHOUGH NORTH VIETNAMESE TROOPS FOUGHT A SERIES OF BATTLES in early 1972 they accomplished little. Since their major defeats in 1968 and 1969 North Vietnam's leaders urgently needed to accomplish two things. They had to improve their deteriorating strategic posture in South Vietnam, and they had to defeat Vietnamization if they were ultimately to win.

North Vietnam's negotiators in Paris later disclosed that their spring offensive had been launched because they needed leverage to strengthen their demands for a coalition government in South Vietnam. They considered it mandatory to control as much of the South as possible to accomplish this goal. So, they risked an all-out offensive, but it failed. Throughout 1972 North Vietnam hoped to achieve a standstill ceasefire as soon as it achieved territorial gains. Then they hoped their negotiators in Paris could end the war on terms most favorable to them. Their campaign failed throughout South Vietnam, and North Vietnam virtually exhausted its manpower and material resources. They suffered more than 100,000 casualties, with the loss of at least half of their large caliber guns and tanks. By the fall of 1972 they were no longer capable of mounting another general offensive. And, not one of South Vietnam's provincial capitals—Quang Tri the only exception and only for a brief period—ever fell into Communist hands. Out of the 260 district towns, fewer than 10 were occupied by the Communists and almost all were in remote areas.

North Vietnam's leaders had under-estimated South Vietnam's armed forces; their ability to sustain combat and their capacity for endurance. This was especially true of their estimate of the Territorials whom they had long held in low repute. They made a strategic error when they underestimated the effectiveness and the extent of American airpower. They made other strategic and tactical miscalculations that caused them to lose in every battle they fought. Their most serious error was in dispersing their main force units and making major efforts on three widely-separated fronts instead of concentrating on a major thrust against a single objective. Although they were successful in gaining territory in each region, only in northern Quang Tri Province did their gains amount to political and military significance. If they had concentrated their offensive in this area they would have gained Hué and continued south, possibly ending the war in 1972.

Although South Vietnam's armed forces fought exremely well in most instances their success was due to support by the United States Navy and Air Force. Without their assistance Quang Tri City could not have been retaken, nor could South Vietnamese forces have held at Kontum and An Loc without Air Force support. South Vietnamese forces became too dependent upon B-52 support, often delaying attacks until targets could be bombed. This became a major handicap later when B-52s were no longer available.

President Nixon replied to a request on June 23, 1972, by the North Vietnamese to resume meetings, proposing July 19 for a private meeting. This time Kissinger learned that the North Vietnamese no longer took for granted either a military victory or Nixon's defeat in the coming fall election. Publicly, North Vietnam's officials called the United States' agreement to return to discussions a great victory. In fact, their own military ineptitude gave them no other choice.

At the August 1 Paris meeting Kissinger told Le Duc Tho that their meetings could no longer be kept secret. The Communist leader made some concessions but Kissinger said they were not sufficiently worthwhile to continue the talks.

After Kissinger and President Thieu later reached a concensus about what to offer North Vietnam, a tentative agreement with Le Duc Tho was reached October 12. They settled on all the principal issues except the right of the United States to replace military equipment for South Vietnam and the question of civilians detained by the South Vienamese. However, a more precise commitment to a ceasefire in Laos and Cambodia was needed. The issue of a coalition government was believed to have been laid to rest. Kissinger and Le Duc Tho agreed to make the announcement on October 22 and to sign the agreement nine days later.

In a meeting on October 17 Kissinger and Xuan Thuy argued about the principal of equality on the replacement of military equipment. Kissinger sought one-for-one replacement of worn-out equipment. Xuan

Thuy accepted this position if the United States would agree to release Communist civilians detained in South Vietnam. This position was rejected.

Kissinger and Ambassador Bunker met with President Thieu two days later to review the latest details of the ceasefire, some of which Thieu had not approved in advance. To the draft of the typed text Nixon wrote in long hand, "Dr. Kissinger, General Haig and I have discussed this proposal at great length. I am personally convinced it is the best that we will be able to get and that it meets my *absolute* condition that the Government of Vietnam must survive as a free country. Dr. Kissinger's comments have my total backing."

Thieu read the statement without comment.

Despite later sessions with South Vietnam's President, Kissinger by October 21 still had not reached a final understanding with Thieu, although the North Vietnamese supposedly had accepted all American demands, including those on Laos and Cambodia.

Earlier, journalist Arnaud de Borchgrave was granted a visa to Hanoi that he had not sought and an interview with Prime Minister Pham Van Dong that he also had not requested. This was bad faith on Dong's part but he also gave an interpretation of the draft agreement that was at variance not only with the American interpretation but with the text of what had been negotiated. In the article Thieu was described as overtaken by events, and Dong discussed a three-sided coalition government that would be set up during a transition period. The article stated that all detainees on both sides, including civilians, would be released, but this point had not been agreed to. And lastly, the article said that the United States had agreed to pay reparations.

Thieu's reservations had already been high but now they turned to grave suspicions about the so-called agreement. He was opposed to any ceasefire that left 135,000 North Vietnamese troops in his country, and he considered this issue basic to South Vietnam's future and he argued for pressure to be applied against the Communist negotiators for withdrawal of all North Vietnamese troops.

In a letter to President Thieu Nixon repeated that he considered the agreement fully acceptable as it stood. He added a warning, "Were you to find the agreement to be unacceptable at this point and the other side were to reveal the extraordinary limits to which it has gone in meeting the demands put upon them, it is my judgment that your decision would have the most serious effects upon my ability to continue to provide for you and for the government of South Vietnam."

The following day—October 22—Thieu again indicated to Kissinger his opposition to the continued presence of North Vietnamese troops in his country. Kissinger handed him Nixon's letter that he read without emotion. He told Kissinger that he understood America's desire to end its participation in the war. "For me," he said, "it is a matter of life and death for my country." He said he would consult with his advisers and the National Assembly.

Kissinger cabled Nixon, "I think we finally made a breakthough." He and Ambassador Bunker were encouraged by their meeting with Thieu.

Laos and Cambodia were to be dealt with in two sets of documents. Now these two countries posed the most significant problem. The United States Congress had limited aid to Cambodia to $300 million. In a meeting with Kissinger, President Lon Nol endorsed the agreement, declared a unilateral ceasefire and called for negotiations. Under Article 20 of the Vietnam Agreement North Vietnam had pledged to withdraw its forces from Cambodia and Laos and to refrain from using the territories of Cambodia and Laos for military operations against any signatories of the agreement. In effect, this was a reference to South Vietnam. The Americans hoped that with North Vietnam's forces withdrawn that Lon Nol could handle the Khmer Rouge.

When Kissinger returned to Saigon from Phnom Penh he met with Thieu who was enraged about American meetings with Thai, Cambodian and Laotian officials. He said the United States had obviously "connived with the Soviets and China to sell out South Vietnam" and that he would not be a party to it. He revealed that his sense of betrayal went back at least a year to the proposal asking him to agree to resign a month before a presidential election. At the time he had accepted the provision without protest.

Kissinger was angered by his response. He told him, in part, "Your conviction that we have undermined you will be understood by no Americans, least of all President Nixon.

"As to specifics, we have not recognized the right of North Vietnam to be in the South. We have used the language of the Geneva Accords since we thought this the best way to work out a practical solution. Had we wanted to sell you out, there have been many easier ways by which we could have accomplished this.

"We have fought for four years, have mortgaged our whole foreign policy to the defense of one country. What you have said has been a very bitter thing to hear."

Kissinger knew there was no point in staying so he told Thieu he would return to Washington.

He wired his deputy, General Alexander M. Haig, Jr., that there were two options available. He could proceed to Hanoi as originally scheduled, present Saigon's changes, and go back and forth until some concurrence was achieved, or return to Washington. Haig was advised to tell Ambassador Dobrynin that he had encountered major obstacles in Saigon and that we were bound to present them to North Vietnam. He said he still hoped to gain the Soviet Union's support in containing North Vietnamese actions.

A message was sent to Le Duc Tho in Paris that Kissinger had been asked to return to Washington for further discussion of problems encountered with the South Vietnamese government.

Before he departed from Saigon Kissinger met once more with Thieu, who was calmer than at their previous meeting, but still adamantly opposed to some parts of the ceasefire agreement. He insisted on 26 changes in the agreement to make it acceptable, and he gave Kissinger a letter for President Nixon stating that his country could not approve of the agreement because of its shortcomings.

Kissinger returned to Washington October 23, the same day he sent a message to North Vietnam's officials that they rejected as not "really serious." They warned the war would continue, and that the United States must bear full responsibility.

This was also the day journalist Arnaud de Borchgrave's earlier interview with Pham Van Dong was released, declaring that peace negotiations in Paris were producing good results and that there would be a three-sided coalition government of transition.

Kissinger sent a cable to Le Duc Tho that the United States was prepared to sign on October 31, but that it might be difficult to stick to the timetable. He informed North Vietnam's prime minister that all bombing above the 20th parallel would cease as of October 25.

President Thieu went on television to tell his people that South Vietnam would refuse to take part in a coalition government.

The North Vietnamese now released their version of the agreement. They revealed the United States messages of October 20 and 26 in which President Nixon had called the text of the agreement "complete" and had expressed satisfaction with North Vietnam's concessions. In their statement, the North Vietnamese strongly denounced the Nixon Administration's "lack of good will and seriousness." They demanded that the agreement be signed by October 31.

With the President's consent, Kissinger spoke to the press on October 26, giving the American side of the negotiations and using the words "peace is at hand." He defended the right of the people of South Vietnam "who have suffered so much . . . who will be remaining in that country after we have departed" to participate in the making of the peace. He said the United States would not be stampeded into an agreement.

A North Vietnamese spokesman said that Le Duc Tho and Xuan Thuy would receive Kissinger again only if the United States was prepared to sign the October agreement, saying, "Peace is at the end of a pen." Kissinger responded that the proposal was ready for final negotiation, and he promised a full bombing halt 48 hours after a settlement.

Nixon's overwhelming victory over Senator McGovern on November 7 prodded North Vietnam to agree to a new meeting on November 20.

The President gave renewed consideration to Thieu's objections to the ceasefire agreement. The major issues were that the Demilitarized Zone should be recognized as the border separating the two countries as determined by the Geneva Accords in 1954, and a token withdrawal of North Vietnamese troops—25,000—was to be reciprocated by a similar reduction in South Vietnam. There was also the question of whether a ceasefire should involve all of Indochina. South Vietnam wanted an international control force strong enough and ready to take up positions when the ceasefire went into effect.

General Haig, Kissinger's deputy, arrived in Saigon to deliver a personal letter from President Nixon to stress the significance of the American aid program. Haig indicated that if South Vietnam kept refusing to accept the agreement that the United States might go ahead and sign separately with North Vietnam.

Progress had been achieved four days earlier when the United States State Department revealed that Canada, Hungary, Indonesia and Poland had agreed in principle to participate in a control commission.

Kissinger and Le Duc Tho met in Paris again on November 20. At first, while new demands were made by Kissinger to honor South Vietnam's terms, all went smoothly. But three days later Le Duc Tho got tough and rejected all American proposals and again demanded the removal of South Vietnam's government. Kissinger insisted that he explain why he had reversed himself. He was told that new demands had brought a change in North Vietnam's attitude. The talks were terminated on November 25 and they agreed to meet again in early December. They met December 4, but no progress was achieved.

After Kissinger talked to President Nixon a cable was sent to Hanoi warning that unless serious talks were renewed within 78 hours that the United States would resume the bombing of North Vietnam above the 20th parallel that had been halted since October.

Kissinger concluded a meeting in Paris December 13 with a warning to Le Duc Tho of growing impatience in Washington. "We came here twice, each time determined to settle it very quickly, each time prepared to give you a schedule which we would then have kept absolutely. We kept the Vice President standing by for ten days in order to start the schedule which we have given you. And we believed that in the last week there had been just enough progress each day to prevent a breakup but never enough to bring about a settlement. I admire the Special Adviser's skill in keeping the negotiations going."

When there was no satisfactory response from Hanoi, President Nixon issued an order December 14 for the reseeding of mines in Haiphong Harbor, resumption of aerial reconnaisssance over the North, and for B-52 strikes against all military targets in the Hanoi-Haiphone area. The President was convinced that now was the time for action, and not further talks. He did not hesitate to make a decision that should have been made seven years earlier. He called in the chairman of the Joint Chiefs of Staff and told Admiral Moorer, "I don't want any more of this crap about the fact that we couldn't hit this target or that one. This is your chance to use military power effectively to win this war, and if you don't, I'll consider you responsible."

The first warning order for a series of raids was issued to the Strategic Air Command on December 15. In the next two weeks 34 strategic targets were bombed in North Vietnam with 15,000 tons of bombs. Sixteen hundred military structures were either destroyed or damaged and 372 pieces of rolling stock met the same fate. Three million gallons of fuel were destroyed—a fourth of North Vietnam's reserves—and 80 percent of her electrical power was destroyed. North Vietnam's imports were reduced from 100,000 tons per month to 30,000. There were probably 1,242 missiles fired at the bombers, or a conservative estimate of 885, and only 24 made hits on the bombers for a 2.7 percent success rate of launches versus hits. Of the 24 missiles that hit aircraft, only 15 B-52s were actually lost. This was a Communist kill rate of 1.7 percent for the number of SAMs launched.

The quality of the airmen who flew the B-52s made the difference. This bomber had been designed in 1949, and was first flown three years later. Despite their valor, there were still some Americans so concerned about the people of North Vietnam that they urged President Nixon to accept any terms to end the war.

Although 15 B-52s were lost, 94 percent of the Stratofortresses released their bombs on assigned targets. These losses actually were far lower than expected, and considerably less than comparable World War II strikes deep into enemy territory.

Of greatest importance, for 11 tense days and nights the United States tactical and strategic air forces delivered a blunt, emphatic response and North Vietnam's leaders accepted it with the utmost seriousness.

The strategic bombing of North Vietnam was almost universally condemned by the world's press. In the United States Congress, criticism mounted and President Nixon had few defenders. Generally the bombing was termed indiscriminate carpet bombing of heavily-populated areas. This was not true. Even the North Vietnamese claimed at most that only 1,600 people had died. Such losses, compared to the bombing of German and Japanese cities in World War II, hardly rated the term terror bombing. It was obvious that the media overreacted and that their reports were based on inadequate and false information.

The magnitude of the bombing effort shocked the Communist leadership. For the first time the full weight of America's aerial might had been unleashed and, with their factories destroyed and their harbors mined, they quickly became more amenable to reason.

The American government had insisted December 27 that it would not stop the bombing until technical meetings were resumed January 2, 1973, and that a meeting between Kissinger and Le Duc Tho must be set for January 8 with a time limit on negotiations.

The North Vietnamese responded in less than 24 hours. The next day they announced approval of the American proposals and asserted "constantly serious negotiating attitude."

The Communists were advised on December 29 that as of 7 p.m. that night that the bombing would cease. They were sternly warned that the United States would make only one final effort to settle their dispute within the framework of the October agreement.

The Democratic caucus in the House of Representatives voted January 2, 1973, 154 to 75 to cut off all funds for Indochinese military operations contingent upon the safe withdrawal of American forces and the release of all prisoners. They made no provision for a ceasefire. The Senate Democratic caucus passed a similar resolution 36 to 12. Neither resolution was helpful, and members who voted for the resolutions acted disgracefully.

On the second day of talks in Paris it was apparent on January 9 that Le Duc Tho had come to settle all differences. A draft agreement was completed on January 13, together with all understandings and protocols. There was a provision for continued military support to Saigon and the Demilitarized Zone was reaffirmed in precise terms according to the provisions established by the Geneva Accords in 1954. One provision was added that the parties of the agreement would undertake to refrain from using Cambodia and Laos "to encroach on the sovereignty and security of one another and of other countries." It was hoped that such language would prevent the use of these countries as sanctuaries by the North Vietnamese. The agreement called for an immediate ceasefire in place throughout Vietnam, withdrawal of all remaining American troops—by now down to 27,000—and the release of all prisoners of war throughout Indochina. Infiltration by the North Vietnamese was prohibited and there would be international supervision. The 17th parallel was again made the demarcation line. The matter of a political settlement between North and South was left up to them for future negotiation.

Le Duc Tho agreed to arrange a ceasefire in Laos after consultation with Communist forces in that country. In fact, the Pathet Lao were totally subordinate to North Vietnam.

The North Vietnamese Communist Leader refused to be specific about Cambodia. He claimed that North Vietnam had little influence over officials of that country. This statement was doubted at the time, but later was proved to be correct.

During the war, America's armed forces were unbeatable and Vietcong and North Vietnamese Army units suffered terrible losses. Although a true figure is impossible to determine, the Communist dead probably reached a total of one million, and possibly more. There is no precise record of those wounded, or the number of civilians on both sides who were killed, but a figure of four million dead and wounded Vietnamese appears realistic—roughly 10 percent of their combined populations. For South Vietnam the military death toll was considerably less—approximately 240,000. But this figure may also be conservative. Of the 3.7 million Americans who served in Vietnam, including 7,500 women, 58,135 lost their lives but this figure includes 10,753 non-combat deaths while another 153,303 were wounded and required hospital care. Another 50,000 had such slight wounds that they were treated at the scene and returned to their units. Desertions were high, totaling 93,250, but 20,000 had served a full term before deserting.

Norman Hannah, a career State Department Foreign Service Officer with long experience in Southeast Asia, wrote in 1975, "In South Vietnam we responded mainly to Hanoi's simulated insurgency rather than to its real, but controlled aggression, as a bull charges the toreador's cape, not the toreador.

"Instead, the United States adopted a defensive strategy that had failed so many times before. Westmoreland believed his strategy would eventually achieve success. The United States was fighting for time rather than space, and time ran out along with the patience of the American people." Actually the United States never had a real strategy to force North Vietnam to stop its aggression. As a result, the American defeat in Southeast Asia was inevitable.

Nixon ended mandatory wage and price controls on January 11, 1973. They had been in effect for 17 months since passage of the Economic Stabilization Act, but they had failed to slow the nation's inflation rate. The President announced that except for controls on food, health and housing that his administration would rely on voluntary compliance with its anti-inflationary guidelines.

The Supreme Court ruled on January 22 in Roe vs. Wade that all state laws that prohibit voluntary abortions before the third month, with limits on prohibitions during the second three months, were unconstitutional. This was a landmark decision, and the nation's feminists greeted it as an important breakthrough but "right to life" groups denounced it.

During World War II, women had taken over much of the job of keeping America's factories humming to produce the necessary goods and services to support the war effort. In the process, they found a new freedom and sense of worth, but with the end of the war most women returned home to take over their familiar duties of running a household. At the time few thought of re-entering the work force, unless it became mandatory to support themselves. Instead the typical American family expanded as most of these women increased the birthrate by 50 percent in the next 10 years.

Some women refused to join the "baby boom" generation and continued their fight for equality with men in the workplace. Betty Friedan published a book in 1963 in which she called for a wider role for women in American society. Her *The Feminine Mystique* touched the hearts and minds of many women who had become disenchanted with their motherhood roles and who had long waited for a leader to liberate them. Many found such a leader in Friedan and gladly joined her National Organization for Women (NOW). The organization's goal of greater political and economic equality for women appealed to them as they became involved in civil rights and anti-war activity. They saw these activities as part of society's sexual discrimination. Not all women believed in the conservative goals of NOW and formed their own organizations. A few of them alienated the rest of American society by some of their outrageous acts such as the "bra-burners," and those who protested that beauty pageants were "sexist." Advocacy of lesbianism as a substitute of heterosexual activities made titillating headlines in the press, but turned off most women.

With abortion now legalized by the Supreme Court in 1973, and contraceptives more easily available, feminists fought for what they called "complete control over their bodies and their lives."

The United States signed a four-party pact in Paris on January 27 to end the war in Indochina. It was signed by North Vietnam, the Vietcong, South Vietnam and the United States and provided for the withdrawal of American troops within 60 days. The signing called for an immediate ceasefire and the release of all American prisoners. Although Americans considered that the war was over, ceasefire violations continued almost daily and American planes continued to bomb bases in Cambodia until August 14. The war's end boosted President Nixon's approval rating to

68 percent after an end to the draft was announced and it was agreed that the nation would rely upon voluntary enlistments.

Although President Nixon hoped that protests about the Watergate break-in would recede, Congress had other ideas. The Senate established a Select Committee On Presidential Campaign Activities to investigate what was termed the Watergate "conspiracy." Sam Ervin was placed in charge, and he announced that public hearings would commence on May 17.

A "conspiracy of silence" had kept the Watergate illegal break-in from involving the White House, although some staff members were rumored to have been involved. James W. McCord, one of those convicted of the attempted burglary, admitted in a letter to Judge John Sirica in March that he and the other six defendants had been ordered to remain silent about the case. He told the judge there were others involved in the break-in who had not been charged with the crime. Specifically, he named former Attorney General and Republican Party Chairman John Mitchell as the "overall boss."

In April, FBI director Patrick Gray admitted that he had destroyed Watergate evidence on the advice of Nixon's aides.

These revelations forced Nixon's hand and April 30 Presidential Chief of Staff H. R. Haldeman, domestic affairs assistant John Erlichman, Presidential counsel John Dean III and Attorney General Richard Kleindienst submitted their resignations. Nixon announced their resignations in an address to the American people, but he disclaimed any personal knowledge of the affair.

Judge William Byrne on May 11 dismissed charges against Daniel Ellsberg and Anthony J. Russo for stealing the Pentagon Papers and circulating them. They had been charged with responsibility for leaking the classified papers to the press. The case was complicated by the fact that two government agents, E. Howard Hunt and G. Gordon Liddy, had broken into the office of Ellsberg's psychiatrist in a futile attempt to steal Ellsberg's medical records. This fact was revealed to Judge Byrne by the attorney general, convincing him that he had acted correctly.

Nixon's strong suit had always been foreign policy and he enhanced his prestige in this field when he began a series of talks on June 13 with Soviet leader Leonid Brezhnev. The talks proved productive as the two leaders agreed to avoid confrontations that might precipitate a nuclear war. They signed an agreement that established rules for negotiation of a strategic arms limitation treaty to replace the temporary one approved in 1972. Before he returned home Brezhnev addressed the nation in a television broadcast. This was the first time that a Soviet leader had done so but the historic broadcast didn't go beyond vague platitudes designed to sooth the distrust between the two nations.

John Dean III, former presidential counsel, accused the Nixon adminstration on June 25 of involvement in the Watergate coverup. In an appearance before the Senate Watergate Committee, Dean charged that the President had authorized payment of hush money to the seven men accused of breaking into Democratic National Headquarters.

Nixon faced another uproar when the Senate Armed Services Committee began hearings on July 16 and claimed that he had authorized secret bombing raids into supposedly neutral Cambodia during 1969 and 1970. Secretary of Defense James Schlesinger told the committee the following day the raids were "fully authorized" and necessary to protect American troops from attack. He admitted that approximatley 3500 individual attacks had been made. The Senators were particularly outraged by this revelation because they had been advised earlier by military leaders that no such raids had taken place.

The Senate Watergate Committee learned to its surprise that all conversations in the Oval Office were routinely taped. This fact was disclosed by Alexander P. Butterfield, former deputy assistant to the President. Chairman Sam Ervin and committee members quickly realized that they had a way to determine the truth of Dean's allegations about the President, and promptly subpoenaed the tapes. Nixon responded on July 23 that the tapes were "privileged" executive information and he refused to release them. He said in his rejection that turning them over would infringe upon the independence of the Executive Branch.

The Mid-East erupted again on October 6 just as the Hebrew holy days of Yom Kippur began. Egyptian troops invaded the Israeli-occupied territory in the Sinai Peninsula while Syrian troops invaded the Israeli-occupied Golan Heights. Israeli losses in planes and tanks were so severe that that nation's leaders feared their armed forces would be overrun.

The United States had long suspected that Israel had a nuclear capability, since the days of President Kennedy all presidents had chosen to ignore this fact, making a mockery of America's plea to all nations to sign a non-proliferation treaty. It is believed that Israel had started production of nuclear weapons in 1968. Now her leaders panicked and literally blackmailed the United States Government into rushing new planes and tanks to the war fronts by threatening to use its nuclear arsenal. Although it is impossible to be precise, well-documented sources indicate that Israel had at least 24 nuclear weapons. With new planes the Israeli Air Force saved the day for their country by striking deep into Syria and Egypt. They destroyed nine bridges across the Suez Canal, trapping 400 Egyptian tanks on the east bank. Eventually Egyptian and Syrian forces were pushed back to the 1967 ceasefire lines. Israeli Premier Golda Meir first rejected a truce proposed by the United Nations, but later agreed to accept a truce with Egypt on October 2 and then with Syria.

The Republican administration in Washington faced a new crisis on October 10 when Vice President Spiro Agnew resigned. He had been charged with tax evasion resulting from illegal payments by contractors who sought his favors while he was governor of Maryland. Agnew pleaded "no contest" to the charge.

Two days later President Nixon nominated House Minority leader Gerald R. Ford to succeed Agnew. Thus he invoked for the first time the provisions of the 25th Amendment ratified in 1967 to permit the President to fill a vacancy in the office of the vice president.

The Arab-Israeli War had cost Israel huge amounts of war material so its government appealed to President Nixon for approval to resupply its armed forces. President Nixon announced on October 15 that he was doing so, in particular to off-set supplies furnished to Arab countries by the Soviet Union.

President Nixon's problems with the Watergate break-in escalated on October 20 when he ordered his attorney general, Elliott Richardson, to dismiss special prosecutor Archibald Cox. The latter had refused to accept the President's compromise offer to release a synopsis of the presidential tapes that he had subpoenaed in lieu of the tapes themselves. Richardson refused and he and his assistant William D. Ruckelshaus resigned. Cox was then fired by Solicitor General Robert Bork. This "Saturday Night Massacre" caused an uproar in Congress and throughout the nation. Now Congress started the first of a series of steps to impeach the President.

Arab oil-producing nations, infuriated by what they considered was the United States's one-sided backing of Israel in the latest war now declared an oil embargo on all exports to the United States and a 10 percent cut in production. This action was taken to put pressure on the United States and its West European allies to force Israel to withdraw from the Arab lands it had occupied.

The Arab oil embargo soon brought the energy crisis in the United States to the critical stage. In the winter of 1973 a lack of heating oil in several mid-western states forced the shutdown of some factories and schools. President Nixon had created the Energy Policy Office in June to improve the management of energy resources but then the oil embargo drastically worsened an already tight situation. The President addressed the nation in November and proposed several energy saving measures such as year-around daylight savings time, a reduction in environmental standards and a cutback on fuel allocations. Later in the month he called for a 50 mph. speed limit and the closing of gasoline stations on Sunday. None of these actions proved useful in resolving the situation.

The United States and the Soviet Union joined forces on October 22 to sponsor a United Nations resoluton to seek a ceasefire in the Middle East War. Both sides accepted a ceasefire, and the fighting ended on the 24th.

President Nixon's problems mounted in the Watergate affair as the House Judiciary Committee was assigned on October 23 by Congressional leaders to begin an investigation into whether the President should be impeached. Cox's firing had resulted in an outpouring of invective against the President and Nixon agreed through his lawyer to release those tapes with subpoenaed evidence. A week later, the White House revealed that two of the tapes did not exist. The uproar over this revelation had barely died down when it was announced on November 21 that there was an 18½-minute gap on another reel that could not be explained. Later Nixon's personal secretary claimed she had accidentally erased that part of the tape. To check whether she was telling the truth a panel of experts was assigned to review the reel. They reported on January 15 of the following year that the gap could not have been erased accidentally.

Despite the President's veto, Congress passed the War Powers Act on November 7. This was an attempt by Congress to restrain a President's power to commit American troops into foreign countries for an indefinite period without Congressional approval.

Three days later six of the Watergate defendants were sentenced by Judge John Sirica for their break-in at the Democratic National Headquarters in June of 1972. E. Howard Hunt received a sentence ranging from 2½ to 8 years and a fine of $10,000. All but G. Gordon Liddy were given lesser sentences. Liddy was sentenced to 20 years for his refusal to cooperate with the prosecution.

America's first earth-orbiting space situation, the unmanned Skylab, was launched early in 1973. Designed to prove that men could work and live in space for extended periods without ill effects, this first Skylab was the spent third stage of a Saturn 5 moon rocket measuring 118 feet in length. The first Skylab to be manned by visiting three-man crews was launched May 25 and Charles Conrad, Jr., Joseph P. Kerwin and Paul J. Weitz were assigned to the space station in orbit. It carried a varied assortment of experimental equipment, and this first crew remained in space until June 22 completing scientific and medical experiments.

Gerald Ford was sworn in December 6 to replace Spiro Agnew as the nation's 40th Vice President. He had been given a thorough background check prior to his nomination in regard to his fitness to assume the Presidency in the event of Nixon's impeachment. His fellow congressmen found nothing in Ford's long record in the house to indicate otherwise, and he was easily ratified.

Arab countries lifted their oil embargo in March 1974, but the problem lingered because its causes went beyond the embargo. Although this was a difficult period for automobile owners, ultimately it had some positive effects. Motorists drove less, manufacturers were forced to produce more fuel-efficient automobiles, and alternative sources of energy were devised.

The Senate Watergate Committee subpoenaed 500 tapes and documents for use in its investigation of the Watergate break-in but President Nixon on January 4, 1974, refused to surrender them. He told Committee Chairman Sam Ervin that to accede would "unquestionably destroy any vestige of confidentiality of presidential communications, thereby irreparably impairing the constitutional functions of the office of the Presidency." Ervin turned to the courts to force the President to surrender the tapes.

Nixon's association with the Watergate break-in became even more apparent on March 1 when seven former White House staff members, including intimate associates H. R. Haldeman, John Erlichman and John Mitchell were indicted for conspiring to obstruct justice. Two weeks later the President was named a co-conspirator. Those indicted were scheduled to stand trial on October 1. Erlichman, Haldeman, Mitchell and Robert Mardian were found guilty January 1, 1975. Kenneth Parkinson was acquitted and charges against Charles Colson were dropped after he pleaded guilty to crimes in connection with the break-in of Daniel Ellsberg's psychiatrist.

With Nixon's problems escalating at home he began a week-long tour of the Middle East on June 12. Since the Yom Kippur War the previous year in October he had tried various means to promote peace. He had taken a personal role in trying to bring the warring powers to the negotiating table. In May, Secretary of State Henry Kissinger had mediated a tense situation when Syrian and Israeli troops had remained in the field despite the ceasefire eight months earlier.

The President went to Moscow on June 27 for five days of summit talks with Russia's leaders. A week later he and Russian leaders signed agreements concerning nuclear weapons but their talks failed to achieve any significant breakthroughs. *Pravda* praised the negotiations as "an essential movement forward on the path of strengthening peace and mutual trust."

But President Nixon was in no position to use his office to influence foreign leaders. This was dramatically brought about on July 30 when the Supreme Court issued a unanimous decision that President Nixon must turn over the subpoenaed tapes to special prosecutor Leon Jaworski. In this historic decision—the first time the Supreme Court ever ruled on a legal action in which a president was accused of criminal misconduct—the stage was set for Nixon's resignation or removal by impeachment. He had no choice, and eight hours after the court's decision, the White House announced that the President would obey the court's decision.

Three days later the House Judiciary Committee approved two Articles of Impeachment against Nixon. He was charged with obstruction of justice and of repeatedly violating his oath of office. Later the committee recommended a third charge of unconstitutional defiance of committee subpoenas.

President Nixon finally realized that he had no further option but to resign. He had lost not only the support of conservative members of his party in the Congress, but the confidence of a majority of the American people. Senator Barry Goldwater had told him three days earlier that he would be impeached and convicted if he remained in office. Such a trial, Goldwater told him, would be long and hurt the country.

Nixon spoke to the nation on August 8 and announced that he would submit his resignation effective at noon the following day.

An emotional Richard Nixon bade his staff farewell the next morning. "Always remember," he said, "others may hate you, but those who hate you do not win unless you hate them—and then you destroy yourself."

He was driven to the airport by Henry Kissinger to whom he handed his resignation as he boarded the plane. While Nixon was in flight to California Gerald R. Ford was sworn in as president by Chief Justice Warren Burger.

The new President faced a nation beset by political and social problems and a world-wide economy that was suffering from severe inflation with dramatic increases in the cost of fuel, food and raw materials. Americans were outraged to learn that 30 of the world's largest oil companies increased their net profits by 93 percent during the first half of 1974. In most countries economic growth was down to near zero. In the United States, the Dow Jones stock index plunged to 663; the lowest level since the 1970 recession. But the well-liked Ford had been chosen for his stability and personal integrity, and these were qualities admired above all else following the debacle of the last year of the Nixon administration.

CHAPTER 27

"La Guerre Est Fini."

NELSON ROCKEFELLER WAS NOMINATED ON AUGUST 21 TO FILL THE vice-presidency after Ford's ascension to the presidency. He had been governor of New York for 15 years and had failed three times to secure his party's highest political office, but it now became an asset to heal the wounds of the nation with two top men representing both sides of the political spectrum.

President Ford's decision to pardon former President Nixon caused an uproar in the United States when it was announced September 8. The pardon was all but inclusive, providing "a full, free and absolute pardon . . . for all offenses against the United States which he . . . has committed or may have committed or taken part in while President." Ford was strongly criticized for his action, and accused of making a deal with Nixon to secure his resignation. Ford denied these allegations saying that the nation's continued fixation with Watergate was detrimental. He cited Nixon's declining health as a reason for his decision.

President Ford caused another storm of protest September 16 when he announced an amnesty for Vietnam draft evaders and military deserters. He established conditions, however, that returning fugitives must take an oath of allegiance and a commitment to work in a public service program for two years. Most veterans groups denounced it but in general the American people viewed his decision as just another step towards putting the war behind them. Americans who had fled to Canada to avoid the draft complained that the program was punitive and implied their guilt. As a result, many of them remained permanently in Canada.

President Ford took a trip around the world in November, with stops in Japan, South Korea and Valdivostok. There he and Soviet leaders reached a tentative agreement to limit offensive weapons until 1985, with the understanding that further negotiations would take place in Geneva. He returned on November 24 after an eight-day trip.

President Ford ordered an investigation on January 8, 1975, of charges that the CIA had been involved in illegal domestic activities. The *New York Times* charged December 21 that the intelligence agency had participated in domestic espionage on a massive scale. Under the CIA's charter such activity was illegal. The President appointed an eight-man commission to investigate the charge, saying he would not tolerate such activities. He appointed Vice President Nelson Rockefeller to head it and report back to him.

Secretary of State Kissinger admitted on March 22 that his shuttle diplomacy had failed in trying to get Israel and Egypt to agree to settle their disputes. He announced that "irreconcilable differences" had caused him to suspend his efforts.

During 1973 and 1974 North Vietnam's armed forces had been unable to occupy any provincial capital in South Vietnam. They had tried to take Kontum and Tay Ninh. Now its generals turned to Phuoc Long, the northernmost capital of III Corps, and prepared to attack it with two infantry divisions augmented by support regiments. The city of Phuoc Long is 37 air miles northeast of Saigon. At the time there were 30,000 people in the city—mostly Montagnards—who worked on the rubber plantations and in lumbering. The terrain is mountainous and covered by dense jungle that denied air observation. Phuoc Long City was linked to Saigon by inter-provincial Route 1A and National Route 14. The latter also connected Phuoc Long with Quang Duc and Ban Me Thuot to the northeast.

Phuoc Long Province was far outside Saigon's defenses, and bounded on the north by Cambodia, so its importance to South Vietnam was primarily political. As long as it remained under their control they could claim possession of all provincial capitals. On the other hand, the presence of South Vietnamese bases deep inside otherwise North Vietnamese-controlled territory was totally unacceptable to the Communists.

After a series of sharp battles, with losses high on both sides, the province chief ordered a withdrawal on January 6, 1975, from the city of Phuoc Long. The retreat was made under constant enemy fire. It was the first province capital to fall since the ceasefire.

The capture of Phuoc Long gave North Vietnam extended control over a large area. Three Communist base areas were now linked in a continuous arc from the Cambodian border across the northern region with access routes toward Ham Tan on the coast. Psychologically and politically the loss of Phuoc Long came as a shock to South Vietnam's government officials and members of its armed forces. The apparent total indifference with which the United States and other non-Communist nations regarded this loss reinforced South Vietnam's doubts about the viability of the Paris Ceasefire Agreement. There was little hope left that the United States would punish North Vietnam for their continued violations of the agreement.

Phuoc Long was not merely a military victory for the North Vietnamese. It was their first big step toward military conquest of South Vietnam. They now believed they could boldly proceed with conquest without fear of any military reaction from the United States.

North Vietnam's Central Military Party Committee prepared on January 9 to expand their offensive in the South. Ban Me Thuot was selected as their army's first objective, and the main effort in a Central Highlands campaign.

While North Vietnamese divisions converged on their initial objectives in Darlac and Quang Duc provinces for a later assault on Ban Me Thuot, the opening guns sounded along Route 19, life-line to the Highlands, during the early hours of March 4. Simultaneous attacks were also launched to close the highway from the Mang Yang Pass in Pleiku Province to Binh Dinh Province. Unfortunately the area's South Vietnamese commander refused to beleive his intelligence officer that the North Vietnamese target was Ban Me Thuot. He insisted that Pleiku was the major objective. As a result his failure to send a sufficient force to defend Ban Me Thuot resulted in its capture.

This disastrous turn of events proved to be the turning point of the war. Although President Thieu considered it important to retake Ban Me Thuot, he believed he had to sacrifice Kontum and Pleiku. He met with his staff on March 11, just prior to the loss of Ban Me Thuot, to give them his assessment of the situation. "Given our present strength and capabilities, we certainly cannot hold and defend all the territory we want." He said the armed forces should be re-deployed to hold and defend only those populous and flourishing areas that were most important. They encompassed all of III and IV Corps plus their territorial waters. In effect he was recommending that the northern part of South Vietnam be relinquished to the Communists without a fight. He said that those areas in the southern regions that were still under Communist control should be re-occupied at all costs. The President explained that these regions contained the nation's most important resources of rice, rubber and manufacturing plants, and that they were the nation's untouchable heartland— the irreducible national stronghold. It included Saigon, its surrounding provinces, and the Mekong Delta.

Thieu and his advisers reached a momentous decision, but they had not analyzed all the ramifications. Some of his military advisers believed it was already too late to make a successful redeployment of such a magnitude. This was a logical evaluation of the situation, but Thieu had waited too long to put it into effect. He still hoped that the United States would intervene with its armed forces. Nixon had promised such a decision, but he was no longer President of the United States.

Thieu should have had no illusions about America's hands-off policy toward the war. Despite North Vietnam's escalation of the war in the past two years the United States had taken no military action. A Congressional visit of Americans had recently made it clear that the United States Congress would not authorize a return to military intervention. It had repeatedly shown that it was in no mood to intervene.

President Thieu's re-deployment plan came too late to achieve success. It should have been done in mid-1974, or at the very latest when President Nixon resigned. Thieu, and many other South Vietnamese officials believed that Nixon was the only American with the moral obligation to enforce the ceasefire. They believed he was the only one in the United States who was bold enough to take forceful action. If the re-deployment decision had been made earlier, South Vietnam would have been far better off with a reduced but more tightly-controlled country. With the loss of Ban Me Thuot it was too late.

The withdrawal from the Highlands should have been orderly, but it turned into a rout. A retreat is the most difficult of all military maneuvers. It requires detailed planning and strong leadership at all echelons. Re-deployment, however, is not a retreat but a scheduled movement of organized convoys with self-defense capabilities. In this instance it was impeded by refugees and civilian vehicles plus the poor condition of the road over which they traveled with its inadequate river-crossing facilities.

Prior to its fall, 60,000 refugees straggled into Nha Trang on the coast almost due east of Ban Me Thuot. Tragically, at least 100,000 others were stranded in western Phu Yen Province without food, water or medical assistance. The withdrawal was the most poorly executed of any in the war as each general looked after his own troops without concern for anyone else's men, and the army as a whole. There was total failure of leadership at all levels. The troops were not briefed, and discipline was not enforced. The soldiers were not even ordered to destroy Communist road blocks that proved to be a major obstacle to their survival. The rout of the South Vietnamese was of massive and strategic proportions, and at least 7 percent of its troop strength was lost. It ended tragically for South Vietnam.

Thieu's position was difficult. He had ordered the re-deployment from the Central Highlands, and it had turned into a rout. Worst of all was the psychological impact the debacle was having on the civilian population. His whole plan to regroup the armed forces into a smaller and more defensible area was not working out. Still, he continued to procrastinate and he did not give his field commanders the answers they sought. They were advised to hold whatever territory they could with the forces available.

The situation in I Corps was particularly acute and Thieu went on television hoping to calm the worst fears of the South Vietnamese people. He told them that Hué would be defended at all costs. But by the middle of March it was clear that an all-out offensive had begun in I Corps. North Vietnamese attacks continued all along the northern front and 400,000 refugees crowded Da Nang. The necessities to sustain life were rapidly disappearing, and on March 24 the government began to move refugees south by every available boat and ship. Thousands made it safely, but many did not. But as Da Nang's defenses started to crumble the city was close to panic as refugees jammed the streets.

All troops were ordered to evacuate Hué, northwest of Da Nang. Those north and west of Hué were told to assemble at Tan My, Hué's port northeast of the city, cross a narrow channel to Thu Thuan and then march southwest down Vinh Loc Island. They were instructed to cross the mouth of the Dam Cau Hai Bay on a pontoon bridge that would be constructed by engineers, and then to proceed along the beach to Highway 1 where they would go through Hai Van Pass and proced to Da Nang. Inasmuch as no trucks, tanks or heavy guns could make the march, they were destroyed or disabled.

The people still left in Hué streamed out in panic toward Tan My to take any boat or ship out of the province.

Just as the withdrawal was getting under way the commanding general was ordered to release his Marine Division for the defense of Saigon. He told the Joint General Staff that he couldn't defend Da Nang without it, and he objected strongly to its removal. The General Staff suggested that Chu Lai, 50 miles to the southeast of Da Nang, should be given up and the division there sent to Da Nang. This was done and the Chu Lai sealift began after dark on March 25 while an embattled column of soldiers and refugees struggled north on Highway 1 from Quang Ngai City toward Chu Lai. Dead and wounded littered the road—a scene reminiscent of the carnage in Quang Tri on this same highway during the 1972 offensive. Once the Chu Lai sealift started, panic engulfed the soldiers who fought for places on the first boats. It was some time before order was restored and 7,000 soldiers embarked for Da Nang.

Although the 3rd South Vietnamese Division still held two Da Nang districts, with morale at rock-bottom, soldiers deserted their units to save their families. Officials lost control of the population as two million people surged through the streets trying to locate their families and escape with them to the south. Police deserted their posts, and those who remained were unable to control mobs of armed soldiers who roamed the streets. There were even instances of shooting between soldiers and police.

North of Da Nang the withdrawal from Thua Thien Province was orderly at first as South Vietnamese forces linked up on Vinh Loc Island and crossed the narrow channel to Loc Tri in the Phu Loc District. Unfortunately for the South Vietnamese the bridge that was supposed to be installed by engineers never arrived. Engineering boats were evidently commandeered by other military units seeking to escape. The withdrawing forces managed to cross by using local fishing boats. The only disciplined units were the Marines. The rest were fleeing like a frightened mob.

With the Communists approaching Hai Van Pass from the North, and Vietnamese navy boats breaking down faster than they could be repaired, the sea movement of people and equipment from Hué was ordered to cease. Now that it was impossible to reinforce Da Nang with adequate strength, the order was given to recover elements of the Marine Division at Da Nang.

North Vietnamese troops attacked on March 27 and South Vietnamese units held at first, but it was soon evident that they could not hold off massive attacks for long so a withdrawal was ordered to man a shorter defense line within artillery range of the city. Attempts to hold this line failed as large numbers of 3rd Division soldiers deserted to save their families.

With defeat imminent, the commanding general ordered all remaining organized units—mostly Marines—be shipped out of Da Nang to Saigon. Da Nang, last bastion of South Vietnam's I Corps, was occupied by the North Vietnamese by nightfall on March 30.

Now the Nha Trang-Ninh Hoa area was the last concentration of South Vietnamese troops in II Corps. If this area could be held the North Vietnamese might be prevented from moving down Highway 1 to Saigon. Despite bitter resistance, the weight of savage attacks forced a rapid withdrawal of all South Vietnamese troops from this area. The Airborne Brigade had fought well, losing three quarters of its men, but the forces against them were too powerful.

The momentum of the North Vietnamese Army was so great that defense of Cam Ranh proved unfeasible, and the Joint General Staff authorized its evacuation. It now coordinated its offensive countrywide as a ring of North Vietnamese divisions tightened around III Corps, and

American military assistance slowed to a trickle. On March 12, the United States House of Representatives had voted 189 to 49 in favor of a resolution opposing additional military aid for either Cambodia or Vietnam before the end of the fiscal year. The following day the House Foreign Affairs Committee rejected a compromise proposal that would have provided additional aid. President Ford urged the Congress to provide more assistance, saying it was essential to South Vietnam's survival, and that its decision to withdraw from the Highlands was due to lack of interest in their fate.

President Thieu met with American Ambassador Graham Martin and asked him whether his resignation would affect the possibility of more aid from Congress.

Martin replied, "It might have changed some votes several months ago, but your resignation now would not change enough votes to affect the outcome." The ambassador added that Thieu's resignation in exchange for more aid "was a bargain whose day had passed, if indeed it had ever existed."

The United States Congress was not to blame, particularly for the loss of the Central Highlands. South Vietnam's predicament was caused by the failure of II Corps' commander to accept his intelligence officer's estimate that Ban Me Thuot was North Vietnam's primary target and his failure to fight with the forces available to him. When the corps commander followed this critical mistake in judgment with two others—inadequate planning and execution of the counterattack from Phuoc An, and a mismanaged withdrawal—he started the entire nation on a downhill slide that not even the valor of thousands of loyal officers and men could reverse. Like an unplugged hole in a dike, the flow of North Vietnam's armed forces started with a trickle and soon became an uncontrollable flood.

As the frontlines contracted, stiff South Vietnamese resistance and strong local counterattacks in the southern provinces caused the North Vietnamese armies to pull back and regroup. During the first week of April, therefore, a relative calm descended on the battlefields that the South Vietnamese used to reorganize their shattered units trickling in from the North. Hurriedly, South Vietnam's military leaders redeployed their forces to meet the certain resumption of attacks. Approximately 40,000 South Vietnamese troops had escaped capture in I and II Corps by April 1, and they had reported for reassignment to camps in III Corps. In many divisions the officer corps had been decimated and morale was low. The 22nd Division, whose resistance to the North Vietnamese at Binh Dinh was one of the war's most remarkable feats of determination, courage and leadership was in better condition that the others. However, it had lost most of its equipment and the division arrived in the South with only a skeleton organization. It was deployed to Long An Province, southwest of Saigon, on April 12, where a critical battle was shaping up.

A major battle was now taking shape at Xuan Loc on Highway 1 east of Saigon. South Vietnamese military men fought so well that the North Vietnamese high command was forced to sacrifice its own units to destroy irreplaceable South Vietnamese forces. While savage battles continued for Xuan Loc, III Corps moved its divisions to the West to prepare for the expected assault against Saigon.

The final decisive battle was waged at Xuan Loc after a week of the toughest, most continuous combat the South Vietnamese had experienced since the offensive began. The 18th South Vietnamese Division was forced to retreat from Xuan Loc and fight its way back toward Bien Hoa. Armored tank forces on Route 1 also had to pull back after half their equipment was destroyed, and the 6th North Vietnamese Division moved north of Route 1 toward Trang Bom.

Between April 20 and 26 there was an uneasy quiet over the battlefields while the North Vietnamese conducted reconnaissance sweeps, and prepared for their final drive. There were now 16 North Vietnamese divisions in III Corps poised for a three-pronged attack against Saigon.

President Thieu was so shocked by events that he went to the palace's bomb shelter and sat alone in despair for 24 hours.

Upon hearing of the President's condition, Saigon's Regional Commander Lieutenant General Nguyen Van Toan flew to the capital the next day to pick up Chief of Staff General Cao Van Vien. At the palace they met a nervous and white-faced Thieu. Toan's words were blunt, "Monsieur le President, le guerre est fini."

Thieu should have been the strong leader that his country needed. He was the son of a humble fisherman, and a graduate of the French Military Academy at Dalta. A convert to Catholicism, he had fought with the French colonial army against the Communists. But after he became president he used his office to provide draft deferments for the rich, the influential and the educated sons of his friends. Officers were frequently promoted to the rank of general more as a political plum for their support than for their ability.

With the forlorn hope that the North Vietnamese might stop their offensive and negotiate a settlement providing for some South Vietnamese representation, President Thieu resigned April 21. He charged there was collusion between officials of the United States Government and those in the Communist governments in reaching agreements at the Paris peace talks. He stated that the United States had sold out South Vietnam to the Communists.

Thieu's resignation had no discernible effect on the North Vietnamese whose successes on the battlefields, and the absence of any prospect of American intervention, left no basis for further negotiation. In effect, South Vietnam's politicians had no bargaining power left.

Thieu's successor, Vice President Tran Van Huong was lame and ill. The 71-year-old Huong had served briefly as premier in the mid-1960s but he had been ousted by a military coup because of his poor administration of the country.

The North Vietnamese resumed their attacks on April 26, focusing on Bien Hoa east of Saigon. Two air bases received heavy artillery fire as North Vientamese divisions moved along Route 1 toward Bien Hoa. The Communists moved forward with confidence, crossing Route 15 south of Long Binh and isolated the southern coast city of Vung Tau.

North Vietnamese Army units in Long An and Hau Nghia Provinces renewed their efforts to dislodge the stubborn South Vietnamese defenders in the west.

Thieu's successor tried to form a new government that might be acceptable to the North Vietnamese for negotiating a settlement but it was proclaimed unacceptable and Huong had to admit defeat on April 27. He resigned and was succeeded by General Duong Van "Big" Minh—so named because he was six feet tall and weighed over 200 pounds—who now openly boasted of his contacts with the North Vietnamese in previous years. A neutralist Buddhist, he had long advocated a conciliatory policy toward the Communists. Any hope that the 59-year-old Minh may have had that his contacts might help him or South Vietnam were quickly dispelled. The Communists soon demonstrated they had nothing but contempt for him. Such futile political machinations were irrelevant in the face of the reality of continued Communist victories.

The end of the long war came on April 30 as Americans hastily fled Saigon in a sea-and-air lift that also took out 130,000 Vietnamese who feared for their lives under Communist rule. This was just the start of an exodus, and eventually more than a million South Vietnamese left their homeland for other countries. The majority of them came to the United States.

The war in Cambodia had been going on for five years during which Cambodia the monarchy (theme was "an oasis of peace") had become a republic and was now an "oasis of war." At the beginning it had been a war against aggression carried out against foreign forces. Now it became a civil war pitting Khmer against Khmer. Morale of the armed forces reached bottom in the spring of 1975. Each year the Communist encirclement of the nation's population centers had grown tighter. This was particularly true around the capital. Internal political differences could no longer be tolerated. Divisions between the Social Republican Party of President Lon Nol, and the other parties had deepened to the point where reconciliation had become impossible. Lon Nol had totally isolated himself from his companions who had helped to found the Republic.

Lieutenant General Sak Sutsakhan, who had been a roving ambassador, was asked to accept the post of Chief of the General Staff and Commander-in-Chief of the Khmer Republic. He reluctantly accepted on March 12. He viewed his country as a sick man who could survive only by outside means. In traveling from one command to another to assess the military situation, Sutsakhan was shocked. There were defections everywhere for a variety of reasons; lack of resupply, inefficiency, misunderstandings and discontent provoked by the conduct of certain senior officers.

The fight for Phnom Penh was concentrated within a nine-mile radius of the capital. The American Embassy evacuated its staff on April 2, along with acting President Saukham Khoy. The United States offered to evacuate other Khmer officials, particularly those whose lives might be endangered, but most declined to leave. The entire cabinet of military and civilian leaders decided to remain with their people.

Sutsakhan checked the military situation on April 12 and he reported to the Committee of Seven who elected him President that an honorable peace must be obtained, and he made a peace offer to Prince Sihanouk.

When no word was received from Sihanouk by April 17 he agreed to establish a government in exile, although remaining somewhere in Cambodia. When a helicopter or plane proved impossible to obtain for his departure he decided to resist to the death in Phnom Penh. Then a cable arrived from Peking that Sihanouk had rejected his peace proposal, branding the seven members of the Supreme Committee as chief traitors, in addition to the other seven who had taken power in 1970.

After a few helicopters were located, Sutsakhan and his family with some members of his government departed for Thailand. With his departure the ancient civilization of Cambodia died at the hands of a cynical Communist dictator. In the next two years at least two million Cambodians were brutally murdered as Pol Pot suppressed all freedoms.

Two weeks after Americans precipitately fled South Vietnam to escape the victorious North Vietnamese Army the American cargo vessel "Mayaguez" was seized by Cambodia's Khmer Rouge Communist government. President Ford ordered a ground, sea and air operation on May 14 to recover it. Although the "Mayaguez" and its crew were rescued, 15 American Marines were killed in a badly-handled operation by the United States Navy. But after the debacle in Vietnam the President was praised by Congress and most Americans for his prompt action in ordering America's armed forces into action. This act of piracy was an indication of what could be expected from the new Communist government of Cambodia. Officials in Phnom Penh charged that the vessel was part of a spying operation against their country. This charge was patently false.

The President earlier had assigned Vice President Rockefeller to a commission to investigate charges of domestic spying by the CIA. The results of that investigation were released on June 10. It was revealed that the CIA had engaged in a wide variety of covert operations in violation of the agency's charter. The commission recommended a joint Congressional committee to oversee intelligence operations.

Evidence of a closer relationship between leaders of the Soviet Union and the United States was demonstrated in July after they agreed to cooperate in a joint space program. On July 17 the American spacecraft "Apollo," with astronauts Thomas P. Stafford, Donald K. Slayton and Vance D. Brand, linked up in space with the Soyuz 19 spacecraft and its Soviet cosmanauts Colonel Aleksei Leonov and Valery N. Jubasov in the first international manned space flight. They shook hands as the spacecrafts joined together and shared a meal during their two-day link-up in space.

The Senate Select Committee on Intelligence on December 4 released its findings on their investigation of the CIA's role in the overthrow of Chile's President Salvador Allende Gosens in 1973. The report claimed that there was no evidence to directly link the agency to the coup itself, but that the CIA had "created the atmosphere" for Allende's ouster. The CIA had earlier been charged with expenditures of $8 million in their alleged attempts to overthrow the Marxist leader.

President Ford concluded a five-day tour of the Far East on December 5 as the Communists united North and South Vietnam as the Socialist Republic of Vietnam. In the process, they changed Saigon's name to Ho Chi Minh City. During his tour the President stopped in China, Indonesia and the Philippines. In Peking, Ford met with Mao Tse-tung. Everywhere he went he was warned by Asian leaders of the potential dangers of appeasing the Soviet Union. Chinese leaders, in particular, said that the United States was making a mistake by reaching any kind of agreement with the Russians.

The year 1975 demonstrated appreciable progress for women of all nations during International Woman's Year. At West Point, 118 women were admitted as cadets for the first time. The Navy and Air Force opened their academies to women, enrolling 81 at Annapolis and 157 at Colorado Springs. The Episcopal Church reversed itself this year and announced that women would be permitted to be priests and bishops.

It had been apparent for some time that the nation's intelligence services were in need of a drastic overhaul to eliminate waste and illegal methods. President Ford drastically revised the way intelligence was gathered when on February 17, 1976, he ordered a reform of all agencies. The most important change involved the establishment of an independent "oversight" board.

The United States celebrated its 200th birthday on July 4, 1976. President Ford participated in Philadelphia and New York City but there were parades and celebrations throughout the land. Six million people watched the "tall ships" from 31 nations parade up the Hudson River.

The Democratic National Convention met in New York on July 15. Despite a last-minute rush for delegates by California's Governor Jerry Brown who won in Maryland, Nevada and his home state, Jimmy Carter emerged with sufficient delegates to win the nomination. His victory in Ohio had cinched it. Carter was nominated by the convention, and Senator Walter Mondale was named as his running mate. The two candidates were promptly endorsed by major labor unions and black leaders.

With the nation in recession, and unemployment still running high at 7.5 percent in June, Congress on July 22 passed a $3.45 billion bill to create jobs. President Ford promptly vetoed it, but Congress overrode his veto.

As expected, President Ford was nominated August 19 at the Republican National Convention. Challenger Ronald Reagan had claimed victory when the convention opened three days earlier, but he did not have the delegate strength.

This year further advances were made in space by both the United States and the Soviet Union. Russia's Soyuz spacecraft docked successfully with the orbiting Salyut space station. Meanwhile, landing vehicles from the American spacecraft Viking I and II set down safely on Mars and transmitted closeups of the planet back to earth. It was hoped that they might settle once and for all the possibility of life on Mars but the data was inconclusive.

On earth the world's first scheduled supersonic passenger service was inaugurated when two Concorde jets took off simultaneously—one from London and the other from Paris—as Britain and France began supersonic transatlantic service to Washington, D.C.

James Earl Carter, who preferred to be officially called just "Jimmy," defeated Gerald Ford on November 2 with a two million plurality although the electoral votes were closer, 297-241. He stressed during his inaugural address that his administration would focus on human rights, the environment, nuclear arms control, and a search for justice and peace.

The following day President Carter gave an unconditional pardon to almost all draft evaders during the Vietnam War.

The previous year the Supreme Court had ruled that, in certain cases, the death penalty was constitutional. Gary Mark Gilmore, who brutally murdered two students at Brigham Young University in Salt Lake City the year before, had won a stay of execution by foes of the death penalty. After the United States Court of Appeals overturned the ruling, the death sentence was carried out on January 17 by a firing squad at Utah State Prison. He was the first person to be executed in 10 years.

The winter of 1977 in the eastern and central states was one of the coldest on record, and Americans in these areas suffered as never before because of persistent fuel shortages. The shortage was so severe in some areas that factories and schools had to be closed.

The new President took his first major step in dealing with the economy, and it was a typical Democratic move during a recession of "priming the pump." He called for allocation of $31 billion to stimulate the economy.

President Carter underlined his dedication to international human rights when he announced on February 24 that aid would be reduced to those nations in violation of rights. Secretary of State Cyrus Vance backed up the President's order by reducing aid to Uruguay, Ethiopia and Argentina, although the reduction was small and largely symbolic. The President's action lost some credibility when it was announced that America's strategic allies would not have their financial support reduced even if they were ignoring basic rights of their citizens. Among such guilty nations Vance included South Korea which still had a large American military presence.

President Carter tried to aid the economy by cutting defense spending, particularly funds for such large programs as the B-1 bomber which, he charged, was costing $1 million in taxpayer's funds to create each job in the program. At the time the airplanes were costing $100 million each. He believed the cruise missile made the heavy bomber obsolete. Unfortunately the cruise missile's limitations for conventional warfare were not understood. There was a super-secret "stealth" bomber in the planning stages, but that wouldn't be ready until the 1990s to replace the aging B-52 fleet. Carter cancelled the B-1 bomber in a move that was incredibly ill-advised in favor of an unproven bomber that wouldn't be available for almost 15 years. When President Reagan re-instated the B-1 after he defeated Carter in 1980, the cost of re-activating the program raised the B-1's price to three times what it had been originally.

In 1973, at the time of the Arab oil embargo, the United States was importing 15 percent of its oil, and the price had quadrupled. Dependence had grown to almost 50 percent—about nine million barrels a day—with energy consumption at a record level. Dwindling oil supplies in the United States now forced President Carter to initiate what he called "the moral equivalent of war," (a phrase used originally by author William James) to resolve the crisis. In a speech to the nation on April 28 the President proposed stringent conservation of fuels, higher energy prices to reduce demand, and the imposition of penalties against those who wasted energy. He claimed the nation would run short of energy supplies in the 1980s unless Americans changed their "wasteful" use of fuel.

The United States and Vietnam began talks on May 3 in an attempt to normalize relations. The two-day talks broke down when the United States refused to provide financial assistance to the economically-depressed nation.

President Carter and Panama's chief of government, General Omar Torrijos Herrera, signed two treaties on September 7, 1977, for gradual return of the Panama Canal Zone and the canal to Panama by 1999. In return, Panama agreed to perpetual neutrality for the canal. In general, Republicans denounced the treaties but they were ratified on March 16 and on April 18, 1978, with only one vote more than the two-thirds majority needed to approve them. The treaties revoked the 1903 treaty under which the United States built the canal and operated it.

Egypt's Anwar El Sadat made an historic trip to Israel in November to speak to the Israeli Knesset on November 21. In calling for steps to end the continual wars in the Middle East, he offered a program of "peace with justice" between his nation and Israel that were technically still at war. "If you want to live with us in this part of the world," he told the Knesset, "in sincerity I tell you we welcome you among us with all security and safety." He insisted however that Israel would have to recognize the rights of Palestinians and withdraw from occupied Arab lands, including East Jerusalem. Israel's prime minister, Menachem Begin, praised Sadat but rejected his call for withdrawal from Arab territories. Begin told Sadat, "We will not be put within range of fire for annihilation."

Sadat's visit to Israel outraged most of the Arab world who denounced him for joining hands with Begin and pledging "no more war."

CHAPTER 28

Carter Mediates Middle East Crisis

THE PRESIDENT SPENT MOST OF 1978 TRYING TO MEDIATE THE DIFFER-
ences between nations in the Middle East. After a 13-day conference at
Camp David, Maryland, that ended on September 17, Egyptian President
Anwar El Sadat and Israeli Prime Minister Menachem Begin reached two
agreements. They agreed to resume diplomatic relations and to establish
a timetable for peace negotiations. Begin also agreed to his country's
withdrawal from the Sinai Peninsula. It was no serious problem to give
up Egyptian land occupied by Israel, but more serious problems involving
the status of Jerusalem, a homeland for the Palestinians and Israeli occupation of the West Bank of the Jordan River were left to future conferences. Although Carter trumpeted the agreement as a breakthrough,
little actually was accomplished. The seeds of further conflict were sowed
by the conference's failure to reach a total agreement.

Later in the year Begin and Sadat were given the Nobel Peace Prize
for their efforts to bring about peace in the Middle East.

Although the nations of the Middle East had settled down this year
to intermittent warfare, violence erupted in many other areas of the
world. In Central America President Anastasio Somoza Debayle invoked
emergency powers in January when disturbances threatened his dictatorial
regime in Nicaragua. By September Somoza had an armed insurrection
on his hands and in a bloody battle approximately 1,500 Sandinistas
were killed fighting against the well-equipped National Guard and police
force. But now it was evident that the Sandinistas enjoyed widespread
support. The Somoza regime had been supported by the United States

since the 1920s. Now President Carter sent an emissary to President Somoza urging him to accept Latin American mediation to end the conflict.

French and Belgian paratroopers were dropped into the town of Kolwezi in southern Zaire in May in an attempt to free 3,000 foreigners trapped by Communist-backed rebels. They found the bodies of 44 Europeans who had been massacred by Katanganese rebels. President Carter sent 18 Air Force transports to Zaire to assist in the evacuation. The Cuban and Soviet forces backing the rebels continued their all-out fight to control the African nation.

Meanwhile Somalia mobilized against Ethiopia to aid the guerrillas fighting Ethiopia's Communist troops.

Violence continued in Rhodesia between government and rebel forces, resulting in the deaths of possibly 1,500 guerrillas during four raids against rebel camps in neighboring Zambia. The raids took place while Rhodesia's leaders were meeting in Washington with American officials to discuss possible peace talks. Approximately 8,000 rebels battled in Rhodesia with government forces, while another 22,000 were based in Mozambique under Robert Mugabe and his African National Union and in Zambia under Joshua Nkomo's Zimbabwe African People's Union.

There had been rising violence against Shah Reza Pahlavi in Iran during the year, forcing him to place his country under martial law. At least a thousand people had been killed as newspapers, radio and television stations were shut down. The Shah promised his people free elections if they restored order but in Paris Ayatollah Khomeini, the Shiite Moslem leader, threatened to start a civil war to topple the Shah. By late December, when millions marched against the Shah, the country was in a state of collapse.

With hundreds of thousands of people fleeing Laos, Cambodia and Vietnam to escape persecution from their new Communist leaders, the United States took action this year to offer sanctuary to more of these desperate people. President Carter and Congress agreed on November 27 to accept an additional 15,000 Indochinese in America. This action raised the ceiling to 47,000 so-called "boat people," because most of the refugees were fleeing their homelands in any type of boat they could find. For a time this decision alleviated the situation caused by Southeast Asian nations who refused to accept any more refugees.

Diplomatic relations with the People's Republic of China were established on January 1, 1979, by the United States while simultaneously it severed such ties with the Republic of China on Taiwan. The Nationalist government had been recognized since 1949 after Chiang Kai-shek's forces fled the mainland. President Nixon had brought about the change in his administration during his visit to the People's Republic. Leonard Woodcock was confirmed on February 26 as America's first ambassador to Peking.

The Shah of Iran was forced to leave his country on January 16. In parting, he said, "I hope the government will be able to make amends for the past and succeed in laying the foundation for the future." Meanwhile, Prime Minister Shahpur Bakhtiar approved the return of the Ayatollah Khomeini from exile who was greeted by millions on February 26.

In a formal ceremony in Washington, Israeli Prime Minister Menachem Begin and Egyptian President Anwar Sadat signed a peace treaty on March 26. They had worked out the details the year before and now their signatures to the treaty ended the state of war that had existed between their countries since 1948.

President Carter authorized a new guided missile system on June 7. The MX was projected to cost $30 billion.

Eleven days later he signed an agreement with the Soviet Union to limit long-range nuclear missiles and bombers of the two countries to 2,250 each. The SALT (Strategic Arms Limitation Talks) agreement was signed in Vienna after six years of negotiations by three Presidents. President Carter signed for the United States and Leonid Brezhnev as President and head of the Communist Party of the Soviet Union. The treaty had posed one particular stumbling block in regard to whether a Soviet supersonic bomber should be included in the agreement. Brezhnev gave Carter oral and written assurances that production of the bomber would not exceed 30 per year. The agreement was sent to the United States Senate for final approval.

The United States formally gave up the Panama Canal Zone on October 1, although it would not revert to Panamanian control until the year 2,000. After much debate, the Senate approved the transfer of the canal subject to Panama's agreement that it would be kept neutral.

Muhammed Reza Pahlavi, who had been forced to leave Iran in 1978, had come to the United States to undergo surgery for the removal of gallstones. Now Iranian students demanded that the United States return him to Iran for trial. When the United States Government refused, 500 Muslim students attacked the United States Embassy in Teheran on November 4 and took its 66 residents as hostages. Although the Iranian government said it had not authorized the takeover of the Embassy, the spiritual leader of the Iranian government, Ayatollah Ruhollah Khomeini said on November 18 that some embassy personnel might be tried as spies. Khomeini earlier that year had returned from exile in France to be greeted with a tumultuous welcome.

President Carter promptly froze all Iranian assets in American banks, cut off oil imports from Iran, and called for deportation of Iranian students illegally in the United States.

The United Nations unanimously approved a resolution on December 4 calling for the release of the hostages, and in early 1980 sent a fact-finding mission to Iran.

In late November the students released 13 American women and blacks but the remaining 53 hostages were often brutally treated. This action by the students at first was expected to be a minor irritation between the two countries, but it went on and on, exploding into a near-war confrontation.

The Iranian hostage crisis in the spring of 1979 had a ripple effect on American business, particularly the automobile business. When the price of gasoline doubled, and the biggest recession in 50 years hit the United States, the impact on the automobile industry was catastrophic—and not just on one company. The Ford Motor Company lost $678 million in the third quarter, while General Motors lost $300 million. Chrysler faced bankruptcy because its banks refused to loan it any more money. The company appealed to the government for a federal loan and President Carter supported Chrysler's appeal. After bitter debate, Congress approved a bill to bail Chrysler out of its predicament.

Meanwhile, Japanese automobile firms were making ever-larger inroads in the American market. At the time, the Japanese government was rebating about $800 per car when it was shipped to the United States. This rebate was legal under the General Agreement on Tariffs and Trade. But Japanese at home, in effect, were subsidizing Japanese manufacturers because the identical car that was sent overseas cost Japanese consumers more money than Americans paid in the United States. Chrysler's Lee Iaccoca hammered at one of his favorite themes that there was no such thing as free trade because other countries placed limits on imports. This was true, but the United States also limited imports of some foreign goods.

With the Communist government in Afghanistan near collapse in late 1979 due to strong attacks by rebel forces, the Soviet Union's leaders flew 5,000 troops into the country on December 26 and mobilized thousands of others to take over the fighting. President Carter denounced the invasion on December 31, telling the leaders of the Soviet Union that their action "would severely and adversely affect the relationship now and in the future between ourselves and the Soviet Union."

In a television interview, the President rejected Brezhnev's statement that Soviet troops had been invited to Afghanistan by the government. He accused the Soviets of engineering a coup that toppled the government, killing President Hafizullah Amin and installing a new president,

Babrak Karmal. Shortly after the new year began the Soviets had at least 40,000 troops in Afghanistan. Amin was a Marxist, but he had been unable to quell opposition to his regime.

The People's Republic of China denounced the invasion, claiming it "poses a threat to China's security," and demanding the withdrawal of Soviet troops. Even Third World countries, normally inclined to support the Soviet Union, denounced the invasion and demanded a meeting of the Security Council.

The Soviet Union had begun to deploy its SS-20 missiles in eastern Europe in early 1977. These were missles with three warheads with a range of 3,100 miles. Thus they were capable of hitting targets anywhere in Europe. In October of that year West German Chancellor Helmut Schmidt warned that these missiles threatened all of Europe. He called upon the North Atlantic Treaty Organization to discuss ways to counter them. In December of 1979 NATO unanimously adopted a "dual track" strategy to counter this missle threat. Western nations of the alliance agreed to deploy 572 American Pershing-2 ballistic missles and ground-launched cruise missiles. NATO officials agreed also to participate in arms control talks with the Soviet Union to reduce intermediate-range missles in equal levels. By the end of this year the Soviet Union had deployed 120 SS-20s for use against the West in the event of an all-out conflict.

Many Senators, already indisposed to seriously consider the SALT II treaty with Russia, now turned distinctly negative. It was soon apparent that the Senate could not possibly muster the two-thirds vote needed to approve SALT II, and Senate leaders left the treaty in the hands of the Foreign Relations Committee and postponed further action until officials of the Soviet Union could agree on improved observance features of the treaty. Actually, the Afghanistan invasion by the Soviet Union was the death knell for SALT II.

The price of gold soared $159 an ounce on January 18, 1980, to reach a value of $802. This was just another indication that the American economy was in dire straits, and that the American dollar had lost much of its real value.

The Soviet Union's armed intervention in Afghanistan prompted President Carter to re-evaluate several decisions. In the past, he had refused to sell weapons to the People's Republic of China. He reversed himself on January 24 and the Chinese eagerly sought various weapons systems to modernize their armed forces. They, too, were concerned that the Afghanistan invasion signaled a more belligerent attitude by the Russians. The Chinese felt particularly vulnerable because of their long border with the Soviet Union.

New labor statistics released on January 25 gave another indication that the American economy was in trouble. They revealed that the 1979 inflation rate was the highest in 33 years.

Iran's retention of American embassy personnel in Teheran proved to be Carter's greatest burden. He tried every possible diplomatic means for their release to no avail. Now he tried a military rescue on April 24. It also was doomed to failure when two helicopters failed to arrive at the rendezvous point in Iran and another developed a leak that prevented it from taking off. Incredibly, there was insufficient backup to replace them and the rescue attempt ended in failure. Eight Americans died in the attempt as another helicopter collided with a transport plane. Secretary of State Cyrus Vance, who had opposed the rescue attempt, resigned. The effort exposed the Defense Department to public ridicule that was well deserved for this inept military exercise.

On May 24 the International Court of Justice demanded the immediate release of the American hostages in Iran, and ruled that that nation would be liable for reparations. A week later the European Economic Community voted to cancel all contracts with Iran negotiated since the seizure of American embassy personnel. Canada and Japan also adopted sanctions against Iran. Canada pleased the American people by smuggling six Americans from their embassy in Teheran during a diplomatic withdrawal of their own people.

With the invasion of Afghanistan by the armed forces of the Soviet Union now reaching massive proportions, and with no possibility of their withdrawal, President Carter took another step to prepare the country for a period of international crises. On June 27 he signed a bill to permit the draft registration of the nation's 19-and 20-year-old youths. Although peacetime imposition of such registration was not well received, there was little opposition to the registration.

The Republican National Convention met on July 16 in Detroit to nominate their candidates for the fall election. Former California Governor Ronald Reagan appeared to be the strongest GOP candidate. He had a reputation as a hard line conservative, although earlier he had been a Democratic liberal. He had tried to become the party's nominee in 1976 by unseating Gerald Ford, but his campaign had failed. This time he was unbeatable and he was selected by the convention as his party's nominee. Party officials tried to talk Gerald Ford into running as the vice-presidential candidate but he refused. George Bush was selected instead.

In July 1980, President Carter dropped the Nixon-Ford plan for destroying the Soviet Union's means of recovery from an atomic war because the huge escalation of atomic weaponry finally exceeded America's ability to economically support such an arsenal. It was also conceded that the plan itself was seriously flawed because it called for 95 percent destruction of all targets whereas half that percentage was militarily justifiable. The new strategy emphasized attacks against "war-supporting" industries, but it still called for massive urban-industrial attacks. Two new types of targets were added, including attacks on the Soviet Union's political leaders, and that nation's emerging mobile missile force. After President Reagan came to power the following year, his administration continued to follow Carter's presidential directive.

Carter's standing with the American people arrived at a new low this summer because of the hostage situation. The former Shah of Iran had died of cancer in July and it was hoped that his death would make the Iranians more amenable to reason. Iranian government officials had announced in the spring that the hostages were under their control and they continued to make new demands. But it was obvious that any agreement would have to wait until after the election.

It was a dispirited Democractic convention that met on August 14 in New York to renominate Jimmy Carter and Walter Mondale. For Carter the months prior to the election became a series of minor disasters that further reduced his popularity as the Iranians figuratively thumbed their noses at his appeals for release of the hostages.

The election on November 2 was an anti-climax as Reagan won almost 51.2 percent of the vote to Carter's 49 percent. The electoral vote was even more impressive—449 to 49. Riding in on Reagan's coattails the Republicans won control of the Senate with a 53 to 47 majority while reducing the Democratic majority in the House to five seats.

American voters had become disenchanted with Carter's failure to get America out of the recession and reduce inflation. Of major significance was the stalemated Iranian hostage situation.

Reagan promised "to put America back to work again." At age 69, the former California governor was the oldest man to ever be elected as President.

Ronald Reagan was sworn in as President on January 20, 1981. During the ceremony 52 American hostages boarded a plane at Teheran to be flown out of Iran after their 444 days in captivity. In the previous November, Iran had presented a series of new demands that served as the basis for the agreement that brought about their release. Algerian officials had acted as intermediaries during the final two months of negotiations. After the United States agreed on January 19 to unfreeze most of Iran's assets in the United States, (some would be held until legal claims were satisfied) locate and unfreeze the late Shah's wealth following his death in July, lift all trade restrictions between the two countries, and refrain from interfering with Iran's internal affairs, the hostages were permitted to leave.

During his speech Reagan did not mention the hostages until the plane carrying them had left Iranian airspace, and then he acknowledged Carter's long efforts to arrange their release. The new President spoke about the goals of his administration. He said "government is not the solution to our problem; government is the problem." As his first official act he said he was instituting a federal hiring freeze. He vowed to "hit the ground running," to slash taxes, revive flagging American industry, speed up deregulation and return functions to the states that he said had been bungled by a sprawling bureaucracy. His speech was long on goals but short on specifics. He emphasized that "we are not, as some would have us believe, doomed to an inevitable decline."

In a considerate gesture Reagan designated Carter as his personal emissary to greet the returning hostages in West Germany.

President Reagan announced on March 2 that his administration would support President José Napoleon Duarte of El Salvador in his country's fight with leftist guerrillas who sought to overthrow his government. The President promised $25 million worth of military equipment, and 20 more advisers to help train the Salvadoran government's army.

Early in the afternoon of March 30, 70 days after Reagan was sworn in, the President was shot in the chest as he walked to his limousine after addressing a labor convention at Washington's Hilton Hotel. Authorities arrested John W. Hinckley, Jr., a 25-year-old resident of Colorado. Reagan's press secretary, James Brady, and two officers were wounded.

Reagan returned to the White House on April 11 saying that he felt "great" although he was pale and walked stiffly. Before he left the hospital his doctors suggested that he leave in a wheel chair. He refused, saying, "I walked in here—I'm going to walk out."

The Space Shuttle was launched for the first time on April 12 at Cape Canaveral, Florida. "Columbia," with astronauts John Young and Captain Robert Crippen, had a minor mishap when a number of heat-resistant panels were torn off, possibly during takeoff. But, the "Shuttle" landed safely at Edward Air Force Base in California two days later. It made its second test flight in November.

During his administration, President Carter had imposed a grain embargo on the Soviet Union as punishment for its invasion of Afghanistan. During his presidential campaign Reagan had promised to lift the embargo. It had served primarily to hurt America's grain farmers, lose precious markets to other countries that gladly filled the grain needs of the Soviet Union, and did nothing to stop the invasion of Afghanistan. Like so many of Carter's actions, this one may have been morally right but actually it placed an unnecessary burden on America's farmers and achieved no positive results.

In February 1980, during the so-called "Abscam" bribery investigation in New Jersey, Senator Harrison Williams had been indicted. On April 30 he was convicted along with seven Congressional members of involvement in the scandal. The following day Raymond Lederer resigned his seat in the House of Representatives to avoid expulsion.

Sandra Day O'Connor became the first woman member of the Supreme Court on September 21 after her nomination by President Reagan. She had long been active in Republican politics in Arizona, serving first as an assistant attorney general and then as a state senator. She became Arizona's Senate Majority Leader in 1973. She gained a reputation as a tough and methodical jurist. During her Senate confirmation she was questioned about her views on abortion and the Equal Rights Amendment. She replied that she was opposed to judicial "activism" such as prevailed during the days of the liberal Warren Court, and made it clear that she was a conservative but not hide-bound to any ideology.

The United States debt reached one trillion dollars in 1980, and for the first time in its history the annual budget deficit reached $100 billion. But it would get worse, with $200 billion deficits common in the near future. President Reagan spoke to the nation on September 29, saying, "We've only balanced the budget once in the last 20 years." In reference to the trillion dollar indebtedness, he said, "If we as a nation needed a warning, let that be it." Unfortunately his administration didn't heed it.

Conservative Republicans had expected that Reagan would balance the budget by cutting out wasteful expenditures. Instead he began to vastly increase defense spending, while cutting taxes later by 25 percent. George Bush, who campaigned against Reagan for the nomination, had said "this is voodoo economics." Now, as vice president, he was strangely silent about his earlier charge.

President Reagan announced a five-point program for strengthening America's defenses on October 2. Except for building up the nation's non-nuclear capability, the program was not needed. But the President called for building 100 B-1 bombers that the Carter administration had cancelled, plus 100 multi-warhead MX missiles although no adequate protective system was ever devised. Carter had approved the MX but he had favored an underground rail system to shuttle missiles between sites to prevent the Soviet Union from pin-pointing them. Reagan rejected this concept, and rightly so. To improve their chances of survival, he advocated placing them in superhardened silos capable of withstanding a direct nuclear strike, but the costs were astronomical. In reality, with the nation's triad nuclear forces—bombers, submarines and ground-based missles—the MX was not needed. During the Carter presidency the neutron bomb, that destroys people by enhanced-radiation weapons but spares structures, was deferred for production. Now Reagan revived the program and production began.

Despite outcries from the Israelis, the Reagan administration received Senate approval on October 28 to sell several million dollars worth of military equipment to Saudi Arabia. Among the items were five sophisticated Airborne Warning and Control surveillance planes.

In Poland, the volatile political situation reached the explosive point on December 28 when the Polish government cracked down on the independent labor union Solidarity. In response President Reagan imposed sanctions against the Soviet Union whom he held responsible for this hard line action. The President called for a ban on high technology equipment to the Soviet Union, along with other measures that were primarily symbolic. Unlike President Carter, who cut off grain shipments when the Soviet Union ordered an invasion of Afghanistan, President Reagan honored this agreement with the Russians.

Argentina's military forces overran the 84 British defenders of the Falkland Islands on April 2 as Great Britain marshalled its armed forces to retake them. Three days later Britain's Foreign Secretary Lord Carrington resigned for what he called "the humiliating affront" of the Argentine invasion. Britain had governed the Falklands for 149 years, and most of the residents were British. It wasn't until April 30 that the United States Government openly sided with Great Britain after being chided for its tardiness by Prime Minister Margaret Thatcher.

After a major sea battle was fought by British and Argentine naval units during May, Argentina's ground forces made their final stand on May 31. The last Argentinians surrendered on June 14.

Although the Israelis removed their last soldiers from occupation duties in the Sinai Desert on April 25, and the land was returned to Egypt, the Israeli army invaded southern Lebanon on June 6. This action was taken, a government official said, to drive out the Palestinians who had shelled Israelis from this area. But the Israeli army continued far beyond this region, battling Palestinian and Syrian forces along the coastal road to Beirut.

After strong international pressure, and a threat by the Soviet Union that they might enter the conflict, Prime Minister Menachem Begin backed down.

Speaking to the Israeli Parliament, Begin offered to let Palestinian guerrillas leave Beirut with their weapons. Two days earlier the Israeli cabinet had demanded that "all of the 15 terrorist organizations . . . hand over their weapons to the Lebanese Army."

Begin's back-tracking was influenced by anti-war sentiment among his own people, and some members of the Knesset said Begin had already gone too far.

The Israeli invasion included 20,000 soldiers and hundreds of tanks and by June 9th it had reached the outskirts of Beirut where they became bogged down in fierce fighting with the Palestinians and the Syrians south of the capital. But in the air the chief Israeli spokesman claimed that the Israeli Air Force had shot down 61 MIGs and five helicopters over the Bekaa Valley.

In its two-and-a-half year war with Iraq, Iran claimed on May 24, that its forces had recaptured the major port city of Khurramshahr. Thus it had re-occupied all of Iran previously captured by the Iraqis. This announcement shocked the Arab world which had been divided in its support of the warring parties.

While the Middle East exploded in renewed fighting, approximately half a million people demonstrated in New York's Central Park for nuclear arms control. They had marched for three miles through the city's main streets to hear speakers such as Coretta Scott King. She told the throng, "We have come here in numbers so large that the message must get through to the White House and Capitol Hill."

In the Middle East, Israeli combat planes twice bombed Beirut on July 27, killing 120 people and injuring 232. Israeli officials said the bombings were ordered to eradicate 6,000 members of the Palestine Liberation Organization who were holed up in the city.

The escalating war drew even more protests from Israelis opposed to the invasion. Earlier, over 100,000 young Israelis demonstrated against the Lebanese war. When it was learned that American cluster bombs were used during the invasion, United States Senator Henry Jackson said their use violated agreements. He claimed that Israel was straining relations between the two allies. The Israelis denied that any treaty involving their use had been violated.

With continuing heavy bombing and shelling of their positions in Beirut, Palestinians took advantage of the Israeli offer to leave. Their departure was delayed because the Israelis had restricted them to one gun apiece while more sophisticated weapons had to be left behind.

Although the Palestinians were forced out, they tried to put a good face on their departure by firing their automatic weapons in the air and shouting, "Revolution. Revolution until victory!" Some flashed the "V" for victory sign, although they were departing safely only because they were permitted to do so.

Christian militiamen on September 17 brutally murdered hundreds of largely defenseless elderly men, women and children in two Palestinian camps in West Beirut. The shooting began about 6 p.m. and went on through the night, leaving a ghastly scene of bodies contorted in death and lying in doorways and streets. The Christian Phalangists, out for revenge following the death of President Gemayel by an assassin four days earlier, blamed the Palestine Liberation Organization. Intelligence sources claimed that 2,500 Palestinians were still hidden in the city in violation of their promise to leave.

Although the Israeli Government condemned the massacre, it could have been prevented by their troops. But the Israeli Army had withdrawn from the two camps before the massacre.

President Reagan announced that he was "horrified" by the tragedy, and he publicly called for an Israeli withdrawal from Lebanon.

Solidarity, Poland's free trade union that had defied its Communist rulers in Warsaw and the Soviet Union, was outlawed on October 26 by the nation's Communist-dominated parliament. The union was replaced by several unions who agreed not to strike.

Workers demonstrated throughout Poland, particularly in Gdansk where Solidarity was first established. The government cracked down on the union's strike of the city's shipyards by using its power to draft striking workers into the military services.

Reagan responded again to this latest attack against Solidarity by suspending Poland's most-favored-nation status.

Leonid Brezhnev, leader of the Soviet Union for the past 18 years, died on November 10 at the age of 75. Tass, in its official announcement said, "The name of Leonid Ilyich Brezhnev, a true continuer of Lenin's great cause and an ardent champion of peace and communism, will live forever." That assessment would be sharply challenged in a few years. Two days after Brezhnev's death he was replaced by Yuri Andropov as general secretary. The former head of the KGB, Andropov had been in charge of foreign espionage and internal security. He soon made it clear that Brezhnev's policies would be continued when he said, "We know that the imperialists will never meet one's pleas for peace. It can only be defended by relying on the invincible might of the Soviet armed forces."

The military buildup in the United States, and the Reagan administration's 25 percent reduction in taxes, put the nation further in debt. It was announced on October 26 that the administration had a record budget deficit of more than $110 billion for fiscal 1982.

Latin America, long characterized by instability and violence, became even worse in 1983. Since a leftist rebellion in 1979 overthrew the Somoza regime in Nicaragua, violence had spread to the neighboring countries of Honduras, Guatemala and El Salvador. The governments of

El Salvador and Guatemala now faced their own leftist rebellions while Honduras was caught in the middle of the United States' support for the contras who were trying to unseat the new Communist regime in Nicaragua. In a region of 22 million people, 15,000 men and women lost their lives in 1983 as a direct result of political upheavals while the economies of these countries were in a state of collapse.

President Reagan spoke to the nation on March 23 and proposed the construction of an invulnerable missile shield for the United States. He offered what he called "a vision of the future which offers hope" that the United States could stop relying on massive retaliation to keep the peace by countering a Soviet nuclear attack. He warned that the technological breakthroughs had not yet been made for such a system, and might take until the end of the century. A White House spokesman gave few details but said the new system might involve lasers, microwave devices, particle beams and projectile beams directed from satellites to destroy Soviet missiles in outer space. The Strategic Defense Initiative, or more familiarly known as the "star wars" defense plan by the average American, undoubtedly could be built although at an unaffordable cost. But no defensive system has ever given any nation complete protection, and the SDI would be no exception. Using the nation's resources for such a modern "Maginot Line" in the sky was both unrealistic and irresponsible.

Members of the Organization of Petroleum Exporting Nations (OPEC) bowed to the reality of the market place on March 14 and agreed to cut oil prices. At their London meeting they set a production ceiling of 17.5 million barrels of oil a day. This was a million barrels below the current ceiling, but 3.5 million barrels more than current usage.

Since 1974 the price of oil had risen from less than $5 a barrel to $35. The newest cut of 15 percent brought the price down to $29 for Saudi Arabian light crude which the industry used as a benchmark price. Past sharp increases had brought demand down far below its peak. The automobile industry's more fuel-efficient cars had helped to bring the price of oil down to its new level, and also helped to improve the sale of American automobiles.

President Reagan defended his covert aid to Nicaragua's contras on April 14, claiming that his administration was complying with recent congressional restrictions. At a press conference he complained that his constitutional powers had been unduly restricted by the Boland Amendment that banned aid to the contras.

Sally K. Ride became the first American woman in space when she returned from orbit on June 24 on board the Space Shuttle "Challenger." The five member crew completed the seventh shuttle flight after deploying two satellites for Canada and Indonesia. During the flight, Ride used the shuttle's robotic arm to place a West German satellite in orbit and then retrieved it. This was a preview to future attempts to routinely remove satellites from orbit to repair them and then return them to space without returning them to earth.

Although President Reagan was stepping up the American involvement in Nicaragua with more assistance to the contras, the region's leaders released a communique expressing their "profound concern for the rapid deterioration" of the situation in Central America. The Presidents of Mexico, Venezuela, Colombia and Panama released the statement after a meeting of their foreign ministers in the so-called "Contadora" group. President Miguel de la Madrid Hurtado of Mexico appealed to President Reagan and Fidel Castro of Cuba to reject the use of force in Central America.

Reagan refused to cease his support for the contras even when the American House of Representatives voted on July 28 to cancel all covert aid to the anti-Sandinista rebels.

Korean Airlines Flight 007 was shot down by Soviet fighters on September 1 near the strategic Sakhalin Island off Siberia. Five days later the Soviets admitted that the Korean plane's pilot had been ordered to "stop the flight" because the 747 was flying in restricted airspace "without navigation lights at the height of night, in conditions of bad visibility and was not answering signals." A Soviet official charged that the civilian plane was on a spy mission and that "the entire responsibility for this tragedy rests with the United States."

Two hundred sixty-nine passengers died, including 61 Americans, in the shooting down of the civilian plane. President Reagan called the Russian action "barbarous."

Menachem Begin resigned from Israel's Herut Party on September 2, and was succeeded by Yitzhak Shamir. Begin refused to give any reason for his action, but he had been reported as melancholy and withdrawn since the death of his wife the previous November. This action placed Shamir in position to become the next prime minister. Like Begin, Shamir was a former guerrilla leader, who was expected to continue Israel's hard line policies in regard to the West Bank. Shamir had also strongly opposed the peace treaty with Egypt.

Two hundred forty-one Marines died in Beirut on October 23 when a terrorist drove a truck filled with at least 2,500 pounds of explosives past sentries and through barricades at Marine headquarters. Two minutes after the Beirut attack another truck filled with explosives slammed into the French compound, killing 58 people.

Two months later President Reagan took responsibility for the lack of security at Marine headquarters in Beirut. "If there is to be blame, it properly rests here in this office." He said he would not discipline officers because "they have suffered enough." His comments followed a report by a special commission that reported security was lax in Beirut in October, and that it was still inadequate.

Six days after the Beirut attack 1,900 American Marines invaded the tiny island of Grenada in the Caribbean to help restore democractic institutions. Their mission, spelled out by President Reagan, was "to defeat a band of Cuban thugs." The first day was marked by poor intelligence, inadequate communications and interference by higher headquarters.

Although many nations denounced the invasion, American troops quickly overwhelmed all resistance although 16 Marines were killed and 77 were wounded in the fighting. Some of these men died unnecessarily due to poor planning.

The island's prime minister, Maurice Bishop, had been placed under house arrest by the commander of the Grenadian military forces, General Hudson Austin. After a group of Bishop's supporters obtained his release, they marched to a military installation to demand the freedom of their colleagues. Bishop was jailed again by Austin and his radical Deputy Prime Minister Bernard Coard. Coard and Bishop, although both Marxists with ties to the Soviet Union and Cuba, had basic differences on the role that private industry should play in the development of Grenada. Bishop believed in private investment. The situation became acute when Bishop was killed, along with many of his aides, on orders of Coard and the army.

This action prompted Reagan to order an invasion. One of the reasons he gave was that an airstrip had been constructed on the island by Soviet and Cuban engineers which, he said, would be used to export Communism to other countries in the Caribbean region. The President also said that he had received calls for help from some members of the Organization of Eastern Caribbean States, and that he was concerned for the protection of 1,000 Americans living in Grenada to attend a medical school. He said they had reported they were in danger because of a "shoot-on-sight" order to enforce the curfew mandated by the radical rulers. Unstated publicly was Reagan's desire to send a strong message to other Latin American countries, particularly Nicaragua, that the United States would not tolerate Communism in the hemisphere.

Officials of the Soviet Union called the invasion "an act of undisguised banditry." Some Latin American nations protested because they considered the invasion another example of "American Imperialist intervention."

Even Margaret Thatcher of Great Britain, long a Reagan supporter, had urged the President not to invade Grenada. France called the United States invasion "a surprising action in relation to international law."

In the United States, newsmen who had been barred from Grenada to cover the invasion, reacted angrily. A *Washington Post* journalist spoke for all when he said, "I think a secret war, like a secret government, is antithetical to an open society. It's absolutely outrageous."

CHAPTER 29

"Four More Years!"

DESPITE OPPOSITION, THE FIRST CRUISE MISSILES WERE INSTALLED IN England on November 14. Defense Secretary Michael Heseltine, in making the announcement in the House of Commons, was greeted with cries of "reckless cynicism" in permitting their deployment. He announced that by 1990 some 572 American missiles would be deployed in Europe to counter the Soviet Union's 252 SS-20 missiles along its frontiers. He told the Commons that Germany was expected to approve the stationing of American missiles in a week's time.

The tense situation in Lebanon eased somewhat on December 20 when Yasir Arafat announced that he had been pressured to evacuate his Palestine Liberation Organization forces. This was the second time in 18 months that such an evacuation had taken place as 4,000 Palestinians quit Tripoli—a port city north of Beirut. The evacuation was arranged by the United Nations Security Council, and they left the port on French ships bearing United Nations flags.

Lech Walesa of Poland was awarded the Nobel Peace Prize, but he was refused permission to travel to Oslo to accept it. Instead his wife Danuta went and read a statement from the Solidarity leader, "We are fighting for the right of working people to organize and for the dignity of human labor."

A black American Navy pilot was released by Syria on January 3, 1984, following his capture in December. He had been shot down over central Lebanon. The Syrian foreign minister said Lieutenant Robert C. Goodman, Jr., was released after intercession by the Reverend Jesse Jackson who had flown to Damascus with a group of 14 Americans who were dissatisfied with President Reagan's attempt to free the pilot. The Syrians, in freeing the pilot, said they hoped his release would "create circumstances that would facilitate the withdrawal of American troops in Lebanon."

President Reagan wired Syrian President Hafez Assad to thank him for Goodman's release. When queried by reporters to comment on Jackson's assistance in freeing the pilot, the President responded "You don't quarrel with success." He said he still opposed withdrawal of American Marines from Lebanon.

The true nature of the Lebanese situation became apparent on January 10 when Beirut gunmen killed an American educator. Malcolm H. Kerr was shot in the head by two unidentified gunmen as he walked to his office.

President Reagan changed his mind on February 7 about a military presence in Beirut by ordering the evacuation of the 1,400 Marines stationed there. His decision was reached when it became more apparent that the volatile political situation would get worse. Many Congressmen praised the move, but some charged that the Marine withdrawal indicated that Reagan's Lebanese policy had failed.

The Soviet Union gained a new leader on February 13 with the elevation of Konstantin Chernenko as General Secretary following the death of Yuri Andropov. A close associate of the late Leonid Brezhnev, his elevation to the top post indicated that the Soviet Union's hard line policy against the West would continue.

President Nixon had opened the door to China during his administration, and President Reagan opened it a crack more when he visited the People's Republic. Near the end of his six day trip he signed cultural and scientific agreements on April 30.

China's leaders chastized the President for not reducing military aid to the Chinese Nationalist government on Taiwan. He responded, "Let us hope, as contacts grow between the Chinese and American people each of us will continue to learn about the other, and this important new friendship of ours will mature and prosper."

Neutral countries felt the effects of the war between Iran and Iraq when their shipping was attacked in the Persian Gulf. The Arab League warned Iran on May 24 to stop firing at its tankers, but the attacks continued. Actually, Iraq had caused even more damage to neutral shipping than Iran but it had not been criticized. Its attacks had been primarily concentrated on ships approaching Iran's Kharg Island. Therefore they were considered legitimate targets because they were in the war zone. Vice President Bush, visiting the region in Oman, criticized the attacks. He said they were "in violation of international law and should be a source of great concern to all nations."

The Soviet Union announced on May 8 that its National Olympic Committee would boycott the Olympic summer games in Los Angeles. This action was taken, a spokesman said, because it anticipated anti-Soviet protests in the city unrestrained by the American government. "Chauvinistic sentiments, and an anti-Soviet hysteria are being whipped up in the country." Cuba and Vietnam were expected to boycott the games. It was believed by American officials that the true reason was the American boycott, along with 59 other nations, of the Moscow games in 1980 to protest the Soviet invasion of Afghanistan.

Walter Mondale, expected to be the Democratic candidate for President in the fall election, announced his choice for vice president. He chose a woman on July 12 when he said that "I looked for the best vice president and I found her in Gery Ferraro." Representative Geraldine A. Ferraro thus became the first woman to be seriously considered for vice president. Daughter of an Italian immigrant, Ferraro was a teacher and lawyer before she was elected to Congress.

Five days later, after both had been selected by the Democratic Party, they promised to wage a strong campaign although pollsters gave them little chance against the popular Ronald Reagan. Mondale told the convention on July 19, "Tonight, we open a new door to the future. Mr. Reagan calls that tokenism. We call it America."

In her acceptance speech, Mrs. Ferraro said, "There are no doors we cannot unlock."

Nine hundred thousand Filipinos demonstrated without violence against President Ferdinand Marcos of the Philippines on August 21 on the anniversary of the death of opposition leader Benigno Aquino. They voiced their hatred of Marcos, and condemned the United States for supporting him. Aquino's widow, Corazon, denounced the nation's economic situation and called for Marcos to resign.

Representative Geraldine Ferraro, Democratic candidate for vice president, denied any wrongdoing on August 21 in regard to criticism of her financial affairs. She had been reported a week earlier as being surprised to learn that her husband had borrowed $100,000 for their real estate company from the assets of an elderly woman whose finances he was overseeing. She insisted the problem was due to "sloppy record-keeping" as she released her financial records.

The following day the Republicans met in Dallas for their convention. Senator Paul Laxalt of Nevada called for the re-election of President Reagan, calling him "a leader who is not afraid." To no one's surprise, the convention did so, and Vice President Bush was re-nominated on the first roll call.

The United States Embassy in Beirut was damaged on September 20 and 23 people, including two Americans, were killed as a car laden with explosives was driven past road blocks and through intensive fire from guards before being exploded in front of the building. Since the earlier bombing of the embassy it had been removed to what was considered a safer place patrolled by Lebanese Phalangists.

Great Britain and the People's Republic of China signed an agreement on September 26 that Hong Kong would be returned to China in 1997. Although the territory would revert to China, it would be allowed to preserve its free enterprise system for an additional 50 years. Hong Kong had long been a successful commercial and financial entity that provided China with lucrative contacts with the West. In Peking on September 30 Prime Minister Zhao Ziyang said Taiwan (the island under control of the Chinese Nationalists) could be reunited with the mainland and remain capitalistic in a similar fashion. "Our proposition of one country, two systems after reunification is most reasonable." he said.

President Reagan met with Soviet Foreign Minister Andrei Gromyko at the White House on September 28 to discuss the deteriorating relationship between the United States and the Soviet Union. The talks were described as "forceful and direct" meaning they had agreed to disagree. Earlier in the week, when he spoke to the United Nations, Reagan had called for "a better working relationship" with the Soviet Union as he sought for "a fresh approach to reducing international tensions."

Prime Minister Margaret Thatcher of Great Britain narrowly escaped death on October 12 when a bomb exploded near her home in Brighton, England. Two people were killed and 34 others were injured. The Irish Republican Army admitted they were responsible.

Indira Gandhi, India's prime minister, was not so fortunate. She was killed on October 31 by two members of her personal security guard. Her death was laid to Sikh extremists, and one of them was killed. She was replaced by her son Rajiv Gandhi.

The People's Republic of China celebrated its 35th year as a Communist state on October 28 despite the fact that it was tending more to capitalistic practices. Deng Hsiao-ping called for a strengthening of the nation's defenses, and economic reforms to provide limited capitalist opportunities and decrease the government's role in the economic field.

Reagan and Bush were re-elected on November 6 by carrying all but Mondale's home state of Minnesota and the District of Columbia. When the triumphant Reagan entered a Los Angeles ballroom, his supporters chanted, "Four more years." "I think that's just been arranged," he told them.

In the mid-1980s the Soviet Union's Navy and the United States Navy kept a careful check on each other's ships. They were both prepared to move to war status on a moment's notice if, upon receiving notice from their respective governments, that a state of war existed between them.

In the past, the Pacific Ocean was left largely to the United States Navy, but with the global-ranging Soviet fleet, this area became one of the most dangerous spots for the United States in the entire world. To repel attack, the United States Navy was prepared to fight in the air, on the surface and deep within the ocean in an area covering half the world's surface. The United States had 44 fast-attack submarines armed with sonar and computers that listened constantly to locate the Russian submarine fleet through a system of undersea hydrophones, while 120 P-3C Orions maintained their constant vigil aloft and attack submarines and destroyers with bow-mounted sonar domes sought Russian ships from Asia to the American mainland and north to Alaska and the Aleutians.

In addition to their own submarines and warships the Russians made extensive use of so-called fishing boats bristling with radar cones and antennae to listen to the thousands of radio and microwave transmissions between United States ships. Russian trawlers routinely cruised four miles off Pearl Harbor, just outside the territorial limits. There were six between California and Midway Island monitoring American naval ship traffic or observing missiles launched from Vandenberg Air Force Base. Word of American ship movements was flashed to the huge Russian base at Vladivostok.

Prior to 1980 Russian ships were seldom seen far from their bases. When the government of the Soviet Union took possession of the abandoned American base at Cam Ranh Bay in Vietnam, they expanded their naval activities throughout the Pacific Ocean after agreeing to build a Navy second to none.

When the United States positioned Pershing-2 missiles in West Germany in 1985, drastically reducing the flying time of such missiles to Russian targets, the Soviet Union countered this threat. They moved their missile-carrying submarines closer to the West Coast. From these submarines, California targets could be hit in six minutes.

The United States Navy now had eight Trident ballistic missile submarines in the Pacific, each equipped with 24 intercontinental missiles. These submarines cruised in deep water, ready to launch if the President should so direct. American submarines in World War II were vulnerable to enemy action because they had to come to the surface to make sightings. Thus one out of every five American submarines were sunk. Modern submarines seldom come to the surface because they are nuclear-powered and therefore without batteries that must be recharged on the surface.

Mikhail S. Gorbachev took over leadership of the Soviet Union on

March 13 following the death of Konstantin Chernenko. The latter was the third Russian leader to die in office during the past two and a half years. A much younger man at age 54, Gorbachev called for immediate changes in the Soviet system of government. He praised detente between the Soviet Union and the Western Allies and called for "real and major reductions in arms stockpiles."

While the Russians were calling for peaceful ways to end differences between nations, the Iranians and the Iraqis were engaged in the fiercest fighting of their war. The Iranians lost heavily in their attempt to ford the Tigris River and to take the highway linking Iraq's southern port of Basra with the capital of Baghdad. The front lines had seesawed back and forth since the war began, and this situation continued.

President Reagan banned all trade with Nicaragua on May 1 as its government continued to follow a leftist path. This action was denounced by Nicaragua, saying it would hurt the ordinary working person more than the government. A spokesman claimed that the embargo would also strengthen Nicaragua's ties with the Soviet Union.

Two gunmen hijacked a Trans World Airlines jetliner on June 14 after its takeoff from Athens. The pilot was forced to crisscross the Mediterranean while the 39 Americans on board were beaten with weapons the hijackers had smuggled on board. Navy diver Robert Stethem was murdered just before the terrorists forced pilot John Testrake to land at Beirut for the second time. Beirut controllers reluctantly agreed to refuel the plane. Radical Shiites, members of Hezbollah or the Party of God, had undertaken the hijacking to force Israel to release 700 Shiite and Palestinian prisoners.

Israel announced that it might free the prisoners if the United States requested it to do so, but the Reagan administration refused to make such a request.

Through the intervention of Syria the hostages were freed on June 30. Vice President Bush greeted them, saying, "You are back and America did not compromise her principles to get you back." Perhaps so, but Israel released 300 prisoners on July 3.

Israel withdrew its armed forces from Lebanon on June 10 which it had invaded in June 1982. An undisclosed number of advisers would remain there, an Israeli official said, until a substantial peace was secured. The Israelis withdrew after 654 soldiers had died during the invasion and another 4,000 were wounded. It had only served to worsen the political tension in the Middle East.

The United States became a debtor nation on September 16 for the first time since 1914. The Commerce Department released figures that showed the nation's deficit on current accounts—trade in goods, services and investment earnings with the rest of the world—was $30 billion. This meant the United States owed foreigners more than they owed the United States. Just a year before the nation had a $30 billion surplus. Thus dividends and interest payments to foreigners now exceeded those paid to the United States. An official of the Institute for International Economics said this condition made America vulnerable to international market fluctuations. "If there was a run on the dollar tomorrow, we'd be hurt."

Hijackers seized the "Achille Lauro" cruise ship in the Mediterranean on October 7 and for a time held its 400 passengers hostage. The Palestinians brutally murdered one of them, Leon Klinghoffer, who was confined to a wheelchair. Americans were outraged by the senseless killing, and Senator Daniel Patrick Moynihan spoke for all when he said the Palestinians killed Klinghoffer "because he was an American, because he was a Jew and because he was a free man."

Heavily armed members of the Palestine Liberation Front commandeered the ship after it left Alexandria, Egypt, and demanded release of prisoners held by Israel. The terrorists surrendered on October 9 after the Egyptian government promised them free passage out of the country. At the time Egyptian officials did not know about Klinghoffer's death. The Egyptian plane transporting the hijackers was intercepted by American Navy jets and forced to land in Italy. After the alleged leader, Mohammed Abbas, was permitted by the Italians to escape the United States Government criticized Rome's officials.

President Reagan met with Soviet leader Gorbachev in Geneva on November 19 to discuss major issues dividing their two nations. After meeting with their staffs, the two leaders met for six hours of private meetings with only interpreters present. Gorbachev announced after the meeting that he would go to the United States in 1986 and that Reagan would go to Russia the following year.

Reagan went to Brussels after the meeting to brief NATO leaders. He told them that he and the Soviet leader had "got very friendly." Meanwhile, Gorbachev gave his version of the Geneva meetings. He called them "Frank, sharp, sometimes very sharp. But it still seems to me they were productive."

It was revealed that the key differences between them was Reagan's insistence on developing the "star wars" missile defense system. Gorbachev told his press conference that the Soviet Union could build a better system of its own. He said he told Reagan, "Mr. President, you should bear in mind that we are not simpletons."

CHAPTER 30

International Reign of Terror

PALESTINE TERRORISTS CREATED HAVOC AT AIRPORTS IN ROME AND VI-
enna as they hurled grenades at Israel's El Al check-out counters, and
then fired machine guns at crowds of holiday travelers. Fourteen people,
including four Americans, were killed while 110 were wounded. Four
terrorists were killed in gun battles with the police and plainclothes
Israeli security men. The PLO denied it had been responsible for the
attack, and police believed it was done by a renegade Palestinian group
headed by Abu Nidal.

The Reagan administration charged that Libya had aided the terrorists
and called for international pressure on Libya to force it to stop its export
of terror.

Terrorist attacks made 1985 a nightmare of vicious killings throughout
the world. Many nations, including the United States, were determined
to stop this reign of terror by tightening their security and imposing
more drastic sentences against the culprits. Not just the Palestinians and
Iranians were involved. The Irish Republican Army, the Basque separat-
ists in Spain, the Sikhs in India, and Latin American death squads were
all contributing to senseless crimes primarily against innocent victims.

President Reagan signed the historic Gramm-Rudman bill on December 12 to establish guidelines to balance the ballooning budget. If followed as prescribed, it would become the Reagan administration's most
important legislation because it mandated the balancing of the budget
in 1991. Unfortunately it was not.

Reagan ordered ties with Libya broken on January 25, 1986, and the
assets of the country frozen. The President accused Colonel Muammar
el-Qaddafi of supporting international terrorism. He charged the Libyan

leader with supporting terrorist raids on the Rome and Vienna airports in December. In imposing trade and commercial sanctions against Libya, the President also ordered all American citizens to leave the country.

This action was followed by a military show of force as an American task force of two aircraft carriers was dispatched to conduct week-long maneuvers in the Mediterranean north of Libya. A State Department spokesman justified this action "to demonstrate United States resolve to continue to operate in international waters and airspace."

The American ships remained outside of the Gulf of Sidra, claimed by Libya as its territorial waters, but not recognized by other countries. This action, however, heightened the growing possibility of a military clash between the United States and Libya.

With millions of Americans watching the launch of the space shuttle "Challenger" on January 28, it exploded 74 seconds after lift-off and killed its seven astronauts. Those who witnessed the diaster at Cape Canaveral and on television were horrified by the disaster. Among those killed were the shuttle's commander, Francis R. Scobee, pilot Michael J. Smith, and astronauts Judith A. Resnik, Ronald E. McNair, Ellison S. Onizuka, Gregory B. Jarvis and Christa McAuliffe. The last was a high school teacher from Concord, New Hampshire, who was to be the first ordinary citizen in space. All shuttle flights were immediately suspended. The accident was later attributed to a fire in the solid rocket boosters caused by a break in their seals.

Ferdinand Marcos was defeated at the polls in the Philippines and forced to step down as President. He was replaced on February 27 by Corazon Aquino, widow of the man who had been murdered upon his return to the Philippines to oppose Marcos. At first, Marcos refused to accept the results of the election. The National Assembly, which he controlled, swore him in earlier as President but Aquino was sworn in as President of a provisional government. When a military standoff developed, Filipinos took to the streets to protect a group of military officers who had broken with Marcos. Then the American government refused to back Marcos' claim, and he fled the country.

Prime Minister Thatcher of Great Britain and President Francois Mitterand of France announced plans on February 20 to build a rail tunnel beneath the English Channel. Work was scheduled to begin the following year, and the tunnel completed in 1991. Then trains carrying automobiles and buses would travel beneath the channel in 30 minutes while high-speed trains cut travel time between Paris and London to a little more than three hours. They announced that a separate motorway would be built, starting in 1990.

American bombers hit Libyan military targets, and some non-military areas including Col. Muammar el Qaddafi's home, on March 15 in retaliation for Libya's alleged international "reign of terror." Although some foreign nations opposed the strike, a poll in the United States the following day indicated 77 percent of Americans supported the raid. Prime Minister Thatcher of Great Britain, who supported the raid and permitted some of the bombers to take off from British bases, was sharply criticized. Qaddafi vowed to continue his "popular revolution." Eighteen Air Force F-111 bombers had taken off from England to strike an airport, military targets and a port outside of Tripoli. In a separate attack, Navy A-6 and A-7 planes struck Libyan bases near Benghazi after taking off from the carriers "Coral Sea" and "America" in the Mediterranean.

In a television address to the nation, President Reagan said he ordered the raid after intelligence officials uncovered evidence of a "direct" Libyan role in the bombing of a discotheque in Berlin earlier in the month in which two Americans were killed and more than 200 people were injured. "Today we have done what we had to do," Reagan said. "If necessary we shall do it again."

In Tripoli it was charged that 15 residents of a residential area had been killed, including the adopted daughter of the Libyan leader.

In retaliation for the American attack terrorists murderd three British hostages in Lebanon, and executed American hostage Peter Kilburn.

Although it was not immediately announced, a major nuclear generating plant at Chernobyl near Kiev in the Soviet Union suffered an explosion and fire when an accident on April 26 destroyed the Number 4 reactor of a four-reactor facility. Deadly radioactive materials were released over part of the Soviet Union, Eastern Europe and Scandinavia. Later, radioactive clouds moved across Western Europe. The first indication that a major nuclear catastrophe had occurred came when monitoring stations in Sweden, Finland and Denmark reported abnormally high radioactive levels. Communities around Chernobyl evacuated their residents and they will never be permitted to return to their homes. The reactor was encased in concrete where it will be forever entombed to prevent further release of radioactive materials.

Details of the Chernobyl diaster were not officially released by the Soviet Union until May 14 when Mikhail Gorbachev said in a television speech that it showed "the sinister force" of nuclear power gone out of control. Although he denounced western nations for their criticism, he admitted that some of it was justified. He offered a four-point program to hasten the exchange of information about nuclear accidents.

The Iceland summit meeting ended in failure and President Reagan and Soviet leader Gorbachev admitted on October 13 that they could not reach agreement on any of the problems dividing their two nations.

Before leaving Reykjavik, Reagan criticized Gorbachev for insisting that the United States abandon its space-based Strategic Defense Initiative but he said he had invited the Soviet leader to visit the United States for further discussions.

Mordecai Vanunu, a Jewish technician in Israel's nuclear center, shocked the world when he disclosed that Israel had produced at least 200 nuclear weapons, and he had photographs to back up his revelations. He was spirited out of England to Israel and sentenced to life in prison for this top secret disclosure.

It was disclosed on November 30 that the Reagan administration had been selling arms to Iran and that some of the money had been diverted to Nicaragua's rebels. Originally an obscure publication in Beirut had published the report and it soon became evident that the administration faced its worst crisis. Although Reagan officials denied that there had been an attempt to sell arms in trade for release of hostages held by terrorists in Lebanon, the implication was clear that they had tried to do just that.

President Reagan tried to stonewall the growing story but finally had to admit that 18 months earlier he had authorized the shipment of military equipment to Iran. Supposedly he had done so to establish ties with moderate Iranian officials.

The President held a press conference on November 19 and announced that no more arms would be sent to Iran "to eliminate the widespread but mistaken perception that we have been exchanging arms for hostages."

After Attorney General Edwin Meese revealed that some of the proceeds from the arms sale had been diverted to aid the contras, Reagan dismissed his National Security Adviser, Admiral John Poindexter, and his aide Marine Lieutenant Colonel Oliver North who had managed the Iran-contra deal. Reagan appointed a three-man panel, headed by former Senator John Tower, to examine the role of the National Security Council staff. Meanwhile, Congress set up its own committee to explore the matter.

Wall Street was in the midst of its greatest boom in history but a scandal threatened to undermine its foundations. Ivan F. Boesky, one of the richest and most famous arbitrageurs in the financial district, pleaded guilty on November 18 to buying and selling stocks and securities based on illegal secret information. He was fined $100 million for his insider trade and was barred for life from trading in American securities.

An experimental airplane, using only a single load of fuel, landed in California on December 23 after completing an historic flight around the world. "Voyager," with Richard G. Rutan and his co-pilot Jeana Yeager, flew 25,012 miles in nine days, three minutes and 44 seconds. They set records for distance flown without refueling and for endurance of a two-person crew. The "Voyager" carried five times its weight in fuel, and its successful flight was expected to lead to more fuel-efficient airplanes.

President Reagan admitted on December 30 that "mistakes were made" in carrying out his policy of selling arms to Iran. He still insisted that he had not known that money from the arms sale was diverted to the rebel forces in Nicaragua.

Meanwhile, Lawrence E. Walsh, former President of the American Bar Association, was named special prosecutor to investigate the arms sale while several Congressional committees held hearings on the subject.

President Reagan's health aroused further concern among the American people when it was revealed on January 5, 1987, that four small non-cancerous polyps were removed from his colon. The previous day another operation had removed obstructive tissue from his prostate gland which had become enlarged. He soon resumed his schedule and made a normal recovery.

While he was undergoing this colon surgery his budget was presented to Congress. Its contents disclosed that he proposed spending $1.02 trillion in the 1988 fiscal year. The Democrats promptly attacked the President's emphasis on proposed military expenditures and his continued plan for deficit financing.

In China, dissidents took advantage of the relaxation of controls to press their demands for democratization of their country. Communist rulers cracked down on January 14 and Wang Buowang, a Shanghai writer and Marxist theorist, was expelled from the party for his part in pro-democracy student demonstrations. Fang Lizhi, an astrophysicist, was dismissed as vice president of the University of Science and Technology and denounced as pro-western and expelled from the party. Two days later, Hu Yaobong resigned as general secretary for a "major mistake" in permitting demonstrations against the government.

In the Soviet Union, the head of the government, Mikhail Gorbachev, proposed sensational reforms on January 27 in an address to the Communist Central Committee. He charged the Communist Party with stagnation and systematic failures. He called for secret balloting and a choice of candidates for government positions. The Central Committee approved his recommendations the following day to provide for more flexible and multi-party rule in the Soviet Union.

The Tower Commission, established by President Reagan to review the circumstances involved in the Iran arms deal, released its findings on February 26, calling the President confused and remote in the management of the Iran-contra affair. The report claimed that the President failed to understand the secret arms deal with Iran, and therefore had to take responsibility for a policy that caused "chaos" at home and embarrassment abroad. The report charged that Donald T. Regan, the White House chief of staff, and other advisers had given Reagan poor advice while ignoring legal and political risks.

Regan was removed the next day and replaced by former Senator Howard M. Baker, Jr.

It was apparent that Russian seapower had scaled back its plans for a worldwide navy that could project itself into Third World conflicts, thereby changing the United States Navy's mission throughout the world. Leaders of the Soviet Union now were stressing defense operations closer to home. This was evident in the design changes in its largest aircraft carrier under construction in the Black Sea. The "Leonid I. Brezhnev" was being equipped with a "ski jump" flight deck for "jump jets" and helicopters, instead of the standard flight deck needed for regular fighters and bombers.

Cuts in Russian shipbuilding programs were evident, along with a reduction in naval exercises around the world. A 15 percent reduction was noted by intelligence sources in deployments of Soviet ships outside of its own periphery waters. This was the first such decline in decades. It was due, in part, to Gorbachev's demand for a cut in the Soviet Navy's huge fuel bills, and also to counter America's strategy of taking the fight to Russia's home waters in the event of war. But Brezhnev started the reduction in shipbuilding. Few ships other than two minesweepers were assigned to the Persian Gulf in 1987. Although its ship-based aircraft were in sharp decline, the Soviet Navy was increasing its naval aviation on land.

This change in Soviet strategy was an abrupt departure from that adopted by Admiral Sergei G. Gorshkov who had assumed command of the fleet in 1956. He had built up the Soviet Navy as a direct challenge to the United States Navy on the high seas. He said proudly, "The flag of the Soviet Navy flies over the oceans of the world. Sooner or later the United States will have to understand it no longer has mastery of the seas."

Gorshkov, and other military leaders, formulated an "interventionist" policy in the early 1970s, as its armed forces were supported around the world. They developed huge amphibious landing ships to permit the movement of Soviet naval infantry, with provision ships that could transfer fuel and supplies to warships while both were underway. Now, in the 1980s, these programs were reduced to token forces of little danger to the West.

It is interesting to note the marked change in strategy of the Soviet Union's armed forces during various crises in the Mediterranean. In 1967 and 1973 the Soviet Union sent large fleets there to sway events by their threatening presence. When the fighting developed in Lebanon during 1982 this crisis was ignored.

Surprisingly, the Soviet submarine fleet was being sharply reduced. The "Typhoon" class, equipped to carry ballistic missiles, was reduced to one a year, instead of the two formerly produced. The "Oscar" class of cruise missile submarines, which had been projected at a rate of three a year, was also down to one. And, the allocation of nuclear reactors for ships was cut in half.

In the Indian Ocean the Soviet Navy maintained 16 to 17 ships in 1987 instead of the 28 average four years earlier. This reduction was noted in the Atlantic with an average of 33 ships on duty instead of 45 in 1984. Ballistic missile submarines on duty in the Atlantic were fewer in number, while Russian carriers like the "Brezhnev" and the "Kiev" were assigned not to attack capabilities but as anti-submarine ships; a purely defensive role.

While Secretary of State George Schultz was in Moscow in April he reached agreement with Soviet leaders that their short-range INF Forces—a category the United States does not possess—would be eliminated. In what Schultz called a "double-zero" option he said this agreement paved the way for an INF treaty. Both sides now agreed to maintain 100 warheads for their medium-range missiles outside of Europe. Reagan announced that effective verification to confirm compliance with such an agreement was the only obstacle to a treaty between the two nations.

President Reagan's advocacy of the Strategic Defense Initiative was challenged on April 22 by a panel of leading scientists. They reported that a decade of intensive research would be needed just to determine the feasibility of an anti-missile space defense system.

President Reagan and Prime Minister Nakasone of Japan met on May 1 in an attempt to resolve problems associated with Japan's huge trade surplus with the United States. Reagan had earlier imposed a 100 percent tariff against Japanese computers, television sets and power tools because of Japan's alleged violation of exports of semi-conductors. They failed to reach agreement. Nakasone, upon his return to Japan, ordered the Bank of Japan to lower interest rates which served to worsen the situation.

Japan was now where the United States had been 60 years earlier—an emerging world power undergoing rapid growth while the world's economy remained stagnant. Eventually Japan would pay a price for its intransigence about imports from other countries. Internal balances such as high prices and shortages of basic materials at home would someday create an economic disaster for Japan.

American industrial power was on the wane by the 1980s while Japan's was on the rise. The United States had become a high-cost producer in many industries, but it was not apparent in the preceding decade because of worldwide shortages of most basic items. Now, with world surpluses, competition intensified and the United States found it unable to compete. Trade deficits by 1986 reached 3.5 percent of the gross national product. For the first time since World War I the United States had become a net international debtor because it had to borrow so extensively. With unemployment stagnating at around 6 percent, under-employment became a serious matter of concern for economists. Until 1987 annual budget deficits remained above $200 billion despite four-and-a-half years of economic expansion.

By mid-decade, Japan had amassed a $100 billion surplus in trading with the United States. But the ratio of stock value to gross national product in Japan was 130 percent, compared to 60 percent in the United States. For example, Nippon Telegraph and Telephone had a price-to-earnings ratio of more than 250 and a market value exceeding that of the entire West German stock market. The Japanaese did not realize it at the time but these values were unrealistic, highly speculative, and dangerous for the long run.

President Reagan's vulnerability in the Iran-contra affair became more apparent on May 13 when Robert C. McFarlane, former National Security Adviser, told a Congressional hearing that he had informed the President "frequently" about the activities of his staff in their attempts to aid the Nicaraguan rebels. Two days later Reagan admitted that he was deeply involved in private efforts to help the contras even during the two years when Congress had forbidden such government aid.

Reagan's reiterated belief "that government is part of the problem, not the solution," lay at the core of what occurred. The report by the majority of the two congressional committees said that it was the President's own disdain for government and its established procedures—the anti-Washington attitude around which he built his campaign for the White House seven years earlier—that fostered the climate in which the affair flourished.

Arthur L. Liman, chief counsel to the Senate panel, reported, "It became almost a theology for these people that government was musclebound, and that for America to be great again, you have to turn to these unorthodox, out-of-government operations."

The House and Senate committees said President Reagan failed to carry out his constitutional oath of office to "take care that the laws be faithfully executed" and that he bears ultimate responsibility for the Iran-contra scandal. The committees concluded that the common ingredients of the Iran and contra policies were secrecy, deception and disdain for the law. "A small group of senior officials believed that they alone knew what was right. They viewed knowledge of their activities by others in the government as a threat to their objectives." Those specifically mentioned were Lieutenant Colonel North, former National Security adviser John M. Poindexter who authorized North's activities and said he kept many of them secret from the President, and former National Security Adviser Robert C. McFarlane and the late CIA Director William J. Casey who, it was believed, directed North's activities.

The frightening implications raised by North's and Casey's dream of creating a private network, free of congressional strictures or scrutiny, that would carry out secret operations around the world, should have been apparent to President Reagan. Some of his top advisers, who protested about what was going on, were deliberately taken out of the chain of knowledge of what was transpiring. The actions by North, Poindexter and others reflected little faith in the American system, according to the findings of the committee.

Lieutenant Colonel Oliver L. North appeared before the Congressional Iran-contra inquiry during the early part of July and told investigators that his secret White House operations were in response to orders by higher officials. He said he assumed, although he admitted that he did not know first-hand, that President Reagan approved the diversion of profits from the weapons' sale to aid Nicaragua's rebel contras. North claimed that the late Central Intelligence Agency head, William Casey, had helped him and that other high officials had been fully aware of his activities. He said that Casey tried to use the profits from the Iran arms sale to set up a secret espionage agency outside the jurisdiction of normal agencies. North's testimony made him a popular folk hero at first because of his boyish manner as he testified in uniform with a left breast liberally covered with medals.

Robert C. McFarlane, former National Security Adviser to the President, returned to the stand on July 14. He contradicted some of North's statements by saying that he had not authorized any of North's secret activities. North was dismissed by the committee with a severe rebuke for his part in the affair that they said was based on "a series of lies."

Admiral John M. Poindexter, former National Security Adviser, testified for a week starting on July 15. He told the Congressional officials that he had personally authorized use of Iran arms sale profits to aid Nicaragua's contras. He said he kept the information from the President to spare him political embarrassment. The admiral disputed North's testimony that he had sent the admiral five memorandums discussing the use of profits from the Iranian arms sale to the contras. Congressmen from both parties expressed incredulity at some of the statements made by Poindexter and North. They challenged the admiral's statement that it was proper to keep sensitive foreign relations matters secret from Congress and other government agencies.

Secretary of State Shultz, during a two-day appearance starting on July 23, said he was deceived repeatedly by top officials who withheld vital information from him and the President during the Iran arms sale. But he denied charges that he was not knowledgeable about other relations between the United States and Iran and Nicaragua. He expressed outrage by relevations that Poindexter and William J. Casey had repeatedly misled him. His candor and forthrightedness was praised by all committee members.

Attorney General Meese appeared before the hearings on July 28 and 29th. He also claimed that the National Security Council's officials had misled him. He said he had no reason to disbelieve them but he now conceded that North must have lied to him as well as to the committee. When counsel accused Meese of failure to press his own investigation of the arms sale, he strongly defended himself although his words failed to convince the Congressmen.

Defense Secretary Caspar W. Weinberger took the stand on July 31 and for four days he told what he knew about the arms/contra scandal. He testified that he had believed he had stopped the Iran arms sale, but that he failed because of official deception and intrigue. He pointed out that he had been excluded from receiving pertinent information.

With Weinberger's appearance the Iran-contra public hearings came to an end. The chairman of the joint House and Senate hearings called the testimony "chilling and depressing."

The committee charged that former officials of the National Security Council staff and private agents acted upon the premise that a "rightful cause" justifies any means; that lying to Congress and other officials of the executive branch was acceptable when the ends are just, and that Congress was to blame for passing laws that ran counter to administrative policy.

An Iraqi warplane created an international crisis on May 17 when it fired two missiles at the United States frigate "Stark" in the Persian Gulf. Thirty-seven Americans died in the unprovoked attack and the next day Iraqi President Saddam Hussein apologized. The ship's commander revealed that the frigate's electronic defenses were turned off because he did not fear an Iraqi attack.

An even stranger affair occurred on May 29 when a West German private pilot flew 400 miles through heavily-defended Soviet territory to land his tiny airplane in Moscow's Red Square. The next day Defense Minister Sergei L. Sokolov was removed from his duties by the Politiburo.

The pilot, Matthias Rust, was convicted for his unauthorized flight and sentenced to prison although he was later released.

The United States had long pressured South Korea's government to change its dictatorial ways and become more democratic. Following weeks of street demonstrations, President Chun Doo Hwan agreed to presidential elections for July 1. Students had rioted in all major cities, thus forcing the president's hand.

The Presidents of five Central American countries signed an agreement on August 7 that each would end restrictions on dissent, decree political amnesty, and press censorship and agree to elections under international supervision. President Ortega of Nicaragua was one of the signators, and it was hoped that the new agreement would go a long way toward defusing the wars in El Salvador and Nicaragua.

The United States and the Soviet Union agreed to hold an arms control summit later in the year. Plans were announced on September 18 for Gorbachev and Reagan to sign an agreement for a world-wide ban on medium and short-range nuclear weapons. President Reagan had consistently urged the reduction or elimination of whole categories of nuclear weapons. The two leaders, however, still had wide differences on the imposition of limits on Reagan's Strategic Defense Initiative.

On September 22 after 20 ships had been damaged, an American helicopter fired on an Iranian ship in the Persion Gulf that was laying mines. Three Iranian sailors were killed, while another 26 were seized. Ten mines were retrieved after the ship had dropped six into the gulf's waters.

Ceremonies in Philadelphia on September 17 climaxed a series of events honoring the 200th anniversary of the Constitution. President Reagan said the "genius" of the American system is the "recognition that no one branch of government alone could be relied on to preserve our freedoms."

Iran's harassment of shipping in the Persian Gulf, part of its war with Iraq, brought retaliation on October 19 from the United States Navy. Its ships shelled two off-shore missile platforms for attacks upon American-registered ships.

The New York Stock Market reversed itself on October 19 and headed down. It kept going down, reaching a 300-point decline, where traders thought it would bottom out. But it didn't stop there. It dropped another 100 points and the precipitous slide did not stop until it was down 508 points for the day. This 22.7 percent loss forever identified the day as "Black Monday."

The New York market was not the only one to suffer because related futures and option markets also dropped precipitately.

The bull market had begun in August 1982, on a wave of speculative buying that was reminiscent of the days and years leading up to the 1929 crash. It was pure greed that caused the debacle. On the "Big Board" that day 604.3 million shares were traded, almost twice the previous one-day record, and three times that of even a heavy day.

In early October, Commerce Department figures revealed another round of disappointing foreign trade statistics and stocks dropped 91 points.

But the euphoria of most traders had fed on itself throughout the year, especially after the Dow Jones passed the 2,000 point in January. In utter disregard to the reality of the economic situation in the United States most traders believed the Dow Jones would go to 3,600 and beyond.

In the years of the Reagan administration, politicians ignored the ever-growing deficit until the market crashed in October, eventually dropping the index 700 points.

Reagan and his administration abrogated their responsibilities to the American people but their persistent attempts to paint a rosier picture of the economy than was justified by true conditions led the nation to the brink of financial ruin. Finally, in 1985, Reagan was forced to reduce defense spending after he had escalated costs out of control. At least 60 percent of the defense money was wasted due to the rapid buildup and the failure to consider whether many of the exotic defense programs were justified by the nation's true defense needs. Reagan officials continued to paint a positive picture of an economy growing rapidly to a 5 percent a year rate or better. This never happened. Instead, the administration's economic policies led the nation into a recession. White House projections of economic growth overestimated the nation's output of goods and services by $700 billion over a five-year period, leaving a shortfall of $200 billion in government revenues. The deficit then widened an additional $58 billion when the economy in 1983 proved weaker than expected. These errors in economic estimates, according to the Congressional Budget Office, added an average of $23 billion annually to the nation's deficit from 1980 through 1987. The administration's fiscal gimmickry, or technical differences, added another $15 billion a year. For example, they sold government assets that helped in the near term but added to the problem in the long run because they eliminated a future source of revenue. The Reagan administration had spent seven years avoiding the tough decisions that should have been made to reduce or eliminate the deficit. It was "voodoo" economics as George Bush had declared while running for President, but now he disavowed his conservative instincts and went along with the "supply siders."

After World War II, when the United States stood alone as the only nation whose industrial and financial strength emerged undamaged from the war, the nation experienced a period of unprecedented growth, and therefore was able to stimulate Europe to put it economically back on its feet. At the time, no other nation had the money to help needy nations.

This all changed in the 1980s. During this decade, like the 1880s, the United States was forced to import capital to maintain economic growth because its assets were insufficient to do it on its own.

CHAPTER 31

The Quest for Nuclear Disarmament

IN THE SUCCEEDING DAYS FOLLOWING "BLACK MONDAY" PRICES ON THE stock markets fluctuated and there was some rallying. What saved the United States this time from a 1929-style depression was the fact that restrictive laws had been passed in the 1930s to control the market. In addition, bank deposits were now protected up to $100,000 and there were far fewer bank failures compared to 1929. The Social Security program helped to cushion the impact on older Americans while unemployment benefits gave the younger generation a fall-back position in times of economic adversity. And, unlike 1929, farm supports prevented a collapse of the nation's farm structure.

There were similiarities between the 1929 crash and the 1987 stock market's fall. Both came as the nation was moving conservatively to the right politically, amidst booming mergers and acquisitions, and right after real estate prices peaked. In 1929 the Dow Industrial Average fell about 39.6 percent from its peak and in 1987 it fell an average of 36.1 percent.

Russia's leader, Mikhail Gorbachev, agreed on October 30 to visit President Reagan in Washington between December 7th and 10th. The meeting was arranged to sign a treaty to eliminate medium and short-range nuclear missiles.

In August, Soviet negotiators had demanded that West Germany dismantle its 73 relatively short-range Pershing 1-A missiles as part of the INF Accord. The United States had refused to agree to this demand, and West German Chancellor Helmut Kohl had backed the Reagan administration. But in September Secretary of State Schultz and Soviet Foreign Minister Eduard A. Shevardnadze announced that the two countries had reached agreement in principle on an INF treaty, following intensive sessions on verification proposals during meetings in Geneva.

Deng Xiaoping became the first Chinese Communist leader to voluntarily leave the Central Committee when he stepped down on November 1. In a sweeping overhaul of the Chinese leadership, it was stated that his policy of economic change would continue. Prime Minister Zhao Ziyang was appointed the next day as General Secretary. Although the new leadership pledged to continue its open policy with western nations, the leadership of the Communist nation made it clear that there would be no change in its hard line policy of control over the Chinese people.

The final summary issued by the Congressional committee investigating the Iran-contra scandal was released on November 18. It charged that President Reagan failed to obey his constitutional requirement to execute the nation's laws and that he bore the "ultimate responsibility" for wrong-doing by his aides in the sale of arms to Iran and diversion of some of the profits to Nicaraguan rebels. The report revealed that nearly $48 million from the arms sale was distributed to the contras.

Soviet leader Gorbachev arrived in Washington on December 7 and immediately challenged President Reagan to lead the way in cutting their strategic weapons stockpiles. The following day Gorbachev and Reagan signed a compact that, for the first time, reduced the size of their nuclear arsenals. Under its terms, all Soviet and American medium and short-range missiles would be dismantled, and their disposition monitored by inspectors from both countries.

They discussed at length the Soviet invasion of Afghanistan, but reached no agreement on demands by Reagan that the Soviets withdraw. Further cutbacks in strategic weapons were discussed but no decision was reached except that officials of the two countries would continue to discuss the matter and make recommendations.

The summit ended on December 10 with the good news that progress had been made toward limiting strategic weapons and a decision not to let "star wars" impede future negotiations.

Palestinians rioted against Israeli-owned banks in Jerusalem on December 19, and seized streets in the Arab district. Rock-throwing youths led the protest movement in a new tactic to protest Israel's occupation of the Gaza Strip and the West Bank. As rioting went on for 13 days, at least 20 people were killed in clashes between the Palestinian youths and Israeli soldiers. Hundreds of thousands of Arabs inside Israel joined others in occupied areas in a general strike to protest Israel's crackdown on the protesters.

The United States and Canada reached a new trade agreement on January 2, 1988, to eliminate tariffs and lower other trade barriers. This landmark agreement signed by President Reagan and Prime Minister Mulroney was viewed with suspicions and skepticism by many Canadians who feared the United States would dominate Canada's economy to its detriment.

Meanwhile, it was revealed by other sources that the British, Germans and Japanese were buying up American companies and real estate and making other investments in America at bargain prices. This was due to the fact that the value of the dollar had long been depressed. The new AT&T building in Chicago was being built with Japanese money. Now, throughout the United States, many Americans were paying rent to overseas landlords, and a growing number of them were getting paychecks from Japanese firms in America.

The Navy had a total of 568 ships in 1988. Since 1981 it had added 120 ships at a cost of $582 billion. This extraordinary growth came at a time when the Navy was faced with the problem of retention of trained personnel. It was retaining only one-third of its pilots as thousands were lured away from the service by the nation's airlines. Soon, the new carriers, and their sophisticated aircraft, would be forced out of commission for lack of pilots and noncommissioned officers to maintain them. While the Navy in particular spent billions for procurement, it reduced or eliminated many of the services such as health care for families, decent housing and other services that had made the Navy attractive for its key personnel.

Since 1981 the Reagan administration had added 100 B-1B bombers, 1,490 bomber-launched cruise missiles, six Trident submarines and 21 new Trident-2 missiles, 66 MX missiles—including 50 in silos. Seven years later after its own buildup the Army had completed only one-third of its modernization while the Strategic Defense Initiative program had spent $13 billion since 1983. There were projections that SDI eventually might cost $770 billion. This huge cost was projected for a system that could never prevent all nuclear missiles from hitting American targets during a world conflagration. It would have little or no effect against low-flying Russian missiles fired by submarines or other types of ships cruising close to America's shores on either the Atlantic or Pacific sides of the continent. Like all Maginot-Line defense proposals its premise was fatally flawed. Finally, pursuit of an uninterrupted expansion of the armed forces with exotic new weaponry for which there was no true military need came under serious questioning this year by responsible members of Congress. The reality that continuance of such spending would surely lead to national bankruptcy prodded some members of Congress to insist upon a scaling down of military expenditures. The fact that this was a presidential election year, and the subject of excessive military expenditures was under intense scrutiny by Democratic presidential candidates, forced President Reagan's hand to reduce his demands.

Panama's ruler, General Manuel Antonio Noriega, was indicted by the United States Justice Department on February 5 on drug charges. He was charged with using his official position to protect drug traffickers and for allegedly receiving millions of dollars in bribes.

Noriega secured his control over Panama on February 26, 1988, by dismissing President Eric Arturo Delvalle after he had tried to oust him. Meanwhile, Panama faced a cash crisis as the United States took financial steps to make it impossible for Noriega to govern the country.

Panama was torn by a general strike on March 2 when opponents of General Noriega sought to paralyze the nation. After the banks were closed, the United States imposed sanctions. Civil disorders followed throughout the month but Noriega's forces eventually crushed the rebellion.

Thousands of Israelis demonstrated on March 13 to support Prime Minister Yitzhak Shamir's rejection of a United States peace plan to end the conflict in the Middle East. Meanwhile, rioting by Palestinians reached new heights as the Israelis savagely fought to end continuing disturbances. In Washington the following day Shamir described the rioting in the occupied Gaza Strip and the West Bank as a war against Israel. On March 30, with 3,000 Palestinians in detention by the Israelis, the death toll of Palestinians exceeded 100.

Lieutenant Colonel Oliver North, Rear Admiral John M. Poindexter, retired Major General Richard V. Secord and American-Iranian businessman Albert A. Hakim were indicted on March 16 by a grand jury on charges of conspiracy to defraud the government. They were charged with illegally providing Nicaraguan rebels with profits from the sale of arms to Iran. Twenty-three counts were filed against them.

President Reagan ordered American troops into Honduras on March 17 after that country's government charged that Nicaraguan troops had pursued contra rebels across the border. The contingent of 3,000 troops was withdrawn 11 days later when they were no longer needed.

Meanwhile, Nicaraguan government officials and contra leaders agreed to a ceasefire on March 23 which was extended through May as peace talks began to seek an end to the six-year war. Nicaragua agreed to free an estimated 3,300 anti-Sandinista prisoners while the contras consented to recognize the legitimacy of a freely-elected government.

America's trade deficit with the rest of the world jumped sharply in March. It was announced on April 14 that it had increased $1.4 billion over February. After the Commerce Department released the figures, the value of the dollar suffered another sharp drop.

Michael S. Dukakis overwhelmed his leading opponent in the Democratic race for President by defeating Jesse Jackson on April 19 by 210,000 votes in New York state. The Massachusetts governor won 51 percent of the vote while Jackson received only 37 percent, while another 10 percent voted for Albert Gore.

A week later Vice President Bush and Dukakis won their respective primaries in Pennsylvania. Bush won 17 more delegates than he needed for the Republican nomination. Dukakis won again over Jackson by a margin of 2 to 1.

The economy had been improving this year, and this became more evident when the unemployment rate fell a tenth of a point on May 6 to 5.4 percent. This level was the lowest since 1974.

Donald T. Regan, who had earlier resigned as White House chief of staff in the Reagan administration after a fallout with the President, published a book on May 8 that caused an uproar in the Republican administration. He revealed that virtually every major move and decision the Reagans made was cleared in advance with a woman in San Francisco who drew up horoscopes to make certain the planets were in a favorable alignment.

Regan's book also related how *Al Shiraa,* an Arabic-language magazine published in Lebanon, had revealed in its November 3, 1986, issue that the United States had supplied military spare parts to Iran, and that McFarlane and four others had visited Teheran in September to negotiate release of the eight hostages held by Lebanese terrorists. This was not exactly true. McFarlane had been in Iran in May. Regan said the President was urged to give the true story to the press, but he adamantly opposed release of these facts.

Later, the *New York Times* ran the first of many stories quoting State Department sources that Secretary of State George M. Schultz had opposed shipping arms to Iran. He argued, the paper said, that such an action was contradictory to American policy but he had been over-ruled.

The Senate ratified the Arms Limitation Treaty on May 27 after four months of debate. It approved the pact to eliminate medium and short-range missiles based on land. The vote strenghtened President Reagan's hand at the summit conference in Moscow where he and Gorbachev had clashed on the issue of human rights. The vehemence of their private discussions was revealed on May 30 after the President appealed for increased civil and religious liberties in Russia, and Reagan met with dissidents, exhorting them to press for changes. Gorbachev complained on June 1 that the President's pursuit of the human rights issue had resulted in "missed opportunities." In parting, he called President Reagan's visit a major event.

In effect, the summit failed to overcome the biggest differences between the two leaders, although the missile treaty approved by the Senate was signed there. Major obstacles, such as space-based defenses and sea-launched cruise missiles, were still unresolved.

Delegates at a Moscow conference approved measures sought by Gorbachev to overhaul the Soviet government. On July 1 they approved partial transfer of power from the Communist Party to a popularly-elected legislature and an end to party dominance over daily governmental decisions. Most importantly, the party approved a powerful office of a President to govern the country.

A United States Navy ship mistook an Iranian airliner for a fighter plane on July 3 and shot it down. The ship's captain defended his action by saying that he was only trying to protect his missile cruiser from what he thought was a hostile plane. President Reagan called the shooting down of the passenger plane a tragic case of mis-identity which, he said, was "understandable" in the turbulent war zone. He announced on July 11 that the United States would compensate the families for loss of the 290 passengers and crew who died in the accident.

Governor Michael Dukakis of Massachusetts arrived at the Democratic Convention July 17 in Atlanta and pledged to seek unity, insisting that he was in charge. The next day he and Jackson agreed to cooperate in the election. But the Massachusetts governor refused to approve a controversial liberal platform backed by Jackson. Dukakis was nominated on the 20th, and in accepting the nomination he pledged to lead the nation to the "next American frontier." Senator Lloyd Bentsen of Texas was nominated as vice-president and he called for a Democratic attack on federal budget deficits. .

Iranian officials told the United Nations on July 18 that it would accept its plan to end the war between its country and Iraq. In approving the United Nations Security Council's proposal for a ceasefire, Iran surprised the world body because it had previously opposed acceptance. The following day Iraq, fearing deception, rejected such a move and vowed to continue the war. But on July 20 the Ayatollah Khomeini confirmed that he had approved Iran's call for a ceasefire. He called the decision "more deadly than taking poison." For the ayatollah, this was a bitter moment, but he was finally forced to concede that Iran could not possibly win the war that had caused Iran enormous casualties, possibly as high as a million men.

In the Middle East, King Hussein of Jordan announced on July 31 that he was abandoning his claim to the occupied West Bank. In so doing he ceded the disputed territory to the Palestine Liberation Organization. The king's Hashemite family had ruled the territory from 1948 to 1967 when the Israelis occupied it.

American labor union membership had started to decline in the late 1950s and early 1960s, and by this summer a series of showdowns with management in several industries had left organized labor in a state of shock. The leadership of the AFL-CIO had never suffered such continuous defeats. Unions now represented just 16.8 percent of the total workforce, a drop of 30 percent in 20 years. In a labor force of more than 100 million workers, union membership was down to 17 million.

Iran accepted Iraq's plan for a ceasefire on August 8. The compromise that was worked out between the warring parties called for direct talks between officials of the two nations to end the war in the Persian Gulf.

Through American mediation efforts, another long, drawn-out war between Angola and its neighbor Namibia ended in a truce on this same date. South Africa, Angola and Cuba agreed to use their best efforts to mediate the conflict.

The Republicans nominated George Bush on August 19 as their party's standard bearer at their convention in New Orleans. Bush chose Senator Dan Quayle of Indiana as his running mate, a wealthy 41-year-old conservative Republican. Soon afterwards it was disclosed that Quayle's father had used influence to get his son into the National Guard during the Vietnam war. Controversy immediately surrounded his nomination. But Quayle was strongly backed by Bush and other top officials and he remained on the ticket.

High-level changes continued this year in the Soviet Union as Gorbachev consolidated his position. Three veteran members of the Politburo were dismissed on September 30, including President Andrei A. Gromyko.

Gorbachev consolidated his hold over the Soviet Union's government on September 30 by his election as President. He was elected to the post by the Communist Central Committee to succeed Gromyko.

The space-shuttle program resumed in late September when "Discovery" was placed in orbit after a smooth launch on September 29. This was the first time since the "Challenger" disaster in early 1986, in which the entire crew was killed, that the space shuttle could resume its flights. It landed smoothly at Edwards Air Force Base in California after four days in orbit.

George Bush was swept into office as President on November 8 after defeating Governor Dukakis in 40 states, although the House and Senate remained solidly controlled by the Democrats.

Yasir Arafat, chairman of the Palestine Liberation Organization, proclaimed an independent Palestine on November 15. He also, for the first time, implicitly recognized the state of Israel as part of a new approach to resolve differences between the Israelis and the Palestinians in the Middle East.

The United States Air Force unveiled its "Stealth" bomber on November 22, but controversy immediately surrounded the costly B-2 about whether it was truly needed. Claims that it was almost invisible to enemy radar were challenged by experts who said it could be spotted by low frequency ground radar units such as were used in World War II. They conceded that high-frequency radar beams would ricochet off its surfaces but all nations still used powerful low frequency radar units.

In speaking to the United Nations General Assembly in December 1988, Russian leader Gorbachev made it clear that his country was breaking with its aggressive, expansionist past. "Freedom of choice is a universal principle that should allow no exceptions," he said. "Refusal to recognize such a principle can lead to extremely grave consequences for world peace." His words offered a hope that the "Cold War" was finally coming to an end, but skeptics wanted actions rather than words before they placed any faith in the Soviet leader. They had heard such promises before.

At the start of 1989 Japan had the world's second-largest economy and it was the world's largest creditor. Since 1985 its currency had almost doubled in value against the dollar. In 1988 the United States had a $55.4 billion trade deficit with Japan, accounting for 40 percent of its world trade deficit. But there was still no consistent policy in the United States Government for forcing Japan to open up its domestic markets to foreign goods. Imports into Japan had become largely non-competitive due to trade restrictions and outright high tariffs. Actually, identical Japanese goods were sold in Japan at much higher prices than in the United States. In the long run this policy, if it was continued, would make it necessary for Japan to raise prices at home to further subsidize its exports. Thus the Japanese people will be forced to rebel against high costs for housing and food, with the result that labor rates must rise with an inevitable lowering of their standard of living compared to democracies in the West.

George Bush was inaugurated on January 20, 1989, as President of the United States. He promised new efforts to heal wounds and to end two decades of divisiveness between the White House and Congress. He also stressed the urgency of dealing with the Federal budget deficit, and he called upon Congress to join him in coping with crime and poverty.

Ronald Reagan stepped down following two terms as President at a time when two-thirds of the American people believed he had done a

good job. This was the highest rating achieved by a President since
World War II. In parting from Washington he spoke about the nation's
economic recovery and the "recovery of our morale." What he ignored
was the price that America and all Americans had paid once the total
bill for his administration came due.

The Soviet Union withdrew the last of its troops from Afghanistan on
February 5, fulfilling a pledge to leave on that date. The war had become
a burden to Russia's economy, and an international embarrassment for a
nation that prided itself on its peaceful intentions.

Speaking to the Supreme Soviet, President Gorbachev said the Soviet
Union's intervention in Afghanistan a decade earlier had been a violation
of international law, of Soviet law, of Communist ethics and of the "universal human values" that he said should be the basis of Soviet foreign
policy.

He called Afghanistan a grievous error, but there were others equally
serious in more recent years—the construction of a large radar station in
Siberia in direct violation of an arms control treaty with the United States
and "continued mass production of toxic agents" despite a halt by the
United States in the manufacture of chemical weapons in 1969, and
the whole arms buildup beyond the minimum necessary for the Soviet
Union's defense.

In admitting that not only the Soviet people had been lied to, he said
so had members of the Communist Party leadership. Gorbachev said the
Afghanistan invasion had been authorized by just a few members of the
ruling Politburo.

The Russian President stated that socialism had veered badly off course
in the Soviet Union under Joseph Stalin and that it was only now being
corrected. He said the Communist Party had acknowledged that its rule
has been undemocratic and its policies frequently and often fundamentally wrong.

He called for domestic reforms under his new policy of "perestroika"
or openness. "Perestroika gives new meaning to the question of what place
socialism and the Soviet Union occupy in the world, of the correlation of
interests, of values, and priorities." He told members of Russia's legislature that "perestroika, in other words, dictates the necessity of a thoroughly new foreign policy." He stressed the primacy of "universal human
values" over Marxist class struggle and traditional national interests alike.
"No national and state interests," he said, "can justify a political decision
or a diplomatic action, however pragmatic, unless they are moral."

These almost incredible comments by the Russian leader were followed
by equally unbelievable actions that stunned the world. The once-impreg-
nable "Iron Curtain" was shredded to tatters in 1989. It all began on

January 11 when the Hungarian parliament legalized freedom of assembly and freedom of association. Then thousands of Czechoslovakians defied their Communist masters between January 15 and 21 by demonstrating for human rights on the anniversary of the suicide of students who protested the Soviet-led invasion in 1968. The Communist Central Committee in Poland called for gradual legalization of the banned Solidarity trade union on January 18, followed in February by talks to negotiate Poland's future between government officials and Solidarity leaders. Hungary took an important step on February 11 by approving creation of independent political parties. Police fought anti-Communist demonstrators in Warsaw on February 24 and 25 and the outbreaks spread to other cities.

Retired senior officials in Romania wrote a letter on March 12 accusing President Nicolae Ceausescu of violating human rights and mismanaging the economy. They were promptly arrested. But the Hungarians, who started the protest movement in January, escalated the crisis for the Communist world on March 15 when 75,000 marchers in Budapest gathered to listen to anti-Communist speakers. Free elections were demanded, plus the removal of Soviet troops. Surprisingly, authorities permitted those demonstrations to take place. Two weeks later the reason became apparent when Communist Party Chief Karoly Grosz announced that Soviet President Gorbachev had pledged not to interfere with reforms in Eastern Europe.

Dissidents now increased their demands in all of Eastern Europe. Talks in Poland between Solidarity members and the government ended on April 5 with agreement on political and economic reforms. Free elections were promised in June, and Solidarity was legalized. The union's leader, Lech Walesa, met with President Wojciech Jaruzelski on the 18th. This was the man who had jailed Walesa earlier for his opposition to the Communist government of Poland.

In Hungary, troops began dismantling the barbed-wire fence along the nation's border with Austria, thus providing open access to the West for the first time since World War II. Bulgaria's tight Communist control of that nation had brought on an economic crisis, particularly on the nation's farms where collectives had been established. Food production had plummeted ever since the nation's leader Todor Zhikov had announced that collective farms would be broken up, and private ownership encouraged.

Rising tension in Poland caused 20,000 copper miners to stage a wildcat strike on May 5. The Communist government stood by helplessly as the nation's first independent newspaper in four decades appeared. Twelve days later Parliament granted legal status to the Roman Catholic Church, the first Communist nation to do so.

In Poland's first open elections in more than 40 years on June 4 the Communists suffered a humiliating defeat. Solidarity candidates took control of the Parliament. Nine days later the government consented to formal talks to establish a multi-party system. Meanwhile, Romanian leaders were running counter to the trend of more freedom by erecting barbed-wire fences along its borders with other countries. Great Britain protested, but so did the Soviet Union which carried more weight with Romania's dictatorial leader. The fence was soon dismantled. Meanwhile, the situation in Hungary was proceeding along more democratic lines by creation of a four-member collective presidency under reformist Rezso Nyers.

On July 4 Poland accepted a new Parliament with two legislative bodies, composed of Solidarity legislators who had won seats in the recent election. For the first time since World War II Poland had a political opposition representing them in Parliament.

For those who still feared the Soviet Union would step in and return these nations to tight Communist control, President Gorbachev's words to the Council of Europe brought instant reassurance. He said that force would not be used against the Soviet Union's eastern bloc neighbors. People in these nations relaxed when he publicly said that reforms in Hungary and Poland were "their affair." A few days later President Bush went to both of these countries to show America's support for these reforms. Further evidence of relaxation came on July 17 when the Polish government restored diplomatic relations with the Vatican. They had been broken off in 1945.

Although Communist leader Jaruzelski was elected on July 19 as President of Poland, his former control of the government was sharply reduced. When he sought to form a "grand coalition" with other Communist groups, the Parliament rejected his proposal.

Events in Poland during August forced a coalition government on Poland. Solidarity leader Walesa proposed the change, and the union had strength enough in the new Parliament to impose their demands.

Meanwhile, East Germans had been rather quiet in their dissent against their totalitarian regime but in August hundreds of East Germans took refuge in West German diplomatic missions in East Berlin, Budapest and Prague. They pressed their demands for political asylum in the West, and thousands began to be accepted.

Czechoslovakian authorities momentarily cracked down on dissidents on August 21 in Prague. Three hundred seventy people were arrested when they demonstrated for reform on the anniversary of the Soviet-led invasion in 1968.

Unrest in Bulgaria escalated, forcing Turkey to close its borders August

22 to prevent ethnic Turks from leaving the country. By this time 300,000 had already arrived in Turkey for asylum.

The first non-Communist government in Eastern Europe came into being on August 24 in Poland. Tadeusz Mazowiecki was confirmed as prime minister. He had long been active in Solidarity's opposition to the former Communist government.

East Germany's leader, gravely ill with cancer, came in for increasing opposition in September. The unrest started as thousands of East Germans traveled to Hungary in hopes of migrating to West Germany. The outflow became so heavy that it caused a diplomatic crisis between East Germany and Hungary. By September 14 more than 13,000 East Germans had left Hungary for Germany through Austria despite protests from East Germany's government.

The strength of the opposition movement in Poland was indicated on September 12 when 23 members of the coalition cabinet were confirmed, but only four Communists were included.

Meanwhile the crisis in East Germany rose during the last part of the month as pro-democracy demonstrators massed in Leipzig. Such demonstrations had been unthinkable a few months earlier, but now 10,000 people marched to show their contempt for the anthorities who watched them helplessly, unable to stop them. Hungary's political unrest simmered down as government and opposition parties agreed to a multiparty system. It was scheduled to take over in 1990.

East German refugees, who had been clogging western embassies in Czechoslovakia and Poland, received permission in early October to emigrate to Germany. Seventeen thousand people crowded trains bound for West Germany after East and West German officials agreed to permit them to leave. But then the East German government closed its borders with Czechoslovakia on October 4. Street protests erupted in Dresden, and hundreds of protesters were arrested. During East Germany's 40th anniversary Soviet leader Gorbachev spent October 6th and 7th in the country. He strongly urged—it was more like an ultimatum—that East German leaders agree to reforms.

The Socialist Workers' Party—despite its name it was a Communist party—of Hungary on October 7 renounced Marxism and announced that it would become a democratic socialist party. Rezso Nyers, who had long called for reforms, became the nation's leader replacing Karoly Grosz.

The new Polish leaders soon found that their new freedoms did not ensure economic success as the nation dipped further into a recession with high inflation. The creation of free markets, they hoped, would solve their economic crisis. But it soon became evident the nation would endure economic hardships, possibly for years, until the economy could be turned around by a free market along western-style lines.

The situation worsened in East Germany when 100,000 people in Dresden demonstrated on October 16 for a return to democracy. Two days later East Germany's leader Erich Honecker was forced to abdicate as the nation's leader. He had served for 18 years and his harsh rule had been enforced by the hated secret police. Communist Politiburo member, Egon Krenz, replaced him.

Hungary became a free republic on October 23. On the anniversary of the 1956 uprising, 80,000 attended a rally to commemorate the occasion without fear of reprisals.

A similar rally in Czechoslovakia on October 28 was quickly broken up by authorities. Ten thousand had come to protest the government's authoritarian policies.

The East German government removed curbs on foreign travel in the early days of November. Thousands left their country, crossing into Czechoslovakia, en route to West Germany. Meanwhile a million other East Germans rallied on November 4 to demand reforms in their government, an action that shocked the nation's leaders. Three days later the country's prime minister, the cabinet, and the poliburo resigned as the result of continuing protests by the populace. And then on the ninth the Berlin Wall was opened for free passage between East and West Berlin, while other border points were opened wide. Hundreds of thousands poured into West Berlin, most of them—to the relief of West Berliners— just came to gawk at the affluent society that they had so often heard about but had not ever seen. The impression on East Germans was devastating.

In Bulgaria, President Todor Zhivkov resigned on November 10 after serving 35 years in office. He was replaced by reformer Peter Mladenov. Eight days later 50,000 Bulgarians celebrated their new government.

Changes in East Germany's government moved with increasing rapidity. The new prime minister, Hans Modrow, announced on November 16 that nearly half of his cabinet would be non-communists. He also advised East Germans that he was instituting reforms. Those who feared that these abrupt changes in the political structure of the eastern bloc were too good to be true were sharply reminded on November 17 in Czechoslovakia when police brutally broke up a student protest in Prague. It all began when the Politburo argued earlier whether to permit the rally because it was designed to commemorate the death of a Czechoslovak youth by the name of Jan Opeltal by Nazi occupation forces in 1939. Communist party leader Milos Jakes had reluctantly agreed to the demonstration. He had recently been under pressure from officials of the Soviet

Union to curb his repressive government. Then he and other members of the Politburo left for their country homes for the weekend.

During the demonstration students carried banners saying, "We want freedom by Christmas." All was quiet at first but then the police violently opposed the students. In the next two days what became known as "the police massacre" aroused the Czechs like nothing ever had before. Some vowed to start a revolution.

By Sunday evening opposition leaders organized a group called "Civic Reform" and devised a list of demands to be made against the government. They announced they wanted a commission formed to investigate the police action of November 17, the freeing of all political prisoners and the resignation of eight senior members of the Communist Party, including its leader Jakes. Now the veteran Socialist Party general secretary, Jan Skoda, joined the Civic Reform group. This was a surprising defection because this party, although small, formed a part of the Communist-dominated National Front.

Incredibly, the nation's leaders did not learn of the budding insurrection because they were away from the capital. When they returned to Prague on Monday they acted without full knowledge of the extent of the anger that had been aroused. When they issued a declaration supporting the police action, the population's anger could no longer be contained. Public defiance of authority was manifested in Prague's Wencelas Square as thousands gathered in protest.

This attitude shocked the authorities. In the past Czechoslovakia's economy had been the best in the Communist bloc, with plentiful supplies of food and clothing, and an economy that was the envy of its neighbors. Most Czechoslovakians owned a car, and even had a second home in the country. The authorities were paralyzed now by the deepening anger against them because they had convinced themselves that it could not happen in Czechoslovakia. But despite the relative good life, compared to other nations in the area, the Czechs had long smouldered a resentment against their government's repressive ways. With the fall of East Germany's Erich Honecker, they felt the time was ripe.

Dissident playwright Vaclav Havel called a meeting of Civic Reform members on Monday morning to announce that "Civic Reform came into existence last night." He read the demands that had been agreed upon and announced a two-hour general strike for the following Monday, November 27.

Meanwhile, student strike committees were formed. With other college and university students they sent envoys throughout Czechoslovakia to spread the word about their demands. Now workers joined the students and the government had a full-blown crisis on its hands.

Wencelas Square was the scene of daily protests. The movement had started out small, but gained credibility when Prime Minister Ladislav Adamec met with Civic Reform. Reassured that there would be no further violence, he agreed to meet with them again.

Communist party leader Jakes did not dare to take violent action against the group, fearing Gorbachev's wrath, so he tried intimidation. He warned Civic Reform of ominous consequences if they perisisted in what he termed their "insurrection." On Tuesday he called units of the party's praetorian guard, the People's Militia, into Prague. Twenty thousand elite troops camped on Prague's outskirts, while other units moved into factories, warning workers not to join the protesters and ripping down their posters. But workers refused to work until the militia left.

On Thursday almost 200,000 people jammed Wencelas Square in support of the protesters. Jakes' leadership was criticized for its lack of flexibility, and his principal opponent in the Politburo, Prime Minister Ladislav Adamec, was praised.

By Thursday at a rally in the Square the crowd chanted "Milos, the game is over."

On September 24 Milos Jakes quit as head of the Communist Party. His support had dwindled to almost nothing. He was replaced by Karel Urbanek. Then the Politburo's Secretariat quit.

On Saturday more than half a million Czechs rallied, despite freezing weather, against the remaining hard-line Politburo members. Opposition was particularly strong against Prague party boss Miroslav Stepan who had called for the police crackdown on November 17.

The Communist Party now convened to take action against the growing strike that was paralyzing the country. They fired Stepan and the most prominent hard-liners, including the hated trade union boss Miroslav Zavadil.

By Monday, the Communist regime was further humiliated by a strike that shut down the country for two hours.

Twelve days after the students gathered to protest at Charles University the government proposed a coalition government. They submitted a draft amendment to the constitution that would dismantle the Communist Party's monopoly on power. With this unexpected turn of events, the protesters held a victory celebration.

In Romania, the Communists maintained their hold on the nation. Nicolae Ceausescu was re-elected as head of the nation and announced on November 24 that he had rejected reform for his country.

In Hungary, the people themselves voted to delay the election for a new president until opposition parties could be formed to be more representative of all the people. The election was set for the spring of 1990. This would be Hungary's first free election since 1945.

Dissidents in Czechoslovakia further extended their control by ending the Communist Party's leading role. The National Assembly made it official on November 29.

Two days later Egon Krenz, who had replaced Erich Honecker as East Germany's leader, found himself without a job. He quit as party chairman, along with the Politburo and Central Committee. Honecker was even ousted from membership in the party. The reformers named an interim panel to take over the leadership. Manfred Gerlach was named acting head of state; the first non-communist to hold that position.

The Communist party officially lost its control of East Germany on December 1 when its 40-year monopoly came to an end.

President Gorbachev now admitted that the 1968 Soviet-led invasion of Czechoslovakia was wrong. This was an admission that somewhat alleviated this tragic period in the minds of the Czechs.

In Czechoslovakia, Communist leaders named 16 Communists and five non-Communists to a new cabinet. In protest, 150,000 Czechs gathered on December 3 to denounce this action. Two days later Prime Minister Ladislav Adamec quit, and steps were taken to form a new government.

Erich Honecker's misuse of office while head of East Germany, and his out-and-out corruption while in office, was revealed on December 8. He and former members of the Politburo were arrested on these charges. Now a pro-democracy lawyer, Gregor Gysi, was elected as Communist Party chairman, and the party announced that it would follow the path of "democratic socialism." East Germany's first non-Communist government in the past 41 years was sworn in on December 10.

Bulgaria was swept by unrest again on December 10th and 11th. The people demanded an end to Communist monopoly, and free elections were promised by June of 1990.

Romania's dictator Nicolae Ceausescu was executed on December 23, 1989, thus ending a vicious regime that had lasted 24 years. His unpopular wife died with him. The dreaded Securitate, however, fought to the end and large numbers of people were killed. Since the early 1980s Romania had lived at the privation level while the country's leader, his family, and his favorites lived in luxury. Ceausescu had tried to pay off the country's $11 billion indebtedness by depriving his people of the barest necessities of heat, food and light. It was a police state unlike any other in Eastern Europe, and the people were literally kept in bondage. Ceausescu had believed his control of the country was so absolute that his regime would never fall the way the others had been overthrown.

But violent death was meted out to him such as he had ordered for so many of his countrymen.

Although the breakup of a monolithic Communist system in eastern Europe dominated the news in 1989, there were other equally exciting developments in all fields. The new openness in the Soviet Union resulted in one shocking revelation. A Soviet weekly magazine revealed that 20 million Russians had died during Stalin's oppressive regime in addition to the 27 million who had died in World War II. The magazine gave a detailed account of those deaths in labor camps, forced collectivization, famine and executions.

Presidents of five Central American nations reached an accord on February 14, 1989, about Nicaraguan contra troops based in Honduras. Agreement was reached to close these bases in exchange for free democratic elections in Nicaragua. The agreement also called for the release of all prisoners.

Japan's Emperor Hirohito, who had died on January 7, was buried on February 22 according to ancient rites. President Bush attended the funeral, giving him an opportunity to confer with other world leaders on East-West relations and military tensions that were still evident in the Far East.

Some relaxation of international tension was noticeable in the Far East after Vietnam announced on April 5 that it would withdraw its troops from Cambodia. Thus ended an occupation that had lasted for 10 years and three months, although the Cambodian rebels who opposed the Vietnam-supported government remained undefeated. It was little noted at the time that Vietnam had made the same mistakes in Cambodia by fighting a guerrilla war as the United States made in fighting North Vietnam, and with identical results. Although the Vietnamese established a government of their choosing in the major cities, the countryside remained in guerrilla hands with Pol Pot's Khmer Rouge as the largest group.

As the totalitarian walls fell in eastern Europe, Chinese dissidents tried to rally their people to overthrow Communism in the People's Republic. As the world watched with excitement and wonder tens of thousands of students took over Beijing's central square on April 19 in a rally for democracy. These protests grew in size and vigor in the following days as marchers defied police who seemed helpless to control them. On April 27 more than 150,000 young people openly defied the police and army by marching through the capital despite official warnings that troops would be brought in to crush the rebellion. At first the government agreed to discuss their demands for democracy and the charges of corruption that had been leveled at high Communist officials. Then thousands of cheering workers joined the students along the parade route to applaud the marching students.

A jury convicted Lieutenant Colonel Oliver L. North on May 4 of shredding government documents and of two other crimes committed while he was President Reagan's covert agent to aid the Nicaraguan contra rebels. Other key points in the government's case against the former aide to the National Security Council were rejected.

Disturbances in the People's Republic of China escalated in mid-May as young hunger-strikers urged the people to provoke a crisis with their Communist rulers. More than a million protesters thronged the nation's capital of Beijing to demand more democracy and the resignations of Deng Xiaoping, the nation's senior leader, and Prime Minister Li Peng. With chaos threatening to engulf the nation, Li and party leader Zhao Ziyang visited Tianamen Square to talk to the hunger strikers. With more than a million people swarming the city's streets in defiance of martial law, they kept troops from the center of the capital. Workers and students continued to block convoys from entering the capital while Zhao was stripped of his powers in the government after urging a moderate line toward the students.

China's Communist officials brutally cracked down on the students in Beijing on June 4, killing possibly thousands of protesters. Troops retook the capital from the pro-democracy demonstrators who fought with their bare hands against rifles and machine guns. There were some clashes between Chinese military units but the majority of the army stood firm with the government. Meanwhile, the United States and other nations ordered the evacuation of their nationals. During the crackdown more than 400 Chinese protesters were arrested, and the leaders were quickly tried and executed. Deng Xiaoping, and other Chinese leaders, announced that their hard line against dissent would continue despite protests against the massacre. Communism again showed its true face with all its inherent brutality.

CHAPTER 32

"Voodoo Economics"

THE NATION'S NEW "STEALTH' BOMBER TOOK OFF FOR THE FIRST TIME on July 20. Its name is derived for its supposed capability of eluding enemy radar, but the $70 billion project was immediately attacked as grossly over-priced and unnecessary. The House Armed Services Committee said it was considering whether to release funds for it in 1990 or force the Pentagon to scale back the program.

A future space plane, the X-30, America's National Aerospace Plane project, was funded at $300 million for 1989. It will pioneer a new type of engine called the scramjet under development by Rocketdyne, Pratt & Whitney and Marquardt. Fred Billing of the Johns Hopkins University's applied physics laboratory described the engine as a carefully-shaped duct to contain the airflow that is fitted with fuel injectors. He said it was expected to use a small rocket engine, mounted within the duct, to provide thrust for takeoff. At 2,000 miles per hour the scramjet will ram into the air, compress it, and force it through the duct. Hydrogen fuel, injected into this airflow, then will be ignited and the hot air produced by this action will be expanded through a rocket-like nozzle to produce thrust.

The X-30 is tentatively scheduled to fly into orbit in the fall of 1996. The Japanese are also moving ahead in this field.

South Africa's President, P. W. Botha, beleagured head of his government that was adamantly opposed to giving equal rights to its black majority population, resigned on August 4. He complained that his cabinet ministers ignored him. The following day F. W. de Klerk, who succeeded Botha as head of the National Party, was sworn in as acting President and later was named to the position. His assumption of power was welcomed by blacks because he had promised to phase out white rule in South Africa.

The Strategic Defense Initiative, or "Star Wars" program, was reduced by Congress in 1989 to basically a ground-based system at a vastly lower cost. This was the program's first sizable cut in funding. Senator Sam Nunn, Democrat of Georgia, and chairman of the Armed Services Committee, acknowledged that "some kind of a limited system" was more realistic. "Star Wars," he said, "has become a perishable commodity in Congress." He said the original concept was just too vague and too costly.

With Russia disarming to a certain extent—announcing a 500,000-man reduction in the armed forces, with sharp cutbacks in Central Europe, it was imperative for the United States to reduce its military expenditures as the Soviets curtailed their offensive capabilities. But the Soviet Union's dramatic, profound and unparalleled reorganization caught the administration by surprise.

Reports now indicated that the Soviet Union, with approximately 33,000 nuclear weapons—40 percent more than the United States—was starting to phase out its older warheads. The United States had done much the same thing at the start of the 1970s when its total equalled Russia's peak. With each power possessing about 13,000 warheads or bombs among their long-range arsenals, any reduction was welcome. The Soviets still possessed about twice as many short-range weapons, but they were discontinuing a number of them or replacing their nuclear explosives with conventional explosives.

President Bush and President Gorbachev met for the first time since the American President took office on December 2 and 3 for talks on board a ship at Malta. Although no new agreements were signed they agreed to step up the pace of arms reductions. Gorbachev was widely quoted for his comment that the "Cold War" had ended.

The United States Government revealed on December 18 that two administration envoys, including National Security Adviser Brent Scowcroft, had made a second visit to the People's Republic of China to discuss relations with its Communist leaders. The first meeting, a month after the Communist government brutally put down a protest movement in Tianamen Square in Peking, had been kept secret until now. Its revelation was widely condemned by Republicans and Democrats who charged the administration with a lack of sensitivity for an oppressed people. President Bush insisted it was in America's best interest to maintain an ongoing relationship with the Communist government and hopefully to convince its leaders they should return to the more open society that they had fostered, resulting in improved relations between the two superpowers.

The first group of 4,500 paratroopers, helicopters carrying Green Berets and Navy commandos descended upon Panama's Torrijos International Airport on December 20, 1989, during the pre-dawn hours in a daring and unprecedented assault to overthrow General Manuel A. Noriega. The early-morning assault came as a shock to the dictator who had often defied the United States while conducting drug operations on a massive scale. A short while later 10,000 troops were airlifted to Panama, some from Fort Ord in California.

The operation went off with only a few glitches: failure to secure the Marriott Hotel in Panama City where Noriega's army seized a number of Americans as hostages—they were released later—and failure to knock out the city's radio transmitter. It had been considered by Army authorities but the radio's transmitter was in a heavily-populated area and it was feared that the civilian casualties would be too high if it was bombed.

Eventually 22,500 troops were used, including the 13,000 already stationed in Panama, and they overcame scattered resistance within days. Twenty-three Americans were killed in the operation and 322 were wounded. Among the Panamanian defense forces at least 53 were killed while possibly 300 civilians died. Fifty-two thousand guns were captured, instead of the 100,000 initially reported. The cocaine supposedly found in Noriega's house proved on closer inspection to be tamale powder.

President Bush's decision to invade Panama, criticized in some quarters, and routinely denounced by most Central and South American nations, came after the brutal slaying of an American officer, and indignities against another officer and his wife.

Noriega sought refuge on December 24 at the Vatican's diplomatic mission in Panama City. After negotiations between the United States, the new Panamanian government, and Vatican officials he was released to the Americans who brought him to the United States to await trial on drug-trafficking charges.

In his first state of the union address President Bush called for cuts in defense programs, and deep reductions in United States and Soviet troop levels in Europe. He recommended that American and Soviet military manpower in Central and Eastern Europe be reduced to 195,000 on each side. This was a sharp reduction from the 275,000 figure under consideration by arms negotiators in Vienna. This would mean an abrupt reduction from 570,000 Soviet troops to 195,000 while only a reduction of 60,000 American troops would suffice to bring the United States total down to that figure.

In regard to the invasion troops in Panama, the President promised the Congress and the American people that by February the number of troops there would be reduced to the pre-invasion level.

Speaking of the events in the Soviet Union and Eastern Europe, the President said, "The events of the year just ended—the Revolution of '89—have been a chain reaction—change so striking that it marks the beginning of a new era in the world's affairs. The time is right," he said, "for the United States to move forward with deeper cuts of conventional arms as part of a coherent defense program that ensures the United States will continue to be a catalyst for peaceful change in Europe."

Bush's proposals were greeted warmly by most members of Congress. House Speaker Thomas S. Foley said, "I don't think the United States should totally withdraw from Western Europe, but very substantial reductions are not only possible but inevitable."

The approaching end to the "Cold War" was viewed by the people of the Soviet Union and its former satellites with mixed emotions when their economies floundered in the switch from a controlled market to one involving the uncertainties of the free market place. Romania disbanded its rebellious police force on January 1, 1990, and Gorbachev visited Lithuania Janaury 11 because her defiant people were demanding total freedom almost 50 years after Estonia, Latvia and Lithuania were forcibly annexed to the Soviet Union. He pleaded with the Lithuanians to remain in the Soviet Union while threatening to take punitive action if they continued to seek independence. In Azerbaijan, mobs committed atrocities against Armenians forcing Gorbachev to take emergency measures and send troops to quell the disorders. During a month of climactic changes, Bulgarian Communists voted to end 45 years of authoritarian rule and permit a multi-party system. Then Polish Communists acted January 29 to form a democratic, left-of-center government.

In Nicaragua, opposition candidate Violeta Barrios de Chamorro won a landslide victory against the Sandinistas on February 5, 1990, defeating President Daniel Ortega Saavedra. Three weeks later Ortega declared a ceasefire with American-supported contras.

Communist Party leadership in the Soviet Union took another step toward democracy on February 7 when it backed Gorbachev and agreed to a western-style presidency with a cabinet. The following day Gorbachev was given broad new presidential powers. While Gorbachev was given authority to rule, the Soviet Union's economic plight worsened and food and household necessities became more scarce throughout the country. Even worse, all 15 Soviet republics declared sovereignty, threatening the very existence of the Soviet Union. Ethnic unrest became an increasing problem for the central government, particularly the near civil war between Muslim Azerbaijanis and the Christian Armenians. Lithuania was the first republic to declare its independence in March, but when gasoline and oil were cut off by Gorbachev in retaliation, the republic agreed to suspend its independence declaration and the blockade was later lifted.

Nelson Mandela, South Africa's black leader, who had served 27½ years in jail for plotting to overthrow the government, was released on February 11. He promptly urged an increase in the pressure upon the white minority government to end apartheid, and urged other nations to keep their sanctions against South Africa in force.

Reunification of East and West Germany moved a step closer February 13 when governments of the Allied nations which had opposed Nazi Germany during World War II agreed to terms for ending the division.

Meanwhile the Soviet Union abandoned its demand that equal levels of troops be maintained in Europe. Gorbachev agreed to President Bush's insistence that the United States should maintain a 30,000-man advantage.

President Vaclav Havel of Czechoslovakia urged the United States to help the Soviet Union on its "immensely complicated road to democracy" when he addressed a joint session of Congress on February 21. In so doing, he said, Eastern European nations will be the prime beneficiaries. He said he realized that such a request might surprise leaders of the western world because the Soviet Union for years "was a country that rightfully gave people nightmares." But he reminded his listeners that such a step should be taken because "the sooner, the more quickly and the more peacefully the Soviet Union begins to move along the road toward genuine political pluralism the better it will be not just for Czechs and Slovaks but for the whole world."

In a statement issued after Havel's meeting with President Bush they said that they both agreed that the presence of American troops in Europe was a factor for stability and security.

The Soviet Union's President, Mikhail S. Gorbachev, had to defend his policy of greater democracy for his country in February as conservative hard liners resisted his demands for further changes. They had long refused to end the Communist Party's dominance of their country's government. In denouncing Gorbachev for his "muddled thinking and incompetence," they blamed him for the deepening economic crisis and demanded a halt to his reforms.

After three days of emotional debate by the policy-making Central Committee they approved amendments to a new party platform for consideration by the Congress of People's Deputies, that members elected to the 2,250 member congress must debate and approve major legislation. Among its responsibilities is the election of the Supreme Soviet—the Soviet Union's full-time legislative body—from among its members.

In the end even the Conservatives accepted Gorbachev's most fundamental reforms—the abolition of the party's constitutional monopoly on power and its consequences, with development of a multiparty political system.

Gorbachev had long since repudiated dictatorial leadership under Stalin, but now he openly turned against the philsophies of V. I. Lenin, the founding father of the Soviet state. He said that Lenin promoted the "dictatorship of the proletariat" 14 years before the 1917 Russian revolution. Gorbachev claimed that the proletariat would only stay in step if led by a small, dedicated core of revolutionaries, and that "for the center . . . to actually direct the orchestra, it needs to know who plays which violin and where, who plays a false note and why, and how and where it is necessary to transfer someone to correct the dissonance."

Lenin also declared the "undivided political supremacy" of the Communist Party. In less than a year he brutally destroyed all non-communist political organizations, or rendered them ineffective. After his death Joseph Stalin further centralized the party leadership, and ruled as a brutal dictator. Now Gorbachev was breaking almost completely with the past in an unprecedented move with worldwide repercussions if he failed.

For Gorbachev the Central Committee's action to alter the whole Soviet political and economic system was a victory of incredible proportions. His persistence and courage were applauded by the world's non-communist leaders.

Meanwhile, Vietnam's leaders made it clear that they would not accept such a return to democracy in their country, and took steps to draw away from the Soviet Union and its East European satellites ideologically, financially and militarily.

Nguyen Van Linh, head of Vietnam's Communist Party, said on February 2 that communism would continue to hold a political monopoly in his country. He told a conference on the party's 60th anniversary, "Apart from the Communist Party in Vietnam there is no other party of any class capable of shouldering that role. It was so in the past history, it is now, and it will be so in the future."

Linh claimed that "present realities" in East European countries underlined the harm done to the prestige of the party. He said that Vietnam must avoid similar mistakes.

Some of the pressure against Vietnam's party leaders was reduced after economic reforms were instituted in 1986. State subsidies were ended, the currency was devalued, and open markets were created. As a result food and consumer goods became more plentiful, and inflation declined from 700 percent in 1988 to 24 percent in 1989. With rural land reforms and control of prices the economy picked up and new homes were being built in quantity for the first time since the war ended. After food shortages in 1988, land reforms created a surplus of rice for 1989, permitting the export of 1.5 million tons. Vietnam is now the world's third largest rice exporter after the United States and Thailand. But recent military demobilizations have raised the unemployment level to an unacceptable 20 percent.

Nelson Mandela, following his release from prison in South Africa, emerged as the top black leader in March when he was named to head the African National Congress as deputy president. President Oliver N. Tambo at age 72 was in ill health and had become ineffective.

Israel's Prime Minister Yitzhak Shamir created an emotional crisis when his coalition government refused to accept terms proposed by the United States for the start of peace talks with the Palestinians. On March 13 the government was dissolved because of failure of the Labor and Likud parties to agree.

CHAPTER 33

Cold War Ends

NORTH AMERICAN ROCKWELL RELEASED DETAILS ON MARCH 1 of a new experimental plane when the X-31 jet fighter was rolled out of its hanger. Under development by the Pentagon and a West German firm Messerschmitt-Bolkow-Blohm, it is designed to eliminate stalls and thus permit it to turn around quickly and fire at a pursuing enemy. If successful, it will revolutionize air combat because other fighters stall if they attempt sharp turns and fall out of control.

Such an airplane could make all the world's other fighters obsolete because they rely upon very high speeds, powerful aerial radars and long-range missiles to engage in combat at ranges well beyond human eyesight. Experts reported that the Sparrow missile was successful in only 10 percent of engagements during the Vietnam War. The X-31 is designed to fight close to an enemy with an unmatched agility to break off an engagement or pursue it.

The new fighter was developed when it became apparent in the late 1970s that missiles could now shoot down aircraft in head-on attacks. Prior to that time a fighter pilot had to maneuver behind an enemy in a dog-fight that was little changed since World War I.

An Air Force SR-71 set a new cross-country speed record on March 6 when it flew from Los Angeles to Washington, D.C., in an official time of 68 minutes and 17 seconds. It averaged 2,112.52 mph.

Thus the Lochkeed "Blackbird" ended its distinguished career on a high note as it was removed from service by the Air Force and consigned to permanent display at the Smithsonian Institution. Its historic final flight was flown by Lieutenant Colonel Raymond E. Yeiling with his reconnaissance officer Lieutenant Colonel J. D. Vida.

Eight other SR-71s were sent to musuems, three others were assigned to the National Aviation and Space Agency for aeronautical research, and the final three will be mothballed at Palmdale.

Oliver L. North, a lieutenant colonel formerly on the staff of the National Security Council, was convicted in 1989 of destroying documents and lying to Congress in the Iran-contra case. He was called as a witness in March of 1990 at the trial of former National Security Adviser John M. Poindexter and subjected to sharp questioning by special prosecutor Dan K. Webb and defense attorney Richard W. Beckler. The prosecution sought to link North with Admiral Poindexter while the defense tried to separate the two men in the minds of the jury.

Poindexter was found guilty on April 7 of five charges of deceiving and lying to Congress. He had tried to conceal the Reagan Administration's actions in the Iran-contra affair. (In December 1992, the Supreme Court overturned the conviction, and shortly before he left office, President Bush pardoned six others who had been indicted.)

For the first time in United States history the national debt reached $3 trillion, the Treasury Department revealed on April 2. Thus every man, woman and child in America owed the government $12,000.

The nation's indebtedness had reached $1 billion in 1916 during World War I, climbed to $278 billion at the end of World War II, and reached its first trillion October 1, 1981. It has quadrupled since then under two Republican regimes.

The Defense Department on April 3 released more details of its secret F-117A "Stealth" aircraft, first revealed in 1988. A spokesman said the new fighter was a "key component" of America's military power. Pictures of its chunky fuselage and its odd angles to avoid reflecting radar images were released for the first time. Priced at $73 million each, it is far below the $570 million price tag for the B-2 stealth bomber.

The F-117A was developed by Lockheed's "Skunk Works" starting in 1978 and it was announced that 57 had been produced, with two more on order under a production contract. A spokesman confirmed that three aircraft had been lost through the years and two pilots killed.

The F-117 was first used in combat during the Panama invasion when it dropped a 2,000-pound bomb on a field near a military airfield to stun and confuse its Panamanian defenders. It is designed to conduct precision strikes on targets at night, and it carries a wide variety of weapons to fulfill its role.

The shuttle "Discovery" carried a $1.5 billion Space Telescope into orbit April 24, releasing it 381 miles above the earth. The Hubble telescope was designed to observe distant stars and galaxies to provide a new and comprehensive view of the universe. Trouble with the telescope developed quickly; first with its solar-powered wing which was fixed, and then with the mirror itself which could not be repaired.

The Sandinistas relinquished their control of Nicaragua on April 25 as Violeta Barrios de Chamorro was inaugurated as President to succeed Daniel Ortega Saavedra. The latter's brother, however, remained as the nation's military leader.

There had been rumors for years, but no proof, that the Russians had killed thousands of Polish officers in the Katyn Forest during 1940. President Gorbachev admitted on April 31 that the killings were done by Russian secret police.

The growing shortage of food and other basic commodities in the Soviet Union reached the point during the annual Red Square Parade on May 1 that President Gorbachev and other Kremlin leaders were jeered. Thousands of protesters shouted, "Shame, shame," and "Resign!" Others carried placards saying, "Down with the Empire of Red Fascism." It was an incredible expression of opposition to their rulers.

In an obvious gesture to tone down criticism in the West, China's leadership on May 10 freed all 211 dissidents. Most had been jailed for taking part in the 1989 democracy movement in Tianamen Square.

Gorbachev moved quickly May 14 when the drive for independence by Latvia and Estonia threatened to start a trend that might break up the Soviet Union. He charged that they had no legal basis for separation, but he delayed the imposition of sanctions until later.

The following day thousands of protesters stormed the Parliament buildings in Latvia and Estonia to demand stronger measures by their leaders to separate from the Soviet Union.

Two days later, the government of Lithuania agreed to suspend laws approved earlier by dissidents demanding a free Lithuania. After Gorbachev had imposed sanctions, this action was taken in the hope that the Russian President would lift the embargo. Gorbachev met with the Lithuanian prime minister and agreed to begin talks if the republic lifted its declaration of independence.

Another important step was taken by the two Germanys on May 18 in their efforts to become one nation once again. Each nation's ministers agreed to approve a treaty to merge their economies and to make the West German mark legal tender in both countries.

In Romania's first free elections on May 20, ex-Communists swept to a surprising victory as Ion Iliescu and the National Salvation Front won a surprise victory.

With the food situation in the Soviet Union worsening daily, shoppers crowded stores on May 25 and bought up everything in sight as panic buying swept the nation. The government announcement that there would be sharp increases in food prices—it had long been subsidized under previous Communist leaders—prompted shoppers to start hoarding. Store shelves were left largely empty, further exasperating the Russian people who were close to the explosive point.

Meanwhile, in Armenia on May 29 some 23 died in clashes between government troops and civilians as unrest spread throughout the republic.

One of Gorbachev's strongest opponents was elected President of Russia, the nation's largest Soviet republic. Boris N. Yeltsin was elected by a four-vote margin in the third round of balloting.

President Bush and President Gorbachev met in Washington June 1, 1990, for their second conference and reached a broad understanding that included a reduction in nuclear arms and chemical weapons. Bush also signed a trade treaty that Gorbachev had long sought.

Bush and Gorbachev signed several pacts and joint statements in which both countries agreed to cut strategic nuclear arsenals by about one-third. Each nation will be limited to a total of 6,000 warheads in their missile, submarine and bomber organizations. Both presidents agreed that their nations would cease production of chemical arms and reduce their current stockpiles to 5,000 tons which is roughly 20 percent of the United States' stockpile. They agreed that chemical weapons would start to be destroyed in 1992 with appropriate on-site inspections.

Protocols were exchanged for two existing but unratified treaties that limit underground nuclear explosions to 150 kilotons.

Presidents Bush and Gorbachev reaffirmed their nations' commitment to complete a treaty to reduce conventional forces in Europe at some future date.

President Bush agreed to the normalization of trade between the two countries, and extended a long-term agreement under which the Soviet Union will buy a minimum annual amount of 10 million metric tons of grain from the United States.

A number of other economic agreements were signed to expand passenger air service between the two countries, end discriminatory shipping practices and provide mutual assistance between customs services to combat narcotics traffic.

With the world's major nuclear powers agreeing to scale back their nuclear arsenals, the United States Department of Defense pushed ahead with non-nuclear weapons such as adaptations of the standard cruise missile into vehicles that could fly long distances and circle a target repeatedly if necessary before homing in on an enemy radar's electronic signals and destroy whatever target they represented. "Tacit Rainbow" has enormous implications for seeking out and destroying hidden targets. Another missile, the Long-Range Conventional Stand-off Weapon, can fly 2,000 miles to destroy railyards, bridges and major industrial targets.

The United States Navy began development of the Tomahawk cruise missile for nuclear or non-nuclear warheads in 1984 and ordered several thousand of them, most of which had non-nuclear warheads. The Tomahawk has a range up to 1500 miles and sells for $1 million to $1.4 million each depending on its warhead.

Cruise missiles with non-nuclear warheads can be carried by ships and aircraft giving them the ability to respond quickly to an emergency. Their use against massed troops, communications centers and dug-in armies gives an incalcuable advantage to the United States.

After President Gorbachev returned home following the Washington conference he was challenged again by Boris N. Yeltsin as president of the Republic of Russia. The newly-elected Yeltsin insisted that the Russian republic had primacy over the central government of the Soviet Union.

Byelorussia, the Soviet republic primarily affected by the Chernobyl atomic disaster in 1986, appealed for international assistance to relocate and give medical aid to more than two million people, including 600,000 children, as officials admitted for the first time that the situation was much worse than first revealed.

Diplomat Vladimir Brovokov spoke for his republic saying that one-fifth of its 10 million people must be moved from areas contaminated by fall-out radiation in 27 cities and more than 2,000 villages, even though Chernobyl is not in the republic.

Israel sought to resolve its growing problems with the Palestinians by forming the most conservative cabinet in its history. On June 8, Prime Minister Yitzhak Shamir established a government of hard liners committed to expanding Jewish settlements in the occupied territories. This action further alienated Israel's relations with the United States. Later, Secretary of State James A. Baker, III, said, "When you are serious about peace, call us." After March Israel was virtually without a government after Shamir lost a no-confidence vote in the Israeli Knesset by refusing to accept Baker's plan for peace talks with the Palestinians. But the Labor Party failed to form a cabinet and Shamir was successful when he aligned his party with several smaller parties. The new government was narrowly approved by the Knesset and the Labor Party was shut out.

Meanwhile the Palestinian intifada continued and the death toll of Israelis and Palestinians passed 1,000. The Shamir government refused to even consider peace talks with the Palestinians and the killing went on without a let-up.

Bulgaria held its first free multi-party election in 45 years on June 10. Ex-Communists among the Socialists surprisingly won most elections.

Three days later rioting broke out in Bucharest, Romania, and troops were forced to fire upon anti-government protesters. The President summoned thousands of miners to the capital to restore order. They did so, but with unnecessary brutality that would later cost the government dearly in public support.

South Africa's black leader Nelson Mandela began an eight-city American visit on June 20. He was greeted everywhere by cheering crowds. He told President Bush that he could not rule out the use of force to achieve racial equality.

Iran, in desperate straits after its eight-year war with Iraq, suffered another kind of tragedy. An earthquake on June 21 killed 40,000 people in the heavily-populated Caspian Sea region in the nation's northwest provinces. Scores of towns and villages were devastated by the temblor that registered 7.3 on the Richter scale.

Ninety-three nations were represented in London on June 29 when a new agreement to control the ozone layer in the atmosphere was signed. The conferees agreed to halt production of chemicals that were destroying the protective layer of the earth's atmosphere. The end of the century was agreed upon as the target date to end such production.

Lithuania reached an agreement with the Soviet Union on June 29 to suspend its independence declaration for 100 days as Gorbachev agreed to negotiate its demands. The Soviet Union reopened the oil pipeline, thus averting a serious confrontation.

The "Cold War" ended officially July 6 at a London conference. President Bush and other North Atlantic Treaty Organization leaders proposed joint action with Moscow and East European nations, saying, "We are no longer adversaries." They solemnly declared they would adopt a new defensive strategy to make nuclear forces "truly weapons of last resort."

With growing opposition to Gorbachev's rule as President of the Soviet Union, he still managed to maintain his party's leadership when the 28th Congress met on July 10. But Boris N. Yeltsin quit the party, as did leaders of the Moscow and Leningrad city councils. Yeltsin had long championed a free-market economy and charged that Gorbachev was proceeding too slowly. Gorbachev survived an outpouring of opposition by remaining head of the Communist Party as General Secretary and President of the Soviet Union.

The USSR and Germany agreed July 16 on NATO membership for a unified Germany. This agreement paved the way for a united Germany. Gorbachev and Chancellor Helmut Kohl also agreed to lift most other barriers to unification.

In effect, Gorbachev chose to trade the security provided by 360,000

Russian troops in East Germany for promises made by Kohl of an enduring Soviet-German friendship.

President Saddam Hussein of Iraq became an increasingly disturbing influence in the Middle East—throughout the world in fact—during July as he pressured the Organization of Petroleum Exporting Countries to raise oil prices. Despite his own vast reserve of oil, the high cost of Hussein's eight-year war with Iran had almost destroyed his nation's economy. But there were other steps that Iraq's president had taken in recent months that caused even more concern to nations in the Middle East and throughout the world. In Great Britain authorities seized devices bound for Iraq that could trigger atomic weapons. British customs also impounded a shipment of giant tubes that experts claimed could be used to make a gun barrel to fire nuclear or chemical weapons hundreds of miles to a target.

Despite Iraq's protestations of innocence, Saddam Hussein moved 30,000 troops to the Kuwaiti border and accused the heads of that country and the United Arab Emirates of undermining prices by producing more oil than OPEC had approved. At first, western leaders believed these accusations were just more bellicose talk from a region known for such threats. But then Iraq threatened violence against Kuwait. Mideast diplomats agreed to boost oil prices by $3 a barrel and Kuwaiti officials met in Saudi Arabia to defuse the situation.

Hussein's true intentions became evident on August 2, 1990, when Iraqi troops, spearheaded by tanks, invaded Kuwait and occupied it in a matter of hours. The emir was forced to flee his unarmed country as hundreds died, and Iraq announced that Kuwait no longer existed and that it had been annexed to Iraq.

Suddenly there was a full-blown crisis in the Middle East and Saudi Arabia's leaders feared they were next to be invaded. Her border with Iraq and Kuwait was fortified, but Saudi leaders knew they would be no match for Iraq's armed forces.

Not since the Korean War had the United Nations moved so expeditiously to counter this blatant act of aggression. While European nations placed an embargo on Iraqi oil, the U.N. Security Council on August 6 ordered a sweeping trade and financial boycott of Iraq and Kuwait. The next day President Bush ordered troops, planes and tanks to Saudi Arabia to protect it. Two days later the Arab League voted to send troops to defend Saudi Arabia. On August 12 Bush ordered United States forces to block Iraqi oil exports and most imports. Some American reservists were called up starting on August 20. The Iraqis, stunned by the U.N. action, and the prompt response by the Arab League, countered by moving Americans in Iraq and Kuwait to strategic sites as human shields.

Then, even more serious for Iraq, the United Nations on August 25 gave the United States and other nations in the coalition the right to enforce the embargo by force. Iraq's President Hussein, with most of the world condemning his actions, permitted foreign women and children to leave.

President Bush's forthright action was approved by the vast majority of the American people, and at this stage he received overwhelming support from Congress.

South Africa continued to seethe with ethnic unrest when more than 500 were killed on August 23 in clashes between Zulu and Xhosa tribes in the black townships east and west of Johannesburg. These factional clashes were caused by differences between the African National Congress and the separatist movement under the Zulus. Four days later thousands of blacks remained home, refusing to go to work, to honor those who died.

Brian Keenan, the Irish hostage who had been held in Lebanon for four years, was released August 25. Meanwhile, the 15-year-old civil war continued. Now it involved rival Christian forces.

The YF-22 fighter, developed by Lockheed Aircraft, was unveiled on August 30 at Palmdale. It proved to be significantly different from the competing Northrop version of the new Air Force fighter.

Air Force contracts worth $80 billion were at stake for the winner of the fly-off competition for 750 aircraft, with the possibility of an additional $40 billion for 450 Navy aircraft.

Lockheed had teamed with Boeing and General Dynamics to design the aircraft at a cost of $1.1 billion for two experimental aircraft. The Air Force funded $818 million of the total and the companies spent the remainder. The YF-22 has a shorter fuselage than the Northrop entry, a smaller wing, two horizontal and vertical stabilizers and conventional jet engine inlets. Lockheed opted for maneuvering and dog-fighting capability whereas Northrop decided to emphasize speed and stealth technology.

The winner of the competition would replace the Air Force's F-15 fighter which had been flying for 18 years and which would be 30 years old when the new fighter was ready to replace it.

In Europe, the two Germanys were reunited on August 31 after officials of East and West Germany signed a treaty of reunification. Ten days later Russian and German officials agreed that the unified Germany would share the cost of withdrawing the Soviet Union's military forces from the former East Germany on a two-year schedule. Two days later the four wartime powers signed a treaty relinquishing occupation rights in Germany. After a treaty was signed on September 20 a formal ceremony on October 3 completed the reunification process.

Meanwhile, the United States' buildup in the Middle East continued as combat aircraft were sent to several Gulf nations to help defend Saudi Arabia. Presidents Bush and Gorbachev pledged joint action to reverse Iraq's conquest of Kuwait. The ring around Iraq was further tightened on September 25 when the U.N. Security Council voted an embargo on air traffic with Iraq.

Lebanon's civil war came to a shaky conclusion October 13 when Christian General Michel Aoun surrendered his military forces. They had been fighting Lebanese government forces but capitulated after Syria introduced airpower to supplement its ground forces.

President Gorbachev's plan to transform the Soviet Union's economy from central planning and state ownership to one ruled by market conditions won approval of the Supreme Soviet on October 19. "Life itself has brought us to the transition to the market," the Soviet Union's President said. "We must give back to the people their natural sense of being their own master. And only a normal economy, the market, can do that."

His plan had been bitterly debated for three years and marked an historic change in the Soviet Union which was now abandoning socialism after it had ruled the nation for 73 years.

Gorbachev said the changes at first would bring hardship but he promised the Soviet Union's 290 million people a better life in the future.

Conservative Communists had long opposed changes but as the vote was taken—333 for the new plan with only 12 against it but with 34 abstentions—one deputy said, "We have to pass something and then get to work."

The United Nations Security Council passed a resolution October 29 making Iraq liable for damages, injuries and financial losses following its invasion and occupation of Kuwait. This was the council's ninth censure of Iraq since the crisis in the Persian Gulf began. United Nations members were invited to prepare claims against Iraq and to gather data on Iraqi war crimes. This U.N. action also demanded that Iraq permit the resupply of besieged foreign embassies in Kuwait.

This latest measure was adopted by a vote of 13 to 0 with Cuba and Yemen abstaining. The voting was delayed while the Soviet Union tried to keep diplomatic efforts from collapsing but to no avail.

Iraq's United Nations ambassador, Abdul Amir al-Anbari denounced the resolution, calling it an "escalation" to permit the United States and its allies to claim they "have exhausted all attempts to achieve peace and that they have failed and that the option of war is the only one left."

At the urging of non-aligned nations, U.N. Secretary General Javier Perez de Cuellar was authorized to "undertake diplomatic efforts to reach a peaceful solution to the crisis."

His later trip to Baghdad ended in failure.

Despite the effects of a troubled economy in the United States, which was anticipated to be damaging to the re-election of incumbents, they won almost all their seats in Congress in the November 6 elections. The turnout proved surprisingly low with only 36.4 percent of eligible voters going to the polls. Only one senator, Republican Rudy Boschwitz of Minnesota, was defeated. Democrat Paul Wellstone, a college professor, was elected to his seat. Democrats picked up only one seat, while they won eight seats in the House. In the gubernatorial races, six out of 23 incumbents were unseated, and party control of 14 governorships changed hands.

The growing American involvement in the Persian Gulf had no impact on the election because most candidates of both parties had supported President Bush's actions.

Two days after the election President Bush ordered a large increase in the number of American units deployed to the Persian Gulf. He announced that he was almost doubling the size of these forces to approximately 400,000 men and women by early 1991. He justified this action by saying that the multi-national coalition opposing Iraq needed "an adequate offensive military option."

Critics protested that the President was changing the character of the U.S. involvement from a defensive position to one permitting offensive operations.

Bush had earlier claimed that Article 5 of the U.N. Charter offered sufficient legal justification for the U.S. to come to the defense of Kuwait by attacking Iraqi forces. Some members of Congress disagreed, along with some U.N. diplomats, claiming that a new Security Council resolution was needed before armed intervention was taken.

The President's action in doubling the American commitment to the Middle East made it necessary, he said, to make the first large callup of Reserves and Army National Guard units.

The following day Defense Secretary Richard B. Cheney said the Pentagon was no longer planning to rotate troops in the Gulf because of the need to expand the region's combat potential for military action.

The five permanent members of the United Nations Security Council agreed in a draft resolution November 26 that Iraq's withdrawal from Kuwait should be accomplished by January 1, 1991. Officials of the Soviet Union protested and, in deference to their pleas that further diplomatic initiatives be taken, the date was moved to January 15.

Secretary of State Baker chaired the final meeting and presided over the vote of Resolution 678 on November 29. He opened the session by quoting the words of the late Emperor of Ethiopia, Hailie Selassie, in his appeal to the League of Nations (the U.N.'s predecessor) in 1936 that his country be saved from invasion by Fascist Italy. "The League's efforts to redress aggression failed and international disorder and war ensued."

Baker continued, "History has now given us a second chance. With the Cold War behind us, we now have the chance to build a world which was envisioned . . . by the Founders of the United Nations."

Sheik Sabah al-Ahmad Al Sabah, foreign minister of the exiled Kuwaiti government, made an emotional plea to save his country from "the atrocities of an Iraqi regime which has run amok."

The resolution was approved and the council agreed to take no military action before the January 15 deadline unless provoked by Iraq.

The Soviet Union's foreign minister said the deadline would give Iraq "one last chance . . . to allow the instinct of self-preservation to work." For the anxious Russian people, he stated that the Soviet Union would not send troops to the Gulf because "the tragedy of Afghanistan is still fresh in the minds of our people."

Several hours before the final vote in New York, Iraqi President Saddam Hussein said, "If war breaks out, we will fight in a way that will make all Arabs and Muslims proud."

After the United Nations voted for the resolution, President Bush said, "I think up to now we have failed to have Saddam Hussein understand how clearly the whole world feels against what he's doing, and I think this new approach will guarantee he does understand."

The following day Bush said he was ready to "go the extra mile" when he announced that Secretary of State Baker was available to go to Baghdad to talk to leading Iraqi officials, and he invited Iraq's foreign minister to meet with him in the White House.

President Hussein accepted the offer on December 6 and announced that he would free all foreign hostages in Iraq and Kuwait.

Bush's action to offer direct talks was motivated by his desire to reduce the concern of America's lawmakers and all Americans who were expressing doubts that the United States had fully exploited diplomatic initiatives.

"In our country, I know there are fears about another Vietnam," Bush said in a television press conference. "Let me assure you. Should military action be required, this will not be another Vietnam; this will not be a protracted, drawn-out war. The forces arrayed are different, the opposition is different, the countries united against him (Hussein) are different, the topography of Kuwait is different and the motivation of our all-volunteer force is superb.

"I want peace, but if there must be war, we will not permit our troops to have their hands tied behind their backs, and I pledge to you there will not be any murky ending. If one American soldier has to go into battle, that soldier will have enough force behind him to win, and then to get out as soon as possible, as soon as the U.S. objectives have been achieved. I will never, ever agree to a halfway effort."

In regard to Baker's trip to Baghdad, the President said it would not be a "trip of concession" but would be aimed at convincing Hussein that the United States was not bluffing about its willingness to use force to liberate Kuwait. "The best way to get that across is one-on-one, Baker looking him right in the eye.

"I am not suggesting discussions that will result in anything less than Iraq's complete withdrawal from Kuwait, restoration of Kuwait's legitimate government and freedom of all hostages."

In response, Iraq's ruling Revolutionary Command Council, said, "We accept the idea of the invitation and the meeting," but it condemned Bush as "arrogant," and contemptuous of Arabs and Moslems, and "the enemy of God."

While these exchanges were going on, Prime Minister Thatcher of Great Britain stunned the world by announcing her resignation. She was taking such action, she said, due to differences between her and members of her own party. She was replaced on November 28 by John Major, the Chancellor of the Exchequer, who promised to continue her policies. The "Iron Lady" had changed Great Britain as few of her predecessors had ever done. She had been elected in 1979 and proceeded to abolish socialism in almost all areas of British life.

Rumors that at least 4,000 civilians were killed in the December 1989 invasion of Panama by American armed forces, despite official denials, persisted this year. The official casualty estimate was that 515 Panamanians were killed, including 202 civilians. One of the causes for the disparity in figures resulted from the fact that hundreds of Panamanian defense force members cast off their uniforms at the start of the invasion and dressed in civilian clothes.

The Government of Panama released figures showing the total death toll was 570, including many who were killed in the looting that followed the invasion. The Committee for Human Rights, a respected independent organization, came up with a figure of 565.

Responsible officials now deny that there were mass graves and hidden cemeteries, allegations made by irresponsible groups who made the claims to further their own political ends.

On December 12, President Bush approved federal loan guarantees up to one billion dollars for the Soviet Union to purchase American food. He also pledged further shipments of food and medical supplies and American support for a Soviet "special association" relationship with the

International Monetary Fund and the World Bank. This would be a step toward full membership.

The President also proposed a summit in Moscow February 11–13, 1991, to sign a strategic nuclear weapons treaty.

The American offer of assistance came at a dire time for the Soviet Union because food shortages had prompted many Russians to hoard food, thereby increasing the problem.

In addition to this American action, many other countries promised public and/or private humanitarian aid.

The President's action came after Foreign Minister Shevardnadze and Secretary of State Baker met in Washington and the Russian official had publicly asked for American aid; the first time a Russian official had ever asked Washington for assistance.

The Soviet Union's Foreign Minister shocked the world December 21 by resigning from his top office, although the Congress of People's Deputies had to approve his action. He did so, he said, because the Soviet Union was headed towards dictatorship.

CHAPTER 34

Desert Storm

AFTER PRESIDENT BUSH AUTHORIZED A BUILDUP IN THE PERSIAN GULF in August, 1990, Navy carriers were soon on the scene. The "Independence" arrived in the Gulf of Oman on August 7 while the "Dwight D. Eisenhower" moved through the Suez Canal with the permission of the Egyptian Government as it headed for the Persian Gulf. Between them they had 164 airplanes that were ready to fight. Their presence undoubtedly proved a deterrent to Iraq's President Saddam Hussein whose goal was to annex Saudi Arabia. President Bush's forthright reaction to the crisis was approved by the vast majority of the American people.

The Air Force and Army needed six months before their organizations could build up sufficient forces to defend Saudi Arabia. If Hussein had moved quickly—a possibility that became a nightmare for American commanders—only carrier aviation would have been available to resist his massive ground and air forces. It would have put up a good fight but without a chance of overcoming Iraq's vastly superior air fleet.

While the buildup continued, the United States Navy and its coalition partners intercepted Iraq-bound shipping under the United Nations embargo so that Iraq's armed forces soon began to feel the pinch as many supplies and spare parts became scarce. Navy sealift ships carried 95 percent of the American military cargo to Saudi Arabia while Marine equipment was prepositioned aboard Navy warehouse ships in the early days of the Persian Gulf War.

After General H. Norman Schwarzkopf took command of United Nations forces in Saudi Arabia he and the leaders of the coalition drew up a plan to defend Saudi Arabia and, if ordered to do so, to defeat the Iraqis. It was a complex plan that relied heavily on airpower and deception. Simply, it was designed to deceive the Iraqi command about the coalition's true intentions by destroying the electronic eyes and ears of its communications system, bomb its key installations into rubble and then encircle its armies and destroy them. One of the plan's major goals was to target Iraq's airfields and air defense networks to deny its air force an opportunity to challenge the Allied air assault.

Major deceptions were devised to use diversionary actions, such as amphibious exercises off Kuwait, and saturation bombing to confuse the Iraqis about the primary focus of a land assault. It was hoped that these moves would keep numerous Iraqi divisions along the Kuwaiti coast to guard against an amphibious assault, and to deploy additional infantry divisions along the Kuwaiti-Saudi border to block an anticipated allied land attack.

The plan's goal was to isolate the Iraqi army in Kuwait by threatening an amphibious assault while the coalition army made a huge, high-speed maneuver with two full army corps 200 miles west of the Kuwaiti-Iraqi border. These army units would then sweep across Iraq to the Euphrates River and trap the Iraqis in Kuwait. It was hoped that such an action might instill a doubt in the minds of the Iraqi commanders whether they were headed for Baghdad.

After Kuwait was invaded by the Iraqis in August the United Nations Security Council passed 12 resolutions calling upon Iraq to withdraw and it imposed a series of sanctions. The last one was passed on November 29, 1990, and authorized the use of "all necessary means" to drive Iraq from Kuwait unless it withdrew by January 15, 1991.

U.N. Secretary General Javier Pérez de Cuéllar made one last diplomatic effort to avoid war by meeting on January 13 with President Saddam Hussein in Baghdad. Four days earlier, American Secretary of State James A. Baker had met in Geneva, Switzerland, with Iraq's Foreign Minister Tariq Aziz on the same quest. Both meetings ended in failure.

War became inevitable when the United States Congress gave President Bush authority to use "all means necessary" on January 12, 1991, when they voted as the crisis headed for a showdown.

These meetings with Iraqi officials were last-ditch efforts to end the crisis without war because President Bush had decided in the previous November not to wait for the embargo to bring Iraq to it senses, and to liberate Kuwait by force. At that time Schwarzkopf and General Colin Powell, chairman of the Joint Chiefs of Staff, insisted that they needed 514,000 American troops to do the job effectively. The President supported their request. Both generals insisted that the policy of "incrementalization" that had governed the war in Indochina must not be repeated because they knew from personal experience that it was a strategy for defeat.

While sealift ships brought the bulk of the troops and their equipment to Saudi Arabia, C-5s, C-141s and C-130s of the Military Air Transport Command flew around the clock to airlift high-priority men and equipment.

The Schwarzkopf plan to invade Iraq was a variation of the Air-Land Battle developed by Army planners to distribute firepower over the whole depth of a battlefield for 100 miles or more. Tanks, armed helicopters, anti-tank aircraft, multiple rocket launchers, self-propelled artillery and "deep-strike" bombers were assigned to meet an enemy strong in tanks.

Analysts of the Iran-Iraq war had noted that the Iraqis had fought a static, trench-type war such as had been conducted in World War I. Against the ill-equipped Iranians this strategy of fighting a war of attrition saved Iraqi lives. Schwarzkopf and his planners knew that the Iraqis were dug into fixed positions to fight his coalition army, and he was confident they were inviting disaster. With his powerful mobile forces, Schwarzkopf gave orders to pound these fixed positions with bombs and ship bombardment until they were, in effect, impotent to withstand his rapid-moving armies.

The theory behind the Air-Land Battle is that successful military campaigns are founded on a few clearly-defined concepts. The most important truism is that mobile armies almost always defeat static defenses and that control of the air and control of communications is essential. Through the synchronization of air, land and sea forces, maximum force can be concentrated against an enemy's weakest point.

From the outset, General Schwarzkopf's plan was "to put the Republican Guard" out of business. Supposedly, Hussein's elite force would be the adversary to beat before victory in the Gulf could be achieved.

Schwarzkopf ordered his air forces to attack during the early morning hours of January 17, 1991 (Iraqi time), and a huge aerial armada of hundreds of coalition airplanes headed for their targets. The attack began less than 17 hours after expiration of a United Nations Security Council deadline for Iraq to withdraw from Kuwait.

President Bush's spokesman, Marlin M. Fitzwater, announced the air attack at 7 p.m. Washington time when he said, "The liberation of Kuwait has begun." He revealed that the operation was being conducted under its code name "Desert Storm."

Air Force F-15 pilot Captain Steve Tate quickly shot down an Iraqi Mirage F-1 in the first kill of the war. The Iraqi aircraft was locked on the tail of another American F-15 when Tate fired a Sparrow air-to-air missile. The Mirage blew up, lighting up the sky, and it continued to burn until it exploded on the ground.

As Tate turned back for home base he could see the city of Baghdad in the distance—"lit up like a huge blanket of Christmas lights. . . . The entire city was just sparkling at me."

Then American, Saudi Arabian, British and French pilots dropped their bombs on the city. Lights flashed as bombs and missiles exploded and tracers lit up the night sky while guns on the ground went into action.

The air war went on throughout the night as cruise missiles and F-117 stealth aircraft sought out the Iraqi high command headquarters to cut communication links, destroy key government ministries and eliminate Iraq's control network. Iraq's airfields were struck repeatedly but the Iraqi air force remained largely on the ground, unable or fearful of defending the air space above their country.

The coalition air forces of the United States, Great Britain, France, Saudi Arabia and Kuwait established air superiority within 48 hours and eventually gained air supremacy when most Iraqi pilots refused to fight.

Iraq responded to these attacks by ordering the firing of a Scud missile at Saudi Arabia and eight others into Israel. Although it was not a member of the coalition, Israel threatened to retaliate, but refrained when her people suffered only a few casualties.

One American plane was shot down that first night and its pilot, Navy Lieutenant Commander Michael S. Seicher, was killed. Two British aircraft were also shot down and one Kuwaiti.

America's high-technology weapons proved effective despite earlier scandals involving Pentagon extravagance, contract fraud and faulty weaponry. The F-117A stealth fighters, which cost $100 million each, easily evaded Iraqi radar and were successful in striking key communications targets.

Tomahawk cruise missiles were used in combat for the first time and these $1.3 million missiles were sometimes effective against high-priority targets but they actually hit only half of their intended targets. More than 288 Tomahawks were launched from ships in the Persian Gulf and the Red Sea.

The Patriot, a radar-guided anti-missile missile costing $1 million each, was used for the first time. The Scud, a Soviet-made, liquid-fueled missile with ranges between 150 and 400 miles, proved to be a terror weapon that was highly inaccurate and of little military significance. But its indiscriminate firing at populated areas in Israel became a highly-emotional issue. The Patriot countered the Scud effectively, knocking almost all of them out of the air but it was not powerful enough to destroy the Scud's warhead. Thus the Scud's warhead often fell into populated areas in Israel, and a few times in Saudi Arabia, and killed quite a number of people as the air war progressed.

Oil prices on the New York Mercentile Exchange plunged $10.56 to $21.44 a barrel in heavy trading on January 17 in what was claimed as the largest one-day drop on record.

United States warplanes began bombing Iraq from Turkey's Incirlik air base on January 18, in effect opening up a second front against Iraq.

In the most intensive aerial offensive in history (the coalition had 1,800 aircraft while Iraq had 750), Iraq's air force was eliminated from combat, anti-aircraft defenses were largely nullified, and ballistic missile launchers were attacked. Among the special targets hit were those storing or producing nuclear, biological and chemical warfare facilities.

During the first three weeks allied coalition air forces flew more than 42,000 sorties. America's six carriers were positioned in the Red Sea and the Persian Gulf. These narrow, restricted waters were normally used by large numbers of commercial ships. As a result the carriers were highly vulnerable and 25 percent of their planes had to be used to protect their task groups. In addition to their self-protective role, they also covered the vital right flank of the Desert Storm operation. Their presence would have been even more crucial if Iran had elected to intervene in the war against coalition forces.

In addition to American Air Force bombers and fighters, there were a large number of Marine tactical aircraft based on the Saudi Arabian Peninsula or aboard amphibious warfare ships offshore. Marine F/A-18 Hornets, AV-8B Harriers, OV-10 Broncos and AH-1 helicopter gunships used air-to-ground ordnance such as the Standoff Land Attack Missile (SLAM) the high-speed anti-radiation missile HARM, the Shrike anti-radar missile, Walleye bombs, regular iron bombs, Rockeye Cluster bombs and Harpoon anti-ship missiles.

The venerable A-6 Intruder and the F/A-18 Hornet bore the brunt of strikes by carrier planes. The last two A-7E squadrons were on board the USS "Kennedy," and the Corsair IIS were on their 26th year prior to retirement.

One of the United States Navy's assignments in the early part of the war was to destroy 36 bridges in Iraq. Carrier planes used old-fashioned gravity bombs and, reminiscent of Vietnam in their attacks against the Dragon's Jaw bridge, they failed to destroy them after 790 sorties. Air Force planes were added to the Navy's strike operations and with their "smart" bombs quickly dropped the remaining bridges. These laser-guided bombs had long proven their effectiveness but only the Navy's

A-6 Intruder was equipped with the necessary kits to permit their use. As a result, Navy aircraft dropped only 10 percent of the "smart" bombs.

As the air war pounded away at targets in Iraq and Kuwait, the level of destruction rose to incredible heights. It took 9,000 bombs in World War II to destroy a "point target" such as an aircraft shelter, and 300 unguided bombs in Vietnam. Only two precision bombs were needed in this war. Air Force B-52 bombers concentrated on Republican Guard divisions, carpet-bombing areas where they were deployed, while Air Force F-117s, F-15s and F-111s sought out precision targets. Later it was learned that some defensive lines were left virtually unmanned as Iraqi soldiers deserted and headed for home. The psychological impact on Saddam Hussein's armies was explosive, causing two out of every five Iraqi soldiers to desert. At first it was believed that the bombings had killed a great number of Iraqis, but this was later disproved. But the impact on Hussein's front-line army, estimated at 540,000 but now reduced to only 183,000, was just as severe as if they had been killed in battle, as Iraqis deserted their units by the tens of thousands. After the war it was learned that Iraqi's, 42 divisions in southern Iraq and Kuwait were severely undermanned, due largely to the 88,000 tons of bombs dropped during the war.

The United States Central Command in Riyadh revealed on February 14 that the allies had destroyed 1,300 of an estimated 4,280 tanks (this number was raised to 2,100 tanks a week later). It was also announced that 1,450 of 2,870 armored personnel carriers were destroyed and 1,100 of Iraq's 3,110 artillery pieces.

With atrocities mounting in Kuwait, and the nation's oil wells set on fire by the Iraqis, plus a 60-mile long, 20-mile-wide oil slick deliberately spilled into the Persian Gulf as an act of "environmental terrorism," Schwarzkopf ordered the ground invasion to begin on February 24. His coalition forces numbered 690,000 men and women against a demoralized enemy about a third of its size. The coalition commander believed that the interdiction of supply lines by his aircraft had weakened front-line Iraqi troops to the point of starvation, while the bombing of bridges had cut off routes for reinforcement or escape. Schwarzkopf decided to seal the trap in which the Iraqi army found itself. With amphibious forces threatening to land on the shores of Kuwait's Persian Gulf, Schwarzkopf ordered the main thrust of his forces to advance into southern Kuwait.

Meanwhile, a Saudi-Kuwaiti mechanized task force moved into southern Kuwait along the gulf and the American 1st Marine Division, in combination with the 1st Brigade of the United States Army's 2nd Armored Division and the 2nd Marine Division, moved forward on their left flank.

Schwarzkopf ordered another mass movement of troops on the extreme western part of the battlefield to move forward because the vast majority of Iraq's ground forces were in Kuwait. With control of the air, he knew that the Iraqi commander would be incapable of moving out to counter this move, even if they were aware of it. He was convinced that Iraq's "eyes and ears" had been destroyed.

The allied main force, the United States VII Corps with its strong armored units, supplemented by British and French tank divisions and two American airborne divisions, covered 200 miles in two days against little opposition. Then they attacked the positions of the vaunted Republican Guards.

The French 6th Armored Division set up a screen even farther to the west to prevent any escape or reinforcement, and to confuse the Iraqis as to whether they might be headed for Baghdad. At one point they were only 150 miles from the capital, with nothing in between to bar their way.

In one of the greatest armored sweeps of all time troops from the 101st Airborne Division secured airfields and blocked escape routes across the Euphrates River. The 24th Mechanized Division then surrounded the Republican Guards. A pause was ordered so that coalition forces could rest, refuel and rearm.

When they attacked the Republican Guards were too demoralized to put up much of a fight and their resistance was broken within 48 hours.

The pre-invasion bombing campaign had quarantined the field of battle, and coalition air forces shifted to the south, to the immediate theater of operations. Bombs were dropped in front of advancing troops to destroy barriers and to burn off oil-filled trenches the Iraqis had dug to slow the advance of coalition troops. Bombs, rockets and missiles destroyed thousands of Iraqi tanks, armored vehicles and artillery guns.

Iraqi troops began to desert as casualties mounted. Some surrendered to coalition units while others fled northward, abandoning their positions.

In eastern Kuwait, while amphibious forces threatened to land from their ships in the gulf (they were not needed), two Marine divisions broke through the lines despite minefields, barbed wire and the threat of chemical weapons constantly from massed artillery. Schwarzkopf said of their advance, "If I use words like brilliant, it would really be an under-description of the absolutely superb job that they did in breaching the so-called 'impenetrable barrier.'

"It was a classic—absolutely classic—military breaching of a very, very tough minefield with barbed wire, fire trenches-type barrier. They went through the first barrier like it was water, then went across into the second barrier line."

American, French, British, Saudi and Egyptian forces followed through their breaches, fortunately meeting unexpectedly light resistance while encountering masses of Iraqis who wanted to surrender.

As the Iraqis clogged the roads into Iraq's interior, coalition airplanes hounded them every mile of the way. The roads north of Kuwait City became clogged with retreating Iraqi trucks and armored vehicles.

American Navy carriers focused their attacks on two roads leading north from Kuwait City to Basra, the stronghold of the Republican Guards. While they bombed the roads, Air Force B-52 bombers devastated the area with thousand-pound bombs.

Navy jets went below the low clouds and dropped anti-tank and anti-personnel Rockeye cluster bombs. After each cluster exploded it sent a deadly shower of armor-piercing bombs that shredded all cars and trucks within their range.

Allied troops were advancing so fast that pilots had to be given new targets as they boarded their planes.

General Colin L. Powell, chairman of the Joint Chiefs of Staff, called Schwarzkopf at night on February 26 and asked him if he had "any problem with halting combat the following morning."

Schwarzkopf replied, "We've accomplished our military objectives, and that's as good a time as any other to cease the war."

The ground war was decided in the first 48 hours. President Bush announced on February 27 that "Kuwait is liberated. Iraq's army is defeated. Our military objectives are met." With these words he said the coalition would suspend offensive combat operations at midnight but he specified certain conditions that must be met by the Iraqis to make the suspension permanent.

"We must now begin to look beyond victory in war," the President said. "This war is now behind us. Ahead of us is the difficult task of assuring a potentially historic peace."

He said the next step was up to Saddam Hussein who must agree to: "Return immediately all coalition prisoners of war it holds, any citizens from other countries, and the remains of America and allied soldiers killed in combat; release all Kuwaitis it had seized, (reports indicated that thousands had been taken to Iraq) inform Kuwaiti authorities about the location and characteristics of any mines its forces planted at sea and on land; and comply fully with each of the 'relevant' resolutions passed by the United Nations Security Council in an effort to force the Iraqi occupiers to get out of Kuwait."

Saddam Hussein agreed to these terms and the ground war ended after 100 hours. This was 209 days after Hussein had invaded Kuwait.

In retrospect it is clear that the war was ended too soon. With coalition forces only 150 miles from Baghdad, with no intervening Iraqi troops to bar their approach, the Iraqi capital should have been surrounded and demands issued for Saddam Hussein's capture so he could have been placed on trial for his war crimes. He would have been quickly turned over if the alternative was occupation of Iraq's capital city. This was not done for political reasons. Other Arab nations were concerned that partition of Iraq would only lead to a rise to power of such nations as Syria and Iran who were considered equally menacing to free institutions in the region. Such reasoning has little merit and the region has had to live with a defiant Saddam Hussein who has increased his control of the Iraqi people. In the long run, this will only increase the problems in the Middle East because Saddam Hussein will always be a threat to peace as long as he controls Iraq.

Prior to the war, American military planners anticipated that there might be 20,000 American casualties so Schwarzkopf ordered that 18,000 hospital beds be set up in 65 hospital facilities staffed by 41,000 medical personnel.

This was considered a "worst-case estimate" and the actual number of casualties was a fraction of that number. During the 43-day war 147 Americans were killed and 357 wounded. Tragically, 35 of these Americans were killed by "friendly fire" from other American forces, while another 72 were injured. (One hundred American service people died prior to the war in non-combat accidents.)

Several months after the war ended Pentagon officials admitted there had been 28 instances of "friendly fire" from other American troops and that total casualties were revised from earlier estimates of six such incidents involving 11 deaths and 15 injured. Thus 23 percent of the death toll—mostly Army personnel—died at the hands of their comrades. Senior military officials said these deaths were due to the fluidity and intensity of the fighting.

Marine Lieutenant General Martin Brandtner, director of operations for the Joint Chiefs of Staff, characterized the revised estimate as "too much." He explained, "If we had plodded along methodically, conservatively, and hadn't gone after the Iraqis in the highly aggressive manner that we did, the casualty rate (from enemy fire) would have been significantly lower. So the very means by which we won the victory did cause to some extent the battlefield situation that resulted in some of these incidents."

He conceded that equipment failures contributed to the toll. He said equipment designed to identify friendly tanks frequently did not work. He said signals emitted by the equipment often could not penetrate the haze, dust, smoke and bad weather that prevailed over the battlefield for much of the conflict. A major contributing factor was the poor communications between units.

American troops were also responsible for the deaths of nine British soldiers and the wounding of 13 others.

Widespread use of shells made of depleted uranium was the key to identification of these instances of casualties due to friendly fire. Depleted uranium, the densest material on earth, leaves a telltale trace after a shell strikes a target that can be identified.

General Schwarzkopf also revealed in testimony to two congressional committees that despite the huge investment in sophisticated reconnaissance satellites it was impossible to get timely information about battle conditions to ground commanders and pilots.

In previous conflicts, he said, pilots on bombing missions were supplied with aerial photographs that were less than 24 hours old. "And therefore, as the battlefield changed, they were up to date on the changes that occurred on the battlefield. We didn't have that capability in this war and that's what we mean by tactical intelligence." He said the nation must invest in new systems capable of delivering "real time" intelligence to battlefield leaders.

He told committee members that during the war his commanders relied on reconnaissance photographs, pilot reports and judgment to make their estimates. He said after four weeks of bombardment he concluded that the Iraqi Army was "on the verge of collapse."

Pentagon officials revealed after the war that American military forces were poorly prepared at the start of the war to counter Iraq's threatened use of biological weapons. It was said that the first American troops "did not have a policy regarding vaccination against biological warfare agents," and that "vaccines were not available in significant quantities until early 1991."

This could have been disastrous because Iraq had weapons employing both anthrax and botulism toxins. Either germ weapon, used alone, could have created enormous numbers of fatalities and overtaxed the medical treatment system.

The Pentagon report claimed that high technology systems, including cruise missiles and stealth aircraft, proved "immensely effective" against Iraqi targets, (not borne out by post-war analysis) but the allied campaign to locate and destroy the enemy's low-technology but highly mobile Scud missiles was "very difficult and diverted significant resources."

The Allies repeatedly bombed targets it had already destroyed, and damaged utilities beyond military necessity. Key segments of Iraq's war-machine—nuclear and chemical weapons complexes—emerged un-seathed.

Defense Chief Cheney admitted that the Patriot missile defense system "worked, but imperfectly" in hitting Scud missiles but not in destroying their warheads. Obviously, he admitted, the Patriot needs extensive modifications.

The F-117 stealth fighter performed well but it is now apparent that it has serious limitations. Its laser-guided bombs hit only 60 percent of its targets. Many of the materials used in such full-stealth aircraft are very susceptible to damage and they are three times as costly as comparable conventional aircraft. Some of their radar absorbent material is actually soft to the touch, making stealth aircraft vulnerable on Navy carriers. This is hardly the type of material to stand up to the bump and grind world of tool boxes, tie-down chains and fender benders so common in the close quarters of a carrier. Such bumps and scrapes on metal aircraft pose little penalty aside from the man hours needed to repair them. On stealth aircraft, many of these small bumps will result in fairly complex repairs due to their exotic materials. If not repaired properly, much of the "stealthiness" will be lost. Even more important is the need for a controlled environment. In part this is due to the bonding material used on the skin of these aircraft. It is subject to accelerated deterioration when exposed to the elements. The manufacture of stealth aircraft involves the bonding of materials with vastly different qualities of expansion/contraction characteristics due to heat. Thus, over a period of time, these stresses weaken the bonding qualities of the airframe. Keeping a stealth aircraft in an environmentally controlled hangar is intended to minimize these stresses. This condition can be maintained on land, but borders on the impossible on ships at sea.

It is apparent that Navy officials should proceed slowly in embracing the concept for its carriers at a time when it cannot afford to fill its decks with first-rate conventional aircraft. Industry may some day develop the capacity to build a suitable, sturdy and affordable Navy stealth aircraft. Until then it would be wise for the Navy to procure conventional aircraft and not spend Naval Aviation into oblivion with a handful of aircraft of questionable capability. One of the lessons of the Gulf War should be kept in mind. Although no F-117s were lost, neither were any A-7s or F-111s that flew similar missions and they were two of the most vulnerable aircraft used in the war.

Coalition air forces lost 36 planes in combat. The American Air Force shot down 32 fixed-wing aircraft, while the Navy accounted for two more, and the Saudi Air Force another two.

Although Iraq has not released official casualty figures, experts believe there were 75,000 to 120,000 military dead with about 33,000 civilians killed.

Kurdish and Shiite Muslim rebels seized an opportunity to gain their independence from Iraq after the ceasefire but thousands were slaughtered by Iraqi troops who savagely put down their rebellion. In northern Iraq the United Nations had to guarantee the safety of the Kurds before they would return home after a mass exodus from their homeland.

Coalition armies have a record of fighting among themselves more than against their enemies. There was almost none of that in the Persian Gulf War. Right at the start when he took over his command Schwarzkopf instilled in each man and woman that they must remain almost unconscious of their specific service or even nationality. At the front, positioning of people relative to one service versus another was almost lacking. Schwarzkopf set the pattern that all services were as one with identical insignia on their uniforms (badges, name and rank), and without squadron or unit patches. These conditions contributed to a sense of oneness that is vital to success in a coalition involving diverse people from 28 nations. They were responsible for an incredible victory that will rank with the most successful battles of all time.

CHAPTER 35

An Old-Fashioned, Tough Recession

DEFENSE SECRETARY DICK CHENEY CANCELLED THE NAVY'S A-12 AT-tack plane on January 7, claiming that its contractors McDonnell Douglas and General Dynamics had mismanaged the program. He said it was obvious to him that the program involving 10,000 workers in 42 states could never meet the government's contract terms.

The two companies offered to restructure the program, build fewer airplanes and thereby save billions of dollars. But Cheney pointed out that $5 billion had already been allocated.

"This program cannot be sustained unless I ask Congress for more money and bail the contractors out," Cheney said. "But I have made the decision that I will not do that.

"No one can tell me exactly how much more it will cost to keep the program going. And I do not believe a bailout is in the national interest. If we cannot spend the taxpayers' money wisely, we will not spend it."

He said the contract was being terminated for "default," based on the "inability of the contractors to design, develop, fabricate, assemble and test A-12 aircraft."

Officials at McDonnell-Douglas and General Dynamics said they were "deeply disappointed" by Cheney's action and promised to fight the default aspect of the cancellation which would make them financially liable and to pursue unspecified financial claims against the government.

The end of the Cold War had one positive effect as the United States Defense Department announced on April 19 that it was removing about 20 percent of the 8,500 Soviet bloc targets assigned to its nuclear retaliatory force of 12,000 atomic and thermonuclear weapons in the event of an all-out war.

A two-year, top-secret review reached this conclusion in anticipation of arms control treaties and Pentagon budget cuts.

About 1,000 of these targets were in the former Warsaw Pact states of eastern Europe, while a similar number were removed from the list of targets in the Soviet Union.

Despite these reductions the Pentagon still had an over-kill capacity that needed to be sharply reduced to sensible proportions. In the past, four or more nuclear weapons were assigned to "high value" targets to assure 95 percent destruction but with new, highly accurate delivery systems that number are no longer needed.

Air Force Major General Joseph Halston told the Senate Armed Services Subcommittee on conventional forces and alliance defense that the Air Force was reducing its tactical fighter wings from 36 to 26 wings and thus would need fewer fighters.

The next day Air Force Secretary Donald Rice named the team headed by Lockheed as the winner of the $72 billion contract.

Lockheed's F-22 will replace the existing "air superiority" fighter, the F-15 Eagle, which will be 30 years old by the time the new aircraft goes into service.

Air Force Secretary Rice claimed that the technological superiority of United States aircraft was critical in the Persian Gulf War and that future threats will require even more advanced capability. He said the F-22's combination of stealth, high speed and agility will maintain the nation's superiority over foreign aircraft that have gained steadily in performance.

In the Soviet Union President Gorbachev fought off an attempt by his hard line critics to oust him as leader of the Communist Party on April 23. He accused them of wanting to return the country to a dictatorship.

He won the support of his radical rival, Russian Federation President Boris N. Yeltsin, on a program to stabilize the Soviet Union's economy. The two agreed on a new union treaty as the basis for holding the country together.

Yeltsin's willingness to support the government's economic stabilization program—which he had recently denounced—was his acceptance of the fact that the Soviet Union faced both an economic and political crisis.

Soviet health and energy officials revealed that their government was spending the equivalent of $16 billion a year on caring for the victims of Chernobyl and cleaning up the still-present radiation. They said the full cost of the disaster could be as high as $350 billion

The United States Air Force's Strategic Air Command, whose jet bombers and atomic weapons have given the Russians pause for more than 40 years in their grandiose scheme of world domination, announced that it was prepared for a new world order now that the cold war had ended. Its commanders envisage an equally important role as a conventional bomber strike force available to fight non-nuclear wars such as the Persian Gulf War.

Unfortunately the Strategic Air Command's failure to develop a new heavy bomber to replace the aging B-52 puts that mission in jeopardy. The B-1 remained out of action during the Gulf War due to engine problems (it was grounded for all but nuclear-alert missions) and the B-2 was unwisely selected as its successor despite its huge cost ($870 million each) and its continuing developmental problems. A "flying wing," the B-2 is inherently unstable and can only be made to fly normally through the use of costly "fly-by-wire" controls that sense its instability and correct the tendency through electronic means.

The United States Navy is now undergoing operational changes by shifting emphasis from open-ocean conflicts to development of expeditionary forces to fight "brush-wars" anywhere in the world. Marines will be used to make beach landings, while task forces of small warships will be created to operate in restricted waters such as the Persian Gulf.

Admiral Frank B. Kelso, chief of naval operations, described the Navy's new role in the post cold-war era by saying, "We've been trying for some time to come to grips with how the world has changed, and we've re-focused from the idea of global confrontation to how we can help operate with one foot on the sea and one on land." He acknowledged that the Congress must provide the funds for resources to equip such forces.

Kelso's comments mark a strategic shift in emphasis, probably heralding the end of the Navy's primary focus on aircraft carriers. It is evident that the Navy's insistence on a force of 12 carriers is now impossible to justify. A more likely number is a maximum of 10. Although this is a one-third reduction, 10 carriers will provide a potent "backbone" for the nation's naval forces with a fleet of more than 700 warplanes.

The United States Army will face a drastic reduction in manpower but it demonstrated in the Gulf War that it has learned its Vietnam lessons well and will need fewer drastic changes.

President Bush and President Gorbachev of the Soviet Union finally reached agreement on July 17 on a Strategic Arms Reduction Treaty that ended nine years of negotiation. Under its terms both nations will reduce their missiles and bombers to 1,600. Each nation will be permitted an accountable 6,000 nuclear devices, with only 4,900 as ballistic missile warheads.

Prior to the treaty the United States had 2,450 intercontinental ballistic missiles while the Soviet Union had 6,665.

The two leaders met in Moscow on July 30 and 31 to sign the treaty. It is the first to require verification of the reduction of warheads.

In early 1991 there were approximately 12,000 long-range nuclear warheads in the United States inventory and 11,500 in the Soviet Union. The new treaty reduced them to 9,500 for the United States and 7,200 for the Soviet Union. Under terms of the treaty, almost 8,000 Soviet warheads and their delivery systems would be eliminated.

In a sense the new START treaty marked little change in the status of nuclear proliferation because the total was back to the number that existed when negotiations began nine years earlier.

American Air Force and Navy personnel and their dependents were evacuated on June 17 from Clark Air Force Base and Subic Bay Naval Station in the Philippines after Mount Pinatubo erupted. The disaster proved so devastating that 100,000 Filipinos became homeless. Later, with the destruction at Clark so massive, the United States decided to abandon the base. Subic Bay was not damaged as severely but the government of the Philippines refused to renew the lease and the United States agreed to abandon the base by the end of 1992.

President Bush approved a list that was sent to Congress on July 10 to close 234 military installations in the United States and realign 48 others. Congress had 45 legislative days to react negatively but it chose not to do so.

CHAPTER 36

The Week That Changed the World

OLD-TIME CONSERVATIVES IN THE SOVIET UNION'S MONOLITHIC COMMU-
nist Party had long fought every attempt to reduce their stranglehold
over the Russian people, and when they sought to oust Mikhail S. Gorbachev as president of the U.S.S.R. on August 18 for sponsoring democracy
they expected the people to meekly accept their decision. When they did
not, turning out instead by the millions to support democratic ideals,
they were shocked by the Russian people's stand against the coup led by
eight key members of Gorbachev's cabinet whom he had appointed.

In less than three days the coup d'etat was broken because large elements of the Soviet Army refused orders to fire on their own people
voicing their dissent in the streets.

While Gorbachev was vacationing at his summer home in the Crimea,
the heads of the army, police and KGB appeared before him with members of his cabinet, the prime minister and Gorbachev's own vice president to demand his resignation. He refused. They placed him under
house arrest and announced that he was too ill to continue in office.

The self-proclaimed Committee on the State Emergency made it clear
that they planned to return the Soviet Union to its former reliance on
the political and economic system in effect prior to the time after Gorbachev adopted "perestroika" as the wave of the future. His advocacy of a
political system based on pluralism, a free-market economy and the return
of power to the republics was anathema to old-line Communists.

The conservatives had miscalculated the mood of the Russian people.
Their decision was based on the assumption that army conscripts would

413

unquestionably follow their officers' orders even if it meant firing at peaceful demonstrators.

It soon became apparent on the streets of Moscow and Russia's other cities that the nation's soldiers owed their first loyalty to the people as they stood passively by and refused to interfere against the protesters.

It might have been otherwise if the conservatives had acted brutally, as in the past, and crushed the rebellious masses. Obviously they did not have the necessary brutal ruthlessness to issue such orders.

Vice President Gennady I. V. Yanayev assumed presidential powers on Monday morning, August 19. He claimed Gorbachev was in poor health and was undergoing treatment for an undisclosed illness. He declared a six-month state of emergency. The press and broadcast media were again placed under official control by the committee.

The committee had planned to seize Russian Federation President Boris N. Yeltsin at the same time as Gorbachev was placed under house arrest. They just missed him, as he gathered his loyal advisers around him in the Russian Federation's Parliament building. Yeltsin appealed to all Russians to resist the takeover and urged a nationwide strike in protest.

While hundreds of tanks, armored personnel carriers and other military vehicles moved into Moscow, its citizens swarmed around them so thick they could barely move. A Soviet military official announced that he was assuming control of the three secessionist Baltic republics of Latvia, Estonia and Lithuania.

The situation grew ugly on Tuesday when the conservatives ordered tanks deployed near the Russian Federation Parliament building where Yeltsin was located. They declared a curfew from 11 p.m. to 5 a.m.

Two people were killed when they tried to trap a military vehicle beneath an underpass near Yeltsin's headquarters, and the vehicle's occupants opened fire. Another man was shot to death during demonstrations.

This unexpected opposition by the Russian people shocked the eight-man ruling committee and reports persisted that some members had resigned.

Throughout the other republics thousands of people rallied to Yeltsin's call to denounce the coup.

President Bush, who had been following events closely, said he had promised Yeltsin that he would continue American support to restore Gorbachev as President.

Bush suspended economic assistance to the Soviet Union, and swore in Robert S. Strauss as United States ambassador to the Soviet Union. He was dispatched immediately on a fact-finding mission, and ordered not to present his credentials to the coup's perpetrators.

The European Community also acted by suspending more than $1 billion in economic aid to the Soviet Union. An official spokesman demanded Gorbachev's return.

Japan's prime minister announced that his country would suspend its aid to the Soviet Union, including a $350-million loan to refinance trade debts.

On Wednesday coup leaders abandoned their takeover attempt in the face of worldwide condemnation and the revolt of the Russian people against them. In Moscow all troops were ordered to return to their barracks.

The Communist Party belatedly denounced the takeover, but the damage to its credibility could not be rectified at this late date.

President Bush, who had tried to no avail to speak to Gorbachev, finally reached him that night. Gorbachev told him that the coup was over and that he now was taking a plane for Moscow.

Later, in a statement read on television, Gorbachev told the Russian people that he was again in full control and he credited the "decisive actions of the democratic process of the country."

Rusan Khasbulatov, chairman of the Russian Federation's Parliament, told an emergency session of the legislature on the 21st that "The defeat of the right was decisive, and the people deserve the credit."

Oleg D. Kalugin, a retired KGB general but now a reformist member of the Congress of People's Deputies, explained that the coup failed because it was poorly planned. "To organize such an operation, they had not only to cut the telephones, the telegraph lines and television and radio, but they had to arrest all the leaders, particularly Yeltsin, who could mount an opposition movement. They did it timidly, and so they failed."

After Gorbachev assumed office on Thursday, August 22, he immediately fired the defense minister, the KGB chief and the 11 other plotters who overthrew him and charged them with treason.

But on the streets, and in the hearts of most of the Soviet Union's people, the man of the hour was Yeltsin who had saved the Soviet Union by his dynamic actions.

That night crowds pulled down the black bronze statue of "Iron Felix" Dzerzhinsky who had created the hated KGB.

Gorbachev's first steps upon returning to power were widely criticized when he named Army General Mikhail A. Moiseyev, the Soviet armed forces chief of staff, as acting defense minister to replace Dmitri T. Yazov who had been one of the plotters. He made other similar ill-advised appointments and was later forced to change them.

Another plotter, Interior Minister Boris K. Pugo shot himself to death.

Six others were placed in custody, while Prime Minister Volentin S. Pavlov was hospitalized and under guard, reportedly suffering from high blood pressure. Vice President Gennady I. Yanayev was arrested in his office.

Now the Communist Party's Secretariat began a probe instigated by Gorbachev of all who participated in the coup.

"It is my duty to the very end to contain reactionary forces in the Communist Party of the Soviet Union and drive them out," Gorbachev said. "We should do everything in order to undertake reforms in the party."

On Friday, when Gorbachev appeared before the Russian Federation's Parliament presided over by its President, Boris N. Yeltsin, he tried to protest a decree to suspend the activities of the Communist Party. Yeltsin, with the applause of the parliamentarians, announced that he was signing such a decree.

The depth to which Gorbachev had sunk in the eyes of the millions of Russians was evident when his appearance at the parliament was greeted with only scattered applause while Yeltsin was given a thunderous ovation.

Yeltsin pressed Gorbachev to read an account of the cabinet meeting on Monday at which all but one of Gorbachev's hand-picked ministers had called for his ouster. Gorbachev protested that he had not read it but complied when deputies demanded, "Read it! Read it!"

"I will," Gorbachev replied with reluctance. "I will do this. I'll read it." And he was forced to read the minutes describing the actions of men who were former colleagues and whom he had considered friends.

After Yeltsin's decree suspending the Communist Party's activities in the Russian Federation (the country's largest republic), and halting the publication of its newspapers including the party's daily *Pravda*, the party's headquarters were closed, the staff removed, and the files sealed to keep them from being destroyed. Even the KGB, which ran the nation's security and intelligence activities, was forced to disband its party cells.

Bowing to the reality of the situation, Gorbachev agreed to a power-sharing alliance with Yeltsin; the first step in a coalition government. He said he and Yeltsin would replace the other if either became incapacitated.

In an address to the Russian legislature, Gorbachev announced that he and Yeltsin had agreed on the appointments of a new Soviet defense minister, interior minister and KGB chief to replace the three men he had appointed a day earlier. He said they would become the foundation of a new government made up of ministers "committed to democracy."

Now key members of the plot to overthrow Gorbachev were identified and criminal charges were made against the self-proclaimed State Emergency Committee, including former Prime Minister Pavlov.

Foreign Minister Alexander A. Bessmertnykh, who had served as ambassador to the United States, was fired for not taking a firmer stand against the plotters although he was not directly involved. It was also announced that one of Gorbachev's closest friends, Anatoly I. Lukyanov, chairman of the Supreme Soviet, would be replaced.

Throughout the Soviet Union "people power" asserted themselves as the pent-up anger of the common people found expression. Statues of prominent Communists were tumbled from their pedestals, party offices were ransacked and their officials driven away.

At first, attempts to drive the Communist Party from power were resisted by Gorbachev because he feared disintegration of the Soviet Union into fully-independent republics. But in the rapidly-changing scene Gorbachev reversed himself and resigned as General Secretary of the Communist Party on Saturday, nationalized the party's property and assets and ordered its cells disbanded in all state organizations.

At the same time Gorbachev revealed that he would dissolve the present Soviet Cabinet and appoint a committee headed by Russian Prime Minister Ivan S. Silayev to manage the country's economy.

Gorbachev denounced the Communist Party which he said had betrayed him, and called for the dissolution of the party's policy-making Central Committee and also urged other parties to assess their roles. Despite these steps he did not quit the Communist Party and he praised its honest members. Indirectly he called for creation of a new democratic party to replace it; one committed to radical reform of the nation's political and economic system.

These decisions were announced at the end of the nightly news on all radio and television stations without further embellishment.

On its own, the Russian Republic announced that it had recognized the statehood of Latvia and Estonia. It had earlier taken similar action in regard to Lithuania.

As this incredible week came to an end, Communism had sustained a deadly blow throughout the Union of Soviet Socialist Republics. Fortunately it had taken place with only three casualties.

The pace of change quickened on Sunday with a wholesale shakeup of the military involving 80 percent of the top officers of the Army, Navy and Air Force. Colonel General Yevgeny I. Shaposhnikov appeared on the Sunday evening news to announce personnel changes to remove generals and other officers who aided or sympathized with the coup's plotters. The former commander of the Air Force, who replaced Marshal Dmitri

T. Yazov, said the new people "should be younger, more loyal and incapable of anti-constitutional acts."

He gave his personal assurance that "as long as I am defense minister, our country's armed forces will never in any circumstances be used against the people."

Meanwhile, Gorbachev's personal military adviser, Marshal Sergei F. Akhromeyev, committed suicide. He had been at the meeting in which Gorbachev's overthrow was approved. He was the second plotter to kill himself rather than face a trial.

Despite the euphoria about the overthrow of communism in the Soviet Union, a sobering development occurred as Byelorussia became the eighth Soviet republic to move toward sovereignty, posing the threat of complete dissolution of the Soviet Union.

A million people gathered in Moscow on Sunday to pay tribute to the three defenders of Russian President Yeltsin who died during the coup attempt. The bloodstains on the pavement were covered in flowers to honor them.

In an historic announcement on August 26 President Gorbachev appeared before the Soviet Union's national legislature to say that the nation's 15 republics must be given the "right of independent choice."

He told members of the Supreme Soviet that "we must take a specific position on republics that are unwilling to sign the Union Treaty." Prior to the coup, the major republics had agreed to terms that would retain each of them as part of the Soviet Union, and a vote was scheduled. It was prevented by the events of the previous week. "Immediately after the Union Treaty is signed," Gorbachev said, "negotiations must be started with those who wish to leave the union. Preparations for this can be started now." But whether the climactic events of recent days had made the treaty an anachronism remained to be seen. Most leaders of the republics believed it was no longer a viable plan.

In a speech to the Supreme Soviet Gorbachev's voice was filled with emotion when he said that the most "tragic result" of the previous week's coup was that it spurred the very "centrifugal tendencies" it was meant to halt. He spoke of a power-sharing plan but most republic leaders said such a union had been superseded by events.

But Yeltsin joined Gorbachev in calling for such a union. A coalition of people calling themselves "centralizers," mostly from the Republic of Russia, had become alarmed by the possible breakup of the huge nation into possibly 15 separate regions most of whom could not survive economically if such a disunion were to take place.

Thirteen top Communists were formally accused on August 28 with attempting to overthrow President Gorbachev, a crime punishable with death by firing squad. Meanwhile, vigilante groups loyal to Gorbachev and Boris Yeltsin searched throughout the Soviet Union for accomplices. Even some members of the Secretariat and the Central Committee were sought for questioning.

The Soviet Union's legislative body, the Supreme Soviet, now acted to ban all activity by the Communist Party, ending an era that began with the Bolshevik Revolution in 1917, and its speaker, Anatoly I. Lukyanov was stripped of his authority and charged with treason.

With the Soviet Union facing disintegration, the two largest Soviet republics Russia and Kazakhstan reached an agreement to respect their common borders and work to prevent the "uncontrolled disintegration" of the nation. This action was taken as two more republics declared their independence. The Central Asian republics of Uzbekistan and Kirghizia were the ninth and tenth republics to take such action.

Meanwhile, Russian troops began to withdraw from the secessionist Baltic republics of Lithuania, Latvia and Estonia.

While leaders of the United States and other western nations applauded these actions in the Soviet Union, they issued warnings that economic assistance was tied to cuts in the Soviet Union's nuclear forces.

On September 16 President Gorbachev and leaders of 12 Soviet republics proposed the creation of a loose federation that would sharply reduce central authority. At first the proposal was greeted with doubt and uncertainty but was finally approved in principle to prevent the Soviet Union's complete collapse. The final agreement called for the independence of separate republics in an economic union. It was agreed that the State Council would be made up of Soviet President Gorbachev and republic leaders acting as the Soviet Union's transitional government. The agreement, however, was contingent upon the drafting of a treaty to establish a common market among the 12 republics. This new union would be based on the principle of free enterprise and private property, with prices established by supply and demand. It called for the free movement of commodities, services and labor throughout the union.

Once this economic union was approved, its leaders agreed to discuss a "union of sovereign states" to become the political successor to the Union of Soviet Socialist States.

It was also announced that the Baltic states Latvia, Estonia and Lithuania would become free and independent states outside of this new union. President Bush had recognized their independence on September 2, a step other nations had already taken.

Then, on September 5, the Soviet Parliament voted to abolish the centralized state established by V. I. Lenin and the czars before him and returned power to the republics.

On Russian television that night the lead story began, "Today, September 5, 1991, we all begin living in a new country. The Soviet Union is no more."

President Gorbachev spoke with great emotion when he said that the nation has given itself "a chance to do everything anew."

The decision had been fraught with angry debate. At one point Gorbachev met resistance in the Congress to approve a law granting central power to three institutions until a union treaty could be signed by the republics. He threatened to dissolve the chamber, amend the Soviet Constitution or simply issue a presidential decree. He finally succeeded in overcoming almost all resistance and the law was approved as a whole by a vote of 1,682 to 43.

It was almost too late to establish any kind of responsible government, with food supplies almost unobtainable, and the Soviet ruble now worth less than three United States cents—down from $1.60 before Gorbachev came to power.

The new government formally gave up the Baltic republics on September 6 and they became free and independent countries.

Oliver L. North, one of the central figures in the Reagan administration's Iran-contra scandal had been accused of setting up an organization to finance the Nicaraguan rebels although Congress had specifically forbidden such aid. He was convicted in May 1989, on three charges involving diversion of funds from the secret sale of arms to Iran to the rebels.

On September 17 U.S. District Judge Gerhard H. Gesell dismissed the case at the request of independent counsel Lawrence E. Walsh who said that recent testimony by North's former boss, Robert C. McFarlane, made it unlikely that North's previous convictions could be reinstated.

North called his long ordeal "five years of fire," and declared himself totally vindicated.

Air Force Lieutenant General Charles A. Horner, who headed the air war against Iraq during the Persian Gulf War, discussed some of the problems faced by his command. He said his command's key objective was to neutralize the threat of Iran's biological weapons. At first, he said, his commanders were concerned that the destruction of factories and warehouses containing biological weapons might spread anthrax and botulism toxins by wind and kill "off every living thing on the Arabian Peninsula." He said an Army report on germ warfare advised him that the bacteria that causes these diseases was vulnerable to sunlight, heat and water and would pose no problem if released into the atmosphere.

Horner ordered a plan drawn up to bomb the Iraqi storage areas where germ weapons were stored with special bombs that could penetrate hardened bunkers.

Bombing runs were then made by other planes to drop mines around the destroyed bunkers to complete their destruction.

The Air Force general credited military lawyers with screening all targets to assure that none of their bombs were aimed at historical, cultural or religious sites in violation of international law.

The American economy strengthened after the Persian Gulf War ended in early 1991, but then began to slump during the summer. A disturbing increase in bankruptcies indicated that for the first time they might reach a million by the end of the year according to Samuel Gerdano, head of the American Bankruptcy Institute (The actual figure was about 960,000). The vast majority, he said, were individuals who misused their credit cards.

The long-delayed first flight of the Air Force's C-17 cargo plane took place on September 15 from the airport at Long Beach adjoining the McDonnell-Douglas plant.

The $35 billion program had long been beset by controversy as its costs skyrocketed and its first flight was delayed a year. The Air Force charged that McDonnell-Douglas had an estimated cost overrun of $700 million, a figure disputed by the company.

About this same time Air Force Secretary Donald B. Rice admitted that its B-2 Stealth bomber had revealed serious shortcomings. He said it would be only 80 percent successful in evading enemy radar as originally envisioned, even after further costly work was done on the bomber.

The B-2 is produced by Northrop Corporation at Palmdale and Pico Rivera. The announcement came after Congress was informed that the $860 million bomber had failed a key test of its stealthiness during recent flight tests.

In the Soviet Union, the new federation drafted a constitution on September 17 that had to be approved by the parliaments of each of the former Soviet republics. It proposed a western-style government with executive, legislative and judicial powers. Part of the proposal was the resurrection of the Duma, Russia's first national parliament, which functioned between 1905 and the 1917 Bolshevik Revolution. Early indications were that it faced a long and involved process of debate with approval a matter of conjecture.

Any doubt that the "Cold War" had ended was dispelled on September 26, 1991, when President Bush addressed the people of the United States and the world to reveal a new plan to reduce the nation's reliance on nuclear weaponry. He announced that he was immediately withdrawing short-range nuclear weapons from Europe and abandoning the Mobile Intercontinental Missile program, and the short-range attack missile

SRAM-2. In particular, he called for the elimination of all multiple warhead missiles.

For 42 years America's nuclear arsenal had been a deterrent to another world war although the United States and Russia had faced one crisis after another during those years. "We can now take steps to make the world a less dangerous place than ever before in the nuclear age," he said.

The President called for the Soviet Union to join the United States in building only one kind of a less-destructive, ground-based missile.

His most revealing statement was that the United States would take some of these steps unilaterally although he called on the Soviet Union to "go down the road with us" by making the same reductions. He warned that if such a step was not taken "a historic opportunity will have been lost."

Prior to his speech President Bush spoke to Soviet President Gorbachev and Russian Federation President Yeltsin, both of whom praised the President's initiative. They had earlier offered to discuss massive reductions in their respective nuclear arsenals.

Since the recent coup that sought to oust Gorbachev from power, Bush had become increasingly concerned about the thousands of short-range nuclear weapons in artillery shells and battlefield missiles located in some of the republics now trying to break away from the U.S.S.R. His fear was that some of them might get into the hands of terrorists.

Prior to his speech, and in discussion with his top advisers, the President told them that he wanted to take advantage of a historic opportunity to dramatically reduce the number of nuclear weapons to enhance the world's stability and to lessen the risk of war.

Defense Secretary Cheney had been charged with developing a program to reduce America's nuclear arsenal but his first proposal was rejected by the President because it did not go far enough. The President wanted a proposal that would cover all tactical nuclear weapons which, he said, were no longer needed to defend Europe as a counter to the Soviet Union's former advantage in conventional weapons and manpower. President Bush claimed that the collapse of the Warsaw Pact made such an approach a logical and defensible alternative. Now, he said, with the Soviet Union beset by internal problems, its threat for the free world was minimal.

But with the President's call for a sharp reduction in nuclear weapons, he continued to call for production of the B-2 bomber and strongly supported the Strategic Defense Initiative that was conceived during the Reagan administration. In an otherwise wise and provocative plan, Bush's support for the B-2 and SDI demonstrated again his mind-set about two unneeded and outrageously expensive weapons systems. His concern that the United States was at risk from some Third World countries dominated by terrorists was valid, but SDI would protect the United States only from a missile attack. Whereas terrorists undoubtedly would use a nuclear weapon that was brought to this country by secret means and detonated inside one of the nation's major cities. Then, too, nuclear devices could be easily brought to the nation's major harbors by ship and detonated on board by remote control, causing enormous damage if such a device was in the megaton range.

President Bush's plan specifically eliminated all land-based, short-range nuclear weapons which number about 850 warheads on Lance missiles. The 1,700 nuclear artillery shells for 8-inch and 155-millimeter guns, now based primarily in Western Europe and Korea, would be destroyed.

Nuclear cruise missiles will be removed from the Navy's surface ships and attack submarines. Many will be destroyed while the others will be placed in storage. Non-nuclear cruise missiles, such as the Tomahawk that was used successfully in the Persian Gulf War, will continue in use.

Under Bush's orders all strategic bombers, which have been on around-the-clock alert for years, will no longer be maintained on alert status. Intercontinental ballistic missiles, scheduled for deactivation under START, will also be taken off alert. These actions were taken two days after the President's speech when Defense Secretary Cheney ordered the crews of 280 strategic bombers and 450 Minuteman II missiles to cease their 24-hour alert status.

The Chairman of the Joint Chiefs of Staff provided additional details. General Colin Powell said that only 40 percent of the Strategic Air Command's 280 B-52 and B-1 long-range bombers had been on continuous alert. These aircraft, he said, can carry "several hundred" nuclear bombs and missiles although he refused to divulge the exact number for security reasons.

In Moscow, Gorbachev called the Bush initiative "very positive." He said of the President's proposals, these are "serious steps forward toward the nuclear-free world." He declined to go further, saying Bush's plan was too complex to respond to immediately and in detail. He did say that he and Bush had already agreed to discuss the proposals at some future date.

In 1991 the Soviet Union had approximately 27,000 warheads, including 10,000 ground-launched, short-range weapons such as were recommended for elimination by President Bush.

President Bush's proposal would eliminate 3,000 American nuclear weapons, leaving the United States arsenal with approximately 18,000 weapons. Two-thirds of those recommended for destruction had already been declared obsolete and were due for retirement.

Defense Secretary Cheney revealed that approximately 500 tactical nuclear weapons aboard Navy ships would be returned to the United States for storage. They included nuclear bombs and depth charges and nuclear Tomahawk cruise missiles carried on surface ships and attack submarines. Half of them he said will be maintained for future emergencies while the rest—including all depth charges—will be destroyed. General Powell said that there were 350 nuclear Tomahawk missiles in the Navy's inventory, with an average of 100 at sea at any one time.

Despite these sharp cutbacks, the United States' nuclear deterrent will remain massive because there will be no change in the status of the Trident and Poseidon ballistic-missile submarines. Twelve of them will remain on alert at all times. They are almost invulnerable.

In Europe, the United States plans to maintain medium-range bombers equipped to launch nuclear cruise missiles and to drop conventional bombs. At home the 50 MX Peacekeeper missiles, each loaded with 10 highly accurate warheads, and 500 three-warhead Minuteman II missiles, will remain constantly on alert.

Two points of sharp difference remained between the super powers. The leaders of the Soviet Union had long sought a reduction in sea-based systems before they would agree to cut their ground multi-warhead missile systems. The United States has repeatedly rejected any limits to its submarine-based multiple warhead missiles because they are considered impossible to target whereas land-based missiles of this nature are considered destabilizing because they present such lucrative targets for a preemptive strike. The other disruptive factor is President Bush's insistence on deployment of SDI defenses against ballistic missiles. The 1972 Anti-ballistic Missile Treaty, signed by the United States and the Soviet Union, would have to be amended to permit such a new defense system. The Strategic Defense Initiative has an enormous price tag despite the fact it can never hope to destroy all incoming warheads, thus making it ineffective to prevent a massive nuclear exchange. In the past, purely defensive systems have always proved ineffective.

A senior Soviet Defense Ministry official announced plans on October 1 to reduce the Soviet Union's armed forces by half during the next three years. Colonel General Pavel Grachev, the new first deputy defense minister, said the reduction would cut the armed forces from 4.2 million to 2.5 million or possibly 2 million service people by the end of 1994.

CHAPTER 37

A Victory for Democracy and Freedom

THE REAGAN ADMINISTRATION'S STRONG BACKING FOR THE STRATEGIC
Defense Initiative or "Star Wars" had almost derailed meaningful plans
to reduce the enormous stockpile of nuclear weapons possessed by the
Soviet Union and the United States. When George Bush became President, he urged Congress to "do its part" by funding SDI "at a level that
will enable us to deploy a ballistic missile defense at the earliest point
feasible." He had retreated from Reagan's expensive space-based missile
defense system to propose deployment of a limited system called "Global
Protection Against Limited Strikes." By itself this was a sharp departure
from Reagan's plan to form an "umbrella" against an attack by thousands
of Soviet intercontinental ballistic missiles. Bush's new system was limited to shield the United States from one or a few missiles that might
be fired by dissidents in the Third World.

When it became evident that Congress would strongly resist even this
limited system, Bush announced on October 14 that he was willing to
negotiate with the Soviet Union to put restrictions on even this new
system.*

With a new round of space and defense negotiations underway with
the Soviet Union in Geneva, the President's new plan was placed on the
table. It was greeted with the same resistance as Reagan's original plan.

The Soviet Union continued its economic free-fall and it was apparent
to leaders like President Gorbachev and Russian Federation President

---

*President Clinton canceled SDI in May 1993, after $35 billion had been spent.

Yeltsin that drastic measures must be taken. Yeltsin took the most decisive step on October 27, 1991, when he recommended specific steps to reform the economy which, he said, would save Russia if its people would only stick with him through a year of excruciating change. He asked Parliament for extra powers to give him direct control of the Soviet Union's most populous republic. He admitted that prices would skyrocket, possibly tripling present levels, and create greater unemployment and deeper poverty.

"The time has come to act—decisively, harshly and without vacilation," he told the Congress of People's Deputies in a speech broadcast live to the federation's 150-million people.

His major recommendation was to lift government price controls before the end of 1991 because they had kept bread and other necessities relatively cheap although in short supply for decades.

Yeltsin said such steps would turn the economy around by the fall of 1992, pledging that prices would drop within six months. He pledged to improve support for the nation's poor by providing soup kitchens and food stamps.

Yeltsin recommended that the government sell off almost all state-owned small to medium-size factories, billions of dollars worth of unfinished construction sites, and break up collective farms. His plan called for balancing the budget by reducing contributions to the Soviet government, removal of obstacles to increase Russian imports and exports, and reduce controls on foreign investments and the conversion of rubles.

His plans won support from all except hard-core Communists and now his reputation was on the line.

Although economic conditions in the United States were not in as perilous a state, the nation remained in recession despite denials by President Bush. This was evident on October 28 when the nation's growth between July and September was announced. In the first sign of expansion in a year, the gross national product rose 2.4 percent. But this was only half what it should have been and private economists warned that this anemic growth rate could be temporary. Some warned of the possibility of a double-dip recession.

A more realistic assessment was given by Federal Reserve Board Chairman Alan Greenspan who told a business group that the economy had turned "demonstrably sluggish" recently and he described it as "moving forward, but in the face of 50-mile-an-hour winds."

During the summer and early fall President Bush had appealed to Israelis and Arabs in the Middle East to put aside their differences and seek peace for the region.

Despite haggling, the Bush Administration's call for a Middle East

Conference was finally realized. He urged conferees to put aside "a history that weighs heavily against hope" and provide a framework for peace in the region. He promised Arabs and Jews that the United States, in conjunction with Western Europe and Japan, would provide economic assistance to assure "that peace and prosperity go hand in hand."

Although the President's remarks were received cooly, top officials of Israel, Syria, Lebanon, Jordan, and the Palestinians for the first time in modern history sat around a T-shaped table and discussed their differences in Madrid's Hall of Columns in the Royal Palace.

The gap between the rich and the poor in America had been growing throughout the 1980s and it was given official recognition on October 29 by Janet L. Norwood, United States Commissioner of Labor Statistics. She charged that the country was being polarized by the growth of the most severe gap between the poorest and richest Americans that she had seen in 38 years of government service.

The Census Bureau's 1990 report on income backed her up, indicating that the top 20 percent of Americans received 46.8 percent of all the household income while the bottom 20 percent received 3.9 percent of all household income.

The war in the Persian Gulf had exacerbated the economic condition although foreign governments had paid most of its $61.1 billion cost. But these payments still left $7.1 billion to be borne by overburdened American taxpayers.

Congress originally had appropriated $15 billion to pay for the war.

Although 19 nations signed an agreement October 23 to end the 12-year-old civil war in Cambodia, concern grew in Washington this month that Pol Pot, former leader of the Khmer Rouge, might regain control of the government because his army was the largest in the fragile coalition known as the Supreme National Council.

Meanwhile, China and Vietnam signed an economic accord on November 7 involving trade and border matters.

Relations between China and Vietnam had fluctuated greatly during the preceding 30 years. China aided the North Vietnamese during their war against the United States but they became enemies after Vietnam invaded Cambodia. They fought a brief but bloody border war in early 1979, and until recently relations between the two nations had been tense.

Secretary of State Baker, during a visit to Japan on November 10, urged its leaders to assume a more active role in international diplomatic relations, and to expand their horizons beyond the economic sphere.

Baker told the distinguished gathering that Japan should begin to take on "broader global responsibilities." He invited Japan's leaders to work together with the United States not only in Asia but around the world.

But Baker warned that the United States would be unhappy with any arrangement in which Japan offered only economic aid and tried to stay out of political controversy.

He called for Japan's leaders to provide leadership not just in economic matters but also in "building democracy, respect for human rights, stopping the proliferation of weapons of mass destruction and in facing transnational challenges in areas such as the environment, narcotics and refugees."

A number of attempts had been made by the European Community to end the civil war in Yugoslavia. The war began on June 25 when Croatia declared its independence and armed ethnic Serbs declared their autonomy in regions of Croatia after capturing a third of the republic.

Since the breakup of the nation began differences between the warring factions proved impossible to reconcile and violent death and destruction went on without abatement.

Lord Carrington, former British foreign secretary who had tried to negotiate an end to the war, met with Serbian and Croatian presidents on November 12 to discuss foreign intervention as a means of ending the bloodshed in the Balkans.

First, he said, a lasting ceasefire must be achieved because there had been 12 previous truces signed by Croatian, Serbian and federal authorities and they all had collapsed; some within hours.

These failures were due primarily to the inability of Croatian, Serbian and Muslim leaders to control their extremist factions. The process was further hampered by broad disagreements between the Serbs and the Croatians about the placement of foreign troops.

As Lord Carrington set out again in mid-November to explore the possibility of a truce, he said he was hopeful because this time "both the Serbs and Croats have asked for an international peace-keeping force either by the United Nations or the European Community. They've not done that before. So I think it's worth going out there to see whether or not we could do something along those lines.

With large areas of Yugoslavia totally destroyed and 200,000 people dead or missing, time is running out. If the fighting does not cease, the economy of the region will continue its free fall, and it will take decades to repair the damage to some cities that have been laid waste like those in World War II, making two million people homeless.

In an attempt to put pressure on the varying factions, the European Community and the United States imposed economic sanctions.

El Salvador's guerrilla leaders announced in November that they would halt all offensive military operations indefinitely. Five commanders of the Farabundo Marti National Liberation Front announced the unilateral ceasefire to begin at midnight on November 15, thus offering hope that the 11-year war that had caused 75,000 lives was finally over. The guerrillas said the ceasefire would last until a peace agreement was signed with the American-backed government. President Alfredo Cristiani said the rebel decision was a "sign of goodwill that allows us to reach a definitive ceasefire in the shortest possible time."

The position of the Soviet Union's central government grew even more precarious as Soviet President Gorbachev and leaders of only seven Soviet republics reached agreement on a new political confederation with sharply reduced central authority. The Union of Sovereign States did not include five other republics who refused to send representatives to the Moscow meeting.

Ten republics had earlier agreed to a common market style of "economic community" but it proved impossible to implement because of the absence of a political union. It was hoped by Russian leaders that the new union would resolve these differences but President Gorbachev and President Yeltsin admitted that many of their differences still were unresolved.

On December 21, 1988, Pan American Flight 103 blew up over Lockerbie, Scotland, killing 259 passengers and crew and 11 others on the ground. Sabotage was suspected and in one of the greatest sleuthing jobs ever attempted clues were found linking intelligence agents from Libya as the ones who placed the bomb on board. The Libyan government was not officially charged with the alleged crime, but two of its intelligence operatives were indicted on November 14, 1991, by a federal grand jury in Washington and charged with 193 criminal counts for placing the bomb on board the jetliner.

Senator John D. Rockefeller IV of West Virginia, chairman of the National Commission on Children, released the bipartisan commission's findings on November 21 on the status of the American family in Twentieth Century America. He said most Americans were pessimistic because financial and time constraints make it much more difficult to raise children than in the past. Incongruously, he said, most families described their own family life as satisfactory.

Rockefeller summed up the commission's findings by saying, "Although parents and America's children are speaking directly to Washington through this survey, they are telling us that they are being tested and torn by too little time, by too little money, by too many absent parents and by their growing fears about crime."

The last hostages held by Shiite Muslims were released on December

4 when Terry A. Anderson, who had been held for 6½ years, was released. He had been the Associated Press's correspondent in Beirut. He gave credit for surviving his long ordeal to "my companions . . . my faith, stubbornness, I guess. You just do what you have to do."

Joseph J. Cicippio and Alan Steen were also released just prior to Anderson's freedom.

President Bush presided over ceremonies at Pearl Harbor December 7, 1991, to honor those who died in the Japanese attack 50 years earlier. He and Mrs. Bush cast flowers into the water over the sunken battleship "Arizona." The President called upon the nation to lift its eyes unflinchingly to its responsibilities across the globe and warned against the urge to withdraw into the isolation of its own problems.

Gorbachev's long political battle to preserve the Soviet Union as one nation came to an end on December 8 when Russian President Yeltsin and leaders of Ukraine and Belarus agreed to establish a new "commonwealth of independent states" with its capital at Minsk instead of Moscow.

In a formal treaty, the Soviet Union was abolished effective January 1, 1992. The preamble stated that "We, the Republic of Belarus, the Russian Federation and Ukraine as the founding states of the U.S.S.R. and co-signatories of the 1922 Union Treaty. . . . state that the U.S.S.R. is ceasing its existence as a subject of international law and a geopolitical reality."

This action was taken in open defiance of President Gorbachev who had warned that disintegration of the union would prove disastrous to the country and possibly the world. He denounced it as "illegal and dangerous."

The Soviet Union had been formed 69 years earlier by V. I. Lenin. Its pretensions as a socialist state of the people were soon unmasked as the U.S.S.R. became a nation governed by dictatorial rulers.

The three republics which founded the commonwealth comprise 70 percent of the Soviet Union's 290 million people. Negotiations were scheduled with other republics who may wish to join it. A number of thorny issues faced the new leadership: what to do with the armed forces, and most particularly the nuclear forces, and the necessity of moving quickly to shore up a collapsing economy.

Gorbachev, the man most responsible for the great changes in the Soviet Union, was now out of a job. But he will always be remembered as the man who destroyed dictatorship in the Soviet Union and created the climate for democratic reforms. Unfortunately he lacked the ability to carry out the necessary drastic reforms. The euphoria of a free society soon gave way to the reality of a free market system. The commonwealth's leaders faced an almost impossible task and it was within the bounds of reason that their days may be limited. They had to translate words into reality or the ever-patient Slavic people of these republics would turn to others to solve the commonwealth's multiple problems. The commonwealth will need massive foreign aid to survive at a time when most nations have economic troubles of their own.

An historic accord was signed on December 10 when 12 West European nations agreed to link their political and economic systems, although Great Britain refused to join the other nations on workers rights and a common European currency. However, before it could become a reality, the voters of each nation had to approve.

In the United States the recession deepened, along with the hopes and aspirations of most Americans. Federal Reserve Board Chairman Alan Greenspan warned that the recovery had "already faltered."

He said that "there is a deep-seated concern out there, which I must say to you I have not seen in my lifetime." He told members of the House Ways and Means Committee, "It is very hard to grasp the depth of the concerns unless you look at it as a problem about their future."

President Bush declared on Christmas Day 1991 that the Soviet Union had passed into history and that the United States was according full recognition to the Russian Federation and five other former Soviet republics which had agreed to form a commonwealth of nations.

Within a few hours after President Gorbachev resigned as President of the Union of Soviet Socialist Republics President Bush went on television to proclaim that "this is a victory for democracy and freedom." He praised Gorbachev for his "sustained commitment to world peace and for his intellect, vision and courage."

Bush said that the United States "applauds and supports the historic choice for freedom of the new states." Despite the possibility of "chaos," he said, "these events clearly serve our national interests."

The President praised the emergence of a free, independent and democratic Russia, "led by its courageous President Boris Yeltsin."

Bush moved quickly to recognize the new commonwealth by giving immediate recognition to Russia, Ukraine, Belarus, Kazakhstan, Kyrgzstan (formerly Kirghizia) and Armenia. These republics, he said, have made specific commitments to the United States on nuclear weapons and internal reforms. He said official recognition would be given to the six remaining republics when "we are satisfied that they have made commitments to responsible security policies and democratic principles." One of these republics, Georgia, was soon involved in a dissident rebellion that overthrew its president, a move that demonstrated the fragility of the new political arrangements.

In regard to economic aid, President Bush had already offered more than $3 billion to the former Soviet Union. Most of this money went for agricultural credits.

President Bush and Russian President Boris N. Yeltsin agreed on June 16, 1992, that neither nation would ever make war on the other. They initialed a preliminary agreement to destroy two-thirds of their nuclear arsenals within the next 11 years. This action significantly reduced the number of missiles agreed to in the 1991 Strategic Reduction Treaty (START I). Under terms of the final agreement for START II, signed by the two presidents in Moscow on January 3, 1993, the United States will have 3,500 strategic warheads while Russia will have 3,000. This status will assure that neither nation will have sufficient nuclear weapons to make a disabling first strike on the other. Although the terms of the treaty give the United States a slight edge, it is not significant. Critics of the treaty in Russia, however, insist that their leaders gave away too much. Yeltsin assured the Russian people that the treaty is not a sellout of their security. He revealed publicly that as of January 1 Russia had 9,915 strategic warheads. But even with a redution to 3,000, he said, his country would still have a "powerful shield which is capable of defending Russia."

The treaty bans land-based intercontinental missiles with more than one warhead. The 10-warhead SS-18, known as "Satan," is Russia's most dangerous weapon. It will be eliminated, along with the United States's MX "Peacekeeper" developed to replace Minuteman III and provide greater range and accuracy with its 10 warheads. The United States agreed to cut its submarine-launched ballistic missiles—the core of its retaliatory power—from 3,456 warheads to 1,750. These reductions will be completed as early as 2000 but no later than 2003.

The Russian Parliament and the United States Senate must approve the treaty. In America, there is little opposition but that is not true of parts of the former Soviet Union, particularly the Ukraine which still has not approved START I. Two other former Soviet Republics, Kazakhstan and Belarus, also have nuclear weapons. Under START I, all three of these nations must agree to give up their strategic weapons. They are included in the new treaty's Russian total. Leaders of the Ukraine are bargaining for economic benefits before they agree to destroy their missiles. They are also seeking security guarantees from Russia and the United States.

Several last-minute changes were approved for START II to address some of the Russian criticism of the 1991 agreement. It was agreed to by American negotiators that Russia can keep 105 of its 170 SS-19 MIRVS, but must remove five of their six thermo-nuclear warheads. In June, Bush and Yeltsin approved their destruction. The Russians also can retain 90 subterranean silos, now used for the 10-warhead SS-18 missiles, and convert them for use by the now-mobile SS-25s with a single warhead.

Russia won the right to inspect 100 American strategic bombers that will be converted to carry non-nuclear payloads. Inspection will also include the B-2 bomber to verify it carries no more than 16 nuclear weapons.

Through the years the United States produced more than 80,000 nuclear and thermo-nuclear weapons of all types. Quite possibly the Union of Soviet Socialist Republics created a similar number. Although wars have not been eliminated in 1993, the danger of a cataclysmic conflict that could destroy the world as we know it has largely been eliminated.

The "Cold War," that lasted almost half a century, came to an end not with the "big bang" most people feared, but with a whimper. Few regretted its demise, although its economic cost will be a burden for all nations for generations to come.

Selected Bibliography

Ambrose, Stephen E., Nixon: *The Triumph of a Politician*. Simon & Schuster, New York, 1989.

Beck, Warren A. and Williams, David A., *California: A History of the Golden State*. Doubleday and Company, New York, 1972.

Burner, David, Herbert Hoover: *A Public Life*. Knopf, New York, 1978.

Cannon, Lou, President Reagan: The Role of a Lifetime. Simon & Schuster, N.Y. 1991.

Caro, Robert L., *Means of Ascent: The Years of Lyndon Johnson*. Knopf, New York, 1990.

Carter, Jimmy, *Keeping Faith: Memoirs of a President*. Bantam, New York, 1985.

Colton, Joel G., *Twentieth Century*. Time-Life Books, New York, 1968.

Chellis, Marcia, *The Joan Kennedy Story: Living with the Kennedys*. Simon & Schuster, New York, 1985.

Chien, Nien, *Life and Death in Shanghai*. Grove Press, New York, 1987.

Drosnin, Michael, *Citizen Hughes*. Holt, Rinehart and Winston, New York, 1985.

Editors, *The Confident Years: The Period Between the Civil War and World War I.* American Heritage Publishing Company, Inc., New York, 1969.

Editors, *Webster's Guide to American History.* Merrian Company, Springfield, 1971.

Eisenhower, David, *Eisenhower at War: 1943–1945.* Random House, New York, 1986.

Farrell, Don A., *Pictorial History of Guam: Liberation 1944.* Micronesian Productions, Guam, 1984.

Fehrenbach, T. R., *Lone Star: A History of Texas and Texans.* Macmillan, New York, 1968.

Grew, Joseph, *Turbulent Era: A Diplomatic Record of Fifty Years, 1904–1955.* Edited by Walter Johnson. Houghton Mifflin, Boston, 1952.

Grun, Bernard, *The Timetables of History.* Simon & Schuster, New York, 1975.

Hersh, Seymour M., *The Samson Option: Israel's Nuclear Arsenal and American Foreign Policy.* Random House, New York, 1991.

Hitler, *Adolf, Mein Kampf.* Houghton Mifflin, Boston, 1943.

Higham, Charles, *The Duchess of Windsor: The Secret Life.* McGraw-Hill, New York, 1988.

Hoffman, Nicholas von, *Citizen Cohn: The Life and Times of Roy Cohn.* Doubleday, New York, 1988.

Iacocca, Lee, with William Novak. *Iacocca, An Autobiography.* Bantam, New York, 1984.

Josephson, Matthew, and Josephson, Hannah. *Al Smith, Hero of the Cities: A Political Portrait Drawing on the Papers of Frances Perkins.* Houghton Mifflin, Boston, 1969.

Lash, Joseph P., *Eleanor and Franklin: The Story of Their Relationship.* Norton, New York, 1971.

———Lash, Eleanor: *Eleanor Roosevelt and her Friends.* Doubleday, Garden City, 1982.

Lord, Bette Bao, *Legacies: A Chinese Mosaic.* Knopf, New York, 1990.

MacArthur, Douglas, Reminiscences. McGraw-Hill, New York, 1964.

Monaghan, Jay, Editor-in-Chief, *The Book of the American West.* Simon & Schuster, New York, 1963.

Morgan, Ted, *Maugham: A Biography.* Simon & Schuster, New York, 1980.

Morrison, Wilbur H., *Hellbirds: The Story of the B-29s in Combat.* Duell, Sloan and Pearce, New York, 1960.

———*The Incredible 305th: The "Can Do" Bombers of World War II.* Duell, Sloan and Pearce, New York, 1962.

———*Wings Over the Seven Seas: U.S. Naval Aviation's Fight for Survival.* Cranbury, New Jersey, A. S. Barnes, 1974.

————*Point of No Return: The Story of the Twentieth Air Force.* Times Books, New York, 1979.

————*Fortress Without a Roof: The Allied Bombing of the Third Reich.* St. Martin's Press, New York, 1982.

————*Above and Beyond: 1941–1945.* St. Martin's, New York, 1983.

————The Elephant and the Tiger: The Full Story of the Vietnam War. Hippocrene, New York, 1990.

————Donald W. Douglas, *A Heart with Wings.* Iowa State University Press Ames, Iowa, 1991.

Nixon, Richard, *In the Arena: A Memoir of Victory, Defeat and Renewal.* Simon & Schuster, New York, 1990.

Nevins, Allan, and Commager, Henry Steele, *A Pocket History of the United States.* Washington Square Press, New York, 1981.

O'Neill, Tip, with William Novak, *Man of the House: The Life and Political Memoirs of Speaker Tip O'Neill.* Random House, New York, 1987.

Perkins, Frances, *The Roosevelt I knew.* Viking, New York, 1946.

Reagan, Nancy, with William Novak. The Memoirs of Nancy Reagan. Random House, New York, 1989.

Regan, Donald T., *For the Record: From Wall Street to Washington.* Harcourt, Brace, San Diego, 1988.

Rhodes, Richard, *The Making of the Atomic Bomb.* Simon & Schuster, New York, 1986.

Roosevelt, Eleanor, *This is My Story.* Harper, New York, 1937.

Roosevelt, Elliott, and Brough, James, *An Untold Story: The Roosevelts of Hyde Park.* Putnam's and Sons, New York, 1973.

Ross, Walter S., *The Last Hero: Charles A. Lindbergh.* Harper and Row, New York, 1964.

Russell, Francis, *Tragedy in Denham: The Story of the Sacco-Vanzetti Case.* McGraw-Hill Book Company, New York, 1957.

Safer, Morley, *Flashbacks: On Returning to Vietnam.* Random House, New York, New York, 1990.

Sann, Paul, *The Lawless Decade.* Crown, New York, 1957.

Seagrave, Sterling, *The Soong Dynasty.* Harper & Row, New York, 1985.

Scaduto, Anthony, Scapegoat: *The Lonesome Death of Bruno Richard Hauptmann.* G. P. Putnam's Sons, New York, 1976.

Shirer, William L., *Berlin Diary,* Knopf, New York, 1941.

————*End of a Berlin Diary,* Knopf, New York, 1947.

————*The Rise and Fall of the Third Reich.* Simon and Schuster, New York, 1960.

————*A Native's Return: 1945–1988.* Little Brown and Company, New York, 1990.

Sperber, A. M., *Murrow: His Life and Times.* Freundlich Books, New York, 1986.

Steffens, Lincoln, *Autobiography.* Harcourt, Brace, New York, 1936.

Swanburg, W. A., *Citizen Hearst.* Charles Scribner's Sons, New York, 1961.

Toland, John, *Adolf Hitler.* Doubleday, New York, 1976.

Truman, Margaret, *Harry S. Truman,* William Morrow, New York, 1972.

White, William Allen, *Autobiography.* Macmillan, New York, 1946.

Index

454   TWENTIETH CENTURY AMERICAN WARS

Strategic Arms Reduction Treaty, 411,
    412, 423, 432
Strategic Defense Initiative, 331, 341,
    349, 358, 359, 376, 422–425
Strauss, Robert S., 414
Struble, Adm. Arthur D., 181
Subic Bay Naval Station, 412
Submarine fleet, (Germany orders attacks
    by), 11
Sudetenland, (takeover of), 74, 75
Sugiyama, Gen. Haime, 108
Supreme Headquarters Allied Powers,
    186
Surplus War Property Act, 138
Sutherland, Gen. Richard, 131
Sutsakhan, Gen. Sak, 314
Suu, Phan Khao, 242
Suzuki, Adm. Kantaro, 149, 155, 158
Sweeney, Maj. Charles W., 157, 159

Tacit Rainbow," 386
Taft-Hartley Act, 170, 194
Taft, President William Howard, 5, 6,
    20, 21, 85
Tambo, Pres., Oliver N., 381
Tani, Viscount, 58
Tanikaze, (damage to), 106
Tannenberg, (Russian defeat at), 9
Task Force 58, 131, 133, 149
Task Force 77, 179, 198, 239
Tate, Capt. Steve, 399, 400
Taylor, Amb. Maxwell, 242
Tay Ninh, 306
"Teapot Dome," (Naval Petroleum Re-
    serve No. 3), 14
Teheran, (conference at), 120
Teller, Dr. Edward, 214, 230
Temple of Music, 2
X Corps, 182, 186
Testrake, John, 340
Tet, 259, 261
Texas Oil Company, 21
Texas School Book Depositors, 236
Thatcher, Margaret, 328, 333, 338, 344,
    345, 394
Thieu, Maj. Gen. Nguyen Van, 242,
    255, 256, 267, 274, 281, 291, 292,
    294, 308, 309, 311–313
Third Army, 135, 139, 143
3rd South Vietnamese Division, 309, 310

Tianamen Square, 374, 376
Tomahawk, (cruise missile), 387, 400,
    424
Tower, Sen. John, 346, 347
313th Wing, 148
314th Wing, 147
315th Wing, 148
Trans World Airlines, 340
Tho, Le Duc, 290, 293, 294, 296
Thurmond, Strom M., 170, 171
Thuy, Xuan, 290, 293
Tibbits, Col. Paul, 156, 158
"Ticonderoga," USS, 239
Timoshenko, Marshall Semën, 109
Tinian, (occupation of), 133
Toan, Gen. Nguyen Van, 312
Tobruk, (surrender of), 109
Togo, Admiral, 4
Tojo, Gen. Hideki, 131, (removal of),
    134
Toyoda, Adm. Soemu, 131, 132
Treaty of Paris, 1
Treaty of Verailles, 66
Trident Conference, 116
Trident missile, 339, 359
Trident submarine, 359, 424
Trotsky, Leon, 31
Truman, Pres. Harry S, 149, 150, 153–
    156, 158–160, 163, 165, 166–171,
    174–179, 182, 187, 188, 192, 194,
    199, 209, 206
Truman Doctrine, 165
Tse-tung, Mao, 67, 72, 174–176, 246,
    284, 285, 315
Tugwell, Rexford, 59
Turner, V/Adm. Kelly, 132
Twentieth Air Force, 145, 148, 149,
    152, 156, 160
XX Bomber Command, 146, 147
XXI Bomber Command, 145, 146
22nd Vietnamese Division, 311
24th Division, 180, 403
25th Amendment, 301
25th Division, 180
27th Infantry Division, 132
Tyneside, (raid on), 13
"Typhoon," class, (submarine), 349

U-boats, (catastrophic war by), 110
Udet, Major Ernst, 54

HIPPOCRENE MILITARY LIBRARY

New in Paperback

KOREA: THE FIRST WAR WE LOST (3rd EDITION)
Revised with Epilogue
Bevin Alexander

The best book ever written on the subject—now in its third printing!

Praise for the hardcover edition:

"[A] well-researched and readable book." —The New York Times

"This is arguably the most reliable and fully-realized one-volume history of the Korean War since David Rees' *Korea.*" —Publishers Weekly

"Bevin Alexander does a superb job ... this respectable and fast-moving study is the first to be written by a professional army historian." —Library Journal

580 pages   6 x 9
index, 82 b/w photos, 13 maps
0-7818-0065-X $16.95pb

HISTORY & POLITICS
FROM HIPPOCRENE BOOKS

STALINGRAD
V.E. Tarrant

By November 1942, the empire of Adolf Hitler had
reached its zenith. It stretched from North Africa to the Arctic,
from the English Channel to Stalingrad deep inside the Russian
interior. The German Army seemed invincible, but then in a
matter of only five days, from November 19 to 23, 1942, the
impossible happened. During a massive Russian counter-offensive
involving over a million men, 1,560 tanks, 16,261 field guns and
mortars and 1,327 aircraft, not only were two Rumanian armies
wiped off the Axis order of battle, but more decisively the
"crack" German 6th Army, under the command of Friedrich
Paulus, was encircled at Stalingrad.

Despite being cut off from the remainder of the Eastern Front
in a huge cauldron *(Der Kessel),* the 269,000 troops of the 6th
Army continued to resist against impossible odds for 72
blood-soaked days. Devoid of adequate winter clothing, enduring
temperatures of minus 35 degrees centigrade on a bare, blizzard
swept steppe, with nothing to eat, but scraps of bread and watery
soup, the doomed army suffered an infinity of agonies including
frostbite, dysentery, and typhus.

When the 6th Army finally surrendered on February 2, 1943,
only 91,000 of the original force remained alive to be herded into
Siberian prison camps—only 5,000 survived captivity to see
Germany again.

MILITARY BOOK CLUB MAIN SELECTION

272 pages, 7 1/2 x 9, illustrations, maps
0-7818-0154-0   *$24.95 cloth*

HISTORY & POLITICS
FROM HIPPOCRENE BOOKS

THE MURDERERS OF HATYN
Vladimir Abarinov

On October 15, 1992, the *New York Times* and newspapers
around the world announced definitive proof that on March 5,
1940, Stalin personally approved the genocide of 15,000 Polish
prisoners—the Katyn massacre.

The historic disclosure provided the missing documentary link
for the courageous Russian journalist Vladimir Abarinov, who
reached the same shocking conclusion in the *Labyrinth of Katyn*,
published in Russia two years ago. Hippocrene presents the
English translation of this unprecedented history—the only book
by a Russian on Stalin's crime—under the title of *The Murderers
of Katyn*.

In uncovering truth behind the Katyn massacre, Abarinov
stripped away 50 years of lies generated by the Soviet propaganda
machine. Stalin's cover-up included the unsuccessful attempt to
have the Nuremberg tribunal convict the Nazis of the crime.
Even Gorbachev, in his public admission in 1990, never revealed
Stalin's complicity.

Abarinov relies exclusively on Russian sources, including
interviews with over 100 witnesses, some of them retired NKVD
executioners. Taking advantage of glasnost, a policy still in
formation during much of his research, Abarinov cites many
documents never before published in any language.

5 1/2 x 8, 250 pages
0-7818-0032-3   *$19.95 cloth*

HIPPOCRENE MILITARY LIBRARY

DARK AND CRUEL WAR
Don Lowry

"In the name of common sense, I ask you not to appeal to a just God in such a sacrilegious manner. You who, in the midst of peace and prosperity, have plunged a nation into war-dark and cruel war..." —Major General William Tecumseh Sherman, USA, to General John Bell Hood, CSA

By the fall of the city of Atlanta to Union troops on September 1, 1864, it appeared as if the Civil War would soon end with a Union victory. And yet, the end was still a long way off. In the long and agonizing months before the moment when arms were finally silenced, terrible depredations the likes never seen before or again in American history were to be wrought, a myriad of bloody battles were still to be fought and thousands who yearned for the end had yet to be killed or maimed.

   Dark and Cruel War is a chronicle of this devastating period of the Civil War. As in his previous two volumes, *No Turning Back* and *Fate of the Country*, author Don Lowry ties together the epic campaigns in the eastern and western theaters of the Civil War in this third volume of the series. His narrative captures the climax of the Civil War, and spans from Sherman's mission to "make Georgia howl" to Philip Sheridan's stunning victories in the Shenandoah Valley.

555 pages, 6 x 9
0-7818-0168-0   *$27.50*

HISTORY & POLITICS
FROM HIPPOCRENE BOOKS

TERRIBLE INNOCENCE:
GENERAL SHERMAN AT WAR
Mark Coburn

In a war of set piece battles, with rivers of blood, General
William Tecumseh Sherman was a striking exception. He
believed that "the time has come when we should attempt the
boldest moves, and my experience is that they are easier of
execution than more timid ones." A master of logistics, he was
most sparing of his men's lives: "night and day I labor to the end
that not a life shall be lost in vain."

He burnt cities, but he saved lives; the terror he inspired
made his victories less expensive in lives and more effective.
Contrary to rumors, Sherman permitted arson and pillage, but not
wanton killing and rape. His army lived off the land, to make
continuing offensives less dependent on uncertain supplies.

A great strategist with an uncanny memory and a feeling for
terrain, General Sherman was a fine writer as well. His orders
were dear and to the point, and his memoirs most readable and
accurate. Mark Coburn's account is as lively and vital as his
subject, and does justice to a general who in his focus on winning
and in his thinking was as modern as General Patton 80 years
later.

An escaped New Yorker, Coburn lives in Durango,
Colorado, and teaches English at Fort Lewis College. He has
written many articles on the American past.

MILITARY BOOK CLUB MAIN SELECTION

240 pages, 6 x 9, 16 illustrations, 6 maps
0-7818-0156-7   *$22.50 cloth*

HIPPOCRENE MILITARY LIBRARY

ANATOMY OF VICTORY
Battle Tactics 1689-1763
Brent Nosworthy
359 pages, 6 x 9, 22 formation diagrams
0-87052-014-8 $16.95pb

BATAAN
Our Last Ditch
Lt. Col. John Whitman
700 pages, 6 x 9, 16 b/w photos, maps
0-87052-877-7 $29.95

BLACK CORPS:
A Collector's Guide to the
History and Regalia of the S.S.
Robin Lumsden
300 pages, 5 1/2 x 8 1/2, 150 illustrations
0-7818-0112-5 $19.95pb

COLLECTOR'S GUIDE TO
THIRD REICH MILITARIA
Robin Lumsden
176 pages, 5 3/4 x 8 1/2, 150 b/w photos and illustrations
0-7101-723-9 $19.95pb

DETECTING THE FAKES
Robin Lumsden
144 pages, 5 3/4 x 8 1/2, 150 b/w photos and illustrations
0-87052-829-7 $19.95pb

ELEPHANT AND THE TIGER
The Full Story of the War in Vietnam
Wilbur H. Morrison
"A comprehensive, hardnosed exploration of the question, how did we win every battle yet lose the war?... Includes a full account of South Vietnamese military operations, an element of the war usually ignored."
—Publishers Weekly
Military Book Club Dual Selection
640 pages, 6 x 9, 16 b/w photos
0-87052-623-5 $24.95

HIPPOCRENE MILITARY LIBRARY

FATE OF THE COUNTRY
The Civl War from June to September 1864
Don Lowry
"An excellent account of the period ... recommended"—**Booklist**
"[Lowry's] frame-by-frame chronology succeeds in heightening the natural drama of the events." —**Library Journal**
555 pages, 6 x 9, index, 4 maps
0-7818-0064-1 $27.50

IMPROVISED WAR
Michael Glover
232 pages
0-87052-456-9 $29.50

INTELLIGENCE OFFICERS
IN THE PENINSULAR WAR
Julia Page
255 pages
0-87052-310-4 $22.95

MILITARY MANUAL OF SELF-DEFENSE
Anthony B. Herbert
0-87052-977-3 $9.95pb

NEW ORLEANS
The Battle of the Bayous
Harry Albright
320 pages, 6 x 9
0-87052-007-5 $8.95pb

NO TURNING BACK
The End of the Civil War
May-June 1864
Don Lowry
576 pages, 6 x 9
0-87052-010-5 $27.50

ORDERS AND MEDALS OF THE USSR
0-87052-989-7 $8.95pb

HIPPOCRENE MILITARY LIBRARY

PATTON'S THIRD ARMY
Charles Province
"This book forms an invaluable work of reference which contains a vast wealth of facts and figures. I'm sure it will be of great interest to both the professional and amateur historian alike." —**British Army Review**
"Had I been able to refer to such a complete work of reference for my *Patton's Third Army at War*, then my task would have been made immeasurably easier." —**George Forty, Tank Magazine**
336 pages, 6 x 9
0-87052-973-0 $22.50

PEARL HARBOR
Japan's Fatal Blunder
Harry Albright
378 pages, 6 x 9
0-87052-074-1 $8.95pb

RIVER AND THE ROCK
Fortress West Point
Dave R. Palmer
0-87052-992-7 $69.50

ROYAL MARINES COMMANDOES
John Watney
0-87052-715-0 $9.95pb

SCOTTISH REGIMENTS
A Pictorial History
P. Mileham
0-87052-361-9 $70.00

SECRETS OF THE VIET CONG
J. W. McCoy
400 pages, 6 x 9, maps, illustrations, formation diagrams
0-7818-0028-5 $24.95

TERRITORIAL BATTALIONS
A Pictorial History
Ray Westlake
7 x 10, color and b/w illustrations
0-87052-309-0 $45.00

HISTORY & POLITICS FROM HIPPOCRENE BOOKS

New in Paperback

THE REAGAN PRESIDENCY
An Actor's Finest Performance
Wilbur Edel

In this carefully documented analysis of the Reagan presidency, Wilbur Edel shows how the 40th president successfully played out optimistic fantasies based on his own black-and-white, good-and evil picture of the world. Although little was made of the Hollywood-in-Washington phenomenon when Reagan was in office, Edel constructs his meticulous argument solely from published sources. The platitudes and double-talk were there for all to see, but the audience seems to have been dazzled by the stage lights. The vertiginous mountain of facts, of word and deed, collected in this impressive book, reveals the true ignominy of Reagan's portrayal of the president of the United States.

Dr. Wilbur Edel is Professor Emeritus of Political Science, The City University of New York.

"A thoughtful, thorough, and devastating critique of Reagan as president ... Highly recommended." —**Choice**
A Choice Magazine Outstanding Book of the Year

360 pages, 6 x 9
0-7818-0127-3   *$11.95pb*

HISTORY & POLITICS
FROM HIPPOCRENE BOOKS

A SHORT HISTORY OF MODERN KOREA
David Rees
0-87052-154-3   *$9.95pb*

THE FORGOTTEN HOLOCAUST
The Poles Under German Occupation, 1939-1944
Richard C. Lukas
This landmark study shows that Nazi treatment of Polish Gentiles
was scarcely less barbaric than that of their Jewish compatriots.
"An absorbing, meticulously documented study." —**National
Review**
"Lively and engaging ... will appeal to scholars and laymen
alike."   —**Polish Heritage**
300 pages, 5 x 7
0-87052-632-4   *$9.95pb*

POLAND
A Historical Atlas
lwo Cyprian Pogonowski
Poland has been a vital force in shaping Europe as we know it
today. This atlas illustrates the central role Poland has occupied
in the history of Europe. With over 170 maps, the book covers
such diverse topics as political history, language evolution,
cultural achievement, and social history.
320 pages, 8 1/2 x 11, 175 maps
0-7818-0117-6   *$16.95pb*

POLISH GENEOLOGY AND HERALDRY
Janina Hoskins
115 pages, 5 1/2 x 8 1/2, 14 b/w illus., photos, maps
0-87052-940-4 $10.00pb

THE YEARS
The Last Decade of Imperial Russia
V.V. Shulgin
0-87052-928-5   *$11.95pb*

HISTORY & POLITICS
FROM HIPPOCRENE BOOKS

BLACK CALIFORNIA
The History of African-Americans in the Golden State
B. Gordon Wheeler
A pioneering work, *Black Calfornia* illuminates every era and every social movement affecting African-Americans in the Golden State, illustrating the key role African-Americans have played in the state's development.
292 pages, 5 1/2 x 8 1/14, index, bibliography, b/w drawings
0-7818-0074-9   *$22.50*

A COLONY OF THE WORLD
The United States Today
Eugene McCarthy
Giving new meaning to the concept of colonization, the fearless and outspoken former senator, and candidate for president in 1968, speaks frankly to the American people as the clear voice of reason at a time when issues facing our country are obscured by soundbites and misleading advertising.
120 pages, 6 x 9
0-7818-0102-8   *$16.95*

DEVIL DISCOVERED:
Salem Witchcraft 1692
Enden Robinson
The only examination of witchcraft based primarily on the records of those convicted.
"The work ... focuses on the people. It is alive with individuals bursting with emotions, foibles, and hidden agendas."
                                     —Library Journal
382 pages, 6 x 9
0-7818-0104-4   *$12.95pb*

HISTORY & POLITICS
FROM HIPPOCRENE BOOKS

EXECUTIVE PRIVILEGE
Two Centuries of White House Scandals
Jack Mitchell
"—Rich in historical detail, written in a lively, irreverent tone ...
guides the reader through a fascinating tour of two hundred years
of high level Washington scandal."
                                    —Jack Anderson, syndicated columnist
"Quality muckraking....Mitchell has unearthed a remarkable
collection of little-known facts, but more important is his balanced
view and his ability to present these leaders in all their complexity
... Telling details, crisp writing, good history."
                                    —Kirkus Reviews
420 pages, 6 x 9, 24 b/w photos
0-7818-0063-3   *$24.95*

George Bush:
An Intimate Portrait
Fitzhugh Green
270 pages, 6 x 9
0-87052-942-0   *$7.95 pb*

TO PURCHASE HIPPOCRENE'S BOOKS contact your local
bookstore, or write to Hippocrene Books, 171 Madison Avenue,
New York, NY 10016. Please enclose a check or money order,
adding $3.00 shipping (UPS) for the first book, and $.50 for
each additional book.

Write also for our full catalog of maps and foreign language
dictionaries and phrasebooks.